The sounds of chanting
reached her ears.

Oh no! One of the Hidden Rites! It has to be . . .

Her mouth went dry. She had never seen one of the secret ceremonies. It was forbidden for her to even stand here and listen. And yet . . . Her path led through a gallery along the top of the huge chamber where the rites were held. There was no other way she could go. For a moment, she hesitated. Dared she try it? If she were caught in the vicinity of a Hidden Rite . . .

With a sudden squaring of her shoulders, Thia began to run. The chanting grew louder, and was now mixed with other sounds, low and muffled, with an occasional shriek or wail rising above the rest of the cacophony.

Reaching the huge archway that led into the gallery, above the enormous chamber, Thia extinguished her light, dropped to her hands and knees, then began inching along. When she reached the first hole in the parapet, she could not resist putting her eye to it and gazing down at the Rite that was underway.

Thia made a low sound in her throat, even as her hands went up to cover her mouth.

Children. Babies. Dressed for the sacrifice.

By all that was sacred—NO!

STORMS OF DESTINY

THE EXILES OF BOQ'URAIN

A.C.CRISPIN

An Imprint of HarperCollinsPublishers

EOS
An Imprint of HarperCollins*Publishers*
10 East 53rd Street
New York, New York 10022-5299

Copyright © 2005 by A.C. Crispin
Song lyrics copyright © Michael Longcor. Used with permission.
Map by Michael Capobianco
ISBN: 0-380-78284-7
www.eosbooks.com

First Eos paperback printing: August 2005

HarperCollins® and Eos® are trademarks of HarperCollins Publishers Inc.

Printed in the U.S.A.

10 9 8 7 6 5 4 3 2 1

This book is dedicated to
Kathleen O'Malley,
friend, teacher, editor, and collaborator.
For the past twenty-seven years,
she's taught me more about writing
than anyone else.
Thanks, Kathy.

Acknowledgments

Many people helped me with information and commentary during the writing of this book. With the caveat that any errors are my own, I'd like to thank:

Steve Osmanski, who helped plan battles, and check my information on antique weapons. I couldn't have done it without you, Steve.

Victoria, my partner in Writer Beware (*www.writer beware.com*), who read the manuscript in chunks and served as a personal cheering section. Without her support and encouragement, I'd have crashed and burned a dozen times—and she also pulled me out of a couple of plot holes, which are even deadlier than quicksand-filled sinkholes for a writer. Thanks, Vic.

Kathy O'Malley, the first person to read the whole manuscript when it was finally finished. Kathy read it and assured me that it kept her reading and made sense—which is the greatest gift a first reader can bestow.

My husband, Michael Capobianco, who drew the maps, helped with the languages of the various lands, and kept my ancient computer running throughout the writing of this book.

Larry R. Kotkin, PhD, who gave me suggestions on how to improve the hypnosis scenes.

My agent, Writers House, Inc., and Ginger Clark, who read the manuscript and made a very useful suggestion.

My Harper editor, Diana Gill, and her assistant, Will Hinton, who were always responsive and helpful.

My friends John (Dino) and Sonia, who happily read whatever I send them and tell me I'm wonderful. Every author needs at least two friends like Dino and Sonia. I'm blessed.

And a special acknowledgment to Michael Longcor, who wrote the songs used in this book. When I first had the idea to write this trilogy, I knew that I wanted the world to have its own music. I spoke with Teri Lee at Firebird Arts and Music. She put me in touch with Michael Longcor, who agreed to provide the music for Boq'urain. Michael designed songs to fit individual scenes in the book, and I occasionally rewrote scenes to incorporate some of his wonderful songs. This relationship between songwriter and author is unique, so far as I know, and it added immeasurably to the project.

If you're interested in hearing the songs and music from this book, visit http://www.firebirdarts.com, or call 1-800-752-0494 (fax 503-255-5703). Or write to Firebird Arts and Music, P.O. Box 30268, Portland OR 97294.

STORMS OF DESTINY

BOQ'URAIN
Boq'urak's World 2,406 S.B.

River Weizin

Pathless

Savage
Lands

PELA

Gen
Talano
Tartona
Minoma
Ombal
Pass
Benini
Omora
Napice
Omora
Pioli
Karithe
Islands

Ikir
Amavav

Tanai Range
Galrai

Steppes
Severez

Kata
Minoma
Strait of
Dara
Pela
Meptalith
Islands

Rain
Forest
Or'zavir
Oriz
R. Sar
Sarsithê
Pathas

Jezzil

A gleam of westering sun pierced the dimness of the forest, turning the light from emerald to pale jade tinged with gold. Jezzil squinted, momentarily dazzled, then straightened in his saddle. Ahead of him lay shorter trees, scraggly underbrush, then the amber gleam of late summer crops. The climate was mild, this far south. The people of Taenareth were justifiably proud of their clement winters. The young Chonao warrior regarded the vista ahead with satisfaction and a touch of relief. *At last! I was beginning to think we'd have to ride through this forest until the end of time.*

His knees tightened fractionally as his hands closed on the reins. Beneath him, Falar halted as smoothly as flowing water. Jezzil raised a hand, and the horsemen behind him drew rein. The young soldier had been raised in the fertile, forested lowlands of Ktavao, and his experience with this kind of terrain had led the captain to appoint the young Chonao the lead scout for this mission—an assignment he'd now completed successfully.

Ahead of them lay a stone fortress at the top of a hill, surrounded by a wide moat. This was their destination . . . the stronghold of m'Banak. Their orders were to take it before sunrise the next morning, take it by stealth, from within. They were the Pen Jav Dal, the Silent Ones, the elite of the Chonao forces. Their leader, the Redai of Ktavao, had led his invasionary forces across the Eastern Sea, bent on the conquest of the large, fertile isle called Taenareth. They'd landed a week ago at Fiere, then ridden north, and m'Banak was the last unfallen fortress. If they took it, the Redai's victory would be complete.

Gardal, Jezzil's Amato, urged his gelding up beside the younger man, then both Chonao dismounted, leaving their mounts' reins dangling as a signal to stay. Placing a finger to his lips, Jezzil beckoned, and they picked a soundless path through the underbrush until they were crouched at the edge of the forest, staring up at their destination.

The stone domes of m'Banak and its slender timbered spires stood outlined against the reddening gleams of sunset. The fortress stood straight and proud, like a warrior on guard . . . and rightly so since m'Banak was the heart of the Taenareth defenses. The Redai, Kerezau, had beaten the island's forces in every battle since they'd landed, but the island's ruler had fled to this spot, the most secure in his land. A massive water channel surrounded the hill, a channel cut, some said, by sorcery. Rumor also had it that the dark waters hosted strange creatures swimming in their depths.

"So that's where Zajares is holed up . . ." Gardal muttered, half to himself. "A snug den, for an old fox."

Jezzil pulled off his helm, enjoying the play of breeze across his scalp, and pushed a sweaty lock of dark brown hair off his forehead. His green eyes narrowed. "It won't be easy, getting inside, much less getting close enough to Zajares to take him out. How many troops does Intelligence say he has in there with him? How many pistols and muskets?"

"A full company is assigned here to guard Zajares," Gardal said. "But Intelligence says he's been sending out raiding parties, preparing for a siege. So there's no telling how many are actually in there with him. He has firearms, but his powder supply is very low. Enough for a few volleys, perhaps. Not enough for heavy artillery." Gardal's eyes narrowed as the grizzled Amato studied the fortress. "And it's not like he'll have a chance to use cannon."

Jezzil nodded. The information about the lack of powder came as no surprise. The Redai had cut Zajares's supply lines weeks ago. "So he could have a hundred soldiers," he said. "We're outnumbered."

"The Pen Jav Dal often are," Gardal pointed out, truthfully. "But a surplus of troops can work to our advantage, youngster."

Jezzil gave him a quizzical glance that he barely kept from being openly skeptical. "How, sir?"

"The more of them there are to be thrown into chaos, the greater that chaos will be," Gardal replied. "The first thing we must do is make them see what is not there."

"But, sir . . ." Jezzil struggled to phrase his question so it would not seem insubordinate. "We have no Caster with us. How can we create an illusion?"

Gardal sighed, shaking his head reprovingly. "Youngster, what are they teaching you nowadays, eh? The Silent Ones can make enemies see what they want them to see, believe what we want them to believe, whether we do it by magic or by stealth and guile. Haven't they taught you that yet?"

Jezzil flushed at the reproof. "Of course, sir. I know that. It just . . . slipped my mind."

Gardal gave him a wry glance. "How many missions have you been on, youngster?"

The scout took a deep breath. "This is my second, sir. Don't worry, I'm ready for this." He patted the pommel of his short, slightly curved sword. "By dawn, this place will be the Redai's for the taking."

His officer nodded. "That's the spirit, Risore Jezzil. You and Risore Barus come from the same Company, yes?"

Jezzil nodded. "We do, Amato. Barus and I have known each other since our first days in ranks. He is my best friend."

Gardal nodded. "You both speak Taenarian? You work well together?"

"We both speak it, sir. And we trust each other as we trust ourselves."

"Good. You will need that kind of trust, Risore, because I am sending the two of you in first. You will be responsible for scouting a way across that moat and into the fortress. You will locate Zajares's quarters and determine how many men he has guarding him there. You will make recommendations as to how we can carry out our orders to assassinate Zajares and open the fortress to the Redai's onslaught. Understood?"

Jezzil squared his shoulders, his green eyes shining at the honor his Amato was bestowing upon him. He threw the officer his best formal salute. "Yes, Amato! I am grateful for the honor, sir!"

Gardal returned the salute. "Ease up. You may not thank me an hour from now—that fortress won't fall into your lap like an overripe pluma. Now get Risore Barus up here and plan your foray."

"Yes, sir!"

Quickly, the young man headed back through the trees to where the forty-nine members of the scouting and infiltration party were waiting. He was very conscious of the honor Gardal was giving him in allowing him to plan this raid. If he were successful, it might mean a step up in rank—possibly even a commendation from the Redai himself. The other Chonao were gathered together, having taken the opportunity to water their mounts from a tiny creek that threaded through the forest. Falar had her head turned, obviously scenting the water, but still obedient to her master's command to stay. The Chonao felt a surge of pride. The Chonao horses were the best in the world, and his mare was the best of the best.

The young Risore was the fourth son of a nobleman whose vast estates included many acres given over to the raising of some of the finest horses in all of Chonao territory. Falar had been by his best stud, out of his finest broodmare. She was not as tall and fine-boned as a Pelanese racer, but she was far more delicately built than the sturdy horses from the Chonao steppes that the other party members rode. With her smoky dapples, dark mane, tail, and points, she was a beauty, from her wide-set dark eyes to her small ears. She pricked them up upon hearing her master's step.

"Are you thirsty, lady?" Jezzil murmured in his southern dialect, picking up the reins. Falar whuffled, turning her head deliberately toward the water. Her master led her to the tiny stream, then slipped the bit from her mouth so she might drink freely. As the mare sniffed delicately, then began to gulp the water, her ears moving with each swallow, Jezzil beckoned Barus over. Signaling his own mount to stay, his friend joined him.

Barus was shorter and slighter than Jezzil, with the swarthy skin of a steppes dweller. His slim, wiry build made him look almost inconsequential when at rest, but he was a master at both armed and unarmed combat; he had the quickest reflexes Jezzil had ever seen. Barus's lank sable hair was longer than his friend's shoulder-length, and had to be elaborately braided and pinned to fit beneath his close-fitting helm. "What's up?" he asked quietly.

Jezzil jerked his chin at the distant fortress. "The Amato has assigned the two of us to scout the place and help plan the attack."

Barus's dark eyes lit up and his teeth flashed briefly in a broad grin. "Superb! I can hardly wait!"

Jezzil's mouth twitched. "Contain yourself. There are over a hundred soldiers quartered there, guarding Zajares."

The junior officer dismissed the thought with a flick of his left hand in a rude gesture. "We are the Silent Ones. We'll cut their throats before they even know we're among them. This is a great opportunity for us. If we do well . . ."

Jezzil nodded. "My thought exactly."

The two scouts quickly checked their weapons and armor, abandoning their swords for the moment in favor of several knives and throwing discs of assorted sizes concealed in sheaths and holders beneath their loose-fitting tunics and trousers. Jezzil slipped a vial of poison into the holder sewn into the top of his riding boot, where it was hidden by the thick tooling on the outside calf. Gathering his shoulder-length hair in his hand, he secured it with a leather thong, then wound a coil of cutting wire around the thong so it appeared to be held by a silvery mesh clasp. He tucked the leather-bound free ends under, concealing them. His leather wrist guards could also be unwound and used as strangling cords.

While he was doing this, the words of the training song all cadets learned in their first year of schooling, "The Arming Rhyme of the Silent Ones," ran through his head.

Helmet rivet solid, plates without a crack
Body armor fastened, front and side and back
Neck and arms and body, free to stoop or stand
Weapons in their scabbards, ready to the hand.

Check if blades are solid; pommel, grip, and guard
Weapon belts all fastened? Check them quick and hard
Jump and see what rattles. Tie and pad it fast
Second chances never come. Fool's luck doesn't last!

Check the shadow weapons, set and out of sight
Steel and cord and poisons, stopped and fastened tight
Skin and face all darkened, metal dulled of shine.
What's your ordered mission? What's your place and
    time?

What's the secondary plan? What way in and out?
Where's the second rally point? What's the hidden route?
Feet and hands are weapons, but number one's your
    head.
Stay relaxed and use it, and you may not end up dead.

As the final words ran through Jezzil's mind, he slipped two ruby studs into the holes in his left earlobe. Each stud had a tiny drop of a powerful soporific coating the inside shaft, which was inserted into the thicker, outside wire. All the young Chonao had to do was twist the inner shaft free of the outer sheath, and he held a tiny, sharp, potent dart. One pinprick would be enough to fell a strong opponent in less than two minutes.

Falar nickered softly and bunted him gently as he loosened her girth and tethered her close to a bush with succulent leaves. "I'll be back, lady," he told her, stroking her satiny neck for a moment. "Wait here for me. *Stay*."

Then the two scouts, clad in their traditional garb that was the color of shadow, eased out of the forest. Meadows encircled the hill where the fortress stood, and the two young warriors moved quickly across them until they came to the narrow fringe of trees and undergrowth that had sprung up on the bank of the moat.

Barus and Jezzil crouched in the shadow of a scrubby oak and stared up at the fortress. The sun had set, and twilight gathered around it like a dark cloak. The spires that had appeared so proud and stately in the sunlight now looked bladelike and forbidding. The stone domes seemed to hunker down between the spires like animals hiding in burrows. Jezzil, who had a lively imagination that he tried sternly to ignore—too vivid an imagination was a drawback for a soldier—repressed a shiver.

"Let's get on with it," Barus said, his voice barely a breath on the evening air. "We know what we're looking for."

The two Chonao began a systematic search in the waning light. Each was equipped with a night lantern, should that become necessary, but both young men had excellent eyesight, and they found what they were seeking before the last light had faded away.

A trapdoor, set into a tiny clearing, was carefully camouflaged with cut brush that must have been replenished only yesterday. Most men would have walked past it without noticing the drooping leaves, but the Silent Ones were well-trained in ferreting out secrets. A moment's investigation revealed the cut branches and the wooden slabs set flush with the ground.

"No ring," Barus said, staring down at the uncovered trapdoor with a frown.

"Of course not," Jezzil said. "They don't want anyone using it to get *in,* they just want to make sure they can get *out.*"

"We'll have to dig and lever it up," Barus said. "And that's going to make noise. I'll give you good odds there's a sentry down there."

"No doubt," Jezzil agreed. "There's probably another at the exit on the other side of the moat. We'll have to take care of both of them before we can get into the fortress."

Barus glanced around the clearing, evaluating it as a site for an ambush. "You start digging, and I'll take care of him when he appears."

Jezzil opened his mouth to protest, then shut it and shrugged. Barus was a better swordsman and hand-to-hand fighter than he was, even on his best day. The steppe warrior was the acknowledged champion of the troop. "Oh, very well," he said gruffly, but he was conscious of a stab of relief. He had been in two battles and fought hard, but there was a difference in deliberately luring a man to his death by stealth, rather than killing him in open warfare. Besides, as long as the job was done, and done well, who was he to protest?

Walking over to the concealed door, Jezzil dropped to one knee and began hacking at the dirt on the opening side with the point of his dagger. There had been little rain for weeks, so it was as hard as stone, but crumbled once it was loosened. He made no effort to disguise the scraping noises he made.

The young Chonao had a brief moment of apprehension then; what if the sentry sent for reinforcements before coming up to investigate? But then, he thought, surely the man would want to assure himself that there wasn't some animal up here digging.

His reasoning was borne out a second later when the door suddenly burst open and an armed guard catapulted himself out of the ground.

Jezzil fell back with a half-genuine squawk of dismay, deliberately lost his footing and went sprawling onto his backside, scrabbling to put distance between himself and the guard. He had only a moment to glimpse a bared sword in the other's hand before a dark shadow flowed across the little clearing and merged with the guard's moving figure. The man was jerked back on his heels, and had barely time for one muted gasp before he dropped limply to the ground.

Barus stood where the man had been, a broad smile on his face, his garroting wire swinging from his hand. Red droplets flowed along it. "You make a perfect decoy, my friend," he said admiringly, extending a gauntleted hand down to help his partner to his feet. "You chose the wrong profession. You should be on the stage. I've never seen anyone look both stupid and scared more convincingly."

Jezzil chuckled hollowly as he stared down at the fallen sentry. The body gave one final twitch, then lay still.

"We've got to hide him, before he's missed," he said.

Barus nodded, then eyed the prone figure measuringly. "He's closer to your size. Take his armor and surcoat. We'll dump him in the moat."

Carefully, Jezzil turned the sentry over and began tugging at the fastenings. Barus had slipped the garroting wire in so expertly that there was little blood; only a few drops stained the top of the surcoat. Jezzil donned the armor, concealing his own weapons beneath the scout's metal-studded leather kilt. Buckling on the short, straight Taenarith sword, he slapped the helm on his head. "How do I look?"

Barus studied him critically. "Stay in the shadows," he advised. "In a dim light, you'll pass."

Quickly, the two scouts grabbed the stripped body and carried it down the bank of the moat. After listening for a moment, they swung it back and forth, then sent it splashing into the dark waters, where it sank with scarcely a bubble or ripple.

"They say—" Jezzil began, only to fall silent and step back hastily as a monstrous, barely seen form slid past in the black water.

"Wh-What was that?" Barus sounded, for once, faintly unnerved.

"I was about to tell you. They say there are monsters in the moat."

"I would say they are correct," muttered Barus. "I wouldn't swim across that thing for a year's pay."

Returning to the trapdoor, the scouts levered it up out of its frame and prepared to descend into the torchlit tunnel at the bottom of the ladder. "You first," Barus said. "If you meet anyone, don't try to talk to him. Your accent would give you away."

Jezzil gave his friend an exasperated glance. "I know that. Stop treating me like a first-year recruit."

"Sorry," Barus muttered.

The Chonao warriors made their way along a stone-blocked tunnel. Green ooze and the faint sheen of oily water stained the sloping walls, ceiling, and floor, making the footing treacherous. They did not speak, only conversed in the Pen Jav Dal's language of signed gestures.

When the tunnel began sloping upward, obviously nearing its end, Jezzil gestured for Barus to stay behind him. His friend gave him a quick victory gesture with thumb and two fingers and dropped back.

Jezzil eased forward, inwardly cursing the clumsy Taenarith boots that made squelching noises in the wet muck on the floor. Mentally, he assessed the armor he had donned, calculating its weak points. The metal strips studding the boiled leather shirt started several inches above the belt . . .

Flexing his right wrist and little finger, he felt the blade strapped to the inside of his forearm ease downward. A hard squeeze and twist would send it sliding down into his waiting grasp.

The guard at the top of the slope turned as he heard a faint splash. Seeing Jezzil, he visibly tensed. "What's going on? It's not time for shift-change."

Jezzil shook his head grimly within the concealing shadow of the helm and, turning, pointed back down the tunnel. "What did you say?" he mumbled in Taenarian, careful to keep his voice muffled so it echoed oddly in the tunnel.

"What?" asked the guard, coming toward him. "Speak up, Carad!"

Jezzil coughed, clearing his throat like a man who was catching a rheum from the dank air. Just as the man reached him, he bent over, hawked and spat. When he straightened, the knife was in his hand, a muted metal flash in the torchlit dimness. Jezzil put the entire force of his body into the thrust; the razor-honed blade entered the sentry's body just above his heavy belt, stabbing upward through leather, flesh, and viscera in one swift stroke. Jezzil's aim was exact; the blade found its target in the left chamber of the man's heart.

The sentry gasped with the force of the blow, gurgled once, and sagged, dead already.

Jezzil stepped back, yanking his blade free with a practiced gesture, then, feeling queasy, he stood looking down at the blood soaking his gauntlet and dripping off his knife. He'd practiced that stroke thousands of times in sparring practice or against wood and sawdust dummies, but had never before used it on another living being.

"Nice work," Barus commented, grinning broadly. "Almost as smooth as if I'd done it. Next time twist your wrist a little harder to the right, and you can get both chambers. Even quicker that way."

"We'd better get rid of the body," Jezzil said. "Do you want to put on the armor?"

Barus turned the man over and regarded the blood-soaked form measuringly. "No, too stained," he said. "You stay here, so they'll think the sentry is still on duty, and I'll scout the fortress, count how many troops."

Jezzil nodded, and together they lugged the body out of the tunnel and dumped it into the moat. As before, it barely sank before something they could only glimpse was upon it.

Then Jezzil took up his supposed station, while Barus stole into the fortress.

The young Chonao fretted as he stood guard, his unfortunate imagination presenting him with images of Barus discovered, attacked, killed, and m'Banak alerted and impossible to take from within—their mission a total failure.

Nobody came near him. Jezzil had little way to judge the passing of the time; only his increasing need to relieve himself made him guess that nearly an hour had passed before a gray shadow flowed down the ladder leading up into m'Banak.

Jezzil repressed a sigh of relief. "What took you so long?"

Barus gave him a quizzical glance. "I came and went as quickly as I could. What's wrong? Place giving you the jumps?"

"Of course not," Jezzil snapped. "Are you ready to report?"

Barus nodded. "Zajares is quartered in the west dome, on the top floor. The guards are all wearing surcoats with his insignia, just as Intelligence said. If we put on the ones we brought with us, taken from those prisoners, we can march right in."

"How many?"

"No more than sixty. They've got patrols out, all right."

"What if one of those patrols returns while we're attacking?"

Barus made a dismissive gesture. "You worry too much."

"What about the security surrounding Zajares?"

His friend shook his head. "That will be harder," he admitted. "They change the passwords with every shift of the guard. But we should be able to divide our force, set fire to the main hall, and use that as a diversion. Then we'll just have to deal with Zajares's personal guard. The door's locked, but we can handle that. We'll get in, never fear, youngster."

Jezzil glared at his friend. Barus was a year older than he, and never let the younger Chonao forget it.

"You'd better get back to Gardal and report. I'll stay here," Jezzil said, with a swift glance up the ladder. "Try to bring the troop in before midnight. I'm betting that's when the guard changes."

"Likely," Barus agreed. "We've got at least two hours before then. We should make it."

"Don't forget to bring my blade. I don't want to have to fight with this," Jezzil said, resting his hand on the pommel of the Taenarith sword. "Clumsy thing."

"You said it," Barus nodded. "Don't worry, I won't forget."

"Good. Hurry."

When his friend was gone, Jezzil walked a little way down the tunnel to relieve himself, then waited impatiently, striding back and forth to keep warm in the dankness of the tunnel. He found the sentry's half-eaten supper and drank the half cup of overly sweet wine, then chewed determinedly at the tough, grainy bread and nearly tasteless cheese. Even though he was not hungry, he knew the food would give him energy.

The faint sound of footsteps finally reached his ears, and he straightened, hand on his weapon. Recognizing his Amato in the lead, he saluted briskly and signed, "Quiet here, sir."

Gardal's fingers moved in answer. "Good. Follow me, Risore."

Jezzil joined the small troop of soldiers, all clad in surcoats taken from captured Taenarith soldiers. His heart hammering, the young Chonao fell into step beside Barus, who handed him his sword. As he belted it on, the other Risore gave him an excited grin and a wink.

The troop of Silent Ones climbed the ladder leading into Zajares's stronghold. They found themselves in a small wooden guard chamber. Outside lay a courtyard. Sentries were stationed on the walls surrounding the fortress, but the doors leading into the stronghold were unguarded. Barus, with Jezzil beside him, moved up to take the lead.

Soft-footed, the Silent Ones scattered and crossed the courtyard, unseen. Stealth was their speciality; each warrior melted into the shadows like something spawned from the darkness. The sentries never heard a thing as the Pen Jav Dal crossed the hard-packed surface.

Barus led them to the western dome. Gardal signaled to the young Risore to take twenty of the men and head right, into the main hall. Jezzil knew the plan. They would fire the hall, making it appear as though there was a troop rebellion in progress.

The other thirty Silent Ones followed their Amato into the western dome. They waited around the curve in the corridor, backs pressed against the stone, for their signal to begin the planned attack.

Despite the chill air, Jezzil was sweating, and he was vaguely sorry he'd eaten. The food roiled uncertainly in his stomach, and the wavering dance of the smoky torches added to his queasiness. He couldn't stop remembering the way it had felt when his knife had punched upward through the sentry's vitals, ending his life.

What had his name been? Had he had a mother, father,

perhaps brothers and sisters? Or a wife, children? Was he young, or old? He would never know.

As they waited, breathing shallowly, evenly, every muscle poised to explode into action, they heard shouts and crashes from behind them, in the direction of the main hall. The others were doing their part.

A minute or so later a dozen or more guards came thundering down the ancient wooden staircase, shouting harried orders and directions at each other:

"Buckets! Get them from the stables!"

"You, Ranla, stand by at the well!"

"Weapons at the ready! This is sabotage!"

"I told you Adlat wasn't to be trusted!"

As Zajares's men charged around the corner, the Pen Jav Dal were ready. Blades flashed, throwing discs whizzed. Meaty thunks, grunts, and a muffled scream or two—

—and it was done. Fourteen guards lay dead. Gardal's troops made no effort to hide their bodies. At this stage in their attack they wanted their work to be seen, to strike fear into the hearts of Zajares's soldiers. The troop merely pulled the bodies out of the way, stacking them up along the wall to leave a clear path, should a retreat be necessary.

All the while, the sounds behind them had intensified. Jezzil smelled smoke, then heard the pounding of running feet. He checked his fighting stance, then relaxed as he heard a familiar whistled signal. Moments later Barus and the others appeared and saluted quickly.

Mission accomplished, the young Risore signaled.

Gardal acknowledged the message, then the Amato pointed to the rightmost corridor, making a questioning sign. The young Chonao scout nodded. Zajares's quarters lay in that direction. At Gardal's signal, the Silent Ones followed their Amato deeper into m'Banak.

In response to a silent order, Jezzil and two other men grabbed torches off the wall and fired the next two rooms they came to. The main structure was stone and would not burn, but there was plenty of wood around, and oil lamps to kindle it with.

Barus pointed to a stairway, then the young Risore's hands moved in quick gestures. "Upstairs. Zajares has the uppermost apartment, right beneath the dome. There's a back stairway down to the courtyard, the one I told you about."

Gardal nodded. "Let's go," he signaled.

With Barus in the lead, the Silent Ones raced up the stairs. Twice they had to pause, and each time when they moved on, a guard's body was shoved to the side. The stairs dead-ended in a huge, timbered door. Barus stood before it. "Locked," he signaled.

Something flashed in Gardal's hand, and the Amato positioned himself before the massive timbered portal. His fingers moved, twisted, slid, twisted . . . and the door swung open.

Gardal did not hesitate. He opened the door halfway, using his body to block off the sight of the troop, and began yelling at the occupants. "Help! They've turned against us!" he screamed, his Taenarian accent perfect. "Adlat has rallied them!"

A babble of questions and orders followed. Gardal's fingers moved in a quick signal, then, without warning, he kicked the door all the way open and leaped in, his troop on his heels.

So far Gardal's bluff had worked—but the officer in charge was no fool. The moment he got a clear view of the newcomers, he shouted, "Kill them! They're Chonao! Call for reinforcements!"

Chaos erupted around Jezzil as the guards fired their pistols. Several Chonao went down. Jezzil tried to stay beside Barus, but they were quickly separated. Chairs and furniture went flying as the Taenarith guardsmen surged forward. Men shouted battle cries and curses, and someone was blowing a horn. He tried to listen for Gardal's voice but couldn't make it out. Jezzil realized he was nearly surrounded by Taenarith troops. So far they had taken him for one of their own, probably because of his stolen armor and helmet.

A hard blow resounded against his helm, and he found himself almost engaged with one of his own troop. Quickly, he shouted at Darin in Chonao, then yanked off the helm to prevent being attacked again. A blade whizzed by his ear, nearly cutting it off, and Jezzil whirled, his sword at the ready.

He found himself engaged with a burly Taenarith guardsman, fighting to stay on his feet and not trip over broken furniture or other men. The man attacked furiously, and Jezzil forced himself to concentrate on watching for an opening in his guard. All around him the Chonao forces were similarly occupied, and he was constantly being shoved and bumped. Jezzil drew his dagger and used it to parry thrusts aimed at his left side. His curved blade flashed in the light of ruby-crystal lamps hung from the domed ceiling on silver chains.

There was a loud crash behind him, then a man's shriek. Jezzil smelled smoke, guessed that someone had knocked over a lamp and started a fire. Out of the corner of his eye he caught a flash of yellow. The tapestries were alight.

His opponent was immensely strong, but Jezzil was faster, far faster. The young Chonao forced himself to concentrate on the work at hand, and a few strokes later an opportunity presented itself. He did not even have to think about it; his blade turned and sought out the opening in the man's guard, slipped through, and slid neatly into his throat like an extension of Jezzil's arm. He gave his wrist a quick twist, then smoothly disengaged and looked for another Taenarith.

Smoke stung his eyes. The shouting intensified, suddenly, behind him. There seemed to be more Taenarith than before—where had they all come from? Jezzil turned in time to see the door behind him, which presumably led into Zajares's bedchamber, slam back on its hinges. Armed figures poured out through the veil of smoke. Jezzil leaped forward, his sword at the ready.

The din was incredible, and it was nearly impossible to tell friend from foe in the welter of fighting bodies and the haze of smoke. A sword rang against Jezzil's, and he half turned to engage again. A pale figure, short, half wreathed in smoke . . .

Parrying automatically, the Chonao blinked sweat and smoke-born tears out of his eyes, trying to clear his blurred vision. At that moment a gust of fresher air swept past his face, parting the clouds of smoke. Jezzil's eyes widened as he caught sight of his new opponent.

She was small, lovely, and naked.

Jezzil hesitated, completely taken aback. He had never fought a woman opponent; indeed, as a Pen Jav Dal, he was sworn to celibacy as a novice priest of the warrior god Arenar. He would serve Arenar as a soldier until he became too old or crippled to fight, then live out his days as a full-fledged priest. Women, especially naked ones, were completely outside his experience.

Yet despite his training, his years of conditioning to reject and despise females, he was still a man, and he could not help noting her beauty—her long black hair, which rippled as she moved, the brown circles that surrounded erect nipples, and the dark thatch of hair between her legs. She must have realized her effect on him, for her teeth shone in a savage grin as she lunged at him inexpertly, swinging the huge sword that was far too heavy and long for her to wield.

Jezzil parried again, automatically. He could not fight her, he decided. It would be butchery. She was scarcely more than a child, she knew nothing of weapons . . . and she was so beautiful. It would be unthinkable to slay her. He blinked stinging sweat from his eyes, forcing himself not to stare at her breasts, her sex. In all his life he had never seen a woman naked, and the sight fascinated him the way a snake's swaying form fascinated a tree vole. He parried another clumsy lunge, his mind formulating strategies for disarming her. There was no doubt in his mind that she would not give up; her entire countenance fairly shouted determination. He admired her courage, even as he twisted his wrist, his blade engaging and then twisting hers from her grasp.

The girl gasped and made a frantic lunge for the sword that was already falling. As she did so, Jezzil found himself shoved violently from behind. His weapon, still extended, pierced her left breast, and her own impetus spitted her on the blade past any hope of survival.

Shocked, Jezzil jerked back, retreating from the spurt of crimson that followed his blade's exit path. He had one final glimpse of her, eyes wide and accusing, before she fell forward and was lost amid the surging melee of struggling bodies.

Even as he stood gaping, he caught a blur of movement out of the corners of his eyes. Only years of training saved him; without having to think about it, he tucked and rolled away from the sweeping slash that would have turned his head into a wall trophy. Coming up to his feet, blade in hand, he engaged for a moment with his opponent before he recognized Barus, even as his friend did likewise. "Sorry!" his comrade shouted, his wide, infectious grin nearly splitting his sweaty features. "Damned smoke's in my eyes! We should—"

Jezzil caught another blur of motion, and leapt forward, but was a fraction of a second too late to deflect the mace that thudded against his friend's helmet. Scarlet blossomed beneath the steel even as Jezzil's sword pierced the throat of Barus's attacker.

Grief-stricken, Jezzil shouted, "Barus!" and threw himself toward his friend. At the same moment a screaming, flaming form hurtled across the room and crashed into him, writhing and shrieking. Jezzil shoved the dying warrior away violently, then tried again to reach Barus, but dead and dying bodies were everywhere and he had lost his sense of direction. As he peered desperately through the smoke, Jezzil was horrified to realize he was the only Chonao still standing. His comrades lay strewn around him like straws from a child's pickup game.

Gasping, half sobbing, Jezzil focused on his Amato's features, grimacing horribly above the gaping red maw that had been his throat. Some of the Taenarith were still alive, and he knew Gardal would have decreed that he should fight to the death and take as many of his comrades' slayers with him as he could.

Jezzil gripped his sword hilt in suddenly nerveless fingers. Across the smoke-wreathed room, one of the enemy had caught sight of him, shouted an order, and three of them staggered toward him, tripping on the bodies of the slain.

Stay and fight! his brain ordered, but his body would not

listen. Whirling, Jezzil bolted away from them, seeking escape, shelter, refuge—he didn't want to die! His mind kept yammering at him to obey his training, to turn and fight, but the panic driving his body was too strong. He tripped over something, looked down, saw a severed arm still clutching a sword, and a shriek burst from his throat unbidden.

Reaching an arras, he yanked it aside, searching for a door, but found none. The shouts of the Taenarith warriors came closer and closer, and he knew he was done for, and part of him was glad. He was a coward, after all, and did not deserve to live.

As he edged along the stone wall, gulping desperately at the cleaner air that had been trapped behind the arras, Jezzil saw a hand grab the curtain and jerk it violently. The entire drapery came tumbling down.

The young Chonao closed his eyes as the folds descended, and, with every particle of his being, willed himself to invisibility. It was a silly thing to do, he knew only too well he was no Caster, but in a moment they would see him, and he would be spitted on their blades like a piglet, and he did *not* want to die, he wanted only to vanish, to disappear, to—

The last of the concealing folds pulled free, and the Chonao braced himself to feel steel sheath itself in his vitals. He had gone beyond fear now, and seemed to be floating somewhere in a state of agonized but passive expectation. He braced himself . . .

And nothing happened.

After a few moments Jezzil opened his eyes, only to find himself confronting the three Taenarith. The central one was barely a foot away, his head moving from side to side as he scanned the area where Jezzil was standing. Then turning to the soldier on the right, he growled, "Where'd he go?"

The man he addressed shrugged elaborately, then pointed to the window in the next room with a questioning expression.

It was only then that Jezzil realized what was happening, and that knowledge shook him to his core.

They couldn't see him.

By Arenar's balls, *they couldn't see him!* He, Jezzil of the

Chonao, was a Caster, one who could cloud the mind of others with illusion, make them not-see what was before them. Some Casters could even Cast illusions and make others see things that were not there. But . . . how was this possible? The ability usually surfaced when the Caster was young, ten or twelve . . .

Jezzil's mind wavered, then reeled at the knowledge—

—and the man before him suddenly blinked, eyes going wide. With a baffled roar, he swung his morningstar. Even as Jezzil's trained reflexes took over and he dodged and ducked automatically, his mind was spinning and he was trying frantically to regain the Casting.

With a shout, the three Taenarith were after him, and he blundered through the room, tripping over bodies, feeling the flames lick at him from the walls. By now half the fortress must be alight, he realized.

With a last, frantic effort, he dived through the door into the next chamber and went rolling across the floor. Flame seared him; the bedclothes were on fire. Hearing pounding feet approaching the entrance, he concentrated, willing, grasping, and holding that center of passive calm, will beyond conscious thought, fear so great it went beyond panic into strength and calm . . .

And this time he could *feel* the Casting settle over him like a muffling blanket of invisibility.

The guards charged into the room and went rampaging around, roaring like dune-cats cheated of prey. Holding the Casting firm in his mind, as he would have gripped the hilt of his sword to defend himself physically, Jezzil rose to his feet, careful to make no sound. He had no idea whether the Casting would cloak him from their ears, but intended to take no chances.

His heart thudding with the effort of holding the Casting around him, sweat pouring off him as though he'd run a league in full armor under a summer sun, he moved cautiously over to the high, barred window. He noted with a stab of relief that the bars were set in a framework that could be swung inward.

The guards, not seeing their quarry, withdrew to the doorway and huddled there, whispering uneasily. Then, making the sign against demonic possession, they vanished into the smoke.

With a gasp, Jezzil released the Casting and reached for the pin holding the barred window shut. When he had it open, he shoved a chest, already sparking and smoldering, into place beneath it and climbed up.

Below him—far, far below him—lapped the waters of the moat. The Chonao remembered those half-seen shapes and nearly gagged with fear, but he knew this was his only way out. He could not possibly hold a Casting long enough enough to go back through that charnel house that held the bodies of his comrades—especially knowing in his soul that he belonged there with them—and down those steep stairs, and fight his way out through all those Taenarith. Where had they all come from? One of the raiding parties must have returned, he thought bitterly. Barus had said there was nothing to worry about. He'd been wrong—and had paid for his mistake with his life.

The fabric of Jezzil's tunic was beginning to smolder. He looked down again at the gray water. It was either the moat or go back into the next room, fall on his sword, and join his comrades.

Jezzil shook his head, hating himself, knowing himself for a twice-damned coward. But by all the weapons in Arenar's Arsenal, he wanted to *live*.

Hearing a shout behind him, he sprang from the windowsill, launching himself into empty air.

He was falling . . . falling . . .

It seemed to Jezzil that all of time and yet no time had passed before he struck foul, chilly water. The shock of his landing drove the breath from his lungs. He thrashed desperately, swimming upward with all his strength, but his heavy sword and armor weighed him down.

He gagged, fighting the water more fiercely than any enemy of flesh and blood, and knew, with a sudden, terrible clarity, that he was going to drown.

Frantically, his fingers found clasps, buckles, and the heavy armor slipped from his shoulders. His lungs were bursting as he discarded the metal-studded kilt. Fortunately, his stolen footgear was loose enough so he could kick it off.

With those burdens gone, Jezzil was able to kick upward, until his face broke water and he grabbed a quick, blessed breath before he sank once more.

His sword—his fingers found his sword belt, just as his thrashing brought him up again. Another breath, longer, deeper, then the flame-edged darkness of the moat enclosed him again.

He unbuckled the heavy sword belt, but hesitated. Abandon his sword to the dark water? He'd as soon leave an arm or a leg at the bottom.

Jezzil drew his weapon, then let the heavy, metal-studded sword belt and the attached sheath go. Kicking hard, he swam back up to the surface, and this time he managed to stay there, though the sword dragged at his arm.

Grasping the hilt, the Chonao warrior began a clumsy one-armed stroke-and-kick, his eyes fixed on the low stone wall that marked the other side of the moat.

He was within a body span of touching it when an oily ripple in the flame-marked water announced the arrival of one of the moat's rightful inhabitants.

In the murky darkness of the water it was naught but a black-scaled shadow. The eyes gleamed fiercely from behind horn-studded ridges, golden and slit-pupiled. Jezzil estimated each of those eyes to be as large as his closed fist.

The creature came straight for him, its mouth opening wide, wider . . .

Jezzil fumbled, trying to concentrate, but this time his effort at Casting flickered like a guttering candle. He tried harder, fighting panic, and felt the Casting work—but he knew he could not hold it.

The approaching behemoth swung its massive head back and forth, seeking its prey. As that huge, barely seen head moved toward him, Jezzil thrust hard with his sword, and the blade slid deep into the creature's eye.

The water exploded in a froth of blood and bubbles. Jezzil almost lost his sword as the creature thrashed violently. He pulled his arm back, felt his sword slide free.

He clawed his way up, up, toward air and sanity, his fingers still gripping the hilt. His arm burned with the effort of keeping his fingers tight. He was barely conscious when his head finally broke water.

He was sobbing for breath as he paddled clumsily along, and the water that washed his face tasted now of blood. Finally his questing hand encountered the edge of the mõat. He grabbed it, hung there, trying to breathe. Even under the threat of another moat inhabitant finding him, it took Jezzil nearly five minutes to regain enough strength to hoist himself and his sword up and over the low stone wall.

He lay on the ground for a while, hearing the roar of the fire, a few scattered shouts and screams, then rolled over and got to his feet. *Falar . . .* He allowed himself to think only of his horse. She was waiting for him. He longed for the silken feel of her coat, for her warm, living breath. *Falar.*

Jezzil glanced back only once as he staggered away from the fortress. The entire place was aflame, though most of the stone walls were still standing.

When the Chonao reached the horses, he went from animal to animal, removing their saddles and bridles and speaking the Word of Release that would free them to behave as horses once more, and not as Chonao war-mounts.

As he spoke the Word, over and over again, each horse snorted, then ambled away toward the field in search of grass.

Jezzil's hands were numb as he tightened Falar's girth. He was further disgraced to find that he hadn't the strength to mount Chonao-style, by swinging up onto Falar in one fluid motion. He was forced to use the stirrup, like a farmer or a tradesman.

As he rode out of the clearing, he heard the distant rumble of thunder, like an echo of the turmoil in his spirit. He had no idea where he was going or what he would do when he got there. He was Chonao, and he had left his brothers-in-arms. He was Chonao, and he had run from a battle. He was Chonao, and his honor was gone. He was Chonao, and his life was over.

Jezzil touched Falar's neck with the reins, and she headed south. The last of his strength flowed from him like water, like lifeblood, and he slumped over his horse's neck and began to weep.

2

Thia

Night gathered around the two stepped pyramids like the folds of demon wings, enclosing them in darkness and dank winter chill. High above the ground, deep within that ancient pile of stone, cold air gusted through a narrow window slit, abruptly extinguishing the flame of a single, guttering candle. Thia, Novice Priestess of Boq'urak, blinked and shivered in the sudden gloom. *Dark already? How could it be so late? I must hurry and finish . . .*

She fumbled as she relit the candle; her fingers were cramped with cold. Thia spared a moment to rub and flex them as she quickly read back over the page she had been copying and illuminating.

The sacred text told of the travels of Blessed Incarnate Balaj, recounting his sojourn among the infidels of the southern regions and of his first days in the northern reaches of Galrai, before Amaran had taken it over and renamed it Amavav. Balaj, dead for nearly a hundred-year, had been an educated man, as well as a lively and astute observer. His tales of his travels were fascinating to read— and, unlike most of the novice scriptorians, Thia *could* read.

A swift glance at the water clock on the wall made her gasp sharply. *Only a quarter-span till dinner? I'll have to run or I'll be late—and I daren't risk another penance!*

Novice priestesses who garnered too many penances did not remain long at the twin ziggurats in the capital city of Verang . . . there was no public disgrace, but they tended to quietly vanish overnight, without farewells. Thia supposed the High Ones did it that way so as not to dampen the spirits of those who remained by exposing them to the sight of the ones who had failed to please Boq'urak . . . but she found it unsettling all the same. And she had no desire to be sent home.

The novice could barely remember her home; she had been given to Boq'urak on her sixth birthday, nearly thirteen years ago. Her parents had wanted a son, and they'd been willing to give their daughter to the god in the hope Boq'urak would heed their prayers.

Thia could no longer picture their faces or recall her family name, but she still occasionally heard their voices in dreams. "Stay here with this~man for a little while, Thia, while we ~~~~~" Mother had said, her head bent so she seemed to study her dusty peasant shoes.

"No, Mama!" the child Thia had wailed. "I don't want to stay here!"

"It's only for a while, child," her mother had said, still not looking up.

"We'll be back for you, daughter," her father had added.

But they'd been lying, of course. Thia had known it instantly. Ever since she could remember, she'd been able to tell when anyone was lying. It was nothing she did consciously; she simply *knew*, the way she knew she had two hands and eyes so dark the pupil could scarcely be discerned from the surrounding iris. It had been a surprise to discover that most people could *not* immediately discern truth from falsehood.

So Thia had known instantly that they were not coming back, not ever. She would never forget the way she'd felt as she stood on the temple steps, her hand clamped in the huge hand of the elderly High Priest, watching as they walked away, melting into the throng of petitioners and worshipers until they were lost to view.

Sometimes, just before she fell asleep, Thia wondered whether Boq'urak had ever granted their wish for a boy. She was as devout as most novices, but she had never been able to force herself to pray for that.

The candle flame wavered in the night breeze, and she adjusted the wind guard, then began putting her work away. The next New Moon would mark her tenth year in the scriptorium, and she knew the routine well.

She picked up the tiny vials of cobalt blue, scarlet, and leaf-green ink and placed them on a tray. The big inkwell held the deep purple writing ink, a hue so dark that it would dry nearly black. Thia twisted the stopper into its mouth with a quick jerk of her slender wrist. Carrying the tray, she scurried over to the cabinet and inserted each vial into its proper slot.

Now for her horn-pens and brushes . . . her steps came faster as she cleaned and stowed her materials away. At last only the texts themselves and the tiny, precious vial of liquid gold remained. Thia scurried to put the gleaming vial in its correct place, then locked the small cabinet with the key she carried on her scarlet cord that girdled her gray, hooded robe. Her bare feet were soundless against the massive yellow sandstone blocks that formed the floor and walls of the scriptorium.

As she examined the day's work, automatically checking each page to make sure the inks were dry, and smoothing out any wrinkles, she forced herself to be careful. If she damaged a Sacred Text, that would be an even worse penance than being late for dinner.

Thia had actually been in the scriptorium on the day that Ryleese had overturned her desk and spilled all her inks onto the text she'd been copying. It had been awful, hearing the other girl's shrieks and wails for mercy as the scriptorians dragged her away. They said she'd been possessed by Outer Demons who had caused her clumsiness to punish her

for sinning, and that under questioning she'd blasphemed.
They said that Ryleese was fortunate that Boq'urak, in His
mercy, had granted her the blessing of cleansing.

All Thia knew for sure was that two days later Ryleese
had been declared Chosen and given to Boq'urak. Thia
swallowed uneasily. *Don't think about it. Concentrate . . .*

As she rolled up the day's work, she felt pride in the neat
rows of precise letters, the beautifully illuminated capitals
that marked the beginning of each page. *Thank you, Master
Varn,* she thought, remembering the first day he'd noticed
her. She'd been sitting on her stool at this very same desk,
eagerly poring over a scroll, wondering about the meaning
of the words and letters on the vellum. Unlike many of the
other fledgling scriptorians, Thia understood the theory of
written language, if not the symbols themselves. Each time
she worked here, she listened intently to all the conversations going on around her, and she'd learned quite a bit that
way. Until that day . . . Her lips curved in a smile as she remembered . . .

She had been on this very stool, at this very same desk.
She was all alone, and so dared to trace the letters with her
finger, wondering what they meant. "What are you?" she'd
whispered softly, under her breath. "What do you say?"

As if in answer to her plea, a deep voice said, almost in
her ear, "That is the letter om-ee."

Startled, she'd swung around in her seat to find Master
Varn, vivid in his scarlet robe, standing beside her. The
priest was a handsome man, with the typical coloring that
betokened Northern blood—like Thia, he was tall and slen-
derly formed, with dark, dark eyes. Like all the priests and
priestesses, his skull was shaven, but he was standing so
close that the girl could see a faint pale fuzz on his pate, just
like the fuzz that she had to remove from her own head. His
hair must be the same color as her own, the color of ashes
just before they blew away.

"And that one there is the letter tyy," he said quietly. He
put out his hand, and his fingers closed around Thia's, warm
and strong. "Would you like to know all of them?"

Thia had stared at him worshipfully. "Oh, yes, Master! What word is that?"

"That word is 'ocean,' " he said.

" 'Ocean,' " she repeated, under her breath. "What is an ocean, Master?"

"A body of water. Like a sea, but larger. They lie on the other side of Boq'urain."

"The other side, Master?"

"The world is shaped like a ball, child."

The child priestess had stared up at the priest who would become her Mentor, her dark eyes wide with amazement. "How can that be? If I look out any window, the world is flat, save for the mountains surrounding us here in Verang. If I look out through the pass, to the sea, it is flat. If the world was shaped like a ball, the sea would pour off it!"

He'd smiled at her, his big white teeth flashing in amusement. "Not only curious, but intelligent," he said, and the approval in his voice made the girl flush with pleasure. "Would you like me to teach you to read, little one?"

Thia could only nod, struck dumb with the enormity of his offer. Young as she was, she'd known it was forbidden for the novices to read, but she wanted to learn so badly that she'd convinced herself that she could do her job better, copy better, for the glory and worship of Boq'urak if she knew *what* she was copying. So they'd met, secretly, late at night, for months, then years, while Varn taught her . . . first to read, then about the world as he knew it. Her Mentor had traveled as a missionary priest in his youth, and he told her all about his journeys as he'd preached Boq'urak's scripture and doctrine.

Thia had learned to be circumspect, to never reveal that she and her Mentor had a relationship outside the ordinary one of Mentor and novice. She knew that revealing their mutual transgression would result in both of them being thrown out of the temple, or worse. And she'd treasured every minute they spent together. Her Master was the wisest, kindest man in the world.

Master Varn had made it possible for her to achieve her

dearest wish—to learn, to understand, to accumulate knowledge. He'd even arranged for her to leave the temple complex on several occasions, to accompany some of the lay workers when they went to buy provisions or other goods. Unlike her sisters, she knew what money was for, and how to count it. The novice had watched the townspeople at work and at play, had witnessed staggering drunks and rowdy fights between street urchins, seen lovers holding hands and embracing . . .

Of course, Thia had averted her eyes quickly from such sights. She was a Sacred Vessel, soon to take her final vows. Such carnal pleasures were not for her.

Thia would not even allow herself to recall the dreams that had come to her after seeing those lovers. Dreams where Master Varn touched her face, her hand, even, once, her breasts . . .

Realizing where her memories had led her, the novice blushed violently. *What is wrong with you? Be careful, or you'll make a mistake! Do you want to wind up Chosen?*

Memories of the daily sacrifice performed before dawn each morning to ensure that the Sun would rise made the novice shiver, her chest suddenly tight. To have a huge hole punched into one's breast, so that the entire living heart could be removed . . .

But she knew it was necessary. Boq'urain needed the Sun for the crops to flourish and the people to thrive, but . . .

But sometimes the Chosen would remain conscious for a long minute as they beheld their own dripping, pumping hearts. Usually they lost consciousness and died quickly, but not always. Thia had learned to look at their hearts, rather than their faces, since it was a transgression to look elsewhere than at the High Priests and their victims.

All of the scrolls were now safely stowed. Thia closed the cabinets, slid the bolts into place, and activated the locking bars with urgent haste. Seconds ticked by in the novice's head as she extinguished the candle and darted out the door, carefully closing and locking it behind her. Then, holding the skirt of her gray habit high, she began to run.

The corridors around her were whitewashed, nearly featureless, and spotlessly clean due to the ministrations of the
acolytes and postulants. Thia's bare feet pattered against
chill stone as she ran, but she was used to it and never noticed
the cold hardness. Verang was a city built in the mountains,
surrounded by peaks on three sides . . . even the summers
were chilly. Winters could be deadly for the unprotected.

Swish-slap, swish-slap . . . the sound of her feet striking
stone warred with the pounding of her heart. She rounded a
corner, darted down a flight of stairs so time-worn that a
faint depression hollowed the center of each step.

Down . . . down. Around another corner. So far she had
not met another soul, and that was a bad sign. That meant the
community was gathering in the eastern ziggurat, where the
refectory was located. Acolytes and lay priests and priestesses would be moving among the rows of tables and
benches, handing out bowls of barley-lamb soup and thick
chunks of bread for sopping up the broth. Thia had not eaten
since the noon repast, six hours ago; her stomach rumbled
loudly at the thought of food.

She hesitated but a bare instant at the tapestry near the end
of an otherwise bare corridor, then lifted it and slid through
the door beyond into darkness. Fumbling with her cold fingers, she lit her tiny travel-candle, shielded from drafts in its
protective cylinder of metal.

No time to run down the ten tiers of steps that led down
from the western pyramid, cross the cobbled courtyard, and
then up the ten tiers to the eastern ziggurat. Instead she
would take the secret way, the way Master Varn had first
shown her all those years ago. It was forbidden—but taking
it would save her so much time that it was worth the risk.

The corridor here was more like a tunnel; the blocks of
gray granite were bare of whitewash. The novice kilted her
habit up into the knotted scarlet scourge that served as her
belt and set off again. The flame from her tiny lantern threw
barely enough light for her to see ten paces ahead, but she
knew these secret ways well; she had been traveling them for
years.

There were crypts down here, and that was not all. Secret conference rooms hidden within mazes, ancient altars and confessional cubbies . . . even abandoned prison cells and places of torture. It was in the first level beneath the western ziggurat that she and Master Varn had conducted their clandestine lessons, hunched together over a single flickering flame as Thia pored over reading scrolls or laboriously worked out the sums the High One set her to ciphering. Varn had warned her sternly against venturing below the first level, but over the years, Thia had explored on her own, becoming braver as she translated the guiding symbols that marked each tunnel.

Each branching tunnel was marked with secret signs, combinations of letters and numbers. Some were in script so old that no one alive could translate it. But overlaying the ancient runes were modern letters and numbers that provided an infallible guide to one lessoned in its use. Even though she had been this way many times before, Thia was careful to check the symbols. All of the tunnels looked alike, and a mistake could mean a slow and torturous death, wandering these hidden ways without hope of being found and rescued.

Forty-two, Sun sign, overscribed with the letter kay, she read, scarcely pausing in the swaying light to dart down the leftmost branch of a triad of tunnels.

She was now far, far below the level of the ziggurat, deep within the foot of the mountain itself. It was so cold that her nipples tightened, and she hugged her arms across her breasts. Her steps came quicker in the chill dankness. This place . . . she had never traversed this section without the sense that someone was watching. The walls were clammy, the floor sloped down, steadily down.

Despite her urgency, Thia came to an abrupt halt when the sounds of chanting mixed with the rush of water reached her ears. *Oh, no! One of the Hidden Rites! It has to be . . .*

Her mouth went dry. She had never seen one of the secret ceremonies. She was only a novice, and it was forbidden for her to even stand here and listen to the chanting. And yet . . . her path led through a gallery that ran along the top of the huge chamber where the rites were held. There was no other way she could go.

For a moment she hesitated, half turning to look back up the tunnel. Dare she try it? Or should she go back all that long, weary way to the western ziggurat? If she were caught in the vicinity of a Hidden Rite . . . She had no idea what would happen to her, and did not even want to think about it. On the other hand, the stone parapet lining the gallery passage was low but thick, with small ornamental patterns cut into the stone. If she stayed low and crept along, the High Ones would not see her. And she was over halfway to her destination . . .

With a sudden squaring of her shoulders, Thia began to run again, down the tunnel, toward the huge, echoing chamber. The chanting sounds grew louder and were now mixed with other sounds, low and muffled, with an occasional loud shriek or wail rising above the rest of the cacophony.

Reaching the huge archway that led into the gallery above the enormous chamber, Thia extinguished her light, dropped to her hands and knees, then began inching along, careful to stay below the level of the ornamental pattern cut into the parapet. The stone of the gallery floor was smooth and chill against her hands. Her robe caught her as she tried to creep, until she kilted it up to mid-thigh. Her feet were toughened by constantly going barefoot, but her hands and knees began to ache almost immediately.

When she reached the first hole in the parapet, she could not resist putting her eye to it and gazing down at the rite that was under way.

The chamber beneath her had been hollowed out over ages by an underground branch of the River Ver. The water rushed through the chamber, cold and dark as the mountains in winter. The chill of the black water reached the novice even in her high perch. Great stone icicles hung from the ceiling and thrust upward from the floor, glistening in the light of dozens of torches.

Beside the rushing river stood a huddled group of children, a full score of them, ranging in age from perhaps ten to

a few that could barely toddle. All were dressed in the white
flowing robes of Boq'urak's Chosen.

Thia made a low sound in her throat, even as her. hands
went up to cover her mouth. Children? *Babies*? Dressed for
the sacrifice? *By all that was sacred—no!*

But there they were. Most of them were crying, and the
ten High Priests moved among them with alabaster bowls,
carefully collecting their tears, encouraging them with
pokes and frowns to cry harder. One youngster, a lad of perhaps nine who stood scornfully tearless, suddenly broke and
ran for the entrance, but was roughly dragged back. He began to weep, and the High Ones scurried to catch his tears,
as though they were to be treasured above all.

Thia had lived with sacrifice as a daily part of her life
since she had first come to Verang. She'd been taught to
think of the Chosen as fortunate, because as soon as they
died, they would be with Boq'urak in the Paradise Beyond
the Sun. It helped that the Chosen were usually enemies of
Amaran, either outlaws, captives, or enemies of the state.
They were not innocent, they were being given a wonderful
opportunity to redeem themselves and to enter Paradise.

But to sacrifice children? Innocent children? It was unthinkable! How could Boq'urak demand this? How could
anyone do this?

Now she knew why the Hidden Rites were shrouded in
such secrecy, concealed in the bowels of the mountain. It
was only because of Master Varn's illicit teachings that
she'd learned the codes that had allowed her to ferret out the
tunnels leading to this place. He'd warned her against going
down to the lowest tunnels, and now she knew why.

The chamber contained a huge obsidian altar-stone, a
solid square block of blackness that seemed to draw the light
of the torches as it lay gleaming and ready.

Ready for what?

Not for the children, it seemed. Thia tried to make herself
crawl on, away from what she knew must be coming, but she
was frozen with horror. She tried to close her eyes as the

High Priest, in his scarlet robe, raised a stone knife to the first little one's throat. But she could not look away.

A quick slash, a hideous, gurgling moan, and the little girl collapsed, twitching, her white robe spattered with scarlet even more vivid than the High Priest's robe. Carefully, the High Ones collected a generous dollop of blood, then poured it into the rushing river, chanting loudly all the while. The remaining children screamed and wailed, and a few of them struggled to break past the line of priests, but to no avail.

Quickly, one by one, each child was sacrificed. They saved the boy who had tried to escape until last. The child kicked and shrieked, bit and fought like a wild snow-cat from the heights, but they held him hand and foot and head, and the knife moved, slicing slowly through his pulsing throat until finally he was still.

Thia bit down on her finger until her own blood flowed sickly sweet into her mouth, making her chapped lips sting as she fought not to be noisily sick.

All thought of dinner and why she had come down here had vanished. The novice knew she was doomed. Boq'urak saw everything, was All-Powerful. Surely He could see her now. Surely any moment a blast from the heavens would strike her, reducing her to a charred heap of flesh and blackened bone. But that would be better than living with what she had learned, Thia thought, blindly wiping away tears.

The children, the children . . . those poor little ones . . .

But the expected smiting did not come. Thia watched dully as one of the High Ones made a summoning gesture, and two more entered, half supporting a swaying figure between them. The novice recognized the young woman . . . Narda, a first-year priestess. She'd been a year ahead of Thia throughout their postulancy and novitiate.

Narda was a pretty young woman with dark eyes, hair the color of winter snow-roses, and a full, womanly figure. Thia did not know her well, but she remembered what an expert cook she'd been while they'd served together in the kitchen.

Now Narda's dark eyes looked twice their normal size. She was smiling, an ecstatic, wide smile of complete bliss.

Drugged, Thia realized.

One of the High Ones threw a handful of dust onto a brazier that was burning near the collapsed bodies of the children, and coils of reddish smoke began eddying up from the coals. Thia pressed herself against the floor, trying to breathe shallowly, lest she lose consciousness from the intoxicating fumes.

Narda's Mentor, a High One whose name Thia didn't know, approached the young priestess, and her smile widened even further as she gazed at his familiar features. The chanting, which had subsided to a throbbing background murmur, picked up tempo and grew louder, increasing in intensity until it made Thia's head pound even worse than the fumes from the smoldering brazier.

Waves of *something* began to fill the air. Thia could not see it, could only sense its presence. It was like sensing the place where lightning had struck only moments before . . . a prickling of the downy hairs on her body, as though some unseen hand had tipped a sacrificial bowl filled with cold, congealed blood and allowed it to engulf her spirit. The novice struggled not to scream aloud in protest against that unseen presence.

When she glanced through the hole in the parapet again, she saw that the High Ones were stretching Narda out on the huge block of black stone, securing her wrists and ankles to rings embedded in the rock. Narda's Mentor bent over her and with one fluid motion, tore the priestess's white robe from neck to ankles, rending it in two. For the first time, Narda's smile faded; her expression of dreamy contentment vanished.

The priestess shook her head, her gaze focusing on her Mentor as he stood at her feet, his voice rising above the others in the chant. She shook her head again, then cried out in fear.

Thia could not see the Mentor's face, but she was aware, suddenly, that he was Changing.

Changing . . .

At first it was as though his shadow had gathered around

the outlines of his body, gathered and rippled in the torch-light. The shape of his head altered, grew broader, more domed. His hands . . . they curled, and ridges of scaled flesh sprouted upward from the backs. The fingers were engulfed, turning to talons like those of a lizard.

By all that is holy—he is becoming Incarnate!

Thia knew that Boq'urak could transform Himself into the bodies of his High Priests for brief periods of time, there to work miracles. She knew that from her illicit reading. But to even reveal that she knew of the Incarnation Rite, Master Varn had warned her, would mean her death. To actually *see* it . . . she stifled a whimper of utter despair.

The chanting intensified, but all of the priests had fallen back against the walls, as though they did not want to be too close to the god when He became Incarnate.

With a muttered growl, the transforming Mentor threw off his robe. He had nearly doubled in size, and was half again as tall as his human height. Tentacles sprouted from his sides, two on each side, flexible tentacles tipped with a sucker at each end. In the depths of each sucker was a viciously curved claw or tooth. His skin darkened, darkened . . . It was now a smoky violet, now a brownish purple . . .

Scales erupted from beneath his skin. A ridge of frilled flesh poked up from his back, ran down to a tail that sud-denly extruded, whip-thin. His body seemed to constantly crawl and shift, as though it were somehow fluid, mutable.

Thia felt her mind reel, and fought to stay conscious. She couldn't afford to faint.

The Incarnate's breathing intensified, changed rhythm, and He growled again, louder, as He bent forward. His trans-formed "hand" came up to rake His talons along Narda's bared body.

The priestess, who had closed her eyes as though she could not bear to see what was happening, opened them. Her mouth opened, and Thia's throat ached in sympathy. Narda was try-ing to scream, but like one caught in a nightmare, she could not force any sound to emerge. Narda began to thrash and struggle as the Incarnate fell on her, between her parted thighs.

Thia saw His body plunge downward, and finally Narda's scream burst free and rang in the air, rising even above the sounds of the chanting. For a moment Thia wondered if the Incarnate was going to devour the young woman, then she blinked in horrified realization. The novice had been only six when she'd left the farm, but farm children grew up quickly, and no effort had been made to keep her away from the sight of the animals mating.

Mating . . .

Thia gagged, choked, and time seemed to slip sideways, away from her. She did not—quite—lose consciousness. Some shred of self-preservation made her cling to a thread of reality. She returned to full awareness to find herself lying with her cheek pressed against the floor, her eyes tightly shut. She had to force herself to open them.

The novice pushed herself upward and managed to crawl a few feet farther along the gallery, forcing herself not to look. She could not shut out the sounds, however, the wet, gurgling noises, the sucking sounds. There was no further sound from Narda.

How could Boq'urak's High Ones lend themselves to such a rite? How could they let themselves be used in that fashion? Had her own Mentor, Master Varn, let that happen to him?

The thought of her esteemed teacher lending his body to be used in that obscene manner made her reel sideways, until she fetched up against the stone parapet again.

If you faint, they'll find you. You'll be punished. The same thing might happen to you. You have to get away. Away from the temple, away from Verang, away from Amaran. Get away, away, away, away from that thing!

That thing, the Incarnate . . . Had it discovered her? She couldn't stop herself from looking down, through another hole in the stonework.

The chanting was now at its height. Plumes of reddish smoke filled the air, curdling and thickening as they wrapped tendrils around the body of the now fully transformed priest. He was enormous—the body of the god nearly eclipsed the black stone altar. With a last, obscene plunge of His torso, He stiffened, then a shudder rippled through the giant frame. The tail lashed like an angry cat's.

Boq'urak reared back, straightening, and Thia could see Narda's body. Her throat was a bloody ruin, and huge puckered circles oozed red along her sides. Her parted thighs were scarlet.

The god raised His head, and for the first time Thia saw the countenance of the being she had been trained to worship above all.

Boq'urak's face was wide, with a frill of flesh where the priest's brows had been, extending across His face to shield slits that had replaced His ears. The god had eyes, two huge, staring, lidless eyes that seemed to see everything. No nose. A sucker appendage with a single tooth served as the creature's mouth. The facial skin was lighter than the body, a pale gray.

Thia stared into those eyes, and knew that Boq'urak saw her. Saw her, and knew her for who she was.

She was dead, and she knew it, but her body refused to believe. With a gasp, the novice scuttled through the doorway and, scrambling to her feet, ran like a hunted animal.

Her mind was whirling, and she barely retained sense enough to check the doorposts for the secret signs. Her flying feet carried her up steps, down tunnels, up more stairs. She turned the corner into the hallway leading out of the ziggurat, breath sobbing, feet like two lumps of ice—

—and crashed full-force against a solid, unyielding form. Her mind gibbered and teetered on the edge of utter madness for a moment, then she realized the newcomer was human.

She staggered back, gasping, and looked up, ready to babble explanations and apologies.

"Master!" she cried. "Oh, thank Boq'urak!"

Master Varn stood gazing at her, his dark brows drawing together in concern. "Thia! Child, where have you been?"

"I . . . I . . ." She dragged in a deep breath, marshaled her wits, forced her mind to cast off its panic and work again. She made the proper obeisance of a novice to a High One, then plunged into the ritual response, grateful not to have to think about what she was saying. "Master, this unworthy one begs forgiveness. I am late to supper. Assign me penance, that I may redeem myself and cast off my sin."

He was staring down at her, and his eyes, behind his hooded lids, were filled with a mixture of exasperation and humor. "Thia, child! What shall I do with you? Late *again*! Do you know how many—"

He broke off as Thia grabbed his sleeve, clutching it in both hands, twisting. "Master Varn, do you know what they're *doing* down there? They killed children! And Narda—"

She stopped, gagging, one hand pressed to her mouth.

Master Varn stared down at her, his black eyes intent. "What? What are you saying?"

"It's true, I *saw* it!" Thia whispered. She was shaking and her knees threatened to buckle. Master Varn put a steadying hand on her shoulder, and gratefully, she rested her forehead against his chest. His warmth steadied her, comforted her.

"You *saw*?" his voice was strained. "Tell me what you saw, child."

"A monster," she whispered into the folds of his robe, whimpering at the memory. "Horrible." She raised her head. "We have to stop them."

"I understand," he said. "We must—" He broke off, eyes widening, then narrowing. His entire body stiffened and he blinked several times. Then his gaze once again fixed on her.

Thia gazed up at him, feeling a chill that had nothing to do with the fact that it was winter and the ancient stones were as cold as well water. "You, you believe me, don't you?"

"Yes I do," he said steadily. "I know you, child. You could never lie to me."

"Have you ever seen . . . it?" she asked.

"No," he said. "No, of course not."

He's lying. Thia knew it immediately. *How could I have been so stupid? Of course he's seen it!* She felt betrayed. Only her realization that she was in terrible danger kept her from collapsing into tears. She bowed her head, hiding her face against his robe, thinking fast. *He's a priest of Boq'urak. They say Boq'urak can communicate His wishes to His priests. Boq'urak is Incarnate even now. Could He be communicating with Master Varn?*

Whether or not the Incarnate was sending instructions to her Master, she couldn't take the chance that Varn would let her leave, after what she'd admitted to seeing. *I have to get away!*

Just then her Master wrapped both arms around her, holding her tightly, rocking her. Once she had longed for such an embrace from him. Now, she shuddered with revulsion.

He was whispering softly, so softly that the novice could barely make out the words. "Child, child . . . what shall I do with you?"

Thia gulped, forced herself to think clearly. *I must get away.* She raised her head and looked up at him. "Master, we can leave together. Fetch your cloak. I will wait here."

Gently, she pulled back, and he released her.

Thia smiled shakily at him. "Hurry, Master!"

He hesitated, and for a moment Thia thought he was going to turn away. Then he shook his head. "No. You must come with me." He took a step toward her.

Thia took a step back.

His eyes narrowed as he took in her reaction. "Child, calm yourself. You trust me, yes? Come, I will take you to a place where you will be safe, and we can talk."

He extended his hand, smiling reassuringly.

He was lying, and Thia knew it as surely as she knew the sun would not rise without the predawn sacrifice of the Chosen each day. She shook her head and backed away farther. "I'm afraid. It was horrible."

"I know," he said, speaking truth. He hesitated, then repeated, "Child, come here . . ." Thia realized that he was torn, truly torn, between his duty to the god and his genuine affection for his protégé.

She stood there, wondering what she should do. He was between her and the way to freedom, the corridor that led outside, to the open air, to the postern gate that led away from the temple courtyard, to the path that was the shortcut down the mountain to Verang.

A brief memory flashed into her mind. Once, in the streets of Verang, she had seen two streetboys fighting, and the smaller one had disabled the other in a most decisive manner . . .

Thia took a step forward, her hands going to the skirts of her habit, still partially kilted up. She took another step.

Varn smiled, his mouth curved upward, but there was no warmth in his eyes. "We will talk, child," he said.

Thia took another step—

—and then her foot flashed upward with all her strength in a hard, swift, kick. Her scrunched-up toes buried themselves in the space between her Mentor's legs, bunching his robe around her. For a second her foot was encased in warmth and softness.

Then she leaped backward, in time to see Varn's eyes roll back in his head. The High One dropped to his knees, then rolled over on his side, gagging and writhing in agony.

"Master Varn, I'm so sorry, please, please forgive me . . ." Thia fell to her own knees, wondering if she had killed him.

But he was still breathing, though he did not seem aware of her or her babbled apologies. The novice made the Sign of the Incarnate over his gasping form, then began to pray.

"Boq'urak Incarnate, save thy servant, heal him, bless him, let him not know pain, only thy blessed succor—" Realizing what she was saying, Thia stopped, shook herself, and scuttled backward. What was she doing? Praying to that . . . that thing? That obscenity? Never again! Not if they sacrificed her a thousand times!

"I'm sorry," she whispered, edging around her fallen Mentor. "Farewell, Master."

Grabbing up her skirts, she began running again. Corridors and doorways flashed by, until she was at the portal leading to the courtyard. She eased the big door open and slipped out, into the yard where patches of frozen slush made her feet burn as she stumbled and slid through them. Across the courtyard, dodging into the blessed shadows, she scurried to stay out of the torchlight. Thia shivered as she felt the first lash of the wind.

Even the mountains seemed to bend down and look at her, making her feel hemmed in as she wrestled with the latch of the postern gate. Surely the god would not let her get away! Surely she would be struck down at any moment in a blast of fire—or perhaps He would turn her to stone, as a lesson to other erring novices.

Through the postern gate, now, and the pathway down the mountain stretched before her. No alarm yet sounded. She was outside at night, and that alone was an offense worthy of being declared tomorrow's Chosen and being offered to the god to ensure the sunrise.

Freezing, snow-laden air assaulted her shaven pate, her bare feet. The first storm of the season had arrived. Pulling up her hood and hunkering low against the blast of the wind, Thia began to run again, her arms wrapped around her, holding her warmth in, holding her life to her. It was all she had . . . and who knew how long Boq'urak would choose to toy with her, permitting her to remain alive?

Perhaps it would be better just to sink down into the deepening snow, stay still for a very few minutes and let the blizzard work its will. It would be a brief, merciful death, compared to what the High Ones would do to her.

But something in Thia's nature would not allow that. While she lived, she would fight to keep on living.

Her jaw tight with resolve—and to keep her teeth from chattering—Thia trotted on, down the path, down the mountain.

She did not look back.

Khith

The ruins of the Ancients stood deep within the Sarsithe Jungle, surrounded by monstrous trees that seemingly challenged the clouds. The ruins were so old that trees had grown and spread amidst them, and the roots of the forest giants cradled, clenched, and, in some cases, crushed the strange building materials of the Ancients. Gnarled gray roots stretched down like talons to enclose the opalescent material of the cracked domes. Broken spires shimmered with bands of oil-slick color amid the lacy green curtains of selshir leaves. The caved-in domes and the ruined spires seemed to sprout from the soil and the broken paving like giant fungi.

None of the Hthras, even Khith, who had been studying them for nearly thirty years, knew who those Ancients had been. They had left no images of themselves. They were not Hthras, that was certain—the dimensions of their buildings, their doorways, their furnishings, proved that. Even a tall human could walk into one of the ruined domes without stooping. Khith was tall for a Hthras, yet the scholar stood barely half the height of one of those vine-tangled doorways.

Khith's people lived in the giant trees, avoiding the ruins as forbidden. But Khith was . . . different. Had always been different. Ever since it had reached the age of responsibility—though not maturity, for Khith had never developed a sexual attraction for another Hthras, and thus remained in the neuter phase—the scholar had made frequent trips into the places other Hthras shunned, searching out the secrets of the ruins.

Unlike most of its people, Khith enjoyed solitude. The scholar's father had been a trader who did most of his trade with humans, and as a result, Khith had spent more of its childhood years interacting with human children than with its own kind. The ruins fascinated the scholar; their mysteries beckoned the young Hthras into defying one of the most basic tenets of the Hthras culture—that the ruins of the Ancients were forbidden ground.

The Hthras authorities had spoken to the young scholar several times, cautioning it against such investigation. Once, the scholar had even been summoned to a meeting of the Council of Elders.

"The Ancients had great powers, but they were reckless, and at the end, wicked," First Elder Nkotha had admonished, shaking a bony digit at the younger Hthras. "They unleashed such destruction as has never been seen, according to our legends. There are even hints that *they* caused the Great Waste that lies to the east of the Sarsithe. Before their time, that land was a garden. Now it is death for any who walk there for more than a handful of days."

Khith stared at the Council of Elders, fascinated. "How could that happen? The Great Waste is larger even than the Sarsithe! And our forest is larger than the islands of Pela and Taenarith put together. The Ancients' sorcery must have been as far above our magic as we are above the animals of the forest! How could they control such power? Elder, if we could but solve their mysteries—"

"Control . . . that is the point, youngling!" old Nkotha broke in, pounding a veiny fist on the table. "They *had* no control! They unleashed what they did not understand, and could not control! We Hthras will not make that same mistake . . . we will *not*!" Nkotha sank back in her seat, panting, and her attendant bent over her solicitously.

"Nkotha is the wisest among us," Second Elder Sthaal declared. "We are determined never again to delve into those forbidden things, lest the fate that befell the Ancients become ours. Cease your investigations, youngling!"

With an aching heart, Khith had bowed its head and spoken the words the Elders wanted to hear. "I shall obey, Elders. I respect your wisdom."

And, for many years, Khith had kept its promise. The scholar had gone back to live with its people among the treetops, in their cities of bell-shaped dwellings Hthras Growers had ripened in their nurseries. Hthras knew plants, knew growing things, as no other creatures did. Rather than maim or destroy the jungle to accommodate their species, they cultivated, coaxed, and "convinced" it to do their bidding.

But after another handful of years had passed, years of frustration when none of the unmated Hthras caught its eye, Khith's curiosity about the Ancients proved more than it could conquer, and one day the scholar went out for a walk . . . and never returned to the treetops. Instead, Khith stole back to the ruins and resumed its studies there.

The Hthras scholar had always been good with the magic of its people: herb lore, healing, a little farseeing, magics to sooth, confuse, or frighten. But the Ancients had delved into so many powerful magics! Deep in vaults beneath the ruins, the Hthras scholar found ancient texts, some crumbling, others miraculously preserved. Khith spent days laboriously copying the most decaying tomes. Slowly, the Hthras worked at deciphering their language, puzzling out their letters and numbers, slowly piecing together words, phrases, and finally reading the ancient texts. It took the Hthras scholar nearly two years to learn to read the language of the Ancients, and longer still to be able to understand and put into practice what it had so painstakingly translated.

At first Khith had maintained some discreet ties with other Hthras villages, trading with them for food and supplies, but then, sensing the disapproval of the Council of Elders and realizing it was under observation, the scholar went underground, literally. The domes and structures still visible on the forest floor represented only a small part of the Ancients' city. Beneath the ground were networks of chambers and seemingly endless tunnels. There were also many record storerooms and several libraries. For the past half-year Khith had ventured out mostly at night to search the jungle for herbs and food.

The scholar had been content with its search for knowledge. Content . . . until the dreams had started.

Dreams held great import for the Hthras. And every night for the past tenday, Khith had dreamed of jaws in the night, of teeth tearing, of trying to run from an unseen foe while weighted down with invisible chains.

Khith knew that such dreams should be taken seriously . . . but these warnings were so vague, so formless. It was not enough for the scholar to sense danger approaching—Khith needed to know what the danger was, and who presented it.

Reluctantly, the scholar had realized that it must find out what those ominous dreams portended.

So it was that one afternoon Khith sat perched atop a tall stool in one of those underground chambers where the Ancients had practiced their version of alchemy. The scholar frowned as it stared uneasily at a bowl of oily black liquid resting on the high table before it.

Hthras foretelling spells usually caused the worker to dream in highly symbolic terms of danger. Such dreams could be useful, but they required interpretation, and they were never precise.

But the spells of the Ancients were different.

Khith had found this spell in a crumbling tome, and it had been extremely difficult to translate the fragmentary and vermin-chewed pages. And even when it had determined the proper ingredients, there was something missing—the correct proportions. For that, Khith had to experiment, trusting instincts honed by years of experience in brewing potions, tisanes, infusions, and teas.

This brew was the strongest it had ever made, the most distilled. Khith stared at the concoction, thinking perhaps that knowledge wasn't worth the risk. The scholar wasn't sure exactly what the effects might be, but it knew lian roots were a powerful hallucinogen. There were tales among the Hthras of magic workers who had taken potions to farsee, only to leap to their deaths from their homes in the forest giants, thinking themselves winged or invulnerable.

But even now the council might be meeting . . .

Khith stared at the dark, viscous liquid, feeling a chill that had nothing to do with the temperature control that still prevailed, deep in the bowels of the ancient city. It had worked for two days to decoct this mixture. But . . . would it work for anyone but an Ancient—whatever they had been like?

What if it poisons me? Khith thought. *I could die down here and no one would ever know.* The thought caused the silky fur on its arms and back to stir and rise up in reaction to danger. Its tail lashed back and forth.

And yet, to have the power to see things happening far away, or possibly even the future . . .

The mixture was a distillation of lian roots and vilneg leaves. The Hthras had combined them, adding a dollop of its own blood to give the spell strength and focus. *But if I haven't the courage to use what I've learned, I might as well go back to my village, give up sorcery,* the scholar thought. *There is no gain without risk.*

Khith stared at the potion for another moment, then resolutely picked up the bowl, balancing it on its slender, four-digited hands. Cautiously, it sniffed the brew, its nostril-flaps quivering at the sharp, bitter odor. It hesitated for only a second. *I must know!*

The liquid tasted every bit as vile as Khith had expected. The scholar's throat tightened, and for a moment it feared its stomach would revolt. Putting down the bowl, it clapped both hands over its narrow-lipped mouth, fighting the urge to retch.

Now to say the words . . .

Khith stared down at the text, and the letters tilted strangely. It blinked, trying to read the words, but its eyes would no longer track.

The Hthras looked up, and slowly, the room swung, rippled, and elongated. It was now long and narrow, like a burial net. Then it contracted, rotated, and widened, extending farther, farther . . .

With some small, still unaffected portion of its mind, Khith remembered that the potion was a powerful hallucinogen. *Must focus . . . speak the spell . . .*

Fumbling atop the table, the Hthras managed to close one narrow-fingered hand around the rune-pieces carved from jagowa bone. Shaking the pieces, it mumbled:

> *"Forest-juice, help me see,*
> *Bones of hunter, let me hear,*
> *Show me those who wish me harm,*
> *Let me farsee, so to warn . . ."*

As Khith spoke the final words of the charm, it opened its fingers and the bone pieces thudded down onto the tabletop. Khith peered at the pattern. *The rune-sign for danger . . . the sign for the present or the near future, the jagowa itself . . .* As it peered down, its vision blurred, swam, then darkness gathered around the Hthras . . . grew . . . enfolded . . .

Khith sighed and closed its eyes, letting the darkness take it.

It opened its eyes and was in a different place, seeing with eyes that were . . . strange. Eyes that did not perceive most shades of color, eyes that were faceted, so that each view was repeated a hundred or more times. Khith tried to blink, tried to focus, but the eyes it was seeing through were so alien, it was several minutes before it could force itself to see through only one of the multiple eye-lenses and make out what lay before it.

The Council of Elders sat hunched around a high table. Their voices sounded odd through the insectoid ears, but

Khith could hear them. ". . . cannot allow this to go on," the Eldest was saying. "Who knows what young Khith has found there, in those ruins? Foolish one! We warned it. In this very chamber, we told it what would happen!"

Third Eldest spoke up. "Shall I summon the Peacekeepers?"

First Elder Nkotha considered, then signaled assent. "Yes, do so. And tell them to bring their Trackers. We cannot have Khith roaming loose after we have angered it. It was a Sorcerer before living amidst the remains of the Ancients. What vile spells may it have learned from them?"

Third Elder made a quick gesture of assent and respect, then stood to leave the chamber.

"Go with the Peacekeepers, Drahnik, Vleth." Nkotha motioned to two of the youngest Elders. "See that no one is harmed. The Trackers can be dangerous when loosed."

The Elders rose and the three of them left the Council Chamber.

Khith made an effort to withdraw its mind from the creature that was hosting it, but the spell still held it in thrall. First Elder glanced around the chamber, then lowered her voice. "The first thing we must do when Khith is back among us is to force the Change upon it. Once safely wedded, it will no longer have these yearnings after dangerous knowledge."

Second Elder Sthaal blinked in surprise and distress. "Force the Change, First One? That is forbidden!"

"We are the Elders," Nkotha said. "Who is to judge what we do? But we shall be discreet."

Sthaal still seemed taken aback. "You know how it can be done, Eldest?"

Nkotha leaned back in her tall chair. "There are ways, Sthaal . . . a tea brewed from uinto berries should accomplish what we want."

Sthaal sat straight up. "But that can be dangerous. Uinto berries can be poisonous if consumed in quantity!"

"Certainly they can. But we have shahmans who know the proportions. Khith will not be harmed, only Changed."

"And who will volunteer to become Khith's mate, First One?"

Nkotha examined her long, double-digited fingers as though she had never seen them before. "That hardly matters, Second One. I am sure one of the unwed laborers can be persuaded. After all, young Khith inherited wealth, did it not?"

"Indeed," the Second said. "Most wise of you, First Elder."

"But first we must capture our young scholar. And that may prove no easy task. We must—"

With a massive effort born of encroaching panic, Khith managed to separate its mind from that of the host-insect. The farseeing spell was still in force, though. Khith discovered that it could, with little effort, "see" the band assembling on one of the massive limbs, ready to step into the powered lift-basket. The Tracker-handlers stood by, a safe distance away, bracing themselves against the lunges of the snarling jagowas. There were four, three with mottled russet and cream coats, their spotted hides bright against the green backdrop of leaves, and one black one that seemed no more than a sinuous shadow.

Khith struggled against the drug's effect. *Must . . . think . . .*

Khith's former village was at least a half-hour journey away. Time enough to escape, to hide any betraying sign, if it did not dawdle.

Khith swung around on its high stool, then slid down. The room tilted and rocked like a boat in a storm, and it had to catch the edge of the table to steady itself. The Hthras shook its head, fighting to throw off the effect of the potion. Staggering, Khith headed toward its living quarters. *Must pack . . . must escape.*

Swaying, weaving, Khith made an unsteady way through the underground warren. It seemed as though hours had passed when it reached its own rooms, but the Hthras knew that blurred time-sense was typical of the hallucinogenic potions.

The scholar grabbed a pack and began stuffing things into it, trying desperately to concentrate. *Scrolls, herbals, the herbs themselves, the Ancient redes I copied, gold to pay my way . . .*

Hthras usually went naked in their own forests, but that

would not do for the outside world. Khith grabbed a hooded robe from a shelf. Soft blue-gray, with red borders: the traditional garb of a physician. Stuffing the robe into the pack, the Hthras spared a moment to "see" its pursuers, calling them up with an ancient Hthras farseeing chant.

> *"Find the center of the self*
> *Hear the heartbeat, feel the breathing*
> *Feed the air and blood to mind*
> *Feel the thought-flow sparking, seething.*
>
> *Sense the Forest 'round us all*
> *Sense its slow and frantic bustle*
> *Sense the Forest and its mind*
> *Sense its bone and vein and muscle."*

This time the Hthras was seeing the hunting party through the eyes of some small animal crouched frozen only a few feet from the trail, its every instinct insisting that safety lay in non-movement. Khith watched the Elders with the Peacekeepers walk by, following the faint trail it had forged all those months ago. The Trackers snarled and lunged on their leashes. Thinking about what jagowa teeth could do to its softly furred hide brought Khith up out of the trance, panting with fear.

Calm, stay calm. You'll only escape them if you can out-think them.

Food and a flask of water went into the now bulging pack. Khith stood looking down at the stacks of scrolls it could not carry. *Best hide them. If they find them, they'd likely destroy them.*

The unsteadiness caused by the potion was waning now. Khith stacked the scrolls, balancing them in a high, tottery stack across its long, furred arms, then the scholar headed out of the room, moving quickly. *The alchemy laboratory—that would be the safest place. I'll bar the door, then get out through the back.*

Minutes later the scrolls were concealed as much as possible, and the main door off the corridor was barred from the inside.

Khith hurried back toward its quarters and the waiting pack. As the Hthras trotted along, it chanted another verse of the farseeing song.

"See with eyes of hunting birds
See the world with eyes of raptors
See that they may not see me
See so they won't become my captors."

The scholar stumbled as another vision unfolded. Again it was seeing through the eyes of another. It was a strange overlay. "Behind" the vision, Khith could still make out the Ancients' corridor, the diffuse lighting following it along as it moved.

But the vision was as close and immediate as if the scholar were standing beside its would-be captors. The hunters were having problems fording a sluggish stream. Tiny, savage swimmers waited there, ready to attack any warm flesh unwary enough to be placed close to their fanged jaws. The hunters tested the water, then wandered off downstream to look for a better, safer place to ford.

I've gained a few more moments . . . must hurry!

When the Hthras reached its quarters, it quickly assembled the makings for yet another spell—this one for confusing Trackers. This spell was an old one it had learned from one of its own kind, not from the Ancients. But the Hthras who had taught this rede to the youngster had died long ago, leaving behind no apprentice. The old magics were being lost. The Hthras Wise Ones these days practiced only healing spells, and few of them.

Khith glanced over the ingredients, mentally checking them off.

Thread, spun from a corpse's hair. Beetle carcasses, and a large, wax-dipped fringe-leaf. And a special distillation of a powerful herb that was as subtle as it was intoxicating.

Quickly, Khith stuffed the ingredients into the belt it wore around its slender waist. Then it grabbed the overloaded pack, swung it up into place, and fastened the harness across its narrow, soft-furred torso.

Out, into the hallway, turn right, two lefts, up a stairway, then left again. Another stairway, and another. Khith raced up the Ancients' wide-flagged stairs, up and up, until it reached ground level. The Hthras paused once again to farsee. This time it was difficult to gain any images. The spell was waning quickly.

Another insect was the best "view" the scholar could find. They had crossed the stream and were making good time, moving nearly as fast as the lunging jagowas that led the procession. Khith's heart pounded. Now they were only minutes from the Ancients' city.

Khith's hastily formed plan called for it to travel west, then north, crossing the Sarsithe, then heading up out of the rainforest into the Steppes that lay southwest of Severez. There were settlements aplenty on both the mainland colony of Kata or on the island kingdom of Pela.

Turning south, it plunged into the jungle, deliberately picking a path along a muddy trail, and making only a cursory effort to smooth out its trail behind it. Even if the Hthras were fooled by this ruse, the jagowas would not be.

Straining its rounded, upstanding ears, Khith listened with every sense for the sounds of pursuit.

When it had gone far enough to reach the banks of the wide stream that its pursuers had crossed upstream, Khith paused to check that there were no killer swimmers there, then stepped delicately into the cool water. The Hthras stood there for a moment, allowing the liquid to flow around its spindly, furred legs.

Quickly it took out the materials from its belt-pouch, arranging them in the middle of the leaf it spread across its hand. Hair, herb, dried husks of beetles, and finally . . .

Khith took a deep breath and sank its sharp teeth ruthlessly into the skin covering its palm. When it drew back, two half-circles of red welled up. Khith held its palm over the leaf, letting the blood drip down until the silver-green was splashed with deep red.

Quietly, it whispered the first few verses of the Chant for Confusing Trackers, tapping time with its wounded hand against its furry belly.

"Searchers <beat, beat>
Seek to find me
Hunters <beat, beat>
On my trail
Forest <beat, beat>
Help to hide me
Help me with the Forest's veil
Help me help themselves to fail.

Slow them <beat, beat>
Glide me farther
Shake them <beat, beat>
While I run
Lose them <beat, beat>
Walk through water
Let this prey their hunt outrun
Slow their searching . . . or I'm done.

Footprints <beat, beat>
Can confuse them
Backward <beat, beat>
Walking false
Streambeds <beat, beat>
Can refuse them
Draw them where the forest calls
Block them with your living walls."

Then the Hthras bent and placed the leaf on the water, releasing it to the sluggish current, watching for a moment as it went bobbing downstream.

Glancing back over its shoulder, Khith took a slow, cautious step backward—then froze, ears alert.

Those sounds! The swish of vegetation, the hushed sounds of voices, the low snarls of the jagowas—

They're right behind me!

Khith forced back panic and took another step back, careful to ease its foot down into the same footprint it had made minutes ago when it had first walked up the muddy path.

Another careful backward step, echoing the existing footprint, then another, and another . . .

Khith's heart was hammering so hard now that it was increasingly difficult to track the progress of its pursuers. It tried to control its breathing, listening so hard it seemed like a physical effort.

And always, those slow backward steps, setting its feet precisely into its prints.

Softly, under its breath, it chanted the next verse.

"Wild pigs <beat, beat>
Root in pathway
Insects <beat, beat>
Buzz and bite
Birds fly <beat, beat>
Up from cover
Spread unease with dying light
Let them dread the coming night . . ."

Khith paused for a moment, feeling the mud squish beneath its bare feet. When it donned clothing to walk the land of men, it would also put on sandals to shield its feet from their hard roadways, but Hthras in their homeland were tree people, climbers, and they never went shod.

All around it the Hthras sensed the forest. Closing its eyes, it concentrated, and was finally rewarded by a blurry image of the searchers amidst the ruins. They had not found the vine-shielded entrance to Khith's lair, or, if they had, they had not entered. Instead they were casting about, plainly searching for a trail.

One of the jagowas snarled, its cry rising into a roar as it surged forward, dragging the handler.

Time to disappear, Khith realized. *They'll be here in moments.*

Slowly, balancing on one foot, the Hthras thrust its right foot backward, full into the blade-brush that encroached onto the narrow trail. Smooth, sharp-pointed leaves raked along its hide, but its fur provided some protection. Then, awkward with its heavy pack, the scholar gave a little hop, leaving the path and crashing back into the blade-brush. It stifled a whimper as the leaves drew blood.

Hastily, trying to ignore the stinging of its palms from the leaves, Khith pushed the screen of brush back into place. Then the Hthras wiped the edges of the leaves to remove the narrow blood-trails. Sprinkling herbs to hide its scent, the scholar arranged the branches as it would a living sculpture. When the brush was back in place, Khith ducked its head to protect its eyes, then backed away on hands and knees, ignoring more stinging little slashes from the leaves.

Finally, when it was at least three body lengths off the trail, it subsided into a little huddle, trying to repress its shivers. This was a calculated risk. The blade-brush might discourage a jagowa, but it would also make flight nearly impossible.

Voices . . .

Khith's ears twitched. *They're here!*

It stiffened with fear as its pursuers came swiftly up the trail, with the jagowas bounding in the lead.

Khith whispered another verse of the chant, its voice so soft that it could barely hear itself.

"Briars <beat, beat>
Tear their clothing
Roots catch <beat, beat>
At their feet
Swamp ground <beat, beat>
Stirs their loathing
Hold them until I can retreat
Hold them so we will not meet."

The Hthras heard the hunting party go past, headed for the stream, then heard the irritated snarls and yowls of the jagowas. The big hunters hated water. Still, from the sounds of it, they splashed right into the stream. Khith heard the hunters exclaim excitedly, and dared to hope that its spell was working and they would be lured downstream.

If only the Hthras trackers trusted their senses! If they did, the spell would work on them, fooling their eyes, their ears. They would follow the leaf downstream, thinking they saw glimpses of a running figure, thinking they heard running footsteps, thinking they smelled the fear of a fugitive.

The spell would not fool the jagowas, of course, but the water would do that . . . or so Khith hoped.

Still whispering, Khith began edging back again, careful not to move the brush more than necessary. Stoically, it ignored the scratches, chanting in a voice that was scarcely more than breath.

> *"Searchers* <beat, beat>
> *Will not find me*
> *Hunters* <beat beat>
> *Lose my trail*
> *Forest* <beat, beat>
> *Help and guide me*
> *Shield me with the forest's veil*
> *Help me that I may not fail . . ."*

It was a long, slow, miserable crawl. Khith backed away for many lengths before it could find a place to turn. Once it could crawl forward instead of scuttling backward, it was a little easier. The Hthras ducked its head, ears flattened with misery, crawling doggedly as insects feasted on its cuts, and its palms, knees, and feet grew sore and abraded, despite the softness of the forest loam.

Finally the Hthras took a chance and crawled out of the brush. Only then did it dare to turn and look back whence it had come.

Dusk was falling, and the searchers must have activated

their lightsticks. There was a distant phosphorescent gleam far downstream.

The spell had worked!

Khith drew courage from that knowledge, feeling the swell of pride. It had studied for years, but never before had a spell been so important. The scholar had feared that the old spells would prove ineffective. Khith had wondered whether Hthras magical abilities had waned over generations, and that was why most Hthras had given up on the old spells.

But that one had worked. Khith hugged itself in triumph.

Then the scholar stiffened, as it heard a different sound. Snarls and growls, followed by a keening, uncanny wail, and it was growing louder!

The jagowas—they've loosed them! They only sound like that when they're coursing free!

Quickly, Khith changed its escape plan. It could no longer hope to stay to the forest paths on its way northwest. No, for now it must go due west. And quickly!

Khith was already tired from its long crawl, but the scholar forced its body into a fast trot. The heavy pack bounced uncomfortably on its back, but there was no time to adjust the straps. Khith glanced up at the treetops, wishing it could travel those byways. To the Hthras, even narrow tree limbs were like roads, and they felt most comfortable traversing the forest canopy.

But if it took to the treetops, its pursuers could send for reinforcements, and in a short time it would be caught. Khith had no illusions about being able to outdistance searchers in the treetops. Only here, on the forest floor, far below the Hthras' domain, might it hope to elude its pursuers.

Unlike most Hthras, Khith knew the forest floor. The scholar had spent so much time down here, where most Hthras never went, that it could sense the green pulse of the forest life.

As the scholar ran, following faint paths that were little more than game trails, Khith strained every sense to its utmost. *Where are the jagowas?*

Dream-memories of sharp teeth assailed the fugitive as

Khith imagined the creatures gaining, gaining, then their bodies arcing up in a huge pounce. Khith shook its head, telling itself to calm down. If the jagowas were within pouncing range, it would have heard them.

The trail grew less distinct, then vanished. Khith was wading through scattered blade-brush now. The tiny cuts and slices smarted and drew insects to feast on the blood.

Gasping, Khith ran faster, abandoning its efforts at stealth. It could hear the jagowas coursing, sensed them drawing nearer. Without their handlers to control them, the beasts would tear it to pieces within minutes.

Khith wished fervently that it had studied spells of warding, spells of defense, spells meant to render an enemy helpless. But such spells were not in its nature. It found the idea of violence abhorrent.

Its world narrowed until there was nothing but the forest and its terrible need to flee the bloody fate coursing behind it. *Run! Run! RunrunrunrunRUN!*

Panic threatened to overwhelm the scholar, but with one small, sane part of its mind, Khith forced itself to look around as it plunged onward. *Where am I?*

The ground beneath its running feet was ascending . . . a good sign. The forest giants were smaller here, mixed with other varieties of trees. Khith's night vision, like that of all Hthras, was acute. Putting on a burst of speed, it managed to gain a minute or so on its pursuers.

With frantic haste the scholar leaped for the bole of a rough-bark tree, swarmed up it halfway. From this vantage point it could clearly make out the landmark it needed—a tall, dead forest giant shone ghostly silver by the light of the Moon.

Khith scrabbled back down the tree trunk, the air tearing its chest with every breath it drew. Altering course slightly, it headed for the dead giant.

As Khith approached the huge, silver bole of the lightning-blasted tree, it could hear the pursuers. They had gained again, and were now only minutes behind. The jagowas were in full cry, maddened by the blood-fresh scent of their prey.

Moving cautiously despite its haste, Khith walked due west of the dead giant. *Fifty paces . . .*

It nearly overshot its goal, despite the moonlight and the thinning vegetation. But its night vision was keen, and it saw the faintly luminescent marker far down the tree trunk, nearly hidden by the giant roots. Pulling off its pack, the Hthras wrapped its robe around its hands as it cautiously searched for the slender cord of spun silk that was fastened to a staple set deep into the tree trunk.

Its questing hands found the narrow length, so fine-spun and translucent that it would be nearly invisible even in daylight. Quickly but carefully, Khith began reeling in the spun-silk cord, winding it round and round the bole of the tree.

Hurry! Hurry!

It seemed that hours had passed by the time the silken cord was replaced by the anchor-rope for the Hthras bridge.

Khith hastily fastened the bridge-ropes to the tree trunk, using the clamps attached to the cords. Only then did it regard the bridge and the chasm that yawned beneath it.

The cliff was a high one, naked rock scored as if a huge blade had slashed downward, creating a deep chasm. Far below, water rushed foaming white in the moonlight. This chasm marked the boundary of the local Hthras demesne.

Digging its narrow heels into the ground, Khith began tightening up the bridge, snugging up each cord until it was taut. The sounds of shouts and snarls from the jagowas closing in lent speed to its exhausted body. The harsh ropes scored the scholar's palms.

It seemed to take forever, but finally it was done. Khith hauled on the bridge until it was taut, then secured the end to the bolts screwed into the tree at the edge of the cliff.

The bridge was visible in the moonlight as a spiderweb of narrow cords, scarcely seeming strong enough to support a single Hthras. But lian vines were strong.

Holding tightly to the two cords that served as handrails, Khith ventured out, its narrow, limber toes curving around the thicker ropes running along the bottom of the bridge.

The bridge swayed and shivered, and Khith stopped,

clutching the hand-ropes tightly. It had crossed this bridge before, in daylight, with experienced guides to shepherd it over the chasm. Never by moonlight. Never when it was already trembling with exhaustion and nearly witless with fear.

Another shout, much nearer now, lent strength, and Khith wavered forward, trying to balance, trying to gain speed. The thick rope beneath its feet seemed impossibly narrow.

The scholar was nearly halfway across now. Below it the river thundered and spray from the white water shimmered in the moonlight.

Hurry! Don't look down!

Khith lurched forward, almost running, fixing its eyes on the end of the bridge. Its world narrowed to those last few strides to be crossed . . .

And then it was there, on the other side!

Khith whirled around, unslinging its pack, only to see one of the jagowas burst out of the forest and leap onto the bridge. The animal crouched low and started forward, snarling.

No!

Khith grabbed its sheath-knife out of the pack and began frantically sawing at the rightmost hand-rope. It was gasping for breath and could not look at the animal that crept so determinedly forward. The scholar had never in its life intentionally harmed another creature.

Hthras did not eat meat, did not even keep animals for fur or milk. Everything they used, they grew.

With a *spung!* the hand-rope parted. The bridge tilted sideways, and the jagowa, with a scream of fear, fell . . .

And fell.

Khith was sobbing as it sawed on the next rope. Minutes later the last of the bridge was severed, and the scholar watched the limp rope structure twist and turn in slow motion before it came to rest against the opposite cliff.

Looking up, it saw its people on the other side of the chasm. They stood there, regarding the scholar across the nothingness, and Khith realized that it had literally cut all ties with its own people by its action. There would be no forgiveness, no pardon . . . ever.

Slowly, stumbling with weariness, Khith managed to shoulder its pack. Then it turned and staggered into the forest, leaving its homeland and its people behind.

4

The Road to Q'Kal

Despite the late winter chill outside, the interior of Shekk Marzet's tent was stuffy from the braziers burning dried yak dung. Seated on a cushion at the back of the tent, where she had a good view of the Shekk and his many guests, Thia blinked and blinked again, fighting drowsiness. It was essential that she stay awake. Shekk Marzet needed her, and the old man had been very kind.

It had been nearly five months since her escape from Boq'urak and the twin ziggurats. She'd staggered into Verang half dead from terror and exposure, aware that her novice's robe and shaven head marked her as a runaway from the twin temples.

The town was nearly deserted, all the good citizens relaxing by their fires after supper. The only other person out on the streets had been Shekk Marzet. Seeing the staggering, exhausted girl, he quickly wrapped her in his cloak and hustled her into his town house before anyone could see her.

At first Thia had been afraid that the old man had unworthy motives in rescuing her, but her fears abated when the Shekk immediately summoned his two daughters to tend her, bathing her numb white feet in warm water, giving her some of their own clothing, and burning her habit. When Thia finally recovered her wits enough to ask why the Shekk and his family had risked so much for her, his eldest daughter, Joyana, had regarded her steadily, her eyes sad.

"Our father hates the priests, and he spits when he hears Boq'urak's name," she replied, struggling to keep her voice steady. "It's because of our brother. When he was only seventeen, he and some other boys in Verang stole some trinkets and sweetmeats in the marketplace. It wasn't the first time Doren had been in trouble with the law. The priests . . . they decreed that the only way he could expiate his sin was . . . was—" Joyana's voice broke and she began to sob.

Her sister, Loisa, finished the grim tale. "They said he must go to the god at sunrise. They took him, and they did it. Cut out his living heart, as though he were a common criminal. Our little brother! Father cursed them, and cursed Boq'urak and His worship on that day. Fear not, Thia. We will hide you. If you have turned your back on that evil god, you are our friend."

Since then, Thia had remained in the Shekk's house, accustoming herself to wearing a thick modesty veil—as behooved a woman of marriageable age—letting her hair grow, and waiting until the search for the runaway novice had died down. Shekk Marzet had treated her as a third daughter; she was intensely grateful to the old merchant, and extremely pleased to be of use to him in his business.

Thia realized that her eyelids were drooping again, and gave herself a vicious pinch. *Wake up! Time for you to be alert!* The company had just finished a huge meal, and belches and other sounds of digestive activity erupted. Marzet clapped his plump, ringed hands. "My friends, we have had our dinner and friendly conversation. Time now for business, by your leave."

The two thin, pale-faced gem merchants nodded. Marzet gestured, and servants hastily cleared a space in the center of the tent, taking away the low table and replacing it with several thick Severian rugs and large, tassled cushions. With surprising ease for one so old and pudgy, the Shekk dropped down onto a crimson cushion and sat cross-legged. "My esteemed guests, I am eager to see your wares."

With a flourish, Dantol, the taller of the two gem merchants, spread a midnight-colored swath of velvet before the Shekk. "We bring only the best for our generous host," he said with a bow, then nodded at Gervej.

Gervej reached into a pouch and brought out a large stone that flashed green fire. "An emerald, Lord Shekk. Nearly flawless, and . . ." he held it out on his palm, "but see the size! As big as a woman's thumbnail, and the color," he made a kissing noise, "it is as vivid as any I have ever encountered."

"Ah . . ." Marzet took the gem, turned it over thoughtfully, then produced a thick lens and peered at it. "The color is indeed vivid. Natural? Or enhanced by magic?"

Gervej shook his head, his expression pained. "Shekk, how can you imply that I would offer you an enhanced stone? Of course not!"

Marzet nodded, then held the stone and lens up to study it in the light of the lantern that hung on a pole to his right. In doing so, his eyes slid sideways to Thia, who was busily adjusting her modesty veil over her left ear.

"Ah, well, a lovely piece, a lovely, lovely piece," Marzet said heartily. "How much?"

Gervej named a sum that was merely exorbitant. The gem merchant smiled, obviously anticipating a good bargaining session.

"No, I regret, too rich for my blood," Marzet said, putting the emerald back onto the cloth. "Next?"

Gervej glanced sharply at his associate, Dantol. "You are not interested?"

Marzet smiled with his mouth only. "Next?" he repeated.

Thia sat watching, now fully alert, as Marzet examined the gem merchant's wares. Thanks to her ability to sense truth from lies, the Shekk acquired two flawless and genuine flame-gems, an opal, and a dozen faceted blue topazes that would be ideal for a necklace or bracelet.

Finally, when the mystified gem dealers had gathered up their rejected wares and were bowing themselves out of the tent, Thia caught the Shekk's eye. Marzat gave her a wink and a grin of thanks.

Quietly, Thia gathered up her skirts and slipped out of the tent. The chill was bracing after the stuffiness of the tent, and she stood gazing up at the night sky, thinking how few days were left until they reached their destination, the crossroads city of Q'Kal. This trade city, larger even than Verang, lay in the northernmost reaches of Kata.

Dropping her modesty veil, she inhaled a breath of cold, dry mountain air. The caravan was traversing the last of the high steppes that came down from the range that bisected Amavav. Within a tenday's journey they would be crossing a narrow stretch of territory claimed by Galrai, then they'd have to journey across Severez before reaching Q'Kal, which lay nearly on the Katan and Severez border.

Hugging her heavy shawl around her shoulders, Thia turned and gazed back at the mountains, which she could only see as dim black shapes, since there was no moon tonight to illuminate their jagged, white-capped peaks. She could trace their outlines only by the way they blocked out the profusion of stars. This far from any city, the stars seemed almost close enough to touch, and they glittered more vibrantly than any gem merchant's wares.

Marzet's party was traveling with a large caravan bound for Q'Kal. The old merchant had explained to Thia that he always traveled with a caravan, never alone. There were bands of fierce robbers in the steppes, and there was safety in numbers.

Thia realized that for the first time in her life she couldn't see the mountains that surrounded Verang. The range behind her divided Amavav from Amaran; these were not the mountains of her birth.

I'm on my way to being free! she thought with a surge of exultation.

The moment of excitement faded quickly, however, to be replaced with apprehension. Thia frowned as she stared into

the darkness. The caravan would reach Q'Kal in only two
tendays. *And what shall I do then? Stay with the Shekk, who
has been so kind? Or go off on my own?*

Thia had never been alone for more than a few hours, had
never earned her own living. For a moment she was tempted
to remain with the Shekk and his family. They spoke her language, they were decent people. The Shekk treated her like
another daughter.

Even as she thought longingly of remaining part of their
family, realization coalesced in her mind. *No. I must leave
them.* The decision was as inescapable as the snow and ice
shrouding the mountains in winter—only if she left behind
every trace of her former life, could she ever hope to be free
of the twin ziggurats. As long as she traveled with the
Shekk, she would be under suspicion from anyone sent by
the priests to track her. Any priest or priestess who left the
temple voluntarily was considered the worst kind of heretic,
and would be hunted and recaptured if at all possible. And if
she were recaptured, Thia had no doubt she would meet
Narda's fate, or one equally harsh.

And . . . worse . . . Thia knew she was endangering Marzet
and his family. If they were discovered to be sheltering a
runaway from the temple, they would be judged criminals,
and given to the god at sunrise. It was the law.

*I can't repay their kindness to me by putting them in dan-
ger,* Thia thought. Her heart felt leaden, sick with fear. *I must
leave them. I must find the courage. When we reach Q'Kal, I
must slip away, without a word of farewell, so if they are
ever questioned, they will honestly be able to say they have
no idea where I have gone.*

Thia tried to picture herself wandering the streets of a
strange city, filled with foreigners speaking a different
tongue. She'd begun learning Pelanese, the language spoken
in Severez and Kata, but she was far from fluent. *I can't
bring attention to myself. I'll have to . . . adapt. Fit in. But I
will be alone, totally alone!*

She forced back panic. *You'll manage. You can do lots of
things.* Her truth-telling ability had proven useful to one

merchant. Perhaps she could find employment with another one. Q'Kal was, by all reports, teeming with merchants.

Or perhaps someone needed a clark. She could read, write, and cypher, and not everyone could do that well. She could cook simple fare, which she'd learned from her days serving in the temple kitchens. She looked down at her hands, pale blurs in the starlight. She could always scrub and clean. Oh yes, every postulant learned that skill.

She heard a soft hail from behind her. "Thia?"

The glow of an oil lamp illumined the night, its yellow light bobbing up and down in time to the quick strides of the woman carrying it. Thia knew that voice, so she did not trouble to raise her veil before turning to face Marzet's eldest, Joyana. "I am here, Joy."

Joyana was carrying a large basket over her arm. "It is time to take the watch their supper," she said. "Can you take care of that again? Father is weary after his bargaining, and has asked me to play my hand-harp for him until he falls asleep."

Thia nodded and reached out for the basket and lamp. "I will," she promised. "Tell the Shekk I said to sleep well."

"Oh, he will," Joyana assured her. "Nothing puts Father in a better mood than making good bargains—and, thanks to you, he made many tonight."

Thia smiled. "It is good to be of service to those who have been so kind to me."

"Nonsense, you paid us back long ago, Thia. We are in your debt."

"You are the one who speaks nonsense, Joy," Thia replied. "I am more grateful for your kindness than I can ever say." She tried to put every bit of conviction she could into her voice, hoping that Joyana would remember her words after she was gone.

The two young women exchanged another smile, then Joyana turned back toward her father's tent.

After raising her veil, Thia went the other way, the light of her lamp providing a small puddle of gold in a vast black sea of night. She trod carefully over the winter-blasted turf, avoiding the prickle-bushes that could deliver a painful sting. One by one she sought out each of the guards at his post and delivered the food. She did not speak, only doled out each meal and a measure of watered honey-ale, receiving each guard's thanks with a dignified nod.

Her heart quickened as she headed for the last guard post. *Is he on duty tonight*? she wondered. She had no way of knowing. *You are acting foolish,* she chided herself. *What is wrong with you? He's just a guard with a beautiful horse; the two of you have barely exchanged a handful of words, because his Pelanese is no better than yours. What ails you?*

Still, as she approached the last guard post, she realized she was holding her breath. He was stationed at the farthest perimeter of the camp, near a large rock outcropping. When her lamplight revealed the swish of a silver tail and she heard a soft whicker of welcome, she smiled, grateful for the anonymity of her modesty veil.

She hesitated, lamp held high, searching for a glimpse of him, but saw nothing. She already knew he could move as silently as a mountain cat. Thia peered into the darkness. "Where are you?" she whispered in Pelanese. She was still not fluent, but she had learned much since leaving the temple.

"Here, lady," came a voice from behind her. Thia started so violently she nearly dropped the lamp. She whirled around, to find him standing scarcely two paces from her.

"I am sorry—I did not . . . have fear not . . ." In his distress, his command of the foreign tongue was slipping. Thia held the lamp higher.

The guard was taller than she, with brown hair pulled back and fastened with a leather thong. He was clad in a horseman's buckskin breeches, high boots, and a leather corselet studded with metal rings. Thia could not see the color of his eyes, and wondered whether they were dark, like her own. Slowly, carefully, he held out his empty hands, palms up, plainly hoping to allay her fears.

"You move too quietly," Thia said finally. She held out the last package of food and the flask from her basket. This guard drank only water, never ale. "Here is your supper. You must be hungry."

"Many thanks, lady," he said.

She knew from experience that he would not sit to eat, nor remain in the lamplight. She gently stroked the gray mare's neck and shoulder while he took the bread, meat, cheese, and dried fruit over to his guard post. He stood there, eating without relaxing, all the while scanning the darkness and listening for any signs of intruders.

When he was finished, the guard came back to stand beside her as she petted his mare, humming softly in a way that seemed to please the animal. "You know horses?" he asked.

"Not much," Thia replied. "Where I was raised, we did not travel, nor did we ride for pleasure. But I like them. She is beautiful, this one. So gentle."

She caught the flash of his teeth in the lantern light as he smiled. "Gentle, not to enemies, no. Falar is battle-trained."

"'Falar'? Is that her name?"

"On her pedigree, it is Chotak Falar-azeen. In my tongue it means 'Chotak's Silver Blade.'"

"Greetings, Falar," Thia murmured, and laughed a little to see the mare's ears flick back and forth in response to her name.

The guard motioned to her. "Time for my round. You will stay until I return?"

Thia hesitated, then nodded.

She spent the minutes petting the horse, wondering what it would be like to ride such a splendid steed. While traveling with the caravan, she'd occasionally ridden a plodding mule, but never a horse.

The guard materialized out of the darkness suddenly, with no warning. Again Thia jumped, startled. "You move so quietly!"

Again that slight smile touched his normally stern mouth. "That is my . . . what is the word? My duty here. I am Pen Jav Dal . . . or was."

She haltingly repeated the unfamiliar phrase. "What is that?"

"The Silent Ones."

"Silent Ones?"

He looked away, and she sensed that he regretted having revealed anything. He did not talk much, not to anyone.

Silent One. It is an apt name for him.

Thia studied him for a moment, then said, softly, "I do not mean to pry. I am not one who asks for truth while withholding it." She drew a deep breath. "My name is Thia. I was raised in Amaran. Until a few months ago I was in holy orders." She looked up at him in the lamplight, and his face held strange shadows, seeming almost a mask.

After a moment she continued, "I wore a habit and went unveiled, because I am not a marriageable woman. If you are skilled at reading faces, you will see that I speak the truth." Greatly daring, she bent over and picked up the lamp, holding it high, then dropped her modesty veil.

The guard held her gaze for a long moment, then spoke in a low tone. "I am Jezzil. From Ktavao."

Her eyes widened. "You are a long way from home, Jezzil."

He nodded. "So are you."

Thia smiled faintly. "Yes, I am farther from where I was raised than I ever dreamed I might be."

"Where were you raised?"

She hesitated for a long moment. Jezzil reached out, his movement uncertain, unlike his movements when handling his weapons or his mount. His fingers brushed the fabric of her shawl where it lay over her shoulder. "I am a Silent One," he reminded her. "You can trust me to repeat nothing."

Thia looked up at him, knowing he spoke the truth. "I was raised in Verang, in the temples. I was a priestess until a few months ago. Then I ran away."

Jezzil's eyes widened. "One of Boq'urak's priestesses? And you dared to run away?"

She nodded, and suddenly found herself fighting back tears. Hastily, she raised her veil and fastened it again, using that moment to try and regain her composure. "I lost everything when I learned the truth," she said finally. "Boq'urak is a vicious, cruel god, not worthy of reverence. I ran away when I realized what I had been serving all those years. If they find me, they will kill me."

This time he reached out and touched her hands as they held her shawl clutched about her. His fingers were rough, callused from rein and weapons. "Sister Thia," he said. "I understand, more than you dream I can. When I was Chonao, I was . . ." He searched for the words. "I was a priest who fights. Warrior priest. Then I ran away too. Now I am no better than a dead man to my brothers, my order. If they find me, they will kill me."

Thia caught her breath and stared at him in the lamplight. "I see," she said finally. "We have much in common, then."

"Yes."

She hesitated, and unable to think of anything more to say, stooped and grabbed her basket. Jezzil stepped in front of her as she turned to leave. "You will come back, Sister Thia? You are . . . I could not speak of this to anyone but Falar . . . but you, you understand. It was good to speak, after so long as a Silent One."

She nodded. "Yes. I'll be back tomorrow. Fare you well tonight, Brother Jezzil."

He stepped back, raising a hand to her in half salute as she hastened away with her lamp, leaving him alone in the darkness, save for Falar.

Khith had traveled steadily for a month now, and still was not free of the forest giants and the warm embrace of the Sarsithe. It knew that in the North it was late winter, and the Hthras was not in a hurry to experience snow and ice again. It remembered winter, from when it had traveled the world with its merchant father.

Khith could barely remember its mother. She was only a soft blur of warm, reddish-brown fur and a lilting voice that had trilled lullabies to her only child. She had died after being attacked by a wild jagowa while gathering river reeds for basket weaving.

Khith had been doing some weaving itself. Knowing that it would face much harder ground soon, it had been gathering reeds and vines, so it could make sandals to shield its long-toed, narrow feet from roads and streets. When Khith and its father had traveled in the lands inhabited by the humans, it had worn protection on its feet, just as it had worn a robe to cover its slender, furred body, and a hood to shield its eyes from the sun.

With the half-finished sandals tied to its pack, the Hthras trudged on, its ears alert for any sound, its large, round eyes constantly scanning the animal trail before it. Khith's people loved the jungle, but were ever mindful of its myriad dangers.

It kept the sun always to its left after noon, and each morning it shed its pack and climbed to the top of a forest giant to check the position of its rising, in order to make sure it was still on track. Khith was trying to gauge its travel so that it missed the arrival of the rainy season, while still not having to travel during the worst of the northern winter.

Its goal was a human port town. Q'Kal had been one of its father's favored places for trade, with ships tying up daily to the quays, vessels containing goods from Pela and other countries lying across the Narrow Sea. Khith remembered Q'Kal as a bustling place, the busiest port in the Pelanese colony of Kata. *It has undoubtedly changed in twenty-five years,* the Hthras thought with a sigh, shifting the pack on its back. *Everything changes.*

A port city, it had learned early on, tended to be more open-minded to newcomers. And where there were ships and sailors and merchants and those who served them, there was bound to be the need for a good physician.

Khith's constantly roving gaze caught a tiny flash of vermilion on a vine weaving across the animal trail it was following, and it froze in mid-step.

A brekiss!

The snake was long and narrow, scarcely bigger around than Khith's finger. But to touch its skin could result in severe shock, convulsions, even death. Khith's people used the brekiss's skin-venom in minute quantities to induce healing visions.

Carefully, Khith stepped back, away from the creature, and took stock. Two faint animal trails led off the main one, one on either side. Khith chose the one leading off to its right, since it appeared to roughly parallel the trail it had been following.

It hadn't gone more than another twenty paces before it saw the shimmer of shattered, opalescent material and the half-melted spire that marked one of the Ancient Ones' ruins.

Khith's eyes widened with joy at the chance to add to its store of knowledge on that long forgotten civilization. The scholar knew that exploring ruins was dangerous, but it could not pass this opportunity by.

It circled the remains, eyeing them carefully. This had not been a large structure, as these things went. Perhaps it had been some kind of remote outpost, or way station.

The Ancients always stored their records belowground. Khith picked its way carefully into the heart of the ruined structure, stepping high over the vines wreathing the ruin, searching for an opening that would lead below. When it spotted a sunken place, it nodded in satisfaction, then waded out of the ruin to locate a suitable fallen branch to use as an improvised excavation tool. After half an hour of digging and scraping the undergrowth away, Khith broke through the overlay of soil and roots into emptiness. Its heart hammering with the thrill of the quest for knowledge, Khith dropped to its knees and cleared away soil, revealing a crumbling stairway leading down into damp darkness.

Khith had explored many of the ancient ruins before, so it knew there was a good chance that the lighting systems had failed. Hastily, it improvised a torch from its trusty branch and some moss, then set it afire with a mumbled word and a hard stare.

The Hthras descended the stairway, torch held high. There was water underfoot, but the Ancients had been marvelous engineers, and the walls and ceilings were mostly intact. Quickly, Khith surveyed the rooms, many of them still containing moldy lumps it knew must have been furniture:

kitchen, sleeping rooms, offices, storage rooms . . . and, yes! One of the storage rooms held, not unused furnishings, but record books! Khith was aware that the Ancients had used methods other than printed paper to store information, but since there was no power for the readers, it could not read them. Still, most of the Ancients had also produced some paper records, perhaps for quick reference.

An hour later it fought its way up the stairs, back into the light above, three crumbling record books held tightly beneath its arm. *What a discovery! Hand-scribed records, the first such ones that I have located! A true treasure!*

The Hthras knew it should push on, make at least some progress toward its daily travel goal, but curiosity and the desire to learn won out. Khith made camp a short distance from the ruin, then sat down after a quickly swallowed dinner to peruse its find.

Translating the handwritten records was much more difficult, it found, than the printed ones it had discovered in the Lost City. The books were actually written by several individuals, it discovered, over a period of years. They were journals of the sentinels who had been posted to this remote outpost, far from the cities that lay to the east.

The last journal was in the worst shape, but it had the latest date, so Khith examined it first. As darkness gathered over the jungle, Khith sat, totally absorbed, attempting to puzzle out the ancient words on the filthy, crumbled, and pest-nibbled pages. Fragments and snippets of meaning surfaced as it struggled to translate:

(Name) was here tonight for scheduled inspection, told me of new (untranslatable) device. I was fascinated, asked many questions . . . (indecipherable smudge) . . . told me it can open (doorways? gates? or was it corridors? hallways? entrances?) . . . Khith puzzled over the word, then resolved to come back to it later. *. . . to allow passage to another (place? plane? world?) . . . experiments commencing . . .*

That cannot be right, Khith thought, perplexed. *I must have translated that wrong. I should cross-check that word with my notes. A passageway to another world?*

For a moment it considered digging out its notes, but decided to read on instead. Perhaps the term would become clear in context. Khith waved the flame of its little torch higher, shedding more light on the damaged pages. The next few were stuck together. With painstaking care it separated them, only to find that they were damaged beyond reading, only a few words visible per page. *This section must have gotten wet at some point, and mildew set in.* Finally it discovered another semireadable passage.

Another message today from (name) in the east. Experiments have been shut down, but now there is trouble. We are not alone, it appears.

The next page was vermin nibbled. Khith clicked its tongue in frustration and turned the page.

. . . damage has been done . . . government crumbling . . . plague in (untranslatable) . . . war in (untranslatable). (Name) says there is a rumor that the (gateway? door? portal?) brought this upon us. Caused us to be noticed. Makes no sense to me, but every day the reports grow worse. I used to curse the day I was sent here to this remote outpost, but now I am glad to be far away from the chaos. What of (name) and (name) . . . fear for them fills me. Will I ever see them again? All is crumbling around us . . .

Khith shivered, despite the warmth of the jungle night. Even in such a battered, mostly indecipherable text, the desperation of the writer came through in those scrawling, hastily written words. The Hthras realized that it might be the first person ever to read about the final days of the Ancient Ones, and shivered again. Turning the page, it saw that only a scant half page of text remained.

More refugees today. I gave them what provisions I could, then sent them on their way north. Mothers holding children. I will never forget their eyes. The world is (coming loose? unraveling? fraying?) more with every hour that passes. (Name) says that they sent a mission through the (portal? gateway? door?) to try and stop it, but they have not been heard of since departing. He calls it the Player, or, sometimes, the Meddler. How could such a thing be? But (name)

*would not lie to me . . . Two days now since I last heard from
(name). The refugees say there was a terrible blast far to the
east. The ones who were the closest to it are sick. Several
died on the way. What should I—*

The text stopped.

Khith turned the page, then forcing its hand to near steadi-
ness, slowly turned the remaining pages in the journal.

Empty.

What did it all mean?

Khith shook its head, hugging itself against the trembling
that assailed it in growing waves. It was frightened, frightened the way it had been when it ran from the searchers and
the jagowas. *Ridiculous!* it thought. *They are the words of a
person who has been dead for thousands of years. How
could they have the power to frighten you?*

Still shivering, Khith carefully placed the three journals
into its pack. Then it drew out its physician's robe, to use for
a blanket. Despite the warmth of the night, it could not stop
trembling, and it took a major effort of will to stare at the
torchlight and quench the flame.

The warm, muffling darkness of the Sarsithe enclosed the
Hthras like a comforting caress, but Khith lay curled around
its pack, eyes wide open, unable to relax, knowing that tired
as it was, it would not sleep. Somehow, in some way the
scholar could not yet comprehend, what it had read held
some personal meaning for it. The realization was becoming
inescapable, no matter how preposterous it seemed. The
words of that Ancient One had brought a premonition of
trouble to come—trouble, and pain, and death. And, most of
all, fear.

Khith tried to dismiss the notion that it was experiencing
a true foretelling. *I cast no spell! I did not scry!* But try as it
would to dismiss the fear, it could not.·

All its adult life the scholar had pursued knowledge, but
this was the first time something from the distant past had
caused such a reaction. *Why this terrible sense of foreboding? I did not even understand most of what I read! How can*

those old words seem like a foretelling of doom and death?
How can what I read be a warning of trouble to come?

Khith moaned and buried its face in its hands as it lay shivering in the warm jungle night. *If only I had not found this outpost!*

As the caravan wound its way past the Galrai peninsula and continued south into the rolling hills and gentle valleys of Severez, Jezzil spent his nights on guard duty and his days sleeping in one of the wagons. During his free time he practiced with his weapons, went scouting on Falar, or joined the hunting parties that went out each morning. Fresh meat to add to the cook pots was always welcome, and helped alleviate the sameness of the fare served to the guards.

The mountains lay behind them now, and the foothills they traversed grew gently rolling, with pleasant valleys lying between them. The threat of brigands abated as they traveled deeper into settled lands, for the King of Severez was not known for his leniency. The gibbets they passed were seldom empty of criminals, left to rot until the next execution, a grim caution to lawbreakers.

To Jezzil, raised in Ktavao, where each landholder possessed vast sweeps of land for his herds and crops, the farms they passed seemed almost like miniatures built for children. But they were tidy and prosperous, and the winter cold had not killed off all the green. Many trees in this land remained green the year round, keeping their spicy, spiky "leaves."

For the first time since he'd embarked from Taenareth, Jezzil felt like a man instead of a walking corpse. He'd thought that his spirit was dead after his courage had failed him in the fortress, but as the days passed, he realized he was glad to be alive. *Perhaps the gods still have a purpose for me,* he thought as he rode Falar alongside Marzet's wagons, looking out across the farms with their stone and shingle cottages.

Part of his renewed interest in life was because, each night, *she* came to talk to him.

Jezzil had left home when his two sisters were little more than babies. His mother and his aunts were the only women he'd ever known well. Until Sister Thia came into his life, young women had been a mystery to him, forbidden and a little frightening.

But now he felt closer to his new friend than he ever had to anyone—even Barus.

Only Thia understood what it was like to have been a member of a holy order and then to be abruptly deprived of the life one had chosen. Sometimes Jezzil thought it was even worse for her than it was for him. He still had his faith, while she had repudiated the god she had been raised to worship. Every evening when he went through his meditation rituals and prayers, he pitied her, deprived of all spiritual solace.

Jezzil thought about Thia's story, wondering what she had actually seen on that night she'd run away from the temple. A god, materializing on this mortal plane? It seemed preposterous. And yet the terror in Thia's eyes told him that she'd seen something beyond his ken.

Chonao males worshiped a number of deities, just as Chonao females had their own goddesses of hearth and home. The Pen Jav Dal were priests of the war god Arenar, and Jezzil had invoked that sacred name before every march, every fight, every scouting party. Yet he had never expected to actually *see* Arenar while still living. And now, thanks to his cowardice at Zajares's fortress, he never would. When he died, Jezzil knew, he would be cast into the Darkness and Emptiness reserved for the most black-souled of sinners.

Jezzil knew that he deserved that fate, but he was not eager to meet it any time soon. So he kept his blades and his warrior skills honed to sharpness.

Several times the road passed through small farming villages, and the caravan masters stopped briefly to trade. Jezzil was fascinated by how different life was on this side of the Narrow Sea. Here in Severez, women walked boldly through towns, carrying their own money or items to barter.

Many of the younger women went unveiled, this far south, and they spoke when they pleased.

Jezzil was stationed to guard Shekk Marzet's wagons while they traded with a small town that lay on the border between the northernmost reaches of Galrai and Severez. Coquillan nestled like a drowsy child in a cozy valley in the foothills. The caravan arrived there a little after dawn on market day, and already the town square bustled with vendors who had set up pushcarts and colorful awnings.

Jezzil was pleased to be able to spend his time near the Shekk's wagons, keeping a watchful eye on the townspeople as they eyed the wares spread out for them to view. Coquillan seemed a peaceful place. Except for the knives they wore on their belts, the men went unarmed. Still, Jezzil knew there were many ways to kill, and so he did not relax his vigilance.

He saw Thia several times accompanying the old Shekk as he traded. Her dark eyes above her modesty veil met his briefly.

After the noon hour the guard commander sent Jezzil's relief to him, with the message that he was off-duty until his night watch. Jezzil glanced at the colorful marketplace, deciding that he'd like to go and explore.

But as he started away from the wagons, he realized that he would rather not go alone. Squaring his shoulders, he turned back and approached Shekk Marzet's personal traveling wagon. Thia, he saw, was outside, stirring something over a cooking fire. Jezzil walked up to her. She looked up at him, and he could tell by the way her dark eyes crinkled at the corners that she was smiling behind her veil.

"I was going to the marketplace for a while," he said. "Would you like to accompany me, and see the wares?"

She hesitated, then glanced toward the wagons. "If the Shekk says I may; he may need me this afternoon."

But it seemed that Shekk Marzet, having eaten a hearty noon meal, had settled in for a nap. Thia came back within moments saying that she, too, was free for the afternoon.

They walked into the town together. Jezzil had seen a number of such towns during his travels to reach Amavav, where he'd hired on with the caravan, but it was clear that much of this was new to Thia. Coquillan was prosperous enough to boast a cobbled main street. The stones were slick with spring mud, and the open sewer ran in a channel down the middle. But there were sidewalks, and raised stepping blocks so people could cross the road without treading in the slippery muck. Pigs and chickens seemed to wander at will, and horses stood hipshot at the hitching posts, drowsing until their owners chose to return. The tiny yards before the two-story brick and timbered houses and businesses were for the most part tidy and swept, and early spring flowers opened like tiny yellow trumpets in brightly painted window boxes. Some of the businesses boasted glass windows displaying their wares, and Thia tapped the glass admiringly, explaining that in Amaran, glass was produced only in small, thick panes.

Jezzil smiled as he watched her exclaim with wonder and delight.

She was particularly entranced by the printer's shop and by several bound books displayed in the window. One was open, showing the printed pages.

"Their scribes are so precise!" she murmured, astonished. "How could anyone write so small, so evenly? Every line is so straight, every letter the same, no matter how many times it is written."

"An invention from Pela," Jezzil explained. "This is done by a machine, not a scribe."

She stared at him. "A machine?"

"Yes. They can print whole volumes, and each is the same. They use lead letters that they can move around to print each page."

"How wonderful!" Thia said. "That way they could print the same page dozens of times. Why, they could make hundreds of scrolls!"

"They bind the scrolls together, see? When they're bound, they call them books," Jezzil said. "We had some Pelanese texts in the library at our cloisters."

"Did you have these printers in Ktavao?" she asked.

"No. The King of Pela, despite his shortcomings as a military leader, has been wise to encourage inventors in his land. Pela is ahead of Ktavao in many ways. They have many inventions that would prove useful to the Redai," Jezzil said. "Their firearms are far superior to the ones I was taught to use. Easier and faster to load and fire, far more accurate, and their range is more than twice that of our muskets."

"Does the Redai know that Pela possesses such weaponry?" Thia asked.

"I believe he must," Jezzil said. "He has his spies, like any leader."

They continued down the street, heading for the town square. When they reached it, they saw the market ranged around the perimeter, with its colorful stalls and displays. A crowd was gathering in the center of the square.

"What is it?" Thia asked.

Jezzil shaded his eyes from the sun. "Some kind of show," he replied. "Would you like to see?"

Thia nodded, her black eyes bright with eager curiosity above her modesty veil. They walked across the square, then made their way through the gathering crowd to the small troupe of traveling entertainers who were setting up a makeshift stage and scenery in the center of the square. They stood in the second row back, watching the preparations curiously until the performance began.

First there came a juggler, who kept daggers flying through the air from hand to hand, with nary a lost finger or even a cut. Thia made a soft exclamation of wonder in her own language. He learned closer to hear better. "What did you say?"

She whispered back, "How does he do that? Is it a skill? Or magic?"

Jezzil smiled. "A skill," he said. "I have seen others do it."

The next performer was a man who proceeded to insert, first, a knife, then a sword, into his mouth and down his gullet. Jezzil had never seen this done, and wondered if it was some kind of illusion. But since his discovery in Zajares's fortress of his own ability to Cast, he'd discovered that magic had a certain *feel* to it—almost an unheard vibration, a tingle in the air. It made the hairs on the back of his neck stir and gave him gooseflesh on his arms.

Several times the young warrior had been able to detect when someone was using folk conjury to heal, charm warts, or rid their crop of pests. Watching the sword-eater, he experienced no such tingle.

But magic or no, the entertainer put on a good show, finishing up by extinguishing a flaming torch in his mouth. The crowd clapped and stamped their feet as they threw coins into the baskets arrayed before them.

The next entertainment was a clown with a troupe of trained dogs that capered and jumped through hoops, barked on cue, and turned flips in the air. Thia's eyes shone as she regarded their antics, and Jezzil heard her laugh.

When the performance was finished, each of them tossed a coin into the basket before turning to walk through the marketplace. "You liked the clown," Jezzil said. "And the dogs."

"Yes," Thia said. "Where I was raised, little was funny or even amusing. The learned priests or the Mistress of Postulants would say that such a performance was frivolous, worldly, possibly even sinful. And yet, I found no harm in it."

"That is because there is none," Jezzil said. "Since I . . . left . . . the Pen Jav Dal, I have realized that most people live the way these folk do. Religion is but one part—often a very small part—of their lives. They have their own gods and goddesses. The gods I was raised to worship—these people know nothing of them."

"Heathens," Thia murmured, as though reciting an automatic response.

"Perhaps," Jezzil said. "But Thia, *you* do not worship my gods, nor I yours. What does that make us?"

She paused in mid-step, then slowly looked up at him, her dark eyes wide and haunted. It was several moments before she spoke. "Exiles . . ." she whispered.

Jezzil nodded. "As good a word as any." He reached over

and awkwardly patted her shoulder. "But I believe it is better to be two exiles together, rather than one exile alone."

She looked down, clearly at a loss for words, and Jezzil quickly changed the subject.

Immersed in their conversation, they turned the corner and left the main street behind. The cobblestones beneath their feet gave way to ridges of dried, rutted mud, and the buildings grew seedier, less prosperous, the farther they proceeded.

When a burst of raucous laughter broke out, Jezzil stopped what he'd been saying and turned. Thia was closest to the narrow walkway that edged the street, and she had to dodge out of the way quickly as the doors burst open and a big man hurtled out as though he'd been tossed by an angry bull.

The man landed in the street before them, perilously close to the midden channel, belly down. They heard him gasp as his wind was knocked out. Moments later he wheezed, caught his breath, then rose to hands and knees, spitting out filth.

Jezzil looked back at the door and saw that it was a tavern. As he watched, the door opened again, and a man and a woman appeared. He heard Thia catch her breath, and glanced down to see her staring uncomprehendingly at the other women.

She was wearing a yellow gown so bright it was painful to the eyes in the afternoon sunlight. It had slipped off her shoulder, revealing half of a rounded breast. Her lips and cheeks were unnaturally red. As she opened her mouth to laugh, Jezzil saw that she was missing several teeth.

The man who held her wrist was as slender and vicious as a stoat. He glared down at the burly man and snarled, "I told you, pay *before* you have your fun, or no deal! Now, do you want her or not?"

The big man lurched to his feet, then stood looking sullenly at the woman and her procurer. Finally, he reached into his vest and took out a small pouch. Scowling, he hurled three coins at the pimp. "All right, but she better be worth it!" he warned.

The woman tittered. "Oh, you'll have no complaints, dearie. C'mon with me, now . . ." She held out a hand, and the burly man, wiping the slime from his face, took it and followed her back inside.

The pimp gave Jezzil a measuring glance, then his gaze shifted to Thia. "Come to sell me your skinny sister, boy?" he jeered. "If you haven't, wait a few minutes. When Amalee's done for the plowman, she'll take you next."

Jezzil felt himself flushing scarlet. Turning to Thia, who was still standing there, uncomprehending, he took her arm and hurried her back up the street.

"What? What was all that about?" she asked, trying to turn back to see.

"Keep walking," Jezzil said tightly. "Come on. I should never have brought you here. I wasn't paying attention."

They headed back toward the caravan. When they left the cobblestones behind and were in sight of the merchants' encampment, Thia abruptly stopped. "You must tell me what happened back there," she said. "You understood what was happening. Everyone understood what was happening, except me. That woman, she was laughing at you, and at me. But not in the same way. Why? And I'm not wearing a slave collar. Why did that man speak of 'buying' me from you?"

Jezzil could feel the heat in his face, and could not meet her eyes. He searched for words, but there were none.

Thia reached out and took hold of his arm. He was surprised at the strength of her grasp. "Jezzil," she said, her voice holding impatience, almost anger, something he'd never heard from her before. "Tell me. I have been shut away from the world, but now I am out in it, part of it, and I must learn its ways, lest I come to harm from ignorance. You are the only person who knows my secret. I have trusted you, and you have trusted me. Now *tell* me."

Jezzil took a deep breath, shook his head. "It is not easy to speak of such things," he said, unable to meet her eyes. "We of the Chonao Brotherhood are told not to even think of them, and if we do, we must enact a penance on our flesh."

"I am no longer in the temple, and you no longer answer

to your brothers," she said, an edge in her voice. "We must survive. *I* must survive. Soon now I will be on my own. I need to learn."

"That woman . . ." Jezzil said. "She was . . . a whore."

"Whore . . ." Thia repeated the unfamiliar word softly. "And what is that?"

"A woman who sells her body—her womanhood—to any man who cares to pay the price. That man who was with her was her pimp. He sells her services, collects the money from the men who, who . . ." Jezzil shook his head and trailed off.

"I see," she said, and, glancing up, Jezzil could tell that she did, indeed, comprehend. "And there are many such women in towns and cities?"

Jezzil nodded. "And sometimes young men. Boys."

Thia shook her head. "I had no idea . . . and that is how they earn their keep?"

"Yes. Hardly a pleasant existence, I would think," Jezzil muttered, still unable to meet her eyes. A thought struck him. "What did you mean when you said you would soon be on your own?"

She hesitated, gave him a sideways glance as they walked on. Jezzil kept his gaze on her, but he did not push, only waited silently.

Finally, she said, "Do not tell, but I must leave the Shekk in a few days, when we reach Q'Kal."

"Why? How?"

She answered the second question first. "I shall wait until we camp near the city, then slip away, leaving no trace of where I am going. I'll find someplace to live, some useful work to do. There must be work for someone who is willing . . ." Her voice was not quite steady as she trailed off.

"Why?"

"I can't endanger the Shekk and his family. As long as I am with them, I make them targets for the priests. They have been kind to me. I cannot let them be harmed."

Jezzil nodded. "I shall miss you, Sister Thia."

"And I you, Brother Jezzil. But there is no help for it."

They walked on together until they were close to the wagons. Then Thia turned to the Chonao, her dark eyes intent above her veil. "Please, I am trusting you. Don't tell anyone."

"I swear," he said quietly. "I am Pen Jav Dal, remember?"

In the mountains of Amaran, winter still reigned. The black peaks and desolate rocky passes wore mantles of shimmering white snow and blue-tinged ice. The cold was a tangible presence. It rode with him, walked with him, lived with him, and clung to him like the lover he had never had.

He had traded in his scarlet robe for a deerskin shirt and leggings with the fur worn inside, plus a hooded fur cloak and mittens, but he was still chilled much of the time. Only when the sun shone brightly at midday, or when he stopped for the night at a hostel or crofter's hut, did he truly feel warm and comfortable. His shaven pate still marked him for who he was, so he was always given the best seat in the house, the one closest to the fire.

The crofters and innkeepers must have thought him mad, traveling by horseback alone in these barren, winter-locked mountains. But they kept their opinions, if any, to themselves and never even looked at him directly, so greatly did they fear him. For a High Priest of Boq'urak to be traveling so far from the twin ziggurats without an entourage and armed escort was unheard of—but nobody challenged him. Even the robbers who infested the heights left him alone. They were all too frightened of the One he served.

How ironic that is, Varn thought derisively. *I am traveling without the permission of my order, much less their blessing. If any of these robbers were to kill me, there would be no reprisal for my death. Why should the council enact punishment for the death of one of their own who is now disgraced? One who defied the orders of the council to search for a missing novice they all firmly believe is dead?*

Oh, they had searched for Thia, searched for months. But the girl had vanished into the blizzard as thoroughly as a single snowflake vanished into a snowbank. In vain had the High Priests invoked the god, asking him to reveal Thia's whereabouts. Boq'urak had remained silent.

At last they had concluded that she must be dead, that she'd gotten lost in the blizzard and wandered off the road. Her body might be found come spring, partially thawed and gnawed by predators. Or, more likely, she had fallen into some crevice in the rocks and would never be found.

Varn was the only one who refused to accept the decree of the council. He had stubbornly maintained that Thia lived, that she had escaped, and that she must be tracked and brought back to the twin ziggurats so she could atone for her sin against the god.

He had no concrete reason for his belief, just a growing conviction that he *must* search for Thia. So when word had come to Verang a tenday ago that an unseasonable early spring thaw had cleared the mountain passes, he filled a saddlebag with provisions and some clothing, took all the money he could lay his hands on from his brother priests' secret stashes, saddled a horse and rode out before dawn.

Since leaving Verang, he'd spent each day in the saddle, chilled but resolute, determined to succeed in his quest.

Now, as his mount picked its way along the downslope of the last pass leading out of the Amaranian heights, Varn realized that the ice and snow surrounding him was not piled quite as high. The Sun was beating down on the hood of his bearskin cloak, and he was actually warm enough to push it back in order to feel it on his face and his naked scalp. Soon after, he dared to slide off his furred mittens.

Three hours later the trail he was following paralleled a narrow rivulet of stream, and the water was actually *flowing*. Varn halted his mount and swung down, his nearly empty waterskin in hand.

Leaving his horse tethered to the spiky branch of a conifer, Varn picked his way across the wet rocks until he could crouch on a small, flat tongue of stone to fill his waterskin. Before him lay an icy section of the cliff, black rock shadowed from the Sun.

After so many days riding through a completely frozen landscape, the rush of flowing water was like a benediction. Trying to keep his hands from touching the icy current, he lowered the waterskin into the stream. As it slowly filled, he looked across the little rivulet to the ice-rimed cliff wall and beheld his own reflection. It had been years since he'd seen himself; mirrors were a symbol of vanity, not allowed by the order.

Varn stared at himself, fascinated. He looked very different as a man than he had as a boy.

As he stared, time seemed to slow, to stop around him. The real world receded, grew distant. His face began to Change.

At the same moment, he felt the touch of the god within his body. Varn had been Incarnate three times, and recognized the sensation of having his body shift and alter when Boq'urak touched it.

His face . . . it was now overlaid with the face of the god. His eyes were his no longer, but Boq'urak's huge, round, lidless orbs. He was not truly Incarnate, for no tentacles had sprouted and his suddenly dry mouth had not actually changed shape, but there was no denying the presence of Boq'urak within him, the stamp of Boq'urak lying like a brand across his own unfamiliar features.

He managed to move his lips. "Lord," he said. "Command thy servant."

The voice spoke. Was it solely in his mind, or was it actual sound? Varn could not tell. *My servant,* it said. *My faithful servant.*

Varn felt a tremendous surge of gratitude and affirmation.

"Lord," he said. "I left the order behind to go in search of the novice, Thia. My brethren did not understand why I did that. I am as outcast as she is now."

They will understand when you return to them, the voice said. *You will be honored for your faith. Nothing moves save by My hand.*

He nodded. "Thank you, Lord. You want me to find her and capture her. That is your will?"

It is My will. She has witnessed the Rite of Incarnation. She has denied Me. She must pay for her impiety. Capture her, and give her to Me. Perform the rite with her.

Varn swallowed, as his throat suddenly seemed to close up. Thia . . . so warm, so alive, lying dead before him? "Must she pay with her life, Lord?" he ventured. "Surely she can be brought back to the way. She is . . . she is so young."

She will be Mine.

Varn nodded. "I will obey, Lord."

Without warning, the external world returned with a rush. The waterskin slipped from his numb fingers, and he pitched forward, his arms going up to the elbows in the stream's frigid embrace. Master Varn gasped, groping for his waterskin. By the time he found it and hoisted it out of the stream, then looked back up, the Sun had gone behind a cloud. The High Priest could no longer see himself in the icy surface of the black rock.

Memories of Thia assailed him as he stood and went over to fasten the waterskin to his saddle, then mounted his horse. Thia as a child, looking admiringly up at him, her huge dark eyes filled with trust. Thia as a girl, gawky and coltish, her intelligence setting her apart from the rest of the postulants. Thia as a novice, her body beneath the shapeless habit ripe with the promise of a woman's curves, a woman's fire . . .

Varn's mouth tightened. She was not for him. Boq'urak had spoken. She would go to the god, and he would be but the vessel that contained the god's essence. It would not be his hands that stroked Thia's nakedness. It would not be his body that mounted her.

Hot resentment flickered. *Boq'urak has spoken. Very well. He will take her body, and her life. But before I relinquish myself to Him, I will take some reward for myself. An embrace. A kiss. I will tell her I love her, and hear her speak of her love for me. And then we shall share a kiss. Boq'urak said I was His faithful servant. Surely He will not begrudge me one kiss.*

Six days after their stopover at the village of Coquillan, the caravan was camped in a large meadow just outside Q'Kal. Thia struggled through the last meal she spent with the old Shekk and his daughters, wishing all the while that she could openly thank them for their kindness and say farewell. She reminded herself fiercely that her actions were for their own good, but in the past months they had become dear to her, and it was hard to know that she would never see them again.

After supper, as the sun was setting in a splash of sullen crimson, she put on all her clothing, layering it on so she would not have to carry it. Lastly, she pulled on her dullest, most nondescript tunic and skirt, then laced on her stout boots. She had no bag, only her shawl, to serve as a pack. Quickly, she arranged her few belongings in the center—the arm bangles and necklaces the Shekk had bestowed upon her, the few coins she'd managed to hoard, and a small parcel of bread, dried fruit, and cheese, then brought the corners together and tied them into a pack that could be slung across her back.

Slipping through the evening shadows, Thia stole away from the familiar wagon, feeling tears threaten. She blinked them back, concentrating only on moving quickly and staying unseen.

She kept to the underbrush until out of sight of the caravan, then resolutely squared her shoulders and struck out on the hard-beaten road that led into Q'Kal.

The caravan had camped on a hill overlooking the city, and as it grew darker, she saw the lights spring up before her as the lamplighters made their rounds. Q'Kal was a large city, far bigger than any she had seen before.

Thia swallowed, fighting down her fear, and forced herself to keep walking swiftly. She had no idea where she might be able to obtain lodging or food, and was terrified that someone would mistake her for a whore because she was alone and friendless. Since Jezzil had told her about whoring as a way for a woman to earn her living, she'd eavesdropped with far greater attention to the rough talk of the guardsmen as they approached the city. The way they talked about whores frightened her—as though they were not women at all, only vessels for their seed, bodies for them to manhandle.

She tightened her modesty veil, determined not to let anything but her eyes show. According to what she'd seen, whores went unveiled, so she hoped her veil would keep her from being accosted.

For a while she'd considered dressing like a boy. Her hair was still barely long enough to touch her ears and collar, and she was slender enough, with small breasts. But since coming to stay with the Shekk, and having more to eat, she would have had to bind her breasts painfully in order to appear sufficiently flat-chested. Her voice was a problem; too high-pitched. And, most important, she had not spent enough time in the company of men or boys to emulate them. So Thia had reluctantly abandoned the notion.

After weeks with the caravan, she was accustomed to long marches. She lengthened her stride, falling into the mindless rhythm of walking, determined to get into Q'Kal before the city gates were closed for the night.

She concentrated on moving swiftly and surely, determined not to think about where she would sleep, how she would live, what would happen. *Let the future worry about itself, the present is where we live,* she thought, remembering an old Amaranian proverb.

Hoofbeats sounded behind her on the road. Thia's heart bounded in her chest. Could the Shekk have missed her?

Quickly, she scuttled to the side of the road, scrambled up the bank and pushed her way into the brush, feeling greenbriers catch her clothing and flesh.

Dropping to her hands and knees, she wormed her way into a thicket, then peered out cautiously.

A rider was approaching, sure enough, a rider astride a horse that moved as smoothly and quietly as a shadow. Thia tensed. *It couldn't be . . . could it? There are many gray horses . . .*

Just as the horseman came abreast of her hiding place, the gray halted, standing obediently in the middle of the road. Thia heard the rider's voice. "Thia? I know you are there. Come out."

She blinked in astonishment, then wriggled forward, losing more skin and snagging her veil so thoroughly that she had to remove it to untangle it. "Jezzil?" she whispered as she struggled with the thin fabric, trying not to tear it.

"Yes . . ."

Finally the veil came free, and she hastily fixed it in place, then slid down the bank, her small bundle of food and her few possessions bumping along beside her.

Falar whickered as she caught the familiar scent. "What are you doing here, Brother Jezzil?" Thia asked as she walked up to pat the mare's neck.

"I came looking for you tonight, and you were gone." The Moon would rise late, and she could not make out his features, only see his form silhouetted against the sky. "You left without saying farewell."

Thia bit her lip, hesitated, then blurted, "Forgive me. I couldn't bear to. I was afraid . . ."

"Afraid of what?"

"Afraid of everything. But mostly afraid that if I tried to bid you farewell, I would lose the will to go. And I *must* go," she said fiercely. "I'm endangering the Shekk and his daughters—perhaps even the whole caravan!—by my very presence. I had to get away."

He did not answer, but dismounted smoothly from Falar's back and walked over to her. Try as she might, she could not discern his features save as a pale blur. "I know," he said. "I do understand. But . . . I found I could not stay with the caravan when you were gone. I had to come after you."

She shook her head dazedly. "Wh-Why?"

"Because, Sister Thia, I understand you. I trust you. And I cannot see you come to harm because you are alone in a strange city." His hand moved to his side and she heard the clink of coins as he jingled them. "I asked for my payout and left."

"You've left your job?" Thia could scarcely believe it.

"Yes. We'll go to Q'Kal together. You'll be safer that way. And I . . ." He hesitated, then chuckled, one of the first signs of amusement she'd ever detected in him. "And I will have someone to talk to, someone who understands."

Thia's mind raced like a herd of startled cattle. "You want to stay with me? For us to . . . live together?"

He took a step toward her. "Fear not, I mean no disrespect, sister. I speak only with respect and friendship. I believe we could . . . help . . . each other."

She backed away a step, hesitated. "You are telling the truth," she muttered, thinking furiously. "I know you are."

"I would never lie to you," Jezzil said.

"You had better not," Thia said dryly.

The movement of his head reminded her of Falar's when she pricked up her ears and gazed warily into the distance. "Aside from the fact that lying is a sin," he said, "and I have enough sin burdening my soul to last me for a dozen lifetimes, what did you mean by that?"

She took a deep breath. "I can tell when someone is lying," she said. "Always."

He did not speak for a moment, then, when he did, his words were slow, thoughtful. "I . . . see. How do you do that? Can you read faces, eyes, that well?"

"I don't know how I do it," she said. "I just can. I don't need to see faces, or eyes."

He made a sound, half amused, half skeptical.

Thia flushed. "I can prove it," she said. "Tell me three things from your past, make one of them a lie. I cannot see your face in this darkness."

"You don't have to prove—"

"Just do it."

Jezzil was silent for a moment, then said, in slow, deliberate tones, "I abandoned my brothers to die in a fire. I have never known a woman. I slew a monster in a moat."

Thia laughed harshly. "You think to trick me," she said. "All of those things are the truth."

Now it was Jezzil's turn to take a step backward. "How do you do it? Magic?"

"I don't know. I just can," she replied. "I have always been able to do it."

"Can you do other magic?"

"No," she said, then remembered that he'd known where she was, even when she was hidden. "Can you?"

"I . . . I . . ." He stammered for a moment, then must have remembered who he was talking to, and said simply, "Yes."

"Let me think for a moment," Thia said. Folding her arms across her chest, she paced back and forth across the road, thinking. *It would be good to have someone to talk to,* she mused. *But . . . he is a man! From what the High Sister told us, even men who are well-intentioned cannot control themselves. There were stories that even the High Priests succumbed to fleshly temptations in Verang at times.*

The thought of the High Priests reminded her that they might be trying to trace her, follow her trail. *But they are looking for a young woman alone,* she reminded herself. *Not a woman who shares a hearth with a man.*

She glanced back at him over her shoulder, heard an impatient sound from Falar, then heard her paw the roadway. Jezzil spoke to her, his voice holding unmistakable authority, and the mare stood still.

If Jezzil were with me, no one could break in and harm me while I slept, Thia thought. *No priest, no drunken bruiser looking for a whore. Jezzil is a warrior. And I must sleep sometime . . .*

Her heart rose a bit within her as she realized she'd made her decision. Her steps swift and sure, she walked back to him. "Let us try it," she said. "I am willing."

He nodded. "Good," he said, and she heard relief and pleasure in his voice. "On to Q'Kal, then." He swung up on Falar and reached down a hand. "Hand me your bundle."

She gave it to him, and he quickly lashed it to one of the ties on the saddle. He reached his hand down again. "Now you."

Thia looked up at him. "Me? Ride with you?"

"It grows late," he said. "We don't want the city gates to close before we can get there."

After a few abortive tries, he rode Falar over by the bank, and Thia was able to climb up, then slide on behind him. She perched uneasily on Falar's round rump, feeling the surge of the strong muscles between her thighs, through her rucked-up skirts.

"Hold onto me," Jezzil directed. "We must hurry a bit."

Thia leaned forward and grabbed his belt.

He must have given some signal, for Falar's hindquarters bunched, and then they were heading down the road at a dizzying pace. Thia had never gone so fast.

She found that she was clinging, not to Jezzil's belt, but had wrapped her arms around his body, hiding her face against his back. Her nostrils were full of the smell of oiled leather, and the edges of the plates in his armor dug into the skin of her forehead, cheeks, and chin.

Falar's hoofbeats sounded like miniature thunder as she galloped, and Thia struggled to hang on, to balance. She clamped her legs tightly about the mare's flanks.

She heard Jezzil shout, "Stop that! Do you want her to pitch us off?" But even before his warning, she'd felt the muscles of the mare's rump tighten like a drawn bowstring. Hastily, she forced herself to loosen the muscles of her calves.

The cantle of the saddle dug into her thighs and groin, the plates from Jezzil's armor scored her flesh, the night rushed past her so fast that she grew dizzy and her head reeled.

And yet Thia had never felt so alive, so *free*. She heard a sound, realized it was coming from inside her, bubbling up like clear water from a mountain spring.

It was laughter. Pure, joyous laughter.

5

Eregard

Eregard Livon Willom q'Injaad, third son of King Agivir of Pela, stood with his brothers on the wall-walk of the ancient fortress that enclosed much of the capital city of Minoma.

The ramparts of the old fortress stood high above the city that had outgrown their limits two centuries ago. The fortress itself had crumbled, as had the castle it guarded. But the outer protective wall remained, enclosing the royal palace Agivir's grandsire had built, along with the Old City.

Eregard leaned on the rampart and sighed as he looked down at the prosperous, bustling harbor town. It was a beautiful vista, and the autumn air was as clear and tangy as a fine Pelanese vintage. The Prince could easily make out the blue-green waters of the Narrow Sea beyond Minoma's sheltered bay. So many ships rode at anchor that their spars and masts resembled the forests from whence they'd come.

If I concentrate on the view, the Prince thought, *I won't have to listen to Salesin gloat about wedding Lady Ulandra. I can just let his voice blur into the whisper of the wind and the cries of the sea birds. I will not allow myself to envision my brother screaming as he plunges down from these ramparts to the street below.*

Salesin, Crown Prince of Pela, Viceroy of Kata, noticed his younger brother's preoccupation with the view. "Eregard! Don't look so sour, this is good news!"

Eregard nodded. "Indeed, brother," he said softly. "Excellent."

"You weren't even listening!" Salesin accused. "Hear me, baby brother! Father says that if I produce an heir within a year, he'll consider relinquishing the crown. He wants to be free to spend more time with Mother." The heir's tone betrayed his contempt for a king who would let a woman— even his queen, the Princes' mother—influence him. "What d'you think of that, little brother?"

Eregard was royal, and he'd learned to control his features before he learned to straddle a horse. Royals did not betray their inner thoughts or emotions . . . not to friends, and most certainly not to enemies. So his expression when he turned to face his brother was neutral, conveying only polite interest. "I think Mother thrives on company, and we should all spend more time with her."

Salesin stared at his brother for a moment, then threw back his handsome head and laughed, long and loud. "Where did you learn to dissemble so well, youngster? In one of your everlasting books?"

Eregard smiled thinly. "Where else, brother? Books are no substitute for your fleshpots, of a certain, but they do teach a few minor lessons."

Salesin's grin broadened, losing all semblance of good humor, until his teeth were bared wolfishly. "Remind me to take you along to some of my haunts, brother. You could use a few lessons in learning to be a man . . . if it's not already too late, that is. You haven't been baring your backside to Lord Malgar and his mincing bunch, have you?"

Despite his control, Eregard felt himself flush hotly, and knew that his brother had not missed that. He shook his head, but held his tongue. *Don't let him bait you. He always wins, and he never stops. Push him, and you will regret it . . .*

As the brothers bristled at each other, Prince Adranan,

whom both had forgotten, stepped between them. "Here, now. Let's have none of that. Mother wouldn't like it."

Salesin's lip curled. "Adranan, try not to be any stupider than you can help. Who cares what Mother would like?"

Eregard looked at his brothers, then shook his head inwardly. *Did our mother cuckold the King? How can we be siblings? We are nothing alike!*

Agivir's sons were all young, but any resemblance between them ended there. At twenty-seven, Crown Prince Salesin was tall, lean, and disturbingly handsome. His men jokingly called him the "Demon Lover," in homage to both his looks and his cold-blooded prowess with women. The Prince had dark, saturnine features and gleaming black hair with a pronounced widow's peak. A short beard and moustache framed his thin lips. His eyes were pale brown, almost the color of amber, startling in his dark countenance.

Prince Adranan was two years younger. He was also dark, but was built like a wine cask, tall with broad shoulders and a gut that betrayed his fondness for ale and rich foods. Despite his bulk, he was a formidable fighter, an excellent shot, and an even more expert swordsman. His good-natured smile was gap-toothed; he'd had two of his front teeth knocked out in a brawl during one of his incognito tavern crawls in Minoma, and refused to wear his false ivory teeth except during state occasions.

Nineteen-year-old Eregard was a full head shorter than his brothers. He had impeccable taste and always dressed in the latest fashion, but his elegant clothing did little to improve his unprepossessing exterior. Pale, freckled skin, lank, mouse-brown hair, and eyes that were an indeterminate shade between blue and gray made him easy to overlook. The spectacles he wore for reading either dangled on a ribbon around his neck or were pushed up onto the top of his head. He was as heavy as Adranan, but without the underlying muscle. His belly bulged over his fine, tooled belt.

Salesin stared intently into his youngest brother's eyes, then suddenly laughed. "Oh, you should see yourself, baby brother. If looks were weapons, I'd be choking on my own lifeblood right now. Watch yourself, Eregard. You just . . . watch yourself."

Rage bubbled in Eregard, and he couldn't disguise his anger. He longed to draw his sword and bury the point in Salesin's throat. Or . . . there was always the rampart. Up and over, yes . . .

But there was no point in trying. Salesin was much stronger, an experienced fighter. The Crown Prince was a master swordsman, while he was barely beyond the basics.

Besides, Adranan wouldn't let him do it, even supposing he could somehow get the best of the heir in a physical tussle. Eregard drew a slow, deep breath. *Control. You must learn control. Salesin will be King, remember. Already he wields almost as much power as Father. Kill him and you commit treason.*

Aloud, he said, "You go too far, brother. But for Adranan's sake, I'll say no more."

The second-in-waiting for the throne of Pela clapped him on the back. "There's the lad! Salesin, what say you? Peace between you?"

The Crown Prince did not reply, but he shrugged, and Eregard knew that was the only concession he would get. Anger stirred in him again, but he repressed it.

"Just wait until I'm King," Salesin said. "There'll be no more buy-offs or ceding of land to avoid trouble. Any country that dares look askance at Pela will face war, all-out war. Father used to be a force to reckon with, but in his old age he's grown as spineless as a jellyfish."

Eregard bit his lip until it stung fiercely, but he did not rise to Salesin's bait, knowing that's what his brother wanted.

Luckily for Eregard, a distraction was approaching at a brisk pace. A group of ladies-in-waiting out for their daily constitutional were almost upon them, so the three Princes fell silent. As each lady drew even with them, she sank down in a rustle of satin brocade and Severian lace, curtsying deeply.

Eregard gave each of them a nod and a polite smile. Adranan had a grin, a guffaw, and something personal to say to each, sending many scuttling away, blushing and giggling.

Salesin gave each lady a brief, cool stare—even those whom Eregard knew he'd bedded.

Following behind the ladies-in-waiting came a gaggle of barefoot serving boys and girls, carrying palm fans, shawls, pomander balls, boxes of sweets, parasols, and squirming lapdogs.

Eregard regarded the colorful display, wishing for a moment that he could be one of those boys, with no care in the world except to carry his lady's lapdog or parasol. *If I were a servant, she would be so far above me that I would not even dare to think of her,* he thought. *I could have followed her all the day long, listened to her voice, and been happy in her presence. I would have been spared the torture of hope.*

The Prince turned away from the crowd to gaze back over the ramparts at Minoma. The Sun had gone behind a cloud; the sea no longer sparkled. Directly below him he could see the dark green tree-lined paths of the King's menagerie. Commoner and noble alike strolled along the paths, gazing at the rare animals in their spacious cages. Faintly, he heard a cry from one of the wild desert cats, a snarl that deepened into a full-throated roar.

Adranan poked him with an elbow and pointed. "Look," he said. "King's messengers, two of them. Odds are they've come straight up from the port, with news from the mainland."

Eregard watched as the two riders approached, seeing they were urging their horses onward with whip and spur. Their mounts clattered up the cobblestoned street, running all-out. Passersby scattered to get out of their way as they recognized the official scarlet tunics banded with black.

As though the Sun's disappearance were a signal, the wind picked up, reminding them this was autumn, and winter was scant weeks away. A chill gust made Eregard shiver as it buffeted him.

Salesin swore as his cloak snapped out behind him. "Thrice-damned wind!" he muttered. "I'm going in before I catch my death. Besides, I need to see what message they brought."

Good riddance, Eregard thought. Despite the cold, he waited, shivering, until his brother was long gone. Adranan stood beside him. Only when Eregard bade his brother farewell did the middle Prince speak.

"Listen, Eregard," he said, his normally jovial features twisted with concern. "Don't let Salesin bait you. He's . . . he can be . . . cruel."

"That's putting it mildly," Eregard said.

"He has spies everywhere. Plot against him—or even *think* about plotting against him—and you'll find yourself exiled. Father may well abdicate in his favor."

"And would that be good for Pela?"

Adranan smiled ruefully. "Depends on your point of view. It would fill up the dungeons with political prisoners, thus providing jobs for many additional gaolers. And on the mainland, those outspoken Katan grumblers would learn to guard their tongues and watch what they print. No more outrageous political ·cartoons or broadsides. Salesin would make short work out of suppressing any hint of rebellion."

"True," Eregard agreed dourly.

"I care about you, little brother," Adranan said. "Heed my warning. Don't cross him."

Sound advice, Eregard thought. He managed to smile at his brother. "Adranan the Peacemaker. Why couldn't you have been firstborn?"

Adranan smiled. "Being heir is not my idea of a good life. I'm content to be the King's arm. I'm not good at intrigue."

"Unfortunately, Salesin excels at it," Eregard observed bitterly.

"Yes he does. And I don't want to lose my favorite brother," Adranan said. "So control your temper, Eregard. There are eyes and ears everywhere."

"Sound advice, brother," Eregard agreed. "I thank you for it."

"I'm going down to the Golden Sail for a pint," Adranan said. "Join me?"

Eregard shook his head. "No, thanks. I should be getting back. I was going to visit Mother before supper."

Adranan nodded, then headed out to meet his personal guard where they stood waiting patiently.

Moments later, Eregard, clutching his cloak around him, hurried down the stairs. A small contingent of soldiers, his personal guard, awaited him on the landing.

Eregard nodded brusquely at the sergeant, then started down the next flight of weathered, oft-mended steps. When he reached the street level, the Prince headed back toward the royal palace. Flanked by his guard, Eregard walked down the oft-repaired streets, automatically avoiding the slimy gutters running down the middle. Smells warred with each other: the stench from the gutters, a pungent reek from an outhouse, the warm scent of bread and ale, the sharp yeasty stink of horse piss, the sweet fragrance from a flower-seller's cart, and the mouth-watering fragrance of gamebird pie.

Minoma's Old Town was old indeed, far older than the royal palace. It was at least as old as the massive wall. The houses were bluestone and weathered wood, with occasional newer structures of half-timbering and whitewashed stucco.

Shops lined the streets, interspersed with residences. A goldsmith's shop, with a beautifully kept exterior, perched uncomfortably next to an old, low-ceilinged tavern, rowdy and full of sailors even at this early hour. A wool-merchant's shop presented splashes of color from the dyed hanks of yarn, and a sail-mender's shop was doing a brisk business.

Eregard strode along, head down, and the sergeant of the guard forged ahead, making sure his path was clear and that no knife or gun-wielding assassins lurked in the alleys. The Prince's thoughts were as bleak and cold as the autumn clouds that continued to block the Sun.

If Father abdicates in favor of Salesin, what will happen to me? I'll be here, stuck at court, having to watch the two of them together. I'll have to watch him treat her badly, for Salesin treats none of his women well, and to him a highborn lady has the same furnishings down below as a tavern wench—

The thought was so distressing that he forced himself into

considering something else, a subject he normally detested—politics.

What if he decides that the Chonao Redai . . . what's his name?—Kerezau, that's it—what if he decides that Kerezau is too powerful for Pela to fight? What if he tries for an alliance with that barbarian instead?

Bleakly, Eregard wondered if Kerezau had any daughters. If he did, that was bad. Adranan was a formidable fighter. He could lead troops. Adranan was valuable. Whilst he, Eregard, was useful only as a potential pawn in a ruler's marriage game.

Scowling, Eregard kicked a loose cobblestone on the edge of a dank pothole, sending it skittering into a narrow, greasy little alleyway. He glanced over at the sergeant. "Notify the street warden to fix that spot."

"Yes, Your Highness."

The Prince lengthened his stride, pulling his cloak tight around him as a chill gust whipped down the streets. *A touch of winter's breath*, he thought. The wind suited his mood, matched the cold desolation growing within his heart. *Soon I won't even be able to think of her without committing treason.*

His dark thoughts accompanied him the rest of the way home, dogging his steps like a relentless beggar. The walk from the old fortress wall to the royal palace was not long, but it was all uphill, and Eregard was not in the best of shape. The Prince was panting by the time he reached the gates and was bowed through them.

Dismissing his personal guard, he started up the raked gravel toward the entrance. The palace consisted of one large square central building with three smaller wings on each side and at the rear. It was built solidly of pale gray stone, with red tiles on its roofs lending a touch of cheery color against the leaden skies.

Soldiers drilled in the courtyard as Eregard walked by. Absently, the Prince returned the Captain of the Guard's salute. Reaching the broad, sweeping staircase that led up to the palace, the Prince plodded up the wide steps.

He was halfway up when some sixth sense made him look up—and then he saw her. She was evidently just back from her own constitutional, and, as he watched, Lady Ulandra's slender form stepped through the palace entrance and vanished.

Eregard's steps lengthened until he was taking the steps two and three at a time. Part of his mind shouted at him to slow down, as befitted royal dignity, but he redoubled his efforts.

The Prince burst through the doors and was rewarded by the sight of the Lady Ulandra, carrying her small dog, just ahead of him in the entrance hall with its black and white marble pavement. Her maid, laden with shawls and a cushion, was just disappearing through the door toward the east wing of the palace.

She's alone! Eregard realized. At the sound of his rapid footsteps, she turned, startled, her hand raised to remove her small, stylish hat.

The Prince halted his undignified rush, then just stood there, staring at her, at a loss for something to say. Color washed the lady's pale cheeks, and she hastily dropped into a deep curtsy. "Your Highness!"

"Lady Ulandra," the Prince said. He walked over to her and held out his hand to help her rise. He felt a thrill throughout his entire body as her fingers met his; he had never touched her before.

Lady Ulandra q'Jinasii was small and slender, with pale, delicate features and thick, flaxen hair that glimmered pale as crystal in the dimness of the hall. Her brows and lashes were light, too, something Eregard had never noticed before. Suddenly he realized that for formal occasions she must use cosmetics to darken them, and rouge to color her cheeks.

Her eyes were light blue, as clear as a winter sky, and often as distant.

But today, as she stood looking up at Eregard, there was nothing distant about them. She was smiling, her small, even teeth echoing her modest pearl necklace.

Her walking dress was a color that Eregard had seen her wear before, the dusky hue of a blue rose.

Eregard forced himself to relinquish her hand, then, realizing that she was waiting for him to speak, he cast about for something—anything!—to say.

"It's turning cooler, my lady. I am afraid winter is just around the corner."

She nodded. "Yes, Your Highness. When I left this morning it was very pleasant, but now it almost seems that a storm is brewing."

"That's what Salesin said," Eregard said, hating himself for stooping to bring his brother's name into the conversation. But he wanted to watch her features when she heard her betrothed's name. *Does she love him?*

An expression flicked across her features, then was gone. *Wariness, apprehension, even. Certainly not warmth.* Eregard's heart beat fast. *Stop it. It's impossible, and you know it.*

She dropped her gaze. "The Crown Prince is, as always, perceptive," Ulandra said. "The weatherwatchers are predicting snows in the mountains, and rain in Minoma by midnight, Your Highness."

Noticing that Ulandra's small, shaggy dog was squirming in her grasp, Eregard reached over to cautiously pat the creature's head. The dog eyed him warily, but used to being fussed over, tolerated the caress. "Poor little fellow," Eregard said. "Always having to put up with strangers petting him. What's his name?"

One part of his mind was shouting that he should give her leave to go, that keeping her talking was an invitation to scandal. But he was drunk on being so close to her, close enough to smell her sachet, close enough to touch her, if he but dared.

She gave a breathy laugh. "You'll laugh if I tell you, Your Highness. His name is Wolf. But it's actually an apt name, for he thinks he's the size of the King's mastiffs."

Eregard chuckled. Ulandra bent over and deposited Wolf on the gleaming marble floor, letting him sniff at an urn filled with lush blossoms from the King's conservatory. *I should let her go . . . but what if we never meet again?*

He pointed at the small book that protruded from the top of her reticule. "Poetry, lady?"

She laughed a little and colored. "Yes, Your Highness. I adore Rimbala. He's so . . ." she hesitated, casting about for words.

"Passionate?" Eregard suggested.

Her blush deepened and she dropped her eyes. "Yes, I suppose that is the correct word, Your Highness. His words, they make my heart beat faster. Do they affect you so, Your Highness?"

With all his being he longed to hear his name on her lips, but court etiquette forbade such informality. He smiled at her. "Yes, they do, my lady." He hesitated, then added, "I have set some of Rimbala's most passionate verses to music. Would you like me to play for you sometime?"

Immediately he knew he'd erred, been too familiar. Lady Ulandra did not look up as she whispered, "Perhaps, Your Highness. Perhaps I might go along when you visit your mother the Queen, and we could both hear your artistry, my Prince."

Eregard knew he'd been rebuffed with exquisite delicacy. He admired the lady's virtue, even as he sighed inwardly. Glancing up at the clock in the wide hallway, he saw that they had been talking long enough to raise eyebrows. *I must let her go.*

He nodded formally at her. "Lady Ulandra, you often walk at this time of day?"

"Yes, Your Highness, often."

Eregard inclined his head slightly, first to her, then, jokingly, to Wolf. "Then I shall hope that our paths may cross again, and soon. It would be a pleasure to have such excellent company on my daily constitutional."

Ulandra blushed becomingly and sank into a deep curtsy. "You do us too much honor, Your Highness. But Wolf and I thank you."

Turning and walking away from her was one of the hardest things Eregard had done in his short life, but he knew it was the right thing to do. He was tempted to turn back and wave, but royal dignity would not permit such a common gesture.

The Prince made his way back to his apartments in the west wing of the palace, alternating between despair and elation. He had never before spoken to Lady Ulandra alone, and that was enough to set his heart leaping. But what if this was the only time? Remembering the faint perfume of her sachet, his head swam.

When he reached his bedchamber, he gestured impatiently at his manservant and the guard. "Leave me!"

They bowed themselves out, and Eregard sank onto a sofa to brood.

The Prince's apartments were cozily cluttered and a bit shabby. He never entertained there, so comfort was his main concern. The bed boasted only a small fabric canopy, and bookshelves occupied every wall. The royal arms were carved into the footboard of the bed, but the rest of the furniture was unadorned. Chairs and sofas were overstuffed and comfortable, with mirrored candelabras providing light for reading at night.

After a few minutes, the Prince opened a chest and removed a stringed balankala. He fiddled with it for a few moments, tuning it, then began to strum a plaintive melody.

Words . . . what words?

He glanced down at the sheet music he'd begun scribbling yesterday. *Ulandra, not an easy name to rhyme, 'tis true . . .* After a few minutes of adding in and crossing out, the Prince began to sing in a trained, resonant baritone.

> *"The world is hard, the world is cruel*
> *It treats me as a lowly fool*
> *I cannot have my own true love*
> *Aside I am unfairly . . ."*

He paused. "Shoved?" he ventured finally.
No! It rhymes, but 'tis an inelegant word.

After trying "moved," and finding that it was completely wrong, the Prince abandoned the first verse for the second.

> *"The world treats me like a clown . . .*
> *'Twere better if I were struck down*
> *If I can't have my destined love*
> *By lightning bolts shot from above."*

That's better, he thought. After a moment's reflection he scratched out the word "destined" and substituted "one true."

Now for the third verse, which was only partly completed:

> *"The world is so unfair to me*
> *I cannot hold her . . ."*

Eregard frowned. *On my knee?* He shook his head. *No! Think!*

> *"The world is so unfair to me*
> *I cannot hold her tenderly*
> *I cannot kiss the girl I love*
> *I'm sure we'd fit—"*

Like hand in glove? he wondered, then shook his head. For a moment he had a wild impulse to hurl the balankala across the room. But it was an old instrument, and a gift from his mother. Eregard set it down carefully, then just sat, head in his hands.

What am I going to do?

Minutes later he was roused from his wretched musings when he heard the scuff of a foot, then a discreet cough. "Your Highness?"

Eregard did not turn his head to speak to his manservant, not wanting Regen to see his eyes. "I wanted to be alone," he said coldly. "Therefore, if you've disturbed me, Regen, it must be important."

"Aye, Your Highness," the servant said. "It is. Your father

the King has asked to see you immediately. He's in the conservatory, my Prince."

Eregard nodded. "I'll be along directly," he said. "As soon as I've made myself presentable. Go ahead and tell my father I am coming, Regen."

The man bowed. "Yes, Your Highness."

Eregard hastily splashed water from the ewer onto his face, then ran a comb through his shoulder-length hair. Quickly, he changed his padded leather outerjerkin for a padded satin one, and buckled a gold-buckled belt around his chubby middle.

A quick glance in the fine Ventanian mirror that hung opposite his bed showed him that he was ready. Eregard quickly left the room.

He threaded his way through the corridors and down several stairways, then more corridors, until he reached the southern wing. The conservatory was built as an extension on the back of this wing. Eregard saw his father walking alone at the end of the glass-walled annex. The guards at the doors opened them and formally bowed him through.

Eregard stepped into the conservatory, smelling the heady scents of exotic blossoms and rich wet soil. Humid warmth surrounded him as he walked down the shallow steps and headed for his father. Urns of plants and trees were everywhere, interspersed with immaculately tended banks of hothouse blooms. The floor was of green marble, so the plants and flowers seemed to have sprouted from the stone pavement.

The King, hearing the footsteps, straightened up from a tub of blooming alandeors and waited for his son to join him.

Agivir Cosomiso Invictos q'Injaad III was a man who had once been tall, broad-shouldered, and imposing in his battle armor. There were traces still of that man in the King's craggy features and painfully straight carriage. But his body had sagged and thickened, his lank hair—what was left of it—was gray, and his beard was sparse and untidy. His gaze, once so direct and unflinching, had a tendency to wander.

His eyesight was failing, so he wore a quizzing glass around his neck on a golden chain.

He wore no crown, no sign of his rank, except for a pendant that bore the Great Seal of Pela: a sea serpent, rampant, silhouetted against the rising sun.

Eregard walked over to his father and, since this was an informal meeting, bowed deeply rather than knelt. "Sire, you sent for me?"

Agivir smiled at his youngest son. "I did. I have something to discuss with you, then, after we have had our talk, I thought you might wish to accompany me to your mother's apartments to visit with her."

Eregard nodded. "I was planning on visiting Mother this afternoon."

"Good. Adranan comes every week, but you are the most faithful. Your mother the Queen is mindful of it, my son."

"How fares she today, my Father?"

Agivir sighed. "The weakness grows worse, day by day. Her hands tremble, and she has pain in her—" the King gestured vaguely at his midsection.

Eregard had been hearing much the same report for the past two years, but it still gave him a pang to hear that his mother did no better. "I shall bring my balankala and play to her until she falls asleep tonight," he promised.

"Good, good." Agivir beckoned to his son, and the two royals began strolling along the paths of the conservatory. Eregard wondered why his father wished to see him, but he held his tongue. Agivir would get to the meat of the matter in his own way, at his own pace.

"Did you see the messengers?" Agivir asked finally.

"Yes I did, sire," he said. "I am assuming they had just landed off one of the ships?"

Agivir nodded. "Yes, my son. They brought . . . disturbing news."

"Tell me, sire," Eregard said. "News of the unrest on the mainland? Or news of the Chonao invasion force?"

Agivir halted and sniffed the sweet-sour fragrance of a blossoming orcjha vine. "Both, actually," he said. "The news is not encouraging, and not nearly as detailed as I need."

"What of the Chonao Redai, Kerezau?" Eregard asked.

"We learned today that Kerezau took the island of Taenareth a month ago," Agivir said, lapsing into the formal "we" and sounding almost as if he were quoting from the formal dispatch. "Our intelligence sources tell us that the Redai is currently negotiating with the independent trading and fishing fleets of the Meptalith Islands to gain passage to the West."

Eregard shook his head. "The Meptalith will never grant them passage, sire. They have always refused it to us, and to Amaran, also. The only ones who dare those waters are the Amaranian pirates."

Agivir ran his fingers through his thinning gray beard. "I would not be too sure of that, my son. Kerezau wields an impressive battle force. The Meptalith may want him occupied with us, rather than them. An alliance is certainly . . . possible."

A sudden thought occurred to the Prince. "Father," Eregard said, slipping into the most familiar form of address, "does the Redai have any daughters?"

Agivir shook his head. "Our intelligence sources say his first marriage was childless, but that he has managed to get a son off his second wife. Why do you ask?"

Eregard shrugged, relieved. "Nothing. Just . . . curiosity." He glanced at his father sharply. "What you have told me is worrisome, sire. If the Meptalith allied with the Redai, they would provide the ships to transport Kerezau's troops. That could be very bad for Pela and Kata."

The King nodded. "Indeed so. I doubt they would attempt an assault on Pela; we are too well defended here, and the Royal Navy could make sure they landed few troops. Our island coasts are well patrolled. But Kata is a frontier colony. The coasts there . . ." The King shook his head. "Our Pelanese troops are spread thin, and the colonial militia is too ill-trained and untrustworthy to make an effective deterrent."

"If the Meptalith ships carried the Redai's army to the coast, they could march north to Amaran, or south to Kata,"

Eregard said slowly, thinking aloud. "Winter is almost here. If they are on the move now, they would most likely march south. Within a few weeks the snows will close the mountain passes of Amaran."

His father smiled grimly and nodded. "Good analysis, my son. Yes, if they make an alliance with Meptalith, they will almost certainly march south, to Kata, once they cross the Narrow Sea. If the Meptalith and Chonao allied, Amaran would not be the best target for an invasion. Our colony would."

"Bloodthirsty as the Amaranian pirates are, they would not let their homeland be invaded without a fight. They may be barbarians, but they look upon us as infidels. Attacking Amaran would start a holy war," Eregard said.

"Yes, and Amaran has historically proven impossible to invade . . ." Agivir trailed off.

"Those cursed mountain passes," Eregard agreed. "And, of course Amaranians claim their god protects them." The Prince hesitated, conscious of a prickle of unease. "Superstition, of course."

"Boq'urak's Chosen," Agivir muttered. "That's what they call themselves."

"Do you think that Kata might ally with the Redai against Pela?" Eregard asked. "Some Katans are fomenting insurrection against the mother country, or so say the rumors."

"So say the rumors," Agivir agreed. "Those two scouts who came in by ship this afternoon spoke of unrest throughout Kata. Ever since I made Salesin Viceroy of the colony, there have been rumblings. Too much taxation, unfair tariffs, always they complain. Nothing overt, mind you. No actual attacks. Boys throwing rocks at the royal governor's carriage. Speeches and broadsides."

Eregard shrugged. "Boys and broadsides. So?"

"But boys reflect the attitudes of their elders. A growing number of Katans are listening to a few revolutionary hotheads, or so they say. They have sent delegations, and each delegation makes wilder demands. This last one had the gall to demand autonomy! When I laughed at them, one of them actually dared to voice hints of rebellion if Pela does not allow them—" Agivir shook his head, visibly controlling his anger. "Well. Suffice it to say that Kata grows above itself."

"Assuredly," Eregard said. "Autonomy? The idea is ridiculous."

"There's one leader in particular whose name is mentioned repeatedly: a fellow named Rufen Castio."

"Have him arrested and brought here in chains," Eregard said. "Salesin is Viceroy. Let him deal with this Castio, as he dealt with that impudent firebrand Petro Tomlia last month. Salesin will enjoy it. He'll make a production of Castio's execution, and such a public spectacle will put a quick stop to this colonial nonsense, mark my words, Father." The Prince considered for a moment. "How far has the unrest spread? Who are this Castio's followers and associates?"

"Those questions bring me to why I called you here today, my son," Agivir said slowly. "The truth is, I don't know. And with the current situation, it is difficult to know whom to trust . . ."

Agivir trailed off and fell silent, then busied himself pinching faded blooms off a lorapel bush. Eregard stared at him. *He's talking about the power struggle between him and Salesin. Father doesn't know who is loyal to him and who is backing my brother in his plans to depose him. Father obviously does not want to abdicate. Salesin is trying to force him out.*

Eregard felt another flare of anger at his brother. *Father is a good monarch, just and merciful. Why does my brother have to be like this?*

"I understand, Father," he said after a long moment. "I know the . . . situation." Unbidden, thoughts of Ulandra rose in his mind, and he forced himself to look at his father, his king. Bitterness tinged his voice. "I know the situation and I hate it. I wish there was something I could do."

Agivir gazed at his son for a moment, and Eregard saw compassion and love in his eyes. He put a hand on the Prince's shoulder. "I know that, my son," he said. "And that is why I am about to ask you to do me a service. These days, there are so few I can trust. So few councillors, and even fewer of our military leaders. The royal governors Salesin has chosen for the Katan provinces are *his* choices, and I know them only a little. My generals, my admirals, those who remember me from the old days, when we fought together for Pela . . . their numbers are growing thin. We are none of us young and fit for voyaging."

Eregard stared at his father questioningly. "Voyaging?"

"Yes, my son. I want you to travel to Kata, and be my eyes and ears there. Go incognito, as a merchant. Meet the Katans. Talk to them in taverns, up and down the coast. Go to public gatherings. Listen to the rantings of this Rufen Castio, if you can find him. If the seeds of revolution are borne on the winds, I want to know. But tell *no one* of what you find—that information is for my hearing only. Do you understand?"

Eregard's heart was hammering with excitement. *A secret mission! Traveling in disguise!* Here was his chance for adventure, to be like one of the heroes in the stories he loved.

His father was regarding him intently. "This will be a hardship for you, my son," he said. "It is an eight-day voyage to Kata, if the winds are kind."

"I'm a good sailor, sire," Eregard said.

His father smiled. "Of course, you are a true Pelanese. But this trip will be aboard a merchant ship, not our royal yacht."

Eregard found the notion of a few privations romantic. He smiled at his father. "I shall assume the guise of a merchant, a wine merchant."

His father considered this, then shook his head. "Wiser, I think, my son, for you to allow your manservant to pose as the wine merchant, whilst you travel as his clark and servant."

Eregard blinked. "A servant? But . . ." He thought for a moment. "What you say makes sense, sire," he said. "No one would believe in a·wealthy wine merchant as young as I am."

Agivir nodded. "My thinking exactly, my son. There will be hardship in this mission. Think carefully about this before you agree. In a few short weeks it will be winter, and sea travel will be curtailed. If storms sweep down from the north, you may not be able to return until spring. You will miss the Festival Season . . . and your brother's wedding."

Eregard stopped short and stood staring at his father, barely managing to keep his expression from betraying his shock. *He knows! How can this be? I never said a word to a living soul . . .*

The King's eyes were tired and bloodshot, but filled with great wisdom and compassion. Eregard swallowed, feeling love for his father, and admiration. *He is a great man, a great ruler. Salesin is not fit to empty his chamber pot.*

Dropping to one knee, Eregard bowed his head. "Sire, anything I can do, I will. I swear that I will discover the truth and reveal it only to you. And," he looked up, "Father, I thank you."

King Agivir nodded, and reached out to lay a hand on his son's head as if in benediction. "Just stay safe, my son, and come back to me. Come back when you can." The King straightened his shoulders. "And now, let us go to see your mother. She will want to bid you farewell."

Eregard nodded silently. His throat was so tight he could not trust himself to speak.

Three days later, traveling incognito and accompanied only by his manservant, Regen, Prince Eregard left Pela behind. He traveled aboard the *Saucy Lass*, a two-master whose scantily clad figurehead sported a lascivious leer and a wink. Stashed in the hold of the ship was a cargo of fine golden Pelanese sherry Agivir had supplied, a cargo that "belonged" to Master Regen, the wealthy wine merchant.

At first it had made Regen uncomfortable to be dressed far better than his Prince, and to have Eregard wait on him, but the prince had been adamant that they must keep up their roles even in private, so he could practice.

The Prince found himself actually enjoying playing the role of a humble clark and valet. Even the scurrying of the rats and the bites of the insects that were an inevitable part of belowdecks life did not dampen his enthusiasm. This was indeed a great adventure!

The distance between Minoma and the coast of Kata was

a bit more than fifteen leagues. The *Lass* headed due east, into the Straits of Dara.

On the second day of the voyage, Eregard went for a stroll around the deck. This was the farthest out to sea he'd ever been, and it was strange not to be able to sight land in any direction. The water here was the deep blue-green of the true ocean, different from the warmer waters in Minoma's harbor and the southern Pelanese coast.

The Prince stood leaning against the railing, watching the sailors swarming up and down the twin masts as they put on more sail. The breeze was chilly and brisk, and they were moving at a good five knots, he estimated—excellent for a heavily laden cargo vessel.

He heard voices raised in song, and, almost against his will, found himself humming along with the crew's ribald chantey:

> *"I got a beauty so fine in my bed*
> *We're bound for the promised land!*
> *Hair down her back, but there none on her head*
> *We're bound for the promised land!*

And then he actually sang along with the chorus.

> *Haul up her dresses*
> *Haul down her stockings-ho!*
> *Haul in your sweetheart dear*
> *We're bound for the promised land!*

> *I got a beauty whose eyes are the best*
> *We're bound for the promised land!*
> *The right one points east and the left one points west*
> *We're bound for the promised land!*

> *Haul up her dresses*
> *Haul down her stockings-ho!*
> *Haul in your sweetheart dear*
> *We're bound for the promised land!*

I got a beauty who's queen of the land
We're bound for the promised land!
I'm lucky she loves me, as mean as I am
We're bound for the promised land!

Haul up her dresses
Haul down her stockings-ho!
Haul in your sweetheart dear
We're bound for the promised land!"

Eregard found himself smiling as the song ended. He stared out across the white-capped waters, feeling better than he had in a long time. It was a relief to be free of court intrigues, of Salesin's needle-bladed gibes and even—Eregard hated to admit it, but it was the truth—the knowledge that Lady Ulandra could be just around the corner.

Strange, he mused. *A year ago, and I had no idea she even existed. And now, just a scant year later, she is the linchpin of my life.* The Prince smiled faintly, liking that image. He'd have to work it into a song sometime.

His smile faded and he sighed heavily. *At least now I won't have to stand there and watch her wed my brother. I don't think I could do that.*

Lady Ulandra was the daughter of one of Pela's foremost bishops, and she had led a very sheltered life, mostly attending schools within cloister walls, taught by priestesses who had retired from the world. And then, when she'd turned seventeen, her father had brought her to court. Eregard wasn't sure exactly when he'd fallen in love with her. But she'd aroused his protective instincts immediately, with her big blue eyes and innocent gaze.

Though the Prince could be rowdy enough with lower-class females, women of high rank tended to intimidate him. Thus Eregard watched Ulandra, watched her covertly for months. He saw that she was gentle, and virtuous, and that she went daily to the Chapel of the Goddess for prayer and meditation. She liked romantic poetry, and children, and animals. There was no vice in her, no cruelty, no shadow of sin.

Compared to his mother's Ladies in Waiting, with their neverending sly intrigues and bedroom adventures, Ulandra was a candidate for sainthood. One spring morning, Prince Eregard had dreamed of the Lady Ulandra, and when he awoke he realized, to his horror, that he had fallen in love with his brother's betrothed.

The Prince had tried to fight his emotions, but how does one fall out of love? He had occasion to wonder that many times over the long spring and summer months, torturing himself with long distance glimpses of her. Eregard found himself inventing impossible scenarios where Salesin was killed, Adranan had found another, and Ulandra was free.

Standing by the *Lass*'s railing, Eregard thought, *By the time I see her again, she will be a married woman. It is time to put her out of your life, out of your heart. Time to concentrate on helping Father.*

A thought occurred to him then. *Did Father send me away to save me from Salesin? Is it possible my brother is plotting my death?* Eregard shook his head, but he had to admit it was possible. *Plots within plots!*

The ship gave a violent lurch as a sudden blast of wind caught her. Eregard had to grab the rail. Jolted out of his reverie, he looked up to see dark clouds boiling up out of the north, racing toward them.

"Storm canvas, lads!" the captain shouted. "Smartly now!"

Sailors were frantically rolling the bigger sails and rigging the smaller, stouter sails. The Prince turned as he heard rapid footsteps, and just managed to get out of the way of one of the other passengers, Dame Alendar, as the heavyset matron headed purposefully toward the rail, hand clapped over her mouth.

After making sure the woman wasn't going to fall over the side as she heaved, Eregard left her to her misery, grateful for his own cast-iron stomach. He stood gazing at the oncoming storm, seeing the bruise-colored clouds lit from within by lightning. The first faint boom of thunder reached his ears.

"You passengers!" shouted the mate, pointing at Eregard and the dame, who was finished with her upchucking. "Get below!"

Eregard nodded, and offered his arm to the shaky dame, who clung to it gratefully.

By the time he reached the small cabin he shared with Regen, the *Lass* was rolling and wallowing like a sow in labor, every timber creaking in protest. Regen, who had done a stint in the Royal Navy during his youth, shook his head as the Prince lurched into the cabin and managed to fling himself on the small trundle bed allotted to him for the voyage.

"I don't like the feel of this, Your Highness," the manservant said. "Feels like it's blowing up for a real tempest, if I'm not mistaken."

"Don't call me 'Your Highness,'" Eregard chided, grabbing the sides of the bed as the *Lass* heaved again. "But you're right, Master Regen. Masses of clouds as dark as the inside of a cask, shot through with lightning. It was traveling faster than the fleetest racehorse in Father's stable."

It was now growing so dark that Regen had to light the ship's lantern, which swung wildly to and fro, casting monstrous shadows. The older man's expression was grave. "From what direction, Your . . ." He paused as Eregard gave him a stern glance, and amended, "From what direction came the storm, my lad?"

"From the north. The captain was calling for storm canvas when I came below."

"North . . . these storm winds will drive us off course, for certain. At least we've cleared the coast and have open water to maneuver in, but this is not good. South of us lie the Karithe Islands, the lair of some of the worst of the southern pirates."

"But they lie many leagues away!" the Prince said. "Surely no tempest could drive us so far off course."

"You are most likely correct, Eregard," Regen said, but his unease was palpable.

The storm continued throughout the day and well into the night. Eregard and Regen occasionally ventured out into the companionway, only to be driven back by the sheets of rain that poured through the edges of the hatches and down the companionway ladder. The wind shrieked, the timbers groaned, and the dripping of the water was enough to drive a man mad, Eregard thought as he lay, damp and chilled, on his trundle bed. He tried to sleep, but it was too noisy, so he lay, staring at the swinging shadows cast by the lamp.

Finally the wild tossing of the ship abated and he fell into an uneasy doze, to awaken to the sound of the cabin door closing. Regen was gone, and the porthole showed early sunlight coming in from the east.

Eregard hastily straightened his clothes, picked a few adventurous vermin out of his hair, then went up on deck. The sun was just clearing a bank of dissipating clouds, and the whole world seemed as clean and bright as a newly washed sheet.

After pissing discreetly off the stern, into the glassy smooth water, he headed forward. Regen was standing on the other side of the ship, speaking with the first mate. He glanced around at the gently rolling sea and saw, to the east, the humped silhouette of an island. Turning further south, he made out another. He hurried across the deck toward Regen, only to have the older man peremptorily wave him away.

For a moment Eregard was taken aback by this temerity on the part of his servant, but after a second he stepped back. *Stay in your role,* he reminded himself.

Finally, Regen turned away from his talk with the first mate and headed toward Eregard. The Prince noted the lines of strain and worry on the manservant's face, and took a deep breath. "What chances, Master Regen?" he asked.

"They have determined our position, and it is as I feared last night," Regen said grimly. "We have been driven off course to the Karithe Islands. We are putting on all possible sail to try and get free before we are sighted by those cutthroats."

Eregard stood staring at the distant islands. "If we can see them, they can see us, is that what you're saying?" he asked, forcing the words past a sudden tightening of his throat.

Regen nodded. "It is possible. After such a tempest, the pirate strongholds will certainly have their lookouts sta-

tioned in high places, scanning the sea for any unlucky vessels such as ours. But . . ." He glanced west, then south. "We
are, after all, a deal smaller than the islands. A ship is an
easy thing to miss, and we are far away. It may be we can—"

"Ahoy, look to the sou'east!" The shout interrupted him.
"A signal!"

Eregard and Regen ran over to the opposite rail and stared
at the island. A plume of smoke was rising into the clear
morning sky, dark and foreboding.

Regen groaned something that might have been a curse or
a prayer. "The saints shield us," he muttered. "It's a pirate
lookout, sure enough. And, look!" He pointed to a plume of
thick, rising smoke. "They've spotted us!"

6

Sea Changes

Eregard stared at the pirate smoke signal, unable to move. His heart seemed to be trying to hammer its way clean out of his chest, so wildly was it beating.

Captain Farlon was shouting for more sail. Barefoot sailors raced around the deck, hastily moving the barrels of cargo lashed to the deck down to the main hold. Two teams of gunners were preparing the six small cannon with small-shot. Eregard stood gaping until Regen grabbed him and jerked him bodily out of the way of a sailor who was dispensing cutlasses and pistols from the ship's arms locker.

"They're quick, they are," Regen muttered, pointing in the direction of the nearest island. Eregard squinted, and finally could make out two ships—sloops, from the look of them— sailing swiftly in their direction.

The two men stood watching tensely as the ships inexorably gained on the heavy-laden merchant vessel. Now Eregard could see the flag the foremost ship was flying, a bloody hand gripping a dagger that was driven through a grinning skull.

"Th-They're gaining on us," Eregard stammered. "Regen, at this rate they'll catch us!"

"Aye, lad, they will," the ex-soldier said, staring at the ships.

Eregard fought for breath. Panic coursed through his veins. "If we can't outrun them, surely we can outfight them!"

"They each have twice as many guns as we do, lad. If Captain Farlon values the lives of his crew, he'll do well to surrender."

Eregard shook his head violently. "Surrender? Regen, you can't be serious!"

"Oh, but I am, Your Highness," the manservant said. "Pirates ply their trade mostly for coin of the realm. They don't want to damage a valuable ship like the *Lass* in the taking of her. They'd much rather have a nice, peaceful surrender."

Eregard stared at the pirate vessels, stunned. *This can't be happening! What shall I do?*

Regen turned his head. "Your Highness, allow me to tell them your true identity. They will hold us for ransom then, rather than impressing us or selling us for slaves."

Eregard's fists clenched. "No! Regen, I order you to hold silent, even if they kill me!"

"But, Your—"

The Prince grabbed the man's arm, shook it fiercely. "Listen to me! Reveal my true identity, and they'll sell me to the Redai, Kerezau! He'll use me as a pawn to make my father grant him concessions! No, I *order* you, on pain of death— hold silent!"

The man bowed his head. "Very well, I obey you, Your Highness."

Eregard swung back around. "Besides," he said tightly, "we may yet escape. We have picked up a good, strong breeze."

"Their ships are lighter, and built to cleave the waves like dolphins, Your—" He broke off at Eregard's warning glare.

Just then one of the ship's officers came running past. He stopped suddenly and wheeled on them. "You passengers, get below! Now!"

Regen gestured toward five of the male passengers, able-bodied men who by their dress and bearing were once soldiers. They had been issued pistols and cutlasses. "I am a fighting man," he said. "Give me weapons."

The officer gazed at him skeptically. "Grandsire, get below. No matter what you were, you are too old to be of aid now."

Regen stiffened with indignation, and Eregard could see that the old servant was about to refuse. He grabbed his sleeve and urged, "Come, Master. We should do as he says."

Regen allowed himself to be led away, though he was muttering something about, "They've but to give me a cutlass, and I'll show these lads how a man fights on heaving decks . . ."

Once below, Eregard headed for their cabin. When they reached there, Regen quickly grabbed up their few valuables and gold coins, placing them in his pouch. "And now, my Prince, we head for the cargo hold," he said.

Eregard started to ask why, but realized that it was the logical place to attempt to hide. "We'll hide there?"

"Until we know what's happened," Regen agreed as they hustled down the narrow walkways. "But if the pirates catch us, there will be no place aboard they won't look for loot. Once we hear them coming, we might as well give ourselves up."

When they reached the main hold, they found many of the other passengers. Some were huddled against the barrels and bales of cargo, others, when they recognized Eregard and Regen, popped up out of concealment.

Eregard left Regen talking to several of the other passengers and began investigating the piles of cargo. He began to see that his hope of concealing themselves so they wouldn't be discovered was unlikely. But what else could they do?

If Adranan were here, he'd go up on deck, fight them to the last vile cutthroat, he thought bitterly, wishing he'd paid more attention to his fencing masters. He knew that Regen carried a small pistol concealed beneath the folds of his loose tunic and overjerkin, but what good was one pistol? Eregard was slightly better with a gun than he was with a sword, but that wasn't saying much.

Finally he located a small cubbyhole beneath a large bale of Pelanese silk, barely large enough to contain both him and his manservant, lying close together.

He beckoned to Regen, and the man came over, glanced down, and nodded. They went back to the other passengers, who were milling around, talking in tense whispers. The only other sound was the groaning of the timbers and the rudders. The light was dim in the hold—only a wan illumination from a few shafts of sunlight filtering down through the cargo hatches. The hold was below the waterline, so there were no portholes.

Time seemed to crawl as they waited. *Blow, wind!* Eregard silently prayed. *Goddess, help us, lend thy breath to the wind! Save us!*

They heard the sounds of running feet from above, then muffled shouts, followed by three sharp *booms!* one after another. The *Lass* lurched to port, then settled back. "We've fired," Regen reported, looking up. "Fired the three portside carriage guns."

"That didn't sound like any cannon I ever heard," Eregard said.

"These aren't big guns, lad," Regen said. "Four- to six-pounders, no more. Not like your father's great guns." He hesitated. "It's not good if they're within firing range."

Eregard could smell the rank smoke from the burnt gunpowder now. *Goddess, help us!*

"Should we go and fight?" asked one of the passengers, a middle-aged tailor who was traveling with his wife and young daughter.

"Not unless you know how to handle a sword or a pistol, and have one to hand," Regen said. "You'll just get in the way and get some honest sailor killed, most likely."

Moments later they heard the distant sounds of the other ship firing on them. Regen listened intently. "Man-killing shot," he reported calmly. "They don't want to damage their prize."

"Prize?" quavered Dame Alendar.

"This vessel."

Above them they heard more running feet, and someone in the distance was screaming, a shrill, high-pitched sound that did not stop for many minutes.

The *Lass* fired again, and again, and again.

Both pirate ships returned fire. The ship was lurching now, the groaning of the rudders louder than ever as she tried vainly to maneuver out of the way of the pursuing vessels. The stench of gunpowder filled the hold, and small leaks had started up where the grapeshot had pierced the hull.

Eregard listened to the dripping water, smelled the rank smoke, and realized his hands were shaking uncontrollably. He gripped the edge of a cargo barrel until his knuckles whitened.

More firing . . . more screams from above.

Loud booms, much closer . . .

And then they heard a prolonged *crack*, and moments later a loud thud. The entire ship shuddered. "Goddess, that's done it," Regen muttered. "That was the mainmast, if I'm any judge."

"You mean we can't run anymore."

The older man nodded. "Right, Your Highness."

Eregard glanced around quickly, but none of the other passengers had noticed Regen's slip. The pale, terrified men, women, and children huddled together, clinging close for comfort.

"Time to hide, lad," Regen said. "Any time now they'll be grappling alongside."

Eregard nodded, and showed Regen their place of concealment. "It's possible Captain Farlon will be able t'fend 'em off, even now," Regen murmured. "Possible . . ."

Eregard wriggled into the little cubbyhole, then moved over to give Regen as much room as possible. "Possible . . ." he repeated. "But not likely?"

Regen grunted as he wriggled into place. "Clever lad."

"Wasn't hard to figure," Eregard said, trying not to tremble. He didn't want Regen to feel him shivering. Panic whimpered and gibbered at the edges of his mind, and he bit his lip, forcing himself to remain silent.

Minutes went by, then came a fusillade of pistol shots and more screaming—followed by a thud. The *Lass* lurched again. But there had been no sound of cannon fire. Eregard glanced at Regen. By now his eyes were accustomed to the dimness, so he could make out his manservant's face. "They've grappled alongside us," the older man whispered.

With howls the passengers could hear all the way down in the hold, the pirates boarded the ship. They were shouting something, some battle cry. "What are they saying?"

Regen hid his face in his hands. "No quarter," he groaned. "Captain Farlon angered them, fighting back. They'll kill the crew if they resist."

And, from the sounds of the firing and screaming, the crew of the *Lass* were putting up a good fight.

Eregard lay there, terror gnawing at him, trying to convince himself this wasn't happening, that it was some nightmare he'd awaken from at any moment. Part of him wanted to run, but he forced himself to lie there silently. Beside him, he could feel Regen, his body stiff with frustration and the eagerness to join the fray. *But he won't leave me,* Eregard thought. *His duty is to me, and he'll stay with me.*

Finally, after what seemed hours but was probably only minutes, the sounds from the deck changed yet again—instead of battle cries and the ringing sounds of steel and firing of pistols, there were shouts of triumph. Some of the wounded were still screaming, but one by one those screams ceased.

Regen's face was naught but a chalky oval in the dimness. "They've won," he whispered bleakly.

Despite Eregard's efforts to steel himself for anything, the Prince felt as though someone had driven a mailed fist into his gut. He gasped, and gulped, and, for a minute or so, could not gain enough air to speak. Finally he forced himself to take deep breaths. "What now?"

Regen put his finger to his lips and pulled himself as far back into their cubby as he could. Eregard, hearing the sounds of bare feet descending the ladders to the lower decks, did likewise.

For several minutes they could hear the crashing sounds of the pirates looting the several small passenger cabins and the crew quarters, then the cry went up. "Passengers! Where are the passengers?"

"Don't hide from us, you're part of the prize!" another attacker shouted.

Running feet approached the hold. Eregard wished he could disappear, the way the warrior priests of the Redai were said to do.

"The captain's manifest lists a cargo of Pelanese sherry!" one loud voice said. Even though he could not see them, Eregard could tell they were now in the hold itself, from the way their voices echoed.

"Good, we'll have one tonight to celebrate taking this fine prize," was the gruff reply. "There are rats in this hold, Laston. Rats. Big ones."

"Really?" Laston finally caught the joke and guffawed. "Oh, of a certainty, rats! Well, we have no cat, so we shall have to turn ratter ourselves!"

Footsteps, more footsteps, then the sound of a bale being shoved aside. A woman's terrified cry.

"Found one, sir!" another voice whooped. "A big fat one!"

Dame Alendar! Eregard thought, feeling a wave of sick horror. *I should do something!* But what could he do? From the sound of them, there were at least three or four pirates in the hold.

The dame was sobbing now. Her captors ridiculed her, hooting and making vulgar sounds. Eregard heard smacks and the sound of ripping cloth. *They're toying with her, as though they were indeed cats and she a mouse . . .*

Another bale moved. He heard a bitten-off scream, then a child's querulous, pleading voice.

Eregard clamped his teeth into this lower lip and tried not to hear.

"Another one, sir!"

For the next few minutes pirates rousted terrified passengers from their hiding places. Footsteps passed their spot several times, but, for a miracle, they were not discovered.

The hold was now filled with wails and sobs from the unhappy passengers. The captives pleaded, telling of those who would ransom them back on Pela.

Eregard lay still as the pirates passed his hiding place again. There was the sound of bales moving, then a muffled shriek.

"Sir, sir! Here we have a pretty one!" The sobbing girl stumbled past their refuge, dragged by two pirates. "Sir, she's prime! We can have our sport now, afore we take her to the captain!"

There was the sound of ripping cloth, a shriek of terror, then the sound of a blow. Laston cursed. The pirate officer's voice was cold. "Leave her be, Laston. She's young, and likely a maiden. She'll fetch more on the block intact—and don't you forget it!"

A shrill scream, and loud sobbing. "No! No!"

Ripping cloth, then the officer spoke again. "Here! This one is no maiden, and she's round enough to make any seaman a comfy couch, Laston. Look at those udders, why, a cow might envy her. You can have this one."

Wails and babbled protests from Dame Alendar. "No! Please, please no, my husband, he's in the colonies, he'll pay, please . . ."

The sound of ripping cloth again, then Alendar began shrieking in earnest.

Beside Eregard, Regen moved. Before the Prince could do more than gasp, the manservant slithered out of hiding in one smooth motion. Eregard crawled after him and caught just a glimpse of Regen's feet and legs, then the older man strode out of his range of vision.

The report of the pistol was shockingly loud in the confines of the hold.

Before Eregard was even sure that he was moving, he found himself halfway out of the hiding place. He staggered to his feet, then stood there, gaping. Dame Alendar, her gown ripped from bodice to crotch, screamed mindlessly as she lay back against a bale of cloth, her lower body pinned by the still-twitching body of a pirate. Regen had shot the man in the back of the head. The manservant stood proudly, head up, not even trying to reload. At a gesture from the officer, two other pirates raced forward.

"Well, here we have a brave old geezer," the pirate officer, a short, strong-looking man with a horseman's bowed legs said. "You just deprived me of a good cooper, sirrah. Unless you can take his place, I'm going to have to punish you in like manner as you punished him."

Regen did not move as the two armed pirates grabbed him and marched him over until he stood before the pirate officer. "Are you a cooper, then? Or something equally as useful? You may join us if you've a skill we need," the pirate said, cleaning his nails with the point of his dagger. " 'Tis a rarity to find a codger so brave, who can shoot straight."

"Regen—" Eregard said, trying to reach him. He was grabbed from behind and halted; the grip on his arm felt like an iron manacle.

Regen did not look over at the Prince. He stared down his prominent nose at the pirate. "I have many skills, but I would rather die than turn pirate," he said disdainfully.

The officer shrugged. "Fine." He nodded at the man on Regen's right, and, with no more care than Eregard would have given to squashing a flea, the man's hand rose and whipped across Regen's throat in a blur of steel and flesh.

Both pirates stood back as the old man turned, grabbing at his throat, his eyes bulging. Regen gave a strangling, bubbling gasp, then his crimsoned hands fell away and his knees buckled. Hot blood sprayed out, catching Eregard and his captor across the face.

Regen fell, twitched once, then lay still. The flow of blood across the deck spread, slowed, and finally stopped.

Eregard stood there in shock, then his stomach revolted and he fell to his knees, retching.

"Boq'urak's balls!" his captor swore, dancing out of the way so his boots would remain unsmirched. "Get up, you!"

Eregard knelt there, his mouth hanging open, a rope of

vile spittle spinning its way down from his lower lip. He stared at Regen and could not believe that he was dead. *This is a nightmare,* he thought. *It can't be happening. It can't be . . .*

With all the will that was in him, he tried to wake up.

Instead of opening his eyes back in the palace in Minoma, however, the Prince was seized again and dragged to his feet. "What shall I do with this one, sir?"

"Take them all up on deck," the pirate officer decided. "And take the guts up, too, and toss them to the fishes. We're taking the prize back with us, and we don't want the hold to stink."

"Aye, sir."

Eregard felt the pirate reach around him and relieve him of the small dagger he wore on his belt, then a hard hand shoved him toward the ladder. He staggered forward, then found himself climbing.

Moments later he stood blinking in the light of day, staring in shock at the carnage all around him. The *Lass*'s crew had fought bravely, and the angry pirates had given no quarter indeed. In places, the deck was awash with blood, and when Eregard's captor pushed him forward, the Prince skidded in one congealing mess and nearly fell. "Move!" his captor barked, shoving him again.

This time he did lose his balance, and fell jarringly onto his hands and knees. When he stood again, his hands were red and sticky. Eregard gagged and retched again, but his stomach was already empty.

He glanced up at the position of the Sun and realized that only an hour or so had gone by since they'd seen the pirate signal. Eregard stumbled forward under his captor's prodding.

The pirates had gathered all the captives on the foredeck, separated into two groups—the passengers who were to be ransomed, and those who would be sold as slaves. Dame Alendar was sobbing as she clutched the rags of her dress around her. Her face was bruised and blood trickled from a torn lip. Yet she was one of the lucky ones, for she was with the prisoners who would be ransomed by their loved ones.

The younger, stronger passengers, especially the servants, were in a second group, and it was there that Eregard's captor took him.

Pirates paced around the passengers like wolves scenting wounded prey. Every so often one would pounce, then retreat with a bauble torn from a woman's ear or a ring yanked from a trembling hand.

Eregard saw one man, not tall, but still imposing, who had a shaven head and wore an expensive silk dressing gown over his bare and muscled torso. His cutlass was a fine one, with a gold-chased guard and grip. The captain, he guessed.

The man strutted up to the cringing slave-captives and looked them over. "Cap'n!" the man behind Eregard said. "Can't we have some fun wi' 'em? We ain't had no fresh arse in a long time. Them whores in Cape Raldi is all startin' t'look alike!"

The captain regarded the two captive serving girls, who cowered back under his gaze. "Not those two," he said. "If they're maids, they'll fetch a fine price. Have your fun with yon dame," he said, jerking his head at Alendar.

Several of the sailors approached the dame with purposeful strides, grinning like fiends from some foul netherworld. Eregard turned his head away when the screams began. Someone must have gagged the woman at some point, because they stopped after a few minutes. There was only the grunting and gasping from the pirates.

Eregard swayed on his feet as spots danced before his eyes. He was beyond horror, beyond terror.

"Aw, Captain," Eregard's captor complained, "I don't want t'stand in line, and I surely don't want *her*. She's too old and fat for sport. Let me have one of the young'uns."

"Use the lads if you want," the pirate officer said. "But no touching the maids, Drenn."

Drenn chuckled, and the Prince found himself seized from behind again. "You heard the captain. How about this one, lads? He ain't pretty, but he's young, and I'll bet his butt's virgin and tight! Let's 'ave a look at ye, lad!"

Drenn grabbed the Prince's jacket, then fingered the material. "Nice! That'll look just fine on me." He began dragging the garment off over Eregard's arm.

"No!" The threat roused Eregard from his daze. He swung at Drenn with his unencumbered arm, driving his fist into the pirate's eye. The pirate's head snapped back with the blow, and he howled with rage and pain.

Eregard backed away, but he was surrounded by a circle of pirates, laughing with coarse good humor. One grabbed him and shoved him staggering back into Drenn's reach.

The pirate was an experienced brawler, and Eregard had never exchanged blows except with the court boxing instructor. The Prince put up his fists and tried to defend himself, but he was lost from the first.

Three hard left jabs that moved with blurring speed split both lips, bloodied his nose, then opened his left cheekbone. The pain was blinding. Eregard staggered back, his hands going up to his face, tears of pain flooding his eyes. A hard right was driven deep into his gut, and he could no longer breathe. He hadn't even known he was falling until he crashed to the deck.

He lay there, gasping like a sea·creature stranded on a rock, struggling for air. Finally his lungs filled again, and it was bliss simply to breathe.

He lay there unresisting as Drenn came over, yanked off his jacket and appropriated it, then dragged off his loose linen tunic. "Fine stuff!" the brigand crowed.

Hauling the dazed Prince to his feet, the pirate dragged him over to one of the barrels of cargo that had fallen on its side, then pushed the younger man down until he was lying over it. Eregard tried to struggle, but it was all he could do to breathe. Blood choked him, flooding his mouth.

He felt the man's hands reach beneath him, grab at his trousers, yanking them open, then pulling them down. The breeze touched his buttocks with gentle coolness.

"All right, lads, line up!" Drenn shouted.

Eregard thrashed in mindless terror.

"Hey, Drenn, sure you want to do that?" one of the pirates hooted, laughing. "That lad's so terrified that he'll let 'is bowels fly loose all over you, see if he doesn't!"

Another pirate hooted. "You want a dirty cock, Drenn? Didn't know that was your fancy!"

More laughter. "Just look at that fat arse of his a'quivering!"

Drenn hesitated, then stepped back. "You're right, lads. I'm not riskin' it. Ugly fat bugger, anyhow. But I'm not let-tin' him off with no punishment for givin' me this shiner. Here, hand me that sword."

The Prince heard the ring of steel being drawn from a sheath, then a line of white-hot pain lanced across his rear, accompanied by a resounding smack. The pirates hooted encouragement as Drenn's blows landed again and again. Finally, whether by accident or design, Eregard did not know, the edge caught him and he felt the blade slice his flesh.

"Damn it, Drenn, enough!" the captain roared. "You've marked him but good, he'll have a scar to the end of his days. I want him *salable*, rot you!"

The slapping blows ceased. Eregard slumped over the barrel, his head swimming with pain and fear.

Drenn kicked his thigh. "Pull up your pants, lad. And don't ever swing on me again."

Eregard pushed himself up to his knees, then managed to yank his pants up. "Get up!" Drenn ordered.

The Prince tried to comply, but his knees buckled. The roaring in his ears was louder than ever, and he could not tell whether it was the pirates, or the blackness that was pressing him down, engulfing him, sending him into blessed oblivion . . .

The next few days passed in a blur of misery, hunger, and pain. The captives were herded onto one of the pirate ships, chained together on deck, then *The Merry Widow* set sail for the northwest.

At first Eregard was barely conscious and could hardly see out of his swollen eyes. His backside throbbed so horribly that he could not sit up, even if he had been strong enough to do it. He lay on his side, or on his stomach, eyes shut, huddled under the scrap of blanket that was his only protection from the chill night air. Days and nights passed in a blur of feverish misery, and he scarcely knew where he was or what was happening.

On the morning of the fourth day he awoke, clear-headed, to find himself shackled at the end of the line of captives. He was hooked to a dark-skinned young man in his thirties who wore his hair cropped, as house servants did in the colonies. Slowly, painfully, he pushed himself up until he was kneeling on the deck. His buttocks were still sore, but no longer throbbing with heat. "Where are they taking us?" the Prince whispered, his voice emerging as a hoarse croak. He hadn't spoken to anyone since the day they'd been captured.

The man turned to regard him with surprise. "Ah, you're with us again!"

"More or less," Eregard mumbled, managing to ease himself down onto his left flank. He winced, but found a way to sit that was only mildly uncomfortable. "Where are we bound?"

"Kata, most likely," the man said. "They'll still need strong backs to harvest the winter wheat crop. Most likely they'll land us at Port Alvar, sell the unskilled labor, then take the rest of us to the big farm auctions in Barslod."

Just then one of the pirates came down the line with a pail of brackish water. He gave each captive a dipperful and a ragged hank of bread, plus a handful of dried figs.

Eregard's mouth was still sore, but he forced himself to chew and swallow the food. It was his first meal since the tempest had driven them off course.

"I just wish Captain Farlon hadn't been killed," the lad, who had identified himself as Grimal, muttered when they'd finished their scanty meal. "He'd have ransomed me, sure. They never sell anyone who's important, who has family, or a place in things."

Eregard smiled wryly. "Oh, yes they do," he said. "I'm a prince, and they're planning to sell *me*."

Grimal gave a muffled snort of laughter. "'Tis a rare man indeed who can joke in a situation like this."

The Prince shrugged wearily. "I'm also the court jester."

More than once Eregard had come within a hairbreadth of identifying himself to the pirate slavemaster, but each time, a vision of how he must look had stopped him. His shoulder-length hair, once well-groomed, hung in greasy strings. His face was crusted with dried blood, he was filthy and covered with bruises, with barely enough rags left to him to cover his loins. And his shoes. He still had his shoes, though his stockings hung down over them, dirty and torn. Eregard had always had small, delicate feet for a man, and, although several pirates had eyed his footwear speculatively, his small size had preserved his shoes for his own use.

The voyage passed in a haze of misery. Many of the new slaves were seasick, and soon the deck was slippery with their heavings. Eregard sat hunched, too dispirited even to look up when the lookout shouted, "Land ho!" from the crow's nest.

Several pirates wandered back and forth among the captives, tossing buckets of seawater over them to clean the worst of the dirt and blood off, joking about how rank they smelled.

Eregard shivered with the dousing, but it was a relief to be free of Regen's blood.

Several hours later *The Merry Widow* was anchored off Port Alvar in Kata. Eregard and the other slaves were shoved and cuffed along the deck to a gap in the rail. Eregard looked down, to see the slavemaster and several guards waiting for the prisoners in a boat. A spindly rope ladder hung down the side of the *Widow*.

In order to climb, the slaves had to be unchained. Eregard reveled in the sensation of being able to move his arms and legs freely as he crawled down the ladder. Moments later he was in the boat, sitting hunched on the plank seat, too dispirited even to raise his eyes to the harbor that lay before them.

The Lass *was supposed to make Port Alvar,* he remembered. He had successfully reached his destination, but he would never be able to carry out his father's wishes. Eregard buried his face in his hands.

In just a few minutes the boat was full. Most of the slaves were too terrified to speak or even whisper, but the pirates had no such compunction. As they rowed with smooth, powerful strokes, sending the boat skimming along the water, they began to sing, bellowing out a cheerful chantey.

> *"Hard as the rocks where breakers roll*
> *Hard as the iron cannon cold,*
> *Hard as the fight for a merchant's gold*
> *Hard as the Royal Judge's soul!*
>
> *Oh . . . we are the sharks of the open sea,*
> *We are the scourge of the King's Na-vy,*
> *We are the hard and the wild and free,*
> *We are the sharks of the open sea!*
>
> *Free to sail wherever we may,*
> *Free to brawl in a bar room fray,*
> *Free to shout what we want to say,*
> *Free to hang on our reckoning day!*
>
> *Oh . . . wild as the waves on the northern coast,*
> *Wild as fur-assed horseman's boast,*
> *Wild as a drunk captain's toast,*
> *Wild as a pirate's wandering ghost . . ."*

Eregard heard them sing, and the music was stirring. But for once even music had lost its power to move him. He sat hunched against the whip of the wind and the chill spray, wondering if it wouldn't be better just to roll over the side of the boat. With his heavy ankle cuffs, he'd be pulled down even if he struggled. *And I won't even struggle,* he decided.

Before he could change his mind, the Prince leaned toward the side, only to have the pirate sitting opposite him reach over and clout him on the side of the head. Eregard slumped back in his seat, his head throbbing, his whole world turned gray and hazy.

He was still unsteady on his feet when the boat bumped

the public dock of Port Alva. "All ashore!" bellowed the pirates cheerfully.

When they were all chained together on the dock again, a pirate with a dirty piece of paper, a pen, and a brush went down the line, painting a number on each captive's shoulder. Eregard was number thirty-two. "Any skills?" the pirate barked at him.

Eregard was still too dazed to make much sense. "Educated . . ." he muttered. "I can read and write, cipher . . ."

"A clark, eh?" muttered the pirate, scribbling a notation. "Best be tellin' the truth, lad."

Eregard shuffled after his fellows as the pirates herded their prizes toward the center of town. After a ten minute walk, they reached a large, brick building and a town square. Along one side of the square, Katan citizens were gathered. They were sturdy, prosperous-looking folk, though their clothes were far out of fashion, Eregard noted, wondering why such a ridiculous detail should stick in his mind.

There was a small podium in the middle of the square, and it was toward this that the pirates pushed their captives. Eregard saw men, women, and a few children standing off to the side, and from their scanty, ragged clothing and downcast demeanor, judged them to be slaves.

It's the slave auction. I'm about to be sold. Eregard halted, knowing he could not force himself to take even one more step toward the platform. *I am a Prince of Pela,* he thought. *This can't happen!*

With all his might he willed himself to awaken from this nightmare.

He was jerked out of his thoughts when a bamboo cane slashed across the rags that barely covered his sore buttocks. The pain was searing. Eregard jumped and cried out.

"Get moving, you!" the pirate yelled.

Eregard forced himself to continue his shuffle toward the sales block. Pain accompanied each movement; he was most certainly wide-awake.

He whimpered, low in his throat, but nobody heard.

Finally, he stood beside the block. The auction was going along briskly. Eregard watched as three or four slaves were sold. Most seemed not to care one way or the other. One woman sobbed and tried to cling to her young son when they were sold to different owners.

Finally, it was Eregard's turn. At the pirate's prodding, he stepped up onto the block.

"And here we have a fine healthy specimen. Young, too!" the auctioneer called. "How old are you, my fine fellow?"

Eregard could not speak, only looked at him, beyond fear, beyond horror. The pirate jumped up onto the block, grabbed his face, stuck a filthy finger in the side of his mouth as though he were a horse, forcing the Prince to open wide. The pirate shouted, "If he's four and twenty, I'll eat my boots! He's prime!"

"Did you hear that, citizens? Young, and strong. And obviously an easy keeper! Claims to be a clark, so he can keep your accounts after a day in the fields. He'll soon sweat off that flab!"

Eregard's cheeks burned, and the audience guffawed as he blushed. "So, citizens . . . what am I bid?"

A man from the front raised a languid hand, flicked his handkerchief at the auctioneer and said, "Five liera."

The auctioneer did not seem pleased at the paucity of the offer. "Citizens, we have a fine young male here. He can read, write, and cipher! Please, do not insult us! Do I hear ten?"

A dark-skinned blacksmith waved a filthy hand. "Ten."

"Very well, we have ten . . . ten . . . ten . . . do I hear fifteen? I can't allow you to steal this lad! Look at him! Excellent health, excellent teeth! Fifteen, give me fifteen!"

A woman laughed raucously. "I'll give you ten to take 'im away and bring out something decent!"

Eregard blushed, and the crowd hooted. A short, bearded man idly flapped a hand. "Twelve."

The auctioneer appeared deeply pained. "Twelve . . . twelve . . ." he chanted. "Twelve . . . good citizens, let me hear fifteen . . ."

But he heard nothing more, and moments later Eregard was knocked down to the bearded colonist for twelve liera.

The Prince stood there quietly, numb with shock, as his new owner filled out the paperwork and paid for his acquisition. He held out the paper to the Prince. "Read that," he ordered.

Eregard tried to wet his lips, but his mouth was too dry. He managed to croak, " 'Male slave, poor condition, number thirty-two, claims to be—' "

"Right," his new owner said. "Good for you that you didn't lie. You can cipher, too?"

Eregard nodded.

The pirate cuffed him. "Yes, *sir*!" he growled. "Show some respect!"

"Yes, sir," Eregard mumbled, his swollen lips barely moving.

When the paperwork was completed, the man glanced over at the pirate guard. "You haven't collared him."

The man bobbed his head in a partial bow. "Haven't had time, sir. But this one oughtn' give ye any trouble. He's been quiet as a lamb ever since he's been handed over to me."

"Well, I want him collared," Eregard's owner said. "Marking them makes them think twice about running away. But I haven't been branding since I lost two to blood sepsis after the brands grew fevered. Collaring is better." He passed a coin and a metal tag to the pirate. "See to it, and I'll return for him in half an hour."

Eregard looked around him dazedly, still half expecting to wake up in his bed in his father's palace. "You can't collar me," he said hoarsely. "I'm King Agivir's son, Prince Eregard. Take me to my father and he'll reward you handsomely."

Both men looked at him in amazement. The guard began to laugh.

"Here now, I didn't bargain for a crazy fellow," the planter said.

"Oh, sir, he ain't crazy," chortled the pirate. "He's just . . . *creative*. Must've been an actor, eh, lad?"

"Is that it? Were you a player?" the planter demanded suspiciously.

Eregard stood there, realizing that it would do him no good to repeat the truth. He would never be believed. If he ruined this sale for the pirates, the guard would likely thrash him and take him back to the boat.

Aboard ship I have no chance at escape, he thought. *At least here I'd be on dry land.*

He took a deep breath. "Yes, sir," he said. "I was lead actor for the Minoma Players."

"I see," his owner said, then, quick as a striking serpent, his hand came up and lashed across Eregard's mouth. "We'll have no more tall tales, no more insubordination, lad," he said, with no particular malice. "Understand?"

"Yes, sir."

The pirate nodded. "I'll tend to him, sir."

The planter turned his back and walked away. The guard glared at Eregard. "Prince, eh? Well, Your Highness, I've had about enough of you, so shut your yap."

Eregard tried to resist when the guard grabbed his arm, but the older man swung around and raised a bony, clenched fist. "Come along, Your Highness!"

The Prince began plodding forward. The pirate escorted him over to the smithy across the town square. The man Eregard had seen bidding was there, hammering out a horseshoe. He looked up inquiringly.

"Need a collar for this 'un," the guard said.

"Very well, I'll be with you directly," the smith said.

Minutes later Eregard sat there, watching as the smith hammered a thin strip of iron into the right shape, attaching a ring to it. Then he heated the metal and attached the owner's tag to the collar.

Then the metal had to be heated to be bent around Eregard's neck, and it was still hot enough, despite the smith's quick dowsing in the bucket, to make the Prince yelp as it touched his neck. Despite his struggles, the guard held him still across the anvil as the smith hammered the iron circlet into place, then sluiced it with cold water.

Eregard lay there, dazed, feeling the throbbing pain from

his burned neck. When they finally let him up, he reached up to touch the iron band, and felt his world crumble into dust and ashes.

Goddess, help me, he thought. *Let me die, rather than live as a slave . . .*

But She was not listening. His sight did not fail, the world did not stop its spinning, and he did not fall dead.

The guard grinned at him and winked. "Looks right proper on you, lad. Now let's go to meet your master."

Eregard rose shakily to his feet and followed the pirate out of the smithy. *Goddess . . . let me die.*

Thia's initial good spirits at reaching Q'Kal did not last. By the time she had been in the port city for a day, she was convinced she'd made a dreadful mistake leaving the caravan. It was all she could do not to grab her few possessions and race out the city gates, back to the Shekk and her friends.

The city oppressed her; she was frightened all the time. The stench of the open sewers, dodging the smelly cascades from flung chamberpots, the crowds, the noise—for the first day or so she was afraid to do more than look out the window.

Jezzil found them lodgings in a spare room over a bakery, rented out by a widow woman whose son had gone off as cabin boy on a merchant ship. The room was small, doubly so because they hung a curtain from ceiling to floor between the two sleeping mats.

The Chonao took a job guarding a warehouse at night, so they managed to pay their rent and to eat, but there was nothing left over. Jezzil's savings from his job with the caravan steadily dwindled.

It took Thia a full tenday to gain the courage to leave the room, to walk the streets and look for work. Q'Kal was far larger than Verang, and much more boisterous. Cutthroats and beggars, pickpockets and whores, abounded.

Their lodgings were on the edge of the city's worst sector. When she looked across her street at lamplighting, Thia could see the whores awaiting their customers.

Reluctantly, she abandoned her veil after just a few days.

Nobody in Q'Kal wore them, and she realized that clinging to her shrouding gray garments and veil would only help searchers to identify her. Instead she traded an amber bracelet the Shekk had given her for a dull-colored plaid skirt, homespun blouse, and loose overtunic. Dressed more like the chambermaids and other women workers she saw passing by, she gathered up her courage and went out to seek work, while Jezzil slept, exhausted from his night watch duty.

She walked along the squalid streets, picking her way over piles of horse dung and splashes of human waste, hardly daring to take her eyes off what lay before her. She crossed the street, barely managing to dodge in time when she heard a shout of "Heads up below!" and someone emptied a chamberpot from an upper story. When she reached the relative safety of the storefronts, she glanced around to get her bearings. Her eyes widened as she realized that a rough-looking man was eyeing her speculatively.

Thia forced herself to drop her eyes, and held her shawl clutched around her so her face was half hidden. *Who is he? Could the priests have sent him? Or does he wish to grab me and take me away to force me?*

She dared another glance, saw the man walking in her direction, and her heart pounded so hard that she feared she might faint. *Don't swoon! If you do, you're finished!* Panic made her dart out into the street, running blindly. Skirts kilted up in one hand, she ran, splashing through foul puddles, leaping over mounting blocks that suddenly appeared in her way, dodging around carts, horses, and people. She ran, scarcely seeing where she was going, her only thought to get away, far away.

Finally, unable to run another step, she staggered over to a nearby wall and leaned against it, breathing in gasps that tore her chest. When she finally dared to look around, she saw that nobody was paying any attention to her, and the man was nowhere in sight.

When she could finally breathe without pain, she looked around her, seeing that she was in a much better part of town. There were no houses here, only tidy shops, with hitching posts before them. As she watched, she saw a carriage clatter down the street, drawn by a team of matched bays.

Wondering how she could find her way back to the loft on Baker's Alley, Thia stood up straight, then turned to look around the corner at the building she had been leaning on. It was a brick building with a glass window, and she recognized what was displayed in the window. A book. Like the one she'd seen in Coquillon.

Jezzil called them printers. They make books without scribes to copy them.

Intrigued, she walked over to the window to get a closer look at the book, which was open and displayed on a wooden stand. Through the window she saw a woman behind a counter, and through the doorway she saw a man's back, standing before several shelves of books. Slowly, she puzzled out the sign. She'd learned to read a little Pelanese when she'd helped Shekk Marzet with his accounts. But they were mostly numbers . . . the letters still gave her pause.

BOOK SHOP AND PRINTER.

Before she could stop herself, Thia gently pushed open the door and went in. Inside there were shelves, and standing upon those shelves were books and rolled scrolls, much like the ones she'd worked on for years.

The woman behind the counter was regarding her warily. She was short, with a round girlish face beneath a beribboned lace cap. "Good morn, mistress," she said after a moment.

Thia nodded. "Good morn to you. I wanted to see the books."

"Well, there they are," the woman said, seeming to relax slightly. She walked out from behind the counter, and Thia realized from the bulge beneath her gown and her ungainly walk that she was far advanced in pregnancy. Thia had rarely seen anyone who was pregnant, and had to force herself not to stare.

"If your hands are clean, you can touch 'em, even," the woman said.

Thia presented her hands for inspection, palms up, thankful for the bucket of cold water Jezzil hauled up the stairs each morning so they could both wash. The woman eyed them, then nodded.

"Were you looking for anything in particular?"

"No," Thia said. "I used to . . . I used to make books myself. Well," she amended, "scrolls. I wanted to see the ones made by the machine."

"Well, go ahead, but be careful."

Thia gently touched the leather covers, then opened the books, eyeing the printed first pages wonderingly, running a fingertip over the watermarked endpapers. Some had real hand-drawn and colored maps inside. She held one book up, studying to see how it was put together. *Sewn into place,* she realized.

"They're beautiful," she said, her voice warm with genuine admiration.

The woman smiled at her. "You can read?"

"Yes," Thia said. "I haven't had much chance to learn Pelanese yet, but I know a little."

"Where are ye from?"

Thia hesitated. "Far north. Amavav."

"Oh, that explains the accent," said the woman. "You was a scholar, you say?"

"Yes. I copied books, so they could be preserved."

The well-dressed man finally selected a book. While the woman waited on him, Thia looked over the texts in several of the books, realizing she could puzzle out many of the words if she sounded them out.

Absorbed in reading the first pages of a Pelanese novel, Thia jumped when she heard a rhythmic pounding from the other room. The woman laughed. "Ah, that's just the press, mistress. Denno is a'printin' up some bills for the new performance over at the theater." She beckoned Thia toward the doorway. "Denno! Can she watch while you print?"

Thia came over to the doorway and stood there, watching as the printer fed the sheets of paper into the machine, one by one. She watched in fascination as he reinked the type, then printed several more. The familiar smells of ink and paper were comforting, and she felt completely warm and safe for the first time since she'd left the twin ziggurats.

When Denno was finished, he turned to regard her, his eyes bright in a countenance that was smudged black in several places. He was not a tall man, but he was solidly built, like a tree trunk, with bushy brown hair and freckles. "So, you're interested in printin', mistress?"

"Yes," Thia said. "This is a wonderful machine."

The woman had followed her in and was standing in the doorway between the bookshop and the printing shop. "She's from Amavav," she said. "Can read and write. Used to be a scribe, Denno."

"Well, well," Denno said. He walked over to a cluttered desk. "Can you show me what you used to do?" he asked. "I might be in need of some help. Beddi won't be able to keep shop much longer, as you can see."

Beddi giggled. Thia decided the pair were husband and wife. *Working in the print shop? That would be wonderful!* Eagerly, she went over to the desk, sat down, took up a pen, dipped it. "What would you like me to write?" she asked.

"The alphabet," Denno said.

Quickly, Thia scribbled down the Amaranian alphabet, then as much as she could recall of the Pelanese. Her fingers seemed to remember her old skills. She forgot everything except what she was doing, enjoying the scratch of the pen, the smell of the inks.

Denno nodded, impressed when he saw her neat, precise script. "Can you do aught else?"

"I can cipher," Thia said. "And I can illuminate."

"You mean you can make them fancy capitals?"

"Yes."

"Draw me one. Pelanese, please."

Thia labored over the unfamiliar character, sketching in its outlines with short, precise strokes. Finally she looked up. "I'll need colored inks to finish," she said.

Denno was nodding. "Very nice. Those hand-colored capitals would add a nice touch to some of our jobs. Invitations, and cards and suchlike. And the first letters of poems and such." He gazed down at her. "You be lookin' for work, mistress?"

Thia nodded. "My name is Thia. Yes, I would love to work here. I want to learn how the machine works. I'll work hard, Master Denno."

"Just Denno," he said. "I can't pay much, but you'll be learnin' a skill. Five half-liera a month?"

That amount was almost as much as Jezzil was making as a guard. Thia nodded. "That's fine . . . Denno."

"When can ye start?"

Thia stood up, smiling. "How about now?"

Working for Denno and Beddi required long hours, but Thia was so happy to be working and earning that she didn't mind. The coins she was earning allowed her to buy and prepare better food, and provided Falar with a ration of grain at the boarding stable.

Her duties for Denno were exacting but not onerous. After Beddi grew so close to her time that she could no longer wait on customers, Thia took over that task, and both she and Denno worked at cleaning the shop and keeping it tidy. Denno began teaching her how to set type for the press, but that was a difficult job, requiring a great deal of experience to do efficiently. Thia was amazed by how quickly Denno could set a page. His hands seemed to move in a blur.

Three weeks after she began working in the print shop, Beddi gave birth to a daughter. Denno invited her upstairs to their living quarters to see the new arrival. Thia gazed at the baby in wonder, never having seen a newborn up close. When Denno placed the squirming, flailing bundle into her arms, she gazed at him nearly in panic. "I'll drop her!"

Denno chuckled, beaming with pride. "Nah. Isn't she a pretty thing?"

Privately, Thia thought the infant looked like a reddish-orange blob, but as she gazed down at the newborn, she felt a tightness in her throat. It felt good to cradle the warm, damp weight of a baby in her arms.

She gazed up at Denno and smiled. "Thank you," she said.

He grinned back at her. "Wait until you have to change her nappies, Thia."

Several times after the baby was born, Thia came into the shop to find Denno red-eyed from lack of sleep. "Baby had colic," he always explained.

But when Thia asked Beddi if little Damris had gotten over the colic, Beddi gazed at her in surprise as she sat nursing her daughter. "Colic? Not this one. She's got the digestion of an ox, and thank the Goddess for it. My mother's often told me that I was a colicky baby, and how she nearly dropped me out a window more than once because of it."

"But Denno—" Thia started to say, then abruptly closed her mouth. Beddi, crooning to her baby, did not notice.

One morning Thia arrived early, only to hear the press running already. When he heard the tinkle of the front door, Denno appeared in the doorway, red-eyed and obviously flustered. "Thia! You're early, lass!"

"So I am," she said, putting her lunch down on her desk and taking off her shawl to hang it on a hook. "I thought I'd give the floor a good scrubbing. All this spring mud—"

"Good idea, good idea," mumbled Denno. "I'll be done in a few minutes."

The press resumed operation.

Thia swept the shop floor, then hauled in water from the public well and added in a few yellow soap shavings, mixing hard until some bubbles appeared. Taking the mop, she began swabbing the floor vigorously, occasionally dropping to her hands and knees to scrub up the worst of the scuffs and marks.

A few minutes later Denno appeared, his arms laden with a box of documents. "I'll be back in a few hours, Thia. Watch the shop."

"Of course," she said. "Go out the back way, so you won't track up my floor. 'Tis still wet."

He nodded at the clean floor. "Looks cleaner than I can ever remember it!"

Moments later Thia heard the back door slam.

After she finished rinsing the shop floor, Thia went back into the press room, thinking that perhaps she ought to try cleaning that floor. *So much spilled ink, mixed with dirt and boot marks.*

She sighed, straightening her back. *Well, it's still too early for customers, so I might as well.*

Grabbing a broom, she began sweeping around the press. As she reached the far side of the big machine, she saw part of a paper sticking out from the bottom, where it had evidently gotten caught from the last print run. She reached out and tugged it free, tearing it in the process.

As she started to toss it onto the trash pile, she stopped, staring down at it, her attention caught by the words Denno had printed.

Thia's Pelanese was fluent now, both spoken and written. Her eyes widened as she read the torn document:

. . . sucks the marrow from our bones. Pela is draining us like a night-demon, and we must fight to preserve ourselves and our families. Fellow patriots, join with me. The time for petitions and speeches is nearly over. Soon, if we value our freedom, we must be prepared to defend it. Someday soon, we must stand united against the motherland, and let our voices be heard for what is just and right. We can no longer allow the King to denigrate our land by shipping the refuse of Pela to our shores. Already we are taxed until we groan under the burden. If we wish to preserve our way of life, we must stand together!

It is time, my fellow patriots, for us to rise up, to defend ourselves and our land from tyranny. Join with me!

Thia gazed at the torn broadside wonderingly, then her eyes fell on the name at the bottom of the document.

Rufen Castio . . .

She stood there, rereading the document. *So this is what Denno stayed up all night printing. Who is Rufen Castio?*

Thia read the thing through again. She had little knowledge of politics, but even she could recognize that what she was looking at would be regarded as treason by the Royal Governor.

Treason . . . She glanced around her, almost as though someone had entered and might be seeing her reading the broadside. *What have I gotten myself into?*

7

Talis

Talis Aloro stood in the midst of the outraged crowd of Katan colonists, rejoicing in their anger. *Master Castio is in prime form today,* she thought, gazing admiringly up at the revolutionary leader. Rufen Castio stood atop a makeshift dais in the town square of North Amis, surrounded by a crowd of nearly a hundred merchants, farmers, and laborers. *He has them hanging on his every word.*

"My friends!" Castio raised his arms and shouted. "Tell me something, my friends! Who are we toiling for, as we work our fields and harvest our crops? Are we working for our wives and children, for their future?"

"NO!" roared the crowd. They surged forward eagerly, carrying Talis with them. For a moment she was squeezed between two burly laborers. The stench of ancient male sweat made her wrinkle her nose as she wriggled free and edged away from them. *Men are such pigs!*

"Are we working for our aging parents so they can live their lives out in comfort beside a good fire?"

"NO!"

"My friends, are we working for our descendants, our children's children?"

"NO!"

"Are we working for *ourselves*, my friends?"

"NO! NO! NO!"

Castio was a tall, spindly man who wore his reddish hair tied back in an unfashionable queue. He slammed one big, bony fist into the other, then raised both hands high. "You are right, my friends! We are working for none of these! Who *are* we working for?"

"The King!" they howled, their rage so tangible Talis could almost see it rising into the air like smoke from a brushfire. "The King, curse him!"

"Curse him, and curse his viceroy!" howled the two laborers, who were so alike they must have been brothers.

"Aye! The King, my friends! The King who has given us his lecherous, scheming son for our viceroy! Do Agivir and Salesin care about us?"

"NO, NO, NONONO!"

"Our esteemed viceroy has taxed us till we groan with the burden to pay for his scandalous parties, filled with debauchery! We have sent delegations to Pela, to explain our position." Castio snatched a paper from the breast of his tunic. "My friends, today I received word about the fate of our delegation. We sent a good man, Petro Tomlia. How many of you know him—*knew* him!"

The crowd gasped and muttered.

"That's right, my fellow Katans! Petro Tomlia was led to the block last month! The rest of our delegation now languishes in a Pelanese prison! And for *what*, my friends? For *what*? For no other crime than expressing our concerns! That's all! For being our advocate, a good man has died! The Viceroy is a butcher, and we his cattle!"

"Butcher! Butcher! Butcher!" Talis yelled, and the crowd took up the chant, which continued for quite a while.

Finally, Castio raised a hand for quiet. "Just last month another shipload of convicts came here! Thieves and rapists and murderers set free to walk our land! By the Viceroy's order! He doesn't want to feed them in his prisons, so he sends them to prey on us! To butcher us!"

This time Talis didn't have to shout, the crowd did it for her. "Butcher!"

"Living here in a new world is not easy, my friends," Castio continued, dropping his voice low, as though confiding in the mob, which immediately hushed, hanging on his every word. "We Katans have to work hard. Every day is a struggle, to till our land, protect our homes and livestock. We love this land, but it does not hesitate to kill us." Castio paused. "It is hard enough for us to keep body and spirit together. We have no luxuries, like the Pelanese do. And who provides them with the wealth to have such luxuries, my friends?"

"We do!"

"And, my friends," Castio's voice was growing louder, slowly, steadily, "how does our esteemed viceroy repay the citizens of our colony for the sweat of their brows, for facing the dangers posed by the renegades he and his constables have loosed upon our new land? How does our viceroy repay us?" Castio leaned forward, his blue eyes bright with anger, "My friends, Prince Salesin *taxes* us! More each year! Today we groan under the weight of the King's tax, but who's to say that by midwinter we won't be *screaming* for mercy? And does Prince Salesin care about how we are faring? Does he listen to his people?"

"NO!"

Castio stood there for a beat, then said, simply, "My friends . . . we can stand here and shout our protests all day and all night, and it will make not one whit of difference to Agivir and Salesin and their lords. They have denied the colonies a proper seat on the council. The time is rapidly approaching, my fellow Katans, when we must do more than speak, more than shout. We must *act*!"

"Yes!" the crowd shouted. "Yes, *yes*, **YES**!"

They went on chanting, each "Yes!" coming with increasing fervor. Talis was relieved there was no royal garrison in North Amis. If there had been, this crowd was angry enough to march on them, and such a display would ill serve the cause.

The crowd was yelling and shaking their fists as they shouted. Castio let them go on for another long minute, then raised his arms high into the air. The crowd hushed, listening.

"My friends, remember this moment, remember this hour. It will not be long before we will be asking for your support—your coins, your harvest surplus—and, mayhap, your very bodies and the arms you can bear. The day is coming, my friends! Soon Agivir will have no choice but to listen to us, if he wants this colony to remain loyal to the Crown! In the meantime . . . in the meantime, my friends, we *will* protect ourselves, our land, and our families. We will march and we will drill, and if Salesin tries his butchery on us, we will not go tamely to the slaughter, will we?"

"NO NO NO NO!"

"Our forces are gaining strength and numbers every day! If the King will not pay heed to us, it will be time to take up our guns and march! And, my friends, if that day comes, I will be proud to march with you!"

"We'll be ready!"

"We'll march, Castio!"

"Fight and win for Kata!"

The shouts of the mob engulfed Talis. She looked up at Castio, saw him looking down at her. He gave her a tiny nod, and she smiled.

Carefully, she stepped back, easing herself out of the crowd. As she did so, she raised her dark red shawl and slid it over her head, hiding the thick, luxuriant waves of black hair that fell down her back, almost to her waist.

Usually Talis wore her hair braided tightly and pinned into a knot at the nape of her neck, but her guise today called for unbound hair to go with the low-necked blouse and kilted-up skirts of a tavern wench. Talis's generous curves and enticing smile often enabled her to gain information for Castio and the Cause. Drunken Pelanese would frequently babble to an attractive, green-eyed tavern slut, where they would guard their tongues in the presence of a Katan male who might secretly be a member of one of the militia groups that were forming all over the colony, or one of Agivir's agents.

A few more cautious steps backward, murmuring "excuse me's," and she was out of the crowd. Pulling her shawl tightly about her face, Talis hurried across the weedy grass of the square, crossed the cobbled expanse of Main Street, then turned onto the unpaved stretch of churned mud that was Bay Lane. She was heading for the White Horse Tavern. Talis was careful to keep her head down, lest she be spotted and recognized by any passersby, who would be shocked to see Gerdal Aloro's daughter dressed like a round-heeled strumpet.

Talis lived on a large farm called Woodhaven, a league from North Amis, where her father raised sheep, cattle, emoria fiber, and vegetables. Talis, more than any of her brothers, was Gerdal's "right-hand man," a term he applied to her with a mixture of pride and chagrin. Her father was a royalist, still. Talis had stopped arguing politics with him three years ago, when she'd become involved with the Katan revolutionary underground.

Yesterday morning she'd found a note in the hollow of a tree on her father's land, warning her that a certain merchant named Levons might have important information for the Cause, and that he would be in North Amis today. Generally, Talis preferred to do her spying and information gathering farther from home, when her father sent her to market with their herds and crops, but this time she'd made an exception, knowing that Castio was planning to come to North Amis and speak.

So she'd been up long before dawn, leaving a message for her father and her gentle, ailing mother: "Gone hunting on the mountain. Don't wait supper for me."

Since Talis was the best hunter in the family, and the flocks were migrating south, she'd hoped her father wouldn't question her absence too much. Of course he'd be surprised and disappointed when she returned empty-handed, but there was nothing she could do about that. She wished she could have ridden into town, that would have made her journey much easier, but she'd worried that some passerby would recognize one of Gerdal's riding horses. So she'd alternately run and walked into town, reaching it a little before noon.

Talis had been glad of the excuse to sneak into town; she hadn't seen Castio for months and was eager to share all the news she'd accumulated. She was a bit shaken by Castio's vehemence today—never before had she heard the fiery-worded orator suggest that war with Pela might prove inevitable. Talis frowned worriedly. She'd considered herself a loyal servant of the Crown until just a handful of years ago. She wasn't sure she wanted Kata to be free of Pela . . . she just wanted Katans to have the rights they were guaranteed under Pelanese law. While Agivir had ruled Kata, there had been stirrings of dissent and grumbles over the ever-present taxes. But it was Viceroy Salesin who had hit upon the idea of "cleaning out" the Pelanese gaols by shipping convicts across the sea to Kata.

When Talis was a girl, Kata had been a safe place to live, a place where nobody locked doors and any stranger was invited in and given a hot meal and a place by the fire to sleep. Those days were no more. Too many robberies, murders, and rapes had terrorized those living on Katan farms. Nowadays, any stranger who approached a Katan farm did so in peril of his life, in the sights of a musket-toting farmer.

Rape . . . The thought made Talis shudder violently and grit her teeth to keep them from chattering. Her stomach clenched.

The young Katan revolutionary would be twenty-one on her next birthday, and she remained unpledged and unwed, much to her family's distress. Talis frowned behind the folds of the shawl. *Marriage, marriage, that's all they can think of. No matter how much I do, I'll never be any good in their eyes unless I marry.*

And that, she would never do. She hated men—well, most

men, Castio being one of the rare exceptions. The very thought of the intimacies of marriage made her want to retch. *Marriage! Not likely! But all the work I do for Dad, overseeing the farm, working alongside the slaves in the fields, doing the buying and selling of the crops, keeping the accounts—Goddess forfend, I manage the whole place these days!—and yet, all Dad can think of is marrying me off.*

Just last week Talis and Gerdal had had a terrible row. Her mouth tightened at the memory . . .

Gerdal Aloro waved his arms in frustration as he paced back and forth. The candlelight gleamed faintly on his balding forehead. "Daughter, this cannot go on! People are beginning to talk! Three men have asked me if they may court you, but you will have none of any of them. 'Tis not right! You're of an age to wed these past three years and more! You need a husband to support you, daughter! Are you intending to be a spinster?"

Talis stared at him stonily. "And if that's what I decide? I have told you and told you, Dad, I have no wish to marry. Are you telling me that I'm a burden?"

"A burden, yes!" he shouted, losing the last vestige of his temper. "A burden to your mother and me! We raised you right! We don't deserve such a willful daughter!"

Talis gazed at him in silence, then turned and walked out of the room.

She had barely spoken to her father since that time.

We used to be so close, she thought sadly. *I knew they loved me. Now I've shamed them and I'm a burden, am I? Well, that's too bad. I work twice as hard as my brothers, but I could work until I dropped and it would mean nothing, I suppose. Only marriage will satisfy them. If I'm now considered a burden, then perhaps I should just leave. I could join the Cause full-time. Nobody there would think I'm a burden. Nobody there would nag me to marry.*

Her face twisted in a grimace as she thought of her father and all the young men he'd pushed at her in the past three years. She'd refused to even dance with them, much less go out walking with them. *No man will ever touch me that way again. I'll die first.*

Talis felt the reassuring weight of the dagger strapped to her calf and was comforted. When she was seventeen she'd vowed to learn to use weapons as well as any man, and she'd kept that promise, learning wrestling, swordplay, knife-fighting and throwing from some of Castio's top military advisers, and practicing whenever she could find an opponent who was willing to coach her without getting any lewd ideas.

She was also an excellent shot with both pistol and long rifle, but it was her father and brothers who had taught her to shoot. The Aloro homestead lay at the edge of the wilderness, and farm children of both sexes were taught to shoot at an early age because of the danger from predators.

If I had to, I could shoot Jasti Aloro dead, cut his throat. I could kill him in so many ways . . . The thought came unbidden, but was accompanied by a satisfying vision of a bloody corpse.

Her breath caught in her throat and Talis had to stop, stand pressed against the wall of the tavern. *Oh, no. It's been over a year. I thought I was over it. I can't let it happen now!*

But it was coming, and Talis knew it. She managed to stumble a few steps farther, until she was hidden by a large rain barrel. Squatting down with her back to the wall, she wrapped her arms around herself and fought to stay calm. *Breathe . . . breathe . . .* She gasped, fighting to draw air into her lungs. It felt as though a blacksmith's vice were being pressed down onto her chest. Her attempts to draw breath resulted in ineffectual squeaks. Black spots danced across her vision.

She closed her eyes, willing herself not to be sick, and for a moment she was back there, on that awful night . . .

She opened the door of the privy and stepped out, ready to head back to the family party. Inside the big, sprawling farmhouse she could hear the music and the stamp of dancing feet, the clapping and the singing.

As she headed back up the path, a large shadow stepped out from behind a tree. Talis stopped dead, then backed up a step. "Uncle Jasti, I told you, no more of your 'games,'" she said, trying vainly to keep her voice steady. "I don't like it anymore. It's nasty. Besides, I'm too old for those games, I'm sixteen now. You leave me alone or I'll tell Dad what you made me do."

Jasti Aloro was a big, broad-shouldered man with graying hair. He was five years older than Gerdal, and his gut revealed his fondness for ale. The yeasty reek of it reached Talis as he laughed softly. "Aye, you'll get no argument from me, niece. You're too old for little girl's games. Time for some big girl games. Come here . . . you'll like it."

For the past three years, he'd been saying that hated phrase to her, and Talis had kept silent out of fear and shame. But not tonight. She glared at him. "Get out of my way. I'm telling my father what you've been making me do."

When Jasti didn't move, she turned, stepping off the path.

The blow to the back of her head stunned her so badly she found herself on her knees, not realizing what had happened to her. As she struggled to rise, another slap caught her across the face. Jasti grabbed her by the hair and dragged her up, and when she cried out in pain, he slapped her mouth, splitting both lips. "Shut up, you whorish little slut! I won't hurt you none! Just want to have a little fun, and you want it, too, you're just too pigheaded to admit it!"

Panicking, Talis struck out, scratching, clawing, kicking, opening her mouth to scream. Two hands grabbed her by the throat, squeezing . . .

Talis did not quite lose consciousness. But all the strength left her limbs, and she sagged and would have fallen had he not swung her up into his arms. She managed to gasp, and he laughed harshly. "Oh, you're not dead, missy. You're not hurt, just relax . . ."

Talis managed a faint cry, but she knew it was hopeless. Jasti lurched along the path, heading for the hay barn.

By the time they reached it, she could breathe again, and again she tried to fight. He slapped her again, so hard that everything went gray and distant.

She was roused by pain, sharp and piercing. The air was chill on her legs, for her skirt was kilted up. He was on top of her, grunting ale-breath into her face. Some vague instinct of self-preservation made Talis keep her eyes closed. Jasti gathered himself and rammed into her again, cursing. "Tight . . . too tight . . . slut . . ." he panted. "Never dreamed . . . you'd be virgin . . ."

She was being torn in two; he thrust again, sending a jab of agony through her.

Drawing breath, Talis screamed at the top of her lungs.

Cursing, he clamped his hand over her mouth, and kept it there while he finished.

Crouched in the alley in North Amis, Talis raised her head from her arms, glad to be able to breathe normally again. *It's over. Over. You're not hurt. Breathe.*

Talis forced herself to exhale, rejoicing that the vise-crushing pain was gone. *Relax. He will never touch you again, and if he tries, he'll die for the privilege,* she reassured herself. *He's older than Father, almost an old man. And I'm young and strong. He could never hold me down and do . . .* that, *again.*

For just a moment Talis found herself imagining meeting Uncle Jasti here on the street, and he would be drunk, so drunk he wouldn't recognize the niece he hadn't seen in years. Not since the night when his brother had heard his daughter's anguished cry and burst through the door of the barn mere seconds after Jasti had finished. One look at his daughter, beaten and bloody, had told the story, and Gerdal had grabbed Jasti and thrashed him thoroughly, then ordered his drunken, babbling brother to never darken his door again. As Jasti had stumbled away into the darkness, Gerdal gathered Talis into his arms and comforted the sobbing girl, pointing out that she had "taken no real hurt."

But Gerdal, not wishing to blacken the Aloro name, had told no one of his brother's act. He allowed his clan to believe that he'd broken with Jasti over money his older brother hád borrowed. So Jasti Aloro continued to attend family gatherings, bold as brass and with a smile for any young girl, always ready to invite them to sit on his knee.

Three years ago Talis had dug in her heels and refused to attend any events where her uncle might be present. Her father angrily expostulated with her. " 'Tis two years past, Talis! He'll never hurt you again, you know he wouldn't dare. He was drunk, Talis. Drunken men do lecherous, unholy things. But you took no real hurt—and besides, who's to say that you didn't give him the wrong idea, eh? Young girls flirt innocently, not knowing how such flirting can inflame—"

Talis had given her father a look so filled with utter loathing that he sputtered to a halt. In silence, she'd turned away, and since that time they had spoken only of surface things. But Talis stopped attending family gatherings, and that was that.

I could get him, she thought. *Just a glimpse of a bared shoulder, a teasing smile, and he'd follow me into the alley like a bullock to the butcher. And he'd never come out again.*

Talis took a firm rein on her imagination. She wasn't here in North Amis today to indulge in visions of vengeance. No, she was here to pick the brain of a certain farmer named Levons, who had sold a flock of sheep to the King's garrison in Venra Bay last week.

Squaring her shoulders, she picked up her skirts and forced herself to hurry. When she reached the White Horse, the tavern keeper, a thin, sour-looking man named Toneo, shouted at her. "Lazy slut! Where have you been? Get busy!"

Talis hung up her shawl and made a rude gesture at the man, bringing guffaws from the patrons. *Time to get into character,* she told herself. She deliberately twitched her hips as she went to pick up the tray loaded with ale tankards, eliciting whistles and catcalls. She smiled at them archly, never revealing the disgust these drunken, lecherous *men* inspired in her. Talis was a good actress, and hence a good spy.

While she picked up the rest of the loaded tankards, Toneo winked at her and whispered, "Master Levons is the one you want. The red-cheeked fellow sitting alone by the fire."

Talis winked back. Toneo was a strong supporter of the Cause.

Hefting the tray, she quickly distributed the drinks, ending up at the portly sheep farmer's table. When she handed him his ale, she gave him a dazzling smile. Levons smiled back and flipped her a coin. Talis made it disappear, then busied herself wiping up a splotch of spilled ale. "Can I get you anything else, Master?" she asked with a coy smile.

Levons shook his head. "The only thing I want in this place, dearie, might be your sweet self."

Goddess spare me. Another lecherous swine. Talis simpered at him. "Oh, sir, you'll turn a poor girl's head, you will. Where are you from?"

It turned out he was from some tiny village in the south that Talis had never heard of, not far from Casloria, which she had. Levons had been on the road now for two weeks and he was feeling lonely. Having a pretty young thing hanging on his every word suited him just fine.

Over the next quarter hour, Talis learned a great deal about sheep and their care that she already knew, and little else. She did manage to glean the fact that the King's garrison was now fully manned, thanks to a shipment of Pelanese soldiers that had come in only last month.

"I swear, I never saw so much spit 'n polish in my life," Levons said, waving the fresh tankard Talis had brought him so energetically that it slopped over. "They spend half the day polishing their gear, and the other half drilling."

"Drilling? Ooooh, how exciting," Talis breathed. "What kind of drilling? Do they march, or do they ride around on fine horses?"

"Oh, they've got at least two squads of cavalry, missy, but most of the soldiers are infantry," Levons said. Raising his tankard, he gulped down the ale, his throat rippling.

Talis giggled. "I just love a man in uniform."

Levons smiled widely, showing a broken tooth that was turning black. "Makes me wish I'd brought my militia uniform, sweetling," he said. "I could stand some lovin' from a pretty minx like you."

"Militia?" Talis said, refilling his cup, careful to keep her tone casual. Castio had told her to be on the watch for certain members of the militia. "Which militia are you with, Master Levons?"

"Oh, from Casloria, m'dear. We march there twice a week. I'm a drill leader." He grinned and gulped his ale. "M'wife says 'tis irreverent, disrespectful to the Crown, but I say we have to be ready. One day the Viceroy's going to decide that he wants the broth off our hobs and the shirts from our backs, mark my—" A huge belch ended his statement.

Talis gazed at the old farmer, her thoughts racing. Was he one of Castio's couriers? He'd mentioned two key words, "militia" and "marching" in close succession, though he hadn't voiced the actual code phrase. *Of course, he's pretty drunk,* Talis thought. *It could be coincidence. Maybe I should test him, see if he makes the proper response.*

Talis drew a deep breath, steeling herself for what she knew she must must do next. She slid into the seat beside Levons, pressing against him, nuzzling his cheek. "We need to talk," she whispered into his whiskery ear, her voice barely louder than a breath. "Master Levons . . . do we march in unison?" It was the code recognition query Castio's couriers learned.

The old drunkard paid no attention to Talis's words at all. Instead, he grunted lustfully as he grabbed her breast.

Talis's mouth dropped open in outrage, then she controlled her features. Her right hand, the hand that was concealed from any onlookers, immediately slid down to the old courier's homespun crotch. She closed it around his left testicle with a grip that could not possibly be mistaken for anything but a threat. "Let go of my tit," she murmured keeping her voice sweet. Their faces were only inches apart. "If you don't, I'll crush it."

Levons withdrew his hand from Talis's bodice with such alacrity that he overturned his empty tankard.

"That's better," Talis cooed, still not releasing his testicle.

Levons, now considerably sobered, regarded her, sweating with sudden anxiety. "Did you say somethin' missy?" he muttered, hoarsely. "I'm hard o'hearin' in m' right ear. Can you . . . can you repeat it? Please?"

Talis's eyes widened. *He didn't hear me?* She nuzzled the left side of his neck. "I said, 'do we march in unison?'"

Levons nodded. "We march on the right side," he whispered, giving the proper countersign. "Please, missy . . . don't hurt me. I was drunk and not payin' attention. I'm sorry."

Talis relaxed her grip. "Get this straight," she murmured, licking his good ear. "Nuzzle my neck and touch my shoulder, but leave my double-damned tits alone, or I'll show you real pain."

Shifting on his lap, she giggled wildly, shaking her fore-finger in his whiskery face. "Naughty man!" she chided co-quettishly. "Now you must be *punished!* Tell me that I'm pretty! Tell me you've fallen in love with me! Tell me *everything!*"

Levons obeyed. As they "fondled" and "snuggled," the old courier gave Talis every detail of what he'd observed of the King's garrison while selling his flock, as well as an update on the ammunition, strength, and training level of the Caslorian militia. She listened intently, as she'd been trained, so she would be able to repeat the information almost verbatim.

Finally, when Levons whispered that he was finished with his report, she suddenly jerked back with a shrill squeal of indignation. "What makes you think you can touch me *there*?" she demanded, then let fly with a resounding slap across the old farmer's pudgy features. She pulled the blow, but even so, a red mark blossomed. "Let me go!"

Leaping to her feet, she tossed her head, picked up her tray, and flounced away from Levons, who sat nursing his red cheek. When she reached the bar, she busied herself tending to the glasses, and didn't look up when Levons, accompanied by guffaws and ribald commentary, left the tavern.

Talis scrubbed tables with more vigor than was strictly necessary, trying to shake off a sense of guilt at the way she'd treated the old man. *So what if he's one of us?* she thought, wielding her scrub brush briskly. *He's still a* **man**. *Just an old drunkard, just like Uncle Jasti. Next time he starts to paw some young girl, maybe he'll think twice and keep his hands to himself!*

The clock chimed the hour by the time she was finished with the washing up, and Talis looked up to see Rufen Castio peering at her from the crack in the back room door. Talis began counting, and when she reached five hundred, she nodded to the tavernkeep, who nodded back.

Quickly, she picked up her shawl, pulled it on, and hurried outside. Afternoon was waning and the breeze had grown chill. The clouds overhead were thickening. Talis realized that if she were going to make it home by bedtime, she'd have to run or catch a ride on a wagon. For a moment she considered just starting for home and coming back tomorrow, but she knew she couldn't do that. Castio needed her.

She darted down the street, moving quickly, but not so fast that anyone would become suspicious. There was a countinghouse on the corner, and she turned right onto the northern road and, still moving fast, headed for a small clearing in the trees bordering it.

Castio was waiting for her, clearly impatient, his tall, skinny form striding back and forth like a nervous horse. His mount, a sturdy chestnut mare, stood tethered to a tree. Talis hastened up to the revolutionary leader, feeling her heart leap, as always, when she saw him. Not with romantic love, no. Talis felt that way about no man.

The love she felt for Castio was, in its way, more profound. He was her leader, the one who had shown her the vision of a free land. Rufen Castio was a great man.

Now she hurried up to him, smiling. "You were wonderful today! You had them all in the palm of your hand. If you'd told them to set sail for Pela to bring back Prince Salesin's head, they'd have launched their boats, Castio!"

He nodded at her, as usual, all business. "I received a message that a courier was headed our way," he said. "Did you get his report?"

"Yes" she said, repressing another flicker of guilt.

"What did you learn?"

"'Tis a standard layout for a frontier fort," Talis said. "Wooden stockade, twelve gun platforms, officers' quarters, line troops barracks, armory, stables, commissary, storehouse, magazine, and a kitchen and scullery building." Squatting down in the dirt, she used a small twig to reproduce what Levons had described to her.

"What's their strength?"

"Levons saw a little over three hundred men, but some were out on patrol, he said. Probably a complement of four hundred, give or take."

"Half a battalion," Castio said. "No surprise there. Supplies?"

"They appeared well-supplied, he said. Plenty of hams in the smokehouse, many sacks of flour, and the dinner he ate with them was edible. No weevils, fresh vegetables. Good ale and cider." She chuckled. "If you'd seen the girth on this fellow, you'd know why he was so interested in the food."

"Edible army food, that *is* worrisome," Castio said dryly. "Did he get any glimpses into the magazine?"

"One of his ewes got loose and just *happened* to wander in that direction," Talis said. "He was able to catch up to her right outside the window of the magazine. He caught only a glance before the guard demanded that he take himself off, but he estimated at least twenty-five kegs of powder, and he said there were some boxes that may have contained cartridges with the new style bullets."

"A well-equipped fort, indeed," Castio said. "And just one of many that infest our land, may the Goddess help us." He sighed, and Talis looked at him, distressed. Never before had she seen Rufen Castio look anything but determined.

"The cannon," she said, continuing with her report, not knowing what else to say, "at least twelve of them, and they fire three- or four-pound shot."

Castio glanced up at her and seemed to return to himself. "Excellent, Talis," he said. "Good work."

Talis felt warm all over. Castio was not one to offer praise lightly. Quickly, she finished up her report, repeating everything Levons had told her. When she first met Castio and he'd considered her for this work, he taught her to use her eyes and her ears, and to remember in detail without the aid of written notes. Talis had been highly motivated, and was a quick and able student.

When she was done, her mouth was dry from talking so much. Castio had a leathern flask fastened to his saddle, and she went over to it and unfastened it. "May I?"

"And welcome to it," Castio said. "'Tis the least we can do for you, after such an exacting report."

Talis drank, long and deep. The water tasted of leather and was tepid, but she was so thirsty she enjoyed it anyway. When she was finished, she wiped her mouth, then gathered up her skirts. "I must go," she said. "As it is, I can't make it home before dark. I'm supposed to be hunting up on Lonesome Ridge. I'll have to make up some story about missing my way or tracking a wounded doe and then losing her."

Castio looked at her, concerned. "You're nearly a league from Woodhaven," he said. "How did you get here, and how will you get home?"

"I ran," Talis said. "I told them I was going hunting on the mountain, so I couldn't bring a horse. I'll likely run back to Woodhaven, unless I can catch a ride on a farm wagon."

"No, not likely. You've done the Cause a service today, and we'll not repay you so shabbily. I'll take you there. Rebel will carry double for that distance."

Soon enough Talis found herself perched pillion behind Castio on the rump of his chestnut, wishing she was wearing her trousers so she could ride astride. She was used to riding either astride or sidesaddle, but sitting sideways on a horse's rump with no anchor save Castio's back to hang on to felt strange and precarious.

"You took quite a risk today, playing the tavern wench so close to home," Castio said as they jogged back into town to retrieve Talis's hunting clothes from the inn, where she'd left them. "Why didn't you wear a disguise?"

"I should have, I suppose," she admitted. "But by the time I received that message telling me about that courier coming to town, I didn't want to take the time. I figured it was worth a chance. Besides," she added grimly, "men don't look me in the face when I'm dressed like this, Master Castio."

Castio shifted slightly in his saddle to glance back at her. "Don't take any more such chances, Talis. You are too valuable to the Cause. We can't risk losing you."

Talis was speechless with joy, and seized by a sudden bout of shyness. She nodded silently, eyes downcast.

They stopped briefly in North Amis for Talis to change in the back room of the tavern. She felt more comfortable in her buckskin trousers, homespun hunting shirt, buckskin jacket, and one of her father's old broad-brimmed hats. She pulled it down low over her brow and stuffed her hair up under it so it was unlikely she'd be recognized. Talis's father acknowledged that she was the surest shot in the family and that hunting required her to wear men's clothing. But he'd have been shocked beyond words to see her dressed in hunting garb out in public.

Then, pleased that she could now ride astride, Talis swung up behind Castio again and they set out for the Aloro farm at a slow but steady jog.

Once outside of town, they met few passersby, and soon they were following a rutted track that led to some of the outlying farms. The afternoon sun cast greenish light through the massive trees that bordered the road. "It's been months since I've seen you," Castio commented, breaking a long silence. "How have you been? Keeping up with your arms practice?"

"These days, we rarely waste powder and shot on practice," Talis said. "With the King's taxes so high, Father has to scrimp to make ends meet. But I do enough hunting to stay in practice."

"Good, excellent. Did you read that pamphlet I lent you?"

"Yes, I did. It was hard going, at first. There were so many phrases I had to think about, and Master Sendith uses so many big words. 'Guaranteed rights of the governed' and such. But I stuck with it, and it got a bit easier." She grinned. "I prefer your broadsides, Master Castio. They're interesting to read, not hard."

"I've not authored a broadside in too long," Castio said. "I've been spending my writing time making up tavern songs. Want to hear my latest one? The further it spreads, the better."

"Sing it to me!" Talis urged.

Castio threw back his head, and, since they were totally alone on the back country road, sang out in his pleasant but untrained baritone.

> *"Hey, nonny, nonny and a ho ho ho*
> *Everyone knows that the King must go!*
> *Agivir the feeble, and the fat and slow*
> *Hey nonny, nonny, and a ho ho ho!*

> *If you pick a fight with Agivir he'll offer you a treat*
> *It's silver coin in pocket you'll be stowin'*
> *He thinks he won't be taken when he beats a fast retreat*
> *If he fattens up the purses of his foemen!*

> *Hey, nonny, nonny, and a ho ho ho*
> *Everybody knows that the King must go*
> *Agivir the purser, with his head hung low*
> *Hey nonny, nonny, and a ho ho ho!*

> *Agivir, he likes his food, it puts him in good cheer*
> *He likes it rich and spicy, bake or boil it*
> *The servants must be careful to keep burning candles clear*
> *The explosion could wipe out the royal toilet!*

> *Hey, nonny, nonny, and a ho ho ho*
> *Everybody knows that the King must go*
> *Agivir the windy, with his farts aglow*
> *Hey nonny, nonny, and a ho ho ho!*

> *Agivir, he has three sons who might lord it over us*
> *Succession is secure, and that's the bother*
> *Who's to choose between the villain, the dimwit, or the*
> *   puss?*
> *At least we can be sure of who's the father!*

Hey, nonny, nonny, and a ho ho ho
Everybody knows that the King must go
Agivir the daddy with his brats in tow
Hey, nonny, nonny, and a ho ho ho!

Hey, nonny, nonny and a ho ho ho
Everybody knows that the King must go
Agivir the feeble, the fat and slow
Hey nonny, nonny, and a ho ho ho!

Talis listened wide-eyed, and when he was finished, she laughed uneasily. "Master Castio! I daren't teach that song in the taverns, 'twould get me dragged off to gaol!"

"I know," Castio admitted. "It's not time for that one quite yet. In six months, a year at the outside, you'll hear scores of men bellowing it in every tavern, or my name's not Rufen Castio."

"So, you're saying it will come down to a . . . fight," Talis said slowly, trying not to let her dismay show. "Revolution? Are you sure?"

"Who can be sure of anything in this world?" he countered.

Talis was not going to give up so easily. "Don't you think we can . . . avoid it? Somehow?"

"No, I don't think we can," he answered, all levity gone.

"But that's not what you tell the people." Talis shifted uneasily on the mare's rump. The horse was sweating now, and the smell of it was sharp in her nostrils. She could feel dampness seeping through the seat of her trousers.

"The people must be led gently, like a flock with a good shepherd," Castio said. "Push them too hard, rush them, terrify them, and they'll turn tail and trample you. The key to revolution is to make them aware of all that plagues them, then let them know there are others who feel the same way. Play your cards right, and soon they'll be talking each other—and you!—into marching off to the revolution."

Talis frowned. "When I talk to folks in the taverns, most of them think that if we can just get past Viceroy Salesin and gain the King's ear, things here on Kata can still be salvaged." She didn't add that she wanted that to be the case. "Do you think that's possible?"

"No," said Castio flatly. "Not possible." He thought for a moment, then added, "If Agivir were to take control back again, I suppose there could still be a chance. But that's not going to happen. Salesin will never give up the power he's gained, and he's constantly gaining more. He's ruthless. I'd wager even Agivir fears him. There are rumors that the King may abdicate."

"Oh, no!" Talis was shocked. She'd always known that Salesin would be King one day, but that had been something for a distant, hazy future. Talis had been born on Katan soil, but Gerdal was Pelanese, and proud of it. Every Holy Day he hoisted a glass to "Good King Agivir, may the Goddess keep him." And every visit to the temple had included a prayer for the King's health, wisdom, and long reign.

"Oh, yes. Agivir isn't a bad man," Castio said matter-of-factly. "I know I rail against him, and I think he's indeed made some very bad decisions. He ceded the Isle of Talano, for example, and gave up Pelanese fishing rights east of Paalu. Those were the actions of a king who has lost his stomach for fighting. A leader must be prepared to back his threats with force, and Agivir has lost that ability."

Talis sighed. "So it seems," she said. "I've heard it said by others, too."

"It's plain to anyone that has watched what's happening. I'll grant you that no man is a perfect villain, and Agivir did many good things, too. But his worst decision of all was to make Salesin Viceroy of Kata. I suspect he did it under pressure, but that doesn't take away the effect."

"Yes," Talis murmured. "All those criminals they've transported. Our land is no longer safe." After a moment she added softly, "Master Castio, if it comes to war, my father will side with the Crown."

She couldn't see his face, but he nodded and his voice was unsurprised. "Yes. He's a staunch royalist, isn't he?"

"Yes he is. I don't dare argue politics with him or my

brothers anymore. I fear I'd give myself away. I'm lucky the only thing my father thinks of when he sees me is finding me a husband."

"It would be a shame to waste a good soldier and an even better spy on some royalist lout," Castio said dryly.

Talis laughed. "Master Castio, you are no ordinary man, that's sure as the sun rising at morn. Most men think that a woman is made only for bedding, breeding, keeping house, and cooking."

"I'm not like most men," Castio said, matter-of-fact again. "I grew up knowing women had minds as good as any man's. My father was a ne'er do well who disappeared when I was ten. My mother raised me, and my brother. She earned our living taking in washing and mending, and she learned to read and write so she could teach us. By the time I was twenty, she had earned enough to buy her own dry goods store, and she's there to this day. Remarkable woman, my mother. She'd give me a good hiding even today if she heard me give women less than their due respect."

Talis had been listening raptly. Never before had Master Castio revealed anything of his personal life, and she was fascinated. "You owe your mother one more thing, Master," she said when Castio was finished.

"I do?" The revolutionary turned in his saddle to glance at her inquiringly. "What is that?"

"Me," Talis said. "I heard you speak three years ago, up in Fiorencia when my father took me with him to buy some cattle. You spoke so eloquently of the price of freedom— and its value. You said that freedom was for everyone. For every man, woman, and child. I'll never forget it. Before that, it was only men that anyone cared about. But you said women should be free, too." *I want to be free! I want to choose where I go and what I do, and I don't want to marry . . . not ever!*

"Ah," said Castio softly. "And you, of course, are a woman. Which means, perhaps, that you have personal reasons for devoting yourself to the Cause."

Talis nodded. "But the thought of war, that frightens me.

I'm learning to fight, and they say I have some knack for it. I know a woman who used to be a mercenary, in the next town over, and she's coached me when I could sneak away to see her. I can throw a punch better than most men, she says. But I've never faced battle. I've heard them talk of it . . . glorious one moment, a horror the next."

"The thought of war should frighten any sane person," Castio said. "It certainly frightens me, too. But the thought of living under Salesin's reign frightens me more."

Talis nodded. "Yes, Agivir can't live forever, and when he dies, Salesin will be free to abuse Kata as he wills."

"He's already started," Castio reminded her. "He executed the leader of our delegation. A good man, one who'd committed no crime, save that of attempting to convey the colony's view."

Talis nodded. They were nearing her farm now, only another few miles to travel.

She shook off her thoughts. "Sing the song again, so I can learn it," she urged. Castio complied, and Talis joined in. Finally, when they were done, she began to laugh. "Oh, that's wicked, wicked! One of your best. I'll look forward for the day when I may sing it in the taverns. How about a duet?"

Again Castio complied, and their voices rang out together, echoing against the thick stands of trees on either side of the road.

Minutes later they came to farmland again. "We're not far from home now," Talis said. "Stop here." She slid off over the mare's rump. "Only another two miles to the farm road, and from there I can make it home in minutes. Master Castio, I do appreciate getting this ride. This way, I should be home soon after sunset."

Castio nodded and gazed down at her. "Talis, call me Rufen, please."

She was taken aback, then smiled shyly. "Very well . . . Rufen."

He slacked the reins on the mare's neck, and she began to crop the grass on the verge of the road. "Talis, I've been thinking," Castio said. "Is there any way I could send you some books for you to read, without your father finding out?"

"Books?" She frowned as she thought. "The pamphlets and broadsides I hide in the barns and read in snatches, when I have the time. A book takes more time."

"Yes, they do. But I think you'd benefit from these books. They range from the philosophy of political systems to battle tactics. I'll need able lieutenants when the war starts. Officers who can plan troop movements and who know tactics. And those officers will need to be people who understand why we're fighting."

Talis could read, write, and cipher, but she'd received less than half the years of schooling her brothers had gotten. During the good harvest years, her father had hired a tutor to educate his sons. His daughter he'd taught himself, but only what men of his generation considered suitable learning for a female. Talis had often lurked outside the schoolroom door, listening to her brothers' lessons, but she knew she was no scholar.

The thought of Castio's books made her uneasy. Talis hated to fail at anything, but she knew how ill-prepared she was for what Castio was suggesting. And there was another, even more important obstacle to what Castio had suggested. If she were to become an officer, Talis knew she'd have to spend all her time in the company of *men*. Men like Levons, men whose first thought was to paw her and violate her.

She shook her head. "An officer? No, Rufen, not I. I'll serve the Cause as a spy. Or an assassin. I work best alone. I'm sure I'd make a good assassin. Assign me any target, I'll kill him."

Castio gave her a quick, penetrating glance. "What if I needed you to kill a woman?" he asked.

Talis was taken aback. She couldn't imagine killing a woman for any reason. She gazed at Castio but could think of nothing to say.

"Talis," Castio said after a moment, "I don't think you have it in you to be an assassin. But I *do* believe you were born to lead. Will you read the books if I send them to you?"

"Master Castio . . ." She hesitated, struggling for words, shifting uneasily from foot to foot. "I will try, truly I will."

"That's all I ask," Castio said. "Talis, you are precious to the Cause—smart, and capable. As for being a leader, we'll let that go for now. Time will tell if I am right."

Talis stood gazing at him, wide-eyed. "I . . . I . . ."

"Don't worry," Castio reassured her. "I will expect nothing immediately. Just do your best with the books I send. I'll stay in contact."

"I will," she said. "And, by the by, Mas . . . Rufen, Father will be likely sending me north to buy seed in the early spring. I can let you know when."

"Won't he send someone with you?"

"My oldest brother, who lives in North Amis, most likely, or the foreman. I'll be in charge, because I'm the one he trusts with his money. No fear, they'll take the chance to drink and gamble, so I'll be able to meet with you or whomever you wish me to contact. I won't be able to do my tavern act, but other than that . . ." She shrugged.

"Where will he send you?"

"Probably Louvas, or possibly East Fentina. If the prices are bad, we may go as far north as Q'Kal."

"There are royal garrisons in East Fentina and Q'Kal," he said. "Good. We can use a report about either of them."

She nodded. "I'll let you know."

Rufen Castio flashed one of his rare, infectious smiles. "Good. I wish I had a dozen more like you, Talis. We'd be free of Pela before next harvest."

She smiled back, waved, and darted away down the footpath she'd indicated.

It was after dark when Talis came home, carrying her long rifle. She'd taken the precaution of loading and firing it once, in case her father checked the weapon.

She was tired as she began the last trek up from the pastures to the house. The lighted windows gleamed soft gold with the candlelight, friendly beacons in the darkness. Talis reached the house, then stood for a moment, going over her story to make sure there were no holes in it.

I hunted on the mountain, managed to shoot a doe and wounded her, tracked her for miles, then finally lost her when she went down Montalin Ridge and vanished into Sunset Gorge. By that time I was too tired to climb the ridge again, so I went north and came back along the roadway . . .

Movement caught her eye, and Talis stepped back, out of the light. It was her mother, coming over to the window to lift the curtain and gaze out. Talis could see her face, her pale, freckled features and graying reddish hair. Talis looked nothing like her mother. She took after her father's side of the family.

Seeing her mother's anxious expression, Talis swallowed painfully. She loved her mother, whose health was not robust. Evonly Aloro depended on her daughter for companionship in a household dominated by men. She loved Talis, but she knew nothing about what Jasti Aloro had done to her daughter. Gerdal had warned Talis that if she told her mother, the knowledge that she had been raped might kill her.

As she gazed at her mother, remembering, anger at her father rose once again. *He denied me justice. He denied me comfort. And if he gets his way, he'd going to deny me happiness and freedom.* Talis knew that, much as her mother loved her, Evonly would never stand against one of Gerdal's commands. If Gerdal arranged a marriage for her, as he'd been hinting he would, Evonly would happily begin making the wedding gown.

Talis had known this for a long time, but today that knowledge, coupled with her growing anger at her father, made her feel as though she had a stone in her breast instead of a warm, beating heart. She loved her mother, but it was too much to ask of any daughter, to give up herself!

I won't marry some disgusting lout just to please them, she resolved, *I'd truly rather die.*

But she didn't want to die, either. So what was left for her? Her talk with Castio was fresh in her mind. *If father tries to arrange a marriage, I'll leave,* she decided. *I will leave and never return.*

Tears flooded her eyes as she pictured her mother's reaction. *Goddess protect her,* she prayed. Her mother was a gentle soul who had always longed for daughters she could dress in silk and lace, and she could teach to cook and weave. Instead she'd borne her husband four stalwart sons and a daughter who was the best shot of all of them.

Talis's mouth twisted as she wiped her eyes. Her jaw tightened as she fought a silent battle for control. She realized she'd reached some kind of inner crossroads and there was no turning back now. In just a moment she would put on a smile and walk into the house, greet her family, eat the plate of food they had saved on the warmer for her, but she knew some invisible line had been crossed. From this day forward she could never really go home again.

We all must make sacrifices. Castio's words echoed in her mind.

Taking a deep breath, Talis wiped the tears from her cheeks and squared her shoulders. She smiled, and, smiling, walked into the house that could never again be her home.

8

The Faces of Slavery

Lady Ulandra q'Jinasii stood in the nave of the temple, trying to stop shaking. Her heart was beating so fast that she felt light-headed. Her feet seemed a long way away from her, and she couldn't make them move. *I can't just stand here,* she thought. *I can't disgrace my family. I have to do this!*

Summoning her resolve, she slowly edged one foot forward. She took another step, and then another. Only when she had managed to take several slow, measured paces did she dare to glance up at the temple and the altar that was her destination.

The Temple of the Goddess was magnificent, decorated with ropes and garlands of spring greenery that matched the traditional color of her bridal garb. The gown was of heavy silk, intercut with panels of fine lace and trimmed with tiny beads of jade. Jade earrings hung from her ears. Her hair was unbound, as befit a maiden bride, and it hung past her waist. On her head she wore a gossamer veil, held in place by a garland of grape and olive leaves, plants sacred to the Goddess.

Far above her head soared the famous ceiling of the temple, white stone carved into lacy patterns, reaching up into the top of the dome. Crystalline panels set into the walls and ceiling admitted light, but not a view. Proper worship of the Goddess demanded that one not be reminded of the world outside.

Ulandra kept her eyes downcast after that one glimpse at the temple. That single glance had been enough—her bridegroom awaited her, magnificent in a tunic and doublet of emerald green satin and velvet. She did not know Prince Salesin well. They had only spoken together a handful of times, always under the watchful eyes of her family or her duenna.

He will be King, she reminded herself. *As soon as I say my vows, I will be a princess. My father will be so proud.*

She swallowed dryness. *It is natural for a bride to be frightened on her wedding day,* she tried to reassure herself. *Soon you will know each other, no longer be strangers. He is well-favored, strong, a great leader. Soon, Goddess willing, there will be children to bind you together.*

Ulandra loved children. She had taken care of many in her days at the cloisters. The good sisters ran an orphanage, and the older girls had been permitted to help care for the little ones.

Ulandra knew her father was waiting for her. He would not be performing the ceremony—the High Priestess would do that. Male bishops had many duties in the temple, but marriages and burials were not among them.

She had nearly reached the altar now. Ulandra glanced up to meet her bridegroom's eyes. Salesin appeared relaxed to the point of boredom, as if he were wed every day. Ulandra, realizing this, took an awkward step that nearly turned into a stumble. *Bored? Surely not!*

His dark eyes, when they met hers, held no warmth. After a moment he smiled at her, but the expression did not reach his eyes.

Ulandra fought a sudden impulse to hike her fine skirts up and race away from the altar, out of the temple.

Stop this! she ordered herself. *You are imagining things!*

As the ceremony began, she raised her hand, and the Crown Prince took it. His fingers were strong and cool and dry. Ulandra was chagrined to realize that her own were cold and sweating.

The High Priestess was talking, but her voice seemed so distant. One of the young acolytes began to walk around bride and groom, carrying a pot of sweet incense. The fragrant smoke curled through the air, making her dizzy.

Ulandra cast her eyes down, modestly, as befit a bride— but it was not modesty that prompted her action. She couldn't stand to see that faintly amused detachment in the Crown Prince's eyes.

It will be over soon, she promised herself.

Now the sacred vine was brought out and draped around the couple, symbolically binding them together. It was time for the marriage bracelets. Twin emerald bracelets, proffered by yet another young acolyte. Ulandra fumbled as she took the larger of the two off the satin cushion, and, to her horror, she dropped the precious cuff.

Quick as a cat pouncing on prey, Salesin caught it, then gravely handed it back to her. Laughter twinkled in his eyes. He was amused by her clumsiness. Her cheeks scarlet, Ulandra slipped the gemmed cuff onto his wrist. Moments later he did the same for her.

Ulandra forced herself to breathe. *I am wed!*

Now it was time for the crowning.

Old King Agivir approached, carrying a slender gold circlet that was studded with emeralds. Ulandra sank down into a deep, formal curtsy and continued without a break into a kneeling position. Much practice paid off—she did not falter, her motion smooth. Slowly, she raised her hands to her head and lifted off her bridal wreath.

The King looked down at her, his aged features gray and worn. There were tears in his rheumy old eyes, and all traces of the once legendary ruler had vanished. It had been a terrible blow for him when young Prince Eregard had been lost at sea last fall.

Just for a moment, as he gazed down at her, Ulandra could

have sworn she saw pity in King Agivir's eyes. "I crown you Princess of Pela," the King intoned. His hands trembled as he raised the crown and placed it on her head. "Princess Ulandra, wife to my son, Crown Prince Salesin. May the Goddess bless your union, my daughter."

Ulandra felt the crown settle onto her head. The King extended a hand, to raise her. She stood, feeling the band of the coronet on her brow. It seemed far heavier than its true weight.

King Agivir released her hand and stepped back, just as Prince Salesin reached over to grasp it. He turned her toward the congregation, and for a moment the two of them stood poised together before the altar. Then, moving with slow, proper dignity, they began the recessional.

The carriage ride to the palace amid the cheering throngs of Pelanese, and the reception that followed, were a blur to Ulandra. She managed to eat a few bites, and sipped a little wine, but mostly she stood beside the Crown Prince, greeting guests, smiling, and chatting—and moments later could not remember faces, names, or what had been said.

Prince Salesin stayed by her side for as long as was proper, then courteously took his leave and vanished. She glimpsed him several times with friends, drinking and laughing.

She heard him mention "Kata," then, a few minutes later, "Kerezau." He was talking about the growing unrest in Kata and the fact that the Chonao Redai, Kerezau, after wintering his forces on Taenareth, was now threatening the Meptalith Islands. Ulandra had heard that the Meptalith had broken off their negotiations with Kerezau. Now they, too, faced conquest.

But all of that seemed far away, too distant to be worth considering. Her feet hurt. Ulandra repressed a grimace. The reception seemed to drag on for hours, and at the same time went by in a rush.

Finally things seemed to be winding down. Her feet throbbing, her bladder uncomfortably full, Ulandra sought out the water closet. It was the first time she had sat down since the carriage ride, the first time she had been alone all day.

After she had relieved herself, she tried to find the strength to rise. Suddenly, without warning, tears overflowed her eyes and began spilling down her cheeks. Hastily she dabbed them off with her handkerchief, mindful of the powder on her cheeks.

When she emerged from the water closet, her lady-in-waiting set her gown to rights again. "I will rejoin the party in a moment," she said, and deliberately stepped out of her high-heeled slippers. Padding barefoot into the small, adjoining chamber, she paced nervously back and forth, forcing herself to breathe deeply, trying to regain her composure. The chamber had windows. Ulandra saw, with a stab of fear, that the light outside was failing. Soon it would be dark.

Her wedding night . . .

She swallowed, summoned a smile, pinched her cheeks and lips to give her some semblance of color, then went back out into the reception.

Her high-heeled slippers were now a torment. Ulandra saw that many of the court ladies were dancing with stocking feet, but she did not dare do that. Her wedding slippers were beaded with jade and tiny emeralds, and she dared not lose them.

Finally, after she had danced with Prince Adranan and a number of young noblemen, her husband returned to claim her for several dances. Ulandra felt the strength in his arms, the solidity of his chest. She looked up at him and ventured a smile. Salesin did not see it. He was looking over her head at someone across the room.

Ulandra swallowed dryness. Soon they would be alone togther. What would happen? She knew so little. She had no mother to ask, and it would not be meet to ask one of her maids. Her great-aunt had taken her aside and cautioned her that the marriage bed was something every woman must endure so she could have children. Ulandra felt Salesin's strength and wondered exactly what it was she was supposed to endure.

She looked up at Salesin again, and this time he was looking at her. Ulandra smiled. "My lord, the ceremony . . . it went well, I thought. I hope . . . the King and Queen were pleased?"

He glanced down at her. "My father takes little pleasure in anything these days, my lady. But yes, the ceremony went off smoothly enough. Now it only remains for us to produce several heirs to the throne, and we will have acquitted ourselves well." He grinned, but again there was no warmth in his eyes.

Ulandra felt the heat in her face, and looked down, unable to think of what to say. *What will happen next?*

"You're blushing," he said, after twirling her and guiding her through an intricate pattern. "Admirable. How maidenly." He chuckled, and there was a note of anticipation in the sound that made her miss a step.

Ulandra was sorry she had said anything.

Later, much later, though the party was still going, Salesin handed her into the keeping of her ladies. He gave them a smile and a wink. "Don't fuss too much, ladies. I need my rest."

The ladies giggled and exchanged knowing glances.

They led her to the official royal bedchamber. It was grand beyond anything she had ever seen. She could not look at the great, gilded bed with its snowy sheets of fine linen.

Ulandra waited, passive, while they removed her gown and her jewelry. She stood there in her voluminous petticoats while they loosened her bodice, then removed it. It was a relief to be able to take a deep breath—but she didn't seem to be able to do that. The ladies noticed how her heart was beating and giggled.

As they dropped the folds of her pale green nightgown over her head, then began arranging her hair, Ulandra had an impulse to grab their hands and demand, "What will he *do* to me? What will happen?"

But such a question would be undignified and unseemly. She sat down on the great bed with its fine white sheets, to allow them to take off her thin silk stockings.

The ladies quickly hung up her clothes, then two of them lifted the coverlets. She slid her icy feet beneath them and sat there, stiff and waxen pale as a doll, until they gently pushed her down onto the pillows. "Lie back, Your Highness. We'll tell His Highness you are abed."

The maids and the ladies, exchanging amused glances, bowed themselves out.

Ulandra was alone.

She clasped her hands on her breast and began to pray. "Lady Goddess, hear my prayer. Make me a good wife. Let me be fruitful, and a good mother. Help me . . . help me . . . to endure."

Endure what? her mind screamed.

It took all her willpower to lie there quietly when she heard the door in the dressing room click open and footsteps come toward her.

Prince Salesin paused in the dressing room for a long moment. She heard two thumps that were undoubtedly his boots hitting the floor, and the rustle of cloth. For the first time, she realized that wedded intimacies might well involve a lack of clothing. Ulandra had never seen a naked male, and had only the haziest idea of how their anatomy differed from a woman's. When she'd seen certain works of art that featured naked or nearly naked people, the males had certainly appeared different . . . down there . . . but it was improper for a maiden to gaze too closely, so she never had.

Besides, her duenna had always hurried her away from "unsuitable" art and sculpture.

Footsteps again. In the light of the few candles left burning, a shadowed shape filled the doorway. It was the Prince—*my husband,* she reminded herself. To her vast relief, he was not unclothed. His chest was bare, but he still wore his breeches.

He gave her a slightly tipsy, mocking bow. "Greetings, my lady. We meet again."

"M-My lord . . ." Ulandra managed. Her mouth was so dry she could barely get the words out.

"Well met, well met by candlelight," he said. "Might as

well get this over with. I've a busy day before me tomorrow, and the hour grows late."

"Y-Yes, my lord." As he moved toward her, Ulandra began to tremble.

She tried not to stare at his wide, bare shoulders, thick with muscle, his chest, matted with hair as black as that on his head.

"You're shaking, my lady," he said, and it was plain the honorific was meant to mock her. "That's right, you're a virgin," he sighed. "Bother."

Going over to a cabinet, he reached into a drawer, took out a small jar.

Then he walked back over to the bed. "Let's get a look at you," he said, smiling. He picked up a strand of her long, pale hair, soft and shiny as any silk. "You are a pretty thing, though not to my usual taste."

Ulandra tried to hold onto the covers, but he pulled them free easily and tossed them off her. He regarded her in her beautiful nightdress, her hair tumbling around her, and nodded. "We ought to be able to manage this, my lady. Just behave yourself and don't be difficult, eh?"

Difficult? Behave myself?

Ulandra saw him reach for his breeches, start tugging them down, and shut her eyes. She could scarcely breathe. She tried to pray but could summon no words.

Moments later she could feel the bed sag as he lay down beside her. She could smell the reek of stale sweat from dancing, the strong, sour ale smell of him. His breath was harsh and hot, and stank of fish and cheese.

He reached down, grabbed the hem of her nightdress and began yanking it up. Ulandra's eyes popped open and she made a faint sound of protest. "My lord!"

"Relax, my lady," he said, looming close to her, dark and very warm. She could feel heat spilling off him, as though she lay next to hot coals. "I've done this before. Just lie still."

Ulandra could not just lie there and be naked with him. She shook her head frantically and struggled slightly, pushing the gown down. "No, wait a moment, please, can't we . . . I don't want—"

"My lady, what *you* want makes very little difference to me. Very well, be difficult."

With a move as quick as the one he'd made when he grabbed the falling marriage bracelet, Salesin grabbed the bodice of her nightgown and, with one swift yank, ripped the thin fabric all the way down.

Ulandra's eyes widened in horror. She made an instinctive gesture to try and roll away from his gaze, but a heavy hand grasped her arm. "Lie still," he ordered. "Lie *still,* and let's get on with this." He made an exasperated sound. "Goddess, I *hate* virgins!"

Ulandra gulped, then squeezed her eyes shut and obeyed. *He's my husband, he's my husband, he's my husband,* she repeated silently.

Now he was running his free hand over her skin, touching, kneading. His other hand still grasped her arm, keeping her from moving away. "Good," he grunted. He was breathing harder. "That's right."

His hand left off fondling her breasts. She heard him fumble with something . . . the little container? Then his hand was back, touching her tightly clenched thighs. His hand felt slippery. "Come on, open up," he said. "Let's make this as easy as possible . . ."

Ulandra gasped, trying to do as he bade. His hand was between her thighs now, pushing . . . pushing at her most secret place! She clenched her teeth, trying not to fight, but she could not make herself move. He solved the problem by swinging one leg over her right one, then yanking her legs apart.

As he did so, Ulandra felt his hand, his big finger, slide upward, into her, until it suddenly stopped. She gasped. It hurt, even though his hand was slippery with some oil. "Please, my lord, that hurts," she whimpered.

"Has to be done," he said, his voice harsh with urgency. "You want a baby, don't you?"

"Y-Yes . . . but . . . please . . . not like this . . . please . . ."

He gave a short bark of exasperated laughter. "I'm sorry, m'lady, there just isn't any other way. Now just hold still."

With one of his quick, pantherlike motions, he rolled atop her. Ulandra felt something large and hard and hot butting at her thigh for a second, then it touched the spot his finger had invaded. "Hold still!" he ordered, and she felt his body gather itself, then he shoved himself into her.

The pain was excruciating. Ulandra's eyes popped open and, without her willing it, her mouth popped open, a scream welling in her throat—but his hand was there, clamping over her mouth.

"Shut up," he snarled, his expression so dark and savage that he looked like a wild beast. "Goddess, you'll bring the guards in here! Lie *still*!"

He thrust into her, harder this time, and his hand slipped until it was covering both her mouth and nose, smothering her. Ulandra tried to move her head, push at his shoulders, but he was too strong, too heavy. Now he was pushing into her again . . . then pulling out partway, then another thrust, another . . .

Ulandra jerked her head, thrashing wildly, and managed to free her nose. She drew breath. That was better . . . but oh, how the invasion hurt!

He was thrusting harder and faster now, panting. He dropped his head, nuzzled her breasts, then bit her nipple. More pain. Ulandra closed her eyes. She couldn't bear to watch his face, his mouth, against her skin.

Seconds later he thrust into her so hard that he grunted with the effort, but this time he did not withdraw. Moments later she felt his whole body quiver. He grunted again, and now the sound was soft, filled with pleasure. She felt him relax. A moment later he rolled off her.

"There," he said. "All done. That wasn't so bad, now, was it?"

He yanked the covers up over himself and turned away, his back to her.

Ulandra lay there, afraid to move. She didn't want to disturb him. *Perhaps he'll fall asleep . . .*

He did fall asleep. Within minutes his breathing had steadied, become regular, and then he began to snore lightly.

Only then did Ulandra dare push herself up and look down at her body. Blood streaked her thighs, and the white sheets were as stained as if she had gotten her monthly flux in the middle of the night and never awakened. She moved her legs slightly, and pain answered. She was lying in a sodden, sticky red mess.

She wanted nothing more than to get up, to leave, to wash all trace of him away. But if she moved, he might awake, and perhaps he would want to do *that* again.

It was cold in the chamber. The fire had gone out.

Greatly daring, she eased her hand down, managed to tug the blanket up over her.

She did not dare weep aloud, lest it wake Salesin, but tears flowed from her eyes, wetting her tangled hair.

Goddess . . . please, help me . . . please . . .

Ulandra wasn't even sure what she was praying for. She lay there, exhausted, her body throbbing with pain. If only she could sleep!

But she hurt too much to sleep.

Why did it have to be like that? she wondered. *Why didn't someone tell me?*

She knew now that her husband cared nothing for her. To Salesin, she was naught but a means to an heir.

Goddess, is it too much to ask that my husband treat me with some respect, some kindness?

As she lay silently weeping, a face suddenly came into her mind. Prince Eregard, as he'd stood looking down on her, that day in the hall of the palace. There had been more than kindness in his eyes—there had been tenderness. Caring.

Why am I thinking of Prince Eregard? she wondered. *He's dead. He can't help me, nobody can help me.*

Finally, when there were no more tears in her to weep, Ulandra had a thought. *Perhaps he has gotten me with child. If he has, this will not have to happen again.*

She lay awake the rest of that endless night, praying to the Goddess with every fiber of her being. *Please, Lady Goddess, let me be with child!*

Eregard lay with his face pressed against the sour dirt of the gaol cabin, his back throbbing with every gasping breath. He remembered hearing his father's judges when they'd sentenced petty thieves and other miscreants to public whippings—five lashes, ten, fifteen, twenty or more. But never, in all that time, had he given even a moment's thought to the pain those people would soon suffer. Pain . . . it was beyond pain. Pain was a stomachache, or toothache. Pain was a throbbing head. This was something huge that filled his whole world. He could feel every stroke as a separate line of agony, like fifteen red-hot bars of iron lying pressed against his flesh.

Fifteen lashes . . .

The Prince had lost track of how long it had been since he stumbled onto the dock in Port Alvar. Midwinter Festival had come and gone. He remembered the day, remembered the decorations that had festooned the entrance to the master's estate. The master had ordered a side of bacon and a jug of ale to be given to each slave, and they had all had a holiday from work. Eregard remembered the other slaves cautioning him to save his bacon, portion it out slowly, rather than devour it as he had wanted to. *Ye'll get sick as a poisoned pup, lad,* the oldest slave, Malfrey, had told him. *Trust me on this. Ye can't live on greens, fello bean mush, and river-mussel broth for months, then fill up on bacon.*

Those bits of greasy, oversalted bacon had tasted as fine as anything he'd ever eaten at his father's table. He had a sudden, vivid image of those Pelanese royal banquets, the tables groaning with everything from roast peacock to airy meringue concoctions filled with creamy ices . . .

Eregard felt tears well up, and gritted his teeth, trying to force them back. Weeping did no good. He'd found that out long ago. His first week at Master Corlena's estate he'd tried

to run away. He'd been caught before nightfall. Master Corlena had not punished him, physically. Instead he'd shown
Eregard one of the slaves, the man who worked the bellows
in the smithy.

"Frin here ran away, too," Master Corlena said. "How
many times, Frin?"

"Two, Master Corlena," the red-haired slave had replied,
not looking up.

"Come over here and show His Highness what happened
to you after the second time, Frin," the master ordered.

Obediently, the slave crossed the smithy, walking with a
painful, lurching gait. He stopped before Eregard, turned
around, then leaned over and rolled up the leg of his
breeches. A hideous, livid scar ran across the back of his
knee. The leg had healed, but it was clear that the man had
been deliberately crippled.

Eregard had not tried to run away again.

The little gaol cabin was dim. Not much light filtered
through the small barred windows, but he thought it must be
almost evening. He must have lain unconscious for an hour
or so after they'd taken him down from the whipping post
and tossed a bucket of brine across his back. He repressed a
shudder at the memory.

Just three mornings ago he'd awakened realizing that
spring was well and truly on the way. As he headed for the
office to work on Master Corlena's accounts, he'd actually
felt his spirits lift as he felt the mild breeze and the warm
sunshine caressing his face. After months of winter, hud-
dling into a tiny cabin and a single bedstead with four other
unwed male slaves, nursing a smoky fire to keep warm, the
spring weather felt like a benediction.

When he'd arrived in the office, though, he found not only
Master Corlena, but Overseer Barlin waiting there, and his
spirits had plummeted. The overseer, a big man with swarthy
features and lank black hair, had smiled, showing stained
and blackened teeth. "G'mornin', Your Highness. You won't
be needed here today, you'll be joining us in the fields. We
need every hand for the planting, make no mistake."

Eregard had stared at him for a moment, feeling the metal collar around his neck seem to tighten. "Yes, sir," he mumbled.

The Prince had worked the fields before, and had come to dread the experience. His hands were rough and callused now, but the rough-handled farm implements could still raise blisters. He could tell that he was stronger than he had been—he was certainly far thinner—but his back still ached fiercely from the endless bending and straightening, bending and stooping.

But he'd learned quickly to say as little as possible, so he silently followed Barlin to the fields. He and the other twenty field slaves had worked hard the entire day, breaking up the winter-hard clods of earth with hoes, hauling barrows full of rocks out of the field, then planting and fertilizing the seeds. Eregard had worked as hard as any of the field hands. He'd also learned that slacking was sure to call the Overseer's attention to him.

Apparently, Master Corlena had told the man about Eregard's claim to be a Prince of Pela, because Barlin never lost a chance to gibe at Eregard, calling him "Your Highness" and burlesquing formal bows whenever he addressed him. Eregard tried to close his ears, but rage built in him, slowly but surely. By the end of his third day in the fields, he found himself hoping that Barlin would trip in a furrow and break his bull neck.

Still, he'd managed to keep his temper until the work was finished, mid-afternoon of the third day. "All right, come on, come on in!" Barlin shouted, waving them to him. Eregard was glad to dump his last load of rocks on the rock pile, then head back. He was thinking about nothing more profound than a long drink of water, then a wash at the pump.

One of the young, female slaves, pregnant with her first child, was slow to return from the field. Barlin had waved at her impatiently as the others gathered around him. "Analis! Hurry up! Run, bitch!"

By the time she plodded, one hand on the small of her back, up to where the work crew was gathered, and reached out for the dipper that stood waiting in the water bucket, Barlin, never a patient man, had been in a black mood. As Analis raised the dipper of water to her lips, the overseer slapped it out of her hand, then cuffed her sharply across the face. "No water for you until you learn to obey orders, you ugly sow!"

Analis had stood there, water running down her face, staring at him in shock. Eregard must've made a sound of protest, for the big man swung around to confront him. "Oh, so you fancy pigs, Your Highness? Well, this one would make a clumsy lady-in-waiting!"

Eregard didn't think; he made no conscious decision. He was as surprised as his fellow slaves when he saw his own fist connect squarely with Barlin's face. As if it had happened to someone else, he heard the man's nose crack as it broke, saw blood gush as the overseer fell back onto the ground, then stood there gaping at the man lying still.

After long moments, Eregard realized that his hand hurt. Absently he stood there rubbing it, unable to believe what he'd just done. Then, while several slaves tended to Barlin, two of his fellows grabbed his arms and marched him back to Master Corlena. Excitedly, they reported the entire incident.

The master had shaken his head. "I knew you'd bring me trouble," he said to his erstwhile clark. Turning his head, he ordered his grown son to go and tend to Barlin.

Corlena had overseen Eregard's punishment personally. First they'd branded him on the wrist with the numeral 1. Striking a master or overseer was not a crime punishable by death . . . the first time. If he ever did it again, though, Eregard knew that brand would mark him for a slow and grotesque death.

"Fifteen lashes," Corlena ordered. "You two—the ones who brought him in—see to it, and stint not. Your reward shall be a jug of ale for each of you."

Eregard had been in such pain from the brand that he offered no resistance as they marched him to the whipping post, then fastened his bound hands to a hook set up high. One of the burly fieldmen swished a long teamster's whip back and forth. When Eregard was securely tethered, his captor stepped back.

The leather lash was narrow, and cut deeply with each stroke. Eregard repressed a shiver as he relived that slow, deadly count. *"One . . ."* and then the hissing of the lash through the air had followed, and the loud crack as it struck.

He tried to keep silent, but by the time they reached *"Five"* he was screaming. By the time they cut him down, he was barely conscious, and so hoarse he could scarcely whimper. They'd tossed the bucket of brine over him, then dragged him to the prisoner's crib and flung him inside. He hadn't even felt the impact with the dirt floor.

Now he tried to raise his head, but even that tiny movement made his vision blur. Eregard moaned; he urgently needed to relieve himself, but he couldn't move. *I will wet myself like an infant, then lie here in it,* he realized.

Behind him, he heard the door creak, then soft footsteps. He managed to open his eyes and turn his head slightly. Two small bare feet were approaching, encrusted with dirt from the fields. Another slave, then.

Someone knelt beside him, and he saw cheap, faded calico spread out—a skirt. His visitor was female.

"Eregard?" a soft voice whispered. "Can you hear me? It's Analis. I've brought some willow bark salve for your back."

His lips moved. "Analis . . ." It was barely more than a breath.

"Shhhh, this will help."

The first touch stung like a brand. He couldn't hold back a whimper. But the cool salve was soothing, and after a few moments it did indeed deaden some of the pain. By the time Analis was finished with her ministrations, Eregard was able to sit up. He gestured weakly at the bucket that rested a few feet away. "Can you . . . can you hand me that, please?"

Analis quickly fetched it, then considerately turned her back as Eregard, repressing a groan, managed to get up on his knees to use it.

"Here," she said when he was done, "drink this." She held out a flask.

It was water, cool and sweet, from the well. Eregard's throat was so dry that he nearly choked on the first swallow. "Drink it slowly," she cautioned. "Sip it."

He did as she bade. When his thirst was gone, she gave him a twist of dried herbs. "Chew on these," she said. "They'll help with the pain, and prevent fever."

The herbs were so sour he nearly gagged, but he managed to chew up several hanks. The pain lessened even more.

Eregard's head grew clearer. He glanced at the door to his cell. "They let you come in to tend me? I'm surprised."

She smiled, her dirty, worn face looking suddenly younger. "Perekin has been set to guard you, and he's a friend of mine." She patted her bulging belly. "He let me in so I could tend you."

"I wonder what will happen now," Eregard said, after taking another drink from the water flask and wiping his mouth on his sleeve. "I hate to imagine."

"You're to be taken north and sold," she said. "The master can't allow keepin' a slave here who's laid a hand on the overseer. Even if he can read and write a fair hand." Her mouth thinned. "Might give the other slaves ideas, y'know?"

Eregard nodded. He had been expecting this. "Any idea where they're sending me?"

"They're sendin' to North Amis to buy seed and more help," she replied. "I'd guess you'll be sent up there. 'Tis a pretty big town, and they have slave auctions every market day."

Eregard nodded wearily. "Goddess help me."

She nodded. "I'll pray for you, Eregard. Tell me somethin' . . ."

"Yes?"

"You don't seem addled in your head. Why did Barlin keep callin' you 'Prince'?"

Eregard stared at her and could find nothing to say. At the moment, he scarcely believed it himself. He was one step away from being convinced that his whole life on Pela, his mother, his father, Adranan, Salesin—all were products of a fever dream. He shook his head wordlessly. "I can't explain," he mumbled.

She smiled, suddenly. "You were out of your head when they carried you in here, and you kept talkin' 'bout 'my father the King.' "

He groaned. "I did?"

Analis nodded, and held out two oiled packets. "Listen, here's the rest of the salve, and some of the heal-herb to chew if the pain gets too bad."

He nodded. "Thank you," he managed to whisper. "I'm very grateful."

She nodded. "Well, just in case it *is* true, you can make me a countess when you get back to court, m'dear." Her expression sobered, became serious. "Thank you for tryin' to help with Barlin. The man is a pig-turd, plain an' simple. Not many of the men have the balls to stand up to him."

Standing up, she gave him a last wave, went to the door of the gaol-crib and knocked on it. Quickly, it opened, letting in the last light of day. Eregard had been in the dark so long that the wan sunlight made him blink and hold up his hand to shield his eyes. The door closed and Analis was gone, leaving him in the dark.

The next two days seemed to crawl by. Eregard alternated between fear and apathy. His back throbbed, but he managed, by nearly dislocating his shoulders, to smear Analis's salve into most of the whip-weals.

As his voice recovered, he sometimes sang to himself, old Pelanese ballads, sea chanteys, love songs . . .

When he recalled his previous attempt at a love-song for Ulandra, it now seemed laughably callow and trite. Humming softly, he composed a new song in his head. When he was done, he sang it alone in the darkness, wondering if he would ever see her again.

"Hair of sunlight kissing grain
Eyes of deepest summer skies
Voice of haunting pipes and strings
Ulandra! My heart sings and cries!

Slender as the youngling fawn
Gentle as the nestling dove
Hands like whitest, flying swans
Ulandra! Oh, my secret love!

Face and form like breaking day
Spirit pure and bright and fine
Fate so cruel, my dreams to slay
Ulandra . . . Who can never be mine!"

9

The Prince of Dung

Talis Aloro stood in the doorway of her father's home, watching as her brothers slung their bags into the carriage and waved a last good-bye to her and their parents. She managed to smile and wave, though inside she was seething. Her brothers were going off to school, Armon to study law, and Benno to study medicine.

Talis glared at the back of her father's head. *And me? I get to stay here and run the double-bedamned farm.*

Last night, unable to contain her rage any longer, she had confronted her father. "Father, Armon and Benno are nice boys, but I'm smarter than either of them! I work harder around here than they do. Why can't *I* go to school? I promise you I'll do you credit! There's an Academy for Young Ladies in Port Alvar. I could go there. They wouldn't teach me as much as the boys would learn, but I could learn to cipher better, and study the classics. Firone went, and they taught her geometry and natural sciences!"

Even before she finished her impassioned outburst, Gerdal Aloro was shaking his head. "Daughter, daughter, I don't deny that you've got wits in that head of yours. But you can read and write, and cipher a bit, too. You've plenty of learning for a girl. Any more and you'll scare off any prospective husbands. Your tongue is sharp enough as it is—we don't need you being able to insult suitors in foreign languages!" He'd chuckled at his own wit, oblivious to her rising anger. "Which reminds me. Young Havier Carino saw you at services last week and he asked me to ask you if he could call on you. He said—"

"Dad, *stop that!*" Talis shouted.

Her father had stared at her, his eyes wide at her outburst.

Talis glared at him, breathing hard. "Dad," she said finally, "what is it going to take to make you understand that I don't *ever* want to get married? Ever! After what your precious brother did to me, the thought of letting any man share my bed is enough to make me . . ." Her mouth twisted. "Enough to make me puke."

Her father shook his head, his brown eyes troubled. "Daughter, I thought we agreed never to speak of that. It happened long ago, and 'tis best forgotten."

"*You* may be able to forget," Talis had said, her voice level but filled with venom, "but I can't. It didn't happen to *you*, it happened to *me*."

Then, turning away, she strode out of the room, slamming the door behind her. She'd slept in the woods that night, rolled in a blanket, rather than face anyone from her family. Talis didn't want to cause her mother distress, and she was honestly worried that if her father mentioned marriage one more time, she might lose her temper and lash out with more than words.

Now the carriage was pulling away, pulled by her father's best team of matched chestnuts. Benno and Armon were crowded together at the window, waving. Gerdal and Evonly waved back.

The carriage reached the end of the drive, then turned east. Seconds later it was out of sight. Talis's shoulders slumped and she fought back tears. *It's not fair.* She thought about the books Castio had smuggled to her, books and pamphlets that she kept carefully hidden. She read whenever she had a spare moment, but it was hard trying to learn it all without a teacher, without someone who could answer her questions.

Gerdal came toward the doorway, his arm around Evonly, who was leaning heavily against him. Talis bit her lip as she saw how drawn and pale her mother appeared. Her father helped her mother inside, turning as he did so. "Stay a moment, Talis. I need to talk to you."

Talis waited while he helped her mother to their bedchamber so she could rest. Hope surged within her. *Could it be that he's thought it over, decided I can go to school, too? Perhaps Mama talked to him, changed his mind . . . after all, we just hired a new overseer. If I could go to school, learn more, I could help Castio and the Cause so much more!*

As she waited for her father, her hands were busy, tidying up the last minute clutter her brothers had left. She had nearly finished when he returned.

He glanced around at the room, nodded. "You're a good girl, daughter," he said. "Even though you should be tidyin' a house of your own, I'm glad of your help."

Talis frowned. This did not sound promising. "What did you want to talk to me about, Dad?"

"Your mother . . ." He hesitated. "Well, I don't think she should be alone in the house. I'll need you to supervise the new overseer and the slaves. I'm sorry, daughter, but you know what needs to be done, and your mother is quietest when I'm with her. You know that. With your brothers gone, she's upset."

Talis knew he spoke the truth, but disappointment stabbed her, keen as a blade. "Oh," she murmured.

"What is it?" he said.

"I thought . . . I thought you had changed your mind about sending me to school." She bit her lip and turned away, unable to face him.

"Daughter, Talis . . ." Gerdal stepped closer, until he could look down into her eyes. "I know you'd love to go to school. I know you'd work hard and be a credit to me. But, Talis, I need you here at Woodhaven now that your brothers are gone. And girl, they *had* to go. Your brothers need schooling so they can earn their living. They'll have to support families. You won't. They *need* the schooling. You don't."

Talis bit her lip and counted slowly to twenty. It took that long before she could speak without losing control. "I understand, Father." Her voice was flat.

"Good." Gerdal took her by the shoulders, then dropped a quick kiss on her forehead. "I'll make it up to you, daughter. When you decide to marry—Goddess pray it be soon—you'll have the finest wedding this parish has ever seen. I swear it."

Talis heard the love in his words, and wanted to scream aloud. But she remained silent. There was nothing to say. Her father would never understand.

"This new overseer I hired, I think he'll be all right, but he's going to need watching," Gerdal said. "He thinks well of himself, almost as though he's gentry. He seems a decent enough sort, but we need to let him know that our livestock and our slaves are to be well-treated, so long as they work hard. This fellow, Darlo Trevenio, came from farther south, and I've heard of farms down there where they solve everything by whippings and hangings. So you keep an eye on him."

"I will," Talis said.

"I bought two new slaves in North Amis yesterday. One of them's an older chap, but a skilled carpenter, so we can use him. The other, well, he's young and looks fairly strong, but he's branded. They say he can read and write as well as cipher, so I thought he could be useful. But be careful. That brand marks him as a troublemaker."

Talis nodded listlessly. "Very well."

After she had finished preparing her mother's medicine, Talis changed into work clothes, then went looking for Trevenio.

The weather was getting warmer, and every available slave was out in the fields, planting seeds or seedlings that had been raised in the small greenhouse next to the barn. Gerdal prided himself on raising some of the best tomatoes in the area. Every fall, before the first frost, Talis oversaw the house slaves as they put up a winter's worth of tomatoes, relish, and sauce. Usually they had enough extra jars to sell and make a tidy profit. With the rest of their crops, plus the sales of salted meat and hides to the King's troops, Woodhaven was one of the most prosperous farms in the parish.

Gerdal was planning to expand his barley crop, and earlier that spring, the logging crew had cleared a new field. As she walked down the farm road, Talis realized that Trevenio already had a crew out there, picking up the rocks, breaking up the clods, preparing the land for plowing.

She walked around the edge of the field, answering the waves of the field hands she'd known for years, heading for the overseer, who was supervising the work while seated on his tall roan gelding. The man wore a broad-brimmed hat to shield his face from the sun. When he caught sight of her, he swept it off, bowing slightly before dismounting. "Fair morning to you! You must be Miss Aloro."

"Good morning, Mr. Trevenio," Talis said formally, holding out her hand to him. "How is the work going?"

To her surprise and disgust, Trevenio did not respond by shaking her hand, but bent to kiss it. Talis yanked her hand away.

Trevenio was young, in his late twenties or early thirties, and was dressed so neatly that he seemed something of a dandy—his boots were mirror-polished, his black hair combed neatly, his narrow moustache meticulously waxed. He was good-looking, in a sharp-featured way. Talis wiped her hand on the fabric of her work skirt, wondering if she would have problems with him. Many males did not like taking orders from a woman.

"Fine, they're doing well," he replied heartily. "You father has a good crew, Miss Aloro."

"Yes, many of them have been with us for years," Talis said. "How are the two new ones doing?"

"The older fellow, the carpenter, Kendalo—he was needed to help with fixin' the cow byre. The other one . . ."

He shook his head. "Well, miss, he's goin' to take watchin'. He was insolent to me, so I set the Prince to muckin' out the pigpen."

"Prince? Insolent?" Talis had no idea what he was talking about.

"One of 'em is a little touched," Trevenio said, tapping his temple. "The slavemaster told me that he told his first owner he was a prince." The man laughed, and his laughter had an ugly edge. "Well, until the pigpen is clean, he'll be Prince of Dung."

"He was insolent? What did he say?"

"He didn't *say* anything, miss. But he gave me the haughtiest look. Can't have that! If you let them get away with looks, next thing, you've got a rebellion on your hands. I've seen it happen before. Though never," he added proudly, "on a farm where *I* was overseer. I served in the King's Navy when I was a lad, and I learned then that discipline is vital."

"I see," Talis said. She realized that the man had moved a step closer to her, and she stepped back a pace, turning to look at the crew. They were working industriously. "Well, here at Woodhaven we have no whipping post. We've seldom had any trouble with our people, because we try to make sure they're well-fed and well-treated, Trevenio. They work better for us that way, my father says."

"Of course, miss," he said. "Treat them well, that's what I always say . . . but maintain discipline."

Talis could hardly argue with that, though for a moment she wished she could.

"Tell me more about this touched slave," she said. "My father said he can read, write, and cipher. He's educated, then?"

"I don't believe a word of it," Trevenio said scornfully. "A slave? Mark my words, miss, you'll find he's lying. You can't trust anything they say."

"Perhaps I'll speak to him," Talis said. "Did you think to test whether what he said was true?"

Trevenio's sharp features reddened. He cleared his throat. "Ummm . . . well, truth to tell, miss, I'm not very . . . well, readin' and cipherin' were never my favorite things. I can read a bit, and help with the accounts, but, ummm . . ."

"I see," Talis said dryly.

Trevenio flushed even redder.

"Well, no mind," she said, then changed the subject. "The fences over in the northernmost cattle fields are in need of repair. When the pigpen and the cow byre are finished, put them to work there. Digging postholes ought to be heavy enough work to keep this prince occupied."

He nodded. "Very well, miss."

Over the next week, Talis kept a close eye on Darlo Trevenio, and was forced to concede that the man seemed to know his business. He had already worked up a plan for the cultivating and planting, and a work schedule, and seemed to treat the slaves well enough.

Talis knew it would soon be time for her to head north to one of the big towns to buy supplies. They produced much of what they needed on the farm, but some things—like fabric for clothing, sugar, salt, and other staples—they had to buy.

One morning when she went to saddle her bay gelding, she found the two new slaves mucking out the horse barn. Upon seeing her, both men nodded, but did not speak, as was proper. Talis watched them work for a moment, then busied herself grooming her horse, applying the currycomb vigorously. Bayberry raised his upper lip in an equine grimace, then snorted gustily, enjoying the massage. Talis sneezed. Springtime meant shedding. Her hand was soon so coated with a mat of winter coat that it resembled a furry mitten. She had to keep picking the currycomb clean.

When she finished the grooming, she looked over the stall door. "You," she said, pointing to the younger of the two men. "What is your name?"

He stopped plying his rake and ducked his head respectfully again. "Eregard, mistress."

"Eregard, please fetch my saddle and bridle. The ones on the lowest rack."

He laid aside the rake and went to get the tack, returning quickly. After hoisting the saddle up onto the lower half of the stall door, he stepped back. Talis gave him a measuring glance. "Thank you."

"My pleasure, mistress."

The slave was certainly well-spoken. His accent was pure, lacking the backwoods twang and slurred vowels many of the slaves used. He was not tall—only a few inches taller than she—with lank brown hair tied back with a bit of twine, and a scraggly beard. His rough work shirt and trousers were stained and dirty, and his feet were bare, like those of all the slaves when the weather was not actually freezing. His eyes . . . gray, perhaps. He was obviously strong, because he'd been lifting the heavy forkfuls of manure without apparent strain, but his shoulders could hardly be called broad, and he was rather pudgy around his middle, though his bearded features were almost gaunt. Talis realized that he was about her own age.

"Are you the one they call 'Prince'?" she asked.

He nodded, looking down. "Yes, mistress."

"Why do they call you that?"

He did not look up. "Because I took fever, and I was raving, I suppose, mistress. I can't really account for it."

"I see," she said. "They say you can read and write. Can you read the names on the stall doors for me?"

"Bayberry," he said without hesitation. "Wind, Moonstar, Tomlin, and Blaze."

Talis nodded. "And you can cipher?"

"Yes, mistress."

"Have you ever kept accounts, Eregard?"

"Yes, mistress. For my former master, I did."

"Very good," Talis said. "I may have use for those skills, helping me keep the books."

"Yes, mistress."

Talis gave him a measuring glance. "You were moving stiffly just now, when you hoisted up my saddle. Is your shoulder sore? Are you injured?"

He swallowed, then glanced up at her cautiously. "No, mistress. Not exactly."

"What's wrong, then? Sore muscles? I have some liniment."

"No, mistress," he said. "I was flogged, and it's not fully healed yet."

Talis sighed. "Oh. That's unfortunate." He glanced up at her, and for a moment she glimpsed something in his eyes, some strong emotion, but it was gone too quickly for her to guess what it was. "Well, Eregard, we don't flog our workers. If you need doctoring for those stripes, come see me. I have salves that will help."

"Yes, mistress. Thank you, mistress."

She gave him a quick, perfunctory smile. "Back to work with you, then."

"Yes, mistress."

Talis quickly saddled Bayberry, then went out for a ride. The work was going well. She could smell the scent of the fresh-turned earth and the sharp odor of the manure and compost the workers were mixing into it. Other slaves were bringing seedlings out of the greenhouse in wheelbarrows. It was a fine day, and some of the slaves were singing, a low, half-chanting song that consisted mostly of nonsense monosyllables repeated over and over.

Seeing the overseer riding toward her, Talis nodded and waved. Trevenio trotted up, smiling, and swept off his hat. "Miss Talis! How lovely you look this morning!"

Talis blinked at him. *Goddess, spare me!* She knew full well that she was covered with horsehair and dirt, and wearing her oldest outfit for riding astride. But she had to work with this man. "Good morning," she said curtly. "How is the work going?"

"The planting is going well," he replied.

They discussed schedules and workshifts for a few minutes. When Talis had reviewed the overseer's plans and approved them, she gathered up her reins to go. Trevenio smiled at her. "Wait," he said. Leaning over, he put his hand on her forearm. Talis froze. *What is he doing?* Something in her expression must have alerted him to her feelings, because he sat back on his roan, then spoke in affable tones.

"Miss Talis, there's a quilting bee and a barn raising the

day after tomorrow over at the Beldano place. Would you do me the honor of accompanying me?"

She shifted her weight while squeezing Bayberry with the muscles of her right calf. As she'd trained him to, the horse sidestepped, sidling away from the overseer. Talis shook her head. "I'm sorry," she said, trying to keep at least a semblance of courtesy in her tone. "I will be busy. Good day to you, Mr. Trevenio."

He took the rejection well, smiling easily, tipping his hat. "I understand. Some other time, then."

Talis rode away, her shoulder blades prickling. She knew without looking back that he was sitting there, watching her. For a moment she considered telling her father about the incident, then decided she was being too sensitive. *I can handle this. Dad needs to know that I'm a woman grown and can handle problems myself.*

Trevenio did not say anything untoward for the next couple of days, and gradually Talis relaxed. She still didn't like the way the man looked at her, but there was nothing she could do about that.

She received a message from Rufen Castio, telling her that he would be in Q'Kal next week and where he would be staying—lodging with a printer who was sympathetic to the Cause. Talis knew she would be sent north to buy supplies, but wasn't sure she could justify traveling the extra distance to Q'Kal.

The weather was particularly amenable to the farmers that spring. The day after the slaves finished the planting, a steady rain began to fall, and it continued for several days.

Talis and Trevenio rode out one rainy morning to inspect the newly planted seedlings. As they neared the cow pasture, she saw the two new slaves working on the fence. "It's really too wet to be digging postholes," Talis said, with a glance at Trevenio. "Did you send them out here?"

"Yes," Trevenio said. "I figured building the fence only to have it fall down when the cows leaned over it would teach the Prince a good lesson in respecting his superiors."

"It won't be much of a lesson if one of the cows gets out

and into the newly planted fields," Talis said sharply. "Not to mention having to replace broken rails."

"I'll make sure the Prince has to cut down the trees," Trevenio said, amused. "You coddle these slaves, if you don't mind my saying so, Miss Talis."

She minded very much, but controlled herself, biting back the words that rose to her lips. "What did Eregard do this time? Was he insolent? What did he say?"

"Oh, he didn't say nothin'—he doesn't have the stones for that. He just gave me that look again. And I swear, if he does it again, I'll give him some more scars on his back."

"I told you," Talis said icily, "we don't whip our slaves here at Woodhaven."

The man gave her a look that went beyond bold. *Talk about insolence!* Talis thought, furious. *An insolent cad, just like most of his kind.*

"So you did, Talis," Trevenio said. "But your father hired me to oversee these workers and to get the most out of 'em."

"Now see here," Talis said, "exactly when did I ask you to call me by my first name?"

"I figured you wouldn't mind, Talis," Trevenio said, with a cheeky grin. "Seeing that we know each other so well."

"I object to your manner," Talis snapped. "We are strangers, and that's the way it will remain. I suggest you remember that." She drew rein, stopping Bayberry just out of earshot of the two slaves.

"Hoity toity, miss!" Trevenio's grin was more like a sneer. "Ah . . . but I *do* know you," he added. "I know a *lot* about you. I know that you're a hot little minx, and I know that you ought to treat me better. You're not getting any younger, *Miss* Talis. And you've brothers, so you're not likely to inherit the farm when your da goes. Any girl with half a wit would be very nice to me, indeed. I've got prospects."

Talis's mouth dropped open with shock. "Wh-Who—" she couldn't even get the words out. She was sputtering with rage. "How *dare* you?"

He shrugged and grinned at her. "Oh, I dare. And if you know what's good for you, you'll shut up and be polite,

Talis. You see, I know things about you that you wouldn't want me telling."

"What things?" Talis said quietly. She had gone beyond rage to a vast, cold anger that seemed to fill the whole world.

Trevenio laughed. "Before I came here, I worked on a farm down south. Did some drinking in Northbend. I met a man there, and we got to talking. Nice fellow, name of Jasti Aloro. 'Twas Jasti who told me what a slut you are, how you seduced him when you were but a slip of a girl. He says everyone knows you're no virgin, thus not fit for a man to wed. But Talis, I'm not a judgmental fellow. I've had some wild times of my own. So I'm willing to overlook that and offer you honorable marriage. From what Jasti told me, marriage with me would be the best you can do. No gentleman would touch—"

Talis shrieked at him, a wordless cry of rage that was as shrill and fierce as the scream of a hawk. Wrenching Bayberry around, she dug in her heels and drove the gelding full-tilt into the roan. As the two animals collided, she kicked her feet loose from the stirrups and flung herself at Trevenio, sweeping him off the staggering roan.

They landed hard on the soggy ground. Talis felt her breath leave her lungs in a giant gust, and for an agonizing moment she could not fill them again. Trevenio, too, was winded. He lay gasping.

"What's going on?"

"Mistress Talis!"

She heard the distant shouts of the two slaves, followed by their running feet. Talis managed to draw breath and roll to her knees—just as Trevenio did the same. He grabbed for her. "Come here, you bitch! I'll teach you to—"

Talis punched him in the mouth, throwing her entire shoulder into the blow. She felt her knuckles grate against his teeth, and felt at least one tooth give. Her hand exploded with pain, but she ignored it. Quickly, she followed up with a hard left to his eye. Trevenio howled, flinging himself back, away from her. She staggered to her feet and went after him.

The two slaves had reached them by now, still carrying

their fence-mending tools. They flung the tools down. "Here now—" the carpenter said.

"Stay out of this," Talis ordered, not taking her eyes off the overseer. "You're a dead man," she told Trevenio. "No. Correction. A dead *pig*."

"Mistress Talis, no!" The Prince of Dung tried to get between her and her prey. Talis brushed him aside as though he were a gnat and moved in on Trevenio. The man's lips were split and a cut below his eyebrow bled freely. He gagged, then spat out a tooth. With one part of her mind she realized that she had won, she had hurt him, and badly, but that was not enough. Trevenio was still alive, still moving—and that would not do.

Talis aimed a kick at his chest, but he saw it coming and grabbed her foot, heaving upward. She fell, and the back of her head thudded painfully against the soggy ground. Rolling away, she managed to break free, and came up on her hands and one knee, poised to spring. Trevenio came after her.

Talis kicked him in the gut, but the blow did not land true. He staggered, but stayed on his feet. And then, suddenly, there was the gleam of metal in his hand. He had drawn his knife from its sheath.

Talis slapped her hand down to her side, but her knife was gone—knocked free during the fall. She backed away from Trevenio, who was moving toward her, his mashed lips and crimsoned teeth bared in a hideous grin. "Now, you die, bitch. But we'll have some fun before that, won't we?"

He swiped at her with the knife, not a serious attack, playing cat and mouse. Talis ducked, then kicked at his kneecap. She missed, but managed to slam her forearm against his knife hand. Hot pain slashed her arm, but the knife went flying.

She ignored the blood soaking her sleeve as she advanced on the overseer again. Now there was fear in Trevenio's eyes. *Good.*

Suddenly, out of the corner of her eye, Talis glimpsed movement. Eregard left the ground, springing toward Trevenio with a shout that caused the man to half turn. The slave

crashed against the overseer, knocking him down with the
force of his charge.

Talis stood there, watching Eregard pull back, get to his
knees, then stumble to his feet, backing away. He stared at
the man on the ground, plainly horrified. Talis looked down,
realizing that Trevenio lay motionless. *Why doesn't the pig
move?* she wondered as she walked over to him. *Move, you
damned coward, so I can kill you!*

The overseer lay sprawled in the mud, face slack, eyes
staring up at the sky, unseeing. For a moment Talis didn't
understand what had happened, then saw the mud-smeared
spade Eregard had dropped. It lay there, digging edge upward, and the back of Trevenio's head rested on the steel.
Blood had trickled over the muddy blade. Talis knelt down
and peered sideways at the spade. The point was buried
deeply in the back of the man's skull.

She looked up at the two slaves. "He's dead," she said, her
voice sounding as though it came from far away.

Eregard went even paler. "Dear Goddess," he whispered.
"What have I done?"

Talis pushed herself to her feet, and only now did she feel
the aches and pains from the fight. Her slashed forearm
burned. She clasped it tightly with her other hand, trying to
stanch the bleeding. "Why did you have to interfere?" she demanded angrily. "I was handling him. I didn't need any help."

"I . . . I was afraid you'd kill him, or he'd kill you," Eregard stammered. "But now, *I* killed him. They'll hang me."

"Nonsense," Talis snapped. The rush of anger was abating, leaving her light-headed and shaking, but rational once
more. "His death was an accident."

He looked at her, and she had never seen such fear in a
man's eyes. "If I were free, it would be an accident," he
whispered. "But I'm not free. I'm a slave. Soon I'll be a dead
slave."

"The law is clear," Gerdal said heavily. "The slave killed a
free man, an overseer. He must hang." He paced around his

office, hands behind his back, shaking his head. "There is nothing else to be done."

Talis took a deep breath and counted to twenty. Slowly, deliberately, she sat down on a hassock, striving for calm. *I can't afford to lose my temper.*

"Father," she said, keeping her voice level, "This is not a case of murder. There was no deliberate attack. What Eregard did was an accident." She held up her bandaged hand and forearm. "Trevenio pulled a knife on me, remember? Eregard was trying to defend me."

"You explained that already," Gerdal said. "And I understand that it really isn't fair to hang the slave for what happened. But I can't keep a slave here at Woodhaven who has caused the death of an overseer, no matter how it happened. It might give the other slaves ideas."

Talis had heard these arguments all her life. All of the estate owners had heard tales of slaves rising against their masters. Murder, looting, rape . . . when slaves revolted, no one was safe. She even agreed with her father, in principle. But this case was different.

"All right," she said, keeping her voice smooth and reasonable, "I understand how it might not be a good idea to keep the slave here. It could give the others ideas, I agree. But I don't think he should be put to death. It wouldn't be right."

Her father gave her an exasperated glance.

"I know, I know, he's just a slave. But," she said, thinking fast, "sign him over to me, Father. When I go north to buy supplies, I'll sell him and buy a replacement. That way we won't do the wrong thing by killing him, and yet the other slaves won't have him around to give them ideas."

Gerdal considered that for a moment. "Very well, daughter," he said. "Make sure you get a decent price for him." He walked over to his big oak desk, opened one of the bottom drawers, took out a file and began thumbing through it. "Hmmmm . . ." He removed a sheet of paper, scribbled for a moment, then blotted the ink carefully and handed the page to his daughter. "Here . . . I've transferred his ownership to you, Talis. Best if you don't sell him around here. The story is bound to have spread by now."

Talis saw her chance and seized it. "I was thinking of going farther north, to Q'Kal," she said. "It's such a big market town, all the caravans stop there. Goods are priced more competitively."

Gerdal thought for a moment. "It's several extra days travel. You'll need a guardian."

"I can take care of myself," Talis said.

"It doesn't look right for a young girl of marriageable age to be traveling with just a male slave to accompany her," Gerdal pointed out. "Your mother would never forgive me."

Talis started to say more, then thought better of it. She nodded instead, not raising her eyes from the slave's transfer of ownership.

"Daughter," Gerdal said hesitantly, "just one more thing . . ."

"Yes, Father?"

"Why were you and Trevenio fighting? Did he . . . did he try to take liberties?"

Talis was tempted to just say yes and let him think that. After all, it was true, in a manner of speaking. *No,* she thought. *I'm not going to lie to protect my vermin of an uncle.* "He asked me to marry him," she said, her voice harsh with remembered anger. "He told me that I would be lucky to get him, since I'm ruined."

"Ruined?" Her father was taken aback. "What did he mean by—" He broke off, realization dawning on his features.

"Uncle Jasti told him, Father," Talis said, feeling a mean enjoyment at Gerdal's expression. "I'm a slut. He's told *everyone* about me."

"He . . . he . . ." Her father was sputtering now.

"And what are you going to do about it, Father?" Talis did not try to gentle the edge in her voice. She was shaking with anger. "I'll tell you what you'll do—*nothing.* Just like before. Well, you do what you have to, and I'll do what I must. I'll say no more to anyone about this, but *you* will never mention the word marriage to me again. Never."

Her father looked at her. "But, Talis, Havier Carino doesn't know. He told me he wants to—"

Without waiting for him to finish, Talis turned and strode out of the room. There was nothing more to say.

Gerdal hired a retired female mercenary named Clo to accompany Talis on her trip north. Clo was a short, stocky woman in her early forties with cropped graying hair, broad, freckled features, and keen blue eyes. She liked to sing as she rode, and told Talis several jokes that would have made Evonly faint dead away if she had heard them. Talis had heard worse, while working for Castio in the taverns, but she was careful at first to stick to her role as a gently raised daughter of a gentleman farmer. She wanted to take the woman's measure, to see if she dared be honest with her, because she could tell that Clo could teach her a great deal about how a woman could become a better fighter.

The three set out early on the second morning after Trevenio's death. Clo drove the farm wagon with the goods they hoped to sell in Q'Kal, and Eregard rode beside her on the seat. Talis rode Bayberry, seated sidesaddle like a proper lady, though she had brought her regular saddle in the back of the wagon, and planned to use it when they were at least a day's journey from North Amis. She didn't want to risk running into people she knew while wearing trousers and riding astride.

They made steady progress that day, good enough so that Talis decided to make camp well before sunset. She hobbled the wagon team and Bayberry to graze, while Clo fixed up their beds beneath the wagon. "I'll start the fire," Clo said. "And then I'll do the cooking."

"We'll share the chores," Talis said. "I was raised on a farm, remember? I'm no city girl. I know how to cook over an open fire."

"All right," Clo said, and her smile told Talis that she'd done something very right. "I'll cook tonight, you cook tomorrow night. The slave cleans up. Fair?"

"Fair enough," Talis agreed.

Reaching into the wagon bed, she took out a couple of

blankets and headed over to a nearby tree. After dropping them at its foot, she went back to the wagon and took out a chain and a lock. Eregard, who was sitting on the wagon, bare feet dangling, gave her a quick glance, then looked away. "I gather that's where I'll be tonight, mistress?"

Talis nodded. "I'm sorry, but I can't take any chances. I had enough trouble convincing my father to sell you, rather than hang you. If you ran away, he'd not be pleased." *And besides, you're my property now,* she thought. *The money I'll get for you will be enough to keep me for a while, if I decide not to go back home.*

In fact, she was seriously considering not returning home. She could just send the wagon and the money for the sold crops back with Clo. The thought of her mother's distress caused her a pang, but what was there for her back there? Only her father trying to push her into marriage, and Uncle Jasti's vile lies.

The slave nodded. "Yes, Mistress Aloro. Is there anything I can do before supper?"

Talis nodded. "Rub down the horses, then give them each a measure of grain."

As soon as Eregard left, Talis reached into her bag and took out one of Castio's books—*The Art of Modern Warfare* by General Serio Beldani. As the smell of wood smoke and then the enticing smell of frying bacon and corn mush filled the air, she read on, puzzling over some of the words, wishing the book had diagrams. It was difficult to visualize General Beldani's battle plans.

As she sat there—her small cache of books, pamphlets, and broadsides beside her—Talis sensed movement and looked up. The slave, Eregard, stood there, looking at the book she was reading. "Good old General Beldani," he said, then looked disconcerted, as though he hadn't meant to speak aloud. "Excuse me, mistress," he said hastily. "I didn't mean to disturb you."

Talis looked at him. "You've read this book?"

"Uh . . ." he hesitated. "Mistress, it's forbidden for slaves to read, unless the master commands it."

"I am not going to punish you," Talis said. "Just tell me the truth."

He took a deep breath. "Yes, mistress, I read it."

"Did you understand it?"

"Yes, mistress." He looked panicky. "I did. But, mistress, I wasn't born a slave."

"So I gather," Talis said. "Well, if you understood what General Beldani was talking about in this chapter, when he discusses the effective deployment of cavalry, could you explain it to me?"

Eregard blinked at her, and hesitated.

"Don't worry," she reassured him. "It will be our secret."

He glanced over at Clo, who was busily cooking, then shrugged. "As you say, mistress," he said. "Now, when the general discusses cavalry deployments against superior infantry forces, he mentions several classic tactical situations. Imagine this is the opposing infantry, here . . ." Picking up a stick, he began sketching in the dirt.

Talis watched, fascinated, as Eregard sketched and explained the military tactics the general was discussing in his book. They were still hard at work when Clo called them to supper.

Talis ate fried cornmeal mush, bacon, eggs, and dried fruit. Eregard, as was proper, waited until they were done and Clo beckoned him forward, then they both piled the remains of their supper onto his plate.

Instead of digging into the food with his fingers, the way slaves usually did, Eregard hesitated, placed his plate on one of the rocks beside the impromptu fireplace Clo had rigged, then went off to the nearby stream. Talis saw him kneel and wash his hands. He came back to retrieve his plate, and on impulse Talis held out a fork. "Here. Thank you for the lesson. Those diagrams helped."

He took the fork, bobbed a quick bow at her, then went off to sit on the tailgate of the wagon while he ate. Clo eyed Talis speculatively. "Something going on, Miss Aloro?"

Talis smiled. "We're going to be together for quite a while, Clo. Please, call me Talis."

The mercenary's eyebrows lifted, then she nodded her cropped head. "All right, Talis. Something going on?"

"That slave, Eregard," Talis said thoughtfully, leaning her elbows on her knees, and idly pitching a wisp of straw that had caught in her tunic into the fire. "I believe he must have been born of gentle blood. He can read, and he understands military tactics."

"He does?" Clo was surprised. "Maybe he was once an officer?" She gave the slave a speculative glance. "Pretty young to be an officer, though."

"I asked him that. He said he hadn't been." Talis took up a charred stick and poked the fire. "Clo . . . did you like soldiering? You had rank, didn't you?"

The woman nodded proudly. "Aye, I was a sergeant when I retired. I loved soldiering. I wished I didn't have to leave it, but m'joints got too stiff from sleepin' on the ground."

"It was a good life?"

Clo smiled. "It is. As long as you stay in shape and stay quick on your feet, you do fine. And when you get too old to do that . . . well, things usually take care of themselves. You don't find too many soldiers droolin' by the fire, eh?"

"I suppose not. Is it hard to be a woman soldier? Aren't the men . . . horrible?"

Clo shrugged. "Well, they might be if'n you let 'em, so you have to prove yourself. You have to show them that you're as tough as they are, or tougher. They have to learn that if they lay a hand on you and you don't like it, blood will spill—theirs."

"Seems to me they're all pigs," Talis said, not looking up as she tucked in a corner of the bandage on her forearm. "Or mostly."

"They're human, Talis, just like you and me, 'cept they're more likely to let their crotches rule their heads sometimes than women are." Clo laughed reminiscently. "But most of 'em are decent lads who'll guard your back. I'll tell you, I'd a sight rather march all day and then sleep in the rain with m'comrades than chase after a brood of brats, cooking and cleaning for some husband who treats me like dog turds."

"What made you decide to become a mercenary?"

Clo began picking her teeth, and it was a moment before she answered. "When I was just a young girl, not much more than ten, I saw the King's Army march by, with the drums a-beatin' and the pipers piping away. I knew then I wanted to be a soldier. They told me girls couldn't be soldiers, but as I grew, I kept my eyes open, and I saw that the mercenary outfits were smarter than the regular military. So I talked some of 'em into showing me how to fight." She spat into the fire. "Turned out I had a real knack for it."

"I think I've got a knack for it, too," Talis said after a moment. "My folks would never understand. All they want me to do is get married."

Clo's weather-beaten features were sympathetic in the flickering light of the fire. "I know exactly what you mean, Talis. Mine were the same."

Talis held up the book she'd been reading. "Do you understand tactics?"

Clo made a derisive sound. "Tactics? Bless you, Talis, tactics are for officers. I just stayed with my unit, and we did the best we could to follow the orders our lieutenant gave us. I suppose there are tactics involved, but when you're in the thick of battle, you don't see the words on the pages, or those little drawings with all those X's and dotted lines. You see your mates, fighting, and you see the man in front of you that you've got to kill before he can shove his pike up your arse or get his musket reloaded in time to blow your face off."

Talis flinched at the blunt words. Clo noticed her expression. "Ah, missy, that's the way of battle. It's glamorous perhaps when you're marchin' along and the crowds are cheerin' you, but when you're digging trenches so you can lie in 'em in the mud rather than bein' blown to bits, that's the way of it."

Talis thought about that for a while. Clo began gathering up the dishes, then beckoned to Eregard, who was looking at them expectantly. "Hey, you! Time for cleanup!"

Quickly, the slave hopped off the tailgate and began tidying the campsite.

Talis thought about what Clo had said that night as she lay in her bedroll. Clo was taking the first watch.

A breeze stirred the topmost branches of the trees, a wind that carried a hint of rain. Talis hoped that it would hold off until morning. Chained as he was, Eregard could not get out of the rain, and if he got soaked, he might take a chill and become ill. And nobody would buy an obviously sick slave.

Would Clo take me to her old unit when this journey is done? she wondered. The thought of never seeing Woodhaven again brought pain to her heart. *What will my mother do without me?*

But her loyalty lay with Rufen Castio and his movement to bring freedom to Kata. Perhaps now would be a good time to join the Cause full-time. *I'll talk to Rufen, see what he says. Just let me take care of Dad's business this one more time, then it will be time for me to do what I want, for a change. If Eregard fetches a good price . . .*

She found herself thinking about Trevenio, and was suddenly, fiercely, glad that he was dead. *If only I could get Uncle Jasti,* she thought.

Talis fell asleep with a smile on her lips, fantasizing about ways to kill her uncle.

They made their way north, bypassing most of the towns. Clo cautioned against drawing attention to themselves. In these days, where Kata was used as a dumping ground for the royal prisons, there were far too many brigands roaming the land—desperate men and even women who would steal their horses and the clothes off their backs, with no more thought than most Katans would give to swatting a blood-sucking insect.

They developed a routine as they traveled, similar to the one they had followed that first night. They camped in remote areas, far from any towns, homes, or farms. Clo and Talis alternated guard duty. Lost hours of sleep were made up the next day, napping in the bed of the wagon as it creaked along. As soon as the horses were unhitched, rubbed down, and hobbled to graze, Talis took out her books, and Eregard joined her. He proved to be a good teacher, though he had to squint to read. "I lost my spectacles when I was captured," he said quietly.

"Captured?"

He gave her a glance that was hard to fathom. Was there a glint of anger? Talis couldn't be sure. Slaves learned to control their expressions in the presence of their masters. "Yes. The ship I was traveling on was taken by pirates. I told you I wasn't born a slave."

Talis smiled ruefully. "Yes, I remember. No native born slave can read, you're right. And the way you talk . . . like someone who has had some education."

A slight, answering smile touched his mouth for an instant. "Some education . . . yes, I suppose you could put it that way."

Talis looked over at Clo, whose turn it was to cook that night. "Clo," she said, "have you ever been in a battle where Beldani's Pincers was used?"

Clo shook her cropped head. "If I have, I don't know about it. I leave the readin' and all those fancy movements to the officers, and just go where I'm told and do what I'm told to do once I get there."

"You can't read?" Talis was taken aback.

"Not much. Just enough to write m'name and to puzzle out a map." She gave Talis a quick, shrewd glance. "Readin's for officers," she repeated.

That evening, after she and Eregard finished their "lesson," Talis went down to the banks of the Bar River to bathe. When she returned, feeling considerably fresher, she found Eregard reading some of the pamphlets Castio had given her. She stopped in her tracks, then forced herself to relax. Even if Eregard were to tell what he'd read, no slave could bear witness against a free person. Talis pulled a towel from her bag in the wagon bed and began drying her long black hair. "What do you think?" she asked when Eregard looked up.

Something flashed in his eyes, and his tone, when he finally answered, was cool to the point of impudence. "Honestly? I think there's a monstrous inconsistency inherent in people who talk about fighting for freedom also owning other human beings, just as they'd own swine, or cattle."

Talis was taken aback. "How dare—" she began, then broke off as Eregard stepped away from her, his shoulders hunched in expectation of a blow.

"I'm sorry, mistress," he said quickly.

Talis took a deep breath. "Stop cringing," she ordered crossly. "I'm not going to hit you. I'm just not used to slaves that were born to freedom."

"Goddess willing, I won't die a slave," Eregard said softly.

Talis thought about the brave words in Castio's pamphlets. She'd had slaves all her life. Everyone she knew owned them. Could it be true that freedom should be for everyone, slave and freeman alike? They said that there were no slaves on Pela, that Agivir's great-grandsire had freed them.

Eregard was watching her, his eyes intent. "Ah," he said, softly. "Mistress Talis is thinking a new thought. I can tell by her expression."

Talis felt herself blush, and that angered her. "You're being impertinent. If I were any other owner—"

"If you'd been on that ship instead of me, our positions might be reversed," Eregard said, not troubling to hide his anger. "Ever think of that? Can you imagine what it's like to be free one minute, then find yourself a slave the next?"

Talis had never thought of that before, either. She'd been speaking to slaves all her life, but this was the first time she'd had an actual *conversation* with one. Giving orders, yes. Handing out extra rations for the holy days, yes. Visiting the sick, admiring a new baby, yes and yes . . . all those things she had done, but it wasn't the same as actually talking to a slave like a . . . like another person. Especially a male slave.

She stared at Eregard. *I own this man,* she thought. *If I ordered it, he would be hanged—whether or not he'd committed any crime or offense. Can it be right for one person to have that power over another?* "That *is* a frightening thought," she said slowly.

"Of course it is," Eregard said. "Because it makes you think of me as a man, not as something you *own*. You don't want to think of me as a *man*. I get the impression you don't like men."

"I hate them," Talis said, surprised into telling the truth. As soon as the words left her mouth, she regretted her candor. Who did this slave think he was?

He nodded, smiling faintly, not at all surprised by her

words. Talis fought the urge to hit him. "Watch your tongue! If it weren't for me, you'd have been hung. I was the one convinced my father to give you to me, so I could sell you. That way you may not be free, but at least you'll be alive!"

He laughed, and the sound was ugly and full of pain and frustration. "Ah . . . so my children's children's children will be free?"

Talis stared at him, hearing the hurt in his voice, and her anger ebbed. *He sounds like me when I talk to Dad.* She knew what it was like to yearn to be free. She'd just never realized that slaves felt the same way. For the first time, she looked at this man that she owned and saw him as though he were a person. Not a male, not a slave, just someone who knew what it was to be hurt, and to long for freedom.

"What do you mean?" she asked quietly.

He looked back down at the page, and she knew he was regretting those words as much as she'd regretted her revelation a moment ago. "Nothing. Just a quote from a song. Nothing for you to concern yourself with, Mistress Talis."

"A song?" Talis sat down beside him. "Slaves have songs, I've heard them singing. Is this a slave song?"

"One of the ones we never let the masters hear," Eregard said. "We never sing the real words except when we are together, and no freeman is near."

Talis was intrigued. "Sing it to me."

He shook his head. "No."

"I saved your life," she pointed out.

He tugged at the iron collar around his neck, gestured at his clothes, his bare feet, and then turned out his pockets to make the point there was nothing in them. "You call *this* living?"

She was surprised into a laugh. "You are a clever one." She remembered her father once saying, *Beware of clever slaves. They can be dangerous.*

"Court jester, in retirement, at your service, my lady," he said, and gave a mocking bow.

Talis stood up. "Let's walk together." She headed for a deer trail leading down to the creek.

Eregard followed her down to the stream bed, where they

began picking their way along the water's edge. They walked for several minutes. The forest was dense here, the trees so old that there was little growth beneath them. This far north, spring was not as far along as it had been in North Amis. The trees still bore new leaves, some still partially curled, of a green so vivid it nearly hurt the eyes.

"All right," Talis said when they had walked for some distance. She sat down on a fallen tree trunk that spanned the stream and looked up at the slave expectantly. "Sing me the song. I swear on my mother's life no ill will come to you for singing it—not to you, nor to any other slave."

Eregard regarded her for a long moment, then shrugged. "Very well."

His speaking voice was soft, rather hesitant, so Talis was surprised that his singing voice was a strong, resonant baritone.

"Take my water, take my sky
Take my air and watch me die
Work me till I work no more, till death gives me relief
Take my children, take my wife
Take my body, take my life
It doesn't mean that I'm a slave, it means that you're a
   thief.

Break my back and break my head
Make blood and tears to shed
I still choose within my mind if still a slave I be •
Break my heart and burn my bed
We're all slave to something, but a slave can still live free
And you'll never touch the free part of me
You'll never touch the free part of me.

Kill my choice of wrong or right
Kill me if I stand and fight
Each slave holds a piece of freedom that the masters
   never see
It all comes from having might

It all ends one coming night
When the pieces come together, and we'll see that we
     are free
And you'll never touch the free part of me
You'll never touch the free part of me."

Eregard drew a long breath and sang the last line, and there was a ringing note in his trained voice that made Talis's heart leap.

"And my children's children's children will be free!"

Talis sat there, stirred by the longing, the feeling in his voice, and the haunting sadness of the song. Eregard stood looking at her, his face flushed, his eyes bright with defiance. She couldn't think what to say, and the only thing she could do was get to her feet and head back to the campsite. She felt as though he had opened up the top of her head and poured in a jumble of new ideas . . . ideas that were as sharp and uncomfortable as pins and needles. The new ideas were jabbing away at all her old assumptions, the preconceptions she'd grown up with—the safe, accepted notions that made up life as she knew it.

She did not speak on the way back to camp, only trudged along.

That night, clouds hung heavy and thunder rumbled to the north, from the direction of the mountains. Instead of chaining Eregard to the tree, Talis tossed the slave an extra blanket and pointed to the wagon. "It's going to rain. You'll sleep between us tonight, beneath the wagon bed. If you snore, I'll kick you."

He smiled. "I'd far rather be kicked than soaked. Thank you, mistress."

Talis didn't reply, only turned away to arrange her own bedroll.

As the rain pattered down, she lay awake, thinking. What did Rufen Castio think of people who owned slaves? Unlike most freemen, who kept a slave to act as a combination groom/valet, Castio did not own any. Talis had an uneasy suspicion that Castio did not approve of owning slaves.

She turned over in her bedroll, punched the rolled-up bundle of her cloak that served as a pillow. *What if Castio told me it was the right thing to do to free Eregard? But if I free him, I won't be able to sell him, and then I'll have nothing except the clothes on my back.*

And Bayberry. She didn't think her father would mind if she kept her horse. For a moment she thought about the bank draft her father had entrusted to her. But no, that money was for the farm supplies. They were depending on her. Even if she didn't go home, she had to make sure those supplies reached Woodhaven. Clo could be trusted, she was sure of that now.

Perhaps I should sell the horse and free the man. But she couldn't sell Bayberry! She'd raised him from a foal, broken him to saddle, trained him herself. If she were going to serve the Cause full time, she'd need a good horse.

All right, I'll have to sell Eregard, but I'll try to arrange a private sale so I can make sure his new owner will treat him well. I owe him that, she decided. *And after Eregard's sold, I'll never own another slave, I swear it to the Goddess . . .*

Talis sighed, thinking that life, once so simple, had now grown hideously complicated. Who would ever have thought she'd wind up in debt to a slave? But she did owe him. She owed him for teaching her about tactics, and for helping her realize that slaves were people. Valuable lessons. She thought of his education, his trained singing voice. *He's so well-educated. His family must be of gentle blood, to be able to afford to send a son for so much schooling.*

For just a moment she found herself thinking about the "title" Trevenio had given him. *Prince of Dung . . .* She grinned sourly. *Maybe he really is a prince. That's just the way my luck runs.*

10

Sparks of Rebellion

Three more days travel brought them over Timberhawk Pass and then down into the valley where Q'Kal lay. As they drove into the outskirts of the city, Eregard realized he was gaping about him like some bumpkin who had never seen one before. Q'Kal was large, but barely half the size of Minoma on Pela.

After driving through the city gates, he kept a sharp lookout for landmarks. The royal governor had a town house here in Q'Kal, and, with Springfest coming up soon, there was a good chance he would be occupying it now. Prince Eregard had met Governor Laurenz several years ago at a state dinner at the palace. Eregard knew he looked vastly different from the perfumed and silken-clad young man Laurenz had met that night, but he was fairly sure that if he could manage to see the man, he could convince him of his true identity in short order. No slave would have any way of knowing the identity of Laurenz's Pelanese mistress and the name of the Governor's natural son.

Only problem was, he'd have to wait to make his escape until just before Audience Day. Once each week, the Governor held a public audience, and, supposedly, no freeman was refused entrance. *Freeman . . . I'll have to get rid of this collar somehow.*

He had managed to steal a file from the farm's toolshed before they left, but he knew he'd need many uninterrupted hours to file through the heavy iron. Eregard had tested the file in secret, on a horseshoe, and now had a rough idea of how long it would take to file through his collar in two places. *Six hours . . . more likely eight. And I should shave and trim my hair so I'll look more like myself.*

As the wagon bounced along over the rutted road, he glanced over at Talis Aloro, who was once more riding sidesaddle, as befit the proper daughter of a wealthy farmer. She was a superb rider, managing the big gelding with a skill Eregard envied.

Some might have called her pretty, with her long, thick black hair, green eyes, and her rounded, ruddy cheeks. But compared to Ulandra, she seemed . . . overblown. *Like one of those big, gaudy roses compared to the delicacy of a pale, perfect orchid,* he thought. Despite his disparaging thought, he couldn't help noticing the way her breasts moved beneath the snug fit of her riding jacket. *Still . . . nice tits,* he thought. *Bet they're firm. Wonder why I never noticed them before?*

Eregard pondered that for a moment, then realized that slaves did not allow themselves to ogle their pretty owners. A male slave who stared too boldly or lasciviously at a lady would be punished if anyone noticed. The prospect of freedom in just a few days time had gone to his head like a potent draught.

One of the first things Talis did when they reached the marketplace was to check when the next big slave auction was to be held. She was visibly disappointed to discover that she'd missed one just that morning, and they'd have to wait over in the city for a handful of days until the next.

Eregard was relieved. Talis had grown careless about chaining him, where a new owner would be extra vigilant with any newly acquired slave.

Leaving Clo to arrange lodgings for them, Talis went off

to negotiate a portion of the bank draft her father had given her. Eregard, ever the dutiful slave, followed her on foot, jogging behind her horse, keeping his eyes open. As they turned onto a large thoroughfare in the most affluent section of the city, he spotted a large, stately residence that had to be the Governor's town house. Nothing else even came close to it in size or elegance.

Good, Eregard, thought, jogging along. *Just past the intersection of Matalino Avenue and Boulevard of Hope.* He leaped nimbly over a huge, steaming pile of oxen dung. *I couldn't have run half this far last year,* he realized.

When Talis reached the Bank of Q'Kal, she slid off her horse, leaving Eregard to hold Bayberry outside the building. "You don't want me to come in?" he asked, wondering if there might be someone inside the imposing financial structure that would recognize him.

"No," she said. "I'll be only a minute. Just stay right here."

With a swish of her plum-colored riding skirt, she headed up the steps and into the building. Eregard stood there, holding Bayberry, absently stroking the gelding's nose. It was strange, after all these months in the wilderness, to be back in a bustling city. Q'Kal was the biggest city in Kata.

After a short while, Talis emerged from the bank, and they headed back for their rendezvous with Clo. The mercenary had found them reasonable lodgings in an area of the town that was marginally respectable. Eregard carried the women's belongings into the rooms and discovered that he would be sleeping on a trundle bed in Clo's room. "I don't mind, miss, and it'll save on the money your father gave you. He doesn't snore, and by this time, he knows better than to mess with me," Clo said, flexing the muscles in her arms. Eregard was in full agreement with her. He wouldn't have tackled Clo in a fight without a brace of pistols to hand, he thought, wryly. *Talis, either, for that matter.*

After the women had washed off the travel dust, they went down to the stables to check on the horses. Eregard kept his ears open as they moved through the tavern, realizing that, ironically, he was now in the perfect place to fulfill the request his father had made of him. *And this iron collar makes me all but invisible,* he thought. *People talk in front of slaves, because we don't count.*

"Talis, I've found something to do this afternoon that you might be interested in," Clo said as she sat cleaning the harness. Eregard was brushing the wagon horses, while Talis groomed Bayberry.

"What's that?" Talis asked as her brush glided smoothly over the gelding's sleek rump.

"There's a young warrior in town, been giving lessons in hand-to-hand," Clo reported. "They say he's quite something to see, and learn from. Want to go by and watch one of the sessions?"

"I'm always ready to learn more fighting skills," Talis said. "I'd like to go. When is it?"

"This afternoon, in a warehouse by the docks."

"Good. We'll have a bit of dinner before we go, then."

Eregard wasn't finished mucking the stalls, so they left him there and went into the tavern. It was the first time he'd been in a town unsupervised, and for a moment he was tempted to bolt. But his hands continued their automatic motions with brush and currycomb and he shook his head. *No. I have to plan this, and plan well. If I ran now, they'd catch me. Broad daylight, with this iron collar? Suicide.*

He was under no illusions as to his fate if he attempted to run away. They'd hang him, with Talis's blessing this time.

When Eregard finished grooming the team, he took a moment to strip off his shirt and wash himself in the horse trough. It felt good to be clean, though there was enough of a breeze to make him shiver.

When he went inside to find Clo and Talis, he was rewarded with a hunk of bread, some smoked mutton and dried fruit, and a tankard of sour tasting wine. He gulped the food and drink thirstily, then waited in the courtyard for the women to appear. *Let her think she can trust you completely: be a good, loyal slave now.*

Talis and Clo wore trousers when they came downstairs.

Eregard followed them at the proper, respectful distance as they headed toward the docks. Q'Kal was a harbor town, and as they walked, Eregard caught the scent of the sea. It stirred him, made him feel more alive than he'd felt in months. It smelled like freedom, like Pela . . . like home. *Be patient . . . soon!*

As they neared the docks, Clo spotted a couple of mercenaries she knew, and hailed them. They, too, were headed for the demonstration, so Talis and Clo followed them. They reached the quays with their vessels tied up at the docks with great hawsers, and headed for one of the warehouses.

The warehouse had bales and barrels of cargo stacked at one end, but the other was open, and was being used as an impromptu arena. Eregard followed Clo and Talis in as they jostled for a good place to watch what was happening. There were perhaps a score of onlookers. In the middle of a roped-off space, two men stood facing each other.

One was a giant, a huge, burly fellow who must have weighed nearly twice what Eregard did. Though stocky and barrel-chested, his weight did not come from fat, but from muscle. Eregard was reminded, suddenly and painfully, of his brother Adranan, though this man looked nothing like him. He was older, in the late prime of his life, and he was obviously an experienced tavern brawler. Both arms bulged with muscle, and the garish tattoos made them seem even bigger. He was stripped to the waist, and the shafts of sunlight from the tall, narrow window-openings gleamed off his bald head and his chest.

Eregard eyed him, thinking he wouldn't want to face such a man even armed with a pistol. *A cannon, perhaps,* he concluded ruefully.

The man facing the giant was young. He was of medium height, slender and wiry, and had dark brown hair tied back at the nape of his neck. He wore loose pants and a sleeveless tunic. His arms were well-muscled, but half the size of the bald giant's, and his feet were bare.

The slender young man made a salute to his opponent, and they began to circle each other. The big man's boots made thumping noises on the wooden floor. The youth moved as silently as a prowling house cat.

With a loud bellow, the giant rushed the youth. Eregard could hardly bear to look—he braced himself to see the young man demolished with one blow. He was completely unprepared for what happened. In a blur of motion, the youth turned, twisted, pivoted on one foot, and the two bodies intersected for just a brief second. Then the giant was flying through the air. He landed, rolled over, and lay still, his wind knocked out.

All around Eregard the audience of off-duty soldiers, colonial militia, and mercenaries were muttering in surprise. "How'd he *do* that? . . . Did you *see* that? . . . What happened? I blinked and missed it!"

In front of him, Clo and Talis turned and looked at each other, and then, as if they'd reached some unspoken agreement, nodded.

The youth in the baggy clothes gave two more demonstrations, and each larger opponent was handled as expediently as the bald giant. When the demonstration was over, the youth spoke for the first time, in fluent but accented Pelanese. He announced that he would be giving introductory lessons starting next week, here in the warehouse, and the cost would be five pesentos per pupil.

The crowd mingled, then began to thin out. Finally, only the young fighter and the man who had arranged the demonstration were left. Clo and Talis started forward, Eregard trailing behind them.

Clo walked up to the young man and gave him a half bow. "That was impressive."

He bowed back. "Thank you. Will you be signing up for lessons, ladies?"

Clo shook her head. "We are from out of town. That's what we wanted to talk to you about. Could we arrange for a private lesson with you, while we're here? Your style of fighting is one that any woman would like to learn, since the fighter who is the fastest and has the best balance can defeat a heavier opponent with longer reach."

He nodded. "The women of my country are not warriors, but I believe you are correct. I could arrange a private lesson for later tonight, if you are willing."

"That would be ideal," Talis said. "I am Talis Aloro, and this is Clo. We came up from the south today, to buy supplies for the farm. Clo is a professional fighter." She shrugged. "I am still a student."

The young man bowed again. "I am Jezzil."

"Well, I'll leave you folks to your negotiations," the manager said. "See you next week, lad."

Jezzil beckoned to the women to accompany him as he, too, headed for the exit. "Walk with me, if you do not mind. My lodgings are not far, and I must check with my landlady to see if I can use the yard tonight for a session."

Eregard trailed behind them as they walked, listening to the conversation. Jezzil had an accent that he couldn't place, though it was vaguely familiar. "I thought I had seen most styles of hand-to-hand," Clo said. "But I never saw that before. Do all the warriors from your country fight so?"

He sounded amused by the question. "The techniques I used tonight are not confined to warriors in Ktavao. Farmers, merchants, even children are taught to defend themselves. Warriors are taught skills that are more advanced, but we never reveal them."

"So we can't learn those advanced techniques?" Talis asked.

"No, I am sworn to keep them secret," he replied.

Ktavao? Eregard thought. *That's north of Bauka, where the Redai launched his invasion force. This fellow is Chonao! Could he be a spy?*

"Well, I'll be satisfied to be able to do what you did tonight," Clo said. "That maneuver you did with that hip-thrust, swing and pivot . . . well, I've been in more than one tavern brawl in my time, and that would come in real handy."

"I can teach you all of the techniques commonly used in my land," Jezzil assured her.

"We want to learn as much as we can before we leave for home," Talis said.

The cobblestone street sloped upward from the harbor, and Eregard glanced around him at the town houses and shops. Q'Kal seemed like a prosperous place, bustling with commerce. Jezzil led them up a hill, past a small, fenced-off park, past an impressive temple, then he turned right, onto Mulberry Lane. The shops were smaller here, more run-down, and there were more taverns. Finally they reached a small bakery, and Jezzil stopped them with a gesture. He opened the door, poked his head inside. "Mistress Bolfini, would you mind if I used the backyard for some lessons tonight?"

Eregard heard a voice say, "Go ahead, but mind you don't knock down my wash lines!"

"We'll be careful," Jezzil promised.

He beckoned them around to the back. The walled yard boasted a vegetable garden, the wash lines, and a small weedy lawn. Jezzil beckoned Talis and Clo over to that area. Both women pulled off their jackets and pulled their loose-sleeve shirts out of their breeches so they could move freely.

Jezzil beckoned Eregard to join them. "You, what is your name?"

"Eregard, sir."

"Good. Since we'll be doing defensive moves, I'll use you as the attacker at times."

Eregard regarded the teacher dubiously, but an order was an order. "Yes, sir."

"Now, listen closely, and do as I do. The first thing you need to learn is proper balance for this style of fighting. The second thing you need to learn is how to fall so you won't be hurt."

Jezzil demonstrated balancing and falling, then had the women emulate him. Eregard admired the instructor's quick, almost feline moves. *If he can fight with a blade as well as he can unarmed, he could probably beat Salesin in a duel,* he thought.

By the time they had managed to fall down to Jezzil's satisfaction, both Talis and Clo were sweaty and grass-stained. The women worked hard, paying close attention. Eregard paid attention, too. He'd never been good at fist-fighting, but the skills Jezzil was teaching depended far more on balance, speed, and skill than on reach or strength.

Several times toward the end of the lesson, Eregard had to "attack" either Clo or Talis. He was glad he'd listened to Jezzil's instructions about falling, because one of the moves the women had learned was a quick over-the-hip throw that, when done correctly, left him sprawled on the lawn.

Finally, Jezzil straightened and looked at his sweaty, flushed students. "That's enough for today," he said. "You don't want to be so stiff and sore tomorrow that you can't work."

"Can we come back for another lesson tomorrow?" Talis asked as she counted out the coins into Jezzil's palm.

"Yes, I'll be here about this time tomorrow," he said. The Chonao led them back to the front of the building.

A young woman, dressed in plain, soberly colored garments, was just walking up to the steps that led up to the second story. When she saw them, she stopped.

Jezzil indicated his new students. "Talis, Clo, this is my . . ." He hesitated a moment. ". . . my sister, Thia."

Sister? Eregard thought derisively. *That's what they all say.*

Thia had pale, thin features, brightened only by remarkable dark eyes. A wisp of hair showed from beneath the scarf that covered her head, pale as ash, pale as newly minted silver. She was thin, but from the way she carried herself, Eregard thought there might be a wiry strength beneath that drab garb.

Her voice was low, musical, with an accent Eregard couldn't place. It was different from Jezzil's. "Greetings to you, Miss Clo, Miss Talis. Hello . . . brother." A faint smile touched her mouth, and her dark eyes brightened with quiet amusement. She looked past them at Eregard. "And you are?"

"My slave, Miss Thia," Talis said.

Still, those eyes, dark as the ocean on a moonless night, gazed straight at Eregard. He found himself coloring as he bowed low—as he would have to a crowned head. "I am Eregard, mistress."

"Your brother has been teaching us his new form of hand-to-hand combat," Clo said. "And glad we are to have the chance to learn from him. Are you skilled in his warrior art, Miss Thia?"

She smiled and shook her head. "The women of my people do not do battle," she said. "It is different in this land, I know."

Talis glanced up the street. "How far away are we from the inn and livery on Avenue of the Blessed? I've gotten turned around. I must check on Bayberry before nightfall."

"Your horse?" Jezzil was quick to ask.

She nodded. "Yes. A fine one. We raise good horses in my region of Kata."

"Jezzil's family raises horses, too," Thia said.

"Jezzil's family?" Clo said, then the older woman closed her mouth quickly, as though she regretted her words.

Thia smiled. "I think we all know by now that Jezzil and I are not related by blood. We are brother and sister in our hearts, though."

Hearing her, Eregard realized she was speaking the simple truth. These two were as chaste with one another as newborn babes.

"Would you like to see my horse?" Talis asked Jezzil. "We could sup at the inn afterward. You and Thia will be our guests."

Jezzil and Thia exchanged a glance, then Jezzil nodded. "Very well. And after supper, I shall show you *my* horse."

"She's beautiful," Talis said, gazing admiringly at Falar. "I don't think I've ever seen nicer conformation. And you say she's battle-trained?"

Jezzil nodded. "Chonao depend upon our horses in battle as much as we do our fellow soldiers. Let me show you," he said, opening the stall door.

At his soft command, the mare trotted out of her stall, bare of any tack, not even a halter. Jezzil led them out toward the paddock. The sun was just setting, and the long blue evening shadows were creeping over Q'Kal, stealing the color from the world. Eregard followed the group out to the paddock, thinking that this was his chance to find out more about the military techniques of the famed Chonao warriors.

Jezzil opened the paddock gate, and Falar trotted into the enclosure, then turned to face him, ears pricked. Jezzil did not even speak, only raised his hand to his chest, then lowered it with a sharp motion. The mare bent her knees, then lay down and rolled over onto her side, lying flat on the ground, motionless.

Talis made an admiring noise and clapped, as did Clo.

The Chonao made another gesture, and the mare was back on her feet. He glanced over at Eregard. "Go and try to lay your hand on her, as if you were going to grab at an opponent in battle."

Eregard went, though he was not happy about the order. But slaves had no choice but to obey.

The moment he drew near the mare, she whirled to face him, ears flattened, teeth bared. When he raised his hand toward her, she reared and plunged forward, and only Jezzil's quick order stopped her.

Eregard backed away, eyeing the horse nervously, determined that if they ordered him to try to grab her again he would refuse. A beating would be better than being struck by those deadly hooves.

But Jezzil was giving the mare other hand signals. As Eregard and the others watched, she walked, trotted, handgalloped, halted, then backed up, all without a single command being spoken. Jezzil went out into the paddock, leapt onto her back with one smooth, flowing motion, then went through a pantomimed fight against an armed opponent. The horse danced beneath him, obedient to his slightest shift of weight or pressure of leg. Finally, she whirled, launched into a gallop and, with a flowing motion, cleared the paddock fence.

Eregard was impressed. *If all the soldiers of the Redai are trained and mounted like that, they will be formidable opponents!*

He stood behind the group, watching silently as they gathered around Jezzil and his mount, talking excitedly, praising his horsemanship and Falar's training. *I've learned a lot today that will help my father. If I can just escape and tell him . . .*

During dinner, Eregard had been consigned to the inn kitchen, and Talis had paid the innkeeper to make sure he was fed. He'd sat there, eating part of a joint that was more than a little overdone, some cheese that wasn't supposed to be moldy but was anyway, and some bread that had failed to rise properly, saying nothing but listening to all that went on around him.

Slaves and servants were far more observant than their masters ever suspected. Eregard had learned a great deal about the Katan colonists and their attitudes toward the Crown from listening to the kitchen gossip. It seemed that Rufen Castio had been seen here in Q'Kal, and that Governor Laurenz had quietly put out the word to the mercenary units that he would offer a substantial reward for his capture. *Probably Salesin ordered him to do that,* Eregard thought cynically. *Laurenz isn't known for either his munificence or his initiative.*

He decided that he was learning so much of what his father had sent him to Kata to learn that he'd stay a slave as long as possible before he ran away. For a moment he allowed himself to think about what it would be like to be back home. He'd tell Agivir everything he'd seen that would help the Crown against these insurgent colonials. And then . . .

Then I'll sleep on clean sheets, wear clean clothes, take nice, hot baths. I'll bask in the attentions of my valet and barber . . . and most of all, I'll eat food that isn't someone else's discarded leavings.

For the first time in days Eregard thought of Ulandra. She seemed as distant and insubstantial as a happy dream. *By now she's certainly married to Salesin, may the Goddess help her . . .*

Princess Ulandra of Pela sat at her dressing table, applying rouge with hands that shook, despite her efforts to control them. *I must hurry. He'll be here soon.*

She'd been brought up strictly, and the holy sisters had taught her that any woman who enhanced her looks with paint was a slut. But when she'd come to court, she discovered that everyone painted. Even some of the men were known to apply a beauty patch or two, or to redden their lips and cheeks.

Still, left to her own devices, she would not have used cosmetics for anything but formal court occasions. But this morning . . .

Her hand shook so much that she smeared a blob of rouge across her lower lip. She took a square of cloth and began dabbing at it. *Hurry, hurry!*

This morning, Salesin had commanded her to join him for a private breakfast. When she'd duly appeared, doing her best to summon a pleasant smile, Salesin looked at her across the table and she knew that, as usual, he was angry. She didn't know why, but then, she seldom did.

"What's wrong with you?" the Crown Prince had snapped, staring at her critically. "You look as pale as a specter. I'd love to think you're pale because you're breeding, but we know better than *that*—don't we?"

The scorn in his tone made the blood rise in her cheeks, but she did not dare look at him, much less reply.

"Well?" he demanded, when she did not speak. "What's wrong with you?"

"I . . . I . . ." She cast about, trying to think of what she could say that would not anger him further. "I am well, my lord."

"Looking at your whey face across the table has ruined my appetite," Salesin said, throwing down his serviette. "When are your courses due this month?"

Every month, the same question. Ulandra thought that by now she should be getting used to it, but embarrassment made her face grow even hotter. She'd seldom spoken of her menses to even another woman—to have to report on them to a male, even her husband, was degrading.

"Any day now, my lord," she said.

Eyeing her calculatingly, he said, "The sooner we know, the better. I know you hate being bedded even more than I hate doing my royal duty by you." He smiled, and for the first time there was a glint of real humor in his dark eyes. "Just give me a few strong sons and I'll trouble you no further, my lady."

The knowledge that he was laughing at her, that she was truly distasteful to him, made her want to crawl away and hide, but she forced herself to simply sit there, silent, as he got up from the table and strode away.

Now she sat there, checking her hair, her cosmetics, dreading the moment when he would arrive. She was wearing a simple boudoir gown of sky-blue satin trimmed with indigo lace, with a short, pale blue silk chemise under it, and she thought she looked well. *Except for my eyes,* she thought, leaning closer to the mirror and studying the shadows beneath them.

Carefully, she dabbed a bit of powder beneath them, trying to conceal the bruiselike marks. She didn't sleep well these days, no matter how many walks she took with Wolf. So far this week, Salesin had spent every night by her side. Even if he did not avail himself of his husbandly privilege, she often lay tense, waiting for him to wake and take her. One of the few times she'd managed to fall into a deep sleep, she awakened to find him atop her, already aroused.

Ulandra longed for the Prince to go off on a state visit, or to visit one of his several mistresses. Oh, yes, she knew about them now. There was Countess Cimiel, and Baroness Rolandra, and probably some others whose names she hadn't heard whispered about . . . yet. At first the thought of those women had angered her. Now she felt nothing but gratitude toward them. When Salesin was with them, he wasn't with her. Sometimes, after he returned from such a visit, he would let an entire day or two pass without taking her.

The agony of that first time had passed with constant repetition, but for the life of her, Ulandra could not comprehend why any woman could find the process pleasant—as some were reputed to do.

As she stared at herself in the mirror, for a moment she

thought she saw a shadow move behind her. She started violently, then turned around to look. The room was empty, and her own shadow, cast by the light of the candelabrum on her dressing table, spread out along the floor behind her. *Stop it,* she thought angrily. *Talk about starting at shadows! Those dreams are only that—dreams.*

Even on the nights Salesin was away, she had not been sleeping well. She had dreams, and dreams, formless as they were, terrified her.

In them, she often seemed to be floating above her own body, gazing at herself through strange, inhuman eyes. Male eyes, she knew that, though how she knew, she could not tell. The body she wore, or shared, was not human, but she had no idea what it looked like—she had never seen it. For that, she was grateful.

Lately she'd sensed that the Other had been drawing closer and closer to her sleeping body. Several times she'd jerked awake as it reached out as though to touch her. The thought of being touched by the Other was frightening, far more frightening than being touched by Salesin, distasteful as that experience was. At least her husband was *human*.

Ulandra could no longer remember what it was like not to be afraid. Some unnamed horror seemed to be part of her now, an integral part of her life. She'd thought once or twice about killing herself, but could not shame her family in that manner.

She started again as she heard the door to her suite open. Hastily, she summoned a smile and rose to her feet, standing there, hands clasped before her, so he would not see how badly they were shaking.

Salesin strode into the room. Ulandra curtsied. "Good evening, my lord. I trust you dined well?"

He waved away her attempt at social chatter and then gazed at her, scowling. What he saw must have pleased him, because slowly his dark features relaxed. He nodded. "That's a pretty robe. If you value it, I suggest you take it off now."

Ulandra flushed. "As you wish, my lord." She headed for the dressing screen that stood against the wall.

"Stop," he commanded, leaning against the doorjamb. "I want to watch."

"But—" Seeing his expression darken, she bit her lip and nodded. "As you wish, my lord."

Hot with shame, she undid the clasps and ties of the gown, then tossed it onto the boudoir chair. She could not meet his eyes as she stood shivering in the short chemise. Ulandra headed for the bed, with its concealing sheets.

"Stop. Take off the chemise, too. I've never gotten a good look at you naked."

She stopped, then turned to face him. "My lord, I am not comfortable with this."

"I'm your husband, and I'm the Crown Prince," he said, sounding more amused than angry. "I suggest you obey, Ulandra."

It was the first time he'd ever spoken her name. Ulandra's hands went to the bottom of the chemise, ready to tug it up and over her head, but she was frozen before his gaze, like a mouse before a snake.

When she didn't move, his temper snapped. With one stride he was there before her, grabbing the garment and yanking it over her head. She gasped, trying not to cry out.

"I've had it with your stupid modesty and your schoolgirl ways!" Grabbing her by both shoulders, he held her steady, naked but for her cloak of hair, and surveyed her up and down. "Too damn skinny, that's your problem. Eat more, and then I'll wager you'll breed!"

Ulandra was terrified, but anger gave her the courage to try and twist away. "Stop it!"

He backhanded her across the face with no more thought than he'd have given to cuffing one of his hounds. "Shut up!"

Her cheek seemed to explode in a white-hot lance of pain, but far worse than that was the stunned disbelief that her own husband would actually *strike* her. She gasped as he grabbed her, threw her on the bed, then fell on top of her, like a forest giant in a hurricane. His hands and mouth were everywhere, hurting her. His fingers dug into her breasts, kneading them, then he sucked and bit them. Tears filled her eyes, coursed down her face, but she was careful to make no sound. *If I anger him further . . .*

"That's better," he muttered. Lifting his head from her breasts, he began kissing her, his tongue thrusting, probing, nearly strangling her. His hand went down to her thighs, and it, too, began probing. "You're wet," he muttered. "Good. I told you you'd learn to like—"

Suddenly he sat up, looking at his hand. Ulandra saw red streaks on his fingers. "Damn! Another month wasted! You barren *bitch*!"

He slapped her face again, bruising her other cheek, then raging, he drew back his open hand and slapped her belly so hard the sound cracked like a lash. "Wake up in there!" he snarled. "I need a *son*!"

Ulandra curled into a ball, cringing away from him. "No, please," she sobbed. "Please, don't . . ."

Abruptly, Salesin seemed to realize what he was doing and stopped. He got up off the bed, then stood there, looking down at her, his breeches hanging open, his thick, engorged organ drooping like a flag on a windless day. He was breathing hard, still flushed with fury. "It's your own fault, my lady," he said coldly. "I hope you learned your lesson. Don't make me teach you again."

Ulandra nodded. "I won't," she gabbled.

Slowly his breathing steadied. He pulled his breeches closed, then looked around him for his shirt and drew it on. When he was dressed, he shook his head at her sorrowfully, almost reproachfully. "You should know better than to defy me, my lady. Nobody defies me."

Then he turned and strode away.

Ulandra lay there in a state of utter shock. For a moment she considered ringing for her maid, but the thought of anyone seeing her like this was not to be borne.

Slowly, she dragged herself off the bed. She was shivering

so hard her teeth clacked together. Fumbling, she rummaged in her drawers, then put on her warmest nightgown. Pouring water into the ewer, she began bathing her face, trying to lessen the swelling.

After she'd done the best she could to cleanse herself, and had tied on a towel to catch her monthly flux, Ulandra knelt before the little chapel to the Goddess that rested in one corner of the room.

She tried to pray but could summon no words beyond, "Help me. Please, help me."

What did I do to anger him? she wondered blankly. She'd been too slow to remove her nightgown. She hadn't conceived a child. And Salesin claimed it was *her* fault he'd lost his temper.

As she knelt there on the cold floor, Ulandra felt the stirrings of hatred. "I did nothing wrong," she said aloud. "By the Goddess, I did *nothing* wrong!"

She knew it was true. She raised her head, straightened her shoulders, caught a glimpse of movement in her mirror and for a second felt the presence of the Other, close to her, as close as her own shadow. In comparison to what she had just been through, the Other's presence didn't seem so terrifying anymore. She climbed stiffly to her feet. *Who needs to fear dream-monsters when I have my very own right here in my bed?*

Strength seemed to be flowing back into her, carried by the hatred that filled her. Ulandra looked down at the shrine. "Lady Goddess," she said in a conversational tone, "I did *nothing* wrong."

For Talis, the time in Q'Kal passed too quickly. She was busy each day from dawn until long after lamp lighting. Each day she went to the marketplace and made arrangements to purchase the supplies her father needed to run the farm. Then, in the afternoons, she and Clo continued their hand-to-hand lessons with Jezzil. After supper, she and Jezzil took their horses to a field outside the city to practice mounted maneuvers. She was in awe of Falar's training.

Having such a mount in battle would be like having a comrade to guard one's back.

Her own Bayberry was a fine animal, as good as any raised in Kata, but the Chonao horses were special—swift, tough, and smart. Within a day of trying to teach Bayberry the special battle-maneuvers Falar performed so easily, Talis knew her bay would never equal the gray. But Bayberry *did* learn, and Jezzil praised her horsemanship. One day he even allowed her to ride Falar, a mark of trust that was a thrill in itself.

She still hadn't decided what to do about Eregard. She knew she would need the money from selling him, but since they'd come to Q'Kal, he'd grown more confident in himself, and tended to act almost like a companion rather than a slave. While she and Jezzil and Clo practiced their arms training, Eregard and Thia often sat on the grass together, talking. Thia, Talis had learned, came from up north, where she had been some kind of scholar. She and Eregard talked about all kinds of scholarly subjects—history, maps of the world, and religion. The few times Talis had bothered to eavesdrop, she'd grown bored quickly. The only history that interested her was military history and tactics.

But Eregard and Thia never seemed to run out of subjects to talk about. Jezzil seemed pleased that his "sister" had found a friend who shared the same interests, even if that friend was nothing but a slave.

Finally, on their fifth night in Q'Kal, the summons Talis had been waiting for arrived. Rufen Castio wanted to meet with her; she was to wait in the alley outside the inn three hours after midnight, and he would send someone to bring her to him.

Talis went to bed early, pleading—truthfully—weariness due to a particularly exhausting lesson with Jezzil that day. She fell asleep, mentally ordering herself to awaken at two of the clock.

Like most farmers, Talis was naturally an early riser, so when her eyes opened in the darkness, she was alert almost immediately. Grateful to have a room to herself, she dressed hastily by moonlight, not daring to light a candle. Then, carrying her boots, she crept out of the room and down the back steps of the inn.

The spring night was chilly, and she was glad she'd brought her cloak. Wrapping it tightly around her, she shivered as she paced slowly down the alley, one hand on the hilt of her dagger. But her tension was unnecessary; the night was peaceful. She saw no one, heard no one, until sometime later a soft hiss caught her attention. Talis turned, her cloak billowing out around her, to see a dark shape at the end of the alley, beckoning.

She moved lightly, warily, toward the figure, remembering the words of the challenge Castio had given her. "Who goes there?"

"Not the Watch," came the expected answer. "Agivir's clock needs winding."

"Then we shall have to tell him what time it is," Talis responded.

A soft sigh of relief escaped into the darkness of the alley. "Thank the Goddess. Be you Talis?"

"Yes," she whispered. "Who are you?"

"Nobody you need to call by name, missy," the voice said. "Just follow me. Castio be waiting."

Talis followed him, squeezing through a hole left by a couple of loose boards in the fence. Her guide moved quickly, lightly, drifting like a shadow through the silent town. It was so late that even the alehouses were mostly closed. They went by the back ways, careful to avoid the routes taken by the Night Watch. At first Talis tried to memorize the route, but within a few minutes she was lost. The buildings were so close together, crowded, with their squalid little back alleys, a contrast to the broad thoroughfares in the better parts of the city.

Accustomed as she was to barnyard muck, Talis had to cover her mouth and nose with a fold of her cloak as she hurried along, trying not to think about what she was treading in. She slipped and skidded more than once, and it was only luck and a fighter's balance that kept her from a fall.

Finally her guide slowed, then stopped before yet another

back entrance, in a section that was visibly cleaner than some they'd traversed. Glancing back to make sure she was still with him, he knocked softly. Two taps, a scratching with his nails, followed by three more deliberately spaced taps.

Then, silently and speedily, the man—was her guide even male? She couldn't be sure—was gone.

Talis stood there before the door, waiting, and was rewarded a moment later when it opened a narrow crack. "Talis Aloro?" The voice was unfamiliar.

"I'm here," she said, moving forward until her features could be seen in the narrow band of candlelight.

"Come in and welcome, then," the man said, opening the door just wide enough for her to squeeze in.

Talis walked in, blinking against the light, even dim as it was. She had been so long in the darkness. The room was dominated by a huge machine, and she smelled ink. Her host was a youngish man of medium height, with bushy brown hair and a stocky build. His sleeves were rolled to the elbow, and his hands, arms, and shirt were spattered with ink stains.

Talis smiled at him. "Talis Aloro, at your service." She gave him the secret hand sign that the revolutionary movement had chosen.

The man returned it. "Denno, printer, at your service." He raised his voice. "Rufen, she's here. Just as you described her."

Rufen Castio stepped out from behind the enormous machine. His lanky frame was unchanged, his queue still unfashionable, and Talis was so glad to see him again after all these months that her throat tightened. "Master Castio!"

"Rufen, Talis . . . remember?"

"Yes, I do. It's good to see you."

"And you, Talis." He came over and gave her a quick, comradely embrace.

Denno pulled up a couple of chairs to a battered old desk and waved to Talis to sit down. Castio regarded her. "So, tell me everything that's been happening."

Talis gave him a quick summary of everything she'd observed in the past few months that related to the Cause. In his turn, Castio caught his two listeners up on his own doings. "Things are moving along," he said in conclusion. "Though not as quickly as I could have hoped. We have molds to allow us to produce the new bullets for the rifled muskets, and we captured the rifling bench intended for the royal fort at Three Notch Bluff, so we've been able to convert many of our smoothbores into rifles able to use the new bullets. But we can't bring every musket in Kata to the rifling bench, and it's slow work rifling the barrels of muskets without it."

Talis was fascinated. *Better, more accurate muskets!* "Where are you keeping the rifling bench?" she asked.

Castio gave her a look. "I'll tell you if you need to know, Talis."

She flushed. "Oh. I understand."

Castio asked her if she could do her tavern-slut act at a popular soldiers' pub in Q'Kal. "The proprietor is not one of us," he cautioned. "He's a royalist. You'll need to be careful. But since there are so many soldiers there, the place is always swarming with whores anyway. Nobody is likely to notice one more. Just keep your ears open, see if you can pick up anything."

Talis nodded. "I'll go there tomorrow, after I register Eregard for the slave auction."

Castio nodded. "Very well." But Talis noticed he didn't look at her when he said it.

She wet her lips. "Rufen, do you own any slaves?"

He shook his head. "Not anymore. I used to."

"You sold them all?"

He finally looked at her. "No. I freed them. One day I realized that it was hypocritical to struggle and yearn for freedom, while owning another human being. That day, I freed my slaves. Two of them are now two of our best couriers, matter of fact."

Talis was troubled by his words. "I've been thinking much the same thing," she admitted. "But if I don't sell Eregard, I won't have enough money to leave home so I can work for the Cause!"

"I understand that's a hard decision," Castio said. "And you're the only one who can make it."

Denno nodded at her. "As someone who freed his slaves two years ago, I can tell you that paying workers puts a hole in your pocket pretty quickly. But," he gave her a rueful grin, "I sleep better at night, and I guess that's worth something, ain't it?"

As the three continued to talk, slipping from actual plans into discussing their dreams for the future, for a free Kata, Denno produced a bottle of wine and blew off three dusty glasses. Talis normally did not drink, but to be companionable, she took a glass of wine, then another.

As they talked and sipped she lost all track of time and things began to blur. At some point she found herself singing Castio's off-color song in harmony with Rufen, while Denno laughed and beat time on the desk.

"What's the title of that one?" he demanded when they were finished, wheezing with laughter.

" 'Agivir's Farts'?" suggested Talis, without thinking.

The two men roared with approving laughter—

—just as the door to the shop opened and a small, slight figure stood silhouetted in the light of day.

Denno was so startled he tried to sit up too quickly. His feet slipped off the desk, and then he overbalanced, trying to save himself. His chair crashed over backward, leaving him upside down, arms and legs waving in the air like an overturned beetle, sputtering with a mixture of laughter and indignation.

Castio rose to his feet somewhat unsteadily, but with great dignity. "Who are you?"

Talis stared owlishly at the woman who stood there. The light was behind her, but there was something familiar . . .

"Thia!" she gasped. "What are *you* doing here?"

"I work here," the other woman said calmly, surveying them all with dark eyes that held both amusement and apprehension. "I beg pardon, Denno, I heard . . . noises, and I thought I should see what was going on. Here, let me help you up."

Advancing into the room, Thia began trying to extricate Denno from his chair. Recovering themselves, Castio and Talis hastened to help her. With all three of them working together, they soon had the stocky printer restored to an upright position.

Castio regarded Thia. The intrusion had obviously sobered him up considerably. "This woman works for you, Denno?"

"Aye, she does," Denno said. "She's a good sort, her name is Thia. Comes from up north. You're in early, girl."

Thia smiled at him and shook her head, amused. "Actually, I'm not. You must have lost track of time. 'Tis morning, Denno. Time to open the shop." She turned to look at Castio. "You must be Rufen Castio. I've read your writings."

Castio was obviously taken aback, but nodded and took her hand, bowed politely. "You have? They aren't generally . . . available."

"Yes. Denno has some of them upstairs in the flat, and when I mind little Damris, I read while she's sleeping."

Castio raised an eyebrow. "Indeed? He has my writings right out in the open?"

Thia shook her head. "Not at all. He hides them under the baby's clean nappies."

Denno's eyes widened. "That's right," he said. "I did. I should have realized . . ."

Talis had been studying Thia's expression, and, slowly, she relaxed, then smiled. "We have naught to fear from Thia," she said. "She'd never betray us."

The young woman with the ash-colored hair nodded. "I like what you wrote about freedom for all," she said, carefully not looking at Talis. "One of my friends is a slave. If you truly believe freedom is for all people, I would like to join your Cause."

Castio nodded slowly. "That might be a good thing. Poor Denno has been working too hard, printing all of our broadsides."

"I know," Thia agreed. "I can always tell when he's been up all night, working for you. Little Damris is *not* a colicky babe," she added, with a smile at her employer.

Denno chuckled shamefacedly. "Rufen, seems to me we can trust her. She's been working here for nigh on two months now, and she's held her tongue about what we do."

Talis barely heard this last exchange. *It's not fair!* she thought. *Sacrificing my chance to work with the Cause, all because of Eregard!* Her mind filled with the memory of the song he'd sung to her, and its haunting refrain.

And you'll never touch the free part of me . . .

"Damn it," she muttered, not realizing she was speaking aloud until the others turned to look at her. "Sorry, nothing," she said hastily. "Just . . . thinking. I had a decision to make, and it seems that I've made it."

Thia looked at her but said nothing.

This is going too slowly, Eregard thought, rubbing the file steadily against one side of his slave collar. *It's going to take hours more than I figured.*

He crouched in the shadows behind the henhouse that flanked the inn's stableyard, hidden from sight behind a stack of half-rotted old boards. The file had scored his hands so badly that he'd had to wrap rags around his fingers as he filed, and his neck burned where he'd managed to score it during the attempt.

The slave auction was tomorrow, and he *had* to have the accursed collar filed off by then, otherwise his whole plan was wrecked. He forced himself to file in short, even strokes. *Don't panic,* he told himself. *You'll think of something.*

"Talis! Clo!" It was a man's voice, shouting, and there was an edge of panic in it that made Eregard's file stroke halt. *Jezzil? Can it be?*

"Talis! Clo!" The breathless shout was more distant now, coming from the direction of the stables. Eregard heard running feet. *What's going on?*

"Master Jezzil!" It was Clo's voice. Eregard inched forward, peering around the edge of the outbuilding. "What is it?"

"Talis, where is Talis?" Jezzil's Chonao accent was much thicker than usual.

Eregard could see them now. Jezzil stood in the courtyard, his face pale and sweating, his hair rumpled and a smudge on his cheek. He had obviously been running.

"She's—"

The front door of the inn banged, and then Eregard heard Talis before he saw her, walking with quick, firm strides. "I'm here, Jezzil. What's wrong?"

Jezzil took a deep breath, obviously struggling for control. "It's Thia. She didn't come home from the print shop. Denno said she left after closing . . ."

Eregard stiffened. *Thia?*

"Well, perhaps she went to do some shopping—" Clo began.

"No!" he shouted, then forced himself to lower his voice. "Please, you must help me. When she didn't come home, I went out and asked along her route—and a boy remembered her. He said she was there, passing an alley, and then she wasn't. Someone must have grabbed her. The lad saw a wagon leave the alley, and there was something in the wagon bed that moved. He'd covered her with a blanket, but the lad was sure."

Eregard's heart was pounding. Thia had told him a little about her life in Amaran. He sensed that she'd left many things—dark things—unsaid.

"Kidnapped?" Talis sounded skeptical. "Who could possibly want—"

"You don't understand. The priests, they will never let her live, if they find her. It must have been one of the priests! She knew they'd search for her!" Jezzil's face twisted. "They'll kill her. We have to find her."

"But—"

"You're the only people I know here that I trust to help," Jezzil said. "Please, help me find her! They'll be heading north!"

Eregard didn't think about his bleeding hand, his scored

neck, and the half-filed collar. He found himself on his feet, running toward Jezzil. "I'll help," he called out. "I'm not much good as a fighter, but I can shoot a pistol."

Talis stared at him, then, suddenly, she was nodding. "We'll help, too. Clo, go saddle the horses."

11

The Chosen

He drove the wagon carefully, scrutinizing the ground ahead of him, hands clenched around the reins. He was not used to driving a two-horse team, especially over rough ground. When he was younger he'd learned to ride, because the temples sent missionaries out into other lands to educate the heathens about Boq'urak's might and power. But riding, he'd discovered quickly, was quite different from driving. The only means of communication with the team was through his voice or the reins, and a team was far less maneuverable than a ridden horse. Now, as a driver, he had to handle the brake on downslopes and plan his path, lest the wagon overturn or overrun the team.

When first he'd left the city, he headed due west, away from the main caravan trail, traveling across the isthmus that linked Kata to Severez. He hadn't gone far enough to glimpse the western arm of the sea, though. Instead he'd turned northwest, heading into Severez, but staying well off the main caravan trail.

Far to the north he thought he could make out a bruise-colored shadow that hinted at the high ranges dividing Severez and Amavav. But his eyes weren't as good as they had been when he was younger, so he couldn't be sure.

The land surrounding him was empty of habitation. The soil was mostly clay, covered with scrub brush and stunted trees. Outcroppings of stone thrust ochre fingers toward the sky. Ravines occasionally split the land, forcing him to detour to find a crossing that would accommodate the wagon.

He glanced to his left, gauging the position of the sun. It would be full dark in a handful of hours.

The horses had slowed to a jog. Leaning forward on the narrow seat, he slapped the reins against their backs. "Get up! Hah!" Reluctantly, they lengthened stride, until they were moving at a real trot. They were growing tired; they'd been moving steadily for several hours, with only brief moments to rest. He knew they couldn't go much farther without water and grazing.

Hearing a faint noise, he turned on the narrow seat to look behind him. The rough gray sacking stirred, then subsided, and he thought he heard a faint moan of distress.

"I'm sorry," he said quietly, knowing she probably couldn't hear him. "I am. But I had to do this. I'm doing it for both of us."

For a moment he thought about what he must do that very night, after sunset, but then resolutely pushed the thought away. *Concentrate on the task at hand.*

He urged the tired horses onward, resisting the urge to glance behind him. He didn't believe anyone had seen him. And even if anyone had, why should they concern themselves with the fate of a young woman from a foreign land, friendless and alone?

He glanced at the sun, gauging its position in the sky, and the thought struck him that Thia would never see another sunrise. Resolutely, Varn fought down the thought. He was Boq'urak's servant, and he was doing as his god bade.

He remembered the first time Boq'urak had spoken to him, in that icy mountain pass south of Verang. *She is Mine.*

He'd been on the trail now for months, keeping his eyes

open, reverting to his role of being a missionary, bringing
the truth to unbelievers in Amavav, Severez, and finally to
Kata. Weeks would go by and he would hear nothing, but
each time he'd thought the trail was lost forever, someone,
somewhere, would remember the quiet girl with the big dark
eyes and the unworldly air.

Tracing her to Q'Kal had been easy, compared to locating
her inside the city. Just as Varn had considered giving up,
wondering if the other priests were right and he was bereft
of his sanity, he'd seen her. Just a glimpse. She looked different in secular clothing. He'd never seen her with hair.

Yet he had known her: her walk, the way she tilted her
head, the way she held herself. He'd followed her for two
days, discovering where she lived, where she worked, mem-
orizing the route she used to go back and forth. And then
he'd made his plans.

Another faint moan reached his ears. Resolutely, Master
Varn did not look around, only clucked to the team, urging
them to even greater speed. Night was drawing nigh. It was
nearly time for the god to claim His Chosen One.

Jezzil was sweating, and only part of it was the warmth of
the afternoon. He wiped his forehead on his sleeve as they
jogged along. *Remember, it's almost summer. This land is
warmer than home.*

He looked about him, studying the landscape, warrior-
fashion, forcing himself to concentrate on it, analyzing it as
he'd been taught. He couldn't afford to let himself think
about what might be happening to Thia. If he thought about
that, he would be no good to her.

*This could be a good land for ambushes, rough and bar-
ren as it is.* It was certainly very different from his homeland. Ktavao was a land of steppes, mountains, and grassy
plains. North and east of Ktavao was, of course, the Great
Waste, but it was death to go there for more than just a handful of days. No humans lived there.

He couldn't imagine people living here, either. It was desolate, though not quite lifeless. Scrub brush dotted the

ground, and there were strange outcroppings of naked stone. Giant cracks in the ground showed where flood channels ran, though most were dried to scarred mud under the sun's relentless assault. Jezzil looked up at one of the rocks as they rode past. Red stone, it thrust upward like a giant's finger pointing at the sky.

For a moment Jezzil found himself thinking about giants, buried in the earth, thrusting their bloody fingers up into the air, unable to break free before suffocating. The thought of suffocation led him to visions of Thia, lying bound in the back of a wagon, heading for who knew what terrible rendezvous . . .

Stop that, he ordered himself, wiping sweat from his forehead again.

"Turn here," Talis, who was riding point, called out. She turned in her saddle to glance back at them, pointing down. "The wagon tracks are heading northwest now."

Jezzil squeezed Falar with the muscles of his left leg, and the mare obediently turned right, following Talis's bay. He was very glad that he'd asked her for help. The wagon tracks were easy to follow now as they led deeper and deeper into the desolate no-man's-land that lay north of the Katan border, but in the beginning the jumble of tracks leaving the city gates had made their task seem impossible.

Talis and Clo had spent time with the city gatekeepers, showing the bored men the glint of coin and questioning them about who had left the city that day. The coins had caused one of them to stroke his chin, frowning, and then recall a two-horse team pulling a small wagon, driven by a silent man with piercing dark eyes. Although the driver had his hood drawn up, the gatekeeper remembered that his head had been shaven. Like that of a priest. Had he been hauling anything? Well, yes, but not very much. Just a few odds and ends, a big bundle of wood and one old gray sack tossed in the back of the wagon bed.

After they moved away from the gates, Talis had slowly walked among the tracks, looking for one set that matched her criteria: a lightly loaded wagon with a two-horse team.

She'd cast about like a hunting dog as the precious minutes crawled by, while every nerve and sinew in Jezzil's body screamed to leap into action. Falar caught his tension and began dancing in place, neck arched. It was only when she went up into a low rear, a battle movement designed to protect her rider, that Jezzil had exerted iron control, forcing himself into warrior mode. From that moment on he had sat as quietly as an equestrian statue, watching Talis, only his eyes moving.

Finally Talis examined one set of tracks, and then looked up. "This is our best candidate, and over here is our second best. I think we should follow these for a mile, see what happens."

Jezzil nodded, and they'd followed the Katan woman's lead. Nobody was particularly surprised when the wagon tracks quickly diverged from the flow of traffic and headed off to the west. As Talis put it, "I suppose it's natural that a kidnapper should want privacy."

It's certainly private out here, Jezzil thought, feeling a sick wash of fear for Thia. *Where is he taking her? And* why?

Eregard urged his mount until he caught up and rode beside the Chonao warrior. "We're heading more to the north now," he said. "Any idea where he might be taking her?"

Jezzil glanced over at him, thinking that the slave would probably prove a handicap during a chase or a fight. He was an indifferent horseman; instead of sitting up straight, he slouched in the saddle, spine curved, heels bouncing against his mount's sides. But so far he'd kept up with the others, and his eyes were intent and steady on the trail they followed.

"I think he is heading for Amaran," Jezzil replied grimly.

"Amaran?" There was a catch in Eregard's voice. "Why there?"

"That's where Thia is from. She escaped from there. She didn't tell you?"

"No," Eregard said. "But she told me she was running from those who meant her harm."

Jezzil nodded. "True enough. And now it seems that they've found her. She told me once that the priests would never stop looking for her. The guard at the gate remembered a man whose head was shaven. Sounds like a priest."

Eregard's brow furrowed. "But if he's heading for Amaran, why would he take this route? The caravan road is much faster and more direct. I've seen maps of this land."

Jezzil gave him a quick, surprised glance. "You can read?"

"Yes."

As Jezzil continued to stare intently at Eregard, the slave hunched his shoulders, as if expecting a blow. The Chonao regarded him, noting a smear of dried blood on the neck of his tunic. "What happened to you?" Jezzil asked. "Your neck. You're wounded."

Eregard shook his head, not replying, only tucking his chin down, hunching his shoulders even more. Jezzil tightened the muscles of his right leg slightly, and Falar sidepassed until they were riding so close to each other that their legs brushed.

The Chonao leaned over in his saddle, eyes narrowed, staring at the slave's neck. "What—" He broke off as he took in the scorings on Eregard's collar. "File marks," he said slowly. "Go ahead, sit straight. You look like a turtle, hunched like that."

Eregard raised a shaking hand to his abraded neck. "Please . . ." he mumbled. "Please don't tell her—she hasn't noticed. I'll wrap something around it."

"I won't tell her," Jezzil said. "But I suspect she'll notice at some point."

"Mistress Talis is going to sell me," Eregard said. "If she does, I'll lose every chance to be free."

Jezzil nodded. "I know. Thia asked me if we had saved enough money to buy you. She wanted to set you free. But we don't have nearly enough saved."

Eregard gave him a quick, incredulous glance. "She wanted to do that? For me? She's—" He shook his head. "I can hardly believe it."

"Thia knows what it is like to be enslaved," Jezzil said.

Eregard nodded. "You can see it in her eyes." He took a deep breath. "If we find her—"

"*When,*" Jezzil corrected sharply.

"Yes, *when* we find her, if you and Thia can use your influence with Talis to persuade her to set me free, I could . . . I could see that Thia was protected. I could take her home with me. Nobody would dare touch her. I swear it."

Jezzil gave him a surprised glance. "Where is your home?"

"Pela."

"I'll con—" Jezzil broke off as Talis halted her bay. He urged Falar into a faster trot, leaving the slave, on his slower mount, behind.

"What is it?" he asked as he drew rein beside the Katan.

"The tracks . . ." She shook her head. "It's almost sunset. He's no longer following even a faint trail, because he's turned and is going west again. He's walking the horses. They're probably tired. I think he's getting ready to stop for the night. We should be cautious."

"If we don't catch them before dark, we'll lose them," Jezzil said. "The Moon won't rise for over an hour."

"We can track," she reassured him. "Though it won't be easy. Unless we cross rock, the prints will be visible. I have a lantern, and so does Clo. We'll have to go slowly, though."

Jezzil nodded. "Let's water the horses and press on. I don't like it that he's changed direction."

"I don't like it, either," Clo said. She dismounted and walked slowly up and down, stretching, then eyeing the tracks. The mercenary's broad, usually good-natured face was set in harsh lines that revealed her true age. She looked up at Jezzil. "I've heard tales about them priests," she said grimly. "Tales about human sacrifice and such. You hear any such thing, Jezzil?" Almost unconsciously, her hands went out to check her weapons: a pair of flintlock pistols, sword, and dagger.

"No," Jezzil replied. "But I am not from this country. I came from across the Narrow Sea, from Ktavao."

"I've heard rumors," Talis said. "They say they sacrifice some poor victim every morning, so the sun will rise."

Clo shook her head. "I don't like it. This doesn't make sense. Why push as hard as he can going west, then turn northwest, then west again?" She gestured in the direction the wagon tracks led. "There's nothing out there but badlands, and then the northernmost arm of the sea. Big outcroppings of that reddish rock, dead-end canyons—it's worthless land, dead land. Nothing lives there except snakes, scorpions, and lizards. Why go there?"

"People do strange things in the name of religion," Eregard said absently. He was staring west, shading his eyes from the Sun. "I don't like this, either."

"Let's water the horses, then move on," Jezzil said, letting some of the urgency he felt be reflected in his voice. He reached for one of the loaded waterskins that hung down over Falar's flank. "Let's *hurry*."

Thia lay in the bed of the wagon, bound and gagged, trying hard not to give in to the waves of nausea that swept over her. She knew if she vomited, she'd choke and die. It was struggle enough just to breathe; luckily, the sack that covered her was coarsely woven, and some air came through, but barely enough.

How long had she been lying here, rolling back and forth as the wagon bounced along? Hours, at least. Despite the rough gray material covering her face, she could tell it was still daylight. It was hot in the bed of the wagon, and thirst was a torment. Her hands and feet had long ago gone numb, and that numbness was spreading. Thia knew with a sick certainty that even if her captor stopped and untied her, she wouldn't be able to run for many minutes.

Her mind continued to torture her with images of pumps spilling gushes of water, of the Narrow Sea down by the docks of Q'Kal, of cold tankards of ale . . .

Stop that, she ordered herself. *You'll drive yourself mad. You have to think. Plan!* But the stifling air and the heat made her head swim . . . coherent thought was so difficult.

She forced herself to try and put the pieces together. It had been afternoon, and they'd finished early with a print run. Denno had told her she could go home early—he was taking his wife and little Damris to the market. Pleased to get away hours before she'd expected to, she was walking back from work, looking forward to spending time with her new friend, Eregard.

He was no ordinary slave, that much was obvious. He was educated, a scholar. He'd been teaching her about the modern world. She'd learned from him just how much history had been repressed or ignored by Boq'urak's priesthood. Master Varn had taught her that the world was round, but Eregard had taught her that it was *huge*. Bigger than she'd ever dreamed.

Master Varn . . . was he the one who had grabbed her as she'd walked past the mouth of the alley near the High Street? All she knew was that she'd been seized from behind in a bone-bruising grip. A hand had clapped over her mouth and nose. She'd twisted and bit down, hearing a muffled cry from behind her, and gotten her mouth free long enough for one aborted shriek of despair. Then the arm enclosing her rib cage had tightened and that brutal hand had clamped over her mouth, pinching her nostrils shut. She'd struggled as she was carried down the alley, but it had been no use. Unable to draw breath, a great roaring in her ears had replaced the sounds of the city . . . then blackness swam up from the shadows of the alley to engulf her, dragging her down.

When Thia finally regained consciousness, she'd been here, in the back of the wagon, rocking back and forth, growing thirstier and more cramped with every mile that passed.

A wave of anger swept over her, leaving her shaking. How dared he do this? How *dared* he? She had just been going about her business, perfectly law-abiding . . . well, except for helping out Castio's group.

And now here she was, tied up, queasy, cramped, and so thirsty she thought she might go mad. Anger swept through her, and for a moment she strained at her bonds, but the effort made her pant, and black spots began to swim before her eyes.

She tried to remember details about her captor. Was it Master Varn? She thought so. He hadn't spoken, and she had never seen him, but something was familiar. His scent, perhaps.

What does he want with me? Will he take me back to Amaran?

That was probably his goal. Boq'urak's priests did not take kindly to being challenged or thwarted. They would meet in tribunal to pronounce judgment. If she were lucky, she'd be given as the morning sacrifice, to ensure the sunrise. If she were not lucky—

Her thoughts bolted away from that subject as her physical body would have recoiled from a deadly viper.

Think, she ordered herself. *Plan.*

Thia remembered all the good times they'd had together. Master Varn had enjoyed teaching her; he'd said so often. Could she remind him of those good times? Share memories of books they'd read together? Perhaps, if she could remind him of what they had shared, he'd let her go.

It wasn't much of a plan, but at least it was something to try.

The wagon lurched and bucked, causing her head to slam hard against something unyielding. Thia saw pinwheels of light, and for a while the world faded away. She roused herself again to full consciousness—and raging thirst—to realize that the Sun was no longer beating directly down on her. She felt cooler. Night must be coming.

Surreptitiously, she began moving her hands and feet, trying to restore circulation. The resultant pins-and-needles in her limbs made her whimper, though the sound was stifled by the gag.

Thia was sweating by the time she allowed herself to rest, but she could move her limbs again, though she would doubtless be stiff and clumsy. *If this is Master Varn,* she thought, *he'll not be cruel. He'll untie me to let me have water. I can say that I must relieve myself, and then I will move in such a crippled fashion that he won't be expecting me to try and run.*

And then what? How could she find her way back Q'Kal? *First things first,* she ordered herself. *Escape.* If she went back to Amaran, her life was forfeit. Anything would be better than that.

She found herself wishing she could pray. The only god that she believed in—because she had seen Him with her own eyes—was a loathsome monster. Never again, she'd sworn, would she pray to Boq'urak.

I have nothing, no one, she thought, feeling a wave of terror and loneliness so profound that her heart ached within her breast. *I have no god.*

Tears stung her eyes, and she fought them back. *Crying won't help. I have to help myself.* For a moment she wondered why she was so determined to try to escape, even knowing it was probably hopeless. She was terrified of Boq'urak and His priesthood, yes, but terror was only part of what drove her. Thia realized that she was determined not to give up her freedom. She'd been Boq'urak's slave all her life, but for the past few months she'd been *free.* Freedom was worth fighting for, even if she died in the attempt. Being killed in a fight with Master Varn was a better fate than being declared Chosen.

The rhythm of the hoofbeats changed, slowed. Thia realized the wagon was stopping. She heard her captor set the brake, then climb down off the seat. Her heart began to pound as it had the night she'd escaped from the twin ziggurats.

She heard footsteps moving away from the wagon, then silence. *What can he be doing?* Not being able to see was torture.

After a few minutes she heard the footsteps again, approaching. "You must be awake by now," a voice said in her native language. For a moment Thia didn't even understand the words, so used had she become to hearing and speaking Pelanese. It took a moment for her mind to translate the meaning. Hands seized her ankles and dragged her sack-encased form across the wagon bed.

When she was lying on what seemed to be the tailgate of the wagon, her captor began pulling the sack off. Fading light struck her eyes, making her squint, after so long in the dark. Thia looked up into the face of her captor. *I was right.*

Carefully, Master Varn untied the gag. She worked her jaw, realizing that her whole face ached. Varn helped her to sit up, her legs dangling off the tailgate. Producing a water bag, he held it up to show her. "Here, child. You must be thirsty."

For just a moment Thia hesitated as he held it to her lips. *What if it's drugged?*

But her thirst would not be denied. She swallowed, gulping, as water dribbled over her chin and onto her dress. The touch of the water, warm and leathery tasting as it was, was bliss. She swallowed greedily, but all too soon he took the water bag away.

"Not too much," he said. "You don't want to be sick."

Thia wiped her mouth and chin on her sleeve as she stared past her erstwhile Mentor, taking in her surroundings. Huge stones surrounded them like sentinels, and the last rays of the setting sun stained them the color of fresh blood. They were in a vast wasteland, barren and sere. Sickly looking brush struggled for survival, but there was nothing else to see except the massive upthrusting boulders. The ground showed signs of water channels, but at the moment it was hard to believe that this land had ever seen rain. The wagon itself held little except another, smaller, bag, a lantern, and a huge bundle of firewood.

Master Varn drank from the waterskin, sparingly, then stoppered it and put it down. He had pushed back his hood, and Thia looked up at him, taking in his familiar features. "Master," she ventured. It felt strange to speak her native tongue. "Why . . . what . . . what are we doing here? Why did you . . ." She decided the word "kidnap" might be too blunt, and searched for a way to express her question. "Why are we here? Why did you bring me here?"

He looked down, his dark eyes full of concern and tenderness. "Thia, my dear, my child, my love, your soul was in danger, living amongst those infidels. *He* commanded me to find you, and to bring you to *Him*. Only in that way can you regain what you have lost."

"Oh," she managed weakly. "Of course. I should have realized."

"You should have," Varn said, a touch of reproach in his voice. "It took me a long time to find you, Thia. Without His guidance, I could never have done so."

Boq'urak . . . she thought, remembering the monster, and fought back a wave of nausea. "Master," she said cautiously, "it is good to see you."

"It is good to see you, too, Thia," he said. "You've grown up in the last few months. You're a woman now, not a child." Carefully, he put out his hand, stroked her hair, which was now long enough to almost cover her ears. "Your hair, it's quite pretty. I had no idea."

Thia managed a wan smile. "Master, I . . . I need to . . . can I have a moment alone?"

He gave her a glance that mixed exasperation with amusement. "Thia, Thia . . . and have you run away again? You think your old Master is a fool?"

"No!" she said, fighting back tears that filled her eyes. *So much for my plan!* "But Master, I have to . . ." She slid off the edge of the tailgate and then stood, swaying, holding onto the wagon for support. It was all she could do to keep from collapsing. "I can't run away, Master, even if I wanted to."

He took her arm, led her away from the wagon, over to one of the large boulders that studded the ground. "Here," he said, "go here." He released her arm. She leaned on the boulder, looking up at him. "Please, turn your back, Master."

He shook his head. "And have you hit me with a handy rock, Thia? You kicked me, child, remember? I'm sorry. I will not turn away."

She felt the hot blood mount in her cheeks, but her body would not be denied. Hoisting up her skirts, she squatted. For a moment she feared that shame would prevent her from going, but she managed, first a slight trickle, then a hot, strong-smelling gush. Master Varn stood facing her as she urinated, but at least he did not gaze directly at her, but stared over her head.

Finally, she was finished and stood up. She was a little steadier now, but she tried not to let him see that. *The weaker he thinks I am, the better.*

The sun had set, and the breeze was growing cooler. The sky to the west was bright with color, but it was fading rapidly. Soon it would be full dark, and moonrise would not come for more than an hour. Thia looked up at Master Varn and couldn't repress a shiver.

She walked a few slow, tottering steps, then had to lean against another boulder. Slowly, she let herself slide down it and sat on the cooling ground. The rock was still warm, and it felt good against her back. She gazed up at Varn earnestly. "Master, you taught me so much. But I have learned even more since I left Verang. There are so many books here that we don't have in our scriptorium! So many volumes of history, and science. So many maps." She held his gaze with her own. "Master, you are a scholar. Surely you can appreciate wanting to learn. I don't want to go back to Amaran. The priests don't want the novices or priestesses to read, remember? It's not fair."

"I know, my child," he said, leaning against the boulder. "I don't agree with that. But Boq'urak's will cannot be denied. He has spoken to me of you. He wishes to reclaim you, in His great generosity."

She had to bite her lip to hold back a cry of utter panic. Thia took a deep breath, forcing calm. *Help him remember the old days. Help him remember how we studied together, kept our secret, protected each other.*

"Master, do you remember the first day I read a whole page by myself?" She kept her voice low, nonthreatening. "You gave me a honeycake from the priest's table as a reward. That was one of the happiest days I knew as a child. Do you remember?"

Varn frowned, then slowly nodded. "I remember. We studied hard, didn't we, all those times in the secret chambers . . ." He trailed off, lost in thought.

Thia wet her lips and went on, bringing up memories, reminding him of times they'd shared, of those hundreds of secret meetings as he taught her to read, cipher, and, later, taught her geometry, and how to tell a planet from a star, and where the Moon went when it was new.

They must have talked for nearly an hour. Varn visibly relaxed and sat down beside her. Turn and turn about, they traded memories. Night crept in around them, and soon she could no longer make out his features, but his voice was so dear and familiar to her that she thought she could read it better than his face. As they talked, greatly daring, she put out her hand and took his, holding it. His long, slender scholar's fingers tightened around her own. During all their years together they had scarcely ever touched, and then only by accident. The feel of his flesh against hers was comforting.

Thia felt increasingly reassured as they talked. *It's working. He could never hurt me. Boq'urak can't be all-powerful, or He would have struck me down long ago. He must need a vessel to work His will. Surely Master Varn would never lend himself to harming me!*

After a few more minutes she said, "Master, did you bring some food? I'm hungry."

She saw his head turn against the brilliant stars of the desert, and fingers tightened on hers. "I'm sorry, Thia, we cannot eat. We must fast before the rite."

Thia froze. *No! He can't mean it!* But she knew he did. She tried to jerk away, but suddenly both of his hands were clamped around her wrist. "No, child," he said. "You cannot leave. As soon as the Moon rises, we must begin."

Despite her efforts to keep it steady, her voice broke. "Please, Master, don't do this. Don't hurt me."

"I don't want to hurt you," he said, his tone earnest and low. "I truly don't. But Boq'urak has commanded me, Thia. He has told me you are His Chosen for tonight."

"But . . . but . . ." She swallowed a sob. "If you do—if you—I saw Narda. Master, Boq'urak killed her. You know that. Do you want me to die?"

"No," he said after a long moment. He sounded shaken. "I

have told Him what you are to me, like my own child. I raised you. But He still demands . . ."

Thia remembered the expression in his eyes when he had stroked her hair. Trying to make the motion seem natural, she leaned against him, putting her head on his shoulder. She dropped her voice to a whisper in the desert stillness. "Master, please, you know how much I care for you. I am yours, not His. *Please* . . . "

He sat still for a moment, then turned his head, and she felt his lips brush her forehead. "For so long I've wanted to touch you," he murmured. "For so long. But it is forbidden, unless He wills it, unless I am His vessel . . ."

Thia tried to imagine what to do next. Kiss him? She had never kissed anyone, and had little idea how it was done. As she hesitated, he abruptly sat up straight, his hand never releasing her wrist. "Come on, get up," he said, pulling her to her feet. "We must prepare. The Moon will soon be up."

She tried to jerk away, poised to run, but his grip never slackened as he headed for the wagon, towing her behind him like a child. Without releasing his grip, he leaned over the wagon bed, and then she heard the muted clink as he lifted out the lantern.

He'll need both hands to light it, she thought, trying to remember where the boulders were that surrounded them. If she could manage to break free, run, lose herself among the rocks . . .

But he pulled her over to stand before him, then pinned her body up against the side of the wagon, holding her in place with his own bulk. Thia felt the rough boards press against the small of her back. Varn fumbled with the lantern, and a scraping sound was followed by a yellow flare in the darkness. It flickered, then steadied as the wick caught. As soon as it was safely lit, his hand clamped around her wrist again and he stepped back.

"Where did I leave that," he muttered, bending over the wagon bed, holding the lantern high. Thia had been so long in the darkness that her eyes watered when she looked at the light. She thought about grabbing the lantern and smashing it over his head, but he was holding it up, out of her reach. "Ah, here."

Again he pinned her against the wagon bed, his body heavy and solid against her own. He reached past her, then straightened up, a coil of rope in his hand. Seeing it, Thia tried to dodge sideways, but his knee rose, prisoning her.

"Hold still, and this will not hurt," he murmured. Placing the lantern on the seat of the wagon, he looped the rope around her wrist.

"Sit down," he said, and when she remained standing, he pushed her down, as he would have pushed a disobedient hound. "Don't make this difficult, child."

Thia caught a glimpse of his face, and was terrified to realize that a shadow of *Otherness* lay over it. The features were still recognizably Master Varn's, but it was as though a mask had closed down over them.

Moving quickly, efficiently, he tied her hands behind her, to opposite sides of the wagon wheel. Then he picked up the bundle of wood, moved far enough away from the wagon to prevent any danger of flying sparks, and arranged it carefully, stacking it so it would burn quick and bright. Reaching into his robes, he took out a pouch, then tossed a handful of powder over the wood.

He came back to squat on his heels beside her. "Soon . . ." he said, his voice deep and rough, as though it, too, were no longer quite his own. "Soon the Moon will rise."

He edged closer to her, his eyes intent on her face, her body. Thia, wild with panic, had to force herself to stay still. *If I scream, he'll gag me. Besides, there's no one to hear. If I kick him, he'll just tie my feet, too.*

Putting out a hand, he began to stroke her hair, her face. "You were so different from the others," he whispered. "Eyes so wide, so bright. You wanted to learn, you thirsted for it."

She swallowed dryness. "Master, I want to keep learning. Let me go. We can go back to Verang. You can be my teacher again."

"I cannot," he said, his voice full of sadness. "He wants you. Even now, He bids me let Him enter, so He can have you. I must obey."

His hand brushed her neck, then gently, hesitantly, he trailed his fingers across her left breast. In the lamplight, she could see that the digits appeared longer, thicker . . . the skin coarse and very dark . . .

The Change! He's Changing!

"It is time," Varn said, his voice harsh with regret. "It will be moonrise in a few minutes. I am sorry, child."

Rising to his feet again, he walked back to the fire and began to chant, swaying back and forth, his eyes closed. Thia had heard that same chant before, from many throats, her last night in the twin ziggurats. Desperately, she twisted her wrists, finding that the rope binding her right wrist wasn't quite as tight. She twisted, pulling, almost dislocating her thumb.

The ropes held. She continued to twist, feeling the pain in her wrist, thinking that perhaps if she could start bleeding, it might help her slide the rope off.

Master Varn was still chanting, and in between bouts of chanting, he prayed to Boq'urak. "Lord of the World, I am here for you. I am your servant, great Boq'urak. Take me, should that be your will. Take my arm, that the ritual fire may burn."

Varn held his right arm up and out, away from his body. The sleeve of his robe fell back, and she saw that jagged ridges were erupting from his forearms; the back of his hand was now thick and leathery. Suddenly, talons sprouted from his fingertips. Varn cried out in mingled pain and ecstasy. He turned to face the pile of wood and held out his hand.

Red fire leaped from his talons to land on the wood, and suddenly it blazed up, hot and bright. Billows of sickly sweet smoke filled the air. Thia twisted and fought the ropes, trying to hold her breath, but eventually she had to breathe, and her head swam from the sacred incense.

The fire, Master Varn himself, the shadowy shapes of the rocks seemed to double, then triple, and she remembered Narda's drugged ecstasy. For a moment she was tempted to stop fighting, to breathe deeply and allow the drugged smoke to carry her away.

No! While she lived, she would fight. She began yanking and twisting at the ropes harder than ever. The pain as they cut her flesh helped her resist the fumes.

Master Varn was chanting again, facing the east. Thia saw that the sky was lighter. *Moonrise!*

Her head was swimming and it was hard to remember why she had to keep trying to get free. All she wanted to do was close her eyes and sleep . . .

For a moment she must have drifted away, because she woke to feel Master Varn stroking her face. Repulsed, she jerked her head back, then saw he was using his left hand, which was still human flesh. She realized he was only partially Changed. His face was broader, his eyes bigger, and ridges sprouted from his brows. Varn's skin was grayish and leathery looking.

But he was still recognizable as her teacher. "Master . . ." she gasped. "Please, let me go. Please don't kill me!"

"Thia, my child, my love," he was gasping, obviously in great distress. "I don't want to harm you . . ."

He slid his left hand over her shoulder, and his fingers fumbled with the laces on her bodice. "I just want to love you, my dear."

Can he stop the Change? she wondered. Anything would be better than Boq'urak's touch. "Master, please, I am yours. Not Boq'urak's. *Yours.*"

Carefully, tenderly, he loosened her bodice and touched her breast. Thia shuddered, half from fear, half because it felt strangely pleasurable . . . warm, down in her vitals. He continued to stroke her, his breathing growing quick.

"She is mine," he muttered hoarsely, sounding as if he were arguing with someone invisible to her. "Mine. It is forbidden, but I am still a man!"

His hand left her bare breast to travel down her body. Grabbing her skirt, he yanked it up to her waist. Thia gasped, but managed to hold still, until he brought his right hand, with those hideous talons, up to tug on her petticoat.

She whimpered and tried to twist away from the leathery touch on her belly, her thighs. Drawing her knees up, she turned partway onto her side, trying to shield herself from his gaze.

Varn's breathing was harsh and rapid now, and he was muttering, half to himself, half to Boq'urak. "Mine, meant to be, I always knew. Master, I am your most faithful servant! Allow me this love, this pleasure. Thia, Thia, my child, my love . . ."

As he began touching her again, using his left hand, Thia whispered, "Master, I am yours. Untie me. I *am* yours! We can go back to Amaran. We can be together there. We can serve Boq'urak together. Either as priest and priestess, or husband and wife."

She was desperate, saying anything to try and get his attention. If only he would untie her, she would run until she dropped and died. Anything would be better than being Boq'urak's Chosen.

"Master! Please, just untie me!"

He shook his head and mumbled, clearly responding to a voice she hadn't heard, "I have devoted my life . . . not so much to ask . . . there are other girls, so many . . . this one is special to me . . . Lord, hear me."

He used his right hand to push her onto her back, even as the fingers of his left hand forced themselves between her legs, probing. Thia cried out in pain. "Master . . . please!"

"Mine!" he muttered. "Mine!" Rising to his feet, he threw off his robes. Beneath them he was clad only in a scant loincloth. Thia saw that his body was partly Changed. Pulsing bulges on his sides made her remember the god's tentacles. And the loincloth moved, changed shape, as though something hideous and living was uncoiling there.

He knelt back down, and she saw that his face had Changed yet again. The mouth was lipless, and the tongue . . .

Varn leaned over to kiss her.

Thia's control broke; she snapped at him like a cornered mongrel, then screamed, shrill and loud and long. "No!" she shrieked. "Get away from me! No!"

Master Varn stretched out his arms, and she saw that they were longer and thicker, rippling with muscle and gleaming with scales. Thia screamed again, screamed until she gasped for breath. Master Varn ignored her. Thia wrenched at her bonds, struggling, whimpering—only to break off in amazement as she heard the drum of racing hoofbeats.

For a moment she thought she had inhaled the smoke and was hallucinating, or lying in a stupor, dreaming. Then she realized that Varn heard them, too. He got to his feet, head turned to the east.

Thia gulped air. "Help me! Please!" she shouted. Her throat was so raw, it was hard to make her voice carry.

Suddenly the firelight was filled with four plunging horses and riders carrying flashing steel. Recognizing Falar, Thia felt a sudden rush of pride as she realized that her friends had come for her. She struggled to raise herself, to cry out and warn them.

"Jezzil! Don't give him time to Change!" she shouted. "He's becoming Incarnate! Don't let him finish!"

"Over here! Clo, Talis! There she is!" It was Jezzil's voice, and she saw him, armed for battle, urge Falar forward.

Varn roared defiance and leaped at them. Jezzil met his rush.

It was hard to see; the fire's light wavered and flickered. The circle seemed filled with horses and weapons. Varn's body appeared even larger, and a dull purplish glow emanated from him, unevenly, in patches that seemed to flash, then fade, only to strengthen again. Jezzil swung a terrible blow at Varn's head, but the blade slid away from the eerie light, leaving the priest unharmed.

Varn was still Changing. Thia saw the tentacles begin to sprout from his sides. His right arm slammed into Falar's neck and the mare fell. Quick as a cat, Jezzil was up, and this time his sword slashed at one of the clear patches of skin. The blade connected, and Varn screamed, a shrill, human cry.

"Clo!" Jezzil shouted. "Avoid that light! Aim for his flesh!"

Clo steadied her pistol. A loose horse darted between Thia

and the combatants just as the mercenary fired, so she did
not see whether the shot struck home. But Varn staggered
and turned away from Jezzil. He headed for the older
woman, who, true to her training, had dropped her empty
pistol and was reaching for her second one.

Clo almost made it. Varn reached her just as she raised the
pistol, then his taloned hand slammed into her midsection.
Clo screamed and the gun went off again, the shot going
wild. One of the horses shrieked. Clo was lifted and flung, as
easily as a child would toss a doll.

Talis and Jezzil moved in again, their movements smooth
and controlled, their blades flashing as they searched for
those elusive vulnerable spots.

As Thia strained to see, her view of the fight was blotted
out. Eregard stooped over her. Deliberately looking away
from her, he reached out and yanked down her skirt, then
pulled her bodice together. Only then did his eyes meet hers.
"Thia, thank the Goddess you're not hurt! What *is* that
thing?" Without waiting for her answer, he began sawing at
the ropes binding her to the wagon wheel.

As soon as Thia's hands were free, she jumped to her feet,
yanking on her bodice-lacings. "I'm all right," she insisted,
giving Eregard a push. "Help them!"

Eregard drew his short sword, then hesitated. Talis and
Jezzil were fighting hard, but Varn's strength was terrifying.
He was fast, too—as quickly as they could strike at an unshielded area, he would twist to avoid the blow. Half a dozen
shallow cuts bled from various parts of his body, but so far
they hadn't even slowed him down.

Suddenly Jezzil took a step back, then sprang forward,
twisting his body in a way that seemed impossible. His feet
struck the priest's midsection, sending the half-Changed
creature reeling back. Jezzil dropped lightly to the ground,
then sprang again, turning completely over in midair. This
time one foot connected with the creature's head. Varn
snarled, lunging at the Chonao. Jezzil danced back, sword
flicking out, slashing Varn's shoulder. He gathered himself
to spring again and—disappeared!

Thia gasped in shock and disbelief. Something struck Varn, sending him staggering back. One huge, taloned hand swept out, raking the air blindly—and suddenly Jezzil was there in his arms, and Varn's talons buried themselves in his midsection.

"No!" Thia shouted, trying to grab the sword out of Eregard's hand. The slave cursed under his breath, shoved her aside and leapt at the priest's back. Talis was already attacking from the creature's front, slashing at the arm that held Jezzil.

Still weak from her ordeal, Thia stumbled back and sat down so hard she saw stars. When her vision cleared, Eregard was in the midst of the fray, his sword biting deep into the priest's unshielded thigh. Varn roared with pain, then flung Jezzil away. The Chonao crashed against a boulder, then slid down it, to lie unmoving. The priest turned to attack the slave.

Thia staggered to her feet, looking around her for a weapon. *Something! Anything!* Her gaze fastened on the lantern, and she seized it. Darting forward, she flung it with all her strength at Varn's head. It struck one of the purplish patches of light, only to shatter and bounce off, but then flaming oil engulfed his shoulder. Howling, he spun around, beating at the flames running down his arm. For just a moment his eyes met Thia's, and they were still her Master's eyes, human, accusing.

"Now!" yelled Talis, and she and Eregard leaped forward, their swords aiming for the unprotected spots. Varn swung a massive arm at them, then turned and ran. Nobody tried to stop him.

Thia watched him vanish into the darkness, realizing that the purple patches had faded and that he seemed smaller. *He has to concentrate to invoke the Change,* she thought. *When he was attacked on all sides, he couldn't concentrate. He couldn't complete the Incarnation.* She felt strange—dissociated, as though she were watching it all from someplace outside her own body.

"Jezzil?" Talis was bent over, gasping for breath. "Clo?"

Thia shook her head, and the world came rushing back—

the firelight, the smell of incense and blood. "Jezzil's here," she called out, stumbling over to the Chonao on legs that shook. She was trembling all over, afraid of what she would find.

Jezzil lay sprawled beside the boulder he'd struck. He was unconscious, but when Thia cautiously touched his face, she could feel his breath on her fingers. She heard a step behind her, turned to see Talis. "He's alive," she said.

"Clo isn't," Talis said heavily, sounding choked with shock and grief. "She's dead. Dear Goddess, what *was* that thing?"

Thia didn't answer, only watched as Talis knelt beside Jezzil in the fireshot darkness. "We're going to have to move him. Get him back to Q'Kal," she said, running her hands down his arms, then running her fingers through his hair. "His leg's broken," she said a moment later. "We'll need to splint it."

"Eregard!" she shouted. "Light Clo's lantern and bring it here! I can't see!"

"I'll see if there's some wood for splints left in the wagon bed," Thia said. She went over to the wagon, felt around inside for any sticks that remained. She found several, and brought them back to Talis. "Do you know how to do this?"

"I've never done it," Talis said grimly, "but I've seen it done. If you're wearing a petticoat, rip it up into strips." As Eregard approached with the lantern, she held up her hand, and Thia saw that it was dripping scarlet. "But first we've got to try and stop this bleeding. There's a wound in his gut."

Thia took the knife Eregard gave her and proceeded to rip up her petticoat. She also cut off the bottom section of her skirt, shortening it until it was barely more than knee-length. Her hands grew raw from tearing the tough homespun into strips.

With Eregard holding the lantern, Talis bound the jagged gash over Jezzil's abdomen, tying her extra shirt down tightly as a pad, trying to stanch the blood flow. "This is bad," she said tightly. "If he regains consciousness, he's going to be hurting. Gut wounds hurt a lot, the soldiers say."

Jezzil moaned as she worked, but did not rouse. Thia acted as Talis's assistant, biting her bottom lip and ordering herself fiercely not to panic. There was so much blood . . .

"Now for the leg, while he's still unconscious," Talis said, wiping her bloody hands on a piece of cloth. "Hold him, both of you. I don't want him waking up and thrashing around."

They held Jezzil's shoulders while Talis stood up, braced herself, and gave one steady, strong pull. Jezzil jerked and grunted with pain, and suddenly his leg was straight again. Quickly, the Katan woman rigged a splint, then she and Thia bound the leg to it. "We'll put him in the wagon," Talis said.

"What about Clo's . . . body?" Eregard asked. "Do we have time to bury her? Or should we take her, too?"

Talis wiped her forehead, leaving a reddish smear. Thia noticed that she had a cut on her forearm, bleeding sluggishly. "I don't know," Talis said. "I don't want trouble with the authorities back in Q'Kal. I can't imagine how we'd answer questions from the Watch."

"Does she have family?" Thia asked.

"No, just her guild, and I know they'd give her an honorable burial," Talis replied. "But they won't want any trouble from the Watch, either." She glanced over at the wounded man. "Jezzil's still alive, he has to come first," she said. "We have to get him to a physician. He may not last the night as it is."

They walked together to look at Clo. The mercenary lay on her back, eyes wide open, arms flung wide. "Goddess, I don't know what to do!" Talis muttered.

"Put her in the wagon," Eregard said. "We can leave the body just outside of town, hidden, and after we find a doctor for Jezzil, I'll come back and bury her. Or I'll bring her guildmaster so he can take charge."

Talis nodded slowly, and the look she gave Eregard was one of sudden respect. "Good idea. Thia and I will rig a litter. Eregard, you give the team as much water as we can spare. We can spell them with the saddle horses when they give out."

As she crossed the circle, still lit by the now dying fire, Talis stopped and gave a choked cry, gazing at something hidden in the darkness. She flung herself down.

"What is it?" Thia asked as she and Eregard hurried over to join the Katan.

Moments later she saw. A bay horse lay sprawled ungracefully on its side, legs sticking out stiffly, eyes staring. Talis stroked the satiny neck. She made no sound, but her face shone wet in the light of the lamp. "Bayberry . . ." she whispered. "Oh, Bayberry!"

"What happened?" Eregard said, dropping to his knees and putting a consoling arm around Talis. She didn't seem to notice, though she leaned against him as if she needed the support.

"That second shot of Clo's," Thia murmured, remembering. "It went wild. I'm so sorry, Talis."

For a moment they stood there, silent. Then Talis straightened. She wiped her hand across her face, smearing it with Jezzil's blood. "Help me get my tack off him, Eregard. We have to hurry."

Moving quickly by the light of the rising moon, they stowed Jezzil in the bed of the wagon, then wrapped Clo in a blanket and put her there, too, using her body as a buffer to keep the Chonao from rolling about. "You ride back here with him, keep him steady," Talis ordered Thia. "If you can get him to swallow, give him sips of water."

Thia nodded, and climbed into the wagon bed. Eregard tethered Clo's horse to the back of the wagon. Falar appeared to be unharmed, despite the fall the mare had taken, so he tied her to the back of the wagon as well. Then Eregard swung up onto his own mount. Talis climbed up on the seat, took off the brake, and clucked to the team.

"Get up!"

Thia felt the wagon bed lurch beneath her as she carefully eased Jezzil's head into her lap. She allowed herself a few sips from the waterskin, then cautiously dribbled a few drops between his lips. His eyelids fluttered, then he swallowed and lapsed back into unconsciousness.

Talis had the team turned now. She slapped their backs with the free end of the reins. "Get up there! Hup!" The wagon lurched forward, heading east for Q'Kal, using the rising moon to set their course.

12

The Power Within

Had he not remained partially Incarnate, he would have died in the wastelands. He was wounded in many places, burned, and he had no food, no water, no clothing to shield him from the sun that rose as he limped determinedly toward it.

Boq'urak sustained him, nourished him, and healed the wounds far more quickly than any magical salve he had ever heard of. By the time he reached the outlying farmlands, the sun was overhead and his partially Changed body was whole again.

As he walked, he had not been aware of the presence of his god, only of the imperative to survive, to heal, to keep moving. But now as he stood looking down on a farm, seeing human clothing being hung on a washline by a farmer's wife, he realized that there was a large cistern to trap rainwater behind the barn.

Quickly he stole down to it, careful to stay out of sight. He had no wish to kill unless his Lord commanded it.

Once there, he put his face down to the water, letting it run up the tube that served as his tongue, sucking greedily. His skin tightened, the scaled places taking on a sheen in the sunlight.

When he finally slaked his thirst, he pulled back his head, retracting his tongue, and stared down into the water, knowing his Lord wished to communicate more fully.

His partially Changed reflection wavered back at him, and then he heard the voice of the god. *My servant . . .*

"I am here, Lord," Varn answered. "The city lies ahead of me. As soon as I resume human guise and covering, I can walk among them once more." His throat tightened as he remembered the previous night's events. "I am sorry, Lord. I was weak. I failed you."

You could not know that the girl had comrades who would ride to her rescue, the god said. *And you have learned a valuable lesson, have you not?*

"Yes," he said to his reflection. "Oh, yes. I must put aside the past, and do thy bidding only, Lord."

You have indeed learned, the god said, *and because of that I am inclined to be gracious.*

"Thank you, Lord," Varn said fervently. "I will dress myself and go into the city. I will seek her out and kill her for her temerity in hurting us."

No, the god said. *Last night's adventure was . . . diverting. She may live yet a little while. There is something else you must do, My servant.*

Master Varn blinked in surprise, then bowed his head. "Command me."

You must go into the town and find a ship. Cross the sea. There is one on the other side of the Strait of Dara that I have chosen as My vessel. An innocent, residing in a place of power. There will be war, and much bloodshed. It is My will that I be present to share in it, to partake of it.

Varn bowed his head. "I shall do as you say, Lord. But there is one thing . . ." He hesitated. "Ship passage will require payment."

Fear not. I shall provide.

Varn raised his head, and felt himself growing smaller,

lessening in every way. He felt the alteration in his bones, his sinews, and then his link with Boq'urak vanished.

But he knew now it would return.

Shivering, clenching her jaw to keep her teeth from chattering, Princess Ulandra paced the royal bedchamber. Despite her fur-trimmed dressing gown, the fire in the fireplace, and the mildness of the summer night, she was chilled to her bones. Halting her restless movement, she stood still as a cramp twisted in her belly. As it passed, she took a deep breath.

He'll be here any minute.

And he would *know*. He would ask her, and she didn't dare lie. Or he'd ask her waiting women; he'd done it before. They would tell him, they dared not lie for her. Salesin's temper was not something anyone wanted to rouse.

As she walked past the casement window, she felt the brush of cool air across her cheek and shivered again. She'd taken Wolf out earlier for a walk in the garden. It was a lovely spring night, with the Moon nearly full. Ulandra thought of the Moon and the roses, bleached to delicate pallor in its light. Suddenly, for no reason at all, poor dead Prince Eregard's face formed in her mind's eye. He would have been a good companion on a moonlight walk.

She felt another cramp uncoil in her belly. Her courses had come on her a day or so early this month. Salesin would know, and he would not be pleased.

At least he wouldn't take her tonight, or for the next few nights. But Ulandra knew she'd far rather endure his rough embraces than his temper when he discovered that once again she had not conceived.

She bit her lip as another cramp assailed her. If only she could just climb into bed, have her ladies-in-waiting bring her a posset and a warm brick wrapped in flannel. She could curl up next to it and, just perhaps, sleep.

How long had it been since she'd had a peaceful night's sleep? She couldn't remember.

Ulandra paused before her mirror. She had lost weight

lately, and was even paler than usual. Hastily, she applied a bit of rouge. She could not afford to show weakness or appear ill. If Salesin thought she was sickly, incapable of breeding, Goddess alone knew what would happen to her.

She felt a sudden hot wave of anger against her husband. There was still fear when she thought of him, but, more and more lately, it was drowned out by hate and anger. *How dare he treat me the way he does? How dare he?*

Her face now had plenty of color. Her cheeks were flushed with anger, and her eyes sparkled with it. But as Ulandra stared into the mirror, she was suddenly aware of that presence, that Otherness. Her features seemed to melt, to lose shape, to rearrange themselves into a countenance out of a nightmare. Huge, lidless eyes stared back at her, and her mouth was not a mouth at all but—

Ulandra cried out in fear, and suddenly everything was back in focus. The face in her mirror was her own.

Her hands were shaking so badly that she could not place the stopper back in her container of rouge. *I was imagining things,* she told herself. *I'm tired. I haven't been resting or eating well for months now. I just need rest.*

A cramp uncoiled within her, and she bit her lip until the pain passed.

She was pale again, and the rouge she'd applied made her look like a street mountebank. Taking up a bit of cloth, she rubbed most of it off. At least that wash of anger had stopped her from shivering. But she knew that wouldn't last. The fear would be back as soon as she heard her husband's step.

Hastily, she stood and walked around the room, quickly tidying it. Salesin didn't like clutter, and would use any excuse to lose his temper.

When she passed the fireplace, she saw that some ash had fallen onto the stone hearth, and quickly she knelt on the stones and began sweeping it up.

She was so intent on her task that she didn't hear his step. "What are you *doing*?" he asked sharply.

Ulandra started so badly that she dropped the hearth

brush. Hastily, she got up, ignoring the cramp that wanted to double her over, and curtsied. "Forgive me, my lord. The hearth needed sweeping."

"Don't your waiting women obey you?" he said harshly. "Or are you such a weak-livered nonentity that they ignore you, the way *I* wish I could?"

"Your pardon, my lord," she said. "Of course they would obey, but the last time you came in and Bethina was here, you were angry at me for having her here to tidy up when you wanted to rest, so . . ." She trailed off, realizing he wasn't listening.

"You're pale," he said, walking over to her. "Even paler than usual. Can it be that you're breeding?"

Ulandra froze, tempted for one wild second to say yes, just so he would leave her alone. *Just one night to sleep peacefully, without pain or fear. Just one night.*

"Well?" he demanded.

"My lord, I . . . I am sorry, my lord, but today . . . today I . . ." She was stuttering, unable to meet his gaze, and shivering .

"Bleeding again? You *must* be barren!" he snarled.

She shrank back, her hands going up to her ears, not wanting to hear the words that felt like blows. "I'm sorry, my lord, I don't—"

She never saw his hand move, but suddenly the blow snapped her head back. Lights exploded against her eyelids, flashes of color, as pain blossomed on her right cheek. He had slapped her before, open-handed, but this time he'd used his fist, and the pain was unbelievable.

The room spun around her, and Ulandra realized she was back on the floor, on her hands and knees. "Stupid, whey-faced *bitch*!" he snarled, and the toe of his boot caught her in her belly, lifting her up, spinning her over, taking her breath.

She lay there, trying to breathe, but all she could do was gasp like a landed fish.

And then she heard the barking.

Oh, no! Wolf!

Ulandra managed to draw breath, rolled over, pushing away the pain. "Wolf! No!"

The little dog must have gotten away from her maid. He raced into the room, a brown blur, and flung himself at Salesin, snapping and growling. The Prince cursed, and his foot moved again. There was a shrill yip of pain, and then Wolf lay stunned, halfway across the room.

"No!" Ulandra moaned. "Please no! Please, I'm sorry!" She began dragging herself across the floor toward the dog, not sure what she was planning to do, only knowing that she had to stop Salesin, she had to save Wolf—Wolf, her only friend. She reached her husband and grabbed his leg, digging her fingers into the hard muscle of his calf. "No! Please! Don't hurt him!"

Salesin knocked her aside with the back of his hand, and she fell back onto the floor. Without even glancing at her, the Crown Prince strode across the floor, grabbed the whimpering dog by the scruff of his neck, then, without a pause, yanked the casement open and tossed the dog through it.

"No!" Ulandra screamed. "NO!"

The royal bedchamber was in the tower, high up. There was nothing outside but a long drop to the cobblestone courtyard.

Ulandra knew her dog was dead. Just thinking of that furry little body sprawled bleeding in the courtyard made her want to die herself. "Wolf!" she whispered. Sobs choked her, and she struggled to remain silent.

Salesin looked down at her, still on her hands and knees. "Get up," he said. "You look ridiculous."

For a moment she was tempted to disobey, to stay where she was. Maybe he would kill her, too, and then she would not have to feel this pain. Something got her to her feet. She glanced sideways at the fireplace, at the poker. Could she reach it before he could stop her?

He's a trained warrior, she thought. *Of course he could.*

Salesin's anger seemed to have drained away, leaving him calm, relaxed. He met her gaze for a moment, then looked away, almost as if he were feeling some shame for what he'd done. "I'll get you another dog, Ulandra. That one wasn't worthy of a queen."

She forced words past the aching tightness in her throat. "No, thank you, my lord. I wish no other pet."

He shrugged, a flicker of anger stirring, then glanced at the window and controlled himself. "As you wish. I'll have my valet see to the corpse later tonight." He turned away, then glanced back. "My lady, pray do not challenge me again. That was most unwise of you. What happened tonight was *your* fault, not mine. I suggest you heed the lesson."

He strode toward the door, but paused just before going through it. "I'll send your maid to tend you. Do something about your face."

The next moment he was gone, and she was alone.

She stared at the door, then straightened, ignoring the cramp that assailed her. Quickly, she pulled on warm riding garb and her boots.

As she opened the bedchamber door, she met Bethina coming in with a bowl of water and some cloths. "Your Highness! Your face! Oh, my lady!"

Ulandra ignored the sympathy, and brushed aside the woman's hand as she attempted to touch her throbbing cheekbone, babbling about cold compresses. "There is no time for that now. Step aside."

"Your Highness," Bethina quavered, "Crown Prince Salesin said you were not to leave your suite."

Ulandra gave her a look that made the maid step back. "I don't care what he said," the Princess said tightly. "I'm going out. You can come with me to help me or stay here, I don't care which."

"Your Highness . . ." The maid wrung her hands fearfully. "I . . . I daren't cross him."

Ulandra nodded. "I understand. Just stand aside."

"Please!" squeaked the woman. "Please don't! He'll have me flogged!"

Ulandra paused for a moment, thinking, then grabbed the woman by her arm and dragged her over to the closet. "Step inside," she said.

"But—"

"Do it!"

"Yes, Your Highness!" Bethina stepped into the closet. Ulandra shut the door, then fetched the key and turned it. "There, now you're protected," she said, raising her voice so the maid could hear her through the panel. "Tell him I shoved you in there when you tried to stop me. I'll corroborate your story. Now I must go."

"My lady, where?" Bethina sounded as though she were weeping. "Where are you going?"

"Down to the courtyard," Ulandra said. "I have to bury my dog."

Khith hated Market Day in Q'Kal. Most of the time the Hthras liked the human city and enjoyed its bustling vitality. But Market Day always meant there would be strangers in town, and many Katans and Pelanese had never seen a Hthras. They stared, whispering rudely, and one burly teamster had even had the temerity to pick it up and pull the concealing hood off its head! Only a quickly muttered warding spell had saved the Hthras from being stripped bodily and exhibited to the crowd like some new variety of beast.

Market Day was also when the slave auctions were held in the town square. Khith's office and lodgings were close enough to the square that it could hardly avoid being aware of the entire distasteful scene. Much as Khith liked humans, it considered slavery an abomination practiced only by savages.

The Hthras was glad that it was now late spring and growing quite warm. It had suffered from the cold during the last of the winter and early spring, and only the fact that its practice was doing well had enabled it to manage. It had kept one serving lad busy for months just keeping the fires in its office, examining room, and bedchamber stoked.

Some Katans would never seek out a nonhuman physician, but many did. Hthras physicians had a far better record of cures than most human doctors. Since arriving in Q'Kal, Khith had treated lung diseases, infected eyes, risky pregnancies, and a host of other human ills.

One of the human physicians had even sent his wife to Khith when she began to bleed during her fifth month of pregnancy. Khith had examined her, then, gravely worried for both her and the child, had "gone inside" by means of drugs and a spell to check on her womb and the baby within it. It had found that the child was alive, which cheered the doctor, but the mother's womb was beginning to cramp with premature labor.

During a long, exhausting procedure, Khith had administered drugs, then managed to calm the poor woman's womb, induce it to cease the cramping. Then it had "gone inside" again, and moved the child slightly so its head was no longer pressing against the birth canal. Over the next few days, the bleeding slowed, then stopped. Khith prescribed strict bed rest for the patient, and it had worked. Three months later the woman delivered a healthy, if small, baby boy, with Khith officiating at the birth.

Success stories like that one had traveled rapidly through the city and even beyond. These days, Khith had a thriving practice. It missed home, though, and even more than the jungles, it missed the City of the Ancients. So much knowledge buried there! It worried that its people, angered by its actions, might attempt to destroy the city and all that lay within it. The city itself had its own wards—no one knew that better than Khith—but the Ancient ruins could not withstand any kind of determined assault. The Hthras was still haunted by the sense of foreboding it had received from reading the Ancient journal, but as the months passed, the terror faded.

Seeing that the humans were gathering for the slave auction, Khith quickened its stride, despite the bulky packages of herbs in its basket. Ahead of it lay the office, with a small, discreet sign hanging beside the door that read, HTHRAS PHYSICIAN. Khith believed in being frank about who and what it was. Humans who wanted human doctors did not make good patients.

Khith narrowed its large round eyes, seeing that two figures were walking up the steps to stand on the front stoop. Despite the masculine clothing, it realized that one of them was a woman. A woman, and a man.

No. Khith peered closer. A woman and a slave.

It hastened its pace, and soon it was close enough to see them more clearly. The woman was of medium height, young, with black hair braided severely back from her face. She wore hunter's garb, trousers and boots, and her skin was tanned with exposure to the sun. A dirty bandage was wrapped around one arm, and her face was bruised and bore faint streaks of what seemed to be blood. *A most unusual woman,* Khith thought.

The slave was not much taller than his mistress, and Khith's expert eye noted that the slackness of his skin indicated that he'd lost considerable weight recently. His features still bore a trace of youthful roundness, softness beneath his bearded jaw and chin, but his arms were muscled from hard labor. He wore a slave collar, though he'd pulled his shirt up so it wasn't visible from most angles.

As Khith approached, its housekeeper, Mistress Lengwill, opened the door. Khith's ears caught the woman's question. "We seek the Hthras physician. We have a badly injured man who needs treatment."

"Master Khith is not here," the housekeeper said. "He . . . it," she corrected herself with a grimace, "went off to the herbalist, and isn't expected back—"

"I am here," Khith called out.

They all turned to regard the Hthras as Khith approached. The woman stepped forward. Khith realized she was trying to conceal her distress, but her eyes and mouth gave her away.

"What is the problem?" the physician asked as soon as it was close enough, careful to speak clearly. Khith had learned pure Pelanese as a youngster, and its cultured, high-class accent was sometimes difficult for Katans to comprehend.

"Our friend," she began. "He's hurt, badly. A broken leg, and a wound in the gut . . ." Now that she was actually facing the doctor, her hard-won composure began to crumble. "He—he's dying, I think." Tears welled up in her green eyes, and she tried to blink them away.

"Where is he?" Khith asked.

The man pointed to the nearby alley. "We have him in a wagon, there. Our friend is watching over him."

Hearing the man's speech, Khith glanced at him, startled. *Pure Pelanese, educated Pelanese . . . from a slave?*

But there was no time for that now.

"Let me get my bag," Khith said.

Minutes later the woman and her slave led the Hthras down the alley to where an open wagon waited. As they approached, Khith saw that there were two humans in the wagon bed. A young woman with ash-pale hair and huge dark eyes cradled the head of a young man in her lap.

Khith reached the wagon and slung its bag up, then nimbly climbed up beside the woman. Expert fingers touched the man's forehead, took his pulse, felt the racing of his heart, and noted the bloody spittle oozing from his mouth, staining his short, trimmed beard. "How was he injured?" the healer asked, carefully removing the makeshift pad of bandage, soaked now with blood, which had been tightly strapped across the patient's belly.

The wound gaped, still bleeding sluggishly. Khith examined the edges, wondering if it was too late to stitch, then realized that there was damage to more than muscle and flesh. It ran its fingers across the wound, not quite touching it, sensing, evaluating, putting forth its other senses to evaluate the internal damage. Calling up its power, it went *inside . . .*

Perforation of the stomach wall and the spleen.

"How did this happen?" Khith repeated.

The young woman in the wagon bed stared at him silently, her eyes glassy with shock and exhaustion.

"I am the physician," Khith said, speaking as if to a child. "Tell me, how was this man wounded?"

She shook her head. "It was Boq'urak," she mumbled. "He was partly Changed . . ."

Khith abandoned its effort to get sense from her, and turned back to the slave. The man spoke up. "We were in a battle, Healer. The enemy grabbed him and clawed his stomach. Then he threw Jezzil against a rock."

Khith blinked. *What kind of enemy could inflict such a wound?* But there was no time for that now. It nodded. "Yes, he is bleeding inside. We will have to transport him to my surgery. Ask my housekeeper to give you the stretcher-board I keep for that purpose. Hurry."

The woman and her slave raced off.

Khith continued the examination, discovering a large lump on the back of the man's head, as well as numerous contusions.

"Please, Doctor, will he live?"

Khith had almost forgotten about the young woman with the strange, silvery hair. Hearing her timid question, it glanced up at her. "I don't know. I will do my best." *I've never seen anyone like this before. Where is she from?*

Something in her eyes, some gentleness, some vulnerability, touched the Hthras. "You are his wife?"

She started. "Oh, no, sir! I am Thia, his friend. Jezzil is like a brother to me."

Khith's fingers were moving again, returning to the worst wound, the one in the belly. "He may live," the Hthras said. "But he is in great danger until such time as I can stop him from bleeding inside."

For the first time, the injured man moved. His eyes half opened, though the Hthras could tell he was not really conscious. His arms and legs jerked, then flailed. "No!" he grunted, striking out at the Hthras. Only the young woman's quick thinking saved the physician from a hard blow.

"Jezzil, no!" Thia gasped, flinging herself across his arm. "Lie still!"

Khith saw the fear and desperation in the patient's eyes, and realized the young man was delirious, probably reliving the battle where he'd been injured. He thrashed and—

—disappeared.

Khith gaped at the place where he had been; was still, judging by the way Thia was lying. But the young warrior was gone.

Magic! Khith realized with a thrill. The Hthras had met a few humans here and there who possessed some abilities, healers and herbalists, mostly, but it had never seen anything like this.

As suddenly as he'd disappeared, the young man was back, lying exhausted and limp in the bed of the wagon.

Khith looked up to meet Thia's wide-eyed gaze. "What happened?" it demanded. "How did he do that?"

Her eyes filled with tears. "I don't know, sir. He did it during the battle, too. He's . . . he's a sorcerer, isn't he?"

"An adept of some kind, doubtless," Khith replied absently. "But all such questions will have to wait. Here are your friends with the body-board."

Minutes later Khith had the young warrior on the table that had been specially made for surgery. Its young human nurse, Beldor, was busily boiling suturing material and instruments, while Khith ground a dark brown substance to a powder in a mortar.

"What . . . what is that?" asked Thia, who was standing beside her friend, lest he thrash around again in his delirium. The patient was much quieter with her present, Khith had discovered.

"Epena," Khith said, measuring the powder carefully. "It will take away the pain of surgery, and keep him still while I work."

The physician took the measured dose and let it sift down into a long, narrow tube with openings on both ends. Stoppering the bottom end with its thumb, Khith took the tube over to the table. "Hold him still," it commanded.

Inserting the end of the tube into the patient's right nostril and pinching the left shut, Khith blew the epena into the young warrior's nasal passages. Jezzil gasped, choked, thrashed briefly, then lay still. His taut muscles relaxed and he lay unmoving.

"You can let him lie now," Khith said. "He cannot move."

Thia stared at her friend's slack features. "Can I . . . can I stay, Doctor?"

Khith regarded her searchingly. "I will have no time for sickness or swoons at the sight of blood or organs. Have you ever seen the insides of one of your kind?"

Thia nodded. "Hundreds, thousands, of times. I shall not faint or be sick."

Khith blinked again. *These people are an odd lot,* the Hthras thought. *When this is over, I shall have to ask them some questions.*

But at the moment it had other, more pressing concerns.

"Very well. Stand out of the way, here. Talk softly to him. He is not conscious, but he might hear you and take comfort from it."

"Yes, Doctor."

Khith was back at work again, mixing up yet another inhalant. "I shall be repairing the internal wounds using the fingers of my mind." It glanced at the nurse. "I shall go inside, as I did for Madame Gendavese. Do not speak to me or touch me. Understand?"

"Yes, Doctor," Beldor replied.

"Are there any questions before I commence the spell?"

The young man indicated a rack of suturing instruments. "Everything has been boiled, including the thread, sir. Will you be needing the tray?"

"Yes. I will close the outer layers manually, so I may check that all the bleeding has been halted," Khith said. "Are there any other questions?"

"No, sir."

"Good. I begin the spell. Let no one interfere. It could be dangerous."

"Yes, sir."

Khith checked the patient's pulse and respiration one more time, then, using the tube, inhaled the snuff twice, once in each flattened nostril. It felt the tingling, the roaring in its ears immediately. The drug worked quickly. It could see the walls of the room pulse in and out, as though they were all enclosed in a giant, beating heart . . .

Taking a deep breath, it closed its eyes and began the focusing chant:

"Still the muscle, bone, and tendon
Slow the heart, the blood, the brain
Bring the sleeping

Bring the nothing . . .

Bring the refuge
From the pain

Let the heart beat
with the tide-time,

Let the lungs
breathe season-slow

Bring renewal,

Bring the peace-time
Hibernating
creatures
know . . ."

Khith repeated the chant, all the while "reaching" with its mind into the stricken human's abdomen. When it did this kind of surgery, it envisioned a hand, a hand of the mind. And that hand was at the end of its own mental "arm." Its mental "fingers" were long, slender, and dexterous past any physical digits.

Khith repeated the focusing chant, feeling the drug take effect. Everything glimmered, glowed, as the life-spirit of each person present shone forth. Looking down at the patient's abdomen, Khith could see that this man's life-spirit was fading, not nearly as bright as it should have been. Over the abdomen was a dark patch that was spreading, growing ever larger, like some dark, malign blossom.

Chanting, Khith concentrated, flexing its mental "hand." Against the darkness that was growing outward from the patient's wound, it saw the hand glimmer, then begin to coalesce. It concentrated, focusing its will, working to strengthen those long digits.

Finally the "hand" was as solid to Khith's eyes as anything else in the room. *Time to begin,* it thought. Slowly, deliberately, it reached inside the man's belly, using its mental "eyes" to find the great tears in the organs. *There, the stomach . . .*

Slowly, carefully, Khith brought the two edges of the rip together, fitting them to each other as it would have pieced together a sheet of ripped parchment. As it drew together the edges, it concentrated, pinching the edges together, then causing the ends of its mental fingers to become white-hot, cauterizing the wound as it fused the ripped edges together. It was slow, painstaking work, but finally the wound in the stomach was sealed.

Now for the spleen . . .

As Khith worked, it could sense the flow of life-force growing stronger as the internal bleeding slowed, then stopped. The man was rallying. Khith sensed his aura growing stronger, brighter. It recalled the way this human had disappeared. *He has the power,* the Hthras thought. *Possibly great power. But untrained, undisciplined. Power without discipline is dangerous—if he does not learn to control it, it will be his undoing.*

Finally the painstaking job was done. The man . . . what was his name? *Jezzil? Yes, that's it.* Jezzil would have to lie still for several days, to allow the tissues to knit completely, but barring infection, the warrior should make a full recovery.

Slowly, deliberately, Khith withdraw its mental "hand" from the patient's abdomen. Now for the external layers of tissue, which would require manual stitching. The cauterization process was exhausting, and Khith reserved that healing technique for serious internal rips.

The Hthras stood braced against the table until the effects of the drug began to dwindle. It had timed the dosage well; it took only a few more minutes until the drug-induced haze was gone.

Slowly, Khith opened its eyes, saw Beldor and Thia staring at it. It held up its physical hands, flexed them. "Cleansing soap, please."

Beldor produced the special soap that Khith had the

herbalist make for just this purpose. It had a strong, astringent scent as the Hthras lathered its hands repeatedly.

Finally the physician was ready. It began removing the pressure pads one by one and stitching up the layers of tissue, then flesh, that were revealed. It was a long, slow process. "He will be scarred," Khith commented. "The wounds are more than half a day old, yes?"

"Yes," Thia replied. "We came as quickly as we could, but we were attacked in the barren lands, and it took us all night to get back to Q'Kal."

Khith took two more stitches, then knotted the gut it was using in lieu of thread. "Finished here," it said. "Now, let us see to these other injuries."

After examining and cleansing the head wound, which was bloody but superficial, and resplinting the broken leg so it would heal straight and clean, the Hthras stepped back with a sigh of weariness. "That's all for now. He must remain quiet and prone for at least a week. Quick movements too early could undo the healing I have wrought."

"We will stay with him," Thia promised. "We will make sure he is not left alone."

Khith shook its head. "Taking him elsewhere would not be wise. I wish him to remain here so I may check him several times each day. I have a few beds in my infirmary, and none are occupied at the moment. For the next day, he must not be left alone. Are you and your companions willing to sit with him, mistress?"

"Of course," she replied.

The Hthras glanced over at Beldor. "You can instruct Miss Thia in what to watch for, and you will administer his medication."

"Yes, Doctor."

"I shall give you a draught to administer if the pain becomes too great. No more than three per day, with at least seven hours to pass between doses."

"Yes, Doctor," Beldor said.

Thia looked at the Hthras, concern shadowing her expression. "Doctor, we have little money."

Khith gave her a stern glance. "Without proper care, your friend could still die. He will stay here. We will discuss my payment later."

She grimaced slightly, but nodded.

Khith looked down at the young warrior's sleeping face. Now that the terrible internal wounds were closed and the bleeding stopped, it had regained a slight tinge of color. *Poor youth,* Khith thought. *Carrying around this power inside him, probably not lessoned in its use . . . what a terrible burden. And dangerous. If he is not taught, the power will consume him, or drive him into madness. As he recovers, we will explore his abilities. To find one with such latent power, it is almost like finding a new discovery in my lost city.*

The Hthras had not felt so intrigued by anything since it had come to Q'Kal. This young warrior, this Jezzil, posed a fascinating puzzle.

Khith looked up to see Thia's anxious expression. "Relax," it told her. "Be calm. Your friend will live, with proper care. He will live, and he will grow. He must. That which ceases to grow begins to die."

Eregard sat in the Hthras physician's parlor, waiting, while Thia and Talis conferred together. With its dull red carpet and heavy, woven draperies, it was a very human room that gave no indications that the proprietor was Hthras. Eregard had seen Hthras before, when a delegation of them came to court when he was a lad. He could remember seeing some of their art in presents they'd made to Agivir, but there wasn't a hint of anything like that in this room, which was so neat and spare it looked like a stage setting in a playhouse. Only the fireplace, swept and empty, showed any sign that it had ever been used.

Eregard strained his ears. He could hear most of what Talis and Thia were saying as they divided up the task of sitting with Jezzil. He was angry. Talis had not included him as one of the watchers.

He's my friend, too, he thought resentfully. *I helped to bring him here.*

He thought of the afternoon he would face, going back out

into the wasteland to retrieve Clo's body so she could be buried by her guild-fellows. *I am trusted to deal with the dead, but not to watch the living.*

He dropped his gaze, so Talis would not see the resentment in his eyes. *You fool. You keep forgetting you're a slave, and thinking you're a man.* Anger rose up in him, and he forced it back. Slaves could not afford to be angry. Anger led to actions like the ones that had brought him here to Q'Kal.

Now the two women were whispering, and Eregard could no longer hear what they were saying. He saw Thia's expression change, and she glanced sideways at him, plainly upset. Eregard tensed. *Oh, no.*

Talis said something else, urgently, and Thia finally nodded, her shoulders drooping. She gave Eregard a quick, distressed glance, then looked away.

A footfall from the doorway made them all look up to see the Hthras physician standing there. "Your friend has been moved to the infirmary and is resting comfortably. Miss Thia, will you go relieve Beldor, please? I will have my housekeeper bring you something to eat."

"Thank you, Doctor," Thia said, and followed the doctor out of the room.

Eregard glanced over at Talis, to find her watching him with a thoughtful expression that made his mouth go dry. He forced himself to stay silent as he rose to face her. *The slave waits for the master to speak.*

Talis came over and stood looking at him. "I'm sorry," she said finally.

"Sorry about what, mistress?"

She reached up to touch the place on his collar that was file-scored. "You need some salve on those raw places. I'll ask the doctor for some."

Eregard's hand went up, reflexively, to cover the place where he'd begun filing through his collar. "I . . . I didn't realize you'd noticed," he said, realizing how inane it sounded.

"Of course I did," she said. "And because of that, you'll have to be shackled at night from now on. I hoped it wouldn't have to come to that, but now I have no choice."

"Come to what?" Eregard asked, his heart thudding so hard he felt dizzy with fear.

"Thia is upset. She begged me not to do this. I had decided against it, but now that Bayberry's gone, I don't have anything else of value. You must understand, Eregard." Talis's green eyes were sad but determined. "Someone is going to have to pay for Jezzil's treatment. Thia can't, and I have little money left."

Eregard stared at her but said nothing. Talis reached up to touch the collar again. "And I see that I can't trust you not to run away, so I'll accompany you to bring back Clo's body."

Eregard flushed angrily. *It never occurred to me to try and run this afternoon! I liked Clo! Goddess! Leave me some honor, Talis!* But he remained silent. Slaves dared not address their owners in that manner.

She took a deep breath. "We've missed the auction for today, so we'll have to wait a week. But next Market Day, I'm going to have to sell you."

Eregard tried to keep his face blank, but something in his eyes must have betrayed him. Thia shook her head grimly. "I wish it could be otherwise. You've served me well, and you deserve better, Eregard." She sighed. "I'll try to see that you go to a good home. I'm sorry, but there's nothing else I can do."

13

Lessons

Jezzil dreamt that he was dead. Over and over, always the same dream, and always he ended up dead.

In the dream he fought, swinging his sword, moving, dodging, trying to connect with that horror that had once been human. The monster, still recognizable as something that had once been a man, swung back at him, and he felt its talons tear his belly, filling it with fiery pain. The pain was so bad that he could not breathe, could not move, could only lie there, aware only of the pain in his gut. His insides screamed that they had been sundered, violated, ripped . . .

Blackness waited for him, all-consuming, and each time he fought it as hard as he had in real life. Fought it . . . and lost.

Even as he cycled through the dream, time after endless time, something else kept trying to surface in his mind. The pain was so bad that he could not remember, could not focus, could not *think*. But each time, he tried. He knew there was something he cared about as much as he cared about the pain, but the pain would not let him think, or remember, or feel anything but the agony of his violated belly.

And then the pain lessened and gradually ebbed. It was

still there, still a throbbing ache, but it no longer filled his mind, his body; it was no longer the entirety of his world. He realized he was lying on a soft surface and that there was light, instead of darkness, touching his eyelids.

He could think again, and remember.

Thia—what happened to Thia?

Jezzil struggled to open his eyes, feeling the grip of the pain, the blackness, loosen further. He willed himself to awaken.

He managed to blink, then open his eyes. As he'd guessed, daylight surrounded him. After so long in the pain-filled darkness, the brightness was dazzling. His lips moved. "Thia?" His voice was so weak that he couldn't tell if he'd actually made any sound at all.

Jezzil realized he was inside a building. That was a ceiling overhead, not the sky. The ceiling was painted white, and there were beams running across it.

He tried to turn his head, but a stab of pain accompanied the motion. Jezzil clenched his teeth to suppress a groan, but the person sitting next to him heard the sound, slight as it was.

"You are awake!" a voice exclaimed in excellent Pelanese, and someone bent over him.

Jezzil blinked and could not repress a start.

What is that?

The being's face was lightly furred, with huge eyes and round, upstanding ears. The fur was light brown on its face, though the eyes were ringed with a darker, almost sable-colored growth. The nose was flat, the mouth small and narrow-lipped. The creature wore a robe that concealed its body.

The being spoke again. "Have no fear, Jezzil. I am Khith, your physician. Your friends brought you to me so I could heal you from the wounds you suffered during the battle."

Jezzil tried to speak, but his mouth was so dry that only a croak emerged. The physician—Khith? Had that been the name?—seemed to realize his problem, and immediately produced a cup. Supporting his head expertly, the doctor gave him water, allowing him only small sips.

Jezzil felt the fur of the creature's arm against his cheek, accompanied by an odor he'd never smelled before. Slightly musky, faintly sweet, it was not unpleasant.

Before his thirst was satisfied, Khith took the cup from his lips. "Enough for now. More in a few minutes. You had a question?"

He tried again, and this time managed sound. "Thia?"

"She is safe. As are your companions Talis and Eregard."

Jezzil started to ask about Clo, but before he could manage it, he realized that the effort of speaking, listening, and simply drinking the water had tired him more than a full day's foot-march.

His eyes closed and he slept. This time there were no dreams.

When next he awoke, he felt much better. Stronger, and the pain in his head had subsided to a dull ache. He opened his eyes and managed to turn his head.

"Jezzil!"

He knew that voice. She was sitting beside him, and, while she appeared tired, worn, she was obviously uninjured.

"Thia," he whispered. "You're safe."

She slid her hand over his, holding it tightly. "Thanks to you," she said. "Thanks to you and Talis and Clo and Eregard. You all risked your lives to save me. I never had friends before." She looked down, and he saw a tear slide down her cheek. "I'm so grateful."

"Is everyone all right?" It was an effort to speak, but he had to know.

She glanced up at him, then her eyes fell again. Jezzil felt a sudden chill. He'd seen that look on the faces of battle comrades before. "What happened?" he demanded, his voice stronger now, rough and fierce.

She swallowed. "The god . . . He took over Master Varn. You fought Him, all of you did. You were hurt: broken leg, a crack on the head, and injuries inside. Dr. Khith saved you. But . . ." Her voice wavered. "Clo, Clo is . . . was . . ."

His fingers tightened on her hand. She was crying now, softly, sounding very young. Jezzil sighed, feeling a stab of grief. "She was a brave fighter," he said, translating the Chonao ritual words into the language of Kata. "She had courage and she kept her weapons clean."

She wiped away the tears on her sleeve, snuffling, then nodded. "I miss her. We all do."

"Where are Talis and Eregard?"

"Talis has been meeting with Castio and some of his confederates. She goes out at night to the taverns where the royal troops go. She's never said, but I suspect she's gathering information for Castio."

Jezzil nodded. "Figures," he said. "She's devoted to his Cause."

"She takes Eregard with her everywhere she goes," Thia said, staring down at her hands. "She's going to sell him, she says. Next Market Day."

Jezzil closed his eyes. "My father always kept slaves," he whispered. "I never thought about them. They were just there. Like the horses, or the stable cats. It wasn't until I met Eregard that I realized . . ." He trailed off, not sure what he was trying to say.

"Realized they were really people?"

Jezzil nodded. "Something like that."

"I don't think Talis wants to do it, but we need the money."

"I have a few coins put by," Jezzil said. "Hidden behind the loose floorboard under my bedroll."

"I got them," Thia said. "I used them to make the first payment to the doctor. I gave up the lodgings. I'm staying with Talis and Eregard now, in their room. It's cheaper that way."

"Oh . . ." Jezzil was tired, but he had one more question he had to ask. "What was—who was—that doctor? I never saw anything like it—him . . ."

"It," she corrected. "Healer Khith saved you. You were injured so seriously, and they told us the Hthras doctor was the best physician in the city. We brought you here, and it saved you. Used magic to heal the tears inside you."

Jezzil's eyes widened. "Magic?"

"Yes. The Hthras have magic that is greater than any I

ever saw before," Thia said. "They look very strange, but Healer Khith is an excellent doctor. We've been talking. When I'm not here with you."

"Talking . . ." Jezzil managed. "About what?"

Thia glanced over her shoulder, and then her lips shaped a word so softly he could barely hear her. "Boq'urak," she breathed. "Khith knows of Him. Khith told me that—"

She broke off as footsteps approached the room. A young man came through the doorway, carrying a small glass filled with a dark liquid. "Time for your medicine," he said.

Jezzil grimaced. He had dim memories of how the stuff tasted. He swallowed it dutifully, though. He wanted to ask Thia what the healer had said about Boq'urak, but the draught made him even sleepier.

When he awoke, hours later, he was able to sit up, propped on pillows, and eat some broth and a bit of bread. Khith came in to examine his wound, and pronounced that it was healing well.

That evening Talis and Eregard came in to sit with Thia, and the four talked in hushed voices about their battle.

"On Pela, we used to hear about the God of the North," Eregard said. "I never thought it was real, though. I never saw anything like that."

"He was not fully Incarnate," Thia murmured. "Be glad."

"The creature we fought was powerful," Jezzil said, "but it could be fought. Its magic was formidable, though." He shook his head, thinking of the force that had picked him up and flung him as though he were nothing more than a stick figure of a warrior.

"And that . . . that *thing* tracked Thia all the way from Amaran," Talis said slowly. "Or caused Master Varn to track her. My question is: we drove it away, for *now*. But what's to keep it from returning?"

The companions sat in silence as the implications of Talis's question sank in.

Eregard glanced over at Thia. "You must not go out alone from now on. He waited until you were alone before. Jezzil

is right, he's not all-powerful, or he'd just have whisked you
away by magical means. Instead he used a man, and that
man drove a wagon into the desert."

Thia nodded. "It takes time and preparation for the Incarnation." Her hands twisted in the folds of her skirt as she sat
beside Jezzil's narrow infirmary bed. "But, my friends, this
is not your fight. You have already done too much for me.
More than anyone has a right to expect. Clo is dead." She
took a deep breath. "I don't know what would be better. To
try and go off farther, perhaps travel down to the Sarsithe, or
go back to Amaran, give myself up to the priests. At least if
I did that, I would be given to the Dawn, to make sure the
Sun rises. A clean death . . ."

"No." Three voices spoke as one.

"But—"

Jezzil struggled up on one elbow. "Thia, stop it," he ordered. "And if you try to run away from us, as you did from
Shekk Marzet, I will find you. We are comrades. I will never
abandon a comrade again."

Thia opened her mouth as though she were going to ask
what he meant, but after studying his face, evidently
changed her mind.

Jezzil looked at her. "Promise us. *Promise,*" he said. He
was tired from sitting up, but he refused to lie down again
until she spoke.

"Jezzil," she began, "you have to understand. Boq'urak . . .
is not to be crossed. He's a *god.*"

"Promise," Jezzil insisted. "Thia, you must promise."

"If I give myself up, He may not bother with you," she
said.

Talis grimaced. "I stuck a sword in him, and Jezzil kicked
him in his ugly mouth. He'll remember us. If you're
doomed, we're just as doomed. But let's not make it easy on
him, Thia. Promise us."

Eregard reached over and took Thia's hand, holding it
tightly. Jezzil felt a stir of resentment as he watched color
rise in her pale cheeks. "Thia, they're right," the slave said.
"Promise."

She looked from one to the other, then sighed. "I can't fight all of you. Very well, I promise."

What little strength Jezzil had abruptly vanished. Stifling a groan, he let himself slide back down against the pillows. His eyes were so heavy he could not even summon the strength to wish his friends good night.

Eregard was heartily sick of smoky back rooms and whispered conversations. Talis always took him with her when she went on her missions, but he was not, of course, included in the actual conversations or planning sessions. Instead, Talis would hobble him as she would have a horse, using a locked leg anklet and a chain.

When she did her "tavern wench" act, he wasn't chained, but instead set to work in the kitchens, under the close supervision of the cook or tavernmaster. Talis wasn't forgetting his half-scored collar, and she took no chances.

His hands, already callused and weathered from work in the fields, grew scratched and chapped from washing cutlery in steaming water, using the harsh soap that was necessary to scour away the cooking grease.

It was in the kitchens that he was able to actually carry out the mission his father had set him. The cook gossiped, and so did the other scullions. Eregard had only to scrub pots and keep his ears open to hear all sorts of interesting tidbits.

"Two soldiers in here last night, and they were talkin' about their pay had been cut, and how any man that protested was likely to be flogged for insubordination. Said there were more floggings every day. Their captain had new orders, from overseas. Untidy uniform, five lashes. Sleeping on guard duty, twenty lashes."

Eregard winced.

"A new troopship docked yesterday. Fresh troops. Even the Governor's personal guard has suffered desertions."

"They say Castio's gaining recruits every day. Every time Prince Salesin dumps another shipload of convicts here on Katan soil and they go to rapin' and killin' and stealin', Castio gains troops. Folk don't like workin', only to have some brigands come along and walk away with it all."

And the next day: "Didja hear the Regent has raised the property tax?"

"*Again*? That's twice since last harvest!"

"The wife and me are thinkin' of moving out to the frontier. Those royal tax collectors don't get out there so often, and a lot of 'em, they say, don't make it back."

"Got room in your wagon?"

"Sure, I can always use another outrider. Can you shoot straight?"

"I can learn!"

"They say the savages are thick as flies on the frontier."

The shorter of the two scullions leaned toward his friend and lowered his voice. "Did you hear?"

Eregard strained to hear him, resisting the urge to turn his head. But he scoured softly and gently, careful not to clang the pots.

"Hear what?"

"They say that now Castio's got militia drillin' in every good-sized town on the coast, he's movin' west. There's talk he has this new kind of musket ball, same as the royalists have. It gets you twice the range, and 'tis far more accurate. Those frontiersmen are deadly shots, they say. And they're not the only ones who'll fight out there."

"He wouldn't recruit *savages*?"

"He's a bold'un. Who's to know what he'd do? But they say he—"

Just then a pot slipped from Eregard's greasy grasp and fell with a loud clanging onto the stone floor. The Prince cursed himself as he muttered apologies and picked it up. Seeing him mopping up the greasy water, the cook curtly ordered him to scrub the entire kitchen floor.

As Eregard scrubbed, the brush moving in ever-widening circles on the rough stone floor, his mind was busy. *I must get home. Father has to take control back from Salesin. He needs to know how close to revolution Kata is. I must escape!*

But Talis was careful. Not once in the week before his up-

coming sale did Eregard get an opportunity. She even hobbled him at night. "I'm sorry," she always said. "Wake me if
you need to use the privy."

Night after night Eregard lay there, curled on his side, listening to the breathing of the two women who shared the
bed. He found himself praying to the Goddess for the first
time in a long time, praying that Talis would sell him to
somebody here in Q'Kal. If he remained here in Q'Kal, he
had a chance of someday getting free and being rescued by
the Royal Governor. If she sold him as a laborer, or farm-
hand, his chances of ever seeing home again—much less of
warning his father about the revolution brewing here in
Kata—were so slim as to be negligible.

The days crept by, as Talis frequented taverns, gathering
information from drunken royal troops by day, then, late at
night, passing on all she had learned to Rufen Castio or his
lieutenants.

Each morning, Eregard awoke realizing he was one day
closer to the next Market Day. Another day closer to standing there on the auction block and being sold like a beast.

If I ever get home, he vowed each night, *I'll do something
about this. It's just not right. People aren't* things *to be sold.*

Jezzil was learning to walk again, hobbling across the infirmary room floor on crutches, under Thia's watchful eye. He
was intent on moving smoothly, testing his splinted leg to
see how much weight it would bear.

"That's good," she encouraged, moving beside him, but
not actually touching him. "Use your hands and forearms
when you walk. Try not to hunch over."

As he moved, using the concentration techniques he'd
learned as a Chonao warrior, adjusting his balance to the
crutches, the door to the infirmary opened and Khith entered. Jezzil glanced up at the little Hthras physician, and the
sudden movement caused his foot to slip on the waxed
wooden floor. He managed to catch himself with a grunt of
effort, but the stab of pain from his leg made the whole
world go gray and dim.

When he returned to himself, he was seated on the bench beside the fireplace, steadied by Thia on one side and Khith on the other. The Hthras reached for his hand, took his pulse, and made a reproving sound. "You must be easy on yourself, young Jezzil. You cannot regain yourself in just one day."

Jezzil nodded, taking a deep breath. "At least I made it across the room," he pointed out. "I have to be able to get around while this heals. I've got to be able to walk and climb stairs."

Khith looked at him, the Hthras's huge, round eyes filled with intelligence and understanding. "Yes, I understand, but if you fall and break that leg again, you will limp for the rest of your life, despite anything I might do to treat you."

The Hthras glanced over at Thia and nodded at the door. "Why don't you get something to eat, my dear? I need to speak with Jezzil in private."

Thia looked curious, but she went without demur.

Jezzil regarded the Hthras with his own measure of curiosity. "Speak to me? About what?"

He had little experience reading Hthras features, but even Jezzil could tell that the physician was concerned . . . nay, worried. "My young patient," the healer began, "please listen to me. And reply with the truth. How long have you been able to vanish?"

Jezzil stiffened. *How can the doctor know about that?* he wondered.

"Or, perhaps I should say, how long have you been able to fling the illusion that you have vanished into the minds of observers? Please, be truthful. Your answer is important."

The Chonao was silent, wondering what to say. Obviously, he must have done a Casting while he was unconscious. He remembered the fevered dreams he'd experienced, dreams of fighting Boq'urak over and over.

Unlike a human, Khith knew how to be silent, and wait. Jezzil looked over at the little physician, and finally decided to be truthful but cautious. "My people call it Casting," he said. "Usually Casters show the ability when they are young, still schoolboys. With me it came late, I don't know why."

"Only males have the ability?"

Jezzil shook his head. "I don't know. I never heard of any women having power. But things with women are different for my people." He smiled thinly. "Women such as Talis and Thia do not exist in Ktavao. The women I have known were quiet, hiding their faces from strangers, living secluded lives, existing only to care for their families. We have no women warriors, or female scholars, for that matter."

"When did you do your first Casting, as you call it?"

"Last winter. Nearly six months ago, now." Jezzil went on to give a bit of his story to the healer—omitting mention of how he had abandoned his comrades to the fire. That, he'd never spoken of to anyone. He dreamed of it, sometimes . . . and in his dreams, Barus was always there, trapped in the smoke, watching with horror as Jezzil abandoned him to the flames.

"I see." The physician's huge eyes were fixed, unblinking, on his face. "Young Jezzil, there are things I sense about you that I must tell you. First of all, you have power within you, and this power will try to claim you. You must be taught to control it, to use it. The lessoning will be hard. It requires great powers of concentration and great courage. You are a warrior, but what I speak of is beyond the courage one learns to have in battle."

Courage! Jezzil had a strong flash of memory, seeing a harmless young woman impaled on his sword, and then he remembered leaping from the window to escape the inferno behind him. He felt himself flush with anger and shame. *I have no courage. I am a warrior in name only.*

He shook his head, refusing to meet Khith's gaze. "I am no adept, Doctor! I am no scholar! I can read and write, true enough, but the idea of spending time with dusty scrolls and rotting tomes makes me shudder. I am only a soldier, skilled a little in the ways of fighting. The road you speak of is not my road to walk." His fingers tightened on the wood of the crutch he still held. "Not my road, Doctor. I can't." His voice sounded thick in his own ears, but he had to make the doctor understand. "I *can't.*"

Khith made a low sound, almost like a moan of distress. Jezzil looked up. For the first time, he could recognize emotion as it flickered across Khith's face. The Hthras shook its head grimly. "You do not understand," it said. "You must—"

"No," Jezzil broke in, "*You* do not understand, Doctor. You say I must have courage?" He shook his head and fought back a bitter laugh. "Courage is not something I am blessed with."

"You fought Boq'urak," Khith countered. "I know a little something of the Ancient One. It is mentioned in some of the scrolls in the ruined city. Even if it was not fully Incarnate, it—He—is a fearful creature. It took courage to engage Him."

Jezzil shook his head. "It's not courage when you don't have time to think. You say that doing magic requires thought, discipline . . . and courage. I'm not good at any of those things. Thank you, Doctor, but I'm not someone who could learn magic." He forced a smile that was meant to reassure. "Just because I can Cast once in a while doesn't mean I'm some kind of sorcerer."

Khith's huge, unblinking eyes held only concern and sadness. "Young Jezzil, it is not so simple as you try to make it. If you do not learn to harness it, control it, as you would control your steed in battle, the power within you will conquer you and kill you, as surely as a blade that cleaves your head from your body."

"*Kill* me?" Jezzil was startled. "This magic, this power, could do that?"

Khith reached over to lay its long, lightly furred fingers over Jezzil's arm. "I swear to you, I am speaking the truth. Listen to me, and I shall explain. This ability is indeed a power. Your potential is great. My people call what you have, what *I* have, avundi. It means the ability of the mind, with proper focusing and conditions, to influence internal and external events. I can sense it within others, as surely as I can smell the ocean when the wind is right. I suspect that you can do the same."

Jezzil stared at the physician. "You say I have this avundi. Does everyone have it?"

"There is no way to know unless it manifests. Many people have a trace of it. They can work minor cures, charm warts, or cast love spells. Simple magics that require only a little lessoning. Unlike you, these people are in little danger from the avundi they possess."

Khith stood up and began to pace the infirmary, moving with a restless, inhuman grace. Jezzil saw the back of its robe move, side to side, and realized, for the first time, that the Hthras had a tail. *Like a cat that lashes its tail when it is upset.*

"Jezzil, listen to me!" Khith's tone was sharp. "I know you don't want to hear this, but you are in grave danger. You have great potential to learn to be a powerful sorcerer. But if you do *not* learn to leash and control your avundi, the avundi within you is quite likely to drive you mad."

The Hthras turned to face the human, and this time the doctor's agitation was plain. "Did you understand what I said?"

Jezzil nodded, then shrugged. "Doctor, I will have to take that risk. I am no sorcerer. I scarcely have the right to call myself a warrior."

"You are willing to risk madness?"

The Chonao shrugged. "You say there is a chance. Once warned, perhaps the madness can be fought, or prevented."

"Jezzil, as a physician, I have been permitted into asylums for the deranged. I could sense the avundi there, in great quantities. It had driven those poor creatures mad. We are not speaking of those who are gently forgetful, or perhaps a bit, what is the word . . ." Khith made a circling gesture with its fingers beside its temple. "I am speaking of people so tormented by their inner demons that they must be bound lest they tear out their own eyes with their own fingers."

Khith's words made Jezzil shudder. "But I—" He broke off, shaking his head. "Doctor, you do not understand."

"Make me understand," Khith said, walking over to put a slender hand on Jezzil's shoulder. The Hthras's huge eyes were liquid with sympathy. Jezzil swallowed. "Tell me, young Jezzil."

The human shook his head again. "I can't," he muttered.

"Jezzil, the fact that you were able to do these illusions, these 'Castings,' as you call them, without any lessoning at all tells me your inherent avundi is great. And so is the danger for you and those around you, unless you learn to control it."

Jezzil considered what the Hthras had said. He knew that the physician was correct in saying that he could sense magic. It was as distinct as an odor that, once smelled, would always be remembered.

Khith watched him in silence. "Harness it, control it," Jezzil said finally. "You mean, learn to become a sorcerer? A witch?"

"Your people tend to regard avundi as something unnatural, to be feared," Khith said. "My people use it as naturally as we use tools to cultivate, or thread to weave. I could teach you," the physician said. "Last night I did a foreseeing. I saw us together in the darkness, surrounded by water. The ground beneath us was unsteady. We were using avundi. Together."

Jezzil regarded the little creature for a long moment. *What would it be like,* he wondered, *to be able to do magic at will? Can a warrior also be a witch? A sorcerer?*

Then the familiar image from his dream was in his mind. Barus was staring at him pleadingly as the flames crept closer. *Khith says this requires courage. You have no courage. You are a coward, and you know it. You will never be anything but a coward.*

"Let me think about it," he said finally. "I will give you my answer tomorrow."

There was a new priest at court, and all of the lords and ladies were whispering about him. Ulandra heard about him from one of her ladies-in-waiting, Marquise Jonala q'Stevrii. "And he's handsome, Your Highness," she burbled as she arranged Ulandra's hair for the Spring Ball. "Too bad this Varlon is a priest." She giggled, then, as Ulandra caught her eye in the mirror, hastily turned the sound into a cough. "I mean, too bad good looks have to be wasted on a priest.

He's tall, with the darkest eyes . . . black eyes that seem to see right through into your spirit, Your Highness."

Ulandra, who worshiped the Goddess—as did most Pelanese—was only interested because the news took her mind off the coming ball. She hated public appearances. She'd been wed for months now, and the whispering and barely veiled glances at her waistline only served to remind her that her life was in shambles.

A barren princess, she thought bleakly. *Is there anything worse?* She thought of her husband's mother, whose sweet, ailing face grew paler and thinner seemingly each day. And yet, Elnorin had produced three sons. *Just one thing . . . a barren queen,* she realized.

"All done, Your Highness!" Jonala said.

Ulandra studied herself in the mirror. Her elaborate hairstyle and the sapphire and diamond tiara made her appear older. Her skin felt tight and dry from the cosmetics carefully painted to enhance her eyes, cheeks, and lips. Still, Jonala had done her job well. "Thank you, Marquise," she said, attempting to inject a warmth she didn't feel into her voice. "You have done well."

"Now you must dress, Your Highness. I will call the others," Jonala said, and slipped out.

Ulandra stood up, stretched, then took a last deep breath. When her ladies returned, they would adjust her corset, and she wouldn't be able to breathe easily until it was loosened, hours from now.

At least she knew that Salesin wouldn't be spending the night with her. She had heard that he had a new mistress, a red-haired countess who was married to one of King Agivir's top generals. With the threat of invasion from the east, as the Redai's forces took island after island, General Goljone was probably grateful that his wife was too occupied with the Crown Prince to demand his attention.

I am becoming such a cynic, Ulandra thought bleakly. *If only I could escape this court . . . this twisted parody of life. If only I could just run away.*

She heard the rustle of fabric and the sounds of footsteps,

then the Marquise, the seamstress, and two other waiting women came through the open door, carrying the voluminous folds of the ball gown.

Ulandra lay down upon the bed so they could fasten the corset hooks down the front. Lying down, it wasn't too restrictive, but when her women pulled her back up and set her on her feet, she had to suppress a whimper of misery. The corset narrowed her waist to nothing, and pushed her small breasts up so high that she actually could wear a low-cut gown without being laughed at, but she felt as imprisoned as any cutpurse in the royal dungeons.

Briskly, as though she were a life-sized doll, her ladies-in-waiting clothed her. Stockings, garters, shoes . . . suddenly she was several inches taller. Underskirt, then two petticoats, one stiffly starched, one with a hoop in the bottom to make her skirt fall correctly.

And then the dress. Maidens were supposed to wear delicate pastels, or white. This was her first ball gown since she'd been married, and it was dramatic in a way none of her other dresses had ever been. It was of a royal blue satin, trimmed with sapphire lace at the bodice, and small lace panniers and a lace rosette in back. The skimpy lace sleeves revealed the tops of her shoulders and most of her arms.

The ladies clucked over the fit of the sleeves and bodice as they made hasty alterations. Ulandra realized she'd probably lost weight since the dress had first been fitted.

When they finally allowed her to examine herself in the looking glass, Ulandra felt faintly scandalized at the amount of white flesh she was baring. She could see the rounded tops of her breasts, and had to fight the urge to cross her arms over her bosom.

"Your Highness, you are beautiful!" the marquise assured her.

"It's awfully low," Ulandra muttered, tugging at the bodice. Her ladies gently but firmly moved her hands.

"'Tis the fashion, Your Highness," Jonala reassured her. "Oh, they'll all want to dance with you!"

Just as long as Salesin leaves me alone, I don't care.

"Thank you, ladies. You have done your work well." Ulandra forced warmth into her voice. "Now, we go." Summoning a smile she'd practiced, so it didn't look like a grim rictus, Ulandra left her room, walking past bowing guards, feeling a bit like a ship under full sail heading into shoal water.

The ladies' predictions proved accurate—even King Agivir took a brief turn around the dance floor with her. Despite her feet and lack of breath, Ulandra actually began to enjoy herself. Salesin had not made an appearance, so she could relax and feel safe.

The son of the Duke of Vestala claimed her for a vigorous row dance, and Ulandra was too busy to do anything except count her steps and try not bump into anyone else. When the dance ended, she was breathless—but actually smiling. She curtsied to the young man. "Thank you, m'lord."

He bowed low, and the motion caused the gold braid on his dress uniform to sparkle. Ulandra had noticed that dress uniforms had replaced evening garb for many of the noblemen. "You do me too much honor, Your Highness. Every man in the room envies me, dancing with the greatest beauty in the kingdom."

Ulandra blushed and had to stop herself from giggling. *No more wine for me,* she thought. *I must keep a clear head, so I can watch out for Salesin.*

Her corset was too tight to allow her to eat much, but she managed to nibble on some grapes and a bit of cheese at the refreshment table. She stood there, balancing a plate, enjoying the swirl of color on the dance floor, swaying slightly to the lilting strains of music from the orchestra.

As she watched, Prince Adranan bowed deeply, then twirled one of her ladies-in-waiting to the strains of a baracole. The Prince was quick on his feet, despite his beer-barrel substance. He bounced and hopped and his stomach performed its own bouncing, swaying movements. Ulandra almost laughed aloud, but covered her mouth and turned it into a cough.

The dance music stopped, and the dancers bowed and curtsied. Conversation in the room swelled to a muted roar.

Without warning, silence fell. The entire ballroom grew unnaturally still.

Confused, Ulandra turned to the marquise to ask her what had happened, but the silence was gone, replaced by an undertone of whispers and titters from the crowd. Ulandra stood there, her mouth half open, and saw the courtiers bowing deeply, in succession, a wave of bowing that rippled along like a whitecap at sea. She stiffened, and something seemed to clench inside her, like a corset squeezing her heart and lungs. *Oh, no!*

She glimpsed her husband's black head, and then—

—time seemed to freeze, along with heart and breath, as she caught a glimpse of red hair piled high in an elaborate coiffure. *'Tis the countess! Denmara Goljone! His whore.*

She felt the blood leave her face, and for a moment she swayed, light-headed. As bad as Salesin had ever been, she'd never dreamed he might do something like this. Escorting his mistress to a royal ball was so far outside the bounds of civilized behavior that Ulandra had no idea what to do.

Her mind demanded that she leave, but her body didn't seem to want to obey her. She stood there, unable to move, staring at the countess.

She was a beautiful woman, tiny and petite. Ulandra had expected her to appear cheap, trashy, but she was dressed with exquisite taste. Ulandra's dress bared more skin than her ivory satin gown. If she was wearing cosmetics, they had been applied so expertly it was impossible to tell. Even though she was probably older than Salesin by half a dozen years, she looked young and fresh. Virginal.

The countess smiled, displaying perfect little teeth. It was a shy, sweet smile.

I must get out of here, Ulandra thought desperately. *I must get away. But how?*

The marquise was looking at her, obviously at a loss for words. The Princess shook her head warningly, then forced words past the knot in her throat. "I must retire," she said. "I am . . . indisposed."

"Your Highness—"

The Princess shook her head. "Stay here," she said. "I command you. If anyone asks, say I stepped out for a breath of air and will be back any moment."

The marquise dropped a quick curtsy. "Yes, Your Highness."

Ulandra's heart was hammering, but she forced herself to take as deep a breath as possible and scan the room for an inconspicuous exit. There it was: a door set over on the west side, not too far from where she was standing. It was half hidden by a curtained alcove, where ladies went to make quick adjustments to slipping garters or pinching shoes.

Ulandra forced her feet to move. She held her head high, but was careful not to make eye contact with anyone as she moved. She'd learned this trick long ago—just unfocus her eyes slightly and gaze at necks or hairlines.

As she moved, hands full of her satin skirts, trying to pick her course carefully so she wouldn't brush against any tables, servants, or guests, Ulandra could feel Salesin's gaze on her back, penetrating her like a dagger of ice. She forced herself to keep moving, praying she wouldn't stumble and fall. The ballroom floor was white and black marble, patterned like a game board, and highly polished. *Don't fall, keep moving Don't fall . . .*

As she reached the alcove, then the door, she risked a quick glance back, and saw several of her ladies-in-waiting following her. *No! Go back! I don't want you!*

She opened the door as narrowly as she could manage, given the breadth of her skirts, and lunged through it. Once through, she looked back at her ladies, shook her head slightly, then mouthed "No."

They stopped, milling in confusion, and she closed the door in their faces.

Breathing a long sigh of relief, the Princess turned away, allowing herself to slump back against the door. It was hard to say which hurt worse—her throbbing head or her equally throbbing feet.

Ulandra regarded the corridor and decided she was in a part of the palace she had seldom visited, in the area near the

King's audience chamber. She hesitated, confused, wondering how to get back to her chambers.

As she stood peering down the long, vaulted stone corridor, a voice spoke from behind her. "Allow me to escort you, Your Highness."

Ulandra whirled around so fast her high-heeled slippers skidded on the polished floor. She staggered and would have fallen if the man had not stepped forward and caught her elbow, steadying her. As soon as she had regained her balance, he let go, stepped back, and bowed deeply. "Forgive my importunity, Your Highness. I feared you might come to harm."

His voice was deep and beautifully modulated, though he spoke Pelanese with an accent. He was a tall man, with deep-set black eyes. His skull was shaven and he wore a robe the color of fresh-spilled blood.

His black eyes were intense as they held hers for long seconds. There was something there . . . something she *almost* recognized. Something . . .

Ulandra shuddered. "I beg pardon, Your Highness!" the man said quickly. "I did not mean to offend."

The Princess shook her head, cleared her throat, and managed to say, "No, no, there's nothing wrong. I was just leaving the ball early, and I found myself in this part of the palace, which I do not recognize."

The man—he had to be the new priest, Varlon—bowed again. "Allow me to escort you back to the royal apartments, Your Highness."

Gravely, he offered her his arm, and Ulandra took it. "My name," he said softly as they walked, "is Varlon. I have come to court at the King's request to teach him about the philosophy of my homeland."

"I have heard of you, Master Varlon," Ulandra said. "Where is your homeland?"

"On the western continent, in Amavav. North of Kata."

Ulandra's knowledge of geography was sketchy, at best. "Amaran?"

He shook his head, his trained voice as smooth as the polished stone floor. "Amaran is north of Amavav."

"You said, 'philosophy.' You mean your faith? The King wishes to convert?"

"Of course we have a faith, Your Highness. But we also have a philosophy that anyone may practice, no matter what deity they worship."

"Oh." In her exhaustion, she tripped on her skirt and nearly fell again. Once more he was there to steady her.

"Your Highness, please do not think me importunate or forward. But I sense your pain. Perhaps you might remove your footwear?"

Ulandra glanced up at him, a rebuke forming on her lips, but she didn't say it. Varlon's eyes held nothing but kind concern. *Better to take off the wretched slippers rather than fall on my face,* she decided, and, holding onto the priest's arm for balance, stepped out of first one, then the other, shoe. The cold, polished stone soothed her abused feet.

Varlon bent over and retrieved the shoes. "I'll carry these for you, Your Highness."

"Thank you." Ulandra picked her skirts again, and they went on. Finally, they reached the door to the royal apartments, and she held out her hand for the slippers. "Accept my gratitude, Varlon, for your kindness."

He bowed, placing the slippers into her hands. "May I enter, Your Highness? I would like to speak with you about something of import."

Of course not! Ulandra thought, but his black eyes held hers, steady and piercing. She found herself nodding. "You may enter."

When they were in her parlor, she sank onto the small brocade sofa, barely repressing an unladylike sigh of relief. Her corset was still too tight, but sitting down was bliss. "What did you wish to speak to me about . . ." She hesitated, "Varlon?" She frowned. "I do not mean to be overfamiliar, but I do not know what the proper address is for a holy man of your country."

"In my land, a priest is called 'Your Reverence,' Your Highness."

"Very well, Your Reverence."

The priest leaned forward in his seat, those compelling eyes glittering like hard coal. "Princess, I know what happened tonight. I deplore the disrespect shown to you, both tonight and recently."

Ulandra's eyes widened. *How could he, an outlander, know all this?* But long years training in decorum won out. She merely inclined her head to indicate she was listening.

"Your Highness, my god is a powerful god, and He tells me many things. He tells me that He has blessed you. You are high in His favor."

"Blessed?" she echoed blankly.

"Yes, Your Highness. Blessed."

"But I worship the Goddess. Why should your god bless me?"

Reaching over, the priest picked up a candle that stood in its holder on the nearby table. Leaning forward, he held it so that its light illuminated his face, especially his eyes.

"Listen to me, Your Highness." His voice was deep, soothing and compelling. It was as easy to listen to as the chords of a wyr-harp plucked by a virtuoso.

"Allow yourself to relax, and let your mind think only of peace. You have not had much rest lately, Your Highness, but my god will bring you rest. Once you have served Him, He will grant you rest."

He went on, but his words were lost to her, only their deep, compelling sound remained. That and his dark eyes . . .

"Rest, Ulandra, rest, let your eyes close . . ."

Ulandra let her eyes close, and, with a sigh, allowed her weary spirit to rest.

"Your Highness, Your Highness, can you hear me?"

Ulandra blinked, and sat up. She was mortified to realize that she must have fallen asleep while they had been talking. "Excuse me," she stammered. "I . . . I was just resting my eyes . . ."

Varlon smiled kindly at her. "Of course, Your Highness. It

was churlish of me to spout dry philosophy at you when you are tired. Let me summon your ladies-in-waiting for you. I believe some of them are outside the door even now."

Ulandra nodded. "Of course. Thank you, Your Reverence, for escorting me back to my rooms."

He stood and bowed deeply. "May I come again, Your Highness? I wish to offer all of the royal family a chance to learn of the philosophy of my homeland."

She smiled at him tentatively and held out her hand. Varlon bowed deeply. Ulandra realized this was the first time she had felt relaxed or at peace since before her marriage.

What harm can a little philosophy do?

The Princess nodded. "Yes, Your Reverence. You may come again."

Jezzil tossed and turned that night, alternately thinking dark thoughts, then slipping into even darker dreams. He dreamed of Barus, and this time the flames were eating his friend's flesh, blackening it, even as Barus reached out to him pleadingly.

Jezzil jerked awake from that dream, mouth open in a gasp that almost became a scream. He lay there, panting, relieved it was just a dream but then filled afresh with guilt and shame.

Courage? You have no courage, that mocking little voice spoke in his mind. *Better to go mad than to fail and betray your friends, because you* will *fail, you know it . . .*

Finally he rolled out of the bed, pulled the blanket off it, tied it over his bare shoulders as a makeshift cloak, and picked up his crutches. His eyes were used to the dimness, and he knew the little room so well by now that he needed little light to cross it. Teeth fastened in his lower lip, he swung himself down the hall, found the back door and maneuvered his way outside.

The three steps leading down to the small, city backyard looked like a cliff. Jezzil didn't attempt them. Instead he clung to the hand railing and lowered himself onto the top step.

Once seated, he hugged the blanket around his shoulders and looked up at the stars. He could see only the brightest of them, for the streetlamps were still lit. Thirty paces away, Khith's cook was already busy in the small, detached building that housed the kitchen and bakehouse; a whiff of baking bread made his stomach rumble.

Jezzil looked up again, staring at the bright stars in the Hunter's Bow until his eyes burned and his neck grew stiff. *What should I do?*

He tried to pray to Arenar, the warrior's god. But what did Arenar know about sorcery? He was the god of steel and bowstrings and barracks life.

Is there a god for magic users?

Hugging the blanket around his bare shoulders, the Chonao thought about what it would be like to work magic, to be an adept, possibly even a sorcerer. *Could I really learn to do that kind of thing? And if I did, would that be a good thing?*

He wondered whether Boq'urak could be defeated by magic. Swords and musket balls certainly hadn't made much of a dent in the creature.

The words of his first tactics instructor came back to him. "Never ignore a potential advantage! It is your duty to investigate and evaluate *every* possibility! Do you know what they call warriors who stick to tried and true battle strategies?"

Jezzil smiled faintly at the memory. Sergeano Deveni had been a crusty old veteran who'd lost an eye and a leg. But he'd been able get around on his crutch so quickly.

That particular day he'd turned to Jezzil for an answer, but when the boy had hesitated, he'd barked it out himself. "*Defeated!* That's what they call them! Beaten! War is a creative art as well as one with established patterns and methods! *Never neglect a potential advantage!*"

Jezzil was shivering now, but he hardly noticed the cold. Could learning magic teach him what he'd need to know to help his friends? To protect Thia from Master Varn? Could one be both a warrior and an adept?

He didn't know. But it seemed that he was going to find out.

"There are two basic kinds of avundi," Khith said the next day. Obviously pleased that Jezzil was willing to learn, the doctor had wasted no time beginning their first lesson. "The first kind involves using the mind to affect the perceptions of others. What you would think of as an 'illusion.' Your 'Castings' are a type of illusion."

Teacher and pupil were sitting together at the table in the dining room. The curtains were drawn, both doors were closed, and the room was dimly lit by a single sconce of candles. Jezzil, who had not had occasion to write anything in years, was painfully taking notes in Chonao. He'd never learned to read or write Pelanese, so it was laborious for him to mentally translate his teacher's words into his native tongue, then to write them down. But he did it anyway, because he was determined to have a record of what Khith taught him. He'd never been a quick learner, but he knew how to study.

"The second type of avundi is far more difficult," Khith continued. "This involves using the mind and spirit and energy—directed and propelled by the appropriate aids and spells—to affect physical reality. What I did when I healed the tear inside your body is of that type. And when I finished, I was so tired that it was as if I had run the length of Q'Kal at full speed."

Jezzil dipped his pen hurriedly and finished a line before looking up. "Casting tires me. I can't do it for more than a few moments at a time."

"With practice, you will be able to hold the illusion for as long as you wish," Khith assured him. "You will be able to do other things, without having to concentrate on it every moment."

Jezzil gave his teacher a dubious glance. Khith caught his unspoken skepticism and nodded. "I speak the truth, young Jezzil. When you are riding at the gallop, do you have to concentrate every second lest you fall off your mount?"

Jezzil chuckled. "No, of course not."

"This will be no different, I assure you. Before we end our session today, I will give you exercises designed to improve your ability to meditate and concentrate. And as you grow more proficient, you will be able to speed your own healing.

If you work at it, your broken bone will knit in half the time it would otherwise take."

"Very well," Jezzil muttered, thinking that between trying to strengthen his leg and studying magic, he'd have little time for anything else.

"At the moment, though, I would like to test your ability to actually affect your physical surroundings by means of avundi," Khith said. The Hthras produced a small vial, a tiny straw, and a small translucent jade plate. "This snuff I prepared will help you to access the part of your mind that controls this type of avundi."

Jezzil eyed the grayish powder Khith poured out. He'd never been drunk or taken recreational drugs. As a priest, all pleasures of the flesh were forbidden. "Do I really need to do this?"

"Perhaps not," Khith said. "Let us try." The Hthras took a gold coin from the pocket of its robe and placed it on the table between them, turning it on edge, steadying it, then letting it go. "Sit back," the doctor instructed. "So you are not touching the table."

Jezzil obeyed.

"Now, topple the coin."

The Chonao simply looked at his teacher. *"How?"*

Khith tapped its forehead. "There is a place inside your skull, in your mind, that holds the avundi to topple that coin. The snuff would help you isolate that place, but you may be able to find it without it. Try."

Jezzil gave his teacher a dubious glance. Fixing his gaze on the coin, he stared at it, trying to will it to fall over. He felt foolish, and it was difficult to stay focused. Somewhere in the house someone female laughed. Thia or Talis?

His stomach gurgled. Jezzil shifted, then forced himself to remain still. *Concentrate! Concentrate!*

He stared at the coin without blinking until his eyes began to burn and water, silently willing it to move, to tip . . .

Nothing.

Finally, with a frustrated swipe of his hand, he knocked the coin over. "I can't," he snapped. "I tried, but I can't do it." He reached over, grabbed his crutches, and levered himself up. "This isn't going to work. I appreciate that you're trying to help me, Doctor, but you just don't understand."

"What do I not understand?" Khith asked.

Jezzil thumped the tip of his crutch into the carpet. "I'm not the type to learn magic! Teach Eregard, he loves poring over books until he goes cross-eyed. I'm a dumb soldier, nothing more. When I try to read things, I fall asleep, or get a headache. I'm no scholar, I told you that yesterday, and I'm never going to be one."

Khith gazed at him levelly. "You are hardly 'dumb.' And Eregard does not have avundi."

"Well, lend him some of yours!" Jezzil snapped.

"It doesn't work like that."

"How do you know?"

"Because I have been practicing magic for nearly forty years. I recognize when someone has the gift."

"Gift!" Jezzil echoed. He laughed hollowly. "Some gift. I don't *want* such a gift. I'm not the right kind of person to have it!"

"Nevertheless, you possess it," Khith said. "And you will discover that learning to utilize your gift will be as difficult, or more difficult, than any physical feat you mastered while learning to be a warrior. *Now sit down, Jezzil.*"

Jezzil wasn't quite sure how it happened, but he found himself back in his seat. He looked around, feeling a bit dazed. *Some kind of mind magic,* he realized. "What just happened?"

"I will teach you to do that, too, in due time," Khith said.

The Chonao grimaced. "You would have made a good drill instructor, Doctor."

Khith did not reply, merely silently indicated the snuff and the small straw.

Jezzil took a deep breath as he regarded the substance. *Do I really want to do this?*

"How do I know it can be done?" he said after a long pause. "All I have is your word on it."

Khith drew itself up with the first flash of temper the human had seen the creature manifest. "Among my people, truth and knowledge are sacred."

Jezzil spread his hands placatingly. "Forgive me, Doctor, but it would help me to see it done."

Khith stared at him for a moment, eyes narrowed, then the Hthras leaned over the table, picked up the straw, and snuffed a strawful of the mixture up one nostril. Jezzil watched as the physician's pupils dilated until, in the dimness, the healer's eyes looked like two holes punched into the furred countenance.

The Hthras did not move, but a low, throbbing hum began to emanate from its throat. Jezzil was staring at the healer in fascination when he caught a flash of movement out of the corner of his eye.

The coin had risen to the level of his eyes and was rotating slowly in midair.

Jezzil stared at it in shock, realizing for the first time that, despite his own Castings, he hadn't truly believed in sorcery, or power . . . or magic. He let out a slow, incredulous breath as the coin moved, still spinning, until it hung right before his face. Then, with a sudden quick movement, it darted forward and gave him a smart rap on his forehead. Before Jezzil could grab it, the coin moved back in a golden flash to hover again over the table.

"By Arenar's sword!" Jezzil muttered as slowly, delicately, the coin descended until it was once more resting on edge on the tabletop. Jezzil regarded Khith wide-eyed. "You did it. This avundi. It's *real*."

"You did not really believe until just now, did you?" The Hthras straightened in its chair and rubbed a hand over its face. "It has been a long time since I did anything so ostentatious," it said, and there was a weary note in its voice. "When I do magic, it is *useful* magic."

"This was useful," Jezzil muttered, staring at the coin. "You've convinced me it's possible."

"Good. Now topple the coin."

Jezzil opened his mouth, then closed it. Khith eyed him. "Now that you believe, it frightens you, does it not? Good. Nobody should try to learn what I intend to teach you unless he is afraid. Fear is good, it keeps us from doing foolish things."

The Chonao nodded slowly. He was trying to imagine himself doing anything like what Khith had just done. All his life he'd felt out of step with others. Back when he'd been a soldier in the Redai's troops, he'd always been told that he had too much imagination. That he *thought* too much, and it slowed his reaction time.

Knowing in his heart that he was a coward had set him apart, too. Still, he'd found more true comradeship with Thia, Talis, and Eregard than he'd ever experienced as a Chonao warrior. It had been good to *belong*. To be a part of a group that valued him.

And now he was about to try and learn a skill that would once again set him apart.

Never disregard a potential weapon . . .

With a sudden movement, Jezzil leaned forward, picked up the straw, and inhaled some of the powder. He snuffed it up into his right nostril, and it seemed to explode into his nasal passages, straight into his brain. His head felt light, then burning hot. He blinked and gasped, realizing he was holding onto the arms of his chair with both hands. His head was so light that for a moment he imagined he had floated clear off his seat.

The drug expanded in his mind like a sharp-edged blossom of mingled pain and pleasure. The blossom bloomed, then began to shrink, becoming ever smaller, until it was a single, hot point of incandescence in his brain.

Blood rushed and sang in his veins. His brain seemed to throb around that spot of light. Dimly, Jezzil became aware that long, bony, extra-digited fingers were grasping his wrist. A voice was speaking. "That place in your mind that is illuminated is the seat of your avundi, Jezzil! Touch it! Find it so you can find it again. *Use it to topple the coin!*"

Jezzil managed to open his eyes, fixing them on the coin. The physical rush of the drug had faded slightly, but he could still feel that spot in his mind. He stared at the coin and tried to focus using that part of his brain.

He visualized the coin leaning, leaning . . . and then falling onto its side.

Sweat gathered on the Chonao's forehead as he stared, not daring to blink. Over and over he tried to touch that place in his mind, the place that was lit like a candle in the darkness. Over and over he pictured the gold coin leaning over and falling.

Sweat stung his eyes, but still he did not blink.

Fall, damn you! Fall!

All at once he felt that he'd touched that warm place in his mind, really touched it.

The coin on the table shivered, leaned . . .

And fell.

Jezzil stared at it, a flat golden disc marked with the image of the King of the Pelanese, lying on its side. Slowly, hesitantly, he reached out to touch it with his forefinger. One touch confirmed what his eyes told him.

A thin-fingered, furred hand reached out, touched his hand, then held it. Jezzil turned to see Khith regarding him with a mixture of pride and happiness. "Excellent," the Hthras said. "Excellent, Jezzil. We have made a good beginning."

Talis was actually relieved when she discovered that she did not have to sell Eregard next Market Day.

Before they'd gone to rescue Thia, she'd written to her father, telling him that she was enjoying the social life in Q'Kal and asking him for funds to buy some new dresses. She'd hated lying to him, but comforted herself by recalling all the unpaid labor she'd contributed to the farm for years . . . and that her brothers, not she, had been sent to school.

The day before Market Day, she received a letter from her father telling her that he had sent a letter of deposit from his bank to be deposited in the Q'Kal branch of the Bank of Kata, in her name. Gerdal Aloro asked her if she'd met any suitable young men, and encouraged her to buy some pretty clothes. There was also a letter for Clo, which Talis opened. She read it, feeling her temper rise.

The last paragraph read:

As you have seen, my daughter is young and foolish. It is up to you to guard her maidenhood, Clo. Never let her out of your sight. Talis has hot blood, and I do not trust her to stay chaste. Innocence is no proof against a nature that bears the brand of wantonness and rebellion. Guard her virginity, Clo. With this I charge you . . .

Wretched, lying old hypocrite!

When she finished reading the letter, Talis slowly, deliberately, stepped over to the candelabra that sat on the dressing table and touched the paper to the flame. She watched her father's words blaze, blacken, then disappear. It wasn't until the fire seared her fingers that she dropped it, swearing under her breath, a foul oath, words that she'd heard in taverns but never spoken.

The next day she withdrew funds from the bank, and her conscience troubled her not a whit.

"You've gotten a reprieve," she told Eregard that afternoon. "Unless you *want* me to take you to the market and put you up for sale."

He shook his head. "No. I . . . I want to stay with you."

Talis's mouth quirked unpleasantly. *Liar. You want to stay with Thia.* She had seen the looks that passed between them, and noticed that they spent hours poring over books together. There was no denying Eregard's educational level. Perhaps he'd been an instructor at some first-class academy? Once, she'd asked him whether that was the case.

"No, I'm not a professor," he'd replied gravely. "I told you, I'm a prince."

Talis had burst out laughing and clapped her slave on the shoulder. "Good one! All right, keep your secrets, Eregard."

Every day, except when the spring rains brought a downpour, Eregard accompanied Talis to the barn where Falar was stabled. Jezzil had asked Talis to exercise the mare, and she'd told him, with perfect truth, that she would be honored to do so.

Eregard had become an expert groom under Talis's tutelage. He'd learned when to use a currycomb, and where on the animal it was never used. He learned to pick up the horse's feet to clean them, and to keep his own feet pointed straight back toward the animal's hindquarters, rather than carelessly standing sideways. He'd learned to comb and braid manes and tails, and how to clean tack.

When he thought of the army of grooms that had presented him with a perfectly groomed mount whenever he wished to go riding, Eregard had to smile; a faint, ironic smile. *At least now I can saddle my own mount, if need be,* he thought as he rubbed saddle soap into the stirrup leathers. *I've learned a lot since I left Pela.*

He had also learned a great deal about Rufen Castio and his rebels, but had no way to get the information to his father. Eregard felt torn. He knew his best chance to regain his freedom lay with being sold to the Governor's household, but he didn't want to leave his friends.

It was doubly ironic, he recognized, to think of his *owner* and her companions as *friends.* Eregard knew only too well that to Jezzil and Talis, born to wealth and slave ownership, he was a possession, scarcely human.

But Thia was different. She knew what it was like to be trapped, to have no free will. In her life in the temple, she'd been a slave in all but name, doing the exact bidding of the higher ranked priests. Thia had told him about Boq'urak, and Amaran, and the religious texts she'd copied. Eregard was fascinated, especially when she confided that she'd spoken with Khith about Boq'urak.

"Khith says there are mentions of the god in ancient texts, buried in a forgotten city," she said. "The Ancient Ones didn't call him by that name, but it has to be the same entity, Khith says."

"Ancient texts? Lost cities?" Eregard was fascinated. "Where?"

"In the Sarsithe. Khith told me there are buildings half buried in the jungle, and that deep beneath the earth there are old vaults filled with books and texts and scrolls. Can you imagine?"

"A scholar's dream," Eregard said, then something occurred to him. "If there is mention of Boq'urak, what do the old texts say about him?"

"Khith says that He has been around for a very long time," Thia said. "The Ancients blamed Him for some terrible catastrophe that befell them." She frowned. "The doctor says that Boq'urak has meddled many times in human affairs. He has great power, but must work through human vessels. Down through the ages, Khith said, men and women have lent themselves to the god to be used, as a man uses a horse to take him places."

Eregard regarded her, half fascinated, half repelled. "So Master Varn wasn't unique?"

"Not at all," she replied grimly. "Khith said it found some old journals during its travels north that made a lot of hints and obscure references begin to fall together. They said terrible things resulted from Boq'urak's meddling, but Khith had to leave its home before it could learn more."

Eregard's imagination was fired with the idea of a lost city half buried amidst jungle vegetation. "I'd like to go there," he mused aloud. "Think what a resource those Ancient texts would be if they could be taken back to Pela, studied by the King's finest scholars."

Thia nodded. "And only Khith knows where to find the place."

Eregard gazed at her, looking into her dark eyes, seeing her narrow features and her short, silvery hair, wispy and flyaway. She was small-boned, small-breasted. No beauty. *And yet,* he found himself thinking, *there's something about her. Something fey. Exotic.* He eyed the pale pink curve of her lips, thinking that there was a touch of unexplored sensuality about her mouth.

"Maybe someday we should go there," he found himself saying. "You and I, with Khith to guide us there."

For a moment there was an answering gleam in her eyes, but then she shook her head. "That would be dangerous, I think. Khith has told me that its people have a very strong taboo against exploring those ruins. They are a peaceful people, but Khith had to escape before they could run it down with hunting animals. It's a strong taboo."

"Evidently," Eregard agreed.

At night, before he fell asleep, tired from the labors of the day, Eregard would touch the filed place on his collar and remember the old days, when servants waited on him, when he had but to express a wish to have it fulfilled. *If I ran away,* he wondered, *could I convince Thia to come with me?*

He knew the ties between the Amaranian woman and the Chonao warrior were strong, but he'd never had the impression that those ties were anything but platonic. Jezzil had described her at one point as his sister, and they did indeed seem to regard each other as siblings. *If she ran away with me, and we could reach the Governor's palace, he would send us back to Pela in style.*

Eregard almost wished he could fall in love with Thia. He certainly didn't feel about her the way he'd felt about Ulandra, now truly lost to him. The news of Salesin's wedding had traveled to the colony. Everyone was speculating on how soon the new Princess would produce an heir.

Thinking of Ulandra in his brother's embrace was enough to keep him awake at night, so Eregard tried hard not to think about it. Still, these days when he thought of Ulandra, it was hard to visualize her face. Sometimes, when he tried, he would find himself picturing Thia, or even Talis.

He wasn't attracted to Talis at all, but she was a compelling woman, Eregard conceded. He would sit on the paddock fence and watch while she exercised Falar, her face flushed with exertion and fresh air, her brows drawn together in fierce concentration. "She's so finely trained," she said, "it's like she is the teacher and I'm the pupil."

As Jezzil healed, he began coming to the stable a couple of times each week and coaching Talis as she rode. Eregard and Thia would watch the two of them together, and, indifferent horsemen that they were, marvel at the bond that could exist between mount and rider.

Eregard would watch Thia as she watched Jezzil, and wonder whether she was jealous of Talis. Talis was a striking woman, after all. As Jezzil continued to heal and was able to put weight on his leg, they began to exercise and train together.

"All right, now, on the count of three, feint, then thrust!" Jezzil stood in the center of the practice ground behind the stable, sword in hand. He had given up his crutches, but still used a cane to walk.

Talis narrowed her eyes in concentration, trying to feel the sword as an extension of her arm, as part of her body. "Don't watch the tip of your weapon," Jezzil had drummed into her during countless drills. "That's the way to get killed. Watch your opponent, and make sure your sword is part of you. You have to know where your sword is without having to look at it."

When she'd first met Jezzil, she thought she was fair at swordplay, but a few lessons had convinced her that she was naught but a beginner. But she was learning. Each day she practiced, repeating all the moves he had taught her, refining her hand-eye coordination, trying to be faster on her feet. She worked on her balance, her stance, her lunges, feints, thrusts, and parries.

On the day that Jezzil was finally able to walk without the cane, Talis was able to slip inside his guard for an instant. He managed to parry her thrust, but it was a last moment thing.

"Excellent!" he shouted. "Excellent!"

Talis stepped back and saluted her teacher, breathing hard, her face flushed with exertion and pleasure. Thia, who was sitting on paddock fence, watching, while Eregard cleaned stalls, cheered aloud.

Talis's exhilaration was short-lived, however. When the group returned to the doctor's house that evening, she found a hired courier waiting for her from her father. She scanned the letter he handed her, her jaw set, lips tightly pressed together.

Talis:

I have made inquiries after you, and discovered that you have lied to me about your reasons for staying in Q'Kal. Blessed Goddess only knows what you have done with Clo, but, according to reports, she has not been seen for more than a month.

Nor have you bought a single pretty gown, or attended a single afternoon party or evening ball. Instead you have been frequenting taverns and wine-gardens, wearing sinful clothing and consorting with Imperial troops. I have heard the reports of your wanton activities directly from my observer, so do not think to try and deny my findings.

You are to start for home immediately upon receipt of this letter. I must tell you that when your poor mother, Goddess bless her, heard of your sluttish antics, she collapsed, and has not been able to rise from her bed since that day. You are needed to tend her, Talis.

If you come straight home, daughter, do not fear that I will insist that you marry. Instead you may stay on here, caring for your mother. That is also a daughter's proper role, and I will not be ashamed to have you living here, unmarried, so long as your mother lives.

I believe in being truthful, so I feel I must tell you that we have a new addition to the household. Daughter, you have been gone now for two months, and during that time, your uncle Jasti has been of great help to me. He tells me that he is sorry for his drunken behavior that night, Talis, and I believe him. He has gotten himself into debt, and I was in strong need of an overseer, as you well know. So Jasti has come to live in the overseer's cottage. But fear not, Talis. He is a changed man. I do not allow him drink, and he attends services with us regularly. He has worked hard and the farm is prospering under his care. He will not accost you again, he has assured me.

You are a good girl at heart, Talis. You have always been a dutiful daughter. I am gravely disappointed by your duplicity and behavior there in the city, but I, too,

*was once young. I am prepared to forgive you, and will
welcome you home.*

*Please start for home as soon as you have finished
reading these words. Your mother longs to see your
face, and I do also.*

> *I remain, your loving father,*
> *Gerdal*

Talis finished the letter, drew a deep breath, and looked up
at the courier. "Return to North Amis," she said, "and tell my
father I will do as he commands. Tell him I am sorry for my
behavior."

The courier nodded impassively.

"Also tell him," Talis added, "that I will start for home in
four days. I must wait until Market Day, because I still have
to sell off that troublesome slave."

14

Truth

"Careful, Jezzil," Khith warned. "The fumes that will arise from this distillation are powerful. Unless you wish to take a nap on the floor, cover your mouth and nose, then hold your breath while pouring."

Jezzil glanced over at the Hthras, took up a length of cloth and tied it across his face. Then, very carefully, he tipped the distillation flask and began filling the six small bottles with the greenish liquid.

"Be sure you get the same amount into all of the bottles," Khith said. The Hthras was perched atop a human-sized stool on the other side of the room it had set up as a laboratory. "My notes say this distillation makes exactly three doses per vial."

Jezzil did not speak. Eyes narrowed in concentration, he poured with great care. Not until he was finished and the bottles were sealed did he step away from the distillation tubes and burners to face his teacher. He glanced at his notes. Khith had begun teaching him its own language, so it could translate the spells and potions with greater accuracy.

As a result, Jezzil's notes were a strange mix of Chonao script mixed with additions in the Hthras tongue. "Used to treat insomnia . . . obviously," he muttered. "A general soporific when used in combination with a strong analgesic, can render a patient unconscious for surgery."

"Correct, Jezzil," the Hthras said, pleased. "You are a good and conscientious student. A minuscule dose can be used to facilitate a dreaming trance state, for possible foreseeing or farseeing."

"How much is a minuscule dose?" Jezzil put down the distillation flask and began stoppering the vials with small corks.

"One thimbleful," Khith said. "Half of a regular spoonful."

Jezzil nodded, then brought the rack holding the corked vials over to his teacher. "Now what?"

"The corks must be sealed with wax," the Hthras said. "The hot wax will keep the mixture fresh for many months."

Jezzil nodded, then gestured at the small brazier that sat on the laboratory table. "Where will I find the wax?"

"Not now, young Jezzil," the doctor said. "You are limping a bit. Sit down. Rest. We do not want to strain that leg."

Jezzil shrugged, then sat down on one of the tall stools. Khith slid down, went over to its student and looked down at his leg. "I want to check for heat and inflammation," the healer said. "Remove your trousers, if you please."

Jezzil sighed. "My leg is fine, Doctor," he said, but obeyed, sliding his trousers down until they were puddled around his ankles and he was sitting on the stool clad in his shirt and underdrawers.

Khith carefully examined the leg, pressing delicately, checking for inflammation, heat, or signs of pain. The physician could feel slight swelling but no heat, and Jezzil showed no signs of pain when it probed the site of the break and the surrounding area. "A bit of massage, then elevation, will help," it said, beginning to gently knead the patient's calf muscle.

Jezzil's skin was very warm, the flesh tight and youthful. The human was not very hairy, as humans went. The Hthras went on massaging, realizing that the touch of human flesh was . . . very pleasurable. Deep within itself, it felt a faint stirring. Its heartbeat quickened, its respiration grew faster.

What is this? Khith wondered, then suddenly realized that

it must be experiencing something it had never felt before . . . the first flush of sexual attraction. *For a human?*

Khith had never felt this way about one of its own people. *How can this be happening to me?*

It felt a sudden urge to lean forward and press its face against the human's bare skin. Quickly, it pulled its hands free, and did not look up at the Chonao. "Now make sure you keep it elevated this evening." it mumbled.

"I will," Jezzil said. "Thank you, Doctor, that feels much better."

Khith glanced at the clock on the wall. "Nearly time for dinner," it observed. "Do you know where—"

The Hthras broke off as the door to the laboratory was flung open. Adept and student turned to see a panting, flushed Thia standing there. "Jezzil," she gasped. "I ran all the way. You have to come!"

Jezzil was on his feet and yanking up his trousers before she finished speaking. "What is it? What's happened? Come where?"

"Talis sent me. There are some men who have been talking with Castio, and they're like you. Chonao. Talis wants you to come to the taproom at the Blue Boar."

"Do you need a translator?"

"Something like that! Hurry, come *on*!"

Jezzil didn't even pick up his cane as he headed out the door. Khith watched his apprentice go, and was relieved for the chance to regain its composure before having to face the young human again.

Can I be falling in love? it wondered as it moved around the lab, automatically making the proper preparations to seal the sleep distillate. *Is that possible?*

It was true that the Hthras felt closer to both Jezzil and Thia than it ever had to any being, since the death its father. *But love? No, it cannot be,* it thought fiercely. *It is impossible!*

The Blue Boar was only a few blocks away. Jezzil followed Thia through streets thronged with sailors and soldiers. Several ships had docked that day, and the taverns were full to bursting.

Why does Talis want me here? Jezzil wondered. He had no intention of talking to any of his countrymen. He knew that if they knew the truth about him, they would despise him for a coward and a weakling. *I don't care what she says, I'm not talking to them!*

He thought about trying to explain this to Thia, but was hard-pressed to keep up with her smaller form as she wove her way through the crowd.

Finally she turned into one of the broader alleyways. The lamplighters had been busy, and there was enough light to see the splashed contents of an emptied chamber pot. Jezzil leaped over it, wincing when his wounded leg took his weight.

Rowdy laughter and bellowing voices assailed them from the tavern. Just as they reached it, the door opened and two drunken sailors reeled out into the alley. Jezzil pulled Thia aside as they staggered along. One of them slipped in the puddle and sat down with a splash and a curse. His companion laughed so hard that he nearly joined him. Jezzil snickered. *Serves the sot right.*

Thia tugged on his arm. "Come on!" Moments later she stopped with the door held halfway open, letting out a blast of hot, ale-scented air and the off-key chorus of a bawdy ballad. She beckoned him to lean closer. "They're over on the other side of the room," she said. Her breath was warm and tickled his ear. "Talis wants us to stay near them, so you can hear if they talk in your language. They want to make some kind of alliance with Castio, but she says some parts of their story don't ring true."

Jezzil hesitated. "Do I have to talk to them?"

She shook her head. "Just listen. We don't even want them to know you're Chonao."

Jezzil glanced down at what he was wearing. Except for his boots, which were those of a Chonao horseman, his clothing was Katan and unremarkable. He nodded, then gestured at her homespun blouse and the laces on her bodice. "Loosen that up," he said, and when she gazed at him in confusion, he reached over and did it himself. "Good, now unbutton a few buttons." Blushing, she awkwardly obeyed. "That's better," he said, "And, Thia, if I act, um, unmannerly toward you, I'm only doing it so we won't be noticed. Play along."

Thia's eyes went wide, then she bit her lip and nodded.

They went into the dimly lit tavern, and Jezzil stopped by the bar to order them a couple of glasses of strong, sourish wine. Thia, who had never tasted spirits before, made a face when she took her first sip. Jezzil shook his head at her warningly, and she squared her shoulders and took a second sip.

The Chonao looked around the tavern. It was so dark that it took him a minute to spot Talis, wearing her ordinary masculine attire, seated beside the printer, Denno. They were in one of the back booths, talking to two men who were plainly steppes-born. Jezzil, who had been raised on the lowland plains, was relieved to see that. He'd been worried that they might be kinsmen, and that he might be recognized.

He waited until the man in the adjoining booth began to slide sideways, then nudged Thia. She followed him to the now empty booth and they slid in, sitting back-to-back with the two Chonao. Jezzil was careful not to catch Talis's eye.

He put an arm around Thia, pulling her close to him, and began to nuzzle her hair, stopping only to sip his wine. She went rigid in the circle of his arm but did not pull away.

". . . cannot take chances with our leader," Talis was saying, her voice pitched low, but not whispering. "Castio will meet with you, he told me to tell you that, but at a place of *his* choosing. We will lead you there, when the watch changes at the Governor's palace. Meet us in the alley behind the Blue Boar."

"Lead us?" the taller of the two Chonao protested, in strongly accented Pelanese. "I like not that. We find our own way—"

"You'll be blindfolded," Talis said at the same moment as the other Chonao said softly to his partner, in their own language, "Shut up, fool. She's our only link to Castio. Let them have their little spy games!"

Jezzil clumsily brushed his lips across Thia's cheek. He'd never realized that women were so much softer-skinned than men . . .

The second Chonao cleared his throat. His Pelanese was even worse than his companion's. "Forgive my comrade," he said haltingly, "soldiers, he and I, not . . . ambassador. We are not accustomed to . . . I forget the word . . . this kind of . . . mission."

"If you want to speak with Castio personally, it must be this way," Denno said. "No exceptions."

Thia had relaxed slightly, curving her back so it fit into the circle of his arm. Jezzil gathered her closer, nuzzled her ear, and found himself touching the skin behind it with the tip of his tongue. She shivered but did not pull away.

"So tell us what is going on with Kerezau," Talis said. "How many troops does your Redai actually have?"

"Many," the first Chonao said curtly.

"*How* many, the lady asked you?" Denno said. "If you've naught but a handful of seasick troops, you haven't a hope of taking Pela, even if we Katans ally with you."

"Pela will be ours, rebel," the second Chonao said curtly.

"And Kata will be *ours*," Talis said, an edge in her voice.

"Of course," the first Chonao said.

"The Redai understands this," the second Chonao added.

Jezzil gathered Thia even closer, almost without thinking. Her hair brushed his nose. It was soft, feathery against his skin, his cheek, his mouth. The soft flesh of her upper arm was warm against his palm.

The first Chonao must have raised his tankard. "A toast!" he exclaimed in Pelanese. "Our friendship."

"To our friendship," echoed Talis and Denno.

"To our victory," the second Chonao said in his own tongue.

Jezzil found himself softly kissing Thia's cheek, his lips moving toward her mouth. Her skin was so soft, so pale, and she smelled faintly sweet, as though she had somehow magicked that sour wine into honey.

She moved suddenly in his arms, pushing at him. "Jezzil! *Jezzil!*"

He opened his eyes and let her go, sitting back in the booth. "What? Wh—" His heart was hammering and he was so aroused he felt dazed, incoherent.

She regarded him, wide-eyed and flushed. "Come on, we have to go."

"Go?" he repeated, trying to buy time. He didn't want to stand up at the moment.

"Did that wine go to your head?" She gestured at the booth behind him. "They're gone! Talis signaled to me to meet her outside!"

"Oh!" Heat scorched his face, but the embarrassment helped his other predicament. She slithered out of the booth and a moment later he followed her.

Outside, the street was empty save for a few drunken sailors. Moments later they heard a soft hiss from the nearby alley and found Talis there, waiting for them. She was pacing agitatedly, using short steps to stay in the shadows. "What took you so long?" she challenged, then went on without waiting for an answer. "Jezzil, did they say anything? I don't trust them. But I can't go to Castio with just a hunch."

Jezzil ran back over the conversation in his mind. "Not really," he said slowly. "But there was one remark, something about you being the only way to reach Castio, so they had to put up with your little spy game. It sounded . . ." He shrugged. ". . . not quite right," he finished lamely.

Talis scowled. "Hell spawn! I need something definite. Were they really Chonao?"

"Yes." Of that Jezzil had no doubt.

"For a while I was wondering if perhaps they were Pelanese assassins, sent here to kill Castio. He'll be surrounded by guards tonight, just in case."

"They were Chonao," Jezzil said. "What would it profit them to kill Castio?"

Thia spoke up for the first time. "They'd gain nothing by that," she pointed out. "They need Castio. The Redai sent them as emissaries to Castio, to forge an alliance. Why should they kill him? That would just benefit King Agivir."

Jezzil glanced at her, experienced a strong flash of memory as he saw her lips, then felt himself flush. He was glad it was dark. She had avoided looking at him, he realized.

"There's nothing for it except for you to take them to Castio, making sure he's well guarded," Thia added. "Then, after the meeting, Jezzil can follow them and listen to them."

"Can you?" Talis fixed Jezzil with an intent glance.

He nodded. "Easily."

"You cannot be seen, much less caught," she warned. "If they suspect, then we—"

"You don't understand," Thia interrupted. "Show her, Jezzil."

Now that he knew the correct place in his mind, it was so easy.

Jezzil stepped back, and as he did so, surrounded himself with the Casting. He saw Talis react, heard her gasp. "Goddess! He's a sorcerer!"

Jezzil dropped the Casting. "Barely a fledgling one," he said. "But in addition to being able to Cast, I was Pen Jav Dal. I will follow them and listen to all they say, and I will not be seen."

After Talis left them, Jezzil insisted on escorting Thia back to Khith's residence. He knew that, even now, she was afraid of large crowds and drunken men, and the streets were full of both. He had just time enough to gulp down the plate of food the housekeeper had saved for him before it was time to go back to the Blue Boar.

He surrounded himself with a Casting and was careful to step softly when he reached the appointed alley. He saw the two Chonao waiting there, smoking pipes but not speaking. Talis came along a moment later, with Denno and another man. Jezzil watched as they blindfolded the two Chonao and escorted them along the back alleys toward the meeting place.

Their destination proved to be a cellar down near the

docks. The closer to the waterfront they went, the more noisome and narrow the alleys became. Jezzil was invisible, but his eyesight was the same as when he was visible, and he was not trailing the others closely enough to be able to pick his way by the faint, shuttered light of the dark lantern Talis carried.

Once, he tripped over a dead cat, and his boot splashed into a pool of foul smelling liquid. Jezzil froze, breathing through his mouth.

The two Chonao stopped dead.

"What was that?" the taller one snapped.

"I heard it, too," Talis said, glancing behind her.

Moving slowly and carefully, Jezzil bent down and picked up a chunk of rotten wood. He drew back his arm and lobbed it over the fence into the nearby backyard of one of the tenements. A torrent of furious barking ensued.

Talis let out a long breath. "Just a dog," she said, tugging on the arm of the Chonao she was leading.

Jezzil followed at an even greater distance.

When they reached the cellar that proved to be their destination, and were safely down the steps and out of sight, Jezzil dared to relax the Casting and lean against the side of the tenement. He was tired, and his newly healed leg was throbbing.

Like any experienced soldier, he could doze standing up, but the moment he heard the door scrape, some unknown time later, he was alert. Concentrating, he resumed the Casting and watched.

Talis and the others appeared, leading the two Chonao, who were again blindfolded. They headed away from the tenement, weaving their way through back streets and alleys, occasionally turning and backtracking, to further disguise their route. Jezzil was growing very tired and by the time they stopped on the edge of the main thoroughfare that led back into the heart of the city, he had to strain his abilities to maintain the Casting.

"And here we leave you, gentlemen," Talis said, removing the taller Chonao's blindfold. "Good evening to you."

The other Chonao had his blindfold off before Denno could remove it. "Good evening to you, mistress," he said.

Talis beckoned to her compatriots, and the three walked away without looking back.

At last Jezzil was alone with his quarry.

It was obvious that the two Chonao were tired. They walked slowly, shoulders slumped. By now the streets were deserted, so Jezzil had to hang far back, lest they hear his boots scrape against a cobblestone. The only light was cast by the streetlamps, and the only sound was the far-off wailing of a wakeful infant.

He followed the two men as they walked in silence, thinking that the entire night had been a waste. Talis must be imagining things. There was no plot here.

The Chonao headed uptown, still not speaking. They approached the better section of town, only a few blocks from Khith's house, and Jezzil considered just going home. He was so tired that maintaining the Casting was becoming painful.

Yet, he had promised Talis. He gritted his teeth and hung on, determined to at least see where the Chonao were staying.

They were quartered at the Seaview Inn, one of Q'Kal's better transient establishments. Jezzil followed them as they approached it, promising himself that he would drop the Casting the moment they were inside.

The taller one spoke for the first time in half an hour. "Succeeding on this mission should bring us both a promotion, you know."

"It had better," his companion replied sourly. "Dealing with stinking traitors isn't my idea of a good time. That old eunuch Agivir is no match for Castio and his crew."

"But the Redai will be," the taller man said, opening the door and fishing in his pocket for a key. "More than a match for Castio and his rebels."

"Shhhh!" warned the other as they entered the inn. "We'll have to—"

The door closed.

Jezzil managed to stumble behind a huge ornamental bush

that was covered with ghostly white blooms before he
dropped the Casting. He sank down, exhausted and panting.
His injured leg cramped, the muscles knotting until he
rocked back and forth in agony. He forced himself to point
his toes up, then massaged his calf, gasping with the pain.

*Talis is right. Something is wrong. Something is very
wrong.*

Eregard lay wakeful, praying as he had never prayed before.
*Goddess, help me. Tomorrow is Market Day. Help me be sold
to the Governor's household. Let me stay in Q'Kal. Please.
I'll dedicate a new altar of the finest green marble to you if
you will only help me!*

He rolled over on his truckle bed, hearing Talis's soft
breathing and Thia's faint snores from the bed above him.
Tomorrow is Market Day. Goddess, help me.

Something struck the window frame. Eregard tensed, then
heard it again. He rose up on his elbow, and the next pebble
sailed through the open window and landed on his leg. It stung.

The slave crawled over to the window, dragging his leg-
chain. The night was dark, moonless. Only the faint glow of
a distant streetlamp illuminated a figure standing in the
courtyard of the inn. Eregard saw the figure's arm move and
managed to dodge the next flung pebble. "Who's there?" he
hissed. "Jezzil, is that you?"

"Of course it is!" The Chonao sounded exhausted and ill-
tempered. "You all sleep like logs! Let me in, I have to talk
to you!"

"We'll come down," Eregard promised. "Just a moment."

When he turned, his chain thunked, then made dragging
noises as he moved across the floor. Eregard cursed under
his breath. He reached the bed and leaned over to shake
Talis's shoulder. "Talis! Mistress! Wake up!"

"Wh—" She rolled over and sat up. She had a soldier's
quick alertness at being awakened suddenly. "What is it?"

"Jezzil is down in the courtyard. He says he has to talk to
you, it's important."

"Tell him we'll be right down," she promised.

A few minutes later the small group was huddled in the hay stall in the barn, away from the night breeze, speaking in hushed voices. The only light came from the starlight coming in through the barred window, and Talis's dark lantern. Eregard listened as Jezzil described his experience following the two Chonao.

"So," he finished, "while I can't be sure what they're planning, it seems evident that they aren't negotiating in good faith."

"It sounds like the Redai is planning to use Castio and our people to help him conquer Pela, then he'll turn around and take over Kata, too," Talis said, brushing her black hair back from her eyes. "I *knew* there was something wrong with those two!"

"If Kerezau is on his way to Pela using the Meptalith fishing fleet as transportation, this will destroy the treaty between Meptalith and Pela," Eregard said. "That means the Redai must have made an alliance with the islands. Their little vessels can sail rings around the big navy ships. They can put in at quiet coves where larger vessels can't. Kerezau could land a lot of troops that way. The northeastern shore of Pela would be ideal for his purposes."

Talis and Jezzil turned to regard him, their surprise at his analysis plain. Eregard smiled grimly. "The question is, what, if anything, should we do about this?"

"I'll have to talk to Castio," Talis said. "Warn him that the Chonao aren't negotiating in good faith."

"What do you think Castio should do?"

"I think he should have those two killed," Jezzil said. "Kill them and dump the bodies where no one will find them. That will delay things a bit, while the Redai waits in vain for their return."

Talis nodded. "Good idea. I'll tell him that. And I think Castio should send an emissary to Pela, warning Agivir that Kerezau is planning an invasion."

Jezzil looked from Talis to Eregard in the dim light. "And who will Kata side with, should that happen?"

"Pela," both said, almost in unison. Eregard glanced at

Talis and gave her a wry smile and a nod. "Better the enemy we know, the enemy that spawned us, rather than a new enemy we have no tie with," Talis added.

"But will King Agivir believe Castio?" Thia inquired softly. "He may think it's a trick."

Eregard took a deep breath. *Goddess, give me strength!*

"Agivir will listen if *I* tell him," he said.

Everyone turned to look at him.

Talis sighed. "This is no time for your silly games, Eregard. I'll speak to Castio first, but then I'm coming back here and it's off to Market Day for us. I'm sorry, but I need the money."

Jezzil made a small, quickly smothered sound of distress, but said nothing. Thia turned to Talis. "What is he talking about?"

Talis grimaced, then her fingers brushed her temple and made a quick circle. "He's talking nonsense. Sometimes he claims to be a Prince of Pela, poor thing. That's why he picked that name. Maybe he was hit on the head."

Eregard took a deep breath. "Goddess be my witness! I *am* Prince Eregard!"

Thia's face was a pale oval in the dimness. She reached over and took Eregard's hand, holding it tightly. "He's telling the truth," she said.

"Give me strength," Talis muttered. "Thia, I know you're fond of him. So am I. But I can't keep him. My father has ordered me to return home, but I've decided I'm not going back. I'm going to stay on with Castio full-time. So I'm going to have to leave Q'Kal, and I need money to do that. I have to sell Eregard today."

Thia turned to the other woman. "Talis, he *is* Prince Eregard. He is telling the truth."

Talis made an exasperated sound and rose to her feet. "I'm off to find Castio," she said. "Eregard, come with me."

Eregard found himself on his feet. He'd learned obedience in a hard school.

But Jezzil had risen, too. "Talis, stop," he said. "If Thia

says he's telling the truth, he is telling the truth. She can always tell. Master Khith says her talent is called Truthsense."

"Jezzil! Don't be ridiculous! He's a *slave*."

"Yes, he is," Thia said. "But he's also who he claims to be. I can tell when people lie. He's telling the truth."

Talis hesitated, then shook her head. "Have you all gone mad? Truthsense? What's that?"

"I asked Master Khith about it," Jezzil said. "It told me that some people have it. And Thia is one of them. See for yourself. Test her."

Thia walked out of the hay stall and stood in the aisle of the barn. She beckoned to Talis. "Come over here, where we can speak alone. You tell me things, things so private that only you would know. I will tell you if they are the truth or not."

Talis hesitated, then reluctantly joined the former priestess at the other end of the stable. In the dark stillness, Eregard could see them only as black shapes against the lighter boards of the barn. He made out the soft murmur of the women's voices, but no words. He glanced over at Jezzil. "You . . . you believe me?"

Jezzil nodded. "If Thia says you are telling the truth, you are. I've never known her to be mistaken. How did a Prince of Pela come to be a slave in Kata?"

"It's a long story," Eregard muttered, straining his ears, trying to hear what Talis and Thia were saying. "I'll tell you later, after I get this be-damned collar off." He touched the metal. "I can't wait."

He stiffened as he heard a low, inarticulate cry from Talis, then saw the dark forms of both women merge, and realized they were hugging each other fiercely. After a few minutes they turned and came back into the lamplight. Talis was wiping tears from her cheeks.

She stopped, and stood staring at Eregard. "I believe you," she said harshly. "But I will never bend knee to one of Agivir's issue."

Eregard nodded. "I understand. If you help me get back to

Pela, I'm going to talk to my father about the colonists' problems, believe me. He can't let Salesin take over the way he has been. My brother is . . . well, he's not fit to rule. He's cruel, and he enjoys being that way."

Talis nodded. She looked as if someone had punched her in the stomach, shocked and shaky, but she was trying to compose herself. Eregard turned to Thia, taking both her hands in his. "My lady Thia," he said, then bent down to kiss her hands. "Thank you. Thank you."

She gently pulled her hands away, looking self-conscious but pleased. "What should I call you, Your Highness?"

"Just Eregard," he replied. Seeing a quick expression flit across Jezzil's face, he found himself stepping back. *What's his problem?*

"The question is," Talis said, "how do we convince Castio of who you are? Are there any pictures of Prince Eregard?"

"In the Governor's palace, I suppose," Eregard said. "But my profile is on the twenty liera piece."

Jezzil stuck his hand into his pocket and drew out some coins. He studied one. "You only have one and a half chins these days," he said dryly. "But I think we can manage to convince Castio."

15

A Passage to Pela

Rufen Castio looked down at the coin in his hand, then back up at Eregard. "Hard to tell because of the beard. There's a slight resemblance, I grant you. Slight, but . . ." He shook his head, and a small breath of laughter escaped. "It can't be. The Goddess wouldn't be that good to us."

Eregard nodded. "It's true. I told you how it happened."

"It's common knowledge that Prince Eregard was lost at sea," Castio muttered, closing his fingers on the coin. He straightened abruptly, squaring his shoulders, then demanded, "What is the name of the King's general in the South?"

"When I left," Eregard said, "that position was held by General Deggazo. He was nearing retirement, though."

Castio looked over at Talis, who spread her hands in a "what can you do?" gesture. "And the King's geographer, who is also the royal mapmaker?"

"Petruce q'Avagne."

Castio shrugged. "The answers to these questions are matters of public record."

Eregard smiled wryly and displayed his callused and scarred hands. "For your average fieldhand?"

Castio ignored the attempted witticism. "The only way to

be sure would be to haul you over to the Governor's palace and give him a look at you."

"First you'd have to let me shave, and even then it's possible he might not recognize me," Eregard replied dryly. "I've changed. Hard work can do that to a man." He gave Talis a half-shamed glance. "Even when I was planning to run away, I realized that it would be difficult for people I knew only casually to recognize me."

Jezzil, who had been standing quietly, arms crossed, in the corner of the room, remarked, "Be grateful, Eregard. Castio is right about this mission being dangerous. It's better you remain unrecognized, and that collar is an excellent disguise."

Eregard turned to the Chonao, his hand going up to his iron collar. "Disguise? I'm not going to travel to Pela in *disguise*. What gave you that idea?"

"It's the sensible thing to do," Castio said. "The Redai would like nothing better than to wind up with Agivir's son to use as a bargaining token."

Eregard was shaking his head. "Oh, no. This double bedamned collar is coming *off*, right now, as soon as you can get me to a blacksmith shop. I'm not wearing it one minute longer than I have to!"

"It's the perfect disguise," Jezzil pointed out. "No one looks at a slave."

"I want it *off*," Eregard said. "I want it *gone*."

"Before we dock at Minoma, I swear to you I'll file it off myself," Jezzil said. "Until then, let's leave it."

Eregard looked from Jezzil to Castio, then on to Talis. Each of them nodded agreement with Jezzil's reasoning.

The Prince glared at them, then turned and headed for the door. "I'll wait for you outside, Jezzil," he snarled, opening it. He stepped outside and slammed it behind him.

"He's furious," Talis said.

Jezzil nodded. "I don't blame him. But I think he knows we're right to leave the collar on until we're out of danger."

"So, what's your decision, Rufen?" Talis asked. "I believe

Eregard's story. I believe Thia. She's a Truthsenser. Try her yourself. And if he really *is* the missing Prince, and we return him to Pela, this could be a boon to our cause, couldn't it?"

"Perhaps," Castio muttered, beginning to pace back and forth. "If we could gain Agivir's ear, tell him what his eldest is doing to the colony . . ."

"He said his father may not have enough support left in the military to face down Salesin," Jezzil said. "Or enough spirit."

Castio had stopped pacing. "All right, he's the missing Prince. I believe you." He looked over at Talis. "I can give you the money for your passage, and a document proclaiming you my emissary. But if *he*"—he jerked his chin at the door Eregard had used—"is a fake, you'll likely wind up on a gallows if you manage to reach Pela."

"We have to do something, or we'll find ourselves not free, but a Chonao colony," Talis pointed out. "Rufen, I want to take Jezzil, too. The Prince should have a bodyguard, and I'll have to sleep sometime."

Castio sighed, but nodded. "Very well. But I wish you'd let me send Bona and Sethe with the Prince. You've become one of my best advisers, Talis. I don't want to lose you."

Talis glanced at Eregard. "I believe in this mission, Rufen. And besides . . ." She smiled wryly. "I have to be the one to go. Remember, I *own* this fieldhand."

"I'm going with you," Thia said, her voice quiet, composed, but as steely as any sword.

"Thia, don't think we don't want you to come!" Talis cried. "But this journey is apt to be perilous. The Redai's forces are massing."

The former priestess gave her friend a long, level look. "You've seen Boq'urak. And I'm supposed to be worried about an *army*?" She turned her gaze on Jezzil, who was lounging in the doorway. "I'll pay my own passage. Dr. Khith will loan me the payment, I'm sure of it."

"What will I do?" The thin, inhuman voice came from the

other entrance to the parlor. Thia, Eregard, Jezzil, and Talis all turned to find the Hthras physician, fur still ruffled from sleep, clutching a bedgown around itself against the early morning chill. "What's happened?"

"We have to leave, Doctor," Jezzil said. "We'll be taking the first ship we can board that's bound for Pela."

"Last night we discovered that Kerezau has offered a sham alliance to Castio," Talis added. "He plans to betray Kata and conquer the colony. And we also discovered . . ." She shrugged, and smiled wryly. ". . . that our friend here," she waved at Eregard, "is actually the missing Prince of Pela. We need to take him back to his father, so Kata and Pela can fight together against the invaders."

Khith blinked its enormous eyes, obviously taken aback. Thia watched the Hthras, wondering how much of the human political situation the little physician understood. "I see," it muttered after a moment. "You certainly had a busy night, didn't you?"

Jezzil chuckled, and Talis smiled wearily. Only Eregard remained sober-faced. Thia watched the Prince, concerned. *He's suffered so much,* she thought. *He was raised to luxury, indolence, and self-indulgence. How has he changed? How does he really feel about us? For months Talis has treated him like a thing, a mere possession. What will happen when he's back with his royal kin?*

"Please, Doctor," she said aloud, "can you lend me the fare for the passage? I can't stay here, not knowing whether they . . ." She trailed off, then finished, "I have to go. They're my friends."

Eregard gave her a quick, appreciative glance, then reached over and brushed his fingertips against her forearm.

Khith was staring at them, each in turn, ending with Jezzil. "And you are all *my* friends," it said. "Jezzil, you are my student, my apprentice. Your training has barely begun. It cannot end yet."

Jezzil nodded. "I understand, Doctor. I've learned just enough to realize how important the training is. But I'll come back, I swear it." He hesitated. "If there is war, I may not be able to travel, but as soon as—"

Khith waved its narrow hand impatiently. "No. Your training is too important. Thia and I will accompany you." It looked over at Eregard and Talis. "With your permission."

"But, Doctor, this is going to be a difficult voyage," Talis protested. "Uncomfortable, possibly dangerous. There are Chonao troops moving on Pela and Kata even as we speak. If something went wrong, we might not be able to protect you."

The Hthras gazed up at her, its huge eyes intent. "I do not need your protection," it declared. "I may not have your abilities with weapons one can see and touch, but I am hardly helpless. I have the ability to protect myself. And, possibly, all of you as well."

The four humans glanced at each other, then Talis shrugged. "All right," she said. "The five of us will go."

"Six," Jezzil corrected. "Don't forget Falar. Where I go, she goes."

Talis clung to the railing of the ship, heaving. Her stomach was long empty, yet still she retched. Finally, gagging, she managed to bring up bile that tasted so dreadful it made her heave all over again. She spat, then spat again. Her legs trembled as she clung to the polished wood, wiping her mouth on her sleeve, eyes closed. *Fine warrior you proved to be,* she thought disgustedly. *Puking your guts up the moment we clear the Q'Kal harbor.*

The Pride of Pela lurched, and, groaning, Talis let herself slip down until she was seated on the deck, bracing her back against the railing. *This is so humiliating!*

"Talis?"

Hearing the soft, reedy voice, she managed to open her swollen eyes a slit, and saw Khith bending over her. "Please, Doctor, I'm not well. I don't want to talk to anyone."

"So I see," the Hthras said. "If you will but place this lozenge under your tongue and let it dissolve, I believe you will be much improved."

Talis gave the little physician a dubious glance, but slipped the large bolus beneath her tongue. Khith placed its hand on her forehead. "Relax," it told her. "Relax . . ."

The Hthras began to chant softly, so softly that even Talis had difficulty hearing over the creak of the ropes and the shouts of the crew. Not that it would have made any difference, for the language was one she'd never heard before.

She sighed, tasting the sharp, astringent taste of the lozenge as it dissolved. Her stomach spasms lessened, then stopped.

When Khith's chanting ended some minutes later, Talis dared to open her eyes. The ship was still rolling, but the terrible vertigo and nausea had stopped. Talis glanced up at the Hthras gratefully. "Thank you, Doctor. You are a wonderful healer."

The corners of the Hthras's mouth turned up, ever so slightly. "You are very welcome, Talis. It would not do to have Prince Eregard's bodyguard incapacitated, would it? Now rest, and then get something to eat."

"Will the seasickness return?"

"No. I have made an adjustment. It will not return."

Wondering what an "adjustment" was, Talis nodded and stood up. The fresh ocean breeze was invigorating, and the Narrow Sea sparkled blue beneath a nearly cloudless sky. A gust of wind tautened the sails, and the deck tilted. Talis braced her legs, but her stomach stayed steady. She took a long, deep breath and grinned with profound relief. "Thank you, Doctor!"

The Hthras did not smile as humans did, but the corners of the creature's mouth quirked and the eyes narrowed slightly. "You are most welcome, Mistress Talis. It would not do for our royal companion to have to go without one of his bodyguards."

Talis nodded. "No, it wouldn't. I'll go and take over for Jezzil."

"First, have a moment to enjoy the sea air," Khith suggested. "My pupil will not mind."

Talis began walking along the rail, feeling the ocean roll beneath the ship's keel as they surged through the water under full sail. It was exhilarating now, like riding a horse at a fast canter. "Oh, yes," she said to Khith, who was keeping pace with her. The movements of the ship didn't seem to disconcert the physician at all. "Jezzil is learning magic from you, right?"

"That is correct."

"He really can do spells and that kind of thing?"

Khith nodded. "He really can."

Talis stopped when she reached the more open deck up toward the bow, watching the sailors as they performed their assigned tasks. One was swabbing the deck, another splicing rope, and still another scuttled up and down one of the masts, making minute adjustments to the billowing white canvas. Khith watched them, too. "A fine day at sea," it said.

She shaded her eyes with her hand, gazing out across the expanse of water. "Wait a minute, is that land? We can't have reached Pela yet! Or is it one of the smaller islands? I thought they lay farther south."

Khith's gaze followed her pointing finger. "That darkish line on the horizon? No, that isn't land, child, it is one of the floating seaweed beds. Some are almost as large as small islands."

"I've heard of them. Some of the sailors told me about how they can get so thick farther south, they have to burn them to open up channels to reach inland harbors."

"They provide a valuable resource for the coastal farmers. Some of them harvest the weed tips that grow above the beds, then dry it to feed livestock. A sort of sea hay, one might call it. Farmers tell me cattle thrive on it," Khith told her. "My people trade for it, and it is considered a delicacy. I've also heard the seaweed is used in some classic Pelanese dishes."

"How do they harvest the weed?" Talis wondered.

"The weed grows in mats that will support human weight, at least to some extent. Women and boys harvest it using a special type of scythe. After it is cut and dried, they bag it up for shipment."

Talis turned to the physician wonderingly. "How do you know so much about human society, Doctor?"

"When I was a youngling, I traveled with my father, who was one of the few Hthras traders who went on regular voyages to human lands. I have visited the Meptalith Islands, Pela, and many ports in Kata. I . . . enjoy human society—" The physician broke off abruptly.

"You enjoy human society?" Talis repeated, making it a question. When Khith did not answer, she prompted, "Is that unusual?"

"Yes. My people are insular. Most of them look down on humans."

"But you like us? That's fortunate for us," Talis said with a smile. Putting out a hand, she touched the doctor's furred forearm. "And bless you for all you've done to help us. Without you, Jezzil would have died. Don't think we don't realize that."

"Do not credit me with too much altruism, Mistress Talis," Khith said. "From the moment I encountered him, I could not allow Jezzil to die—and that was for my own selfish purposes. I realized immediately that he was very special, that his abilities, if trained properly, might one day exceed my own."

The Hthras stared off into the distance, across the deep green of the ocean.

"Really? I knew Jezzil was an expert warrior, but I never dreamed . . ." She shrugged.

"Oh, yes," Khith replied. "If he is properly trained, I believe Jezzil could someday become a very powerful Adept. And it is the duty of an ethical mage to encourage and nurture a talented pupil. My people call the ability to control and use what you would term 'magic' avundi. The possession of avundi carries a heavy price for those who are not properly trained to harness and employ it."

"I understand better now why you didn't want to be separated from Jezzil," Talis said. "And, Doctor, you've certainly been useful on this passage. I can swear to that!"

The little healer's mouth quirked in what Talis now recognized was its version of a smile. "Thank you, Mistress Talis. If only all ills of this world were as easy to cure as a case of seasickness."

* * *

The fair weather continued, and *The Pride of Pela* made good time toward Minoma harbor. Having demonstrated Falar's obedience, Jezzil was permitted to lead her around the deck for a little exercise. The captain had originally wanted to stable her down in the hold, where they carried a cargo of cattle, but extra coins had convinced him to construct a makeshift stall amidships, on deck, beneath a hastily erected awning.

Jezzil found his days full. In addition to caring for Falar, he gave Eregard lessons in beginning swordsmanship, and practiced each day with Talis, who was becoming quite proficient. He also continued her lessons in unarmed combat and knife-fighting.

Most taxing of all, however, were his sessions with Khith. The Hthras was teaching him to conjure fire, and that was no small undertaking.

Now that he could "touch" the place in his mind that was the center of his avundi, he realized that he could affect the air enough to move objects . . . small ones, to be sure, but Khith assured him his mastery would grow with time and experience. But creating fire involved changing the air itself, causing its nature to alter, to *accelerate* what Master Khith referred to as its "elementals." The theory behind the entire concept was more than Jezzil could comprehend, but he was beginning to learn how the feat was accomplished.

Their sixth day out, sweat pouring down his face, he caused a candle wick to smolder for a few seconds. The next day the wick ignited and burned steadily. Scarcely able to believe what he was seeing, Jezzil slumped over, exhausted but exhilarated. Khith reached over and grasped his hand, raising it in a gesture of victory.

"You make your teacher proud, Jezzil," the Hthras said solemnly. "You have accomplished in little more than a week what it took me more than a fortnight to learn."

Jezzil smiled. "I suspect I have a better teacher than you did, Master Khith."

"Nonsense," Khith replied, but Jezzil could tell the Hthras

was pleased. The bond between them had grown, so that Jezzil thought of the doctor as his new Amato, his leader, his battle comrade. There was no higher honor recognized among his people. He cared more for the Hthras, he realized, than he had even for Barus.

As they neared the coast of Pela, he learned to summon light without heat, a feat Khith referred to as "coruscation."

Just one day out from Ninoma Harbor, they entered a dense fog bank. The captain reduced sail, then reduced it more, until the ship was barely moving. "Shoal water ahead," Eregard said. "Many captains would have to heave-to and wait it out. It's a good thing our navigator is Meptal-ith. They have their own methods of navigation. With them it's an art, or perhaps some type of magic. They keep their secrets closely guarded."

Jezzil stood with him at the bow-rail. "I've never seen such a dense fog."

"I have," the Prince said. "Pelanese fogs are legendary, and this one is a fine example. It's so thick you can't see from one end of this ship to another."

Something large bumped gently against the bow, then slithered away to become part of their wake. Jezzil caught only a glimpse of a dark mass, so thick was the mist. "Was that a sea creature?"

"No, one of the seaweed mats," Eregard told him. "We've gone a bit north of what should be our course, to make sure we stay far away from any shoal water."

"Will this fog delay our arrival in Minoma?"

"Probably, unless we pick up a very good wind tomorrow. Assuming the fog is gone when we wake up."

"Is that likely?"

Eregard chuckled. "There's an old Pelanese saying: if you don't like the weather in Minoma, just wait. It will change."

Jezzil laughed. "We have the same saying in my homeland."

"I suspect everyone does," Eregard said. "Jezzil . . ." He hesitated.

"What is it, Eregard?" He looked at his companion, then

smiled wryly. "Or should I get used to saying 'Your High-ness'?"

The Prince made a dismissive gesture. "Certainly not when we're alone. I wanted to ask you, that is, make sure . . ."

"What?"

"Well, Thia. You two are friends, right? Just friends."

Jezzil stood there, taken aback, unable to think of a reply. Eregard seemed to take his silence as confirmation, for after a moment he nodded. "That's what I thought. Like brother and sister, or a priest and priestess. Which is, from what I understand, what you both are."

Jezzil shook his head. "I used to be what you might call a priest, but no more. I broke my vows."

Eregard raised an eyebrow. "Oh? Tempted by a woman?"

Jezzil turned back to the rail, stood looking out into the smothering grayness. "Not exactly. It's a long story."

"Well, if you ever decide to tell it, I'd like to hear," the Prince said.

Jezzil cleared his throat, spat over the railing. "Why did you ask about my relationship with Thia?" *What is my rela-tionship with Thia? That night at the tavern, I felt so strange. It was more than simple*— He groped for a word, finally set-tled on one the priests had used incessantly to warn them about the dangers of women: lust. *Or was it? Could it have been the wine?* He shook his head. He couldn't remember when he'd been so confused.

"When I reach Pela, I'll be expected to take back up where I left off. All those powdered, perfumed court ladies, all the dalliances, and the backstairs gossip about who's cheating with whom . . . it's all so tawdry." Eregard turned, and leaning against the rail, regarded the Chonao. "I must have changed, Jezzil, because I can't stand the thought of all those nobles throwing their daughters at me. It would be good if I arrived home with an affianced bride."

Jezzil stared at him, incredulous. "You—You can't mean Thia?" he managed finally.

"Why not?" Eregard asked. "It seems to me she'd make a

fine Princess of Pela. She's educated, scholarly, a lady with good manners and delicate sensibilities. Why not Thia?"

"She's not wise in the ways of the world," Jezzil said after a long moment. "She grew up in a cloister."

"I know that. So did my brother's wife. Princess Ulandra. That was no bar to her marrying him." Eregard fell silent. Jezzil studied him, thinking that there was obviously more to the story than that, but the Prince volunteered nothing more.

"Thia is very shy," Jezzil said. "She's not had . . . I mean, she's never . . ."

"If you're trying to tell me she's a maiden, I already guessed," Eregard said dryly. "That's actually considered an advantage in a royal match—for the bride, that is."

Jezzil stood at the rail staring down at the black water he could barely glimpse through the grayness. The fog seemed to hang on him like a shroud. Finally he said, "You don't love her."

Eregard drew breath, then let it out slowly. "You're right," he admitted. "But I care for her. I am very fond of her. If she agreed to be my bride, I would be the best husband I could be, Jezzil. No court dalliances for me. I leave that sort of thing to my brother," he added, and Jezzil heard the bitterness in his voice.

"Besides," Eregard added after a moment's consideration, "they tell me love often grows after the marriage vows are spoken."

Jezzil's throat was tight. He swallowed to ease it, thinking he should just remain silent. Thia would never again have to hoard a handful of coins and live for a week on mush, beans, and wild greens gathered from the pastures, as she'd had to sometimes in Q'Kal. But the words erupted, heedless of his wishes. "She deserves someone who loves her!"

Eregard was regarding him, eyes narrowed.

Jezzil turned away from that steady gaze. "She does," he said, his voice even and controlled.

"I agree," the Prince said. "But, Jezzil, there are many kinds of love. The kind of love you're probably thinking of is something I feel for . . . someone else. Someone I can never have. I don't think I'll ever feel that way about anyone else. But that doesn't mean I couldn't come to love Thia, and she me."

"Of course," Jezzil said, his voice a monotone. "I understand. But would court life agree with her? It all seems very devious from what you've said."

Eregard gave a grunt that might have been ironic laughter. "Good term. You're right, of course. But there are those who stay above that sort of thing, even in the court. My father never had a mistress, nor my mother a lover. They've been happy with each other for . . ." He paused to think. ". . . thirty years, it will be, in just a few months." He sighed. "My mother hasn't been well for a while, and usually keeps to her apartments. But when I was younger, the entire family would go to the country, or sailing on the royal yacht . . . We really were a family."

"That's good," Jezzil said. "In my country it's different. Little boys live with their mothers, shut off from the rest of the household except for meals and religious observances. Later, when I was older, I was with the men, and hardly ever saw my mother or sisters. Then I left my family when I was seven, to become a warrior apprentice."

Jezzil sighed, remembering the day he'd left home, how he'd caught a glimpse of his mother at the upstairs window, peering out from behind the curtain. "Later, I was chosen out of a hundred boys to try out for the Pen Jav Dal, the Order of the Silent Ones. It's hard now to remember my family. I haven't seen them in more than ten years."

"The soldiers of the Redai aren't granted leave from duty?"

"Regular troops, yes. But not the Pen Jav Dal. We're priests as well as warriors, and we are supposed to remain cloistered, no contact with the outside world except when on duty, and no contact at all with women."

Eregard grimaced. "What a price to pay for being one of the elite! Women are one of nature's greatest blessings . . . some women, at least."

"So I have been learning," Jezzil muttered. "But I still practice my religion. For me to even befriend Thia and Talis was . . ." He hesitated. "Well, it wasn't something I'd ever expected to happen."

"You know what they say. 'Expect the unexpected.' "

The Chonao smiled wryly. "I suppose so. Do you . . . do you think Thia loves you?"

"I don't know. I think she cares for me. I suppose I'll find out."

He sounds confident, Jezzil thought sourly. *But why shouldn't he be? He's a prince.*

"When do you plan to ask her?"

Eregard thought for a moment. "Tomorrow. When the fog is gone and the harbor of Minoma lies before us. It's a beautiful city, built on a mountainside. The palace is built of pale gray stone, with black granite pillars. The roofs are red tiles." He sighed happily. "There's a huge fortress wall runs around the Old City and the palace. The New City spills out down the hillside, all the way to cliffs that lead down to the harbor. The houses are pink and white and pale green stucco."

Jezzil nodded. "It sounds beautiful."

"Oh, it is. It's almost summer; there will be flowering trees and bushes everywhere. Little cafés with tables outside on stone patios. Colorful awnings, and everywhere the smell of the flowers . . ." He smiled. "I've missed it so much."

"Naturally," Jezzil said.

"Tomorrow," Eregard said, staring off into the fog, still with that faraway expression. "Tomorrow I'll ask her. After the fog lifts."

The fog did indeed lift shortly after sunrise, revealing blue skies with a few puffy white clouds, a blue-green ocean—

—and seven small but heavily armed Meptalith vessels surrounding *The Pride of Pela.*

It was Thia who first saw them. Trained from childhood to rise each day before sunrise, she awoke early, as usual. Dressing quietly, she slipped out of the small cabin and went up on deck, hugging her shawl around her as she strolled back and forth, watching the eastern horizon. As the Sun rose and the ships materialized out of the fleeing darkness, she cried out to a passing sailor, pointing. Thia didn't recognize the ships, but the fact that they were surrounded indicated unfriendly intentions.

Her fears were quickly confirmed. The sailor she'd summoned took one look, swore, then went racing away, yelling. Within moments the deck resounded with the pounding of feet and the shouts of seamen and officers.

Thia huddled against Falar's stall, trying to stay out of the way. *I have to warn the others,* she realized, and carefully made her way to the narrow ladder that led below. First she entered the tiny cabin she and Talis shared and shook the Katan woman awake. "Wake up! The ship is surrounded!"

Talis's green eyes opened, then she sat up, cursing as fluently as any of the sailors. "I knew it was too good to be true!" As Thia left, she was yanking on her clothes.

Next she darted into the cabin where Khith, Eregard, and Jezzil slept in their hammocks. "Wake up!" she gasped. "Come on, wake up! There are ships out there. I counted seven, and they're all around us."

Jezzil swung out of his hammock in one fluid motion and stood there, bare-chested and clad only in his drawers. Thia glanced away, feeling her face grow hot. She'd never seen so much male flesh in her life.

Eregard raised himself on his elbow, eyeing her blearily. "Wha . . . ? What?"

"Ships!" she said. "Hurry, get dressed! We're surrounded by ships!"

Eregard snarled a word in Pelanese that Thia didn't recognize, and slumped back into his hammock. "Goddess," he added. "Not *again!*"

Thia whirled and raced out of the cabin, then up the ladder and back onto the deck. The sun had lifted past the low-lying clouds now, and the ships surrounding them were all too clear. One of them had broken the ring and was under sail, approaching *The Pride of Pela.*

As the ship drew nearer, she could make out a man in armor standing in the bow, the wind of the passage blowing his long black hair out behind him.

Moments later Talis joined her at the railing. "Are we going to fight?" Thia asked.

"I doubt it," Talis said. "The *Pride* is outgunned and surrounded."

Khith came up to join them. The little Hthras was shivering in the early morning air, despite the protection of its wool robe. "That man . . ." The doctor pointed at the black-haired man Thia had noticed. "He is . . ."

When the Hthras hesitated, Thia asked, "He is what, Master Khith?"

The Hthras shook its softly furred head, its huge eyes holding apprehension and sadness. "He is . . . important to us in some way. Now, and in the future. If I but had the time, I could scry out what he means, but—"

"Of course he's important to us," Talis said. "He's the Chonao leader of this fleet. I wonder if he's the Redai himself?"

"No, he's not." Jezzil's voice came from behind them. They turned to see him shading his eyes against the eastern light. "Kerezau has much lighter hair. And he always wears a battle helm with a scarlet plume, so the troops can recognize him."

Thia watched as the Meptalith vessel drew closer, Jezzil standing beside her. As the boat approached and she leaned against him, she felt the muscles in his arm grow rock-hard. Looking up at him, she saw his green gaze fixed on the boat and the man standing in the prow.

When the boat was within earshot, they heard the leader demanding that the *Pride* surrender. Captain Garano replied that they would surrender without a fight as long as passengers and crew were taken to within sight of Pela and allowed to leave the ship in the lifeboats, unmolested.

The leader gave his assent, then ordered them to drop a boarding ladder.

Moments later a contingent of Chonao soldiers had swarmed aboard, then stood, swords in hand, as their leader made a more leisurely, dignified assent.

When the man with the long black hair finally stepped onto the deck, Thia realized that Jezzil was so tense he was nearly trembling. He was muttering under his breath, and she couldn't tell whether he was cursing or praying.

Then, before she could move or speak, Jezzil lunged forward, nearly babbling in his own language. Thia heard what she thought was a name. *Barus?* Jezzil lunged at him, arms out, obviously ready to embrace him.

When the man he called Barus did not move, or speak, or smile, Jezzil slowed, then halted, obviously confused and hurt. He spoke again, using that same name, Barus, but this time he seemed to be asking a question.

Barus—if that was indeed his name—abruptly smiled, his teeth flashing, and raised both arms. Jezzil let out an exultant sound, half sob, half laugh, and went to embrace him.

Without warning Barus's armored fist flashed forward like a striking snake, to smash into Jezzil's face with an audible *crack*. Jezzil staggered back, blood erupting from his nose, eyes wide with shock. He crumpled to the deck and lay still, unmoving save for the blood trickling down.

Barus looked down at him again, and the wide smile had turned cruel and mocking. He raised his foot, then kicked Jezzil viciously in the side.

"No! Stop that!" Thia made no conscious decision, was barely aware that she had bolted toward the motionless pair—until Talis and Eregard grabbed her and restrained her.

"Thia! No!" Eregard ordered. "You can't help him!"

Barus turned to look at them and smiled slightly. "That's right, you can't," he said in accented Pelanese. "How interesting to discover that my former friend has new comrades." He smiled. "Two women, eh? You are his concubines?"

Talis muttered an oath. This time she was the one who had to be restrained.

Barus laughed, obviously enjoying their distress. He issued orders to his men, and several of them scattered to begin tying up the captain and his officers. He gestured to Jezzil, who was beginning to stir, and gave orders. With a sideways glance at the onlookers, he translated them. "You two, pick up this cowardly sack of pig guts and confine him to an empty hold. Post a guard."

The men saluted and sprang to do his bidding.

Thia turned a despairing glance at Talis, who was standing with eyes narrowed, obviously considering and then discarding possible actions. She turned to see Khith regarding Jezzil with distress as one of the Chonao tossed a bucket of saltwater into his face. Jezzil's eyes opened and he choked, gasped, then moaned as the others hauled him to his feet. His knees buckled. Thia mouthed, "Help him! We have to help him!"

Khith shook its head ever so slightly and whispered, barely above a breath, "Later."

As the guards dragged Jezzil away, Barus turned to another of his men and gave rapid orders in his native tongue.

"What did you tell them?" Thia blurted helplessly.

Barus turned to translate again, smiling broadly. "I told them to go to the flagship and tell the Redai we have captured a traitor. As soon as he arrives to sign the order for execution, I'll have the distinct pleasure of hanging my old friend." He pointed upward. "From *that* yardarm."

16

Blood Magic

"*Hang him*?" Talis blurted, "for *what*?"

Barus regarded her as though she were some new and not very interesting variety of insect. "Desertion, for one thing. And probably treason." He glanced at another of his guards. "These people who were traveling with Jezzil, escort them belowships and lock them in a cabin. I'll let the Redai deal with him when he arrives."

As the guard moved toward them, Talis stepped hurriedly to the fore. "Wait!" She fumbled for the leather packet she carried beneath her tunic. "My name is Talis Aloro, and I'm the Special Envoy from Kata to the Redai." Hastily, she pulled out a paper, checked that it was the correct one, and handed it to him. "This is my authorization."

Barus scanned the paper. Talis wondered briefly whether the Chonao could read Pelanese script, while thanking the Goddess above that Castio had supplied her with two sets of papers—one for King Agivir, the other for the Redai, in the event their ship was captured.

Finally the Chonao leader looked up. "And who are these others?" He fixed his dark gaze on Khith. "And what is *that*?

A Hthras?" He studied the physician. "Never saw one before. Not a live one, anyway. My father had a stuffed one mounted on his wall."

Talis glanced at Khith, willing the doctor to remain quiet. The huge eyes remained fixed on Barus, but the Hthras said not a word.

"Yes, Dr. Khith is traveling as my personal physician," Talis said, thinking fast, "and Eregard here is my slave. Thia is my maid."

He gave her a long, raking stare, his gaze traveling up her body from her men's riding boots, to her buckskin breeches, to her man's shirt and jerkin, ending finally at her hair—hastily braided, hairpins sticking out of her bun. The Chonao smiled mockingly. "If she's your lady's maid, you need to dismiss her, Mistress Aloro."

Talis felt an angry flush warming her face, but she forced her voice to be steady, neutral. "I ask that my entourage be accorded the same courtesy you accord me."

He laughed. "You travel in bad company, Mistress Aloro. And this," he waved Castio's document at her, "says nothing about anyone but you. In deference to our alliance with your leader, I shall not confine you with the others. You may keep your freedom aboard ship, but the Redai will want to question you, of that I am sure." He turned to the others and gestured. "Take them away, lock them in one of the small cabins. See that they come to no harm. Post a guard."

The soldier he addressed snapped to attention, responded in their own language, and obeyed. Talis watched as her comrades were marched off, disappearing belowdecks.

Barus turned away from her to direct his men. Talis was left standing on the deck. *What now?* she wondered forlornly.

She took a turn around the deck, careful to keep away from the Chonao soldiers. *I have to do something! Why did this have to happen, just when we were almost to Pela?*

She wound up beside Falar's stall, then slid down to sit with her back against the boards. The mare, scenting a familiar presence, came over to snuffle at her hair. Idly, Talis stroked her questing nose. "What am I going to do, girl?"

she muttered. "We're all in a pretty mess, and I have to do something!"

What would Jezzil do? What would Rufen do?

She swallowed, then sat up straight, glancing around. Nobody was paying her any attention. The Chonao warriors were swarming all over the ship, and some of the Meptalith vessels had set sail and were heading away. *We're captured, they don't need all the vessels,* she realized. *They're heading for Pela, carrying troops. How many troops?*

There was no way to know. She watched between the slats of the stall as Barus scribbled a message on a tiny scrap of parchment and bound it to the leg of a messenger bird. The bird went up in a blur of wings, circled once, then headed west.

The morning was now well advanced, and a rumble in her stomach reminded Talis that she hadn't eaten since last night. Searching in the pocket of her jerkin, she found a few scraps of dried fruit and chewed them, hoping they would give her energy, clear her mind.

He said the Redai was coming. Kerezau himself.

She stopped chewing as her answer presented itself, then nearly choked when she tried to swallow. Despite the fruit, her mouth had gone utterly dry.

I have to kill him.

Kill the leader of the world's most formidable army? Could she? Could she even get close enough? How to do it?

He'll be surrounded by bodyguards, warriors trained the way Jezzil is trained. Expert swordsmen and assassins . . .

And yet, Barus had said the Redai would see her. And she knew from Jezzil that there were no warrior women among his people. Kerezau might not be suspecting a female assassin.

I'll wear a dress, she thought. *But still, they'll search me. There's no place to hide a pistol, sword, or knife. How can I get close enough to him with a weapon?*

Falar nuzzled her hair again, the mare's hot breath gusting down the back of her shirt. Talis reached up absently to pat the horse, and her questing fingers brushed one of her hairpins.

She pulled it out and sat staring at it intently. It was longer than her forefinger, made of steel, and quite sturdy. But it was blunt, not pointed. *But if I sharpened it, it would be long enough to stab out an eyeball and enter the brain, or pierce the carotid, or the jugular.*

Talis looked around again, then casually tucked the hairpin into the pocket of her jerkin. There was bound to be a whetstone down in the galley, and the cook had smiled at her each morning when serving breakfast. He'd be thrilled if she wandered into his galley for a little chat.

Whether I succeed or not, my life will be forfeit, she realized. *Can I do it? Knowing I'll die?* She shivered, though the sun and the breeze were warm. Suddenly the taste of the dried fruit seemed cloying, and she swallowed fiercely. She would *not* vomit!

If Castio were here in my place, what would he do?

She knew. Rufen Castio would do what he had to do in order to save his country from a ruthless conqueror. She remembered the way Clo had charged into battle. Surely she had known she might die.

Talis grimaced. There was a world of difference between "might" and "would."

But she couldn't overlook this opportunity. The chance to kill Kerezau had been given to her, and to her alone. She had to act.

Jezzil had taught her some of his warrior philosophy, and she remembered one of his warrior's credos: *Better a dead target than a live assassin.*

Talis got up and walked over to the railing, staring out to sea. Her father and mother would probably never know what happened to her. Her brothers would miss her, all right, because they'd have to do her work. But that would be the only thing they'd miss, she concluded cynically. And if she died, she lost all chance at revenge on her uncle Jasti.

For a moment a wave of the old panic swept over her, but, teeth gritted, she forced it back. Making Uncle Jasti suffer and die was the least of her problems at the moment. If the old demon lived to rape other maidens, there was nothing she could do about it. Killing Kerezau would save hundreds, possibly thousands, of Katans, not to mention her kinsmen, the Pelanese.

Thinking about Jezzil made her remember another thing he'd said. Even a casual scratch could be made fatal. Jezzil himself no longer had access to his assassin's supplies, but what about Master Khith? Surely the doctor had potions that could harm as well as heal?

She wondered how closely her friends were being guarded. Time for a little trip belowdecks, to reconnoiter the situation.

Thia sat on the edge of the bunk in the small third mate's cabin, crying silently. Tears flooded her eyes, slid down her face, and every few moments she swiped at them with her free hand. Her eyes already felt sore and hot.

Khith sat beside her on the narrow bunk, holding her other hand, gently stroking it with its delicate, long digits.

Eregard sat on the floor, knees drawn up, his face buried in his arms, muttering softly in Pelanese. Thia didn't know most of the words, but from his tone, she assumed they were curses. She wished she knew a few herself. Before thrusting them into this tiny third mate's cabin, their captors had patted them down in a rapid and cursory fashion, searching for weapons. They'd confiscated only two things: her firestriker and Eregard's knife. It was obvious they considered the three no threat, as they'd laughed and joked in their own language the whole time.

She'd looked, but hadn't gotten even a hint of where they'd taken Jezzil. Images of him bleeding and barely conscious, being dragged off by his countrymen, tormented Thia. Where was he now? How badly was he hurt? That man—Barus? Was that his name?—had said he would have Jezzil executed, hanged! Thia shuddered.

Khith's fingers tightened on hers as the little Hthras gave her hand a sympathetic squeeze. She turned to look at the physician, on the verge of breaking down completely. "Doctor, did you understand what that man Barus said? That Jezzil will be hanged when the Redai signs his death warrant?"

"Yes."

She shook her head, swiped at her face with her sleeve. "We can't let that happen!"

Eregard raised his face from his arms and regarded her bleakly. "What can we do? There's a guard posted outside this door. The cabin is stripped bare, not so much as pair of drawers left. Talis is still free, but they certainly are going to watch her, so we can't count on her to break us out."

Thia frowned. "There has to be something we can do. Maybe one of us could pretend to be sick. When the guard comes in, we can . . ." She hesitated.

"Break the chamber pot over his head?" Eregard suggested sarcastically. "Thia, this isn't some bardsong or epic lay. That sort of thing only works in stories."

"There has to be something," she insisted. "What have we got between us? Anyone have anything sharp?"

"Just my knife," Eregard said. "And they took that."

"They didn't take everything. Empty your pockets," she ordered, scrabbling through the folds of her skirt. "Let's see what we have."

Eregard laid out his contents on the bare boards of the floor with a sigh and an eye roll. Two small coins, a bit of string, a bandanna that had been used to clean Talis's tack in the past, and two pieces of endpaper he'd torn from a book and folded carefully, planning to use them to write a note to his father in case he had trouble getting past the palace guards.

Thia didn't do much better. She had a small pouch of coins, a chapbook of Rufen Castio's writings that Denno had given her as a farewell present, a stub of candle, and a small waxed parcel of dried fruit and nuts she'd bought from a vendor on the docks before boarding *The Pride of Pela*.

When both humans were finished, they turned to look at the Hthras. "Master Khith?" Thia asked, wondering if the Hthras even had pockets in its robe. "Do you have anything that could help?"

The Hthras's huge eyes gleamed in the dimness of the little cabin. "Let us see," it said, reaching into the folds of its physician's robe. "What do we have?"

Thia watched in growing perplexity as the Hthras crouched between the bunk and the wall, adding objects to the small pile. Five brightly colored scallop shells, tightly closed. Seven large acorns, their little caps still in place. A piece of charcoal, and a stub of chalk. A short piece of string, and a small tube that looked like a pipe with the bowl broken off.

Thia regarded this depressing collection dejectedly. "Oh, well," she murmured. "It was just an idea."

Khith sat down on the deck beside Eregard, arranging its robes prissily around its skinny shanks. The Hthras looked up at her, and the corner of its huge eyes crinkled. "Oh, I don't know, Thia, my dear. I believe we have done rather well, all things considered."

Eregard raised his head to look again at the little pile, then glanced up at Thia. It was plain from his expression that he was wondering, as she was, whether the little healer had lost its wits.

"Master," she said hesitantly, "you see something in this collection that will help us?"

"Quite possibly," Khith said. "It depends on our course of action. What is our first priority?"

"Free Jezzil—" Thia began, but Eregard raised his voice to speak over her.

"Warn my father of Kerezau's invasion."

Now it was Thia's turn to give him a scathing look. "There's no way to do that!"

"Do not be too sure, Mistress Thia," Khith said. "I secreted some of my powders and potions in these"—it touched, first, the shells, then the acorns—"and many things are possible."

"Sending a message to my father?" Eregard jumped up so quickly he nearly stepped on their little pile of "treasures." Khith made a warning hiss as it raked the pile onto a fold of its robe. "Caution, Your Highness! My containers are fragile."

"Yes," Eregard said, moving with exaggerated care. He dropped onto the narrow bunk beside Thia. "Excuse me, Master Khith. I don't mean to seem skeptical, but *how*?"

Khith regarded him. "There are invisible cords that bind us to those we love . . . and, sometimes, those we hate. Tell me, Your Highness, which member of your family are you closest to?"

Eregard considered for a moment, "Well, my mother, I guess . . ."

"Can you see her face clearly in your mind?"

The Prince closed his eyes, then shook his head. "No, she's been ill for some time. I can't visualize her."

"Whose face *can* you see?"

Eregard smiled wryly. "The Princess Ulandra. My brother Salesin's wife. I—" He gave Thia a look that she couldn't read. Embarrassment? Defiance? "I love her," he said after a long pause.

"Love is good. Love is the strongest of bonds, I believe, more so than even hate or fear. Does the Princess return your feelings?"

He looked down. "No. But she knows I'm her friend. I think she has some affection for me . . . at least, I hope she does. But she probably thinks I'm dead, along with everyone else."

"That does not matter. If this works, she will know that you are alive. She will be within you, inside your mind. She will see through your eyes."

Eregard stared at the Hthras, wide-eyed. "You can *do* that?"

"It can be done among my people. Whether I can accomplish it with a human subject is another thing. It would be better if Jezzil were here. He has the potential for great power, and he is of the same species. But we will do what we can, at this time." The little physician raised its head, sniffed the air. "I sense a change in the weather, and not far off. There will be a storm by nightfall, a bad one. We had best hurry."

Quickly, they scrambled to obey the doctor's instructions. Thia found herself hanging the faded old sheet from the bunk on the wall, struggling to catch it on splinters in the ship timbers. Finally the task was done to Master Khith's satisfaction. The Hthras handed her the tiny chunk of charcoal, and told her that she and Eregard would be writing with it, so that Princess Ulandra would be able to read their message. "Write clearly," it instructed. "She will not receive a verbal message, only what you write."

"First of all," Eregard said, "we need a map."

The Prince sketched busily with the charcoal for several minutes, drawing a rough outline of Pela, labeling the port of Minoma on the western side, across the Narrow Sea from Kata. Then he made small sails with half-moons below them to indicate the presence of Kerezau's fleet. "My best guess is that he'll attack from the north," he muttered. "It wouldn't make any sense for him to sail all the way around the island to come in from the south. That way he'd have to cross the Goddess's Crown, and that range is still snowcapped. No, he'll come from the north, or perhaps northeast." He drew an arrow to indicate the direction the symbolic fleet was heading, then handed the charcoal to Thia.

"Not much left," she said, looking down at it. "What shall I write?"

Khith told her, and she obeyed. The charcoal ran out in mid-word.

"It will have to do," Khith said. "Now, we must have a source of flame . . ."

Thia held up her candle stub. "But they took my firestriker."

"That does not matter," Khith reassured her. Using the tip of one taloned forefinger, the Hthras carefully pried open one of the scallop shells. Inside the shell was a fine, purplish powder. Khith picked up the little tube, then, with two loud sniffs, inhaled some of the powder into first one flat nostril, then the other. The Hthras sat there, hand over its eyes, head bent. Thia could hear it breathing.

Finally it raised its head and stared at the candle stub. Without warning, the wick flared with bright yellow flame.

Thia yelped, so startled she nearly dropped the candle. "You did it!" Eregard exclaimed.

"That was the easy part," Khith said slowly, its voice thicker, deeper. *Drugged,* Thia thought, and felt a surge of fear. She tried to reassure herself that Master Khith surely knew what it was doing.

"Now for you, Eregard. We must strengthen that invisible cord, so your minds can meet," Khith said. Carefully, it opened one of the other scallop shells, and there was a grayish powder inside. "This will be difficult," Khith murmured. "If only I had my laboratory instruments." With a quick twist, it took the cap off one of the acorns and handed it to Thia. She held it, seeing a pinch of dark brown powder within. "When the gray powder melts," Khith told her, "pour the brown powder into the scallop shell."

"Yes, Doctor," she said, gripping the acorn.

With exacting care it took Eregard's two coins and the bandanna, then inserted one of the flattened flanges of the scallop shell between the two coins until it was stable. Using a fold of the dirty bandanna, it held the two coins tightly together and moved the scallop shell until it was nearly touching the flame. "This powder will melt, my Prince," it said, "and it will do so suddenly. When it is melted, Thia will add the brown powder. The mixture will then turn red. You must be prepared to take the shell and swallow its contents before the mixture can solidify. You will have only a handful of seconds before the mixture begins to harden. Understand?"

"Yes," Eregard said apprehensively. He caught Thia's eye and squared his shoulders. "I understand."

The three crouched over the candle flame, staring at the powder. The flame burned, and hot wax dripped down over Thia's fingers. She did not move; her training in Boq'urak's temple stood her in good stead. Staring at the powder, she gripped the candle and the little acorn, scarcely daring to blink.

For what seemed like many minutes, nothing happened. The candle was shrinking at an alarming rate. *What if it goes out?*

Just as she decided that Master Khith had made a mistake about the powder, it happened. As the Hthras had predicted, the change was sudden. One moment the grayish power lay there, inert, the next the powder had darkened around the edges . . . and by her next breath it was all dark, an iron gray now, plainly liquid.

Biting her lip with concentration, Thia tipped the contents of the hollowed out acorn into the scallop shell. The brown powder lay there for a second, then Khith carefully tilted the little shell to mix the contents.

Red blossomed like a wound against pale flesh. Even as Khith said, "Now!" Eregard was already snatching the scallop shell. He hissed at the heat, but then his head was bent over it and he tipped it up, pouring the hot contents onto his tongue. He gagged, but mastered the reflex. Thia saw his throat move as he swallowed.

Hastily, Thia blew out the candle flame. They might need light later on.

Eregard moaned and raised his scorched fingers to his mouth. "By all the hells!" he whispered.

Khith grabbed his shoulders and turned him to face the map. "Concentrate!" the Hthras hissed. "See her face!"

Eregard faced the white sheet. Khith inched forward so it was behind Eregard and rested its furred, taloned hands on the Prince's shoulders. The Hthras leaned over and pressed its face against the back of Eregard's neck. "Concentrate!"

Thia sat in silence, watching, afraid to move. For long minutes nothing happened. Then, slowly, Eregard's breathing changed, became deeper, slower. His eyes closed.

She looked over at Khith and could see tension in every line of the Hthras's small body. Softly, the doctor began to whisper a chant. The words were nonsense syllables to Thia.

Khith's voice strengthened, grew deeper, slower. Eregard twitched, shuddered, then began to whisper "Ulandra" over and over.

It's happening, Thia thought. *Khith is doing it!*

More minutes passed as the two figures crouched together next to the narrow bunk. Khith chanted, Eregard muttered, and time crawled by. Thia sat still, forcing herself not to squirm.

Without warning, Eregard moved, pulling away from

Khith's half embrace. The Prince slid forward and began tracing the words she'd written on the sheet in Pelanese, muttering the words as he did so. "This is Eregard, alive, off the northeast coast. Kerezau's troops will invade within hours or days." He looked up. "I need to tell her more!"

"Here!" Thia cried. "Here, finish!" Grabbing Khith's limp hand, she raked the Hthras's talon across her palm. Blood welled up, pooled in her palm. She held her hand out to Eregard. He dipped his finger in the blood and began writing again, "Tell Salesin! Tell my father! I am held captive on ship," he said as he wrote, and painted a hasty red X on the map with his finger. "Send help. Send help . . ."

His hand trembled and then dropped as Khith quietly slumped over, unconscious. Thia gave a muffled cry and reached over to feel the doctor's pulse. Eregard slumped against the wall of their prison and regarded her dazedly. "Is Khith all right?"

"Yes," she whispered. "Khith is breathing, its pulse is strong. My guess is that the doctor fainted from the strain."

Eregard nodded, then stared at the blood- and charcoal-splotched sheet. "I can't believe it worked," he whispered. "I was really there, inside her mind. I was in the palace. Goddess!" He buried his face in his hands. "My brother was there, somewhere close. He had just . . ." He glanced up, then trailed off. "He has not been a kind husband."

Thia watched him. "Surely your brother will be glad to know you are alive?"

He gave a harsh bark of laughter. "I doubt it. He'll probably send the Royal Navy to sink us to the bottom. But he's not stupid. He'll muster the troops."

At her feet, Khith mumbled something, and then its breathing grew deeper. Thia looked at the Hthras. "Sound asleep."

"I'm not surprised. I could feel the effort it cost to open that link. I could sense the strain. I'm tired myself."

He inched over to the sheet, pulled it down off the wall and, turning it over so the message did not show, used it to cover the Hthras. "Let the doctor sleep. How is your hand?"

Thia had forgotten about it. She held it out, seeing that the bleeding had mostly stopped. Eregard used the cleanest corner of the bandanna to wipe away the blood.

Khith continued to sleep as the rest of the day passed. They were fed by the taciturn guard, who replaced their chamber pot with a more utilitarian bucket.

Eregard fell asleep soon after they had eaten their meager allotment of food. Thia read for a while, till the light faded from the porthole, then she, too, fell asleep.

She was awakened abruptly, in total darkness, when the *Pride* suddenly wallowed like a sow in a fresh mudhole. The deck rose beneath her feet as she sat up with an exclamation, then dropped away with sickening abruptness. Outside, she could hear the howl of wind, the lash of rain.

Khith's promised storm had arrived.

17

Bone Magic

When Jezzil opened his eyes to utter blackness, his first thought was that he'd been buried alive. He was lying on his side, on something damp and unyielding, and couldn't seem to breathe.

Moments passed, and then he felt movement beneath him. Not a grave, then. Graves didn't move.

The fight with Boq'urak, he thought. *I'm in the wagon . . . but why are there no stars?*

He remembered that Thia had been there, with him, cradling his head in her lap as the wagon bumped along, and reached out for her. His groping hand encountered only boards, damp boards.

He lay there, fighting to breathe, then managed to turn his head to look up through slitted eyes. *Where are the stars?*

The boards beneath him heaved gently, not sharply like the jouncing of a wagon.

"Thia?" The name was only a ghost of a whisper, so soft and distorted that he could barely hear himself. He tried again. "Thia?"

There was no answer, and he realized he was alone.

It was a struggle to breathe. His entire face hurt. He tried to open his eyes all the way, but could not. He realized that his face was swollen, and that the center of the pain was his nose.

But Boq'urak didn't hurt my face . . . he broke my leg . . . hurt me inside . . .

He tried to move his head, but the pain was so intense that he stopped immediately. *Think. Where are you? What happened?*

Slowly, memories began to trickle back. He remembered Khith. Remembered walking on crutches. Remembered shadowing the two Chonao, overhearing them plotting to betray Kata. Remembered boarding a ship . . .

He let out a grunt as the rest of the memories surged back. *Barus! Barus in command of a ship!*

Jezzil remembered his joy at seeing his best friend, remembered approaching him, but nothing after that. *What happened to me?*

With an effort that left him sweating and wrenched forth a groan, he rolled onto his back. Slowly, cautiously, he raised his hand and touched his face. His eyes, swollen nearly shut. His nose, the pain was so excruciating that even the slightest touch of his fingertips made him gasp. His nose was broken, badly. He'd been hit in the face. With his other hand, he touched his side, and found more pain.

Nose is broken, and ribs, too. Or possibly ribs just cracked . . . Barus. Must have been Barus. But why?

The thought brought a wave of betrayal, anger, then, almost as quickly, the anger subsided, replaced by guilt. *Of course he hit me. I'm a deserter. How could I have forgotten?*

But he *had* forgotten, for that crucial second. He'd been so glad to see Barus, to realize that his friend was still alive! And now he was in solitary confinement, awaiting the fate meted out to a deserter. Chonao hangings were slow, and cruel. There was no scaffold, no "drop" to dispatch the condemned quickly. When Chonao hung someone, they put a rope around his neck, then hoisted him up, slowly, an inch at a time, until he strangled. It could take several minutes before the victim lost consciousness, even longer to die.

This is it, he thought. *I ran away from my fate, but you can't escape destiny. I should have died at m'Banak with my comrades. I deserve to die.*

He closed his eyes, willing himself to just lie quietly until they came to get him. It would be a relief, he told himself, to have it over and done with. He would pay for his crime with his death, and then he would not have to suffer the guilt that had plagued him ever since that terrible day. He should have died. Everyone else had died, after all.

Except Barus. How could he be alive? Did he abandon our comrades, too? Even so, he didn't desert.

He willed himself not to remember. What did it matter now? *Soon it will be over.*

Even as he tried to relax, faces filled his mind's eye. "Thia," he mumbled. "Khith, Talis, Eregard . . ."

What would happen to them? Would Barus realize that they had been traveling in the company of a deserter? Jezzil groaned softly. Of course he would realize! He knew as surely as if he'd seen it that his friends had betrayed themselves when he'd been struck down. Barus might even be planning to execute them, too!

There's nothing I can do to help them, he thought. *I can't help them, or myself. I deserve to die, but they don't . . .*

He thought of how terrible it would be to see Thia or Talis or Eregard hanged. Barus had a mean streak. He might well force him to watch his friends hang first, knowing that would cause greater torment. For some reason, Jezzil found that he wasn't as concerned about Khith. He'd seen enough during their lessons to make him fairly confident that the little mage could take care of itself. Could Khith possibly help the others escape?

He tried to raise his head, but the pain was so great that he subsided, sick and dizzy. His mouth was dry and tasted of old blood. Was there water in this cell? Where was he? In the bowels of the ship, most likely.

Jezzil resolved to face his execution with as much courage as he could. He would offer no explanation, make no plea for mercy. *I deserve to die . . . I betrayed my comrades, betrayed my country. Betrayed the Redai.*

For some reason, he kept thinking of the conquered people of Taenareth, as he'd seen them on his way to take ship for the western lands. Kerezau's royal governors were at least as bad as the Pelan king's Viceroy, Salesin, seemed to be. They enforced the Redai's rule harshly. The slightest infraction of Kerezau's many laws was punishable by maiming, or death.

Talis's friend Castio says that people have a right to rule themselves. That they should not be subject to the whims of despots.

Jezzil groaned softly. *I'm a warrior, not a philosopher. I shouldn't have to concern myself with all of this!* Resentment against the world surged up. *Why me? Things were going along pretty well, and then all of this has to happen!*

Perhaps he'll let Thia and Talis and Eregard go. Perhaps they won't be harmed.

But he knew they were all likely to lose a hand, at the least. Or perhaps they'd be hamstrung. Or blinded.

Maybe if I talk to Barus, confess, I could beg for mercy for them.

But that would be the worst thing he could do. If Barus knew how much he cared for his friends, he'd be twice as likely to torture, maim, or even execute them.

What if I could escape?

The thought crept in unbidden. Jezzil angrily tried to push it away. He couldn't even raise his head, much less break out of this cabin, which was undoubtedly locked and guarded. Escape? Might as well wish to be healed and have his sword returned to him!

Healing . . .

Jezzil lay there, staring up into the blackness. *I do know some healing chants, some ways to focus avundi on the body to speed healing . . .* Khith had taught him to do this for himself to speed the knitting of his broken leg.

But healing required focus and intense concentration, skills that at present were beyond him. There was no way he could tap his avundi when he was in such pain, barely able to breathe. Besides, his nose was badly broken. If he applied avundi to try and heal it in its present position, it would heal crooked, and he wouldn't be able to breathe normally.

Thirst was a torment now. Jezzil lay there, wishing he could fall asleep. *I might as well sleep, there's nothing else I can do. Sometimes, there's nothing you can do, and this is one of those times.*

After all, what could anyone expect of a man locked into a tiny cabin? An injured man, alone in the dark?

Jezzil lay there, his harsh mouth-breathing the only sound, willing himself to fall asleep. Sleep was his only escape.

He was actually beginning to drift off when he realized that he needed to relieve himself. His eyes opened as wide as possible as he stared into the darkness.

It's not fair! I can't even move, he thought angrily. *Maybe there is a bucket in here, but I can't move. I'll just have to piss myself.*

He pictured himself hauled out for his hanging, the front of his britches soaked, smelling like a sewer. *What difference does it make? I'll lose control of everything when I'm hanged, anyway! Might as well piss and shit myself.*

But somehow, he couldn't make himself let loose. Instead, gritting his teeth, he managed to lever himself up from the floor, using both hands. His head throbbed, his injured side screamed a protest, and he broke into a sweat—

—but moments later, groaning, found himself sitting upright. His head spun, and he held still, not wanting to faint and lose what he had gained. Slowly, the dizziness subsided, though it was hard to be sure, since he couldn't see.

Jezzil raised both hands and began feeling along the floor as far as he could reach.

Nothing.

After a few moments, he hitched forward on his knees and tried again. This time his questing fingertips brushed something cold and metallic. A bucket.

After relieving himself, he moved until he was sitting

with his back braced against the wall. He rested for a while, then slowly, delicately, began exploring his face with his fingertips.

His nose seemed to be canted to the right, and there was a definite bump on the bridge that had not been there before.

He took a deep breath, and then, fumbling in the dark, took off his belt. He folded over the thick leather strap and clamped his teeth on it. A warrior did not cry out in pain.

Jezzil raised both hands to his face, thinking of how filthy they probably were. Khith had emphasized the importance of cleanliness in healing, but there was nothing he could do about that.

He raised his knees, grunting with pain as his injured side protested. With his knees up, if he passed out he'd fall on his side, not on his face.

Gripping the belt with his teeth, he put both hands up to his nose. With his right fingers he pushed sideways, and with his left he pulled down.

Pain! Jezzil's harsh breaths burst out past the belt, and for a moment he thought he couldn't stand it long enough to accomplish anything. His ears rang; spots danced before his eyes.

He couldn't breathe! Jezzil spat the belt out of his mouth and sucked in air, half sobbing in agony. But his efforts had worked, at least partially. Now he could draw air into his nostrils. Tentatively, he explored his face. He groaned aloud. *Not again! I can't face that again!*

He gave himself to the count of a hundred to prepare himself. Then, steeling himself, he repeated his manipulation.

He'd forgotten the belt, and a strangled cry burst forth, despite his clenched teeth. Sweat burst out on his face and his fingers skidded in it.

But many breaths later, when he dared to explore his face again, his nose seemed almost straight. Jezzil wished he had some cotton wadding to shove up his nostrils, but he didn't.

But I have avundi, he reminded himself. *I have avundi.*

Part of his mind argued that he wasn't supposed to be doing this, he was supposed to accept his fate, a just fate. After all, he *was* a deserter. He had left his comrades to perish in the flames of m'Banak.

So did Barus, he remembered, with a scowl that hurt his face. *So maybe I will accept my fate . . . and just maybe I won't . . .* Jezzil used the tail of his shirt to wipe the greasy sweat off his face. *But, by Avenar's fist, first I'll help my friends escape.*

Escape to where? the mocking little voice demanded. *You're in the Narrow Sea, remember? Pela is still at least ten leagues away, too far to swim.*

"I'll ride that mare after I catch her," he muttered.

Calming himself, ignoring the pain, he sank deep into himself, controlling his breathing, closing his eyes, commanding himself to focus on his avundi.

He touched the now familiar place in his mind, and was comforted to realize that his physical injuries had not affected it. Carefully, he created a mental picture of his injuries, their precise location, and then sent warm waves of avundi out toward those places. He envisioned bone knitting, swelling ebbing away, torn skin and flesh pulling back together, then closing, closing . . .

He realized he was breathing better, more easily—that it was working—but repressed his exultation. Emotion had no place in the use of avundi.

He was still in the half waking trance, submerged in the healing process, when the door opened. A guard stepped in with a lantern, raising it high. Blinded, Jezzil covered his face with his arms.

The guard gave a grunt of satisfaction, seeing that his prisoner was still safely locked away, and slammed the door shut. Jezzil heard metal bolts slide into place.

He groped his way forward in the dark and found a rough crust of bread and a waterskin. The water was warm and tasted of the cured goatskin that contained it, but it was the equal of any wine he had ever sipped. Jezzil forced himself to ration it. No telling how long it would be before he got any more. He managed to down the bread by soaking it with water and letting it dissolve in his mouth. His face was too sore for chewing.

Then he crawled back to his corner and went back to healing himself. He'd heard the bolts click. It had been weeks now since it was all he could do to lift a simple coin. Lifting the knob on a door-bolt should be easy.

He was trying to decide where they might have imprisoned his friends, when he realized that the ship was beginning to roll and pitch. The swells were growing now. The deck heaved. Even buried in the bowels of the ship as he was, Jezzil could hear the wind howling outside.

Suddenly, the ship dropped, then wallowed side to side like a sweaty, rolling yearling. The waste bucket fell over with a clang. Urine splashed. Jezzil tried to brace himself in the corner as the ship lurched again.

A storm, he thought. *A big one.*

He crouched in the corner, hissing with pain every time his ribs protested, determined to ride out the tempest.

Ulandra lay beside her prince, stiff with loathing, silently cursing her bad luck. Why had she decided to stay in the royal apartments at this time of day, mid-afternoon, instead of going out for a walk with her ladies-in-waiting, as she usually did?

She knew why. She had wanted quiet time alone to read and to think about the new priest's teachings. Varlon had taught her how to meditate, how to relax her mind. His deep, beautiful voice and dark eyes were easy to lose herself in.

But just as she'd donned an old, comfortable robe and settled down to reread one of the letters he'd written her—discussing how hectic the life of a royal was these days, how meditation techniques could help even if one had only a few minutes to relax—Salesin had come trooping into her suite without even knocking. He'd not even bothered to address her ladies-in-waiting, but merely glanced at them, his glare so fierce that they nearly ran over each other heading for the door.

He'd turned his scowl on her. "Strip."

Quickly, she'd obeyed. The sooner it was over with, the better.

Now he lay beside her, snoring lightly, relaxed, sated. She, on the other hand, was as stiff as a corset, muscles aching with tension. Ulandra grimaced as she felt his seed spilling out of her, wishing she dared reach down and pull the sheet over herself. But doing so might wake Salesin, and that she would not risk.

She closed her eyes, deciding to try and meditate. Perhaps if she could relax, she, too, might be able to sleep. If she could fall asleep, there was the chance that Salesin would leave her alone when he awoke.

As she had been instructed, she slowed her breathing, making it smooth, deep, and regular. In through her nose, out through her mouth.

She thought of her private focus-word. It was a nonsense syllable that Varlon had given her, to help her focus and quiet her mind. *Bokurak . . . bokurak . . . bokurak . . .*

Silently, Ulandra repeated the word to herself, controlling her breathing, trying to make her mind a blank—

—when, without warning, she discovered that she was *somewhere else.* She was seeing with the eyes of another.

For a moment terror flooded her, as she remembered that other presence she had sometimes sensed and had once half glimpsed in her mirror. But she quickly realized the presence in her mind was not that inhuman horror.

This was someone she knew. Eregard. Prince Eregard.

Ulandra wasn't quite sure *how* she knew his identity, but she was sure it was he. *But Eregard is dead!* she thought blankly.

She sensed negation, then reassurance. Eregard was alive, alive and well. They seemed to be in a tiny room, and the room was moving. A wagon? No, the movement was too regular.

A ship. She was seeing with Eregard's eyes, and she was on board a ship. Ulandra felt his presence, felt his caring for her, felt his . . . love? Yes, love. It was there, as tangible as the breath in her lungs, the blood in her veins.

She tried to frame her thoughts to reach him. *Eregard? I am here. Where are you?*

But there were no words in this sharing. No actual speech. No answering message. She could hear nothing, but then her attention was focused on a rough square of cloth. There was a crude map drawn on it. As she watched, a hand that she knew belonged to Eregard began tracing a message, letter by painful letter.

THIS IS EREGARD, ALIVE, OFF THE NORTHEAST COAST. KEREZAU'S TROOPS WILL INVADE WITHIN HOURS OR DAYS.

The message stopped. Ulandra lay rigid, willing the contact to continue.

A moment later it did just that.

TELL SALESIN! TELL MY FATHER! I AM HELD CAPTIVE ON SHIP. The lettering was different now, reddish instead of black, blurred and smeared . . . but still readable. She saw an X appear on the crude map. SEND HELP. SEND HELP.

She felt the contact fade. The words blurred. "No!" she gasped. "Eregard! Don't go!" Forgetting completely who lay beside her, Ulandra sat straight up in bed, snatching for her nearest garment, the comfortable old robe she'd been wearing.

Swinging her legs off the bed, she began to dress.

A hard hand fell on her shoulder. Salesin was sitting up on the edge of the bed. "What's going on?"

Ulandra heard the undertone of anger in his voice, and knew that whatever answer she made would be wrong. Silence would anger him even more. She was not a good liar, and she knew it. Nevertheless, she tried. "I . . . I am sorry, my lord. A dream. Only a dream."

"A dream? What kind of dream? I heard you say my brother's name." He gave a short bark of laughter that held nothing of good humor in it. "Have you been cuckolding me with my dead brother in your dreams, Princess?"

"No, my lord, of course not. I dreamed . . . I dreamed of Prince Eregard. 'Twas nothing, really."

Salesin pulled her around to face him. "You're lying, Princess," he said. "And you're hiding something. My brother is dead. So why call out his name? Who have you been talking to? My father?"

"Just a dream!" she stammered. "I . . . I must go, my lord.

I need the water closet." It was not a lie. Her bladder suddenly felt full to bursting. She didn't want to disgrace herself in front of him.

He shook her shoulder lightly. "You're still lying, dear heart. What's this all about?"

Ulandra gave a sudden twist, broke free, and headed for the door. She had to reach King Agivir with Eregard's message!

With a wild lunge, Salesin threw himself off the bed and came after her. She heard his feet hit the floor, and redoubled her efforts, but her long, unbound hair betrayed her. He caught it, yanking her around to face him. "What happened just now? Tell me!"

Tears flooded her eyes, but her mouth was so dry she could not have spoken if she'd wanted to. Salesin slapped her, lightly but stingingly. "Tell me!" His grip on her hair made the skin of her face so taut she could hardly move her lips.

"Please, let me go!"

He open-palmed her on the ear. Pain lanced through her head, drew an arrow of agony from her cheekbone up into her eye.

"It . . . it was . . ." She was babbling and crying now as she tried to get the words out. "Please, Eregard on a ship . . . there was a ship, I think . . . he sent a message . . ."

Two more stinging slaps stopped her. Her left eye was swelling; she could barely see out of it.

"You just have to have attention, don't you?" he shouted. "If you can't get it, you tell lies, stupid lies about my brother who is *dead*, thank the Goddess! Bitch! Lying bitch!" With a roar, he shook her, then punched her in her chest. "What do you know of my brother! What nonsense is this? My brother is *dead*!"

Ulandra's vision swam and she was barely able to stand. "Please, my lord, no—"

Another blow . . . then another. Ulandra reeled, blackness closing in; the only thing keeping her on her feet was Salesin's grip on her hair. He shook her, then punched her hard in the stomach. "You barren *bitch*! There's nothing in there that could carry a child! I ought to throw *you* out that window!" He stopped for a second, and she saw the anger recede, leaving a cold viciousness that was the most terrifying thing she'd ever seen. Her bladder released, and she felt warmth streaming down her legs.

Without another word, Salesin began dragging her toward the window, his hand locked in her hair.

I'm going to die, Ulandra thought, *just like Wolf.* For a moment she felt nothing but resignation. *Anything would be better than living like this, even death . . .*

Without warning, she felt her legs stiffening, bracing against the pull. She cried out as Salesin jerked her hair, but her body did not seem to be fully under her control. Dizziness flooded her. Blackness as thick and impenetrable as smoke trickled into her mind. Her legs braced harder. She was being pulled past the huge armoire now, and she flung out a hand, caught the edge.

Ulandra's good eye widened as she glimpsed her own hand. It was huge, dark, and what seemed to be talons suddenly sprouted from her fingertips. She tried to speak, but her mouth would not obey . . . it, too, was changing. Her teeth seemed too large for her face, and they hurt her lower lip. She tried to scream, but the sound she made was not human.

Goddess help me, she thought, as that wave of hideous Otherness engulfed her. *Help me!* Then there was only the darkness, and she was falling into it . . .

Ulandra awoke to find herself sprawled on the floor of the bedchamber, her robe half torn off, her body so stiff, so aching, that she could scarcely force herself to move. She turned her head, and saw Salesin's foot protruding from the other side of the bed. *Get out, get out before he wakes!*

With a groan she couldn't suppress, she managed to sit up. Looking down at her half nude body, she saw darkening bruises on her stomach and breasts. Her fingers told her that her face was swollen. Blood caked her chin and was smeared around her mouth.

Grabbing the bedpost, she managed to gain her feet, though the room swung around her sickeningly. She gripped

the gilded wood and kept her eyes closed until the worst of
the dizziness had passed. *How long was I unconscious?*

Pulling her robe closed, she shuffled closer to her husband. He was lying on his back, one leg bent beneath him,
his arms flung out like those of a doll tossed across the
room. His face was even more bruised than her own, and the
Princess could see scratches—actually, oozing gouges—as
well as what appeared to be deep bites on his chest.

Dear Goddess, what happened to him? Who did this?

Ulandra remembered the blood around her mouth. She
had a faint memory of talons erupting from her hand. She
stared at her fingernails. Could that rust-colored substance
be dried blood?

Salesin groaned aloud, then relapsed back into his swoon,
or was it sleep? Ulandra could not tell. He was alive, and that
was enough.

Who did this?

She swallowed, tasting blood. *He was hitting me . . .* She
felt her head, and sure enough, there was a lump over her
ear. *Blows to the head can cause hallucinations, everyone
knows that.*

That vision must have been some trick of her mind, as she
struggled to avoid being thrown to her death. There was no
other rational explanation.

Ulandra dismissed the whole subject from her mind. Her
fight with Salesin was over. She had to talk to King Agivir, to
give him Eregard's warning. An invasion . . . *Dear Goddess!*

With shaking hands, she dragged on a loose day-gown.
Despite the sunshine streaming in the window, she couldn't
stop shivering, so she pulled a woolen shawl around her
shoulders. With trembling hands, she washed the blood from
her face and hands. She tied her hair over one shoulder, so it
half hid her swollen eye.

She thought about wearing shoes, but she was so unsteady on her feet that she was afraid she'd fall, so she remained barefoot as she stole out of the silent suite and into
the corridor.

As Ulandra moved down the hall toward the King's apartments, one of her waiting women, Merindra, approached. Seeing the Princess, she stopped and clapped her hand over her mouth to stifle a gasp of horror. Ulandra shook her head at Merindra. "Help me find the King," she said. "I have a vital message for him."

"Your Highness! What *happened*?"

"Help me, or go take care of Salesin, I don't care which," Ulandra snapped, still moving.

It seemed a long walk, with Merindra twittering in distress beside her, but at least the woman did offer a strong young arm to support her faltering steps.

Finally they reached the entrance to the royal apartment. Two guards stood with crossed pikes before the door, pistols in their belts.

"Your Highness!" one exclaimed, stepping forward.

"I *must* see the King," Ulandra said, realizing her mouth was bleeding again. Little red spatters decorated the bosom of her day-gown. "I must see him immediately. I have information for him."

"Your Highness, I will take him a message. Let your woman take you back to your rooms—"

Ulandra's fragile control snapped. "I have to see the King!" she screamed, then lunged forward, pounding her fists on the door. "Please! King Agivir! Your Majesty!"

Both guards grabbed her, then Lady Merindra cried out and wrapped both arms around the largest, trying to pull him away. Both men grabbed Ulandra's shawl, and she let it go. With Lady Merinda scratching and clawing at his face, one of the guards tripped over his own feet and fell. The Princess flung herself forward again, landing full force against the door. The other guard grabbed her shoulder, and she heard her dress rip. As they began to drag her away, down the corridor, she shrieked at the top of her voice. "Please! Your Majesty!"

"What's all this?" a voice bellowed from inside, and suddenly the doors opened. They saw the King with yet another royal guard inside. For once Agivir did not look distracted and melancholy—his eyes were alert and his voice held the ring of command. "What chances here? We demand an explanation for this uproar!"

All of them froze. Ulandra gave a great sob of relief and sank to her knees, her hands held out in supplication. "Your Majesty, I beg you, I have vital information. I must be allowed to speak!"

King Agivir made a peremptory gesture to the closest guard, who hastily handed Ulandra back her shawl. Then he made another gesture to the guards, who carefully helped Lady Merindra to her feet. "Speak you shall, daughter. Come inside." He looked at his own guard. "Leave us."

With his own hands, he raised her. Ulandra staggered into the room, and he carefully seated her on a brocade couch, wrapped her shawl around her shivering shoulders, then sat on the matching ottoman before her, holding her hands. "What happened to you? I will send my personal physician to you. Your face, daughter, who did this?"

She fought back a sob. "Your Majesty, I think you know. But that is not important now. I can have the doctor later. Right now, I must tell you what I know."

His expression tightened, then, slowly, he nodded. "Very well. Tell me."

Her voice shaking, Ulandra told him of her vision, and of how sure she was that the information was true. She put every bit of conviction she could manage into her voice. When he fetched paper and pen for her, she managed to sketch out a rough version of the map that had been on Eregard's wall.

Agivir watched her, his faded eyes lighting with joy. "My son is alive? You truly believe he is alive?"

"Sire, I do." She looked at him. "Have there been sightings of an invasion fleet?"

"I have not heard of any, but I will order the navy to put to sea, headed north. And I will instruct the army to prepare for invasion."

"You believe me . . ." She was so grateful she nearly wept. Raising his hands to her battered mouth, she kissed them reverently. "By all that is holy, I thank you, Your Majesty. I know not how Prince Eregard managed to contact me, but I swear to you—I was inside his mind, seeing through his eyes, and it was truly he."

Agivir nodded. "Yes, daughter. I believe you. I knew that someone would come today."

Ulandra gazed at him in amazement. "You *knew*, sire?"

"In a manner of speaking, daughter. The new priest, Varlon, was here just this morning, and he read my stars. He told me that today would bring an important message, and I should pay heed to that message."

Ulandra closed her eyes in relief. "I know him, sire. He has been teaching me how to sleep better, how to relax at night."

The King gave her a searching glance, then reached up to gently touch her cheek. "My poor child, has this happened before?"

Ulandra nodded, too exhausted to dissemble. "Yes, sire. Today was the worst, though."

"Why did my son do this to you?"

Ulandra closed her eyes and swallowed. "I was on my way to come to you, but in my trance I had spoken aloud of Eregard. He demanded to know why. When I was reluctant to tell him, he was angry. Prince Salesin hates his brother, sire. It is probably a good thing that he did not believe me."

Agivir's features sagged like old wax. "As I feared," he whispered. "We did our best to raise him—what did we do wrong?"

The Princess felt her eyes fill with tears. They overflowed and spilled down her face, hot and stinging on her bruises. "Sire . . ." She dared to reach out and take his hand again. "You and Queen Elnorin are kind and decent people. But sometimes . . . sometimes children are born who do not take after either parent. You must not blame yourself. Both Prince Adranan and Prince Eregard are fine young men."

"I know, but neither is the leader Salesin is," the King replied with a sigh. "We will need him to lead the battle that is coming."

Ulandra nodded. "Your Majesty, may I stay here tonight? In the royal apartments? He is unlikely to look for me here. I could read to Her Majesty. Play the harp for her, perhaps.

She likes it when I do that. Her vision is not good, she will not notice my face."

King Agivir stood up and nodded. His old shoulders were held as straight as he could manage, and there was again that look of command in his faded eyes. "Yes, daughter, do that. Her Majesty loves you like the daughter we never had."

Ulandra slid off the divan and knelt. "Thank you, sire."

The King put out a hand, rested it on top of her tumbled hair. "May the Goddess bless you, daughter. And may she bless Pela. I will send the doctor to you."

Then, without another word, he strode away. Ulandra could hear him shouting for his messengers, for his generals, for his admirals. Sounds of running feet ensued.

Slowly, aching in every joint, Ulandra pulled herself back up onto the couch. She was cold and trembling, and at the thought of his hand atop her head, fresh tears welled up. These moments of kindness after so many months of hatred and abuse were too much. *And Eregard is still alive, thank the Goddess* . . . She pictured his face, round, youthful, and his soft, rounded, nonthreatening physique. *He loves me, truly loves me,* she thought. *If only* . . .

She began to weep softly then, careful not to disturb Queen Elnorin.

18

Night Excursions

Talis stood at the railing of *The Pride of Pela*, watching the massive bank of inky storm clouds racing toward the ship. The wind was rising, cold and dank. She shivered. Behind her the crew was racing around like insects boiling out of a disturbed nest, reefing the sails and battening down the hatches. She could hear the thud of their bare feet, mixed with the shouts from the officers.

A hand fell on her shoulder. "Mistress Aloro!" a gruff voice barked.

Talis jumped and spun around to see Captain Garano, accompanied by a Chonao guard. "Captain!"

"Mistress, the deck is no place for passengers. We face a major blow, no doubt about it. Get below, and stay there."

Talis nodded meekly. "Yes, Captain."

She headed for the belowdecks ladder. As she reached it, she glanced back at the deck, and saw Falar half rear in her pen. Her wind-tossed mane looked like tarnished silver; her eyes were white-rimmed with fear.

I can't leave her alone, she thought. *The crew won't do anything for her, they're too busy.*

She glanced over to see the captain still watching, and hastily made her way down the heaving ladder.

Once belowdecks, she went to her small cabin and pulled on her oiled weather-cloak and her boots. Then, holding tight to the ladder, she cautiously crept back out on deck. Scuttling, keeping low, she made it to Falar's pen and hid behind the bales of hay stacked there.

I can't help Jezzil, she thought, *but perhaps I can help Falar.* The ship plunged as the first of a series of massive waves smashed into her bow. Talis hesitated. *Maybe the captain was right.*

But one look at Falar, sweating and wild-eyed in her makeshift enclosure beneath the flimsy overhang, and she knew she couldn't leave the frantic animal alone. She crawled over to the stall, petting the mare as the ship's pitching worsened. As the wind grew strong enough to send waves lashing at the railings, she realized that anything that wasn't fastened to the deck would probably be washed overboard.

Talking soothingly, she fetched the heavy rope harness that the *Pride* had used to hoist the mare over the side. Usually it was attached to a winch, but, crouching behind bales of hay so she wouldn't be seen, Talis worked to modify it. Finally she had it rigged to her satisfaction.

It took all her skill as an experienced horsewoman to sling the harness over Falar's back, then fasten it between her forelegs and around her girth. All the while, the nervous horse tossed her head, pawed, and skittered around the limited confines of her pen. Despite Talis's best efforts, Falar managed to stamp on both of her feet. The woman blinked back tears of pain, thankful that Jezzil had the mare's shoes pulled before bringing her aboard. And if she hadn't thought to don her boots . . .

Gritting her teeth, she worked doggedly, trying to soothe the horse as her fingers skidded on leather, metal, and rope made slick with wind-driven spray.

Finally the harness was rigged. Talis stretched the two heavy ropes out to each side and fastened them to the anchoring posts of the pen. The pen itself might not survive intact, but it was the best she could do. Then she crouched just outside the enclosure, where Falar could see her and take comfort from her presence. By the time she'd tied the last length of rope around herself and secured it, the storm was at gale force. Talis faced Falar, talking soothingly, then pulled her cloak over her head—small good it did, she was already as soaked as if she'd been dipped into the sea—and hunkered down to ride it out.

The tempest raged. Talis hung onto her post as the ship heaved. There was no way to tell how much time had passed; it was so dark she could hardly tell when night fell. Falar was nothing but a pale bulk in the dimness. Waves washed over the deck, sending everything not tied down over the side. The hay vanished. The barrels of feed and water were gone. The awning ripped loose early on.

Massive waves sent *The Pride of Pela* bouncing from swell to swell like a ball thrown by two small, clumsy children. The captain and crew did their best to keep her headed into the waves, and their efforts paid off. The *Pride* stayed upright, though at times she listed so far over that the tips of her masts nearly kissed the whitecaps atop the massive swells.

Talis clung to her pole, barely conscious, nearly drowned. She struggled to breathe, holding a fold of her cloak over her mouth and nose. Even so, she retched up seawater she'd swallowed, though she felt no return of seasickness, and silently blessed Master Khith. How were her friends faring belowdecks? At one point there was a momentary lull in the storm, and Talis thought about making a run for it. But when she investigated the ropes that bound her, they were too water-swelled to budge. And the Chonao had taken her knife.

It seemed it would never end, that the *Pride* must capsize and sink, but somehow the ship did not founder. Once, Talis faintly heard a long, agonized scream over the demon howl of the wind. The cry stopped abruptly. She clung to her post, trying to pray, but kept getting the words mixed up.

She knew she must have lost consciousness at some point, because she came back to herself and realized the storm was abating. The waves showed blue-green now, topped with whitecaps. Day had broken.

Slowly, painfully, she unwrapped her arms from around her post and looked up at Falar. The mare stood sagging in her harness, exhausted, but very much alive and unharmed. Talis slid down on the now gently heaving deck, laid her head on her arm, pulled her soaked cloak over her and fell asleep.

She was awakened sometime later by one of the sailors, shaking her shoulder and asking her what she thought she was doing up on deck. Talis maintained just enough presence of mind to remind the man that the horse needed fresh water.

Then, slowly, painfully, she untied the ropes from around herself and unfastened Falar's harness. Looking around, she saw that the Sun was nearly overhead and the sea as smooth as glass. There was hardly a cloud left in the sky.

"Mistress Aloro! What are you doing up here?"

It was Captain Garano, accompanied by Barus. Talis blinked at them both, wondering if she were still dreaming.

"I came up when the storm broke," she said slowly. "I knew the horse would need attention."

Just then the crewman hurried up with a bucket. Falar, scenting the water, nickered and moved over to drink thirstily. Talis looked over at Barus. "It is my understanding that your people take good care of your mounts."

The soldier nodded. "You are correct, Mistress. I will take Falar for my own string after we are finished with the traitor."

Talis did not permit her expression to change. She addressed her next words to Garano. "Captain, I must check with my people below to see that they are unharmed by the storm. May I be permitted to visit them?" She spread her hands wide. "They have been accused of no crime. They are guarded by warriors. In addition to being a duly appointed emissary to the Redai, I am unarmed, and a woman. What harm can it do?"

The captain turned to look at Barus. The Chonao considered for a moment, then shrugged. "Our guests below will need to be fed anyway," Barus said. "Allow her five minutes with the three of them."

Talis kept her expression blank, but relief made her knees even weaker. *Five minutes with Master Khith is what I need!*

She followed the Chonao guard below. The man was burly, stolid, and Talis suspected he did not speak Pelanese. When they reached the cabin where her friends were confined, she gave her escort a wide and winning smile. "I'm so glad your leader assigned you to me. You seem like an incredibly stupid chap. Oh, and by the way, I heard that your leader fondles donkey organs," she finished liltingly. "How perverted."

The man's expression never changed. He simply smiled faintly, shrugged, then shook his head. *He might be smarter than I am, and a better actor,* she thought, *but I don't think so. I'm going to risk it . . .*

The guard unlocked the door, then opened it. Talis stepped into the tiny cabin, her nose twitching at the stench from the spilled chamber pot. Seeing her, Thia leaped up off the bunk and rushed over to her. Talis threw her arms around the other woman and, while they hugged, whispered, "Keep talking as loudly as possible in your own language while I'm speaking to Khith. Tell me all about the big storm and how scared you were."

Thia stepped back and burst into a high-pitched, noisy barrage of Amaranian, gesticulating, as Talis went over to look at Eregard. He gave her a wondering glance, and she mouthed, "Trust me," careful to keep her back to the guard.

Finally, she turned to Khith and went over to the little physician. The Hthras stood, and she bent over to give it a hug. As she nestled her face into the silky, furry skin of Khith's neck, she said, as softly as she dared, "Master, I will be taken to meet with the Redai. I have a sharpened hairpin. I need you to give me something poisonous to put on the tip."

The Hthras tensed in her grasp, and she heard its thready voice in her ear, hard to make out over Thia's excited declamation. "Mistress, I cannot. As a healer, I am pledged to save life. Not end it."

"Do you have something?" she hissed fiercely, clutching at the sleeves of its robe.

"Yes, but—I cannot."

"But Master—" She let out an exasperated breath, and just then the guard tugged at her sleeve, indicating by gestures that it was time to go. She stepped back, holding Khith's eyes with her own. The Hthras shook its head, its huge eyes sad. Talis scowled and turned back to face the guard.

Moments later, when the guard had escorted her out, she continued down the narrow corridor toward the better passenger cabins. She did not go into her own cabin, though. Instead she headed for the cabin Jezzil, Eregard, and Khith had shared.

When she reached it, she discovered it was locked, but the simple lock proved no match for her hairpins—the two unsharpened ones. She'd learned to pick locks years ago, under the tutelage of one of Castio's supporters who had been a transportee from a Pelanese prison.

When the catch clicked, Talis glanced over her shoulder, then carefully entered. The small cabin boasted a porthole, so she could see Eregard's and Jezzil's possessions, stowed beneath each of the bunks. *Just let everything be here,* she thought, kneeling to find Jezzil's duffel.

She knew that he carried some vials of powder, and once, he had told her that the Chonao were masters with poison, and also with sleeping powders.

Talis dug through the duffel, finding several false seams, a false bottom, and a number of hidden pockets. She was careful not to touch any of the edges of the weapons she uncovered. Finally, in one of the false seams, she located two narrow vials of powder. One powder was an ashy, pale gray. The other was darker, with a brownish tinge. The tiny stoppers were marked with a single letter—in Chonao script.

Talis sat back on her heels, cursing under her breath. *This is a fine bushel of beets!* For a wild moment she thought about trying to capture a couple of the big rats she'd heard scurrying around the ship's hold at night so she could test each powder, but she had nothing with which to make a trap.

Casting her mind back, she recalled what Jezzil had talked about when they relaxed in the stable after weapons and un-armed combat lessons. They'd been grooming their horses . . .

"Poisons and soporifics, both can be very useful if used at the right time," Jezzil had said. "But you have to be careful. Use the wrong substance, or mix two substances, and you can have a totally different effect." He'd glanced at her over Falar's mane. "Some sedatives will actually cancel each other out. Some poisons, when mixed, become harmless."

"Damn . . ." she muttered now. For a moment she'd con-sidered mixing the powders and coating the end of the hair-pin, but what if that rendered one or both of them ineffective? She didn't want to give Kerezau a good night's sleep, she wanted that miserable, lying tyrant *dead*.

Cautiously, she managed to pry out the stoppers of first one vial, then the other. Cautiously, she sniffed the ash-colored powder. It was astringent; she wrinkled her nose, but felt no illness, no sleepiness. Even more cautiously, she sniffed the other vial. This one was bitter, acrid, and left a foul taste at the back of her throat.

Tapping the stoppers back into the vials, she sat for a long time regarding them. *Which one?*

Finally she fell back on a childhood rhyme. Tapping each with her finger in turn, she intoned, "Two choices here/which one to fear?/I pick the one/that looks like fun." Her questing finger had landed on the ashy colored vial.

"Damn," Talis whispered, then quickly secreted the ash-colored vial back into the false seam and tucked the other one into the inside pocket of her shirt. After stowing away the duffel bag, she rose, left the cabin, and relocked it.

Now all we do is wait for the Redai, she thought grimly. It was a shock to realize that she might have only another day to live. *At least I'll die in battle,* she thought. *Poor Jezzil won't even get to do that.*

After Talis left, Khith went back to trying to get out of their tiny cabin. It wasn't proving easy. The keyhole for their door was blocked from the outside . . . and, of course, there was always a sentry. But Khith had developed a plan. It had discovered a burl in the wood of the cabin door, just the right size and height. If that rounded burl could be removed, the Hthras knew it would leave a nice little hole.

Using its longish, talonlike nails, Khith had begun digging into the wood around the potential knothole. Patiently, hour after hour, it scratched softly, wearing nail after nail down to the quick in its efforts. When Eregard or Thia asked if they could help, the Hthras gazed pointedly at their small, rounded, and quite dull fingernails and silently shook its head.

Fortunately the light in the cabin was dim, so the guard hadn't noticed the slightly lighter color of the wood around the burl. Khith had been working for nearly a full day now, not pausing to sleep, eating only when Thia pushed food into its empty hand.

The groove around the potential knothole was nearly deep enough now to allow Khith to pry at it with the small tube. The Hthras worked on, stopping only when the guard brought their dinner and emptied the slop pail.

Finally, late that night, Khith had dug a deep enough hole around the burl that it felt confident in trying to prise out the rounded chunk of wood.

On the third try, it gave, and the rounded burl tumbled into its hand.

It had been totally dark to human eyes in the cabin, but a faint light now shone through the new knothole. A dark lantern hung in the passageway where the guard was stationed. Khith crouched down and peered through the hole. It could see the guard standing across the narrow walkway. The man was slumped against the wall, thumbs hooked into the front of his belt, plainly bored and nearly dozing.

Perfect, Khith thought.

The Hthras had much better night-sight than any human. Even in the dim light streaming through the little knothole, it could assemble its weapon.

The little tube was not quite as long as the blow-tubes the

Hthras used for defense in the jungle, but fortunately, the distance to be covered was not great. Khith took up the plug of wax it had fashioned from the stub of the candle. It was tipped with a splinter of sharp wood prised from the deck, and the Hthras slid the makeshift dart into the end of the tube. The doctor had coated the little splinter with its most powerful soporific, a powder concealed in one of the seemingly innocuous sealed scallop shells.

The main problem was that Khith could look to aim and could adjust the position of the tube, but not do both at the same time. The hole was too small. So the Hthras took its time, checking and rechecking the positioning of the tube in the knothole. It wanted the splinter to strike the guard on the back of his hand since the splinter wasn't long or sturdy enough to pierce the guard's leather breeches or tunic.

Finally, after many cramped, tense minutes, Khith was confident that the angle and position of the little tube were correct. Keeping its hand perfectly steady, it sucked in the biggest breath its slight body could contain, placed its thin, inhuman lips against the end of the tube, and blew.

The doctor felt the tiny dart leave the tube, hastily yanked it out of the hole, then looked for the results. The guard had opened his eyes and pulled his right hand free from his belt, as though to look at it. But before he could raise his hand, his knees buckled and then, gently, he slid down the wall and slumped there, his deep breathing rapidly growing louder, until he was snoring.

I did it! Khith thought, feeling a surge of excitement. The Hthras took a pinch of its avundi-enhancing snuff, then stared at the door. Moments later there was a click as the latch unlatched itself.

Khith laid a hand on the door, ready to pull it open and tiptoe out, only to stop when it heard a soft whisper. "Master Khith? What's happening?"

In one stride the Hthras was standing beside Thia's narrow bunk. "Shhh . . ." it cautioned. "Eregard is sleeping."

Her voice was a bare thread of sound. "I heard the latch click."

"I opened the door. I must go out for a while, see to a few things. If we have to abandon ship, I want to be sure I have my physician's bag."

In the darkness, the Hthras could barely see her, but it heard her quick intake of breath. "Go *out*? The guard—"

"The guard is enjoying a well-deserved nap," Khith said. "He will awaken in an hour or so, none the worse for his slight dereliction of duty."

"But if you can get out—" Khith heard the excitement in her voice. "We can escape!"

"And leave Jezzil?" Khith asked bleakly. The thought of never seeing Jezzil again was physical pain.

"*No!*" Thia's voice scaled up.

"Shhhh!" Khith placed a hand gently over her mouth, and as Eregard stirred and muttered in his sleep, the Hthras slid into the narrow bunk beside her. "Don't wake Eregard."

"I'm sorry, Master," she said. "But of course we can't leave Jezzil. You can put his guard to sleep, too, can't you?"

"Unlikely," Khith said. "I overheard the guards talking outside—"

"You understood them?"

"Jezzil has taught me a bit of his language. The Chonao guards who watch his cell are changed every two hours. He is the prized prisoner—we are merely an afterthought. And besides, if we all crept out tonight, where could we go?"

"Steal one of the lifeboats?" she asked, plainly realizing how unlikely that scenario would be.

"We have been blown off course and are somewhere in the Narrow Sea. Who will navigate for us?"

She sighed, and her warm breath tickled the doctor's ear. "All right. You made your point. But why are you going out?"

"I need my bag. If I have my herbs, my potions, I can farsee tomorrow morning, try to discover where we are, how far from Pela. Doubtless the storm blew us off course, so where are we?"

"Farsee?"

"I will borrow the eyes of a seabird, Thia. I can do that. As soon as it is light enough to see."

"Oh." She was silent a moment, then her arms slid around the Hthras's slight form and hugged the physician tightly. "Be *careful*!"

As her young body pressed against its own, Khith was conscious of a rush of intense physical pleasure. "I will be," it assured her as it pulled away. "Shhh!"

Hastily, the doctor got up and tiptoed out of the room, passing the snoring guard. That rush of feeling it had experienced . . . it had never felt anything like that before, except . . . except during moments with Jezzil.

The Hthras gave itself a mental shake. *Pay attention to what you're doing! Now is not the time to obsess about either Thia or Jezzil!*

Khith could not "Cast" the illusion of invisibility as Jezzil could, but the Hthras had other ways of remaining unnoticed, using avundi to blur its image so the eye could not focus. The little physician tiptoed up ladders, then down the narrow corridors of the ship to the passenger quarters. Once inside, it retrieved its bag, stuffed with medicinal and alchemical potions, and quickly went through it, keeping only the rare, the difficult to find and distill ingredients, those that were well-stoppered to protect them from the elements.

It removed only one of its surgical implements . . . its smallest scalpel went into the pocket of the Hthras's gray robe, along with a vial of pale pink powder.

Carrying the bag, the Hthras went up into the chill night air. After taking a moment to locate its destination, it began to move, gliding along as silent and unnoticed as a shadow drifting across the *Pride*'s dark deck.

The *Pride* was still heaved-to, and even at night repairs were going on. Sailors were mending sails, splicing lines, and doing other work to repair the damage from the storm. None of them noticed the faint haze of gray fog that passed outside the circles of light cast by their lanterns.

Khith was searching for the ship's fishing gear. All the

ships it had ever sailed on with its father had supplemented
the dried ship's provisions with fresh caught fish, and the
Pride proved no exception. The fishing nets and rods were in
a large, oilcloth-covered storage box not far from Falar's pen.

It was the work of a moment for Khith to locate the cork
fishing bobbers and detach them from the lines and nets. It
stuffed the round pieces of cork into its bag, fastened the
latch securely, then concealed the bag behind the fishing
locker, pulling an edge of the oilcloth over it.

After securing its bag, the Hthras went down one deck to
the gunnery. The gun ports were, of course, closed, but there
was sufficient light for Khith's excellent night vision. The
Pride boasted four cannon, two for each side, each securely
lashed to the deck atop their wheeled gun carriages.

The door to the tiny munitions compartment was locked,
but it, too, yielded to Khith. A rack filled with pistols hung
on one wall, and a rack with muskets on the other. One box
held grapeshot, and another cannonballs. And there, in specially built wooden kegs that had no metal fittings, were the
casks of black powder. Twelve of them.

Khith hefted a couple of them, experimentally, realizing
that it would not be able to carry one for more than a few
steps. And rolling the keg would be too noisy. For a moment
it wished Jezzil were there; a human's strength could have
handled the casks easily.

Taking a deep breath, Khith picked up a keg and managed
to stagger nearly to the door of the compartment before it
was forced to put the black powder down gently. It carefully
edged the keg out the door, then relocked it.

It took the doctor four tries to get the keg over to one of
the starboard cannons. Panting, it gently lowered the cask.
Carefully, Khith prised off the lid and sprinkled the pink
powder from the vial onto the top of the black powder. The
pink powder was its own concoction, highly flammable,
even more volatile than the black powder. An avundi-
generated spark would set it off nicely.

Khith replaced the lid, tapping it down but not securing it
too tightly. Then, moving with great care, it carefully posi-

tioned the powder cask beneath the cannon barrel. With a little grunting and straining, it managed to wedge the keg into the gun carriage beneath the cannon. Seeing the cannon secured in place with thick ropes, it took the scalpel and sawed a little more than halfway through each strand.

Finally, the Hthras left the gunnery deck and crept up the ladder to the main deck. It peered cautiously out. The eastern sky was visibly lighter, which meant their guard would be rousing soon. *Time for this captive to return to captivity . . .*

Once more inside the cramped little cabin, Khith lay down on a blanket spread on the floor. Thia was asleep again. It could hear her gentle breathing intermixed with Eregard's snores.

For a moment the need for sleep seemed overwhelming, but Khith fought it back, blinking hard and rubbing its eyes. *Time to farsee.*

The spell and snuff worked just as well as it had back in the Sarsithe. Khith was able to see through the eyes of a gull, swooping amid the air currents high above the ship.

The seagull's eyes showed the doctor that there was another ship approaching, almost within visible range of the *Pride*. Khith exerted its will, and the gull dove down for a closer look at the inhabitants. What it saw made it struggle to get free of the vision.

As soon as the drug fumes cleared away and it could stand without weaving, Khith was at Thia's bedside, shaking her gently. "Wake, Thia," it said softly. "Wake up."

She stirred, muttered, then her eyes opened. "Master? What . . . what . . ."

"We must awaken and plan," Khith said. "The Redai's ship will be here within the hour. And the first thing they will do—"

Now fully awake, she sat up. "The first thing they'll do is execute Jezzil! Barus said so! We have to stop them."

"Exactly," Khith agreed. "So, what are we going to do?"

"I don't know," she whispered. "How can we fight all of them?"

"We cannot *fight* them," Khith said. "But there may be other ways. Wake Eregard. We must talk."

19

Abandon Ship!

After three days in the dim, windowless cabin, the Sun struck Thia's eyes like a blow. She hesitated at the top of the ladder, squinting, shielding her eyes, until the guard behind her gave her a poke and a curt order to move along. She pulled herself up the last few steps, then stood on the deck. Eregard was the next one up, followed by Khith. The Prince looked around the deck, blinking, then nudged Thia. "That must be Kerezau. The one in the middle, wearing the—"

"Silence!" one of the guards barked in Pelanese, giving the Prince a shove.

Thia could see the man Eregard referred to. He was not tall, but there was something about him that made him stand out. Physically, he was ordinary enough, with black hair, black eyes, a trimmed beard and moustache. His armor had plainly seen hard usage, but it was polished to a mirror sheen. Thia realized after a moment that he was literally set apart—no one stood too close to him. He was like a little island of command amidst the throng of Chonao warriors. She could see the ship that had brought him already moving away from the *Pride*.

In response to an order from the guards, she, Eregard, and Khith were brought up to the outskirts of the crowd. Thia lost sight of Kerezau until someone barked a command in the Chonao language. Within moments the troops had assembled into precise lines, standing at attention.

Kerezau and Barus stood together, with Barus barking orders. Thia caught the name "Jezzil" amid the unfamiliar words and knew that this was it. Her palms were sweaty, but she resisted the urge to wipe her hands on her skirt. *Do nothing to draw attention to yourself,* Khith had told her, *until the time is right.*

She wet her lips. It was hot standing there in the sunlight, after so many days below in the hold. She wished desperately she'd been permitted to change her clothes before being brought up on deck. *Might as well wish for a bath while you're at it,* she thought disgustedly.

Nevertheless, she'd done her best to make herself look as feminine as possible, on Khith's orders. She finger-combed her dirty hair and tied it up with a bit of ribbon. She unbuttoned the blouse she wore beneath her laced-up overtunic to display a hint of cleavage. She brushed the dust and cobwebs off her skirt . . .

. . . and tore strips off her petticoat and used them to strap Khith's little scalpel securely to the underside of her forearm, thankful that her blouse had long, full sleeves.

Now she stood waiting tensely. *Can I do this? What if it doesn't work?*

Khith caught her eye and gave her a hint of a nod. Thia knew the doctor believed she could handle her part in the plan, and she hoped the Hthras was correct.

Guards appeared from belowdecks, half dragging, half carrying another prisoner. It took Thia a moment to realize it was Jezzil. His long hair fell over his face, and he was so filthy that it was hard to even recognize him.

He was hauled before the Redai, so weak he couldn't even stand on his own. Despite his weakness, they were taking no chances. The guards bound his hands behind him as Kerezau addressed him in their own language, evidently reciting a list of charges, then made a single statement in a cold voice. Barus smiled.

The Redai turned to face the three other prisoners, and there was a shuffling in the group of people surrounding him. Suddenly, Talis was there, standing to Kerezau's left, next to one of his bodyguards. Thia's eyes widened. The Katan rebel was wearing one of her best, most feminine outfits—an embroidered white silk blouse, a wine-colored velvet laced-up bodice, and a full skirt of crimson silk taffeta. Ruffled petticoats peeked out beneath the hem of her skirt. *Why is she so dressed up?* Thia wondered, seeing that Talis's long black hair was pinned up high on her head, baring her neck and shoulders.

Kerezau addressed Thia, Eregard, and Khith in strongly accented Pelanese. "I have just sentenced your friend to die by hanging. The execution will be carried out immediately."

Thia let out a shriek of anguish and plunged forward, falling on her hands and knees before the Chonao leader. "No! No, no, *no*! Please, my lord, spare my husband! I cannot live without him! Please! Spare him, for the sake of his babe that I carry!"

Halfway through her speech, guards had grabbed her and hauled her upright. Frowning, Kerezau turned to Barus, who muttered a quick translation.

"This man," Kerezau pointed at Jezzil, who was standing stock still, his mouth hanging open, "is your husband?"

"Yes!" Thia wailed, burying her face in her hands despite the guards' grip on her upper arms. "Oh, yes, my lord! He is my husband, and I love him! I cannot be parted from him! He is everything to me!"

She broke into a noisy storm of weeping and blubbering, tearing at her face with her hands, and, to her own surprise, felt real tears start.

Jezzil, who had been barely able to stand, shook back his hair, revealing a filthy, bruised face. His beard was matted. He took a step toward her. "This woman is mad," he said loudly. "I don't even know her. She's *not* my wife!"

Thia shrieked again, piercingly. "No! Don't deny me, husband! Don't deny your wee babe that I carry!"

She flung herself at Jezzil, and this time the guards, who seemed to be laughing, let her go. Thia scrabbled toward him on her knees, wailing aloud, and grabbed him around his thighs, pressing her face against him. The stench was terrible. "My love!" she howled, looking up at him beseechingly. "My husband!"

Jezzil raised his leg, trying to push her away. "Get off me! Your Excellency, I never saw this woman before now! She's mad, anyone can tell that! I am not married, I have no wife!"

Thia let herself be pushed away, and sprawled on the deck, yowling wordlessly, like a singed cat. "Don't deny me, my love!" she cried. She could feel her own face, hot and swollen with tears as she writhed, holding her belly. "Don't deny our babe!" To her own surprise, she realized that she was actually enjoying her own performance. She'd never behaved like this in her life, and there was something freeing about it. "I love you!"

"Shut this hyena bitch up," Barus said, looking as though he wanted to cover his ears. "What difference does it make if she's his wife? We're still going to hang him!"

Suddenly Talis was there, crouching beside her. "Thia!" she shouted, raised her hand and slapped her. Thia reeled back from the force of her slap. "Thia, what's wrong with you?"

The stinging blow helped bring more tears. Thia sprawled back on her rear, her skirts rucked up around her, and began shrieking again. Kerezau gestured, and two guards pulled Talis away. Another gesture, and Thia was dragged to her feet. "Silence, you stupid slut!" he ordered. One of the guards slapped a hand over Thia's mouth. She subsided, gulping noisily.

"You say you do not wish to be parted from your husband?" Kerezau asked.

Her mouth still covered by the guard's huge, grimy paw, Thia nodded.

"Very well. We will hang him, and then we will hang *you*. You can be together in death." He made a dismissive gesture. "Take them away."

Behind the guard's hand, Thia allowed herself a faint
smile, then sighed, threw up her hands and swooned. The
guards did not let her fall. She made herself stay limp as
they dragged her over to the mainmast, where they had taken
Jezzil. Her pretense paid off; they did not bind her hands.

The guards had already run a long thick rope up through a
pulley set into the rigging above the boom of the mainmast.
Thia saw that it had a noose on the other end. Two guards
grabbed the free end of the line and pulled it down. They
stood holding it, ready to begin hoisting when the noose was
in place.

Thia tensed inwardly but kept her body limp, relaxed.
They had to believe she was harmless. She began keening,
but softly. She didn't want them to gag her.

Barus stepped forward, nodded to the guard, looked
straight at Jezzil and spoke in their language. From his tone,
his comment was evidently an admonition to the guards.
They stiffened, and tightened their hold on Jezzil.

Barus smiled, and it was a terrible sight.

The guard pushed the noose over Jezzil's head, then tightened it so it couldn't slip off when the executioners began
hauling on the rope.

When the noose was secure, the guard stepped back and
nodded to the other two. They grasped the rope and began to
pull. Jezzil's body went up . . . up . . . until he was teetering
on his tiptoes. The guards looked to Barus for the command
to pull him up higher, but Barus did not seem disposed to
make a quick end. He stood there smiling, watching Jezzil
sway on his tiptoes, back and forth, back and—

Without warning, there was a loud *BOOM* belowdecks.
The *Pride* shuddered and heaved; smoke and flame belched
from the side of the ship. Thia was thrown to her knees.
Jezzil's guards staggered. She heard loud, reverberating
metallic crashing from below, mixed with the crackle of fire
and the shouts of sailors.

*Just as they are about to hang Jezzil, there will be a dis-
traction,* Khith had told her.

This is it! she thought. Her guards had both been thrown

to the deck, and neither of them paid her the slightest attention as she scrabbled forward on her hands and knees. She didn't know exactly what the little mage had done, but at least she'd been warned to expect something. She knew she must move fast, while everyone else was distracted.

Jezzil's guards, like everyone else on the deck except for Thia, were now looking off to starboard. She reached Jezzil, stood up and began sawing at the ropes binding his wrists with Khith's scalpel. She could hear him gagging, choking from the taut-drawn noose.

Beneath her hands, Jezzil's wrists suddenly vanished. She could still *feel* the ropes and his flesh, but could no longer see them. She sawed frantically at the last rope, seeing blood smear her hands. She had cut him.

A second later she could feel nothing—he was gone. The noose swung, empty. Thia looked around her at the chaos that had been the well-ordered Chonao troops.

What now?

Talis staggered, nearly thrown off her feet. She smelled acrid smoke and heard loud, metallic clanging from belowdecks. *What in the name of the Goddess was* that? Like everyone else, she turned to see smoke billowing out of the *Pride*'s starboard side. Chaos reigned on deck as the captain shouted for all hands to go below and fight the fire.

Talis turned back to see what had happened to Jezzil, only to realize he was gone. His guards were shouting and flailing the air with their swords. *He disappeared! He's free!*

Kerezau and his men were milling around, everyone shouting and pointing, clearly caught off guard. *Now's my chance!* she thought, and her fingers went to the buttons of her skirt. It took but a moment to unfasten it and the petticoats beneath it, then step out of them. She bunched them up and tossed them overboard. Clad in the breeches she'd worn underneath, she eased her way through the gesticulating, shouting crowd surrounding the Redai.

Just as she'd thought, Kerezau's guards were not paying attention to what was going on behind them. She sidled closer, her hand going up to her hair. Her gaze fastened on the back of Kerezau's neck. Could she try for such a small target, or would it be better to work her way around to the side, so she could go for the artery?

The sharpened hairpin, its point shrouded in fabric, was in her hand. Carefully, using a fold of her shirt, she pulled the protective fabric away. The metal point was dulled from the solution she'd dipped it in. Was it the poison or the soporific? Or was it some other type of powder that would prove harmless?

Step by step, Talis eased forward, keeping her hands down, guarding her gaze. She decided that the top of the spine was too small a target. Kerezau's armor had a thick metal collar that concealed much of his neck and throat, but it dipped a bit in front. That would be her target . . .

And afterward?

Talis told herself that she couldn't afford to think about afterward. Perhaps she'd have a fighting chance if she could grab Kerezau's sword.

She was only two steps away now, and everyone's attention was still focused on the smoke billowing out of the *Pride*'s side.

One step . . .

Talis leaped, her hand flashing out and toward the Redai's throat. But her blow did not land true. Somehow Kerezau managed to twist at the last possible second, and the hairpin scraped along the top of his armored collar. He slapped his hand to his neck as if stung. "Assassin! Katan *whore*! You are a dead woman!"

Had she scratched him at all? Drawn blood? Talis couldn't tell. The Redai whirled, drew his sword and came after her. He waved the others back. "Somebody give her a blade! I want her for myself!"

Talis leaped back just as the nearest guard tossed her his sword, hilt first. The blade was long for her, the curved shape not as familiar as the straight Katan swords. She had practiced with Jezzil's sword a time or two, but . . .

With a shout, Kerezau rushed her and they engaged.

Talis had been a passable swordswoman before Jezzil came into her life. After several months of his training, she was much improved, probably able to best most Katan soldiers. But the Chonao were a different breed. Within moments she was pressed hard just to keep herself from being spitted.

Their blades wove a clashing symphony of bright silver in the sun, hissing and ringing and clanging. She used every trick she'd ever learned, feinting, sidestepping, parrying ... anything to keep Kerezau's sword from hitting her body. Talis kept backing up, trying to remember the way the deck had looked behind her, hoping there was nothing there for her to trip over. One stumble and she was dead; she knew it.

After a minute or two she realized that Kerezau was deliberately prolonging the fight—he intended to cut her to pieces, little by little. A cat playing with a mouse.

Her chest was heaving now as she parried yet another thrust, and her arm was growing tired. *What should I do?* she wondered as she saw a quick opening and lunged. Kerezau stepped aside easily, though, and laughed. "Not bad for a Katan slut!"

Suddenly, she heard a bellow from a voice she recognized. "Talis! There's a plan! Jump! Swim southeast!"

That's Eregard, she thought as she automatically parried another lunge, only to discover it was actually a feint. Kerezau could have slashed her throat, but he only laughed and brushed the top of her shoulder with the tip of the blade. *Jump?*

She could swim, but . . . wouldn't that be sure death?

Exactly what are you facing here and now, my girl? she thought, and then, before she could allow herself to think further, she flung the sword at Kerezau with all her might, turned, ran four long paces and leapt over the railing.

Eregard saw Talis go over the railing with a feeling of relief. His apportioned task for their escape was to make sure everyone knew there was a plan, and that plan was to swim southeast of the *Pride*. He turned and ran across the deck, dodging sailors and Chonao. There was still a lot of smoke, but the fire did not seem to be spreading. He knew that Khith had designed his "distraction" so it would cause pandemonium on deck but would not, with luck, sink the ship.

He reached Falar's pen, then crouched on the other side, out of sight, wondering whether to open the gate and let her go. He knew Jezzil was bound to end up here at some point . . . he would no more abandon Falar than he would one of his human companions. The Prince shaded his eyes from the sun, looking across the deck, searching for his friends. He saw Khith, clutching its medical bag, over on the southeastern side of the ship, climbing the railing. The little Hthras looked back at him as it straddled the railing and dropped its bag. With a quick nod, the doctor was gone, over the side.

Two down, Eregard thought. *Where are Jezzil and Thia?* He was a bit concerned about Talis. She had jumped over on the northwest side of the ship, which would necessitate her swimming quite a distance to get clear of the *Pride* and then all the way around her. He told himself to relax, Talis was probably as competent at swimming as she was at everything else. He couldn't believe she'd managed to hold off Kerezau for as long as she had.

Without warning, the door to Falar's pen opened. Eregard leaped up. "Jezzil! Khith has a plan—swim southeast! There's one of the seaweed islands, we can regroup there!"

He heard Jezzil's voice, though no one was visible. "Did Khith cause that explosion?"

"Yes," Eregard said. "It planned the whole thing, but we couldn't get word to Talis."

"Where is Talis?"

"She fought with the Redai, held him off, then I told her to go over the side. Khith just went. It's your turn, my friend. Can you swim?"

Eregard heard a low chuckle. "Anything to get off this cursed ship, my friend."

Eregard suddenly focused and pointed. "There's Thia. I'll go get her."

"Let me," Jezzil's voice came back. "You've done your part. Over you go."

Eregard sketched a half salute. The door to Falar's pen burst open and the mare bolted out at full stride. The Prince turned, ran for the railing, and executed a clean, precise dive into the Narrow Sea.

Thia stood on the deck, wondering how soon one of the Chonao guards would spot her and kill her. The tumult over Master Khith's explosion was dying down. There wasn't as much smoke streaming out of the hole in the *Pride*'s side, and the loud clanging as the cannons rolled around belowdecks had stopped.

She'd seen Talis leap off the ship, and Khith, too. She knew that was the plan, but couldn't make herself jump, no matter how hard she tried. She had never learned to swim, and the green-blue depths surrounding the vessel frightened her beyond reason.

She wondered what the others would think when she didn't join them. Master Khith said they could reach one of those floating islands of seaweed not too far away. If only she could make herself jump!

She took a hesitant step closer to the railing, then halted. *I can't. I just can't.*

As she stood hesitating, shielding her eyes from the sun, trying to spot her friends in the water, Thia heard the drum of hoofbeats. She looked up to see Falar bolting toward her at what seemed a full gallop.

She tried to throw herself aside, but as the mare swooped past, an invisible hand grabbed the back of her dress, jerking her off her feet. Thia emitted one short-lived scream as she was dragged up across the horse, then the mare launched herself—straight over the railing.

They were falling, falling . . .

Time seemed to stop, then rushed past at a speed even more dizzying than the horse's. Equine and passengers hit the water with a tremendous splash.

The water was cold and salty—it seemed to shock her entire body like a bolt of lightning. Thia threw up her hands as she felt herself plunging down, down. Her skirts weighed her down, pulling her ever deeper, until she was lost in the cold, wet darkness. She opened her eyes, felt seawater sting them, but couldn't see anything except silvery bubbles and dark green water.

Soon she would have to breathe, and it would all be over.

She hung there, weightless, suspended in time and water. If not for the increasing need to breathe, the pressure in her chest, the sensation might have been pleasant.

Then something grabbed her hair and yanked her upward.

Thia's head broke the surface, coughing and choking, too ecstatic at having real air to breathe to even notice her rescuer for a moment. Blinking water out of her eyes, she gasped. "Jezzil!"

"At your service," he said, grinning at her. She'd never seen him smile so widely, look so carefree. He was holding her up on the surface seemingly without effort, moving his legs and one arm lazily.

"You saved me," she said stupidly.

"I was just repaying the favor," he replied. "That was quite a show you put on. I don't imagine that Kerezau has seen too many like it."

Despite her situation, Thia managed a weak laugh. "I was surprised how much I enjoyed myself," she admitted. "But, Jezzil, what now? I can't swim."

"You don't have to," he said. "We'll lighten you a bit, get rid of some of those skirts, then Falar can tow you."

"How will you—" She broke off as he held up a knife. "How did you—" But he was already gone, slipping under the surface as smoothly as a sea creature in one of the ancient texts she'd copied.

She let out a squawk of protest as she began to sink, but then she felt his grasp, supporting her from beneath. There were tugs at her skirt and petticoats. A final, hard tug and the petticoats were gone altogether. Jezzil surfaced. "One more time," he said, gasping in a huge breath.

Moments later she realized that about half of her skirt was gone. Her legs from the knee down were unencumbered.

Jezzil bobbed up again. "And now to regroup," he said. Quickly, he towed her over to Falar, who had been swimming back and forth beside them. "You're going to hold her mane," he said, "and kick your legs. Keep kicking, or you might sink and she might strike you with her hooves. Understand?"

Thia managed to nod, then grasped the mare's soaked, coarse mane with both hands. She began kicking.

Effortlessly, Falar towed her through the water. It took only moments before they reached Khith. The little Hthras leaned on its medicine bag, which was floating very well indeed.

"Ahoy!" Jezzil called out as they approached. "Master Khith! Where are Eregard and Talis?"

Khith shook its head. Its fur was slick as a sea lion's, plastered against its head. "I know not, Jezzil," it said. "When Talis did not join us, Eregard went to look for her. She jumped into the sea on the wrong side of the ship." It lifted an arm to point. "Our destination lies that way."

Thia narrowed her eyes and could barely make out a line on the horizon.

Jezzil was looking back at the *Pride*. They had drifted a little way from the ship, and Thia could see the concern on his face. "Perhaps I should go look for them," the Chonao said.

"I am concerned," Khith admitted. "But let us wait a few more minutes."

They waited . . . and waited.

Jezzil spent his time teaching Thia to tread water, as he termed it. It was a relief to no longer have to depend on an outside source to keep her from sinking.

All the while she was occupied, however, Thia felt her fear building. Where were Talis and Eregard?

Eregard was swimming. It had been a long time since he'd been in the water, but as a boy growing up on an island, he'd learned to swim as well as the rest of the Pelanese children, and better than many. Swimming was the one thing he'd been able to beat Salesin at, and the first time he had, Salesin refused to compete with his younger brother anymore.

His long strokes and rhythmic kicks carried him alongside the *Pride* quickly and nearly effortlessly. His work on the plantations had hardened him, made him much stronger, and that paid off now.

Where is Talis? he wondered, pausing to tread water and look around. *This is close to the spot where she jumped overboard.*

He scanned the water's surface over and over, and finally saw her. She was swimming in the wrong direction, and, from her movements, nearing the end of her strength.

Eregard swam after her. He was afraid to call her name loudly; they were still within arrow range of the ship. In all the confusion, no one had seemed to take much note of their departures, but there was no point in calling attention to themselves.

Talis's strokes were slow now, leaden. It was plain she was exhausted. *No wonder,* Eregard thought. *All that swordfighting, then having to swim for it.* He knew how easily a swimmer could become disoriented and swim in the wrong direction. Talis must have been swimming alongside the *Pride* for half an hour; an inordinate distance for a novice swimmer.

Just as he came within hailing distance of her, Talis's strokes shortened even more, then degenerated into aimless thrashing. He could hear her struggling to breathe, then she swallowed water and went under. She surfaced again a moment later, but all pretext of swimming was gone. She was fighting to stay on the surface, with little success.

Eregard paused. A panic-stricken, exhausted swimmer was the most dangerous variety. He called softly, "Talis! Talis, I'm here. I'll help you. Take it easy."

She didn't hear him. Lost in her struggle to breathe, she fought the water.

Eregard steeled himself, then went toward her. He could tell that she didn't recognize him, only saw him as something to climb up on so she could keep breathing. She lunged at him, grabbing, trying to climb atop him.

Eregard felt a surge of fear before he remembered the old guardsman who had taught him to swim. "If they sees yeh as nothin' but a rock t'climb on, give 'em a duckin'. Works ever' time."

He raised his arms and took them both under. The moment Talis felt the water close over her head, she let go of him and began trying to reach the surface again.

Eregard came back up with a rush, and then, as she threw herself at him again, raised his fist.

Talis's trajectory took her straight into it; she went limp.

Eregard wrapped one hand in her long hair, streaming out around her like the tresses of the fabled Sea Maidens that would follow ships, crying and wailing for sailors to take them as their wives.

He began swimming again, a resting stroke on his side, stroke and kick, then glide, heading around the *Pride* toward the others. He'd been swimming for several minutes when he heard her voice. "Eregard?"

He stopped, treaded water, and tentatively let go of her hair. "Yes, mistress?"

"I'm sorry," she said, looking at him. "I don't even know what happened. I lost my head. I couldn't breathe."

"I know, mistress," he said. "It's all right. Happens to even good swimmers sometimes."

"I thought I could swim well, but I learned in the fishpond," she said ruefully, brushing a long strand of hair off her face. "I was never in the sea before. It's so big. And so deep."

"Yes, mistress, it is," Eregard said.

Talis made a face. "Goddess smite you, stop calling me that!"

Eregard fought not to smile. "Very well, mis—" He trailed off, then grinned. "My apologies."

Talis grinned back ruefully. "From now on it's just Talis. I think I can swim a bit now."

"We'll go together, then," he promised.

Something flashed into the water between them, then another streaking shape fell short. Eregard beckoned to Talis. "Arrows! Swim with me!"

They headed out, away from the ship and the small crowd of crossbow-carrying Chonao that lined the railing.

As they swam, Eregard coached Talis, and when she tired, he towed her until she regained her strength. Seeing that they were out of range, the Chonao quickly lost interest.

By the time they reached the others, they'd nearly been given up for dead. The little group began swimming, with Thia and Talis clinging to Falar's mane and kicking, one on each side. They swam for nearly an hour, taking breaks to rest, and then suddenly the seaweed island that Khith had spotted with the borrowed eyes of a seabird was directly in front of them.

Khith, who was the lightest, was the first one up onto the mat of seaweed. Thia and Talis followed. Despite their exhaustion, they moved as briskly as they could, gathering driftwood to reinforce the seaweed, so Falar would be able to find purchase.

By late afternoon all five, plus Falar, were perched on the dubious safety of the seaweed island. They could move around, except for Falar, whose hooves were so sharp she tended to cut through the interwoven, matted growth. Jezzil made the mare hunker down with her legs folded beneath her, then brought her handfuls of the most succulent seaweed to eat.

The rest of the group simply sat, half dozing, trying to regain their strength.

Finally, Eregard sat up straight and looked around. All sight of the *Pride* had vanished. They were alone, with no land nearby for many leagues in any direction. They had almost no food or water, no warm clothing, and no prospect of rescue.

"There's an old Pelanese phrase," he said, "something about 'out of the kettle and into the coals.' Seems to me that applies now, doesn't it?"

Four faces turned to him. He smiled wryly. "So, what now, my friends?"

20

Seaweed and Sea Serpents

"What now, indeed?" Khith asked, echoing Eregard's question. The Hthras gazed at its companions, thinking that they were hardly a prepossessing lot, though their long swim had rendered Jezzil, Thia, and Eregard considerably cleaner and more pleasant to be near. "Now we must think about ways to signal for rescue. We are in a well-traveled shipping lane. Surely a ship will happen by within the next few days."

"Next few *days*?" Jezzil looked down at the handful of seaweed he had wrung out and was feeding to Falar. "What are we going to do about food and water? Eat this stuff?"

"If animals eat it, we can, too," Talis pointed out. "Maybe if we pick it and dry it in the Sun it won't be so slimy."

Khith shifted on the piece of driftwood, easing away from a splinter. The board was uncomfortable, but better than sitting on the wet seaweed. "We can remove extraneous articles of clothing and spread them to catch the dew. We can get a little moisture that way."

Jezzil nodded. "Yes, and we'll need to gather more driftwood to sleep on."

"Indeed," Khith agreed. "It makes a hard bed, but better that than the dampness."

"We can eat the seaweed?" Thia asked, holding up a tuft. She grimaced. "It smells awful. Like rotting fish."

Khith nodded. "Yes, we can eat the seaweed. There are also . . ." It hesitated, staring intently down at the dark gray-green mat of vegetation at its feet. ". . . kelp grubs!" The Hthras's slender digited hand flashed down, to emerge with a small white creature that wriggled.

Popping the grub into its mouth, Khith chewed and swallowed. "Eminently edible," it announced.

Thia shook her head, her pale features even paler than usual. "I don't think I can," she announced. "I'm sorry. I'd rather go hungry."

Khith waved a hand. "You may feel different tomorrow, my dear. It is certainly possible to mix the grubs with the seaweed, so they will not be so . . . visible."

Thia just shook her head wordlessly. But she joined in to help with the search for more driftwood and to spread any clothing they could spare to catch dew. Khith stripped off its robe, and tried not to notice the covert glances the humans gave its body. *Perhaps it is a good thing that I am still a neuter,* it thought wryly.

By the time the dew-catchers were arranged, the Sun had dipped below the horizon, staining the sky with colors so vivid they seemed to have come from the pallet of some demented artist. They sat in silence, watching the sunset fade, as a cool breeze sprang up.

"We are all tired," Khith said. "May I suggest that we retire early?"

Jezzil signaled to Falar, and the mare lay down on her side, then closed her eyes with a weary sigh. He arranged driftwood beside her, then beckoned Thia to approach. "She will act as a wind barrier, and help keep you warm."

With a wan smile, she moved over to lie down with her head pillowed on the horse's neck. Khith nodded, then curled up against the animal's back. The Hthras could hear Jezzil settling down next to Thia.

Having had no sleep at all the previous night, and little for the past few, Khith pressed itself against the mare's warm hide and felt sleep descend as inexorably as nightfall.

"I envy them," Talis said, stifling a yawn. "I'm so tired, but I'm too keyed up to sleep."

She and Eregard sat together on a driftwood plank a little distance from their slumbering companions. Eregard smiled. "They sleep because they're pure of heart," he said dryly. "The rest of us may need a bit of help." Reaching inside his overjerkin, he pulled out a slender flask.

"What's that?" she asked. "Where did you get it?"

"Brandy," he said. "I filched it from Khith's medical supplies."

"Should we?" Talis started to reach for the flask, then hesitated. "What if the doctor needs it?"

Eregard shrugged. "I figure a swallow or two apiece won't be missed. It'll help us sleep." He handed her the flask. "After you, mis—" He stopped, then finished, "Talis."

She took the flask, unstoppered it, then took a sip. She lowered it, coughing a bit, and offered it back to the Prince. "Oh, my! Burns . . . all the way down."

Eregard took a swig. "Oh my, yes," he sighed. "This is good brandy. Pelanese, by the taste of it."

Each of them had another swallow, then sat in silence, watching the last light fade and the stars begin to appear. "I wonder if the *Pride* sank," she wondered, breaking the silence at long last. "I hope not. I liked Captain Garano. Maybe he can figure out a way to retake his ship."

"By the time I went overboard, the crew seemed to have the fire under control," Eregard said. "I don't think she sank."

"They didn't even put a boat over the side and try to recapture us," she mused. "They shot a couple of arrows, then gave up. I wonder why?"

The Prince laughed. "Put yourself in Kerezau's place. You have some troublesome prisoners that jump off a ship into the sea, leagues from land. Do you care whether they die from a well-placed arrow or from drowning? The Redai had no way of knowing about Khith's little floating refuge here."

Talis smiled. "When you put it that way, it makes sense. Do you think Khith's right, and we're in a shipping lane? And that someone will see us?"

He sighed. "No way to tell. If we're lucky . . ." He shrugged.

The wind was picking up, and Talis, still clad in her thin blouse and trousers, shivered, rubbing her arms. "Here," Eregard said, slipping off his jerkin and giving it to her, "this should help."

"Oh, I can't," she said. "You'll get cold, sitting there in your shirtsleeves."

"Not with this . . ." He took another sip. ". . . to keep me warm. Go on, take it."

She pulled the homespun garment around her. It felt good. After a moment she said, hesitantly, "Um . . . Eregard, I wanted to say . . ." She trailed off, searching for the right words. They eluded her, though.

"Say what?" He turned to look at her. It was full night now, and Talis thought that she had never seen so many stars. Their illumination was enough so she could discern his face, a pale oval against the night.

"I . . ." She shrugged. "I wanted to thank you." She took a breath. "For saving my life today."

He shook his head. "I'm just glad I found you. One little piece of ocean looks a great deal like another. I could have missed you so easily. Gone right past you and never known it."

"You're a good swimmer."

He chuckled ruefully. "I am, I suppose. Most Pelanese children grow up half fish. Comes from living on an island, I suppose. I'll wager you were surprised to find that I was good at anything physical." He chuckled again, but now there was a hollow ring to it. "You're certainly not the first."

Talis realized that surprise was exactly what she'd been feeling, and found herself blushing. She blessed the night. "Of course not. I just . . . I just . . ."

He handed her the flask. "Think nothing of it. Here, it's your turn."

Talis sipped again, and this time did not sputter. The brandy slid down her throat and sent a wave of warmth washing through her.

They sat in silence for another long while. Talis heard the Prince sigh, then curse under his breath. "What is it?" she asked.

When Eregard spoke this time, his voice was harsh, thick with emotion. "The thing that just about kills me is that I was so damned *close*. We were almost to Pela. Almost within sight of Minoma harbor. Then that wretched storm and that wretched tinpot tyrant, Kerezau, had to come along. Just my luck," he finished bitterly. "Just my double be-damned luck."

She put her hand on his arm. "Maybe we'll be rescued. Don't give up hope just yet. At least we're free, not Chonao captives."

"I suppose you're right, mis-" He broke off. "Ah, hells. My mother is sick, you know. I was always the one she wanted to come visit her. I would play and sing for her. Read her stories, tell her court gossip. It comforted her, having me there." He drew in a breath, and the sound was so full of pain that Talis's heart ached to hear it. "What if I never see her— or any of them—again?"

"You will," she said. "If you weren't meant to see them again, we'd never have met. We'd never have met Jezzil, or Thia, and I'd have never realized who you really were . . . are."

"You really believe that?" he said raggedly.

"Yes, I do," she said, surprised to realize she was telling the truth. She strove to put conviction into her voice. "I do believe it."

"I wish I could," Eregard said, and she heard him trying to choke back a sob. He rubbed his eyes roughly on his sleeve. "Damned brandy was supposed to cheer me up, not start me sniveling."

"You're not sn-sniveling," she insisted, trying not to slur.

"I'm supposed to be a double be-damned *prince,* and all I can do is whine and snivel," he continued, plainly not listening. "Talis, when I was small, I believed that I must be a changeling. That the real Prince Eregard was someplace safe, hidden away, and that he was strong and noble and a true royal."

"That's silly," she said. "Of course you're Prince Eregard. Everyone says you look just like your mother when she was a girl."

"Oh, I suppose I stopped believing that fantasy about being a changeling at some point," he said, "but I'm not like my brothers, not at all. I don't look like them. I'm no warrior. I'm no good at court intrigue, either. My father was afraid of my brother, and what did I do to help him? Nothing but get myself sold into slavery. Better if I die out here than betray the family honor any more than I already have—"

"Stop that!" she said, pulling him around to face her on their piece of driftwood. "You're royal, but you are also human, Eregard. You've been given a great gift, to see and understand the other side of things. What it means to work with your hands, how it feels to go hungry, what it's like not to have enough firewood, so you have to sleep shivering."

She drew a deep breath. "That gift makes you the best of them, Eregard. Pela needs you, and so does Kata." She gave him a brief, comradely embrace, then pulled back, holding his face in her hands. "Listen to me. I believe there is a reason for what you've suffered, and someday you'll know what it is. You have a destiny. I just *know* you do. You should pray to the Goddess for a sign, so you'll know it, too."

She could feel dampness from the tears, and his beard was thick and harsh beneath her hands. It seemed to take him forever to focus on her face, hear what she was saying. "Talis," he muttered, and then his hand rose to touch her face in turn. "You think so?"

"Yes," she said. Their faces were now so close together that she could feel his breath, warm and smelling of the brandy. She felt light-headed, doubtless from the liquor. *Pull back,* she ordered herself. *Pull away.*

But her hands did not seem to obey her mind. Her fingers

cupped his cheek. "Oh, Talis. Thank you," he breathed, and turned his head to kiss the palm of her hand. His mouth was warm, and she could not believe the jolt of sensation that simple caress sent through her entire body.

What's happening to me? Talis realized she was drunk, but it wasn't just the brandy. She'd never felt this way before. Eregard's hands slid down to her shoulders, and he pulled her close to him, holding her tightly. He was big and solid, and his warmth felt good.

He was stronger than she had ever realized; she could feel the muscles in his arms and chest. Her head swam, and she turned her head to tell him to let go of her, tell him to stop . . . stop!

Before she could do more than open her mouth to say the word, he was kissing her.

He tasted of brandy, and salt, and his mouth was gentle but insistent on hers. For years just the thought of Uncle Jasti's kiss had been enough to make her vomit, but this was different. So different!

Talis realized dazedly that she was clinging to Eregard and that she had returned the kiss. His tongue touched hers, and it was a fire that ran through her. No one had ever told her that there could be pleasure in this, a pleasure so profound it seemed to fill her body. She could not break away from that kiss, it seemed to go on and on, and she thought she would die if it ever ended.

But it did end. He drew back a little, then began kissing her face, her ear, her throat, murmuring to her, his words slurred but understandable. "Talis, you are so beautiful, so beautiful. You're beautiful when you fight, when you laugh . . ."

She found herself seeking his mouth again, kissing him, and realized that he was touching her breast through the thin blouse, his hand expertly squeezing, his thumb exciting her nipple. Another jolt of pleasure arrowed through her, and she ran her fingers through his hair, traced them down the side of his neck . . . encountered the cold iron of the slave collar—

—only to feel Eregard pull away from her with a jerk so sudden that they both slid off the piece of driftwood, landing on the soggy, cold seaweed.

The cold wetness acted like a slap in the face for Talis, bringing her up short. *What am I doing?* she thought, horrified. *I swore I would never, never let any man touch me again!*

She scrambled to her knees, realizing her heart was pounding as hard as it had when she'd fought Kerezau . . . was it only hours ago? Years seemed to have gone by.

Eregard cursed softly under his breath as he heaved himself back up onto the driftwood. His voice was unsteady as he turned to offer her his hand. "I'm sorry, Talis."

She avoided his hand as she scrambled back to sit on the opposite side of the log, as far away from him as she could get, wrapping her arms across her still-tingling breasts. Falling back on her spy training, she managed a fairly convincing laugh. "Sorry for what? Getting sloshed and pawing me? It's not like it's never happened to me before."

"But—" He broke off, and she saw him shake his head unsteadily. "Well, leave it at that. My apologies, mistress. I bid you good night."

She watched him get up cautiously, then head back toward their sleeping comrades, his dark shape silhouetted against the multitudes of stars.

It meant nothing, she told herself fiercely. *Forget it. Forget it and go to sleep.*

They awoke at dawn, still tired, cramped, and stiff from sleeping on the driftwood. They managed to suck a small bit of moisture from the dew that had collected on their clothes, but it did little to satisfy their thirst. Khith moved around, collecting grubs and seaweed, then rolling the seaweed around the grubs in bite-sized pieces. "Let us break our fast," the Hthras suggested, laying out a row of the morsels. "Jezzil? Eregard?"

Eregard shook his head. "I'm not hungry," he muttered. "I've got a demon of a headache."

"Can't be any worse than moldy field rations," Jezzil said wryly, picking up a couple of pieces and popping them into his mouth. He chewed once, twice, then swallowed, grimacing. "Well, at least it's not moldy."

Talis sighed. "Later. I'll let mine dry out a bit."

Thia just shook her head, turned, and walked away.

Khith followed her. "Please, at least try."

She shook her head. "I'm sorry. I don't feel well. I'm not hungry."

Khith lowered the morsel of seaweed. "Very well. Your skin, it is so fair. Yesterday's Sun reddened it. We must protect you from it today."

The doctor spent several minutes swathing Thia in some of their castoff clothing, using its own robe to cover her head and arms. "I'm going to try and sleep again," she said, and went back to the chunk of driftwood she'd claimed the night before.

Eregard glanced over at the sun, still low in the east. "We'd all better cover up before long, or we'll burn like a roast when the spit stops turning."

Jezzil gestured at the seaweed. "Ordinarily, we'd use mud in the field if we didn't have protective clothing. But there's no mud here, so the seaweed will have to do." He glanced down at his own weathered skin. "I'll be fine for a few hours. Then I'll cover up."

Talis poked desultorily at the seaweed mat. "How does it live, with no earth to sustain it? What keeps it afloat?"

"I don't know," Jezzil said.

"I've heard sailors talk about it. They say that they've seen these things set afire," Eregard said. "How could wet seaweed burn?"

"It is not the seaweed that burns, but the bladders that keep it on the surface," Khith said. The doctor sat down on a plank of driftwood with a sigh. "The weed produces a gas as it takes in sunlight and air, and that gas is incendiary."

"A gas? Bladders?" Eregard poked the seaweed, trying to dig down through to see what lay underneath.

"Yes, membranes of tissue, very tough, but nearly transparent, like those of some anemones," Khith said. "They inflate with the gas that the kelp produces as it digests light and air."

"How do you know so much about it?" Talis said. "You are from the deep forests of the Sarsithe, you said."

Khith drew its slender, furred body up. "I am a scientist, as well as an alchemist and adept. I studied the natural world in the abandoned city of the Lost Ones. When I left, I had learned to translate their language, albeit poorly. The Ancients created this form of seaweed as an adjunct food source for livestock."

"Tell me about this city," Eregard said, fascinated. "Who are—or were—the Lost Ones?"

"They are the people who built the ruins in the Sarsithe," Khith said. "I believe they looked much like humans. They once ruled our world; they had great power. Their science was far beyond even the science of my people, much less yours. And in their last years, they learned to *fuse* magic and alchemy with science. It gave them incredible powers. Before their destruction, there were Adepts among them whose abilities were beyond anything my people ever dreamed possible. They controlled their world, even the weather. When they battled, they did so with weapons that could smite an entire city and leave nothing behind but smoldering, toxic rubble and dust."

Jezzil glanced up. "What you describe sounds like the Great Waste, which lies east of Chonao lands. They say a man can safely travel there for three days, but if he stays much beyond that, he is doomed. Treasure hunters scavenge there for precious metals and gems, but they can reach only the edges of the deposits in a day. That gives them a day to search and to collect, and then a day to return. If they take longer, they fall ill, and often die, of a wasting illness."

"From my reading in the Lost City, I believe that the Lost Ones were responsible for the Great Waste," Khith said. "But their records grew so chaotic at the end, one cannot be sure of anything."

Eregard leaned closer. "Do you think they wiped themselves out? Reduced their cities to ruins, buried in the jungle?"

"It is possible that they were responsible for what happened to them . . ." The doctor paused.

"Or?" Eregard breathed.

"But some of their records seem to indicate that they faced an enemy even greater than they were—a terrible enemy that was not of this world. There are hints in their texts that this may have been so." Khith paused. "It was very difficult for me to decipher their language, and often I was uncertain as to the meanings of words."

"Lost cities and lost history! I'm intrigued," Eregard said. "I'd love to go there."

Jezzil gave him a glance. "I'll never be a scholar, I'm afraid. If you go there, I'll be your bodyguard, and do some hunting. That sounds far more interesting to me than poring over dusty records."

Eregard glanced up. "Thia's sitting back up. I'm going to go check on her." He picked up several of Khith's seaweed concoctions, grimaced, then manfully gulped one of them down, trying to chew as little as possible. It was salty, chewy, and slimy, but he managed to swallow it. "Maybe I can get her to eat something. We have to stay strong enough to watch for a ship."

"I'm worried about her," Jezzil said. "She's too thin as it is."

Eregard rose and slogged over the seaweed, trying to ignore the way the footing underneath rose and sank as it took his weight. It was the first time he'd been alone since he'd awakened, and his "repast," noisome as it had been, seemed to have cleared his head.

The events of last night came rushing back, so vividly that he stumbled and almost splashed down into the seaweed. He managed to catch himself at the last moment, but he was frowning as he realized that not once had Talis looked at him today, much less spoken to him.

He sighed. *Is she angry because I started, or because I stopped?* From observing the way Talis acted around men— as opposed to women—the complete absence of any flirtatiousness in her manner, or any sexual component to her interactions, he feared it was the former. For a moment anger surged. *For the love of the Goddess, I'm only human! And what was it, after all, but a kiss and a bit of groping? It's not as though I raped her!*

He vividly remembered the way she had felt in his arms, the passionate response of her mouth, the hardening of her nipples. *It's just as well we stopped,* he thought. *Ulandra is the one I love, and it's Thia I'm going to ask to marry me, if we get out of this.*

He glanced down and scowled at his groin. "Down, you fool. Get down." He slowed, almost stopping. *Can't let Thia see me like this . . .*

Why *had* he stopped? Up until the moment he released her, Talis had plainly welcomed his attentions. He'd felt her shudder with passion when he caressed her. She'd returned his caress, putting her hand up and stroking his cheek, his hair, his—

Eregard stopped dead, and just as it had last night, his arousal died as he remembered. *It was the collar. I felt her touch this be-damned collar.*

The Prince put his hand up to his slave collar, felt the groove he'd worn in the iron. *I should have made them take me to a smithy so I could get it taken off,* he thought bitterly. He began walking again, and in a few more strides reached Thia. She was huddled on a silvery plank of driftwood, with Khith's robe pulled over her head, shielding her face and arms from the Sun.

"Good morning," he said, sitting down beside her. "I brought you breakfast, m'lady."

Thia peered out at him, turtle fashion, her face in shadow from the shrouding garment. "I'm sorry," she said. "I don't think I can."

"You have to try," Eregard urged. "I felt much better after I forced a little something down. And we need to stay alert, watch for any ships that might come along."

Carefully, he picked at one of the little bundles and offered her a scrap of seaweed that was fairly dry. "See if this will go down. It's just a bit of seaweed."

Thia hesitated, then took the bit of vegetation. She regarded it, resolutely closed her eyes, popped it into her mouth and tried to swallow. She gagged, clamping both hands over her mouth. Eregard could see her jaw muscles working, and finally saw her swallow.

"Good!" he said. "In a few minutes you can try another bit. I've managed to get it down, see?" He popped another tidbit into his mouth, chewed once, then swallowed. "Nothing to it, and it made me feel much better."

Thia smiled wanly. "You shouldn't worry about me. I'll be fine."

"You will if you eat a bit," Eregard said. "Here, just a bit more seaweed now."

They sat together, talking desultorily, while Eregard got Thia to eat nearly a handful of the damp seaweed. She refused to try the grubs, though. In a few minutes her color improved and she looked a bit livelier. The Prince told her about the Lost Cities of the Sarsithe, which captured her attention.

The day dragged on. Eregard wrapped his shirt around his head, feeling the prickly tightness that meant sunburn on his cheeks. He'd never been so thirsty. After a few hours it was difficult to think about anything but water, or cold beer, or ale, or tea, or . . .

Resolutely, he forced himself to watch the horizon. They were sitting back-to-back, with each castaway responsible for watching a designated quadrant. His back was to Talis, and he was uncomfortably aware that not once that day had she spoken to him, or even looked at him. It pained him to be on the outs with any of his companions. In some ways, Khith, Jezzil, Thia, and Talis felt more like family to him than his own family ever had.

As the Sun lowered toward the west, Thia, sitting next to him on the plank, made a tiny moan and slumped over into his lap. "She's fainted! Doctor!" the Prince cried.

Khith hurried to her side to examine her, pinching the skin of her wrist, smelling her breath, and peering into her eyes. "She is unconscious," the doctor said. "She needs water. I have been saving a few swallows for all of us in my water flask . . ."

The Hthras took out the flask and looked questioningly

around the circle. "Give it to Thia," Jezzil said. "My share anyway."

"Mine, too." Talis and Eregard spoke as one. Eregard hadn't spoken in some time, and just moving his mouth made his cracked lips split. He tasted blood.

Khith nodded, and carefully gave Thia the last of their water, sip by slow sip. She did not rouse, but swallowed.

"That is the end of it," the Hthras murmured, stowing the empty flask back into its bag.

"What about the brandy?" Talis asked.

"It would do more harm than good, in her condition," Khith replied. "Besides, there is almost none left."

"Oh," Talis murmured, looking away. She cleared her throat. "Another beautiful sunset," she said, gazing westward. "We should—"

She broke off and leaped to her feet, pointing westward. "Look! Look!"

"A ship?" Jezzil was beside her in an instant. With his soldier's training and physical conditioning, he'd fared the best of all of them, except for Khith. "Where?"

"Not a ship!" Talis said. "A sea serpent!"

Eregard shaded his eyes against the setting Sun, scanning the water, and a moment later saw it. It was coming straight for their seaweed island.

"In all the times I've sailed the Narrow Sea, I've never seen one," he breathed. "Some of our court naturalists have claimed they're extinct."

The creature grew larger as it approached. Eregard, Jezzil, and Talis stood together, watching in fascination. It was enormous, nearly the length of the *Pride*, its body as thick around as a ship's wheel. The head, which was held up, out of the water, resembled that of a frilled lizard more than a snake. Its scales were a deep golden-amber, and its frills a brilliant green. As it drew even nearer, they could see its eyes, large, lidless, and black.

The creature propelled itself by undulating its tail back and forth in the water, and it moved as fast as a ship under sail.

Eregard stood enthralled, watching it glide by their refuge. At one point he thought it turned its head to look at them, but he couldn't be sure.

"A marvel of the natural world," Khith, who was still crouched over Thia, observed. "We are truly blessed."

"It's the symbol of your royal house, isn't it?" Jezzil asked.

Eregard nodded. "The sea serpent, rampant, against the rising Sun, upon a field of azure." He lowered his voice, pitching it for Talis's ears alone. "Talis, about last night . . ."

She gave him a quick, hard glance, and whispered, "Eregard, nothing happened, remember?"

"All right," he said after a moment, feeling obscurely disappointed.

"Good," she breathed, and gave him a wry smile. Eregard was so relieved that she was speaking to him again that he tried to smile back, which hurt. She turned back to watch the creature, which was now receding rapidly into the east. Scant minutes later there was no sign that anything had been there, yet Talis continued to stare fixedly into the distance.

Eregard dropped down beside the doctor and his patient, teetering on the driftwood. "How is she?"

Before Khith could reply, Talis's hand shot out and gripped the Prince's shoulder. Her voice was harsh with tightly restrained emotion. "By the Goddess, the symbol of the royal house. Eregard! Do you remember I told you to pray for a symbol?"

"Yes," the Prince answered, and glanced worriedly at Khith. Had the Sun gotten to Talis, too? "I remember. I forgot to do it, though . . ."

"Well, the Goddess must have heard," she said, still in a half-strangled voice, "because I see a *ship*!"

Eregard stood up so fast he overbalanced and splashed into the seaweed, soaking himself to the thigh. "What?"

"Where?" Jezzil demanded.

"Over there! See the sails, all pink with the sunset? Heading southwest!"

The companions stood there, scanning the darkening eastern horizon. Khith saw it first, then Jezzil and Eregard at the same moment.

"A ship!" the Prince shouted. "We're saved!"

"Only if we can signal it," Khith said. "Unless we can attract their attention, they will sail right past us, never knowing we are here." The doctor turned to the Chonao. "Jezzil, we must work together." The Hthras glanced at Eregard and Talis. "Take care of Thia."

In response, Eregard crouched beside Thia, taking her hand in his, rubbing it, talking to her soothingly, telling her that rescue was at hand. She did not rouse.

"What do you want me to do?" Jezzil asked the Hthras.

"I am going to use my avundi to open some of the bladders on the far side of this mat," Khith said. "When my fingers tighten on yours, use yours to ignite the gas that escapes."

Though hovering over Thia, Eregard watched Khith as the little mage grasped Jezzil's hand, staring intently at the other side of the seaweed island. Khith's fingers tightened on Jezzil's hand as Jezzil stared intently at the seaweed, his lower lip caught in his teeth. Eregard could see beads of sweat gather on his forehead, trickling down his face. The two of them continued to stare.

Long moments passed. A minute, two minutes. . .

Khith made a sudden gesture of impatience. "The gas has all escaped from that pod," it said. "It was one of the smaller ones. We will have to try again. Do you need the snuff, Jezzil? Remember the lessons with the candle!"

"Give me the snuff," Jezzil said tautly, and Khith complied. Jezzil snorted the powder up first one nostril, then another.

"Hurry," Talis urged. "A few more minutes and they'll be past us!"

"Concentrate, Jezzil!" Khith grasped the human's hand again. Once more the two stared intently at the seaweed.

VAA-ROOOM! A gout of flame shot up from the far side of the seaweed mat. Falar squealed in fear and lurched to her feet, floundering in the spongy footing. For once, Jezzil did not go to her.

"Another! The one beside it!" Khith cried.

Jezzil grunted in assent, and another gout of flame exploded, then another.

The flames from the escaping gas made a bright orange beacon against the darkening sky. They reached high enough so Eregard had to tilt his head far up to see their apex.

"Another!" Khith said.

A fourth gas bladder went roaring up in flames. By now the entire far end of the seaweed mat was spewing flame.

"That ought to do it!" Eregard shouted.

Thia murmured incoherently and opened her eyes, bewildered to see the orange inferno against the deep cobalt of the sky.

"Wh-What?" she stammered.

"There's a ship" Eregard soothed. "We're signaling it. Lie still. It's all right." He could feel heat against his left side now.

Suddenly, another segment of the seaweed burst into flame.

Khith turned to Jezzil. "Did you do that?"

"No, Master!" Jezzil had to shout to be heard above the roaring release of gas and flame. "Did *you*?"

"Not I," Khith said, backing away, measuring the distance between them and the lapping seawater. "Tend to Falar. We may have to take to the sea again if this continues . . ."

"Eregard, help me up!" Thia said. "I want to see." Carefully, the Prince helped her sit up, then putting an arm around her, he heaved and she was standing, teetering on the driftwood plank

"Thank you, Goddess!" Talis yelled, and turned to wave both arms at her companions. She was jumping up and down, sending up sprays of water. "They're coming about!" she shouted. "They're turning! They're coming!" She slipped and skidded over to Eregard and Thia and grabbed both of them in a fierce embrace. "They're coming—we're saved!"

Another section of seaweed exploded into flames.

Thia eyed the narrowing distance between them and the fire. "They'd better hurry," she observed, then smiled, a small, wry smile. "And let us hope it's a Pelanese ship, not one of Kerezau's."

Talis stared at them, eyes wide. "By the Goddess, I never thought of that."

Eregard squinted into the distance. Even though the ship was bigger now, the Sun had set, and it was hard to see in its afterglow. "Too much rigging to be Meptalith. It's *got* to be Pelanese. Might even be Royal Navy!"

With a roar, another section of the seaweed mat erupted in flames. Half their refuge was now ablaze, and the heat was growing uncomfortable.

Jezzil and Khith joined them. The Chonao was clinging to Falar's halter, grinning like a fool. "Looks like we overdid it a bit."

"Looks like," Eregard agreed with a laugh. Excitement coursed through his veins, stronger even than the brandy. He gestured at the water. "Anyone feel like a swim?" He bowed to Talis and Thia. "Ladies first."

21

Homecomings and Leave Takings

Carrying a bowl of hot water, a borrowed razor, and a pair of scissors, with a towel thrown over her shoulder, Thia approached the first mate's cabin of Royal Navy Ship *Sea Eagle*. Hearing footsteps within, she stepped back hastily a moment before the door was flung open. Eregard, rubbing his neck and carrying the two pieces of his slave collar, burst out, nearly running. As Thia watched, he reached the ship's rail and with a mightly heave flung the detested iron collar into the sea.

Jezzil, file in hand, stood in the doorway. He nodded at Thia's load. "I didn't know you were an experienced barber."

She smiled. "I spent more than a decade shaving my own head, and, often, the heads of my fellow postulants and novices. I'll manage."

Jezzil, seeing Eregard on his way back, his expression now more cheerful, nodded to her. "I'll leave you to your task, then," he said. He started to leave, then paused, rubbing his own beard. "Um, could I prevail upon you, also? When you are finished with Eregard?"

Thia laughed. "Very well. Before we dock, I promise."

Eregard sat quietly as Thia spread the towel over the

shoulders of his borrowed naval uniform and set to work. By
the time she was finished, the Prince resembled his profile
on the coin—except for the loss of an extra chin, Thia
thought, amused.

She handed him a mirror, and the Prince regarded himself
wonderingly. "Better than my valet ever managed," he pronounced finally. "Thia, you are a woman with many talents."

She laughed, then curtsied. "Why, thank you, Your Highness."

Eregard watched her, smiling, then his expression
sobered. He stood up and walked over to her, his blue-gray
gaze intent. "Don't call me 'Your Highness,' Thia," he said
softly, reaching out and taking her hand. "Not when we're
alone, at least. Things between us are the same as ever."

She nodded. "I know. I was but jesting, Eregard."

"I'm not," he said, and his expression brought a wash of
color into her cheeks. "There's something I've been wanting
to say to you for days, Thia, but things keep happening to
prevent me."

She stared at him, and felt a sudden urge to bolt before he
could go on. But his grasp on her fingers was strong, and that
would have been rude and hurtful. "Eregard . . ." she began,
but couldn't think what to say, how to stop him.

"I like the way you say my name," he said, and glanced at
the cabin door. "I'd better just say this, before a storm blows
up or we're attacked by the Redai's fleet." Swiftly, he raised
her hand to his lips, kissing her fingers.

Thia stepped back, hoping he'd release her hand.

Instead, Eregard dropped to one knee before her. "Thia,
will you marry me? I swear that I will be a good and faithful
husband to you, for so long as we both shall live."

Tears flooded her eyes, and her throat was so tight that she
could hardly swallow. *Oh, no! No, oh why did he have to do
this?* she thought wildly.

He was watching her, eager for her reply. *I must say something,* Thia thought frantically. *He is my dear friend, and I
must say something that will hurt him as little as possible.*

She cast about for words. "No, Eregard," she said sorrowfully. "I cannot marry you."

A cloud of disappointment rolled across his features, obscuring the light that had been there only moments ago. "Why not?" he said.

"Because . . ." She swallowed, thinking fast. "Because I have sworn never to marry. I swore an oath of celibacy."

Eregard dropped her hand and got to his feet, all the while staring at her incredulously. "What?" he gasped. "You're not a priestess anymore! That oath no longer binds you."

"I embraced it willingly, you see," she said. "Because I've never felt; uh . . ." She stumbled to a halt, tried again. "I mean, I n-never w-wanted . . . to, you know . . ." she stammered, and realized that she was lying. That night in the tavern, with Jezzil, something had awakened in her, something that made her knees go weak and left her feeling half drunk with longing. That night, she had wanted to, indeed yes.

"It's not you," she added desperately. "I'm very honored! Any woman would be. And I'm very . . . fond of you. But I don't want to marry anyone."

Eregard took a deep breath. "I confess I'm surprised," he said. "I've never made a decent proposal to a woman before, but I've made plenty of indecent ones." He gave a short, bitter-sounding laugh. "And they were all accepted."

Thia stepped over, took his hand and held it in both of hers. "Eregard," she said, "you don't love me."

She had him there, and they both knew it.

He gave her a crooked smile. "That Truthsense of yours is damned inconvenient at times," he said. "All right. We'll leave it at that, then."

She nodded, then squeezed his fingers. "Friends?" she asked.

He smiled. "Friends forever. I swear it."

Ulandra sat beside Queen Elnorin's bedside, holding the older woman's wasted hand in hers. Since coming to the royal apartments, she had scarcely left the Queen's bedside. Despite the shocked protests of the Queen's nobly born attendants, she'd insisted on helping the nurses care for the sick woman in the most basic ways: bathing her, dressing her, changing her bed linens, coaxing her to eat a few mouthfuls, reading to her, then singing softly until she drifted off into a shallow sleep.

As the Queen eased into slumber, Ulandra's song grew ever softer, until she was humming quietly. Finally, the weak fingers slackened, relaxed, and the Princess was able to lay Elnorin's hand down on the counterpane. Her humming trailed off, and as the Queen's breathing deepened, she pushed back from the bedside and stood up.

"She's asleep," Ulandra mouthed to Countess q'Venisa, the Queen's head lady-in-waiting.

The countess curtsied deeply. "Bless you, Your Highness," she said, her voice only a breath in the sickroom. Ulandra nodded to the day nurse who would remain in attendance, then picked up her skirts and headed for the bedchamber door. Once in the sitting room, the two women spoke in normal tones. "Where is the King?" Ulandra asked. "Her Majesty was asking for him."

"Meeting with Prince Salesin, Admiral His Lordship Nevila, and Rear Admiral Barzil, Your Highness," the countess replied. "The word is that carrier hawks were received this morning from the fleet. There have been several naval engagements with the invaders. Our ships were victorious, Goddess be praised!"

Ulandra tried not to let her features change at the mention of her husband. She hadn't seen Salesin in six days. When the Queen had suffered another of her debilitating episodes, Ulandra had seized on that excuse to avoid going back to her own apartments.

If Salesin is meeting the fleet commanders, she thought, *I should use this moment to go back to my rooms to bathe and change. I can have my women bring some clothes to the Queen's apartments . . .*

She nodded at the countess. "Very well. I am going to my rooms to change. Please have a light lunch prepared for me, and send some bread and meat and cheese for the King, in case he comes directly to Her Majesty's rooms after his meeting is concluded."

"Of course, Your Highness," the countess replied, sinking into a curtsy. "I shall see to it immediately."

"Thank you, Countess," Ulandra replied as she picked up the skirts of her morning gown and headed out the door.

It was the first time she had set foot outside the royal apartments since coming there, and as she headed toward the adjoining wing and her own rooms, she was startled to see the courtiers wearing not their court clothes, but military uniforms. Many officers bustled down the corridors carrying dispatch cases, bowing perfunctorily to her as they hurried by with a murmured, "Your Highness . . ."

She nodded to them, but with each greeting her heart pounded harder. *War. The invasion that Eregard warned the King about is really happening.*

She wondered where the Prince was. There had been no news of Eregard since that fateful day when she'd found Salesin unconscious on the floor, clawed and bitten.

Dizziness engulfed her as she remembered that time, and she had to stop and lean against the door of her apartments. *What really happened that day?* The unspoken question, like a persistent thief, crept into her mind, snatching at her sanity. Ulandra forced herself to concentrate on what she was doing. *Open the door. Step inside. Summon your women . . . Salesin has many enemies . . . you know that. Anyone could have done that to him. Anyone . . .*

Two of her ladies were in her suite, Marquise Jonala and Bethina. Both leaped to their feet when she entered, then curtsied deeply. "Your Highness!" the marquise exclaimed. "We have not seen you in days!"

"You know I have been attending Her Majesty," Ulandra replied, trying not to snap. Just being here in her own rooms made the fear uncoil and rise within her. "Bethina, I wish to bathe. Have hot water brought, please."

"Yes, Your Highness." Bobbing a curtsy, the woman scurried off.

Ulandra went over to the first of her wardrobes, opened it, and quickly chose five everyday gowns of muted colors and conservative cut. "Here," she said, piling them into Jonala's arms. "And these," she added, piling on some night shifts and two more morning gowns. "Take these to the room I am occupying in Her Majesty's apartments and hang them there."

"Yes, Your Highness," Jonala said, stretching her neck to peer over the top of the pile. "I shall see to it."

"And send in my other women," Ulandra said. "I need my hair washed and brushed."

"Yes, Your Highness."

With a swish of satin and a flutter of plum-colored lace, Jonala was gone. Ulandra began to pace, wondering when Salesin's meeting would be over. She knew that military tactics were time consuming. There would be lists of provisions and ammunition to go over, plus rosters of troops from other Pelanese villages . . . Napice in the far south, Vencal, Pioli, and Berini. She'd heard something whispered last night about foreign ships being sighted off the coast of Gen, to the northeast of Minoma, but hadn't been able to overhear much of what had been said.

How long can I stay in my rooms? she wondered. *How long will I be safe?*

She could have ordered bathwater from the Queen's servants, but knew that would cause suspicion. It was all well and good for a royal daughter-in-law to devote herself to caring for the ailing Queen, but Ulandra didn't want to arouse any more speculation than there already had been about her marriage. It was hard enough to ignore the whispers, the sideways glances, and the presence of Salesin's mistresses in his rooms.

She busied herself picking up some shoes, a book, a fan, and other personal items to be taken to her new room in the Queen's apartments. *While I am with the Queen, I am safe.*

Her fingers tightened on the soft kid of a boot. *But the Queen is fading fast. What will happen after she dies?*

Ulandra shook off the thought, ordering herself not to let

such negative notions enter her mind. Even thinking about the Queen's death made her feel disloyal. *She has been so kind to me. Goddess, help her rally!* Ulandra resolved to say an extra round of prayers that night.

Sounds of sloshing from the next room interrupted her reverie, and she went into her bedchamber. The bathtub was standing in the middle of the room, nearly filled with steaming water. Ulandra handed a maid her possessions, and after her ladies had undressed her and unbound her hair, stepped up onto the wooden step and into the tub. She sank down into the water with a sigh.

Her ladies began washing her hair, soaping and rinsing, then soaping again. Her hair was so long that by the time it was clean, the water in the tub had cooled until it was no more than pleasantly warm.

Ulandra took the sponge they handed her and began washing her private places. She knew her maids considered her odd for refusing their ministrations, but she had bathed herself in the convent, and having anyone else touch her there reminded her painfully of Salesin's assaults.

While she bathed, her women carefully combed out her hair, drying it gently with towels.

By the time Ulandra stood up and slid her arms into the robe her maid proffered, the water was tepid, and she felt more relaxed than she had in months.

The Princess pointed to one of her dresses, a pale blue trimmed with dark blue velvet ribbons, and Lady Jonala picked it up and spread it on the bed. Ulandra dropped the robe and extended her arms over her head so Amaryla could slip her silk chemise on.

Just as the silk slithered into place, the bedchamber door opened and Salesin stood silhouetted in the doorway. He was holding one of his ceremonial swords of rank, which had hitherto hung above the mantel in the sitting room.

The ladies gasped with surprise and not a little fear. Ulandra flinched, forcing herself not to take a step back. "Your Highness!" she exclaimed, snatching up her robe, sliding her arms into it. "Forgive me, my lord. I did not know you were there."

Salesin's eyes met hers, and Ulandra recognized a familiar expression in their dark depths. She swallowed. *And now he will order my ladies to leave, as he has done before, and then he will take me . . . as he has done before.*

She steeled herself. She would offer no resistance—that just made things worse, and prolonged the act.

But as she stared at her husband, she saw a different expression flicker in his eyes, crossing his features so quickly she wondered if she had imagined it.

Fear.

Salesin took a step back, then made an abbreviated bow. "My lady," he said formally. "Your pardon, I did not know you were here. I was told you were attending on my mother."

Ulandra nodded. "Yes, my lord."

"How is she?"

She hesitated, then gave him the truth. "I regret to say that she is failing, Your Highness. She had another of her episodes just yesterday, and it left her very weak."

He nodded. "So I have heard." He straightened. "I have duties, my lady, and must take my leave. Pela is going to war."

Ulandra managed to bob a curtsy, holding the skirts of her robe up. "Of course, my lord," she murmured. "We shall all pray to the Goddess for a great victory."

With a curt inclination of his head, Salesin was gone.

Ulandra gasped with relief, feeling her legs grow weak. She sat down with a thump on the edge of the big bed where so much suffering and degradation had occurred for so many months. "Dear Goddess," she whispered. "Dear Goddess . . ."

"Shall we all pray now, Your Highness?" the marquise asked.

Ulandra struggled to regain her composure. "Certainly," she murmured. Holding onto the bedpost for support, she slid down to kneel on the floor, assuming the proper posture for prayer. "Let us pray for a speedy victory against the invaders."

Even as she led her ladies in a prayer for victory and deliverance, part of Ulandra's mind was still reeling from the discovery she had just made. *He's afraid of me. He didn't come near me. What does this mean? Why should he be afraid—what did he see that day?*

By the time she was back in the Queen's bedchamber, it was lunchtime. Ulandra ate her own light repast, then dispatched a servant to fetch soft bread and broth for the Queen. Her chair by the Queen's bedside awaited her. After she was seated, she gently touched the Queen's hand. "Your Majesty?" Elnorin's eyes fluttered open. They were blue-gray, soft and a little vague. *Just like Eregard's,* Ulandra found herself thinking.

Her patient smiled. "Daughter. Back again? You should be off dancing at balls, not sitting here with me."

Ulandra squeezed her hand. "Your Majesty, there is no place in this world I would rather be than here with you. You have become the mother I barely knew."

The faded old eyes filled with tears, and Elnorin squeezed Ulandra's hand in turn. "May the Goddess bless you, my dear, for your kindness to me . . ." She turned her head restlessly on her pillow. "Ulandra, where is my son?"

"Prince Salesin and Prince Adranan are meeting with . . ." Ulandra trailed off. The Queen didn't know about the impending war, so why worry her? "They are in meetings with the royal governors, Your Majesty," she finished, which was at least partly true. The King had summoned several of his provincial governors to accompany their levies of troops, and four days ago he had dispatched Adranan to meet with the governor of the northern province, in the provincial capital, Gen.

"No, not Adranan," the Queen murmured. She smiled, a faint, ironic smile. "He's a good boy, Adranan—kind, honest—but he lacks subtlety. Not good in a royal. He blunders straight ahead, when cunning is called for. He came to see me, was it yesterday?"

"Yes, yesterday," Ulandra agreed. Actually, it had been four days ago, before Adranan had set out for Gen, but what did it matter?

The Queen's expression grew fretful. "And not Salesin. The Goddess must have been angry with me when I conceived him. There is such cruelty in him . . . he thinks only of power."

"Yes, I know," Ulandra said, but so softly she doubted the distracted woman heard her.

"No, the son of my heart, dear Eregard. Where is Eregard? I want him. He plays so well, and sings so sweetly."

The Queen's eyes closed. Even that short speech had exhausted her. Ulandra wet her lips, half tempted to tell the Queen that she'd had a message from Eregard less than a week ago. But they hadn't heard anything since . . . and how would she explain the nature of that message?

Best I not say anything, she decided. *It would only excite her, and might bring on another of her episodes. They weaken her so much.*

Moments later the food arrived. Ulandra did her best to rouse the Queen and get her to eat. She succeeded better than the trained nurse had managed, but the bowl was still more than half full when the Queen waved away the spoon feebly. "No more, no more. Thank you, my dear. I am full."

Knowing that the Queen would soon slip off into sleep, Ulandra quickly checked her swaddlings, and finding them wet, changed them. "You should not be doing this," Elnorin said, faintly. "'Tis no task for a princess."

"It is a task that a daughter would do for a beloved mother," Ulandra replied. "Hush, now, Your Majesty. Soon you can—"

With no warning, no announcement, the bedchamber door was flung open and King Agivir rushed into the room. He was holding a slip of parchment in his hand and his eyes were wild with excitement. He flung himself down beside his wife, and taking her hands, kissed them. "My Queen . . ." he whispered hoarsely, his voice filled with a mixture of joy and amazement, "My Queen, I have news sent by carrier hawk from our ship *Sea Eagle*. They will be docking before day's end. My love, Eregard is aboard her! He is coming home!"

Ulandra gasped. "Sire!"

The King spared her a glance. "'Tis true, daughter. My son is coming back to me."

The Queen's eyes opened and she gazed at her husband questioningly. "Eregard?" she whispered.

"Yes!" Agivir kissed his wife's hand again. "Hold on, my dear. Our son will be with us tonight."

The Queen's lips moved. "Goddess . . . thanks . . ."

"Don't try to talk, Your Majesty," Ulandra said. "Save your strength."

The Queen managed to nod, and then her face twisted with pain. Without warning she trembled violently and jerky spasms ran through her limbs. Her heels drummed on the feather mattress. "Nurse!" Ulandra called urgently. "Nurse, she's having another episode!"

Quickly, she went down on her knees, scarcely realizing she had pushed the King out of the way as her hands went to the Queen's shoulders. She held her as still as she could, so Elnorin would not harm herself while in the throes of the seizure. The nurse hurried over and managed to hold the Queen's head steady and keep her from choking.

It was all they could do.

The seizure was over quickly; Queen Elnorin was too weak to endure such a struggle for long. She slumped back, exhausted. Carefully, Ulandra and the nurse bathed her face and sponged her, then changed her nightgown and the wet bedding.

All the while, King Agivir stood across the room, anguished and silent. Ulandra went over to him when they were finished. "Forgive me, sire, for my importunate behavior."

Agivir shook his head distractedly, and Ulandra saw that tears streaked his cheeks. "I told her too suddenly," he said. "I caused her spell."

Ulandra shook her head. "Your Majesty, there is no way to predict what will cause an episode. She sleeps now. Do you wish to sit with her?"

The King nodded and came forward. He sat beside Elnorin's bed, holding her hand, telling her softly, repeatedly, that her youngest son was coming home. The nurse sat on her stool, folding swaddlings and bed linens. The room was utterly silent, save for the Queen's halting breath. Ulandra stared at the old woman, her chest so tight it was painful. *She cannot last much longer.*

She said a quick prayer to the Goddess that Eregard would arrive in time.

The servants had just lighted the candles when a messenger arrived, gasping, having run all the way uphill from the port. The King and Ulandra met him in the outer salon. The young seaman went down on one knee. "Your Majesty! *Sea Eagle* has just docked! I saw the Prince. He bade me run ahead and tell you that he and his companions are on their way."

The King glanced at Ulandra. "Companions?" he asked the young man.

The youth nodded, still breathing hard. "Sire, the Prince bade me tell you these people saved his life. He begs you to make them welcome."

The King nodded. "And we shall, of a certainty. But the Prince must be brought to the Queen's chamber immediately. Immediately! The Queen . . . the Queen . . ." He cleared his throat. "Intercept Prince Eregard and tell him that his mother is waiting for him. Tell him to *hurry*."

The messenger bowed. "Yes, sire."

As soon as the lad was gone, the King signaled to one of the maids. "Find the royal chamberlain and instruct him to locate Prince Salesin. Have him inform the Prince that he should come to see his mother immediately. Time is of the essence."

The servant curtsied so deeply that her gray skirt spread around her like a pool of quicksilver. "Yes, Your Majesty."

After she had scurried off, there was nothing to do but wait. The King paced restlessly about the bedchamber. Ulandra sat by the Queen's side, holding her hand. The change in the old woman's breathing disturbed her—it was louder now, more stentorian. She glanced up at the nurse and pitched her voice low. "She breathes with such effort."

The nurse nodded, and her voice was barely audible. "It is a sign that all too soon, breathing will cease altogether, Your Highness."

The clock on the mantel had just struck half past the hour when they heard footsteps in the salon adjoining the Queen's chamber. The royal chamberlain opened one half of the big double doors and bowed. "Prince Eregard requesting audience, sire."

"Bring him in!" Agivir bade.

Ulandra sprang to her feet, her heart thudding in her breast. *He is back! After so long!*

As he filled the doorway, she realized she would hardly have recognized him. Eregard's once pasty features were as tanned and weathered as any soldier's. He wore the uniform of a royal naval officer, and the buff-colored breeches and sea-green coat suited him as his court clothes never had. His face was thinner, tighter-jawed, and his sun-streaked brown hair was neatly trimmed, pulled back and tied at the nape of his neck. He was stocky, as she remembered, but no longer plump. His shoulders were broad, and the gut that had once hung over his belt had vanished.

As she approached him, staring in amazement, she realized that they were still nearly the same height—it was his carriage that made him appear taller. His gaze was clear and direct as he stood in the doorway, regarding his father.

The King held out both hands. "My son! May the Goddess be praised!"

Eregard flung himself forward, kneeling, his hands going out to clasp his father's. "Sire, Father!"

Agivir raised him, and the two stood locked in an embrace for long seconds. When Eregard raised his head from Agivir's shoulder, he was smiling, but there were tears in his eyes. The King wept openly. "My son, my son," he muttered, holding Eregard's arms tightly. "How you've changed!"

"Father," Eregard said. "How does my lady mother?"

Before the King could respond, the nurse cleared her throat urgently. "Your Majesty!"

They all turned toward the bed. Ulandra heard the Queen's voice, so faint that she knew the others, farther away, could not have discerned it. "Eregard?"

Ulandra stepped forward. "Your Highness," she said, dropping a quick curtsy. "Your lady mother calls to you."

Eregard glanced a question at his father, who nodded wordlessly, his features gray and haggard with remembered grief. "Go to her, my son," he whispered. "She has been holding on, waiting for you, I believe."

Eregard's eyes closed and his features hardened. Then he straightened, squared his shoulders, and crossed the room with swift strides, smiling. Reaching the bed, he dropped down into the chair the nurse hastily vacated. "Mother?" he said softly, taking the Queen's hand in both of his. "Mother, I'm here!" His tone was light-hearted, teasing. "I've had so many adventures, wait until I tell you! I'll be writing songs for a year." He chuckled. "You'll get tired of hearing me singing them the live-long day."

Ulandra saw the Queen's eyes open, and she smiled. "My son . . ." she whispered.

"I'm here," he said, and this time his voice broke. He leaned over to kiss her, first on both cheeks, then on her forehead, then a light brush across the faded lips. "It's wonderful to see you. I've dreamed of this moment for so long."

The Queen's reply was inaudible to Ulandra, but she saw the Prince's features tighten as he struggled for control. "Don't say that, Mother. You'll be up and about in no time."

The rasping breaths grew shallower and more rapid. The Princess glanced at the nurse, who wordlessly shook her head. The Queen tried to lift her hand toward Eregard's face, but she was too weak. He lifted it for her, kissing it, laying it against his cheek. "Thank the Goddess," Ulandra heard her whisper.

Eregard glanced up at his father. "Where are my brothers?" he whispered. "They should be here."

Agivir nodded, speaking quietly. "I've sent for Salesin, but Adranan is in the North. He saw her before he left, however."

Ulandra picked up one of the chairs from the other side of the room, and, before the servants could move, carried it over to the opposite side of the bed. "Your Majesty," she said, indicating the chair.

The King nodded a quick acknowledgment, then came over to sit beside his queen.

Ulandra glanced at the nurse and the servants and gestured toward the Queen's sitting room. They followed her, leaving the family members alone.

The Princess picked up a piece of the Queen's embroidery that she had adopted and sat down with it. She stitched like an automaton, listening for any sound from the bedchamber, but there was none. *Where is Salesin?* she wondered. *Does he now dare to disobey his father's summons?*

Time seemed to alternately drag and fly. Ulandra found that she was counting her stitches, though the pattern was not a counted-stitch one. *Three hundred sixty-three . . . three hundred sixty-four . . .*

The maidservants began dusting the sitting room in a desultory fashion. The nurse busied herself folding yet another set of clean bed linens brought to her by one of the laundry maids.

Four thousand six hundred ninety-three . . . four thousand six hundred ninety-four . . .

The door to the Queen's bedchamber opened, and Eregard stood there. His eyes were reddened, but his voice was steady. "She is gone."

Ulandra nodded, put down her embroidery and stood up. Distantly, she wondered why she was not weeping. Surely Queen Elnorin, who had been so kind to her, deserved her tears. Perhaps she had wasted them all on Salesin and her failed marriage.

Walking over to the Prince, she put her hand on his arm. "Your Highness, I am so sorry. But thank the Goddess you are home safely—and that you arrived in time."

He nodded, then suddenly seemed to focus on her. He bowed, the brief bob used between equals in rank. "Sister," he said, taking her hand and kissing it, "my father told me how kindly you cared for her. Thank you."

Meeting his eyes, Ulandra felt self-conscious, wondering if Eregard would start up the old flirtation again. But he released her hand. "My father needs some moments to himself. He and my mother were devoted. I must see to my friends. They are waiting in the salon. I want you to meet them."

Ulandra accompanied him into the formal room with its pale green walls and ivory and rose brocaded furniture. Four strangers awaited them: two women, a man, and a hooded creature—a Hthras, she realized after a moment. The Princess had never seen one herself, but she had heard them described. The two women and the Hthras were sitting on the sofa, speaking quietly as they entered. The man was pacing restlessly across the opulent carpet. As they saw the newcomers, all four of them stopped talking. The three on the sofa rose to their feet.

Eregard held Ulandra's hand, presenting her as formally as though they had just arrived at some grand ball. "Princess Ulandra, my comrades and friends: Thia, Talis, Khith, and Jezzil." As he spoke their names, each of his friends acknowledged her in turn . . . Thia with a curtsy, Talis with a stiff, jerky little bow, Khith with a graceful dip and wave of its hand, and Jezzil with a warrior's salute.

Ulandra smiled at them, thinking them an odd lot. Thia was small and slight, with hair so pale it was almost white, and huge dark eyes. She wore a much-worn and mended skirt, blouse, and laced tunic. Talis, dressed in a midshipman's uniform, was tanned and fit, with long black hair caught back in a heavy braid. *She's a beauty,* Ulandra thought. *Dress her in women's garb, and men would be throwing themselves at her feet.* Her gaze traveled to Jezzil, with his weather-beaten skin, greenish eyes, and sun-streaked hair tied back from his face. Despite his battered, threadbare clothes, there was something about his carriage, the way he moved, that bespoke a kind of quiet, potential danger.

Ulandra's features did not change as she regarded Eregard's companions. She nodded to them graciously. "Be welcome here to Minoma, friends of Eregard. My thanks to you for your help to my royal brother." She glanced over her shoulder. "The King will wish to meet you, but he is occupied at the moment. Please, sit." She gestured. "You have traveled far and are doubtless weary." She caught the eye of the footman who was standing across the room and added, "Refreshments for our guests, please. Food and wine."

The young woman named Thia approached Eregard, concern written across her thin, pale features. "Eregard, how does your mother?"

Eregard tried to speak, then simply shook his head. "At least I was in time to say farewell," he added after a moment.

"Oh, Eregard!" She stepped over to the Prince and put her arms around him, hugging him tightly. "I'm so sorry!"

Ulandra was moved by her voice and her gesture. *She genuinely cares about him,* she thought, and when she saw Eregard's expression as he returned the embrace, she knew that the Prince returned her caring. The Princess felt a pang of . . . *Jealousy?* she wondered. After a moment Ulandra realized that she wasn't jealous of Eregard so much as she was jealous of anyone who was genuinely loved and respected.

Jezzil, Khith, and Talis also offered low-voiced condolences. Ulandra could see that the five of them were more than just casual friends, they were comrades, sharing a friendship that had been forged by shared peril and a common goal.

If only I had such friends, she found herself thinking wistfully.

Minutes later, the refreshments arrived. At Ulandra's urging, the newcomers sat down and applied themselves to the food. Thia glanced up at Ulandra. "Join us, please, Your Highness."

Ulandra smiled at her. "I ate not long ago. You must be very hungry. I'm told it's the sea air."

"Eating weevily bread, salt pork, and dried figs for four days can do that," Eregard said. "Not to mention the grubs and seaweed, mind you." He gestured at the bread, meats, cheeses, and fruit spread out before them. "Back when I was a slave, I used to dream every night about—".

"Slave?" Ulandra gasped, horrified. "You were a *slave*?"

"Thanks to the pirates that captured me," he said. "It certainly gave me an interesting perspective on life in the colony."

Ulandra stared at him, aghast.

The door opened then and the King emerged from the Queen's chamber. Agivir was gray-faced with exhaustion, his strides, once so brisk and sure, slow and hesitant. His haggard features lightened when he beheld his son.

Eregard hastily stood and made introductions. Jezzil bowed, Thia curtsied, Khith touched its forehead and bobbed a greeting, and Talis gave a stiff little nod. When Eregard looked a question at her, she gazed back at him with defiance. "I bow to no royalty," she said.

"And who is this?" the King said, coming over to stand before Talis.

"I am Talis Aloro, King Agivir," she said. "I am here as an emissary from Rufen Castio. He wishes me to tell you that, should it become necessary, we Katans will fight the invaders with our brothers, the Pelanese. Better an overlord we know than a strange one."

Agivir regarded her flushed, earnest expression—half defiance, half fear—then inclined his head graciously. "We are grateful to you . . ." He glanced at the others, including them. ". . . to all of you—for your help to our royal son," he said. "Mistress Talis, to thank you for your aid to him, we hereby exempt you from formal protocol in our presence."

Talis's flushed features lost some of their defiance.

"But," Agivir continued, his voice heavy with grief, "I warn you, child, that we cannot protect you if you fail to extend full sign of fealty to Crown Prince Salesin." The King gazed at Talis sorrowfully. "My child, I have just lost the person most dear to me in the entire world. Please do not cause me to lose my son Eregard, for, knowing him, he would spring to your defense, and face grave trouble from his brother on your behalf. Surely that cannot be your desire?"

Talis's eyes glistened, then brimmed over. A tear trickled down her cheek. "Your Majesty," she whispered, and gave the old man a true bow. "I am so sorry for your loss. I will do nothing to cause you more sadness."

Agivir nodded at her. "Thank you, child. Thank you."

The King turned to Thia and studied her. "You have the look of one who has come from far places. My court seer, His Reverence Varlon, has such a look to him."

Ulandra saw the young woman's dark eyes widen. "Truly, sire? I would be interested to meet His Reverence."

"You shall, child, you shall."

Agivir paused before Khith. "A Hthras . . . It has been many and many a year since I have encountered one of your people. You wear the robe of a physician."

"Yes, Your Majesty. I am a healer."

"Ah, I have heard that Hthras healers are among the best to be found. It is a pity that you did not arrive sooner." The King's voice roughened. "Perhaps you might have been able to help my queen."

"I would certainly have done my best, sire," Khith replied. "But no physician can hold back the inevitable. Sometimes, it is just . . . time for departure from this existence."

The King nodded. "Sometimes, that is indeed true."

When the King reached the man Eregard had identified as Jezzil, he said, "My son tells me you are his friend, but are also Chonao. I must advise you that we face an invasion force from your people."

Until now, the young man had been expressionless, but suddenly his features worked, as though he were in the grip of some strong emotion. He drew a deep breath—the kind a man might take before plunging into predator-infested waters—then abruptly dropped to one knee, bowing his head deeply. "Your Majesty," he said in a voice that shook. "I am—I *was* Chonao. I never thought to hear myself say this, but since leaving my people, I have . . . learned so much about this world. What I have learned compels me . . ." He trailed off, and finally looked up. "I want to—that is, I must . . ." He swallowed hard.

The King put out a hand to him, nodding encouragement. "We are listening, Jezzil. What is it you want?"

"Your Majesty, I wish to pledge fealty in this coming war to you and your island comrades. I wish to pledge my sword to Pela." The words came out in a rush, but Ulandra never doubted their sincerety.

The King stood motionless for a long moment before stepping closer to the young warrior. Putting out a hand, he touched his face, then slid his hand down to lift his chin so their gazes could meet. The King stared deeply into Jezzil's eyes for many moments.

Agivir finally spoke. "I see that you mean what you say, young warrior. What made you decide this?"

Jezzil drew a deep breath. "Part of it was seeing the world outside my own land, Your Majesty," he replied. "I have seen the people that Kerezau has conquered, for no reason other than to expand his desire for power and land. Their lives are the worse for it."

The Chonao glanced over at his companions. "But mostly I have come to realize that my people's ways are wrong. In Ktavao, women are not friends or companions. They are possessions, valued for their beauty or their fertility, but not for themselves. Knowing Talis and Thia has taught me that my people are wrong to make chattel of women."

"I see." Agivir gazed down at the Chonao and suddenly, abruptly, nodded. "We accept your fealty, young Jezzil. Rise."

Jezzil stood up in one lithe movement. A smile flashed across his face but was gone almost before it could be seen.

"We face an impressive force of your former countrymen," the King said. "Will you advise us on how best to counter their offensive during the coming attack?"

"I will, sire," Jezzil said.

The King nodded. "Good. Of course, Salesin will not trust you, lad. But he is too canny a tactician to disregard your counsel, if he can tell it is based on experience. There will be—"

The King broke off as the door opened and Salesin rushed

in. Ulandra tensed, but her husband did not even look at her. His sharp, piercing glance took in his brother, dismissed him, then focused on his father. "Sire, I was out inspecting the artillery fortifications in Ombal Pass when your messenger reached me. How fares the Queen?"

Agivir simply stared at him, then his haggard features sagged. Shaking his head wordlessly, he turned and left the salon. Eregard stepped forward. "Our mother is gone, brother. If only you . . ." He trailed off with a sigh. "Never mind. She understood that you had duties, I am sure. She knew what it was to be royal, better than anyone else."

Salesin hesitated, and for a moment Ulandra thought he might embrace his brother. But he contented himself with a slap on Eregard's shoulder that was surely meant to stagger the younger Prince. But Eregard stood firm. "Well spoken, little brother, well spoken. I shall raise a new chapel in her name." He glanced over his shoulder at the others in the room, and again his gaze slid over Ulandra as though she did not exist at all.

"Who are these people, Eregard?"

"My friends, the companions who helped to rescue me from slavery and danger in Kata." Eregard went on to make introductions. Ulandra was relieved to see Talis make a proper, formal bow, though she did not miss the tightness of her mouth and jaw as she did so.

"This is my friend, my comrade, Jezzil. He has left the Chonao homeland and sworn fealty to Pela, my brother," Eregard concluded. "The King has accepted his oath of service. I believe he could be of great help in planning the defense of our land against Kerezau's forces."

Salesin stared at Jezzil for a long moment, clearly taking his measure. Finally, he nodded. "Very well. Pela needs advisers familiar with Chonao tactics. Ride out with my brother tomorrow to familiarize yourself with the lay of the land and our force, then you may join us for the afternoon briefing, Jezzil."

Jezzil bowed. "I shall, Your Highness. Thank you."

Ulandra tensed again as Salesin headed toward her, but he

walked straight past her, then paused at the door to the royal
bedchamber and turned to regard Eregard. "Come, brother.
We have much to discuss."

Eregard nodded, and looked at Ulandra questioningly.
She answered his look, saying, "Do not concern yourself,
Your Highness. I shall see to our honored guests."

Eregard nodded, a look of relief in his eyes, then followed
his brother into the chamber where their mother lay, still and
pale in death.

22

Call to Arms

The next day, as promised, Eregard took Jezzil to inspect the royal armory and the parade grounds where the Pelanese infantry and cavalry were drilling. Then they saddled their horses and made the two hour ride up to Ombal Pass, passing contingents of soldiers transporting cannon on caissons, ammunition wagons, and squads of army engineers. When they reached the pass, they found that the battle line had already been established. Engineers were overseeing crews busily digging trenches and preparing gun emplacements.

At all times, Jezzil and Eregard were accompanied by five taciturn Pelanese guardsmen. They'd been introduced to the Chonao as Prince Eregard's bodyguards, but Jezzil knew they were there to watch him as much as the Prince. Salesin was no fool. He would take no chances that Jezzil's defection from the Chonao forces was not genuine.

When they reached the pass, they rode to the front of the battle line. The Pelanese had the high ground. Eregard and Jezzil halted their horses on a small raised hillock just to the left of the road that ran through the pass.

Ombal Pass spread out before them as they sat there, gazing at the lay of the land. The guardsmen, at a gesture from

Eregard, lagged back a few horse lengths to allow them to speak privately.

Jezzil dropped Falar's reins on her neck. "Stand, lady."

A good place to defend, Jezzil decided, assessing the terrain through the eyes of a warrior. Ombal Pass was narrow, less than a league across. The ground was mostly upland grasses, broken by gray thrusts of jagged rock outcrops and stone shelves. The road they had followed up from Minoma stretched before them, cutting a broad swath through the tall green sward. Falar, scenting the breeze, stretched out her neck and snorted, begging to run. "Hush now," Jezzil said in his own language. "There will be another day to run."

He gazed from side to side, estimating that a man afoot could cross the width of the pass in less than an hour. On both sides, rolling foothills led up to bare black mountains and then to jagged gray peaks, their crowns of snow mostly melted in the summer Sun. Ombal Pass was nearly featureless, save for the road before him. As he peered into the distance, he saw a timeworn stone building. He pointed. "What's that?"

"It's an ancient traveler's shrine," Eregard said. "Used to be an abbey, hundreds of years ago. Now all of that is in ruins, and just the shrine is left."

Jezzil assessed the building, then dismissed it as of no tactical importance. It was too far away from where the Pelanese lines were being established to be significant.

Turning in his saddle, he squinted into the distance at what appeared to be a depression. Brighter green vegetation marked the line of it. *A ravine or gully? How deep?* he wondered. *That might provide cover for an incursion.*

"What do you think?" Eregard asked. Beneath him, his black gelding began to paw at the grass, wanting to graze. "Stop that!"

"I think this is a good place for defense," Jezzil said. "How many troops will you be able to field?"

"Probably three brigades of five thousand troops each," Eregard said. "Salesin usually prefers to take the right brigade, Adranan is likely to be assigned the left, and, traditionally, the King will take the middle. But I've been talking to my father about putting General His Lordship Osmando-Volon in command of the center, while he stays back at the command center. I think I have him convinced that he's too precious to troop morale to risk. But the truth is, he's just too old and frail for true battle."

Jezzil nodded agreement. "What about you?"

"I'll fight," Eregard said grimly. "I'll ride with General Osmando."

Jezzil had to respect the coürage that vow took. Eregard was better than he had been, but he was far from being a good shot or swordsman. Still, it was the Prince's duty, and he could not argue with that. He changed the subject. "What about that ravine over there? Can we take a closer look at it?"

"Surely," Eregard said. "It's too deep and rough for troops to climb, though."

They jogged the horses the mile or so to the ravine. Once there, they dismounted, leaving the guardsmen to hold Eregard's horse. Falar, trained to stand, watched them curiously as they walked over to the edge.

Jezzil stood looking into the ravine. It was fairly deep and quite narrow, scarcely more than half a musket shot across. As he peered over the edge, he could see the blue thread of a stream at the bottom. The sides, as Eregard had said, were steep and rocky, studded with clumps of tough grass and twisted scrub oak. "See? I told you," Eregard said. "Too steep to climb."

"I could climb it," Jezzil said absently.

Eregard gave him a look, half amused, half exasperated. "Oh, of that I have no doubt. You could probably turn invisible and *fly* up it, with all the wizard tricks Khith has been teaching you."

Jezzil felt his face grow warm. "I didn't mean it like that. And I certainly can't fly." Abruptly, he grinned, seeing the humor in it. "If I could, that would make things much easier, wouldn't it?"

Eregard chuckled. "Without a doubt." He looked back

down at the precarious slope. "Well, I suppose I could climb it, too, given enough time and maybe some rope. But there's no way it could be used to mount a flank attack."

"I don't know about that," Jezzil said, serious once more. "If you used knotted lanyard attached to embedded stakes to make guide ropes, and cut away the brush blocking the secure footholds, well . . ." He shrugged. "The Pen Jav Dal specialize in this kind of operation. When I was in the seminary, we were taught to scale fortress walls, rock cliffs, ice cliffs, and forest giants." Squatting down, he tossed a fist-sized rock over the side. They could barely hear the splash it made. "How far does this ravine run?"

Eregard looked west, toward Minoma. "In this direction, not too much farther. It gets shallower and shallower as it runs downhill, until there's just the stream left. The stream joins into the Min River, which empties into the sea, north of Minoma."

"And heading east?"

"It runs all the way up into the mountains, where it becomes a deep gorge," Eregard pointed to the mountains before them.

"Parallel to where the Chonao lines will be," Jezzil said.

"I suppose so," Eregard said. "But the higher it gets, the deeper. Where it begins in the mountains it's called Carsini Gorge. My father named it after old Duke Carsini, who commanded the Royal Fleet for decades. There's a big waterfall at its head, though it mostly dries up in summer."

Jezzil stood up, gazing at the northern mountains. "This gorge . . . it can't be crossed?"

"Not unless you're a goat," Eregard said.

Behind them one of the horses snorted. Jezzil turned back to Falar. "I've seen what I needed to see. Let's look at the other side."

They rode back to their vantage point in the middle of the pass, near the road.

"If there's no crossing Carsini Gorge, then the mountains on the northern side of the pass are blocked," Jezzil said. "What about to the south?" He turned in his saddle to look to his right. Falar shifted her weight beneath him, pawed restlessly for a moment, then quieted when he spoke a soft order.

"There are trails all through those southern foothills that run parallel to the pass," Eregard said. "Shepherds use the alpine fields for summer grazing, and some of the farmers terrace the land up there to grow ruta roots. Lots of trails. Most of them join together, eventually, and run down, past this point, where they come out of the forest into the western part of the pass"—Eregard turned around to point—"almost a mile back that way."

Jezzil nodded thoughtfully. "Noted. Could be a problem."

As they turned to ride back to Minoma, Eregard said, "Did anyone mention to you that there is to be a welcome home feast in my honor tonight?"

"Princess Ulandra told us about it this morning when we broke our fast with her," Jezzil replied. "She said you were with your father."

"Yes. Well, it won't be very festive, because we're all in mourning, but you should plan to attend," Eregard said. "Pelanese chefs are rightly famous the world over."

"I will be there," Jezzil said.

They rode in silence for a while, then Jezzil spoke again. "Eregard, when last we spoke, the night before the *Pride* was taken, you said you were going to ask Thia to marry you. Did you?"

He'd been watching Thia for days now, on the *Sea Eagle* and here in Pela, but she hadn't seemed to act any different toward the Prince. And surely she would have if she'd agreed to be his wife, wouldn't she? On the other hand, Jezzil had been shocked to discover that Thia had acting talents he'd never expected. Her "performance" before Barus had been memorable.

He turned in his saddle, watching Eregard, waiting for his answer, and realized he was holding his breath. He forced himself to exhale.

Eregard reached over and rearranged a wayward lock of his mount's mane, not meeting Jezzil's eyes. "Yes."

The Chonao searched Eregard's face, realizing that Eregard didn't look like a man who was happily affianced. Relief flooded him, followed immediately by a stab of guilt. Eregard was his friend. It was unworthy to feel joyful when his friend was obviously unhappy. But he couldn't help himself.

"She said no," Eregard added after a long pause.

"Oh," Jezzil said. "Did you ask her why?"

"I did," the Prince said. "She told me she was very fond of me—that's the word she used, *fond*—but that she couldn't marry anyone because she had sworn to remain celibate."

Jezzil blinked. "But she's not a priestess any more."

"I pointed that out. She said a vow was a vow. Frankly, she wasn't making a lot of sense, but I could tell she was distressed by the subject, so I dropped it." He shrugged. "She also pointed out that I'm not in love with her, that I love someone else. I'd have denied it," his mouth twisted wryly, "but this was *Thia* I was talking to."

"You love someone else," Jezzil said, making it a statement. He hadn't given the matter a moment's thought until now.

The Prince shrugged, then gave Jezzil a sideways glance. "I try not to give myself away, but I guess anyone who knows me well can tell. I'd hoped that time would help, but the moment I saw Ulandra, there it was all over again. The only woman I love is the one I can never have."

He loves Ulandra? Jezzil nodded as though he'd known all along. "She's very pretty."

"She's beautiful," Eregard said. "But I don't dare treat her as other than a sister. If Salesin knew how I felt he'd use that knowledge against me. He enjoys playing games with people. One of the court gossips took me aside this morning and told me that Ulandra's waiting women have said that she is often bruised, and that he goes out of his way to humiliate her. Curse my brother!" He straightened in his saddle, staring straight ahead, and his voice was low and bitter. "Last night I prayed that he'd be killed in the battle. My own brother!"

"He hurts her? Why?" Jezzil asked. "She seems so quiet, such a good wife. Surely she hasn't been unfaithful?"

"Of course not," Eregard said. "She's a sweet, decent girl.

But she hasn't shown any signs of producing an heir to the throne. Knowing my brother, he would take that as a personal affront."

Eregard sighed. "It's just as well Thia refused me. She's as innocent as Ulandra, and even more inexperienced in courtly life. If she were to become my wife, she'd become a target for Salesin's plots. Thia is intelligent, but she doesn't know how to be devious."

"Is that all?" Jezzil said. Something in Eregard's voice told him it wasn't.

"No," the Prince admitted. "Something else happened . . ." He trailed off, staring straight ahead.

"Between you and Thia?"

"No," Eregard said, a faint edge in his voice. "Nothing to do with Thia or Ulandra." When Jezzil glanced at him curiously, he added, curtly, "Nothing I can talk about, either."

"Oh," Jezzil said.

Eregard gave him an ironic look. "Curse it, why do things between men and women have to be so be-damned *complicated*?"

"I don't know," Jezzil said. "I haven't been around women long enough to be able to figure out how they think, what they want."

Eregard laughed hollowly. "Jezzil, my friend, welcome to the world. I haven't yet met a man who has figured that out."

When they reached Minoma again, Eregard took Jezzil to the target range, where they both practiced using muskets with the newly rifled barrels that used the new, conical bullets. Jezzil was awed by the range and accuracy of the weapons. "Imagine every soldier of the line having one of these!" he marveled, stroking the weapon. "Able to fire as fast as a smoothbore, but with the range and accuracy of a rifle. My people have used rifles for hunting and assassin's weapons, but we have nothing like these."

"They say the royal gunsmithing shops have been working for months, producing them," Eregard said. "Almost all of the military here at home is equipped with them."

"These weapons will make the traditional Chonao cavalry

charge impossible," Jezzil mused. "Kerezau will probably try to compensate for that by using flank attacks. He's a master strategist, and he's trained his leaders well."

"Speaking of leaders," Eregard said, glancing at the westering Sun, "it is almost time for the strategy briefing my brother mentioned. We are both expected to attend."

The briefing was held on the top floor of the officers' barracks. Eregard and Jezzil, still escorted by the silent guardsmen, climbed the stairs and went into the large room. It was long, with a fireplace at one end. A portrait of Agivir, wearing full military regalia, hung over the mantel. Maps of every Pelanese province and colony, plus the surrounding lands, covered the walls, interspersed with portraits of famous Pelanese military heroes. A long, long battered table stood in the center of the room, with quills and parchment placed before each seat. Eregard indicated a seat, and Jezzil sat down, just as the Prince was surrounded by well-wishers.

As Eregard exchanged greetings with the officers who crowded around him, Prince Salesin entered the room. The Crown Prince glanced over at his brother and the assembled officers, obviously not pleased by the attention his younger brother was receiving. He strode to the front of the room, then cleared his throat loudly.

The officers quickly dispersed, bowing to the Crown Prince as they scattered to their seats. Jezzil studied Salesin covertly, noticing that the Crown Prince was in full, formal uniform, ceremonial sword at his side. This was in contrast to Eregard and most of the other officers, who wore field uniform.

Salesin made a show of looking at the ornate clock that hung on the wall. The appointed time for the meeting had arrived. Eregard's brother began pacing the room, moving like a large, feral animal. Jezzil was reminded of the moorland cats that preyed upon Chonao herds. After a few moments of pacing, the Crown Prince halted, then addressed Eregard with a scowl. "Where, pray tell, is our father, brother? Must I once again assume his duty?"

Eregard flushed, but before he could reply, the door to the meeting room opened and a servant hurried in. Bowing hastily to Salesin, he said, "His Majesty bids you begin without him, Your Highness."

"Where is he?" Salesin snapped.

The servant was too well schooled to react, but Jezzil, trained to watch an enemy's reactions minutely, saw him tense. He bowed again. "He is meeting with the bishop about the Queen's lying-in-state and funeral. He bade me tell you that he will come if he can."

Salesin's eyes narrowed and he nodded curtly, waving dismissal. "Very well. Once again it falls to me to lead our country in my father's absence."

Jezzil glanced at Eregard, seeing the Prince's eyes narrow with anger.

Salesin strode to the ornate head chair, then stood behind it, his hands grasping the golden crown that adorned the back. Addressing the assembled officers, he began. "Intelligence reports indicate that the Meptalith fleet carrying the Chonao forces has regrouped after the storm that dispersed them. Reports from Captain Stroma of the RNS *Sea Eagle* and other naval commanders indicate that the storm claimed several dozen ships. Even so, nearly four hundred vessels have made port on our northern shore. This morning we received a carrier hawk with a message from Prince Adranan, who is leading a scouting mission in the North. Gen has fallen to the enemy."

A soft murmur of consternation ran through the room.

"Prince Adranan estimates the troop strength of Kerezau's force to be approximately twenty thousand infantry and nearly nine thousand cavalry."

The Pelanese are outnumbered, Jezzil realized. His tour today had indicated that Pela's infantry numbered about fifteen thousand and no more than three thousand cavalry.

Salesin went on to summarize recent events: Eregard's return, a mention of which provinces had sent troops, reports from naval vessels that had engaged and sunk several of the Redai's troop transports that had been blown off course by the storm. He concluded by introducing Jezzil as a Chonao "consultant" familiar with the enemy's battle tactics.

As one man, the high-ranking officers seated around the

table turned to look at Jezzil. It was all he could do not to drop his eyes and sink down in his seat under the force of their regard. Eregard looked at him and nodded encouragingly, and that helped.

As the meeting progressed, Jezzil's mind was busy, filing away facts and figures. *As many as three hundred fifty Chonao ships confirmed. That's a large force they landed. Ten thousand cavalry, twenty thousand infantry . . .*

The Pelanese were significantly outnumbered. *But they have those guns with the rifled barrels. They can shoot more than twice as far as an ordinary musket . . . will that even the odds?*

He watched as Salesin unrolled a map of Ombal Pass, showing the surrounding foothills and mountains. As Eregard had guessed, the Pelanese forces would be divided into three brigades of infantry, with cavalry held back, along with the infantry reserves. Each brigade would be under the command of one of the royals, Salesin declared. Crown Prince Salesin would command the left flank, King Agivir the center, and Prince Adranan the right flank.

The King has not shared his decision with his heir, then, Jezzil thought, remembering what Eregard had told him earlier. *I will ask to ride with Eregard,* he decided. *His fighting skills are not what they should be, though they have improved. I will guard his back. Perhaps Talis will ride with me.* From what he'd seen of the Pelanese army, women were a minority of the force, but they did serve. Most female Pelanese soldiers were ex-mercenaries, specialists in artillery, sharpshooting, scouting, or intelligence gathering. Talis would qualify.

He listened as Salesin summarized the battle plan, the number of cannon, how much ammunition, how many reserves would be held back, information that could mean victory or defeat. Pela might be outnumbered, but they definitely had the advantage when it came to munitions.

As Salesin finished his summary, the Crown Prince glanced over at Jezzil, fixing his dark gaze on the Chonao.

"And at this time, I would like to ask our Chonao consultant if he has comments to make on our battle plan?"

Jezzil froze for a second, then when Eregard nudged him, he rose to his feet and bowed. "Your Highness, only two. If I may?" he indicated the map of Ombal Pass, and the Prince nodded permission for him to approach.

Stepping up to the map, Jezzil pointed to the foothills on the southern side of the pass. "Your Highness, flank attacks from unexpected quarters are one of Kerezau's most favored strategies. Prince Eregard tells me that there are trails throughout these foothills that would allow a company led by a cohort of the Pen Jav Dal—Kerezau's reconnaissance, infiltration, and assassination experts—to bypass your army and attack your southern flank. I would recommend that you station several companies here," he touched the map, "to block any such attack. This in addition to blocking all of the trails wide enough to admit a mounted force by means of deadfalls, abatis, and the like."

Salesin nodded. "Our engineers are in those foothills as we speak, creating exactly those obstacles you mention, plus others."

"And you will station a reserve force to prevent any flank attack?"

Salesin's eyes narrowed. "With the trails blocked, there will be no need to deploy soldiers to guard a few sheep trails."

Jezzil opened his mouth to protest, only to trail off as Salesin's features hardened. He nodded instead. "Of course, Your Highness. As to my other concern . . ." He hesitated, determined to choose his words carefully.

"Yes?" Salesin was clearly growing impatient.

"This ravine here," Jezzil said, pointing to it. "It concerns me. It is deep enough that a regiment of Chonao could make their way down it in relative secrecy, even in the heat of battle. Then, if that force scaled the sides of the gully behind your front lines, it would be another way for the enemy to flank you."

Salesin waved a hand dismissively. "Obviously, you have

not seen that ravine. It is far too steep to be scaled by any significant amount of troops."

Jezzil wet his lips, remembering long days—and nights—spent in training from boyhood. Climbing that ravine and anchoring rope guidelines so infantry could go up the side would be child's play for the Silent Ones. Seeing Salesin's expression, he realized he would be wise to say no more.

But he found himself speaking anyway. "Your Highness, the Pen Jav Dal are trained in climbing. Securing posts and attaching rope guidelines that would enable troops to scale this ravine quickly, in great numbers, is part of their training."

"I have heard of these so-called Silent Ones," Salesin said, smiling slightly, as if Jezzil were a child that had tried to take part in an adult conversation. "They are regarded with superstitious terror by their own countrymen, which doubtless acts to their advantage. Tales abound of them being able to fly, vanish like ghosts, or walk up walls like flies in summer. But we are talking real battle here, not tales to dominate peasants and children. Thank you for your concern. I shall consider what you have said."

Jezzil bowed, quietly returned to his seat and said no more for the remainder of the briefing.

That night he, Thia, Talis, and Khith attended the banquet given in honor of Prince Eregard's homecoming. The Prince introduced his friends, and they all had to stand while Eregard told the gathered nobles and dignitaries a suitably edited version of how his friends and comrades had rescued him and helped him return home. The resulting applause made all of them, except for Khith, blush. Luckily, no one expected them to give a speech. Jezzil could tell that Talis and Thia were as intimidated as he was. Faced with these glittering courtiers in their jewels, silks, and satins, he felt dull, shabby, and tongue-tied.

The sumptuous banquet hall was dazzling, lit by hundreds of candles in crystal chandeliers. Eregard had told Jezzil that the feast would be a subdued affair, by court standards, since the court was officially in mourning for the

Queen. "Subdued" was not the word Jezzil would have used.

The Chonao was awed by the tables groaning with food and the constant flow of wine. Even though he tried to be careful, he ate too much, and drank more than one goblet of the excellent Pelanese wine. By the time the feast ended, Jezzil was light-headed and had trouble finding his way back to the "visiting dignitaries" wing of the palace where he, Talis, Thia, and Khith had been quartered. He finally had to stop and ask his silent escort which of three possible corridors to take to reach his room.

He reached his chamber and closed the door on his escort, glad to be alone at last. With a stifled groan, he sank down into a chair, struggling to take his high riding boots off. *Why isn't there a bootjack about when you need one?* he thought disgustedly, panting and swaying slightly in the brocaded, gilded chair. Finally, with a sucking sound, the last boot yielded, and Jezzil slumped back in the chair, feeling exhaustion wash over him in waves.

This court life is more wearying than taking point in an undercover attack, he thought grumpily, wishing he could go back to Ombal Pass and bed down there, in the waving grass, with his head resting on Falar's neck. That was the way for a soldier to rest, not eating himself into a stupor and drinking until his head threatened to swim.

He found himself thinking of his public dismissal by Salesin earlier in the day, and his cheeks reddened. *Be damned to you,* he thought sourly. *What do I care if Kerezau's flank attacks wipe out a bunch of Pelanese I never met?*

But he did care. He cared about Eregard, and Talis, and the King. *If only there were some way to see the future,* he thought. But Khith had already told him that it knew of no foolproof way to foresee future events.

Jezzil sighed and leaned back in his chair, propping his bare feet on a leather-topped footstool. It was the plainest piece of furniture in the room, and even so, its legs and sides were carved to look like those of a fanciful beast. The candle burning on the table beside him gave a clear, smokeless light. Jezzil stared at it, half mesmerized by the dance and flicker of the flame.

It was good today to be back in the company of soldiers, to deal only with what can be seen and touched, he mused. *For so long now I have struggled to use avundi, but what place does it have on the battlefield?*

Of course the ability to Cast was useful for stealth operations, assassinations, and such . . .

As he gazed into the glow, Jezzil found himself envisioning those mountain trails Eregard had described. *Will Salesin's precautions be enough?* he wondered. *Or will it be as I fear, that the Silent Ones will find ways around them?*

Thinking of the Pen Jav Dal made him recall his instructors. Sergeano Devini had been the most colorful of them all, faster on one leg and his crutch than many men with two good legs. His face was marked with two livid, pulpy scars, his front two teeth were missing, and he had a habit of whistling through them as he waited for some hapless student to give an answer.

Jezzil remembered how terrified he'd been of the old one-eyed soldier when he'd first arrived at the seminary where the Pen Jav Dal candidates were taught. He'd been how old? Eight? Something like that.

"Never neglect a potential advantage!" Devini had shouted, his harsh voice echoing in Jezzil's ears.

Never neglect a potential advantage.

It was almost as though he could see Devini, hear the raspy growl that served him for a voice.

Jezzil blinked, then looked away from the candle flame with an effort. "You're right, Sergeano," he muttered, climbing wearily to his feet. "You were always right."

Barefoot, he went to the door of his chamber and turned the knob. Two guardsmen stood outside. The sentries were wide awake, ready for action. Both tensed when they saw Jezzil, then relaxed somewhat when he held out both hands, palms up. "What can we get you, sir?" asked one.

"Nothing," Jezzil replied. "I just want to go next door."

The ranking guardsman nodded, and Jezzil went over to the Hthras's door and tapped softly. "Master Khith?"

From inside he heard the familiar voice. "Enter, Jezzil."

Jezzil went into the room, finding the little Hthras perched on a human-sized chair at the small table, scribbling busily on a sheet of parchment. The table was high, and Khith had to sit on a thick, gold-tassled pillow. Jezzil smiled, despite his agitation. The Hthras's medical bag sat open, and various vials and bottles were ranged before it. "Thanks to the help of the Pelanese physicians, I have managed to replenish most of my lost supplies," it said, not looking up. "They have some interesting variations on some common herbs used in tinctures. I am just making a few notes."

"I'm sorry to disturb you," Jezzil said.

Something in the tone of his voice must have alerted the Hthras, for it put down its quill.

"What is it, Jezzil? I sense that you are troubled?"

He crossed over to sit beside the Hthras, and kept his voice low. "I've been thinking about the battle," he said. "And I need you to teach me how to see with the eyes of a flying creature, as you did aboard *The Pride of Pela* before we made our escape."

Khith regarded its pupil curiously. "Very well," it said, "but may I ask why?"

"Let's just say it could be a major advantage in battle to be able to see something miles away," Jezzil said. "And my drill instructor taught me never to neglect a potential advantage. Will you teach me, Master?"

"Of course," Khith said. "Let us begin."

Jezzil and Eregard spent the next day in target practice, up on Ombal Pass. The day was hot, sultry, with heavy clouds hanging threateningly. They rode back slowly, sweating nearly as much as their horses. The silent guardsmen, as before, followed at a respectful distance.

"Have you spoken to your father again?" Jezzil asked after they had ridden a long way in silence.

"Yes. He has agreed not to lead the troops himself, but to

allow General Osmando-Volon to lead the center brigade. He knows in his heart that he's not fit for battle. He's also been consumed with planning my mother's lying-in-state and her funeral. He wants to do her all honor."

"When will it be? Soon?

"Her . . . body . . ." Eregard's voice faltered on the word, "has gone to the preservers. It is likely the obsequies will be delayed until after we have dealt with this invasion."

"Eregard," Jezzil said, "I would like to ride by your side, if that is permitted. Guard your back."

The Prince smiled. "I could have no better protection, I know that. But it will be up to Salesin, as military commander, I fear."

Jezzil nodded, then glanced back at the mountains. "I wish the storm would come. The air is so thick, I can scarcely breathe."

Eregard nodded. "It's probably storming up in the mountains, but I've known clouds to hang like that over the peaks for a day or more."

They lapsed into silence and did not speak again until they reached the stables. "Where now?" Jezzil asked. "If there is nothing more required of me, I will head off to clean my new weapons and adjust the fit on the cuirass your armorer supplied."

"There is another briefing," Eregard said. "I must be there, but you don't have to attend."

"I will go," Jezzil said. "As my old Sergeano used to tell us, 'Never miss a chance to gather knowledge about enemy movements.' "

When they reached the conference room, they found the same group as before. Again King Agivir was not present.

This time there was no waiting. Salesin immediately rose and took control of the council, discussing the final disposition of troops, the posting of scouts, and all the other details that went into a battle plan.

Jezzil sat there, making notes, scribbling diagrams filled with arrows, and saw that Eregard had put on a pair of spectacles and was doing likewise.

He heard a sound on the landing then—the running tread of booted feet, accompanied by shouts of greeting. Salesin broke off as the doors were flung open wide and a burly travel-stained man burst in, trailing several others in his wake. His bearded features were grimed with dust and gray with weariness, but his whole face changed when he looked across the room and saw Eregard. "Brother! May the Goddess be praised!"

Eregard leaped to his feet with a glad cry. "Adranan!"

The two princes flung themselves forward, then Eregard was enveloped in a bone-crushing embrace, lifted clean off his feet and spun in a circle by his brother. Their affection was so tangible that Jezzil smiled.

Finally they broke apart, and Prince Adranan seemed to remember the formalities. He bowed to the Crown Prince. "Brother," he said. "Forgive my lack of decorum. I have ridden without rest for the past two days to bring you the news from the North."

Salesin inclined his head. "Your news is most welcome. Please . . ." He waved at the head chair. "Be seated and make your report."

"I shall," Adranan said. "And I fear my news is not good. But first, may I say that to arrive here and see my brother again has put new life into me."

He looked at Eregard. "When I came through Ombal Pass, they told me that you had returned." His shoulders sagged. "And they also told me of our mother's passing."

Eregard nodded silently.

Adranan made his way to the head of the table and sank into the chair with a sigh. "The Chonao are coming," he said without preamble. "We had to ride both day and night to stay ahead of them, so swiftly do they march. If they continue at the same rate of speed, they will reach Ombal Pass by early afternoon tomorrow."

"We shall be ready for them," Salesin assured him. "What of their numbers? Their weapons? Give us all the details."

Adranan launched into a summary of the Chonao forces and weapons. He was able to fill in a few details they did not know. "When they first landed," he said, "they had no more than six thousand horses, at best. But now, by dint of scouring the countryside and taking as they wished, they are in possession of every ridable mount between here and Gen, bringing their cavalry numbers to about ten thousand."

"We will be ready for them," Salesin promised. "Our troops will be in place by mid-morn."

Hearing this, Jezzil urgently tapped a corner of Eregard's parchment, and when the Prince turned to him, gave Eregard a despairing look, mouthing "No!"

Eregard gave him a long, steady look, then rose, bowing to Salesin. "My brother," he said. "Jezzil has important information for you."

Salesin's mouth tightened, but seeing that his officers had turned to the Chonao, he nodded. "Speak, Jezzil," he said brusquely.

Jezzil rose and bowed deeply. "Your pardon, Your Highness. I would recommend having Pela's troops in place by dawn. It is a favorite trick of Kerezau's to take the enemy unaware by leading troops on an at-speed march during the last hours before battle. The Chonao will press on, double time, one hundred paces walking, one hundred paces running, throughout the night, hoping to fall upon Pela before they could reasonably be expected."

"And the Chonao can do this, and then still fight effectively?" Salesin was openly skeptical.

"They can and they do, Your Highness," Jezzil said. "I swear to you that I have been a part of such marches in the past."

Salesin inclined his head. "Very well, we thank you, Jezzil, for your counsel. Pela will stand ready for battle at dawn."

As he bowed again and sank back into his seat, Jezzil glanced at Eregard, and saw that he was pale with fury. He looked a question at the Prince.

Eregard's voice was shaking with fury as he whispered, under his breath, "My brother uses the royal *we*! He has no right . . . he is not King!"

Jezzil gave him a sympathetic glance.

Again they heard footsteps on the landing outside, and a

moment later the doors were opened by bowing servants. "All rise for the King!" came the ringing announcement.

King Agivir swept into the room just as Adranan sprang out his chair and went down on one knee to receive his father's blessing. Agivir raised him and the two exchanged a few quiet words and embraced quickly.

The King regarded the assembled company, then took his chair. "Be seated," he said, and everyone sank back into their seats.

"Let us say that we are grateful for the help of our Crown Prince in this difficult time, for taking over the planning of this battle," Agivir said. "In order to see our dear, departed Queen given proper honor, we have been attending to planning her lying-in-state and funeral." The King's voice shook as he mentioned his dead wife.

"But we thank the Goddess for our stalwart sons, who have taken up our duties with the army so capably," Agivir continued. "We have heard that we face battle tomorrow. So be it. Pela shall prevail, this we swear to you!"

Eregard leaped to his feet, drawing his sword, holding it out in salute across the table. The assembled officers followed his example, as did Prince Adranan. Last of all was Prince Salesin. "All hail Agivir, King of Pela!" Eregard shouted amidst the ring of the blades crossing over the long, timeworn table.

"Hail King Agivir!" came the response, but Jezzil could not hear Salesin's voice among the others, though the Prince's lips moved.

The King inclined his head graciously, obviously touched by Eregard's tribute.

As the last echoes of that heartfelt cheer faded away, Salesin stepped forward, his sword held straight up before his face in salute. "May the Goddess be praised that we have such a king to lead us into battle on the morrow." He lowered his sword and turned to the assembled officers, smiling broadly. "Good news, comrades and friends! My father plans to personally lead the center brigade!"

Eregard blinked, then stiffened, and Agivir looked up at Salesin, taken aback. *Oh, this Crown Prince is devious,*

Jezzil thought, dismayed. *By Arenar, there is now no way for Agivir to allow his general to lead in his stead, lest he seem to be a coward.*

"But . . . but I thought—" Eregard stammered, then broke off when Jezzil stepped down hard upon his foot. The Prince clamped his mouth shut, his eyes smoldering.

Agivir cleared his throat. "Indeed, yes," he said slowly. "We will, of course, lead our troops tomorrow." He glanced at his servants. "See to it that our warhorse armor is polished and that Banner is suitably arrayed."

The servants bowed and withdrew.

"And now, to business," Agivir said. "We shall review the battle plan. Salesin, will you begin?"

Eregard sank back into his seat, his features cold and impassive. But Jezzil saw his eyes before the Prince lowered them, and they were filled with fear.

23

The Battle

As she stood peering into the gloom of Ombal Pass in the predawn darkness, Talis shivered. The wind coming down from the mountains was chill, and she shivered again, worse than before. Like all of the cavalry, she was in uniform, cap, padded undertunic, metal and leather cuirass, then her uniform jacket, breeches and high boots. It was summer . . . she shouldn't have been cold. But she was.

She cursed softly as she stood beside the horse she'd been assigned, a sedate, overfed chestnut mare that had to be kicked into a trot. "I can't believe this," she muttered to Jezzil, who was standing beside her, holding Falar. "My first be-damned battle, and do I get to fight? No! I get stuck back behind the lines with the First Battalion, Company Two, of the Royal Dragoons. Who are being held as *reserves*. And that means we're downhill from the front lines, and we can't even see. It's not fair!"

Jezzil grunted noncommittally.

She shifted restlessly. "I feel like a mouse shut up in a corn bin. How do we know the enemy is even out there?"

"Scouts," Jezzil reminded her.

"Scouts, yes, of course," Talis admitted sourly. "But we're

back here, and we'll be lucky if we can even see what's happening. Much less get to fight. And after I spent all that time training with you. I should—" Hearing herself, she broke off with a faint snort of laughter. "Listen to me, I haven't heard such whining since my horse stepped on the hound's foot."

There was a long pause, then she sighed. "I can't seem to stop talking," she whispered. "Or shivering."

His head turned and he glanced at her. "You're just keyed up," he said. "You'll be fine."

Minutes crawled by as the reserve company stood to horse, waiting. A faint glow in the eastern sky appeared, growing steadily brighter. Finally, the commanding officer of their Cavalry Reserve Unit, Major Sir Arcoli q'Rindo, rode down the ranks. "Company Two, mount up!"

Talis's heart slammed in her chest, and she barely had the presence of mind to check the girth and tighten it. The mare, who went by the unimaginative name "Lady," backed her ears and swung her head around as she felt the strap tighten. "Don't even *think* about biting me," Talis muttered, raising a fist. Chastened, Lady turned away.

Moments later she was up, sitting beside Jezzil, checking to make sure her weapons had not been displaced during her mount. *Both pistols, sword, knife, all in place.* She pulled her cap down over her forehead, adjusting the strap under her chin. Her hands were shaking, and she was glad that, in the darkness, no one could see.

Major q'Rindo was more visible now, astride his handsome bay, wearing his broad-brimmed, plumed hat. Talis thought she could almost make out the bright blue of his jacket, with its scarlet facings and gold braid.

At the sound of a cantering horse she glanced to her left. A dark shape approached, a runner. The man drew rein before Major q'Rindo and saluted. "Sir, Colonel His Grace Bilani requests his officers to join him in a personal reconnaissance of the field."

The colonel was in command of all the reserve cavalry units, Major q'Rindo returned the salute. "Acknowledged,

Adjutant." Then the major turned his head and looked directly at Talis and Jezzil. "You two, come with me."

Talis had realized early on that the officer was watching them, probably under orders to do so. Of course the Pelanese didn't trust either her or Jezzil—she was a known rebel, and Jezzil was Chonao. *What does this mean?* she wondered. *Has he changed his mind about having us in his company? Or does he just want to keep us near him?*

Jezzil was already urging Falar forward, out of ranks, and Talis chirruped to Lady to follow them. The stodgy mare resisted for a second, then as Talis thunked her in the ribs with her heels, grudgingly moved out. "What does this mean?" Talis hissed to Jezzil as they followed the major. "Are we in trouble?"

"Shhh!" he admonished, but under his breath added, "It means you get your wish, and we'll be able to see what's happening."

They moved forward and to their left, riding behind the infantry units until they were a long stone's throw downslope from the nearest artillery crew. When they reached the highest point on the slope, they found the colonel and the other officers, and joined them.

Mounted, on the highest ground, they had an excellent view of the Pelanese infantry, spread out before them in neat ranks. Talis could see the pass, now that it was light enough to make out shapes. She picked out the lighter swath of the road, off to her right. Straining her eyes, looking east, she made out two large, dark blobs perhaps a mile away. They seemed to be moving.

Glancing at Jezzil, she whispered, "The Chonao army?"

He nodded. "Advancing."

In the east, facing her, the darkness grew lighter . . . lighter. Time suddenly seemed to be rushing by. As she watched, a thin streak of crimson fire touched the eastern horizon, illuminating the bottom of a massive cloud bank. *Sunrise. Now it begins.*

From her vantage point, she watched as the Sun's rays illuminated the mountain peaks. The snow on the highest peaks gleamed pink as the Sun rose.

Talis watched the dark blobs on the field, still in deep shadow, creeping forward. Then, as the newly risen Sun's light touched the Pelanese forces, throwing long shadows, she heard it—a deep, booming drum, sounding a clear pattern. *Boom da da BOOM . . . Boom da da BOOM . . .*

Falar reacted immediately, snorting, dancing in place, ready to spring forward. Jezzil kept her still, muttering what sounded like imprecations in his own language. The air was full of voices now, Pelanese officers issuing commands to "Load and stand ready!" and the artillery officers barking orders to their gunnery crews.

"What's happening?" Talis said, turning to the Chonao. She could see him now, his features shadowed by the helmet, saw the tightness of his jaw.

"They've signaled a cavalry charge!" Jezzil replied, and she heard the strain in his voice. "I can't believe it! What do they think they're doing?"

Below them, the dark blobs were surging forward as the Chonao lines moved faster. Talis could hear the riders urging their mounts on. They were trotting, then cantering, then galloping . . .

"Arenar blast them!" Jezzil muttered. "What was Kerezau *thinking*?"

Sunlight flashed golden on the tips of lances and raised swords as the Chonao cavalry hurtled toward the enemy front line, now barely half a mile away. Two thousand troops running flat out, heading straight for the Pelanese.

Talis's breath caught in her throat as the enemy charged up the gentle slope, bursting into the sunlight as they did so. The light found them, bright colors flashing from the uniforms of the various units. Their horses were magnificent, the pounding of their hooves shaking the earth beneath Lady's feet.

The riders were yelling their battle cry now. Lancer units leveled their lances.

Talis's breath caught in her chest as she stared, half mesmerized by the power and majesty of that charge. She realized that if she'd been in the front lines of the Pelanese infantry, she'd have turned tail and run, and was ashamed to realize it.

The riders charged, and they were closer, closer . . . the ground shook with the thunder of galloping hooves.

Then the air around her erupted with the voices of the Pelanese artillery officers, all shouting more or less at once. "Fire! Fire! Fire!"

To Talis's right and left cannons belched flame and smoke as they discharged, straight into the oncoming charge. The sharp smell of burned gunpowder filled the air. Gaps appeared in the Chonao ranks as horses and men went down. Talis saw scarlet splashes of blood, mixed with hunks that must have been severed limbs and chunks of flesh, all flung high into the air.

Men and horses screamed in agony.

Oh Goddess!

The sight was so horrible that she felt dizzy and faint. She clung to her saddlebow with both hands, closing her eyes, shaking her head to clear it.

As the cannons fired again and again, she heard the Pelanese officers. "First rank, fire!" A volley of shots, then moments later, "Second rank! Fire!" Then "Third rank! Fire!" And then over again, and over again, the volleys of gunfire cracking sharply in the dawn air.

Even though they were firing into the rising Sun, the sharpshooters took deadly toll, picking off individual riders, felling horses by the dozens, the hundreds. Talis glanced over at Jezzil, saw that he was slumped, staring down at Falar's neck, and remembered that these were *his* people. *Goddess, oh, Goddess, make it stop!* Talis found herself praying.

But the slaughter went on and on.

The Chonao lines were ragged now, their ranks diminished to less than half . . . and still they came on, and still the cannons and the gun volleys cut them down. It was harder to see now, because the air was filled with smoke so acrid it stung Talis's eyes, making them water. Or was it tears? The roar of the cannons went on, nearly deafening her, making her head throb with each salvo.

In the end, only perhaps five hundred Chonao riders reached the front lines, driving into them like a lance point into living flesh. The Pelanese infantry lines sagged and folded in places, and all Talis could make out were flashes from the muzzles of pistols and the gleam of swords against swords as they met in fierce hand-to-hand combat. It seemed to take only a minute before the remnants of the Chonao were engulfed, and the ranks of the Pelanese surged forward again in a wave of blue tunics.

Talis coughed, rackingly, as a heavy cloud of smoke rolled over their position. Leaning to the side, she spat, trying to catch her breath. When she could see again, the only trace of that brave, foolhardy charge was a few riderless horses galloping madly between the two armies, amid the scattered bodies. The screaming, much diminished, continued.

Now the two armies were firing at each other, volley after volley, as the Chonao infantry advanced and the Pelanese held their ground.

Major q'Rindo coughed genteelly into a handkerchief, then signaled to Talis and Jezzil. "Well, that's that," he said. "Time to return to reserve position."

Talis was only too glad to turn Lady's head and urge her back to rejoin Company Two. The Sun cast her shadow before her, elongated and dark, and she realized that it had been bare minutes since she was complaining about not being able to watch the fighting.

Well, you wanted to see, she thought miserably, wiping her stinging eyes as another cannon salvo sent more smoke to join the pall already hanging in the air. *So much for the glory of war.*

Eregard, too, had been sickened by the carnage, but as the morning wore on, he was too busy to dwell on the past. He rode at his father's side, behind the front lines, in the middle rank of the central infantry brigade with his father's Royal Guards. This was his first time in battle, but he'd listened to war stories all his life from veteran soldiers, so he was at least somewhat prepared. They sat their horses on the left side of the brigade, only a short musket shot from the ravine he and Jezzil had examined the day before yesterday.

So far things were going according to plan for the Pelanese, and, despite the fact that they were outnumbered, their front line was holding fairly steady. They had been pushed a little farther up the slope by yet another Chonao cavalry incursion into their front lines, this one far better orchestrated than the disastrous one at sunrise. The Chonao infantry had moved in from the side, at an angle, and before they could be stopped, got close enough so the artillery could not fire directly at them because Pelanese troops were in the way. Once in place, they'd fought fiercely, doing considerable damage to several front-line infantry ranks before Pelanese sharpshooters cut them down.

Now King Agivir sat his great white war-horse, caparisoned with the royal blue and crimson, orchestrating the battle and consulting with Prince Adranan, Prince Salesin, and his other commanders by means of runners mounted on Pela's swiftest steeds. Eregard gazed at his father with pride, thinking that years seemed to have fallen away from his sire. Agivir sat his charger straight-backed, effortlessly controlling the spirited gelding with one hand, gesticulating with the other as he gave orders and received information. He wore a flowing cloak over his old-fashioned armor, brightly burnished, except that he wore no battle helm or hat. "Our troops take heart when they see this old white head and beard of mine," he'd told his son early that morning, when Eregard had begged him to run the battle from the rear. "They must be able to see my face, know that I am with them."

Eregard wondered how Adranan, commanding the left brigade, and Salesin, commanding the right, were faring. The reports coming in, and his own eyes, confirmed that the fighting was heavy, with many casualties on both sides. From what he could tell, the Pelanese forces were better drilled and more organized, but the Chonao warriors fought with a fierce skill that eclipsed that of his country's infantry.

Now that the fighting was at closer quarters, the Pelanese rifled muskets afforded them less advantage, though it was still evident. If not for those muskets, Eregard thought, the Chonao cavalry would surely have flanked them by now, which would have meant disaster.

Thinking about flank attacks made him recall Jezzil's warning to Salesin the day before. *Salesin is overconfident to think that he has those southern trails under control,* he thought. *I could make sure they will not prove our undoing.*

Eregard could hear his father shouting orders to the runner he was sending to General Osmando-Volon. "Tell him to bring up reserves to bolster our left and central brigades! We must push them back!"

"Understood, sire!" the runner said, saluting, before wheeling his horse and speeding off, weaving his way between the ranks, back to the central command tent near the supply wagons.

Eregard edged his gelding over until his black's flank was nearly touching the white charger's. "Father!" he shouted. "Let me lead a reserve unit into the foothills to guard against a contingent of Chonao coming through the southern hills to flank us."

The King turned his head. "Salesin reported that all significant trails had been blocked," he said.

"Anything that man can block, other men can unblock!" Eregard argued. "The more I think about what Jezzil warned might happen, the more I fear it will come to pass. Give me a few companies of reserves and I shall see that it does not happen!"

The King considered for a moment. "Stay with me but a while longer," he said. "If things go as I hope, we will regain the ground we lost, as the battle tide turns our way. Then you shall guard the foothill paths for us."

Eregard saluted. "As you command, sire!"

Thia stood at the eastern window, gazing out at the mountains, their tops gleaming white in the morning Sun. The battle had started, and she knew her friends were up at Ombal Pass, fighting. She wished she had someone to pray to, but Boq'urak had left her nothing.

She thought of Jezzil, of Eregard, and of Talis, and wondered if they were still alive.

Surely they are. If one of my friends died, wouldn't I know?

But she knew, with a terrible certainty, that she would not. Master Khith might—the Hthras had magical powers that constantly surprised and amazed her. But she had nothing of the sort, only the small ability to tell truth from lies.

What if Jezzil dies? What if I never see him again?

The thought brought a wave of fear so powerful that she cried out softly, pressing her hands to her breast. *No! No!*

Unable to stand still any longer, she whirled away from the window and began pacing, her clasped hands twisting restlessly. The silk of her gown swished softly, and her new slippers, creamy kid, finer than any she'd ever touched, much less worn, glided across the elegant carpet. She was not used to such finery. She'd been embarrassed by the roughness of her hands when she smoothed them against the fabric. One of the Princess's waiting women had donated the gown, barely worn, from last season, and the Princess had her seamstress cut it down to fit Thia. The soft, sea-green silk was flattering to her pale features and hair, and the plain, unruffled style suited her.

In the past few days, Thia had spent time with the Princess, and the two of them talked, cautiously at first, then more freely, sharing information about Eregard, the court, and Ulandra's life with Salesin. Ulandra had actually said little, but Thia could tell that the Princess was desperately unhappy and terrified of her husband, with good reason.

As she paced, Thia tried to make her mind blank, remembering how she had been able to do that for hours back in Amaran when bad things happened. It was simply a matter of letting all conscious thought go, of putting a blank screen between her mind and all that troubled her.

Thia tried, but strive as she might, she could not stop her mind from imagining Jezzil splashed with blood, moaning in pain, perhaps calling out for water. *When he was hurt before, I was there to comfort him,* she thought. *But not today . . . If he dies . . . if he dies . . .*

A soft footfall sounded behind her, and Thia turned to find Princess Ulandra standing in the corridor, her features drawn and anxious. "Is there any news?" Thia cried.

Ulandra shook her head. "I know not how the battle progresses, but wounded are beginning to be brought in to the infirmary tents. I have spoken to my ladies-in-waiting and told them I am going up to tend the wounded, and that they may, if they wish, join me."

Thia regarded her, surprised. "A princess, tending wounded?" she said. "That is . . ." She searched for a word. ". . . the custom among your people?"

Ulandra laughed, though there was little humor in the sound. "Hardly," she said. "My ladies were shocked, I believe. My husband sent me a message that I must stay here, in the palace." Her chin rose. "I am therefore going, with all dispatch."

Thia had seen Prince Salesin. He was not a man she would willingly have crossed. "You are brave, Your Highness," she said admiringly.

"I am *learning,* Thia," the Princess said. "Besides," she added, trying for a light tone, and not quite succeeding, "one cannot call it courage when one merely does one's duty, can one?"

Thia looked at her levelly. "I would. Your Highness, I'd like to go, too. I have had some experience at treating wounded."

"Good. Your friend, the Hthras physician, will also be accompanying us." The Princess smiled at her, and the sight of her lovely face, still marred with fading bruises, wrenched Thia's heart. She managed an answering smile, though her eyes were misty. Ulandra came toward her, put out her hands, and took Thia's roughened ones in her soft clasp. "Thia, be strong. Have faith."

Thia gave a bitter, choked laugh. "Faith in *what*? I am

sorry, Your Highness, but all my faith was reft from me last winter, most cruelly. I have nothing to believe in anymore. And I fear for my friends, and for Jezzil."

"He is a warrior, Eregard tells me. A remarkable warrior."

"He is," Thia agreed. "But—"

"I know," Ulandra said. "I fear for all my friends today, and for the soldiers I do not know. I have been praying since dawn to the Goddess." Ulandra turned to head back toward her rooms, arm and arm with Thia. Her touch was a comfort. "But let us dress now, so we may go up with the supply wagon. We cannot tend the wounded in silk gowns."

Thia nodded, brushing her free hand across her eyes. "Yes, just doing *something* will help. It is the waiting that is hardest."

When they reached Ulandra's rooms, Thia discovered that the Princess had plain black gowns waiting for them, with sleeves that could be rolled up. There were also gray aprons and scarves to bind up their hair, such as Pelanese nurses wore.

The two women changed quickly, helping each other with the buttons instead of summoning servants. When they were ready, Ulandra left the chamber for a moment, while Thia gathered up food, water, bandages, needles and thread, and blankets, packing them into baskets.

When Ulandra returned, her step was brisk. "I sent my ladies-in-waiting, and my maids, on ahead. Your Master Khith is with them. I have summoned my carriage to take us up to the pass. It will be waiting by the side door."

Carrying the heavy baskets, the two women left the rooms and headed down the corridor. When they reached the intersection, Ulandra turned left, and Thia followed her. She had just turned the corner when she heard the Princess call out, "Your Reverence!"

Thia looked up and saw, halfway down the corridor, a tall man with a shaven head and dark, dark eyes. He wore a scarlet robe that made his pale skin appear even paler. Her breath stopped as their eyes met.

"Master Varn!" she whispered, then, remembering the last time she had seen him, fear set in. Her basket slipped from her hands and she found herself backing away.

She need not have worried. As soon as her erstwhile Mentor recognized her, he turned and fled down the corridor. Moments later the slam of a door eclipsed the sound of running feet.

"Thia? Thia, what is it? Thia?"

Thia staggered, and if it hadn't been for Ulandra's grasp on her arm, she might have fallen. The Princess was staring at her, shaken, her voice shrill with concern.

"That was Master Varn," Thia said blankly. "What is he doing here?"

"I don't understand," Ulandra said. "Master who? That was His Reverence Varlon, who has been spiritual and philosophical counselor to King Agivir these past few months. He is also something of a soothsayer, or prophet, to hear the King tell it. What has he done to upset you so? You are as pale as a specter!"

Thia looked at her new friend. "How do *you* know him, Princess?"

"He has been my counselor, my friend," Ulandra said. "He told me that his god had chosen me . . ." Seeing Thia's expression, the Princess trailed off. "Tell me, Thia. What is going on?"

Thia shook herself like a dog tossed into a snowbank. "It is a very long story," she said, with a catch in her voice. Dropping to her knees, she hastily picked up her basket and repacked it. "And we have made a promise to join the others in the infirmary tents. Let's find that carriage, and I will tell you on the ride up to Ombal Pass."

Once they were seated in the carriage, with its contingent of guards, Thia recounted the story of her life: how Master Varn had been her Mentor, what she had seen that terrible night in the depths of the ziggurat, and finally, how Varn had kidnapped her and been prepared to sacrifice her as Chosen to Boq'urak.

Ulandra listened with an expression of growing horror and fear. When Thia was finished, she leaned forward on the padded velvet seat of the carriage and sank her head into her hands. Shudders ran through her entire body.

"What is it? Thia asked. "What has Master Varn done to you?"

Ulandra sat back up, still trembling. She did not raise her eyes, but stared down at her clasped hands. In a soft, lifeless voice she recounted what had been happening to her over the past few months, ending with a description of that last dreadful scene with Salesin. "I . . . thought . . ." She choked on the words, struggling for composure. "Earlier, I thought I saw something in the mirror. Something that was not I, but instead something . . . else. Something unhuman. And it must have been that same—creature—that emerged when Salesin threatened me. Thia, he was hurt, bitten and clawed." She held out the soft hands Thia had so admired. "I think I remember my fingers, my fingers *changing*, becoming clawed. Oh, Goddess! Save me!"

The Princess began to weep aloud, great, wracking sobs. Thia moved over to sit beside her on the seat, and, without thinking about the difference in their rank, put her arms around the other woman, holding her close, murmuring words of comfort.

Finally, Ulandra sat up and dried her eyes. There was a new determination in her features and in the set of her jaw. She put her head out the window of the carriage and called out to the driver, "Please, stop a moment."

The carriage halted on the road and Ulandra stepped out to face the commanding officer of her guardsmen. "Captain," she said, "I have an order for you."

He swept off his hat and bowed. "Yes, Your Highness?"

"Send a messenger back to the palace, and tell the commanding officer of the Palace Guard to detain the priest, Varlon. Tell him not to harm him, but to lock him up in some secure place and to post a guard. Do you understand?"

"Yes, Your Highness," the captain replied, bowing again. "It shall be done."

"Thank you, Captain," Ulandra said with great dignity. Picking up her black skirts, she climbed back into the carriage. When she was seated, the Princess rapped her knuckles against the door and called, "Drive on! Make haste!"

"Yes, Your Highness! Hup! Get hup!" Thia heard the driver shout, followed by the snap of his whip. The carriage jolted into motion again, rattling as it bounced along the road leading to Ombal Pass.

Back behind the lines, Jezzil sat waiting on Falar, wondering if Company Two of the Royal Dragoons would be called into battle. What would it be like to actually fight his own countrymen? He thought he'd been prepared for the battle, but seeing that brave, foolhardy charge had shaken him to the depths of his being. Watching the horses fall, hearing the screams . . . he had been as upset as Talis, though able to conceal his reaction better.

Still, he could not regret his decision to fight for Pela. His friendship with Thia, Talis, Eregard, and Khith was stronger than any comradeship he had ever felt for his Chonao countrymen, even Barus. Remembering Kerezau's casual cruelty, he shook his head. *I am no longer Chonao. I am not sure what I am, but I know that, of a certainty.*

Smoke from the battle was rising high into the hot summer air, but here, behind the lines, it was easier to breathe. He could hear the volleys, unceasing, punctuated by the booming of the artillery.

The sun was well up now. Jezzil judged that it must be an hour or so short of noon. From what he could tell, the Pelanese were holding up against the Chonao superior numbers, due to the superiority of their firepower, but it wouldn't take much to change the tide of battle.

For the hundredth time Jezzil looked over at the green of the ravine, a quarter mile as a hawk would fly from where he sat. Narrowing his eyes, he peered through the pall of smoke. He stared so intently that his eyes began to water, and he was about to wipe them when he glimpsed a patch of brown against the dull green of the vegetation. A patch that *moved*.

Jezzil rubbed his eyes like a child, fiercely, then stared hard. He could still make out the brown, moving patch, and as he stared, there was another. And another, and yet another!

Scarcely daring to shift his gaze, Jezzil turned to Talis. "Look over there!" he said, not troubling to keep his voice down. "See that ravine, where those green trees break the ground line?"

She gave him a puzzled glance, then looked. "Yes, I see it. What of it?"

"Look along the ravine, even with the midpoint in the Pelanese troops, maybe a quarter mile from us in a straight line, do you see men standing there? Brown uniforms?"

Talis stared along Jezzil's pointing arm. "I don't see anything," she said.

Jezzil turned back, half convinced that he'd imagined it. For a moment he couldn't locate the incursion point, but then he had it again. More brown figures than before!

"You don't see it?"

"No, I—" She broke off. "Wait, yes I do! Brown uniforms, there are men there! On the edge!"

Jezzil felt a wash of relief as he waved to her to follow him, and urged Falar forward, searching for the major. He located him, receiving a report from a runner, and put Falar into a strong trot.

Moments later he was saluting Major q'Rindo, who stared at him, obviously not pleased. "What do you think you are doing, trooper?" he demanded. "Get back in ranks!"

"Sir," Jezzil said, "have you a spyglass? I believe I've spotted an incursion by Chonao troops. They are coming up from that ravine over there." He pointed.

"I saw them, too, Major," Talis said.

The major reached down and took a leather case off his saddle, extracted a spyglass and extended it. "Point it out, trooper."

Jezzil signaled Falar to sidepass until the two horses stood shoulder-to-shoulder, flank-to-flank. "Over there, sir. Follow the line of my arm. Brown uniforms, against the green trees. There must be twenty or more of them now."

The major took long moments positioning the spyglass, adjusting it, while Jezzil waited anxiously. Finally, just as Jezzil was about to speak, he took the spyglass away and telescoped it back to its smallest size. "I see them. Good work, trooper." Turning to the runner, he quickly ordered him to spread the word that he was taking Company Two to deal with an incursion along the ravine and was requesting reinforcements.

Moments later the company was trotting briskly after the major. Jezzil carried one loaded pistol in his hand, guiding Falar mostly with his seat and legs. Talis rode at his side, flushed with excitement.

Company Two threaded its way past the ranks of Pelanese infantry, riding faster to follow the major, until they were cantering. The distance was too short and the disposition of the ranked infantry too close to allow a faster gait.

Jezzil's heart was beating fast. *The last time I was in an attack force, I abandoned my comrades and ran,* he thought. *Will I have the courage to stand and fight to the end this time?*

Beneath him, Falar cantered, gliding like a gray specter through the smoke and the screams. Jezzil sat poised, his pistol gripped in his sweating hand, and sent up a brief prayer to Arenar.

Grant me courage, O Lord of War. Grant me courage!

Eregard took off his hat and wiped his brow on his sleeve. It was nearly midday, stifling. Midnight's neck and flanks were wet with sweat, just from standing under him.

The Pelanese had regained a bit more of the ground they had lost, and the right brigade had fought back another cavalry attack. King Agivir sat on his now quiet war-horse, scanning a dispatch from Adranan on the status of the left brigade.

Eregard looked around at the battle through eyes stinging with smoke. They had lost one of the Royal Guardsman to the heat. The young man had passed out, tumbling off his mount like a sack of wet sand. Quickly, two other guardsmen had slung him over his horse and taken him back to the infirmary tent.

Eregard's gaze turned to the southeast. Dark, heavy-bellied clouds were beginning to crowd in over Royal Peak, whose crest was jagged like the spires of a crown. *Hold off,* he thought, to the storm. *Hold off.* Rain would hurt the Pelanese, because in a downpour the muskets would not fire, and the advantage gained by their better weaponry would be lost. If it came down to hand-to-hand combat, the Chonao still had the greater numbers.

His mouth was so dry his lips stuck to his teeth. Eregard leaned over, unfastened his water flask from the saddle and tilted it up, allowing himself a few swallows. He didn't want to drink too much, for fear he'd have to relieve himself. Bending back down, he slipped the flask back into its holder.

"Eregard!"

The Prince sat up, turning his head to see who had called him. It was his father, who was looking at him, his hand out-stretched. "Water?" the King said, smiling a little. "I'm parched. This is thirsty work."

Eregard smiled back at him as he bent over again, his hand groping for the flask.

He had no warning. His ears had become accustomed to the constant volleys of shots, and he heard nothing different. One moment his father was sitting there, smiling at him, and the next, his father's smile, nay, his entire *face*, had vanished in a smear of red. Hot saltiness exploded outward, splashing Eregard from head to waist.

At almost the same moment, one of the Royal Guards-men shrieked, high and shrill, and dropped like an anchor. The Prince felt something smash into his upper arm, into the muscle, like a punch, and he fell, landing hard on the ground. If he had not bent down, it would have struck him mid-chest. Gasping for breath, numb with shock, Eregard raised his hand, staring at it stupidly. It was red. Out of the corner of his eye he glimpsed a flash of white as the King's war-horse bolted away. His own Midnight shied, nearly stepping on him, as something heavy slammed against the gelding, then slid unresisting to the ground.

Father!

Eregard pushed himself up with his good arm and managed to stand. He ducked under his mount's neck, and then he saw it, sprawled gracelessly in the dirt, facedown: his father's body.

"Father!" he gasped, and threw himself down. Knowing the truth, he still couldn't help turning the old man over—and wished he hadn't. The features he had loved were gone, the white hair and beard streaked red. He clasped his father's body as well as he could and bowed his head, whispering the Litany for the Dead.

When he opened his eyes, the first thing Eregard saw was the body of the Royal Standard bearer, staring sightlessly at him. The proud flag of his country lay in the dirt. The rampant sea serpent swam through a crimson ocean.

Eregard raised his voice. "Guardsmen! To me!"

Moments later two of them were there, one weeping openly.

Eregard gently laid his father's corpse down. "You two—tend to your liege," he said. "Convey him off the field and see that he is laid out with dignity, covered by a shroud."

"Yes, Your Highness," the captain said.

Eregard tried to get up, only to have his legs buckle. "Your Highness, you are wounded!" exclaimed the other guardsman. "Let us take you to the medical tent."

"No," Eregard said. His arm was throbbing, but he welcomed the physical pain—it helped eclipse the pain from the lump of rock that seemed to have replaced his heart in his chest. He forced himself to his feet, stood steady.

As he did so, one of the guardsmen who was still mounted called out, pointed. "Look! Over there! Chonao uniforms in the midst of our lines!"

Eregard turned to the highest-ranking of the guardsmen. "Colonel Delfano, leave these three men here to assist with my father. Take your remaining men over to deal with this new attack. You *must* stop them."

The man saluted. "Yes, Your Highness!" Signaling to his men, he drove his spurs into his mount's barrel and leaped forward.

Eregard turned back to the other two guards, who were busily removing his father's armor so his body could be transported. Wincing at the pain, the Prince managed to catch the reins of a nearby horse. "Here," he said, handing the reins over to the guardsman standing next to him. "Get him up over its back. Use his cloak to cover the body."

"Yes, Your Highness."

Eregard took a deep breath, then heard voices crying out . . . heard them spreading through the army like ripples on a pond.

"The King! The King has fallen!"

"I saw it! King Agivir is down!"

"The King is dead?"

"What do you see? Is the King alive?"

"Head-shot! Agivir is dead!"

"The King has fallen . . . long live the King!"

"Are you sure? What did you see? Is he really dead?"

"The King . . ."

"The King!"

They must not lose their will to fight, the Prince thought. *Morale is crucial in warfare. They must know they still have a leader who will bring Pela to victory.*

He wondered where Salesin was, realizing, with a shock that felt like an actual sword-thrust, that his brother was now King. *Where is Salesin? He must rally them!*

But Salesin was not there. There was no royal leader there to rally the troops.

Except me, Eregard thought dully. *I'm royal. I may not feel like it, but I have to at least* act *like it.*

Wiping his face with his sleeve, he walked over to the Royal Standard, bent over and picked it up with his good hand. *They can't see me,* he realized. *I have to get up higher, so they can see me.*

"Where's my horse?" he asked. Looking around, he spotted Midnight, reins dangling, wandering free. He pointed. "Bring him, and help me to mount."

The guardsman saluted and sprang to obey.

* * *

By the time Company Two reached the ravine, at least fifty Chonao had climbed out and were forming into fighting units, readying their muskets. Seeing them, Major q'Rindo shouted, "Charge!" and spurred his bay.

Jezzil squeezed Falar with his legs, and the mare shot out in front of the rest. Within a few strides he was stirrup-to-stirrup with the major. Sighting one Chonao who was pointing his musket at q'Rindo, Jezzil aimed and fired his pistol. The Chonao went down.

There was no time to reload. Jezzil jammed his pistol into its holster and drew his sword. Responding instantly to the pressure of his right leg, Falar swerved to the left, and Jezzil slashed down at another soldier. The man screamed as the sword sliced into him between neck and shoulder, then he, too, was down.

The next Chonao's musket misfired, and before he could draw his sword, Falar slammed into him, knocked him down, then the man was behind them, rolling and screaming. Jezzil laid about him with his sword, and his training stood him in good stead. A minute into the fight, he did use his reserve pistol—to bring down a Chonao whose sword was aiming for Falar's neck.

All the while that Company Two was fighting, more and more Chonao came swarming up out of the ravine, weapons ready. Jezzil's unit found themselves hard-pressed for several minutes, until a contingent of Royal Guardsmen arrived. They were well-mounted and well-armed and made short work of the remaining infiltrators.

By the time Major q'Rindo's requested reinforcements arrived, Jezzil and his compatriots were climbing off their horses, reloading their pistols and heading for the rim of the ravine. The entire skirmish had taken only a minute or two.

Jezzil looked over the rim and felt sick, realizing what was to come. The ravine was filled with Chonao, hundreds of them. As he'd suspected, guide-ropes led up the side. All a soldier had to do was pull himself up, and the climb could be accomplished in a matter of minutes.

Seeing the Pelanese uniforms silhouetted against the Sun,

the Chonao that were halfway up the slope turned and began scrambling back down, yelling, "Retreat! Run!" Other Chonao looked up, turned, and tried to flee back up the ravine, only to be pushed back by the press of those who were still advancing.

Jezzil shook his head, and when a voice said, "Move aside, lad, 'tis work for the long guns, here," he was glad to make way for a Pelanese infantryman with his musket. As Jezzil turned away, reinforcements began firing down into the ravine. These soldiers were well drilled and could get off as many as three shots per minute.

Screams erupted, and the firing kept on, and on, and on.

Jezzil walked back to Falar and picked up her reins, glad that it was not his responsibility to deal with the men down there. For a moment he imagined what it would be like to be among them, trapped, trying to run, clawing and fighting to get out of range, desperately struggling for footing in a stream that was running red—and then he shook his head and shut out that vision.

A hand touched his arm, and he turned to see Talis. Her face was filthy, but she was grinning broadly. "I'm glad to see you made it!" she exclaimed.

Jezzil smiled at her. "I'm glad to see you did, too."

They heard, then, the sound of men shouting, in unison, the sound issuing from hundreds, thousands, of throats.

Jezzil turned to look for the source. He could make out the words now—a battle cry, growing ever louder. He stood on tiptoe, but that was no good, so he leaped up on Falar. What he saw made him smile. Not far from him, he saw a familiar black horse, and on it, a familiar figure. Prince Eregard was standing in his stirrups, waving the flag of Pela high, and shouting . . . and the troops were shouting with him.

"PELA FOREVER!" they roared.

"Good work, Eregard!" Jezzil muttered, proud of his friend.

Something struck his leg, and Jezzil looked down at Talis. "What's going on?" she demanded.

"It's Eregard. He's got the flag, and he's rallying the troops."

She nodded. "Oh. Yes, I heard it from one of the Royal Guardsman. King Agivir was killed a few minutes ago."

Jezzil felt a wave of sorrow for the old man he'd known only a few days. "Oh," he said. "I'm sorry."

She nodded as though he'd said far more. "I know. I'm the last person to say anything kind about a royal, but he was a good man. He wasn't a good king anymore, but he was a good man."

Jezzil nodded, then looked around. "Where's your horse?"

Talis shook her head. "Lardbutt got creased by a round across her fat rear," she said. "She'll recover, but she's lame in her right hind. I sent her back to the remuda."

"Here, come up with me, then," Jezzil said, taking his left foot out of the stirrup. He pulled her up behind him on Falar, and when Major q'Rindo gave the order, they headed back behind the lines.

As he rode, Jezzil was thinking furiously. *I was right about one flank attack, suppose I was right about both of them? What if Chonao are coming through up there?* He glanced over at the southern foothills. *Eregard said the main trail comes out at the supply wagons and infirmary tents. A thousand cavalrymen could catch the army from behind, crack them like a mouse in a vice. I have to do something.*

When Jezzil reached the Company Two lines, he turned to Talis, offering her his hand to aid her as she slid off over Falar's rump. "I need your help," he said quietly. "Follow me as soon as you can slip away. Meet me back by the supply wagons."

Her mouth opened, then closed, and she nodded, once.

Jezzil spotted his commanding officer, dismounted, and made a show of picking up Falar's off fore and examining it. Then he led the mare over to the major and saluted. "Sir, my mare's got a loose shoe. Request permission to have it seen to before it can cause trouble."

Major q'Rindo nodded. "Permission granted, trooper, but make it fast," he said. "And my thanks for the quick shot back there."

"Yes, sir!"

Feeling guilty about the lie he'd told, Jezzil led Falar away, heading for the rear of the encampment and the supply wagons. When he reached them, he took a moment to step between two wagons to relieve himself, then drank from his flask. The heat hung over the battlefield as tangibly as the smoke from the guns.

When he lowered the flask, Talis was there. "I didn't even have to sneak off. Major sent me to go get a remount," she said. Moving over to Falar, she patted the mare's shoulder, then slid her hand down and picked up her right foreleg. "There's nothing wrong with this shoe," she said, looking up. "What's going on?"

Quickly, Jezzil explained his fears about another Chonao flanking attempt, this time coming through the southern foothills.

"And you intend to ride up there and scout?" Talis said. "If you're right, by the time you reconnoiter, then try to make it back here without them seeing you, it will be too late to stop them."

"I don't intend to physically scout the foothill trails," Jezzil said. "I won't have to, if I can do this spell correctly. But I need you to keep anyone from finding me. I won't be in my own head for a while."

Talis looked scared, but after a second nodded. "All right. Where are you going to try this spell?"

"I'll crawl under the wagon," Jezzil said. "I should be mostly out of sight there."

"All right," she said. "How long will it take you?"

"I don't know. Several minutes, at least."

"You'd better get started."

Jezzil nodded. "When I come back out, I may not make much sense for a few minutes. Make sure I tell you exactly what I've seen. Do whatever you have to do to bring me out of it. Understand?"

"Yes," Talis said, and added, nervously, "I don't like this."

"Neither do I," Jezzil said, "but I don't see an alternative."

Quickly, he dropped to the ground and crawled under the wagon. He discovered that there was enough room for him to

lie on his side as he fumbled for the small vial of black, viscous liquid Khith had decocted for him last night, and the
tiny piece of hollow bone it had wrapped in a piece of silk.

Jezzil recalled the ingredients that Khith had taken from
its bag—lian roots and vilneg leaves. Then, after it had
brewed the decoction, it had pricked Jezzil's finger and
added several drops of blood. He also recalled Khith's
words of warning. "I have no idea whether this substance
will work on one of your people . . ."

Jezzil pried out the stopper, cautiously sniffed the mixture
and gagged. His stomach was empty. Could he even keep the
stuff down?

Only one way to find out, Jezzil thought. With a sudden
movement of his wrist, he put the vial to his lips, tossed back
his head and gulped down the contents.

It was touch and go for a moment, as to whether the liquid
would stay down. Jezzil gritted his teeth, counting in his
mind. He reached fifty before he dared to unclench his jaw.
Picking up the tiny bone, he held it clenched in his fist.

The potion was working. The sounds of the battle seemed
magnified, then very far away, fading in and out. He could
feel every blade of grass that touched his skin.

The ground seemed to rise up beneath him, then drop like
an ocean swell. Jezzil rolled onto his belly, resolutely shut
his eyes and put his hands over his ears.

Must . . . concentrate . . .

Now what were the focusing words Khith had recited?
Ah, yes . . .

Forest-juice, help me see,
Bones of hunter, let me hear,
Show me those who wish me harm,
Let me farsee, so to warn . . .

He thought the words because he could not make his
tongue cooperate enough to speak them aloud. Thought
them over and over . . .

All at once, he felt himself moving—seemingly floating, moving fast and light. Jezzil dared to open his eyes, and realized that the spell had worked: he was seeing through the eyes of a feathered hunter—a hawk, a vulture, or perhaps an eagle.

Beneath him the alpine fields lay green with summer. Beneath his wings, the wind blew, chill and dank, presaging rain. The clouds above him were black, filled with flickers of greenish light and distant rumbles. A storm was coming, sure enough.

Jezzil induced his host to look down again. The creature's vision was remarkable, so much sharper than his own could ever be. He was high up, near the treeline. That would not serve—he must go lower, lower . . .

The bird whose mind he shared responded to his urging and banked, heading north, away from the mountain peak. A moment later he was gliding over the foothills, watching, waiting, looking for any flicker of motion . . .

Yes! There! Living things, moving!

Jezzil pushed gently with his will, and the bird spiraled lower, keening its cry.

Yes, moving things, white and black, puffy fleece . . . a herd of sheep.

Jezzil wrenched his host's attention away from a wobbly lamb, then sent the bird soaring again, circling. He spotted a trail running through the foothills and sent his host winging along it, watching, always watching . . .

Movement!

Again, movement, and this time there was no doubt that he had found his quarry. Men, many men, riding, no more than two or three abreast, along a narrow trail. They were trotting along, completely at their ease. It was hard to tell how far they had traveled along the trail, but Jezzil was sure it would bring them out into Ombal Pass and allow them to crush the Pelanese army between two sides of a vise.

Jezzil sent the bird soaring again, flapping a time or two, the powerful wings pumping, seeking the head of the column. It took only a second for his host to catch up to the leader.

There was something about the set of the man's shoulders, the way he sat his mount, that was disturbingly familiar.

One more flap and he was gliding past the leader, nearly on a level with his face, close enough to startle the man's horse.

Barus.

The shock of seeing that familiar face threw Jezzil out of his trance. He came back to himself lying on the ground, his face pressed against the earth, his fingers clawed into it as if seeking purchase. Had he fallen asleep? He couldn't tell. The effects of the potion seemed to be wearing off. Khith had told him it was fast-acting, but did not linger.

He crawled forward, out from under the wagon, and found Talis there, waiting for him. When she saw him, her expression lightened. "Jezzil! Can you talk? Are you all right?"

"I think so," he muttered, using the side of the wagon to get to his feet. He felt almost normal, though tired.

"Thank the Goddess," she whispered. "I was afraid to disturb you, but you looked almost dead."

"How long was I out?"

"Not too long," she said. "A quarter of an hour? Perhaps a bit more."

"There's no time to lose, then," he said, and went over to Falar. He checked his girth, then loaded both pistols. "Barus is leading a fairly large force of cavalry along the trails up there." He pointed at the southern foothills. "If nothing stops them, they'll come through somewhere near here, *behind* the Pelanese troops. The battle will be over if they succeed."

Talis had turned pale beneath her tan. "Goddess! What are you going to do?"

"I'm going up there, as quickly as I can. I'll scout their position, try to delay them. Use magic to start a fire, maybe."

Jezzil yanked off his cap, then his uniform jacket. Quickly, he tugged at buckles and straps and pulled off his cuirass.

Standing there in his sleeveless undertunic, he glanced up at the mountain peaks. "There's a storm coming, and a hard rain would prove very bad for the Pelanese. We have to make sure this attempt to flank the army doesn't succeed." He swung up onto Falar. Catching his urgency, she danced and snorted.

Talis flung herself forward, grabbing Falar's bridle. "Wait! Did that potion drive you mad? You're going *alone*? One soldier against a whole regiment of cavalry? At least let me come with you!"

"No," he said. "I need you to alert the major, get him to bring reinforcements. I spotted that other incursion—tell him I went off scouting and spotted another one, or something. Damnation, tell him anything, just get reinforcements up those trails as fast as they can ride!"

"But—"

Jezzil leaned forward, grabbed her shoulder and shoved her away, forcing her to release the bridle. "Just *do* it!" Loosening the reins, he shouted, "Hah!" The gray mare sprang forward, running like a creature possessed.

Talis didn't stay to watch Falar disappear into the trees. Gathering her wits, she thought to head back to Company Two's position, then hesitated. Her path would take her close to the remount pen. She'd need a horse if she were to accompany her unit.

She began to run.

When she reached the remount pen her mouth opened in dismay. There were only about twenty horses milling around, and they were the dregs of the cavalry's ridable mounts. An old soldier, evidently the hostler, laughed out loud as he took in her expression. "Not much to choose among 'em, is there?" he said. "We've got more remounts coming up from Pela, but they haven't got here yet."

He gazed at the choices and shrugged. "I'd say take the roan. He's got a few years on 'em, but at least he's sound and fully broke."

Talis looked at the horse in question, noting the hollows

over its eyes and the way its back was beginning to sag. "He's got to be close to twenty," she said. "I've got to have something with some speed and stamina."

"Sorry, young lady," the hostler said. "You'll just have to wait."

A flash of white caught her eye, and she saw a horse standing behind the nearest tent: a big, strong gelding, decked out like a parade horse, with an old-fashioned, heavy saddle. She pointed. "What about that fellow?"

"I've been tryin' to get near him for an hour, missy," the man said. "He won't let nobody get close. There's blood on that old saddle. Poor beast, some of them take it hard when their rider buys himself a farm."

Talis was already moving toward the big horse. "Get me a courier saddle," she said.

The horse snorted and rolled his eyes as she approached, and she moved slowly, speaking softly. "Hey, big fellow." She held out her hand so he could catch her scent. "You poor thing, what happened?" Another step closer. The horse tossed his head uncertainly and sidestepped, eyes rolling. But he did not run. "Hey, listen, fellow, you've got to help me out." The horse extended his neck, and she felt his breath across her knuckles. "That's it, good fellow. I really, really need a good horse, one just like you." The horse continued to sniff her. "Easy, easy now . . ."

And then, as calmly as if he were walking into his familiar stable, the big white horse took two steps forward, until he was standing close to Talis. He sniffed her arm, then butted his head against her, the way Bayberry used to.

Talis smiled with wonder and delight. "Hey, good boy!"

The hostler eyed her admiringly as she led the big horse back to the temporary corral. "You got a way with horses, that's for sure. Here's your saddle, missy."

"Thank you!" she said, hastily stripping off the fancy caparisons and the old-fashioned saddle. There was a red streak running down the animal's shoulder, but she could find no wound. It wasn't his blood, then.

It took her but a second to tack up the big charger with a light courier's saddle. "Give me a leg up?"

The hostler obligingly grabbed her leg and gave her a boost. The white horse snorted and reared, but Talis brought him down. "None of that, now," she said sternly. "You're going to need all your energy for running. Let's go find Major q'Rindo!"

I can't let her keep running like this in this heat, Jezzil thought, *or she'll founder long before we can find Barus.* He eased back on Falar's reins, curbing her forward rush. The breeze was cool, under the trees, but the trail was ascending most of the time. So far, he'd been trotting fast up the slopes, then hand-galloping down, and alternately galloping and cantering on the straightaways. Falar had already run nearly two miles in the sweltering heat.

At the crest of the next hill, Jezzil halted to give Falar a minute to breathe, and to mark his trail. Whenever the path forked, he would break off a branch and leave the end hanging, as a sign for Talis to follow him.

As Eregard had said, there were multiple trails up here in these mountains. When he jumped Falar over one large deadfall of trees, close to Ombal Pass, his aerial vision was confirmed—he saw that a barricade had been removed, the logs chopped in half and dragged off to the side. The Pen Jav Dal had been at work clearing this trail. Jezzil could only hope the flanking attack was still far back in the foothills.

How long would it take Talis to convince the major that there was another attack on the way? Would she even be able to do it? Jezzil shook his head as he cantered down the trail again. He couldn't worry about that now. He had to concentrate on what he was doing, and trust Talis to do her part.

He patted Falar's neck, slick with sweat. *How much farther to go?* "Come on, girl, keep moving . . ."

By the time Talis returned to Company Two, she had reached an understanding with the big white horse. It was just a matter of patience mixed with firmness. She trotted up to Major q'Rindo and saluted smartly.

He glanced at her. "Good mount," he said. "What took you so long? And where is Trooper Jezzil? He should be back by now."

"Major, I have something important to tell you," Talis said. "The Chonao are attempting another flank attack."

The major sat up straighter on his bay. "Where? Report, trooper."

"Sir, they're coming through the foothills up there." She pointed to the southern mountains, noticing as she did so that dark clouds were gathering. "Trooper Jezzil discovered their plan and went on ahead to reconnoiter."

"Discovered their plan?" Major q'Rindo echoed. "How?"

Talis swatted at a fly on the white horse's neck, trying to think of a reply. The major glared at her. "Trooper Talis, just how did Trooper Jezzil discover the Chonao plan?"

This was the part Talis had been dreading. She'd racked her brain trying to think of a reasonable explanation, one that didn't include magic, but no inspiration come to her. "Major q'Rindo, sir," she said, her mind racing, "Jezzil realized what the Chonao were planning because of . . ."

She hesitated. *Goddess, help me!*

The major was plainly losing his patience. *"Yes?"*

Talis felt her mouth move, but had no idea what she was going to say. Words came tumbling out, though. "Because of smoke signals, sir! He saw them rising into the air up on the ridge, and was able to interpret them. It's how the Chonao send long distance signals during secret attacks."

Talis sagged with relief when Major q'Rindo blinked at her in surprise. "Please, Major," she added, "we need to go after him right now. We'll need lots of reinforcements. There's a whole regiment coming. If we can't stop them, the Chonao are going to be attacking from our rear!"

The major hesitated, then shook his head. "That will be Colonel Bilani's call, not mine," he said. He signaled to a soldier. "You there! Take this news to the colonel, and tell him I shall be there in a moment to receive his orders."

"Yes sir!" The trooper was off.

Talis wanted to scream with frustration. "Major, sir, we can't wait for orders! You have to bring this company, and leave word for others to follow us!" she insisted. Her tension was communicated to the white charger, who began to dance beneath her. "If you don't, everything that's happened to Pela today will be for nothing! King Agivir will have died for nothing! We can't let Kerezau win!"

Still the major hesitated, though he was plainly torn.

"Damnation, sir!" Talis shouted, "If you won't go, then I'll go alone. I owe that to the brave men and women who died here today! I owe that to King Agivir, who is doubtless still hovering over this battlefield, waiting for a Pelanese victory to bring him the peace he needs to go to the Goddess!"

She drew her sword, and the familiar ring of steel made the white horse snort and rear. Talis brought him down. "Whoa, boy!" She turned to look at the line of men, her fellow troopers, her *comrades*. Her throat tightened. *I have to appeal to them, get them to follow me! Goddess, help me convince them!*

She raised her sword. "Comrades in arms . . . who will ride with me to save Pela?"

One of the troopers in the front row was staring at her as if he'd seen a ghost. "Look at her!" he said, pointing. "Look what she's riding! That's Banner, by the Goddess—King Agivir's charger! 'Tis a sign!"

Now the major, too, was staring at her mount. He rode his bay over and leaned over to look at the silver and gold markings on the headstall of the bridle. "It is!" he said. "This is indeed Banner!" He glared at Talis. "Where did you get this horse?"

Talis sat up straighter. "He came to me, sir." Realizing that she was sitting astride a dead king's mount made her almost feel as though some of King Agivir's leadership ability was flowing through her, strengthening her. She turned back to the troops. "Who's with me?" she shouted.

Now voices were running through the ranks. "'Tis a sign, I tell you! A sign from the Goddess! We must go!"

Major q'Rindo made his decision. "You three"—he
pointed quickly to three of the troopers—"each of you inform two of the reserve cavalry companies. Tell their commanders where we are headed. Tell them we need them to
join us. You"—he pointed to another trooper—"locate General Osmando-Volon. Tell him what has happened. He needs
to station reserve infantry along the perimeter of Ombal
Pass to prevent any incursion. Is that clear?"

"Yes, sir!"

Once the runners were away, Major q'Rindo turned to his
troops. "Company Two, prepare to move out!"

He turned back to Talis. "Trooper Aloro, we will follow
your lead." He threw her a smart salute.

Talis barely kept her mouth from dropping open in astonishment. She gathered her scattered wits and raised her
sword high. "Pela forever!"

"Pela forever!" the major echoed.

"PELA FOREVER!" Cheering, the company followed
her lead.

There is definitely a storm coming, Jezzil thought. The wind
was whipping his hair as he rode, ducking under overhanging limbs, watching the path before them with every bit of
alertness he could summon. At this speed a big rock or a
limb in the path could prove disastrous. Falar was still galloping gamely on, but the mare no longer wanted to run. He
could hear her breathing in hard, fast gasps.

Jezzil knew if he kept pushing her, she would fall and hurt
them both, or she'd founder and that would be the end of her.
They had come nearly three miles in the heat, much of it uphill, at speed. *When we round the next corner,* he thought, *I'll
stop her and get off and lead her. I can run for a mile or two,
and then get back on. I can—*

They rounded the next corner and did stop, abruptly, because facing them was a large contingent of Chonao cavalry,
with Barus in the lead.

Jezzil pulled Falar up, but it was too late; he'd been spotted. He hesitated, wondering what to do. Set the trees on

fire? Could he summon enough magic without the avundi-enhancing snuff, tired as he was? He cursed himself for not realizing that the attack force was so close.

Barus had halted his horse, too, and was staring at Jezzil with such amazement that, under other circumstances, it might have been funny.

"Jezzil!" he said blankly. "How did you get here? We thought you drowned."

Jezzil smiled and shrugged. "The last time we met, I was about to ask you the same question when you slugged me. I thought *you* died at Taenareth. I was glad to see you when I found out you were alive. Too bad you didn't feel the same."

Barus made an impatient gesture. "I don't find your feeble attempts at wit amusing. I ask you again—how did you get here?"

Jezill grinned at him. *Keep him talking.* "I got here on Falar, as you can see," he replied.

Barus ignored the jest. He gestured, and in the next moment a score of pistols were leveled at Jezzil. "Tell me why you're here."

Jezzil thought fast. "I came to warn you. There's a regiment of Pelanese cavalry on the way to intercept you. Turn back now and you might be able to get away."

Barus stared at him for a moment, then laughed. "You expect me to believe you?"

"We were friends once. I'm telling you the truth," Jezzil said, hoping fervently that he was, indeed, telling the truth.

"I don't count cowards and deserters among my friends," Barus said.

Jezzil flushed, and had to force himself not to react to the taunt. "Listen to me, Barus. If you don't want another massacre like the one this morning, turn around and head back down that trail."

"People with no honor are liars, as well as cowards," Barus said. "I'm under orders, and I'll obey them."

"By the way," Jezzil said, "what fool ordered that charge at dawn?"

Barus gestured at his troops to stay back, then rode his

sorrel closer to Jezzil. He stopped only a horse length away and lowered his voice. "As a matter of fact, Kerezau did," he said softly. "But don't worry, we made sure he won't be issuing any more such orders."

"Kerezau? Has the Redai gone mad?" Jezzil asked.

"He's become increasingly erratic ever since that skirmish on the ship with that black-haired Katan bitch," Barus replied. "We had to actually restrain him this morning. Whatever she did to him, it's been the ruin of a great leader. But we still have able commanders. Pela will be ours."

"I don't think so," Jezzil said. "Those rifled muskets are cutting you to pieces. If you don't want to face them up here, turn around and head back down that trail before the Pelanese arrive."

"You're lying. There's no one up here but you, and why you came, I can't imagine. Not that it will do you a bit of good. First I'll kill you, then I'm going to attack the rear of the Pelanese army and end this cursed battle before we run out of ammunition."

"Oh-ho," Jezzil said. "You're running low?"

"Just between you, me, and the horses here, yes we are. Bad intelligence. We didn't expect this much resistance. King Agivir is old and toothless, more prone to bargain than fight."

"Attack a man's homeland," Jezzil said, "and he'll fight. Kerezau should have realized."

"It didn't help that we lost two of our supply ships, carrying mainly ammunition, in that be-damned storm," Barus said. "But Kerezau was determined to attack."

"I see," Jezzil said.

"At any rate," Barus said, "I have things to do, so I'll thank you to dismount. If you surrender quietly and give me Falar, I may even let you live."

"I don't think I can do that," Jezzil said evenly.

Barus raised an eyebrow. "Oh? Want to make me a counterproposal, then, or should I just have you shot now?"

Jezzil put his hand on his sword and raised his voice, to be sure the Chonao soldiers could hear him. "I challenge you,

Barus. Single combat. You always claimed you were better than I was. Let's find out."

Barus's swarthy features darkened. "Enough wordplay and games, Jezzil. I don't have time for it."

"You always claimed you could beat me easily. Are you afraid to prove it?"

The soldiers murmured to each other. Barus flushed. He had always been quick-tempered, and Jezzil was counting on that.

"Come on, Barus, how long could it take? To beat one coward? Or are *you* the coward?"

With a wordless yell of rage, Barus drew his sword and put spurs to his horse. Jezzil was half a second late in reacting, but Falar, despite her weariness, was not. As she'd been trained, the mare reared back on her hind legs, then launched herself forward. Her fore hooves crashed into the sorrel's chest, knocking the other mare off balance. With a surprised squeal, the sorrel went down. Falar nearly fell, too, but managed to lurch to her feet at the last second.

Barus's extraordinarily quick reflexes saved him from being pinned. He reacted instinctively, kicking his feet loose from the stirrups, and landed standing, astride the struggling mare. He jumped clear and moved in on Jezzil.

Responding to leg pressure, Falar spun around, and Jezzil blocked Barus's sword slash with his own blade. But the angle of fighting an opponent on the ground while mounted was awkward, though height gave him an advantage. Jezzil also knew that Barus might well try to disable him by bringing down Falar. He kicked his feet loose from his stirrups and leaped down.

With one part of his mind, he heard the Chonao troops cheering their leader. Jezzil resolutely ignored them, concentrating on what he was doing. Barus was a formidable opponent, faster and more experienced than he was. Jezzil was a little taller though, and heavier, with a slight advantage in reach.

Barus came in again, and they began to circle, testing each other, their blades kissing and sliding away. In the distance, Jezzil heard a rumble of thunder. *The storm is coming.*

With a shout meant to distract, Barus feinted, then swung low, aiming for Jezzil's legs. Jezzil swung his sword down, striking the blade aside. Their weapons rang out as they both came back up from the stroke, trying to press the advantage, blades sliding together until both guards touched. They paused for a second, breathing fast, close enough to embrace. "You fool," Jezzil gritted, "I'm trying to save your life. Take your men and run."

When he spoke the words, he wasn't even sure if they were true, but he knew one thing: even supposing he could, he didn't want to kill Barus.

"You were always soft, Jezzil," Barus spat back. "And this time it's going to get you killed."

They disengaged, both of them leaping backward, and this time it was Jezzil who feinted. He thrust at Barus's midsection, then turned his sword at the last possible moment, aiming for his opponent's wrist, trying to disarm him.

Barus's blade nicked Jezzil's upper arm just as Jezzil's blade reached its target. Barus cried out as his fingers loosened, and his sword spun away.

With a bellow of rage, he flung himself straight at Jezzil. It would have been child's play to run him through, but Jezzil found he couldn't do it, though he had no doubt that Barus would have shown no such restraint. Instead he stepped to the side and, as Barus went by, brought the guard of his sword down on Barus's head, sending him crashing to the ground, stunned.

"I don't want to kill you!" Jezzil burst out.

Barus struggled up onto his elbow, blinking. "Then you're a fool as well as a coward," he spat. Turning his head, he shouted, "Kill him!"

Jezzil flung his sword at the mass of riders, ducking as he did so—

—and Cast.

He was so tired, so drained from all that had gone before, that it was hard to maintain the illusion, but, grunting with effort, he forced himself to hold the Cast.

A few steps brought him to Falar, and he swung up. She flung up her head and neighed in surprise. *She couldn't see me, either, just like the creature in the moat,* he thought. But his hand on the reins and his weight were familiar, and she obeyed him as usual.

"He's a Caster!" Barus was screaming. "Aim for the horse! He's on her! Shoot him!"

Jezzil hung low on Falar's neck and drove his heels into her sides as he did so, turning her nearly at right angles to the trail. Having caught her breath, she leaped forward immediately, crashing through a thicket of low hanging branches. Jezzil flung up an arm to protect his eyes.

Musket fire filled the air. At any second Jezzil expected to feel Falar collapse beneath him, and he wished with all his being that he could extend the illusion to cover her, too.

But she was still moving, crashing through greenbriers and limbs. Bullets whined all around them, but so far none had struck her.

The moment he'd put a screen of greenery between them, Jezzil wrenched Falar's head back toward the trail. He couldn't run through the woods.

The moment Falar burst through the trees onto the trail, the Chonao soldiers began shooting again. They were still within musket range. A bullet slammed into a tree an arm's length away, and one whined over Jezzil's head, close enough that he felt its passage.

Quickly, still holding the Casting in his mind, Jezzil slipped off his saddle into a right side hang, leaving only his left knee and leg slung over the cantle, his arm thrown over Falar's neck. Using the pressure of his arms as he would have used reins, he made the running mare weave back and forth along the trail. Bullets sang around him, but Jezzil knew only too well how difficult it was to hit a fast-running target.

We're going to make it, he thought. *We're—*

The bullet plowed into his thigh just above his knee and Jezzil cried out. The pain was searing, and he felt his left leg starting to go numb. Quickly, he pulled himself up and over so he could hang by his good right leg.

Waves of pain made it so difficult to hold the Casting.

Was he visible?

Just a few more seconds and we'll be out of musket range. Just a few more seconds . . .

Gritting his teeth, Jezzil signaled Falar to keep swerving, clinging to her with all his strength. She responded gamely. Musket fire slowed to a trickle. They were losing the range, and they knew it.

The shouts from his pursuers grew more distant.

With a grunt of effort, Jezzil pulled himself up onto Falar's back, struggling to stay there. He couldn't get his foot back into the stirrup—his leg seemed numb from the knee down.

He realized, with one part of his mind, that he'd lost the Casting.

Falar was slowing, her breath labored. White curds of foam covered her neck and shoulders. "No, keep going," Jezzil said. "Keep going!"

He slapped her with his free hand, and she stumbled, then picked up her pace.

Thunder boomed, so close it startled him. A drop of rain splatted against his face.

The only thing saving them was that they were heading mostly downhill. Jezzil held the laboring mare together with his hands, his body, talking to her. "Just a little farther. A few lengths more . . ."

He could still hear his pursuers as they swung around a curve and started down another long downslope.

Jezzil stared, incredulous for a long second, then raised his hands and sat back, bringing Falar to a staggering halt.

Before him, filling the trail, was a large contingent of Pelanese cavalry. A big white horse led the charge, its rider shouting encouragement, waving a sword as it urged its companions on.

Jezzil peered downhill. There was something very familiar about that yelling lunatic in the lead.

Just as he recognized Talis and Major q'Rindo, the storm

struck, bringing howling winds, booming thunder, and drenching rain.

The rain had slowed to a steady patter by the time Talis, leading Banner reached Ombal Pass again. Wearily, she reflected on the past hours. Jezzil had barely gasped out his warning when the glint of sword blades and the flash of musket fire announced the enemy's presence.

Company Two had been heavily outnumbered, but the Chonao cavalry in the woods never stood a chance, caught as they were under the trees, unable to spread out into formation. The Pelanese troopers she'd led had kept them bottled up with ferocious sword-to-sword combat until the arrival of the rest of the battalion. At some point infantry reserves joined them, attacking with bayonets against an enemy that was mostly confined to the narrow forest trails, where mounted men could barely maneuver.

And then, suddenly, they were gone, the Chonao falling back in disorderly retreat.

The path she'd followed back from the foothill trails was a shortcut. The major had told her it would bring her out about even with the Pelanese front line. When she stepped out from behind the last screen of trees, Talis stood there for a long moment, staring in disbelief.

Someone had told her that the battle had ended several hours ago, with some Chonao throwing down their guns and surrendering and others simply taking to their heels, but she didn't believe it until the evidence lay before her.

It was late afternoon, and clouds masked the sun, but Talis guessed it was only a few hours before sunset. Ombal Pass lay stretched out before her, its terrain so altered by what had gone on that day that it bore little resemblance to the grassy upland it had been in the morning. Bodies lay scattered everywhere, both human and equine. Cannon fire had scarred the land, leaving huge gashes in the earth, gashes that had now turned to mud. The grass was nearly gone, trampled by thousands of feet into a brownish-green slurry.

Still leading Banner, Talis began walking, picking her way over the wounded earth.

She saw medical teams running back and forth with stretchers, carrying men who screamed and babbled for their mothers, men who cried out in agony with every jounce. Banner snorted the first time they stepped around a dead horse, but after five or six more, he no longer reacted, plodding after her, his wet white coat streaked with dirt, mud, and blood that was neither his own nor Talis's.

When Talis at first stepped over a severed leg, still clad in its boot, she gulped, feeling the urge to retch, but after a few minutes she was numb to them.

For a moment she wondered about Eregard. Had he survived? Or had he been killed, like his father?

When she'd seen him up there on his horse, waving the Royal Standard, rallying his troops, she found it impossible to believe that they'd ever kissed, that his hand had touched her breast. *It never happened,* she reminded herself. *It will never happen again, either.* The thought brought a dull pain she didn't want to examine too closely.

As she plodded on, splashing through puddles, wet to the skin, hair unraveled from its neat braid and hanging in strings around her shoulders, she passed a contingent of Pelanese soldiers helping wounded comrades who could still walk off the field. She gave them a halfhearted wave, though the effort seemed too much to make.

Two of the officers stared, and then one did something odd. He saluted her. The other officer stared at him as they helped their wounded comrade along. "She's not an officer," Talis heard him protest.

"Don't you know who that is?" the captain who'd saluted said. "That's her. The one called Talis, who led the charge up in the foothills. See, that's old King Agivir's horse she's leading."

How strange, Talis thought as she plodded on. *They know who I am?*

She spent a moment wondering where Jezzil had gone. He'd been wounded; she remembered that. But she didn't think it had been serious. By the time the fight with the Chonao cavalry was over, he'd disappeared.

By now she'd almost reached the infirmary tents. Soldiers sat huddled on the ground, some eating or drinking, others simply sitting, too exhausted to move. Under an overhanging boulder, a few were trying to kindle a fire, without much success.

I must see to Banner, Talis thought. *A good rubdown and a hot mash, then I can . . .*

She shook her head, realizing she was too tired to even imagine what to do next. Wearily, she staggered on.

"Ouch," Jezzil said. "That hurts."

"Of course it does," Khith said calmly. "I used up the last of my pain-numbing tisane to get the bullet out. It's wearing off now, and I am still stitching."

The former Chonao lay on a table in the infirmary tent, trying to ignore the screams, the stench, and the pain as his teacher tended to his wounded leg. He jerked involuntarily when Khith set another suture, and when Khith gazed at him reproachfully, he nodded. "Sorry. I promise I'll be still."

"You should not have walked on it," Khith said. "That caused the surrounding flesh to tear."

"I didn't have much choice," Jezzil said, then gritted his teeth, feeling the needle go in. He forced himself not to move. "Falar was almost dead on her feet. I knew I couldn't help them in the fight, so once I was sure they were going to win, I started walking back to the pass. I had to take care of Falar."

Khith made a small sound of exasperation as it tugged, then knotted. "There, that's the last," it said. "Now I'll bandage it and check your arm."

"The arm is nothing," Jezzil said. "Barely a nick. I got one of the soldiers to bandage it."

A nurse hurried up to the little Hthras. "Healer, we need you. There's a case been brought in, a belly wound, a young lieutenant. None of the other doctors can treat it."

Khith nodded wearily as it finished the bandaging. "I

know. I will be there." The Hthras looked at its apprentice. "As soon as you have had time to rest, I will need you here. I am the only one who can use avundi to help the wounded, and I cannot be everywhere."

Jezzil sighed. "I understand," he said. "I just need some food."

"And sleep," Khith admonished. "You may put your breeches back on. I will see you at first light, Jezzil, and I will teach you so that you may help."

"I'll be here," Jezzil said. "But, Master, where is Thia? Back at the palace?"

"No, she is here, along with the Princess—or rather, the Queen, I suppose—helping in the infirmary."

"Which tent?"

"I do not know, Jezzil." Without further ado, Khith turned and followed the Pelanese nurse into the back of the tent.

Jezzil fastened his breeches and stood up, a little wobbly, but Khith had wrapped his leg well and it bore his weight. He limped out of the infirmary tent, glad to be away from the stench.

Outside, he stepped over the guy lines holding up the tent and walked around a huge barrel crammed full of severed limbs. Flies buzzed so loudly they nearly drowned out the screaming.

Jezzil walked over to where several soldiers sat, passing a flask back and forth. A broken lance lay beside one of them. "Mind if I borrow this?" Jezzil asked, picking it up.

The soldiers looked up at him. "They took it out of Garando's chest," the closest said. "That funny little doc, he saved him, they say."

"Yes, Khith is very good," Jezzil agreed absently. "I need to find a friend of mine. I could use something to lean on."

"Sure, take it," said the soldier.

Having the lance to lean on helped. Jezzil began limping from one infirmary tent to another. He would duck inside, scan the people there, and then, when he didn't see Thia, leave. He did see Ulandra, wearing a plain black dress and a blood-splashed apron, but there was no sign of Thia.

His urgency grew. Jezzil's rational mind told him that she was all right, she was fine, that he would see her soon, but he found himself unable to sit down, unable to stop searching. He had to find her. He had to find her *now*.

And find her he did, in the sixth infirmary tent he tried. She was standing beside one of the doctors, helping to hold down a patient for an amputation. For a moment he just watched her, thinking that many men wouldn't have had the courage to do what she was doing. The soldier, a woman, was screaming, high, piercing screams that made his own throat ache. It was a relief to all present when she finally passed out and lay silent.

The doctor continued sawing in relative peace.

Jezzil stood there quietly as Thia and the Pelanese surgeon finished their work, bound up the stump, then transferred the soldier to a cot.

Carrying the severed limb and a basin of bloody water, Thia ducked through the back entrance to the tent. Jezzil hastily backed up and made his way around it, avoiding the guy ropes, pushing himself faster. He had to see her.

By the time he reached the rear of the tent, she'd almost completed her gruesome task. The limb had been deposited into a barrel, and Thia had just finished dumping the bloody water into a stained hollow in the ground that had obviously served that purpose many times. She had her back to Jezzil, and as he moved toward her, she straightened, put a hand to the small of her back and stretched, making a weary little sound that tore at his heart.

"Thia?" Even though he hadn't spoken loudly, his voice seemed to ring through the noisy camp.

She whirled around, and the basin dropped from her hands. "Jezzil! You're alive!"

He laughed, now that he was here, not knowing what to say or do. "I am," he admitted. "Only a bit the worse for wear."

She ran to him, but just as he thought she was going to fling herself into his arms, she stopped, her eyes going to his bandaged leg. "You're wounded!"

"It's not bad," he said. "Khith took care of it. It told me

where to find you. I . . . I couldn't stop thinking about you. I had to see you." He reached out and touched her shoulder, feeling awkward and confused. "It's so good to see you," he added idiotically.

She was staring at him, and there was something in her eyes that made him feel more light-headed than his wound had. "I couldn't stop thinking about you, too," she said. "All day I've thought, 'What if the next one they carry in is Jezzil? What if he's dying?'" She reached over, picked up his hand from her shoulder and held it to her cheek. He felt a warm droplet amidst the raindrops. "I thought I'd rather be dead myself than see that."

He didn't know who made the first move. Perhaps they both did. Somehow she was in his arms and he was holding her. The pain from his leg was gone, and the sounds of the camp faded away. They held each other so tightly it hurt, and the hurt felt more wonderful than anything he'd ever felt before.

She was mumbling his name as he awkwardly kissed her cheek, her forehead, her nose. By the time he found her mouth, she was half laughing, half crying.

Their first kiss was clumsy, tentative, but the second was much better. They were learning fast. Jezzil had not known that kissing felt like this, that such an intimate act could feel so natural. He kissed her until his head swam, and by the time they finally pulled away from each other, they were both learning by leaps and bounds.

He stared down at her. "Is this what love feels like?"

"It must be," she gasped, and pulled his head back down.

"Thia! Thia, where are you? I need you! *Thia!*"

It took a long time for the sound to penetrate Jezzil's fogged brain, but finally he could no longer ignore it. He lifted his head and looked around, to see the Pelanese doctor standing there, staring at them.

"I'm sorry," the doctor said in a more moderate tone. "It's obvious this is important . . . but I do need you, Thia."

She nodded at the surgeon, then looked back up at Jezzil.

"I have to go. Besides, you must rest." She stepped back, away from him, smiling. "I'll see you soon, though."

Jezzil half raised a hand and smiled back at her. "Soon," he echoed.

And then she had ducked back into the infirmary tent, and he was alone, wet from the rain, his wounded leg throbbing—and he'd never felt such joy in his life.

Jezzil turned his face up to the rain and, not sure exactly who he was addressing, whispered, "Thank you . . . thank you."

Epilogue

Thia, Jezzil, Talis, and Khith stood on the old battlements, looking out at the harbor of Minoma, waiting for sunset. It had been four days since the Pelanese victory over the Redai's forces, and the work of healing the wounded and burying the dead was still continuing.

Three of them were still working in the tents housing the wounded: Khith and Jezzil using Hthras medical techniques to heal internal injuries, Thia helping to care for the injured. Talis had ridden out on the expeditions to patrol the countryside, lest any fleeing Chonao soldiers turn renegade. But it seemed that the vast majority of Kerezau's surviving army was even now marching back to Gen under guard. Salesin had promised the rank and file soldiers amnesty if they would set sail back to Ktavao, which is what almost all of them elected to do.

Eregard was in mourning for his parents, and they saw little of him. Salesin had put his brothers in charge of the army and the prisoners of war, so the new king could devote his time to planning his coronation.

King Agivir and Queen Elnorin had lain in state side by side for two days, in closed coffins, while the people of Pela passed by in droves to pay their final respects. Then, yesterday, there had been two memorial services, one a huge state funeral that took hours, and the other a quieter, private service for the family and members of the court.

Eregard had spoken with Prince Adranan in private before the family service, his expression bitter. "You realize that Father was almost certainly assassinated."

Adranan's eyes widened. "How can you say that? It was a *battle,* Eregard!"

"Did you *look* at him?" Eregard asked, his voice harsh with grief.

"No," Adranan admitted, "I couldn't bear to."

"I was with him when it happened. Adranan, you've been in enough battles to know how a bullet acts on flesh and bone. Father's *face* was destroyed, not the back of his head. That shot came from our own ranks."

Adranan gazed at his brother, his expression sad but not particularly surprised. "It could have been a stray bullet. An accident," he said, but Eregard could tell even he didn't believe it.

"The Chonao weren't in range or position to make that shot. The bullet came from *behind* us—the Chonao attack was off to the side. The shots that killed the Standard Bearer and the guard were just to make it look good. Father was the target—and so was I. If I hadn't bent over to get Father water at just that moment, I'd have been killed, too." Eregard raised his bandaged arm. The wound, thanks to Khith's ministrations, was healing well.

His brother gazed at Eregard for a long moment, then sighed. "Bullets do go astray during battle," he said simply. "There is no way to prove anything."

"You're right," Eregard admitted. "But I know what I know, Adranan. First Salesin set it up so Father would have to personally go to battle, then he made sure he would never live through it."

Adranan gazed at his brother sadly. "Eregard, we both have to walk a tightrope from now on. Until Salesin gets himself an heir, we're both in danger. I don't want to lose you again, brother. Please say nothing of what you suspect. Please. For my sake."

Eregard had sighed and nodded. "Very well, Adranan. As you say, there is no way to prove anything."

But the Prince did find some outlet for his feelings by composing a song that he sang at the private memorial service. Eregard did not dare to look at Salesin as he played and sang, so he had no idea how much his brother understood of what he was trying, subtly, to say.

> "Strength and beauty, dwelt apart, met and wed at last
> Strong through test of war and creeping villain Famine's fast
> Beautiful together through the lush and festive years
> Shielding sons and kingdom from grim danger, crippling fears
> Setting founding stones beyond our might of mortal ken
> Sudden now a world without them we must comprehend.
>
> Elnorin, Mother, queen and noble lady fair
> Taken at her height of questing mind and gentle beauty rare
> Queen and Mother, both in fullest measure, she
> Who surpassed all gentler measures bringing us to be
> Elnorin the Queen, see the ringing heavens blaze her name
> Yet it is for loving Mother we must mourn and yet remain.
>
> Now Agivir, our king and father, killed in blaring battle's song
> He whose seed gave strength and life to us, his struggling sons
> Violent more than troubled birth was our great father's death
> His life and fame and regal power robbed of hearty breath
> The golden fruit falls early, rudely shaken from the tree
> As all Life and Power know but bitter brevity.
>
> Truthful Strength and gentle Beauty long were met and wedded strong
> Wedded fast, alas, but not for us forever long

Now for us a world less strong, less beautiful displays
For us to keep their honor by our poorer deeds and ways
Stark see we now how lesser Power fleeting passes on
Let Strength and Beauty grow to be their greater standing
      stone."

This morning they had buried the King and Queen in the family vault, side by side.

Now, standing on the battlements, waiting for sunset, the four companions looked out on the bustling harbor town, each busy with his, her, or its private thoughts.

Knowing that Thia had spent yet another exhausting morning in the infirmary tent, Khith reached out a narrow-fingered hand to touch the former priestess's face. "I sense great weariness," it said softly. "You must not make yourself ill, Thia."

She gave the Hthras physician a wan smile. "I'll be all right. It's just that sometimes they die. And it's terrible when that happens."

"It is," Khith murmured. "I know."

Jezzil was still gazing out over the harbor. "I wonder if any of Kerezau's forces will be able to regroup. He had some strong subcommanders."

"I don't think so," Talis said. "Major q'Rindo told me that we captured most of the top leaders. And do you know what they found in the command tent?"

Jezzil shook his head. "I've been so busy in the infirmary, I've scarcely had a chance to talk to anyone who was unwounded. What did they find?"

"Kerezau's body, bound and gagged. He'd been dead most of the day, the major said."

Jezzil nodded. "Barus said he'd gone mad, and that after he ordered that suicidal cavalry charge, his commanders hustled him away and restrained him, to make sure he couldn't issue any more such orders."

Talis gazed up at Jezzil. "They also said he had an inflamed spot on his neck. Right about here." She touched the side of her own throat. "That poison in your bag . . . what effect would it have on someone if it touched the flesh but did not actually pierce the skin?"

Jezzil thought for a moment. "It could be absorbed through the skin, I suppose, unless immediately washed off, and that substance does cause victims to go mad before they die."

Talis nodded. "I think," she said quietly, "that I may have succeeded after all. Pity it didn't kill him before he could order that charge."

Jezzil shrugged. "That charge was the kind of thing that can have a huge effect on an army's spirit to fight. Without it, who knows how things might have gone that day?"

Seeing Thia leaning over to look down off the battlement, Jezzil went over to her and took her hand. "Be careful," he warned. "You don't want to get vertigo."

Thia smiled. "I've always had a head for heights," she said. "I don't know why. When I was a novice, I was always expected to climb up the tallest ladders in the sacristy to dust the top shelves where the most ancient icons were kept."

The two smiled at each other, but then, conscious that they were not alone, Jezzil changed the subject. "Have you seen the Princess?"

"You mean the Queen," she reminded him. "I saw her this morning, after the burial. She told me that the Captain of the Watch reported to her that Master Varn—also known as His Reverence Varlon—seems to have vanished without a trace. He's nowhere to be found in Minoma."

"He's had more than four days to run," Khith, who had been listening, pointed out. "This island is not that large. If he stole a horse and rode hard, he could be many leagues away by now."

He awoke late in the day, having slept the sleep of exhaustion after his long ride. For three days he'd ridden, all day and most of the night, not at a fast pace, for that might have attracted attention, but steadily.

He'd sold his stolen horse for enough coins to keep him here at this cheap inn for days. While in Napice, he planned to sell the small objects he'd stolen from the palace for enough money to take ship for K'Qal, and from here he would take the caravan back to Amaran. He was relieved that it was over. His service to the god was done.

Varn groaned aloud as he sat up on his lumpy cot. Getting a private room in this run-down inn had not bought him a decent straw tick on the bed, or a pillow with more than a few feathers left in it. And after four days in the saddle, his entire body was as sore as if he'd been roundly thrashed.

Fumbling under the cot, he pulled out the chamber pot and used it, then covered it and slid it back under.

He regarded his travel-stained breeches, shirt, and over-jerkin distastefully, but had nothing else to put on. He'd buried his incriminating red robe the second day he'd traveled south. Varn had no idea whether the citizens of Napice, the southernmost port city on Pela, knew anything about the priests of Boq'urak, but why take chances?

He'd always been fastidious about his personal habits and dress, though, and it was almost physical pain to wear dirty clothes. At the moment he could do nothing about them, but at least he could do something about his own body.

Rising, Varn wrapped himself in his cloak and went to the door. A few shouts brought the innkeeper, and a few coins brought a promise of a tub and hot water.

Afterward, it felt good to be clean again.

His chin and cheeks itched, and he wished he could shave, but a beard was one of the quickest ways a man could change his appearance. Varn felt the stubble that was growing on his head. He would stay here in Napice until he had enough hair and beard so no one would think "holy man" when they looked at him. Then he would find a ship.

The twin ziggurats awaited him. He would go home and devote himself to his god and his fellow priests. He'd had enough of the outside world to last him a lifetime. Varn found himself longing for the peace, order, and silence of the monastic life.

Slowly, distastefully, he dried himself on his dirty cloak, then slipped into his clothes. He would go to the market-place and buy new ones as soon as he had broken his fast.

In the darkest corner of the room there hung an old mirror, warped and stained with dirt and age. When he was dressed, he walked over to it to adjust his traveler's hood so it would hide his shaven pate.

The moment he regarded himself, Master Varn knew that he was not alone. His features began to Change, to flow, in the way he'd experienced before.

His voice, when he spoke, was shrill with fear and awe. "Lord?" he said. "Why do you visit your servant now?"

He heard the answer, not sure whether he was hearing it from his own throat or within his mind. His lips moved, but did sound emerge? He couldn't be sure.

Faithful servant, the words came. *You have done well, but it is not finished.*

"It *is* finished," Varn dared to say. "Pela triumphed, as you wished. The Queen will bear no children. Life-force flowed to you in great numbers. All went as you decreed unto me."

It is not *finished.* The voice was inexorable. Varn could see that his own eyes were gone, that Boq'urak's huge orbs filled his face. His hands . . . He regarded the leathery talons with their huge claws, and for just a second, the part of him that was still Master Varn had a terrible urge to use those claws to rip out those dreadful eyes.

"Lord," he pleaded in a hoarse whisper, "forgive me, but your servant is weary. I can do no more."

There are those who are aware of Me. They have escaped Me. They have flouted My wishes. They do not worship Me as they ought. They challenge Me, simply by living. They must die. Attend to it.

"Who?" Varn whispered, though he already knew.

You know them. The five must die. Eregard, Jezzil, Khith, Talis . . .

The voice paused. Varn tried to choke back a whimper. "No."

Yes. Thia. She is Mine. Her death belongs to Me. You must be My arm and My sword, My servant. Kill them all.

"I can kill Jezzil, Talis, Khith, and Eregard," Varn said.

"But a good servant needs a reward, Lord. Thia is mine. She will be mine."

She can never be yours, the god said, and as His voice filled Varn's mind, a vision filled his eyes.

Thia. He recognized her, wearing a blood-spattered apron, her hair tied up in a scarf. She was standing with her back to some kind of tent, and she was not alone. Varn recognized the other figure in the vision. It was that wretched soldier lad who fancied himself a magic-worker. The priest watched as they drew together, then embraced, kissing. At first they were clumsy as puppies, but within moments they had learned, and their kisses grew long, deep, and passionate—kisses like the ones Varn had yearned to give her for so long now.

As the vision filled his mind, his body reacted to it, arousing him painfully. Anger flooded him. If they'd been before him at that moment, his hatred would have caused him to strike them both dead—and, so closely were they entwined, one sword thrust would have served.

Varn blinked, and suddenly the vision was gone.

The voice spoke again. *Thia must die.*

"No," he said, choking with fear at his own temerity. "Without the others, she is nothing. A girl-child. When she is mine, she cannot possibly be a threat to you. She will be mine. She is all I ask."

No. Thia must die.

Varn let out a moan of anguish. "Please, Lord. Please." He stared into the mirror again, and was startled to see only his own features. With shaking fingers, he ran his hands over his face. It was his own flesh, warm, firm, and living. Human.

Master Varn swayed as he stared into the mirror, and he had to clutch the back of the room's rickety chair for support. Had it really happened? Had Boq'urak really been here?

Or was he still in his bed, dreaming?

Master Varn raised his own hand and slapped himself smartly in the face. He staggered, his cheek burning, then slid to the floor.

"It was real," he mumbled. "Real."

Burying his head in his hands, he began to weep.

Hearing a soft hail from behind them, the four friends turned away from the battlements and the fine view of the harbor of Minoma to see Eregard and Queen Ulandra approaching on the walkway.

"Eregard!" Thia stepped forward to hug the young Prince. "How are you? I've scarcely seen you since the day of the battle."

"I'm well," he said, returning her quick embrace. He turned to Jezzil and Talis. "Ah, the heroes of Pela. Ironic that neither of you is Pelanese, isn't it?"

Jezzil laughed. "I suppose it is," he said. "How goes the aftermath of the battle?"

"They're still interrogating some of the high-ranked officers," Eregard said. He cocked an eyebrow at Talis. "Do you know what they call you, Trooper Talis?"

"No," she said apprehensively. "What?"

"The Katan bitch that killed Kerezau," he said. "It has a certain assonance, doesn't it? Like the beginning of a song. Perhaps I should write it . . ."

"Goddess, no," Talis said fervently. "All I want is to go back to Kata and tell Rufen Castio that I accomplished my mission. And help *you* work to redress some of the wrongs done to my country by the Viceroy—I mean, the King."

Eregard's mouth twisted. "You know I will do what I can," he said. "But Salesin is not one to listen to the counsel of others. Except . . ." He paused. "He did listen to several of his military leaders today, including Adranan and I. You are to be awarded a sign of the Crown's gratitude for your actions, Talis."

She looked, if possible, even warier than before. "I am? What about Jezzil?"

"After publicly proving my brother wrong on two occasions," Eregard said dryly, "Jezzil is lucky that he won't be hanged for treason, I suspect. Prophets who turn out to be correct are usually the most unpopular."

Jezzil chuckled. "It's a good thing I can't really foretell the future."

"So nobody mentioned an award for Jezzil," Eregard continued. "But there is one for you."

"What is it?"

"Banner is yours," Eregard said. "The King has decreed it. A small reward for your services."

Talis looked amazed, then delighted. "He's mine? That's wonderful! He's a beauty! I'm surprised Salesin doesn't want him for himself."

Eregard's mouth was twitching, and even Ulandra began to smile. "I think the fact that Salesin tried to ride him this morning and got royally thrown might have something to do with it," Eregard said.

Talis's mouth fell open and she began to giggle. "Oh, dear!"

Jezzil was laughing out loud. "Smart horse!"

The comrades shared a moment of amusement, then Eregard reached over and took Ulandra's hand. "Master Khith, Ulandra needs your help," he said.

Khith extended its small, narrow hand and laid it on Eregard's sleeve, then reached over to grasp the Queen's hand. "Anything that is in my power, I shall do," it said gravely. "You know that."

"Healer Khith . . ." Ulandra spoke in a low, hesitant voice. "I have been told that you can help to heal sick minds, as well as sick bodies. Is that true?"

"Yes, it is," Khith replied.

"I want you to look into my mind," the Queen said. Her voice was soft, almost a whisper, but there was a firmness to it that held nothing of the childlike creature she'd been before her marriage. "Something is wrong with me. There's something inside me. Thia told me about Boq'urak. I think that whatever is inside me is linked to it . . ." She took a deep breath. "Or perhaps I've been possessed by Boq'urak itself. Whatever it is, I must know what it is, and what it plans."

Khith studied her, then nodded, and glanced around the battlements.

"We are alone," Eregard reassured it. "And will remain

undisturbed. I left guards stationed at the bottom of the stairs leading up to the battlements."

"Very well," Khith said. "Be seated." It indicated a stone bench.

Ulandra seated herself, her hands in her lap, her blue eyes fixed on the Hthras's face.

"Relax . . ." Khith said. "Let your mind relax. Your mind and body are at peace. My voice will help you to relax and find peace."

As it continued to speak of relaxation, peace, and comfort, Khith's voice took on the cadence of a soothing monotone.

Jezzil watched, studying the senior adept's movements. Was this magic? Not quite . . . it was a healer's technique, but it did not have the feeling of magic associated with it.

A few minutes later Ulandra sat on the bench, hands limp in her lap, eyes closed, breathing heavily. Khith turned to Jezzil. "She entered the trance state easily. I suspect that this is not the first time."

"Master Varn?"

"From what Thia has told me, yes."

"Now what?" he asked.

"While she is in a trance, I may be able to make contact with what she fears without arousing it or making it aware of us. But I will have to stop if I sense that it is becoming aware."

Jezzil nodded.

"Ulandra . . ." Khith's voice was soothing. "What lies inside you that you fear? There is a darkness there, you say. Without touching the darkness, look at it, and tell me what you see."

She shivered. "I'm . . . 'fraid . . ."

"You are safe. I will not allow you to be harmed. Just look. Tell me what you see."

She took two more deep breaths, then said, slowly, "He is powerful, so strong. Ugly, so ugly . . ."

Thia gave Jezzil a quick, alarmed glance.

"Who is he, Ulandra? Where is he from?"

"He is many names. In the north He is Boq . . . Boq'urak.

He lives somewhere else. Not here. Not there. Somewhere else. Through a door . . ."

"A door? What kind of door?"

"Door, portal . . ." She was groping for words to describe a concept she didn't fully understand. "Other places, not this world. Portals that go back and forth. He comes back and forth, when He has a vessel to do His bidding."

Jezzil heard Khith's indrawn breath. Ulandra's words meant little to him, but they obviously held meaning for the Hthras.

"And you are one such vessel?"

"He's trying . . ." It was half moan, half sob. "Oh, He's ugly, I don't want Him."

"Why does He come here, to this world?"

"To play," she said, certainty returning to her voice. "He plays here."

Khith looked at the other four, seeing their expressions. "Plays?"

"Amusing fun to bring it down, build it up, bring it down. A game."

Thia drew in a short, sharp breath, and Jezzil put an arm around her. She leaned against him.

Ulandra was continuing without prompting. "Fun to make them fall, and rise. Great sport to bring down the Redai . . . love the look of battle, the gush of blood . . . oh, the blood, spill the blood . . . blood is power, blood is strength . . ." She was moaning now, obviously in distress. "Bring the little creatures down, great sport . . . blood and death and war . . ."

She moaned again, a sound of such pain and distress that Thia cried out softly, "Don't!"

"Queen Ulandra," Khith said sharply. "When I speak the word 'awake,' I want you to awaken to this sunlit day. You will remember what you saw, but it is *not* part of you, and you will remember that, too. I am going to count, and you will rise up, away from that darkness . . . Do you hear me, Ulandra?"

She was calm again. "I hear you."

"As I count you will rise up, back to this world, and you

will awaken. One . . . you are rising. Two . . . you have helped us, dear lady. And three, you have helped your kingdom. And you are now ready to . . . awake."

Ulandra's eyes opened and she sat there blinking.

"Rest for a moment," Khith said. "Move slowly. Do you remember what happened?"

She gazed up at the Hthras. "Yes, I do. That thing, it's amusing itself with us, as though we were pieces on a game board."

"Yes," Khith said heavily. "I have studied the writings of the Ancients. Boq'urak hs been with us for a long, long time. It has done this before. Civilizations rise, only to tumble back to barbarism. Species evolve, only to revert to the animals they sprang from. There is the Great Waste . . . some disaster happened there, so terrible it is still death to walk those sands for more than a scant handful of days. All done at Boq'urak's doing. We amuse Him."

"Goddess!" Eregard was pale and shaking. "Then that battle—we fought so hard, yet our victory, it wasn't . . . real."

"The battle went the way He wanted it to go," Ulandra said.

"And now, He knows who we all are," Thia murmured. "Before it was just me He wanted. But now we all had parts to play in bringing about the Pelanese victory. We have become His game pieces."

They stared at each other as a breeze gently tossed their hair, rustled their clothing.

The setting Sun seemed to have lost its warmth.

"Boq'urak has already tried to kill Thia," Jezzil said. "I doubt it likes being thwarted. I suspect none of us have long to live."

Talis drew herself up. "We fought it once, and won," she said, a warrior's gleam in her eyes. "We can fight it again."

Eregard nodded. "I agree. We must fight."

"What choice do we have?" Jezzil said bleakly. "I am a warrior, as well as an apprentice Adept. I would rather die fighting."

"If it were all-powerful, none of us would be here now," Thia pointed out. "We can't give up, or the game is over."

"There are ancient texts," Khith said. "Perhaps they would tell us more."

"Where are they?" Thia asked.

"In the Ancient City I fled before coming to Q'Kal," Khith said. "It will be perilous to go back. My people have exiled me."

"We're *all* exiles," Thia said, her dark eyes flashing. "But even exiles have a right to live, and a right to fight. We found each other. We have skills, each of us, and we sent Him running once before, remember. Perhaps Boq'urak isn't as powerful as He likes to believe!"

Jezzil looked down at her with an expression that made her pale features flush. "You have more courage than all of us, my lady," he said softly.

"It will take more than courage," Khith said somberly. "Soon enough, I suspect, we will discover whether we have what it will take to prevail in the face of this evil . . . and what it will cost to save our world."

There seemed to be no more words. As one, the comrades turned to stare out at the harbor, where the sun was setting, painting the ocean with streaks of fire.